Forests of the Heart

Also by Charles de Lint from Tom Doherty Associates

DREAMS UNDERFOOT

THE FAIR AT EMAIN MACHA

GREENMANTLE

INTO THE GREEN

THE IVORY AND THE HORN

JACK OF KINROWAN

THE LITTLE COUNTRY

MEMORY AND DREAM

MOONHEART

MOONLIGHT AND VINES

SOMEPLACE TO BE FLYING

SPIRITWALK

SVAHA

TRADER

YARROW

Forests of the Heart

Charles de Lint

A Tom Doherty Associates Book
New York

FORESTS OF THE HEART

Edited by Terri Windling

A Tor Book
Published by Tom Doherty Associates, LLC
175 Fifth Avenue
New York, NY 10010

www.tor.com

Tor® is a registered trademark of Tom Doherty Associates, LLC.

Library of Congress Cataloging-in-Publication Data

De Lint, Charles
    Forests of the heart / Charles de lint.
        p. cm.
    "A Tom Doherty Associates book."
    ISBN 0-312-86519-8 (hc)
    ISBN 0-312-87568-1 (pbk)
    1. Artist colonies—Fiction. I. Title.

PR9199.3.D357 F67 2000
813'.54—dc21   00-027679
                                                         CIP

Printed in the United States of America

0 9 8 7 6 5 4 3

Grateful acknowledgments are made to:

Miss Anna Sunshine Ison for the use of her *cadejos* poem, and for allowing me to make a slight adjustment in it to fit the story. Copyright © 1998 by Miss Anna Sunshine Ison. Printed by permission of the author.

Ani DiFranco for the use of lines from "Pixie" from her album *Little Plastic Castle*. Copyright © 1998 by Ani DiFranco, Righteous Babe Music. Lyrics reprinted by permission. For more information about DiFranco's music, contact Righteous Babe Records, P.O. Box 95, Ellicott Station, Buffalo, NY 14205-0095.

for
Karen Shaffer and Charles Vess

the stars shine brighter
where you walk

Contents

Author's Note

Special thanks to Mary Ann for helping me find the time to write this through a couple of years that were inordinately busy; Charles Vess for providing me with some of the Green Man material (though I hasten to add that my take on that venerable figure is far different from the usual folkloric depictions); Miss Anna Sunshine Ison for *los cadejos*; Mardelle and Richard Kunz for putting up with far too many questions by e-mail—and for tracking down the answers to them; Jim Harris for the lexicon; Rodger Turner and Paul Fletcher for valiantly helping me through some rather severe computer woes (and thanks as well to Rodger for that early reading of the manuscript); Barry Ambridge for straightening me out on tires; Swain Wolfe for explaining the difference between power and luck; Lawrence Schmiel for vetting the Spanish (any errors are mine); Amanda Fisher for once again helping with the bookmarks; and the folks at Tor for being *very* patient this time.

I've been taken to task by a number of readers for not noting the music I was listening to when I've written my last few books. So, this time out my ears were filled, my toes tapped, my spirit was made more full by . . . well, too large a number of fine musicians to list them all here. But briefly, of late I've been listening to a lot of Steve Earle, Fred Eaglesmith, Dar Williams, Ani DiFranco, Stacey Earle, Buddy Miller, Tori Amos, the Walkabouts (including their "Chris and Carla" recordings), and all the various incarnations in which Johnette Napolitano finds herself, one of my favorites being the CD she recorded with Los Illegals.

When I'm actually writing, however, I lean more towards instrumental music where the words in my ear don't interfere with the words going down on the screen. For this book that involved less Celtic music than usual, though Solas was never far from the CD player. Mostly I found myself playing some of those neo-Flamenco artists such as Robert Michaels, Ottmar Leibert, Gerardo Nunez, and Oscar Lopez, while towards the end of the book, Douglas Spotted Eagle's *Closer to Far Away* and Robbie Robertson's last two albums (*Music for the Native Americans* and *Contact from the Underworld of Redboy*) were in constant rotation.

But man does not live by worldbeat alone. Many of the hours spent on this novel found me nodding my head to Art Tatum, Oscar Peterson, Miles Davis, Bill Evans, Charlie Haden's duet albums, Clifford Brown, and this wonderful ten-CD set that my friend Rodger gave me: *The Complete Jazz at the Philharmonic on Verve.*

If you decide to try any of the above, I hope you'll enjoy them as much as I have.

And as usual, let me mention that the city, characters, and events to be found in these pages are fictitious. Any resemblance to actual persons living or dead is purely coincidental.

If any of you are on the Internet, come visit my homepage. The URL (address) is http://www.cyberus.ca/~cdl

—Charles de Lint
Ottawa, Spring 1999

In the middle of the journey of our life,
I came to myself within a dark wood where
the straight way was lost.

—DANTE ALIGHIERI,
from *The Divine Comedy*

1

Los lobos

El lobo pierde los dientes más no las mientes,
The wolf loses his teeth, not his nature.
—MEXICAN-AMERICAN SAYING

Like her sister, Bettina San Miguel was a small, slender woman in her mid-twenties, dark-haired and darker-eyed; part *Indio*, part Mexican, part something older still. Growing up, they'd often been mistaken for twins, but Bettina was a year younger and, unlike Adelita, she had never learned to forget. The little miracles of the long ago lived on in her, passed down to her from their *abuela,* and her grandmother before her. It was a gift that skipped a generation, tradition said.

"¡*Tradición,* pah!" their mother was quick to complain when the opportunity arose. "You call it a gift, but I call it craziness."

Their *abuela* would nod and smile, but she still took the girls out into the desert, sometimes in the early morning or evening, sometimes in the middle of the night. They would leave empty-handed, be gone for hours and return with full bellies, without thirst. Return with something in their eyes that made their mother cross herself, though she tried to hide the gesture.

"They miss too much school," she would say.

"Time enough for the Anglos' school when they are older," Abuela replied.

"And church? If they die out there with you, their sins unforgiven?"

"The desert is our church, its roof the sky. Do you think the Virgin and *los santos* ignore us because it has no walls? Remember, *hija*, the Holy Mother was a bride of the desert before she was a bride of the church."

Mamá would shake her head, muttering, *"Nosotras estamos locas todas."* We are all crazy. And that would be the end of it. Until the next time.

Then Adelita turned twelve and Bettina watched the mysteries fade in her sister's eyes. She still accompanied them into the desert, but now she brought paper and a pencil, and rather than learn the language of *la lagartija*, she would try to capture an image of the lizard on her paper. She no longer absorbed the history of the landscape; instead she traced the contours of the hills with the lead in her pencil. When she saw *el halcón* winging above the desert hills, she saw only a hawk, not a *brujo* or a mystic like their father, caught deep in a dream of flight. Her own dreams were of boys and she began to wear makeup.

All she had learned, she forgot. Not the details, not the stories. Only that they were true.

But Bettina remembered.

"You taught us both," she said to her *abuela* one day when they were alone. They sat stone-still in the shadow cast by a tall saguaro, watching a coyote make its way with delicate steps down a dry wash. "Why is it only I remember?"

The coyote paused in mid-step, lifting its head at the sound of her voice, ears quivering, eyes liquid and watchful.

"You were the one chosen," Abuela said.

The coyote darted up the bank of the wash, through a stand of palo verde trees, and was gone. Bettina turned back to her grandmother.

"But why did you choose me?" she asked.

"It wasn't for me to decide," Abuela told her. "It was for the mystery. There could only be one of you, otherwise *la brujería* would only be half so potent."

"But how can she just forget? You said we were magic—that we were *both* magic."

"And it is still true. Adelita won't lose her magic. It runs too deep in her blood. But she won't remember it, not like you do. Not unless. . . ."

"Unless what?"

"You die before you have a granddaughter of your own."

Tonight Bettina sat by the window at a kitchen table many miles from the desert of her childhood, the phone propped under one ear so that she could speak to Adelita while her hands remained free to sort through the pile of *milagros* spilled across the table. Her only light source was a fat candle that stood in a cracked porcelain saucer, held in place by its own melted wax.

She could have turned the overhead on. There was electricity in the house—she could hear it humming in the walls and it made the old fridge grumble in the corner from time to time—but she preferred the softer illumination of the candle to electric lighting. It reminded her of firelight, of all those nights sitting around out back of Adelita's house north of Tubac, and she was in a campfire mood tonight. Talking with her sister did that, even if they were a half continent and a few time zones apart, connected only by the phone and the *brujería* in their blood.

The candlelight glittered on the small silver votive offerings and made shadows dance in the corners of the room whenever Bettina moved her arm. Those shadows continued to dance when the candle's flame pointed straight up at the ceiling once more, but she ignored them. They were like the troubles that come in life—the more attention one paid to them, the more likely they were to stay. They were like the dark-skinned men who had gathered outside the house again tonight.

Every so often they came drifting up through the estates that surrounded Kellygnow, a dozen or so tall, lean men, squatting on their haunches in a rough circle in the backyard, eyes so dark they swallowed light. Bettina had no idea what brought them. She only knew they were vaguely related to her grandmother's people, distant kin to the desert *Indios* whose blood Bettina and Adelita shared—very distant, for the memory of sea spray and a rich, damp green lay under the skin of their thoughts. This was not their homeland; their spirits spread a tangle of roots just below the surface of the soil, no deeper.

But like her uncles, they were handsome men, dark-skinned and hard-eyed, dressed in collarless white shirts and suits of black broadcloth. Barefoot, calluses hard as boot leather, and the cold didn't seem to affect them. Long black hair tied back, or twisted into braided ropes. They were silent, smoking hand-rolled cigarettes as they watched the house. Bettina could smell the burning tobacco from inside where she sat, smell the smoke, and under it, a feral, musky scent.

Their presence in the yard resonated like a vibration deep in her bones. She knew they lived like wolves, up in the hills north of the city, perhaps, running wild and alone except for times such as this. She had never spoken to them, never asked what brought them. Her *abuela* had warned her a long time ago not to ask questions of *la brujería* when it came so directly into one's life. It was always better to let such a mystery make its needs known in its own time.

"And of course, Mamá wants to know when you're coming home," Adelita was saying.

Usually they didn't continue this old conversation themselves. Their mother was too good at keeping it alive by herself.

"I am home," Bettina said. "She knows that."

"But she doesn't believe it."

"This is true. She was asking me the same thing when I talked to her last night. And then, of course, she wanted to know if I'd found a church yet, if the priest was a good speaker, had I been to confession . . ."

Adelita laughed. "*¡Por supuesto!* At least she can't check up on you. Chuy's now threatening to move us to New Mexico."

"Why New Mexico?"

"Because of Lalo's band. With the money they made on that last tour, they had enough to put a down payment on this big place outside of Albuquerque. But it needs a lot of work and he wants to hire Chuy to do it. Lalo says there's plenty of room for all of us."

"*Los lobos.*"

"That's right. You should have come to one of the shows."

But Bettina hadn't been speaking of the band from East L.A. Those *lobos* had given Lalo's band their big break by bringing them along on tour as their support act last year. The wolves she'd been referring to were out in the cold night that lay beyond the kitchen's windows.

She hadn't even meant to speak aloud. The words had been pulled out of her by a stirring outside, an echoing whisper deep in her bones. For a moment she'd thought the tall, dark men were coming into the house, that an explanation would finally accompany their enigmatic presence. But they were only leaving, slipping away among the trees.

"Bettina?" her sister asked. "*¿Estás ahí?*"

"I'm here."

Bettina let out a breath she hadn't been aware of holding. She didn't need to look out the window to know that the yard was now empty. It took her a moment to regain the thread of their conversation.

"I was just distracted for a moment," she said, then added, "What about the gallery? I can't imagine you selling it."

Adelita laughed. "Oh, we're not really going. It's bad enough that Lalo's moving so far away. Chuy's family would be heartbroken if we went as well. How would they be able to spoil Janette as much as they do now? And Mamá . . ."

"Would *never* forgive you."

"*De veras.*"

Bettina went back to sorting through her *milagros,* fingering the votive offerings as they gossiped about the family and neighbors Bettina had left behind. Adelita always had funny stories about the tourists who came into the gallery and Bettina never tired of hearing about her niece Janette. She missed the neighborhood and its people, her family and friends. And she missed the desert, desperately. But something had called to her from the forested hills that lay outside the city that was now her home. It had drawn her from the desert to this place where the seasons changed so dramatically: in summer so green and lush it took the breath away, in winter so desolate and harsh it could make the desert seem kind. The insistent mystery of it had nagged and pulled at her until she'd felt she had no choice but to come.

She didn't think the source of the summons lay with her uninvited guests, *los lobos* who came into the yard to smoke their cigarettes and silently watch the house. But she was sure they had some connection to it.

"What are you doing?" Adelita asked suddenly. "I keep hearing this odd little clicking sound."

"I'm just sorting through these *milagros* that Inés sent up to me. For a . . ." She hesitated a moment. "For a fetish."

"Ah."

Adelita didn't exactly disapprove of Bettina's vocation—not like their mother did—but she didn't quite understand it either. While she also drew on the stories their *abuela* had told them, she used them to fuel her art. She thought of them as fictions, resonant and powerful, to be sure, but ultimately quaint. Outdated views from an older, more superstitious world that were fascinating to explore because they jump-started the creative impulse, but not anything by which one could live in the modern world.

"Leave such things for the storytellers," she would say.

Such things, such things. Simple words to encompass so much.

Such as the fetish Bettina was making at the moment, part mojo charm, part *amuleto*: a small, cotton sack that would be filled with dark earth to swallow bad feelings. Pollen and herbs were mixed in with the earth to help the transfer of sorrow and pain from the one who would wear the fetish into the fetish itself. On the inside of the sack, tiny threaded stitches held a scrap of paper with a name written on it. A hummingbird's feather. A few small colored beads. And, once she'd chosen exactly the right *milagro*, one of the silver votive offerings that Inés had sent her would be sewn inside as well.

Viewed from outside, the stitches appeared to spell words, but they were like the voices of ravens heard speaking in the woods. The sounds made by the birds sounded like words, but they weren't words that could be readily deciphered by untrained ears. They weren't *human* words.

This was one of the ways she focused her *brujería*. Other times, she called on the help of the spirits and *los santos* to help her interpret the cause of an unhappiness or illness.

"There is no one method of healing," her grandmother had told her once. "Just as *la Virgen* is not bound by one faith."

"One face?" Bettina had asked, confused.

"That, too," Abuela said, smiling. "*La medicina* requires only your respect and that you accept responsibility for all you do when you embark upon its use."

"But the herbs. The medicinal plants . . ."

"*Por eso,*" Abuela told her. "Their properties are eternal. But how you use them, that is for you to decide." She smiled again. "We are not machines, *chica*. We are each of us different. *Sin par*. Unique. The measure given to one must be adjusted for another."

There was not a day gone by that Bettina didn't think of and miss her grandmother. Her good company. Her humor. Her wisdom. Sighing, she returned her attention to her sister.

"You can't play at the *brujería* all your life," Adelita was saying, her voice gentle.

"It's not play for me."

"Bettina, we grew up together. You're not a witch."

"No, I'm a healer."

There was an immense difference between the two, as Abuela had often pointed out. A *bruja* made dark, hurtful magic. A *curandera* healed.

"A healer," Bettina repeated. "As was our *abuela*."

"Was she?" Adelita asked.

Bettina could hear the tired smile in Adelita's voice, but she didn't share her sister's amusement.

"*¿Cómo?*" she said, her own voice sharper than she intended. "How can you deny it?"

Adelita sighed. "There is no such thing as magic. Not here, in the world where we live. *La brujería* is only for stories. *Por el reino de los sueños*. It lives only in dreams and make-believe."

"You've forgotten everything."

"No, I remember the same as you. Only I look at the stories she told us with the eyes of an adult. I know the difference between what is real and what is superstition."

Except it hadn't only been stories, Bettina wanted to say.

"I loved her, too," Adelita went on. "It's just . . . think about it. The way she took us out into the desert. It was like she was trying to raise us as wild animals. What could Mamá have been thinking?"

"That's not it at all—"

"I'll tell you this. Much as I love our *mamá*, I wouldn't let her take Janette out into the desert for hours on end the way she let Abuela take us. In the heat of the day and . . . how often did we go out in the middle of the night?"

"You make it sound so wrong."

"*Cálmate*, Bettina. I know we survived. We were children. To us it was simply fun. But think of what *could* have happened to us—two children out alone in the desert with a crazy old woman."

"She was *not*—"

"Not in our eyes, no. But if we heard the story from another?"

"It . . . would seem strange," Bettina had to admit. "But what we learned—"

"We could have learned those stories at her knee, sitting on the front stoop of our parents' house."

"And if they weren't simply stories?"

"*¡Qué boba eres!* What? Cacti spirits and talking animals? The past and future, all mixed up with the present. What did she call it?"

"*La época del mito*."

"That's right. Myth time. I named one of my gallery shows after it. Do you remember?"

"I remember."

It had been a wonderful show. La Gata Verde had been transformed into a dreamscape that was closer to some miraculous otherwhere than it was to the dusty pavement that lay outside the gallery. Paintings, rich with primary colors, depicted *los santos* and desert spirits and the Virgin as seen by those who'd come to her from a different tradition than that put forth by the papal authority in Rome. There had been Hopi kachinas—the Storyteller, Crow Woman, clowns, deer dancers—and tiny, carved Zuni fetishes. Wall hangings rich with allegorical representations of *Indio* and Mexican folklore. And Bettina's favorite: a collection of sculptures by the Bisbee artist, John Early—surreal figures of gray, fired clay, decorated with strips of colored cloth and hung with threaded beads and shells and spiraling braids of copper and silver filament. The sculptures twisted and bent like smoke-people frozen in their dancing, captured in mid-step as they rose up from the fire.

She had stood in the center of the gallery the night before the opening of the show and turned slowly around, drinking it all in, pulse drumming in time to the resonance that arose from the art that surrounded her. For one who didn't believe, Adelita had still somehow managed to gather together a show that truly seemed to represent their grandmother's description of a moment stolen from *la época del mito.*

"Not everything in the world relates to art," Bettina said now into the phone.

"No. But perhaps it should. Art is what sets us apart from the animals."

Bettina couldn't continue the conversation. At times like this, it was as though they spoke two different languages, where the same word in one meant something else entirely in the other.

"It's late," she said. "I should go."

"*Perdona*, Bettina. I didn't mean to make you angry."

She wasn't angry, Bettina thought. She was sad. But she knew her sister wouldn't understand that either.

"I know," she said. "Give my love to Chuy and Janette."

"*Sí. Vaya con Dios.*"

And if He will not have me? Bettina thought. For when all was said and done, God was a man, and she had never fared well in the world of men. It was easier to live in *la época del mito* of her *abuela*. In myth time, all were equal. People, animals, plants, the earth itself. As all times were equal and existed simultaneously.

"*Qué te vaya bien,*" she said. Take care.

She cradled the receiver and finally chose the small shape of a dog from the *milagros* scattered across the tabletop. *El lobo* was a kind of a dog, she thought. Perhaps she was making this fetish for herself. She should sew her own name inside, instead of Marty Gibson's, the man who had asked her to make it for him. Ah, but would it draw *los lobos* to her, or keep them away? And which did she truly want?

Getting up from the table, she crossed the kitchen and opened the door to look outside. Her breath frosted in the air where the men had been barefoot. January was a week old and the ground was frozen. It had snowed again this week, after a curious Christmas thaw that had left the ground almost bare in many places. The wind had blown most of the snow off the lawn where the men had gathered, pushing it up in drifts against the trees and the buildings scattered among them: cottages and a gazebo, each now boasting a white skirt. She could sense a cold front moving in from the north, bringing with it the bitter temperatures that would leave fingers and face numb after only a few min-

utes of exposure. Yet some of the men had been in short sleeves, broadcloth
suit jackets slung over their shoulders, all of them walking barefoot on the
frozen lawn.

Por eso. . . .

She didn't think they were men at all.

"Your friends are gone."

"Ellos no son mis amigos," she said, then realized that speaking for so
long with Adelita on the phone had left her still using Spanish. "They aren't
my friends," she repeated. "I don't know who, or even what they are."

"Perhaps they are ghosts."

"Perhaps," Bettina agreed, though she didn't think so. They were too
complicated to be described by so straightforward a term.

She gazed out into the night a moment longer, then finally closed the door
on the deepening cold and turned to face the woman who had joined her in the
kitchen.

If *los lobos* were an elusive, abstracted mystery, then Nuala Fahey was one
much closer to home, though no more comprehendible. She was a riddling
presence in the house, her mild manner at odds with the potent *brujería* Bettina could sense in the woman's blood. This was an old, deep spirit, not some
simple *ama de llaves*, yet in the nine months that Bettina had been living in the
house, Nuala appeared to busy herself with no more than her housekeeping
duties. Cleaning, cooking, the light gardening that Salvador left for her. The
rooms were always dusted and swept, the linens and bedding fresh and sweet-
smelling. Meals appeared when they should, with enough for all who cared to
partake of them. The flower gardens and lawns were well-tended, the veg-
etable patch producing long after the first frost.

She was somewhere in her mid-forties, a tall, handsome woman with
striking green eyes and a flame of red hair only vaguely tamed into a loose bun
at the back of her head. While her wardrobe consisted entirely of men's
clothes—pleated trousers and dress shirts, tweed vests and casual sports jackets—there was nothing mannish about her figure or her demeanor. Yet neither
was she as passive as she might seem. True, her step was light, her voice soft
and low. She might listen more than she spoke, and rarely initiate a conversation as she had this evening, but there was still that undercurrent of *brujería*
that lay like smoldering coals behind her eyes. *La brujería*, and an impression
that while the world might not always fully engage her, something in it certainly amused her.

Bettina had been trying to make sense of the housekeeper ever since they'd
met, but she was no more successful now, nine months on, than she'd been the
first day Nuala opened the front door and welcomed her into Kellygnow, the
old house at the top of the hill that was now her home. *Kellygnow* she learned
after she moved in, meant "the nut wood" in some Gaelic language—though
no one seemed quite sure which one. But there were certainly nut trees on the
hill. Oak, hazel, chestnut.

There were many things Bettina hadn't been expecting about this place
Adelita had found for her to stay. The mystery of Nuala was only one of them.

Kellygnow was much bigger than she'd been prepared for, an enormous rambling structure with dozens of bedrooms, studios, and odd little room-sized nooks, as well as a half-dozen cottages in the woods out back. The property was larger, too—especially for this part of the city—taking up almost forty acres of prime real estate. With the neighboring properties ranging in the million-dollar-and-up range, Bettina couldn't imagine what the house and its grounds were worth. Its neighbors were all owned by stockbrokers and investors, bankers and the CEOs of multinational corporations, celebrities and the nouveau riche—a far cry from the bohemian types Bettina shared her lodgings with.

For Kellygnow was a writers' and artists' colony, founded in the early 1900s by Sarah Hanson, a descendant of the original owner. She had been a respected artist and essayist in her time, a rarity at the turn of the century, but was now better remembered for the haven she had created for her fellow artists and writers.

The colony was the oldest property in the area, standing alone at the top of Handfast Road with a view that would do the Newford Tourist Board's pamphlets proud. There was a tower, four stories high in the northwest corner of the house. From the upper windows of one side you could look down on the city: Ferryside, the river, Foxville, Crowsea, downtown, the canal, the East Side. At night, the various neighborhoods blended into an *Indio* traders' market, the lights spread out like the sparkling trinkets on a hundred blankets. From another window you could see, first the estates that made up the Beaches; below them, rows of tasteful condos blending into the hillside; beyond them, the lakefront properties; and then finally the lake itself, shimmering in the starlight, ice rimming the shore in thick, playful displays of abstract whimsy. Far in the distance the ice thinned out, ending in open water.

The view behind the house was blocked by trees. Hazels and chestnuts. Tamaracks and cedar, birch and pine. Most impressive were the huge towering oaks that, she learned later, were thought to be part of the original growth forest that had once laid claim to all the land in an unbroken sweep from the Kickaha Mountains down to the shores of the lake. These few giants had been spared the axes of homesteaders and lumbermen alike by the property's original owner, Virgil Hanson, whose home had been one of the cottages that still stood out back. It was, Bettina had been told, the oldest building in Newford, a small stone croft topping the wooded hill long before the first Dutch settlers had begun to build along the shores of the river below.

Adelita had never lived in Kellygnow, but before moving back home to Tubac and opening her gallery, she had studied fine art at Butler University and some of her crowd had been residents. It would be the prefect place for Bettina, she said. Let her handle it. She would make a few calls. Everything would be arranged.

"I'm not an artist or a writer," Bettina had said.

"No, but you're an excellent model and in that house, one good model would be more welcome than a dozen of the world's best artists. *Créeme.* Trust me. Only don't tell Mamá or she'll have both our heads."

No, Bettina had thought. Mamá would definitely not approve. Mamá was already upset enough that Bettina was moving. If she were to know that her youngest daughter expected to make her living by being paid to sit for artists, often in the nude, she would be horrified.

Bettina had thought to only stay in the house for as long as it took her to find an apartment in the city. She was given one of the nooks to make her own—a small space under a staircase that opened up into a hidden room twice the size of her bedroom at home. There was a recessed window looking out on the backyard, overhung with ivy on the outside and with just room enough for her to sit on its sill if she pulled her knees up to her chin. There was also a single brass bed with shiny, knobbed posts and a cedar chest at its foot that lent the room a resonant scent. A small pine armoire. A worn, black leather reading chair with a tall glass-shaded lamp beside it, both "borrowed" from the library at some point, she was sure, since they matched its furnishings. And wonder of wonders, a piece of John Early's work: a gray, fired-clay sculpture of the Virgin wearing a quizzical smile, blue-robed and decorated with a halo of porcupine quills cunningly worked into the clay and painted gold. In front of the statue, that first day, she found a half-burned candle—someone had been using the statue as the centerpiece for their own small chapel of the Immaculata, she'd thought at first. Or perhaps they had simply enjoyed candlelight as much as she did.

Either way, she felt welcomed and blessed.

The one week turned into a month. Adelita had been right. The artists were delighted to have her in residence, constantly vying for her time in their studios. They were good company, as were the writers who only emerged from their quarters at odd times for meals or a sudden need to hear a human voice. And if their intentions were sometimes less than honorable—women as well as men—they were quick to respect her wishes and put the incident behind them.

The one month stretched into three, four. She needed no money for either rent or board, and had barely touched the savings she'd brought with her. Most mornings she sat for one or another of the artists, sometimes for a group of them. Her afternoons and evenings were usually her own. At first she explored the city, but when the weather turned colder, she cocooned in the house, reading, listening to music in one or another of the communal living rooms, often spending time in the company of the gardener Salvador and helping him prepare the property for winter.

And she began to trade her fetishes and charms. First to some of those living in the house, then to customers the residents introduced her to. As her *abuela* had taught her, she set no fee, asked for no recompense, but they all gave her something anyway. Mostly money, but sometimes books they thought she would like, or small pieces of original art—sketches, drawings, color studies—which she preferred the most. Her walls were now decorated with her growing hoard of art while a stack of books rose thigh-high from the floor beside her chair.

The few months grew into a half year, and now the house felt like a home.

She was no closer to discovering what had drawn her to this city, what it was that whispered in her bones from the hills to the north, but it didn't seem as immediate a concern as it had when she'd first stepped off the plane, her small suitcase in one hand, her knapsack on her back with its herbs, tinctures, and the raw materials with which she made her fetishes. The need to know was no longer so important. Or perhaps she was growing more patient—a concept that would have greatly amused her *abuela*. She could wait for the mystery to come to her.

As she knew it would. Her visions of what was to come weren't always clear, especially when they related to her, but of this she was sure. She had seen it. Not the details, not when or exactly where, or even what face the mystery would present to her. But she knew it would come. Until then, every day was merely another step in the journey she had undertaken when she first began to learn the ways of the spirit world at the knee of her *abuela*, only now the days took her down a road she no longer recognized, where the braid of her *Indio* and Mexican past became tangled with threads of cultures far less familiar.

But she was accepting of it all, for *la época del mito* had always been a confusing place for her. When she was in myth time, she was often too easily distracted by all the possibilities: that what had been might really be what was to come, that what was to come might be what already was. Mostly she had difficulty with the true face of a thing. She mixed up its spirit with its physical presence. Its true essence with the mask it might be wearing. Its history with its future. It didn't help that Newford was like the desert, a place readily familiar with spirits and ghosts and strange shifts in what things seemed to be. Where many places only held a quiet whisper of the otherwhere, here thousands of voices murmured against one another and sometimes it was hard to make out one from the other.

The house at the top of Handfast Road where she now lived was a particularly potent locale. Kellygnow and its surrounding wild acres appeared to be a crossroads between time zones and spirit zones, something that had seemed charming and pleasantly mysterious until *los lobos* began to squat in its backyard, smoking their cigarettes and watching, watching. Now she couldn't help but wonder if their arrival spelled the end of her welcome here.

"You might not know them," Nuala said as though in response to her worries, "but you called them here all the same."

Bettina shook her head. "I doubt it," she tried, willing it to be true. "They are spirits of this place and I am the stranger."

But Nuala, *la brujería* less hidden in her eyes than Bettina had ever seen it before, shook her head.

"No," she said. "They are as much strangers as you are. They have only been here longer."

Bettina nodded. The shallow rooting of their spirits said as much.

"How do you know this?" she asked.

Nuala hesitated for a long moment before she finally replied. "I recognize them from my childhood. They are spirits of my homeland, only these have been displaced and set to wandering after they made the mistake of following the emigrant ships to this new land. They watched me, too, when I first arrived in Kellygnow."

Bettina regarded her with interest. "What did they want?"

"I never asked, but what do men ever want? For a woman to forsake all and go running with them, out into the wild. For us to lift our skirts and spread our legs for them."

Bettina tried to imagine Nuala in a skirt.

"But they grew tired of waiting," the older woman said. "They went their way and I remained, and I haven't seen them now for many years." She paused, then added, "Until you called to them."

"I didn't call them."

"You didn't have to. You're young and pretty and enchantment runs in your veins as easily as blood. Is it so odd that they come like bees to your flower?"

"I thought they were part of . . . the mystery," Bettina said.

"There's no mystery as to what they want," Nuala told her. "But perhaps I am being unfair. As I said, I've never spoken to them, never asked what they wanted from me. Perhaps they only wished for news of our homeland, of those they'd left behind."

Bettina nodded. Spirits were often hungry for gossip.

"Sometimes," she said, "what one mistakes for spirits are in fact men, traveling in spirit form."

"I've never met such," Nuala told her.

Nuala might not have, but when she was younger, Bettina had. Many of them had been related to her by blood. Her father and her uncles and their friends, *Indios* all, would gather together in the desert in a similar fashion as *los lobos* did in the yard outside the house here. Squatting in a circle, sharing a canteen, smoking their cigarettes, sometimes calling up the spirit of the mescal, swallowing the small buttons that they'd harvested from the dome-shaped cacti in New Mexico and Texas.

Peyoteros, Abuela called them.

At first, Bettina had thought it was a tribal designation—like Yaqui, Apache, Tohono O'odham—but then Abuela had explained how they followed another road into the mystery from the one she and her *abuela* followed, that the peyote buttons they ate, the mescal tea they drank, was how they stepped into *la época del mito*. Bettina decided they were still a tribe, only connected to each other by their visions rather than their genes.

"Where I come from," she told Nuala, "such men seek a deeper understanding of the world and its workings."

"But you are no longer where you come from," Nuala said.

This was true.

"And understand," Nuala went on. "Such beings answer only to themselves. No one holds you personally responsible for their presence. I'm simply making conversation. Offering an observation, nothing more."

"I understand."

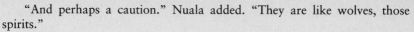
"And perhaps a caution." Nuala added. "They are like wolves, those spirits."

Bettina nodded. *"Los lobos,"* she said.

"Indeed. And what you must remember about wolves is that they cannot be tamed. They might seem friendly, but in their hearts they remain wild creatures. Feral. Incorrigibly amoral. It's not that they are evil. They simply see the world other than we do, see it in a way that we can never wholly understand."

She seemed to know a great deal about them, Bettina thought, for someone who had never spoken with them.

"And they are angry," Nuala said after a moment.

"Angry?" Bettina asked. "With whom?"

Nuala shrugged. "With me, certainly."

"But why?"

Again there was that long moment of hesitation.

"Because I have what they lack," Nuala finally said. "I have a home. A place in this new world that I can call my own."

The housekeeper smiled then. Her gaze became mild, *la brujería* in her eyes diminishing into a distant smolder once more.

"It's late," she said. "I should be in bed." She moved to the door, pausing in the threshold. "Aren't you sitting for Chantal in the morning? You should try to get some rest yourself."

"I will."

"Good. Sleep well."

Bettina nodded. *"Gracias,"* she said. "You, too."

But she was already speaking to Nuala's back.

What an odd conversation, she thought as she went over to the table and began to put the *milagros* back into the envelope she had taken them from earlier. Nuala, who so rarely offered an opinion, little say started a conversation, had been positively gregarious this evening.

Bettina's gaze strayed to the window. She couldn't see beyond the dark pane, but she remembered. After a moment, she took down someone's parka from the peg where it hung by the door and put it on. It was far too big for her, but style wasn't the issue here. Warmth was. Giving the kitchen a last look, she slipped out the door.

It was already colder than it had been earlier. Frosted grass crunched under her shoes as she walked to where the men had been watching the house. There was no sign now that they'd ever been. They'd even taken their cigarette butts with them when they'd withdrawn from the yard.

She considered how they would have gone. First into the trees, then down the steep slope to where these few wild acres came up hard against the shoulders of the city. From there, on to the distant mountains. Or perhaps not. Perhaps they made their home here, in the city.

She closed her eyes, imagining them loping through the city's streets. Had they even kept to human form, or was there now a wolf pack running through the city? Perhaps a scatter of wild dogs since dogs would be less likely to attract unwanted attention. Or had they taken to the air as hawks, or crows?

Knowing as little as she did about them, it was impossible to say.

She walked on, past the gazebo, into the trees where, in places, snow lay in thick drifts. The cottages were all dark, their occupants asleep. A thin trail of smoke rose from the chimney of Virgil Hanson's, the only one of the six to have a working fireplace. She regarded it curiously for a moment, wondering who was inside. In all the months that she had been living here, that cottage had stood empty.

Past the buildings, the trees grew more closely together. She followed a narrow trail through the undergrowth, snow constantly underfoot now, but it had a hard crust under a few inches of the more recent fall, and held her weight.

There was no indication that anyone had been this way before her. At least not since the last snowfall.

There was a spot at the back of the property, an enormous jut of granite that pushed out of the wooded slope and offered a stunning view of the city spread out for miles, all the way north to the foothills of the mountains. Bettina was careful as she climbed up the back of it. Though there was no snow, she remembered large patches of ice from when she'd been here a week or so ago. In the summer, they would sometimes sit out near the edge, but she was feeling nowhere near so brave today. She went only so far as she needed to get a view of the mountains, then straightened up and looked north.

At first she couldn't tell what was wrong. When it came to her, her legs began to tremble and she shivered in her borrowed parka with its long dangling sleeves.

"*Dios mío,*" she said, her voice a hoarse whisper.

There were no lights from the city to be seen below. None at all.

She felt dizzy and backed slowly away until she could clutch the trunk of one of the tamaracks that grew up around the rock. For a long moment, it was all that kept her upright. She looked back, past the edge of the stone where normally the glow of the city would rise up above the tops of the trees, but the sky was the dark of a countryside that had never known light pollution. The stars felt as though they were closer to her than she'd ever seen them in the city. They were desert stars, displaced to this land, as feral as *los lobos*.

Myth time, she thought. She'd drifted into *la época del mito* without knowing it, walked into a piece of the past where the city didn't exist yet, or perhaps into the days to come when it was long gone.

"It is easier to stray into another's past than it is to find one's way out again," someone said.

The voice came from the trees, the speaker invisible in the undergrowth and shadows, but she didn't have to see him to know that he was one of *los lobos*. "We are wise women," Abuela liked to say. "Not because we are wise, but because we seek wisdom." And then she'd smile, adding, "Which in the end, is what makes us seem so wise to others." But Bettina didn't feel particularly wise tonight, for she knew what he'd said was true. It was not so uncommon to step unawares into myth time and never emerge again into the present.

"Who's to say I strayed?" she said, putting on a much braver face than she felt.

With a being such as this, it was always better to at least pretend you knew what you were doing. Still, she wished now that she'd taken the time to invoke the protection of Saint Herve before going out into the night. He would know how to deal with wolves—those who walked on two legs, as well as those who ran on four.

El lobo stepped from out of the shadows, a tall, lean form, smelling of cigarette smoke and musk. There was enough light for her to catch the look of mild amusement in his features and to see that he was indeed, oh so handsome. After all those nights of watching him from the window, his proximity, the smell and too-alive presence of him, was like an enchantment. She had to stop herself from stepping close, into his embrace. But she had enough *brujería* of her own to know that there was no enchantment involved. It was simply the man he was. Dangerous, perhaps, and far too handsome.

"Ah," he said. "I see. And so it was simple delight at your success and not surprise that made you dizzy."

Bettina shrugged.

"And now?" he asked.

"Now, nothing. I'm going home to bed."

"Indeed."

He leaned back against a tree, arms crossed, smiling.

Bettina sighed, knowing that *el lobo* was now waiting for her to step back into her own world, confident she wouldn't be able to. And then what? When he decided she was helpless, what would he do? Perhaps nothing. Perhaps he would bargain with her, his help in exchange for something that would seem like *poquito, nada*, yet it would prove to cost her dearly once he collected. Or perhaps his kind had other, less pleasant uses for *las curanderas tontas* who were so foolish as to stumble into such a situation in the first place. She remembered what Nuala had said about the wolves who'd come to watch her, how they were waiting for her to lift her skirts, to spread her legs. Handsome or not, she would not let it happen, no matter how attracted to him she might be.

She stifled another sigh as the quiet lengthened between them.

He could wait forever, she knew, amused and patient. *¿Pero, qué tiene?* She could be patient, too. And she could find her own way home. All she needed was a moment to compose herself, enough quiet for her to be able to concentrate on the threads of her spirit that still connected her to the world she'd inadvertently left behind. She needed only the time to find them, to gather them up and follow them back home again.

Behind *el lobo* there was movement in the forest, a small shape that darted in between the trees too quickly for her to see clearly. There was only a flash of small, pale limbs. Of large, luminous eyes. Here, then gone. A child, she thought at first, then shook her head. No, not in this place. More likely it had been some *espíritu. Un deunde*—an imp, an elf. Some creature of the otherwhere.

Eh, *bueno*. She would not let it bother her.

She unzipped the front of her parka and let it hang open.

"It's warmer here," she said.

El lobo nodded. His nostrils flared, testing the air. "The air tastes of autumn."

But what autumn? Bettina wanted to ask. Though perhaps the true question should be, whose autumn? And how far away did it lie from her own time? But then a more immediate riddle rose up to puzzle her.

"You're not speaking English," she said.

"Neither are you."

It was true. She was speaking Spanish while he spoke whatever language it was that he spoke. It held no familiarity, yet she could understand him perfectly.

"*¿Pero, como . . . ?*"

He smiled. "Enchantment," he said.

"Ah . . ."

She smiled back, feeling more confident. Of course. This was myth time. But while he might appear mysterious and strong, in this place her own *brujería* was potent as well. She wasn't some hapless tourist who had wandered too far into uncertain territory. The landscape might be unfamiliar, but she was no stranger to *la época del mito*. She might find it confusing at times, but she refused to let it frighten her.

El lobo pushed away from the tree. "Come," he said. "Let me show you something."

She shrugged and followed him into the forest, retracing the way she'd come earlier, only here there was no snow. There were no outlying cottages, either. No gazebo, no house with its tower nestled in between the tall trees. But there was a hut made of woven branches and cedar boughs where Virgil Hanson's original cottage stood in her world, and further on, a break in the undergrowth where the main house should have been—a clearing of sorts, rough and uncultivated, but recognizably the dimensions of the house's gardens and lawn.

Bettina paused for a moment at the edge of the trees, both enchanted and mildly disoriented at how the familiar had been made strange. She could hear rustlings in the undergrowth—*los mitos chicos y los espíritus* scurrying about their secret business—but caught no more glimpses of any of them.

El lobo took her to where, in her time, Salvador kept his carp pond. Here the neat masonry of its low walls had been replaced by a tumble of stones, piled haphazardly around the small pool water, but the hazel trees still leaned over the pool on one side. Lying on the grass along the edges of the pond was a clutter of curious objects. Shed antlers and posies of dried and fresh flowers. Shells and colored beads braided into leather bracelets and necklaces. Baskets woven from willow, grass, and reeds, filled with nuts and berries. On the stones themselves small carvings had been left, like bone and wood *milagros*. Votive offerings, but to whom? Or perhaps, rather, to what?

When they reached the edge of the pool, her companion pointed to something in the water. Bettina couldn't make out what it was at first. Then she realized it was an enormous fish of some sort. Not one of Salvador's carp, though she'd heard they could grow to this size.

The fish floated in the water, motionless. She had the urge to poke at it with one of the antlers, to see if it would move.

"Is . . . is it dead?" she asked.

"Sleeping."

Bettina blinked. Did fish sleep? she wondered, then put the question aside. This was *la época del mito*. Here the world operated under a different set of natural laws.

"What sort of a fish is it?" she asked.

"A salmon."

She glanced at him, hearing something expectant in his voice, as though its being a salmon should mean something to her.

"And so?" she said.

El lobo smiled. "This is a part of the mystery you seek."

"What do you know of me or what I might be looking for?"

"Of you, little enough. Of the other . . ." He shrugged. "Only that the older mysteries play at being salmon and such in order to keep their wisdoms hidden and safe."

Bettina waited, but nothing more was forthcoming. Fine, she thought. Speak in riddles, but you'll only be speaking to yourself. Ignoring him, she leaned closer to look at the sleeping fish. There seemed to be nothing remarkable about it, except for the size of it in such a small pool.

"If it were to wake," *el lobo* went on. "If it were to speak, and you were to understand its words, it would change everything. *You* would be changed forever."

"Changed how?"

"In what you were, what you are, what you will be. The mystery that you follow could well swallow you whole, then. Swallow you up and spit you out again as something unrecognizable because you would no longer be protected by your identity."

Bettina lifted her gaze from the pool and its motionless occupant to look at him.

"Is this true?" she asked.

As if he would tell her the truth. But he surprised her and gave what seemed to be an honest answer.

"Not now, perhaps. Not at this very moment. But it could be, if you bide here too long. We should go—before *an bradán* wakes."

An bradán. She understood it to mean the salmon, but whatever enchantment had been translating their conversation passed over those two words. Perhaps because they named the fish as well as described it?

"Would that be so terrible?" she was about to ask.

For she found herself wanting to be here to see the salmon wake. To call it by name. *An bradán.* To watch its slow lazy movements through the water and hear it speak. To be changed.

But the question died stillborn as she turned back to the pool. On the far side of the water, a stranger was standing—a tall, older man, as dark-haired and dark-skinned as *el lobo*, but she knew immediately that he wasn't one of her companion's *compadres. Los lobos* were very male and there was something almost androgynous about the angular features of the stranger. He seemed to be a priest, in his black cassock and white collar, and what might be a rosary dangling from the fingers of one hand. There was an old-fashioned cut to his cassock, his hair, the style of his dusty boots. It was as though he'd stepped here directly from one of the old missions back home. Stepped here, not only from the desert, but from the past as well.

His gaze rested thoughtfully on her and for a long moment she couldn't speak. Then he looked down at the water. She followed his gaze to see the salmon stirring, but before it could wake, before it could speak, *el lobo* pulled her away from the fountain and the priest, out of myth time into the cold night of her own world, her own time.

They stood beside Salvador's carp pond, the water frozen. From nearby, the windows of the house cast squares of pale light across the lawn. Bettina shivered and drew the loose flaps of her borrowed parka closer about her, holding them shut with her folded arms.

"Who was that man?" she asked.

"I saw no man," *el lobo* replied.

"There was a padre . . . standing across from us, on the other side of the pool . . ."

Her companion smiled. "There was no man," he said. "Only you and I and the spirits of the otherwhere."

"*Bueno.* Then it was a spirit I saw, for he was nothing like you or your friends."

His smile returned, mildly mocking. "And what are we like?"

Bettina merely shrugged.

"You think of us as wolves."

"So now you read minds?" Bettina asked.

"I don't need to. I can read eyes. You are wary of us, of our wild nature."

"I'm wary of any stranger I meet in the woods at night."

He ignored that. "Perhaps you are wise to be wary. We are not such simple creatures as your Spanish wolves."

Bettina raised her eyebrows. "Then what are you?"

"In the old land, they called us *an felsos,* but it was out of fear. The same way they spoke of the fairies as their Good Neighbors."

They were no longer in myth time, so there was no convenient translation for the term he'd used to describe himself. She still spoke Spanish, but he had switched to an accented English. She hadn't noticed until this moment.

"What do you want from me?" she asked.

"I could be a friend."

"And if I don't want a wolf for a friend?"

Again that smile of his. "Did I say I was your friend?"

Before she could respond, he turned and stepped away. Not simply into the forest, but deeper and farther away, into *la época del mito*. Bettina had no intention of following him, though his sudden disappearance woke a whisper of disappointment in her.

She stood for a long moment, looking down at the frozen surface of the pond, then into the trees. Finally she shook her head and began to make her way back to the house. As she crossed the frozen lawn, she caught a flutter of movement in one of the second-floor windows, as though a curtain had been held open and had now fallen back into place. It took her a moment to remember whose window it was. Nuala's.

She kept on walking, eager for the warmth inside. In the few brief moments since *el lobo* had brought her back into her own time, the bitter cold had already worked its way under her borrowed parka and was nibbling deep at her bones. But she was barely aware of her discomfort.

There was so much to think upon.

Qué extraño. How strange the night had turned.

2

Musgrave Wood

We live in a fallen world where good people suffer
because of the actions of others.
—OVERHEARD AT A FUNERAL

1

TWO NIGHTS LATER; TUESDAY, JANUARY 13

The media couldn't stop discussing the see-sawing weather.

Not so long ago, it was all talk of the Christmas thaw, but then it snowed again last week and for the past two days the deep freeze that had gripped the city through most of December had descended once more. The thermometer registered a bitter minus-twenty Celsius yesterday as commuters began their exodus back into the 'burbs. By midnight the mercury had dropped to almost minus-thirty, not taking into account the wind-chill factor. With the biting northern winds factored in, you could subtract at least another twenty degrees tonight.

It was the kind of cold that gave Ellie Jones nightmares. She'd dream she was one of the homeless people they were trying to help with the Angel Out-reach program, that she was stumbling for block upon frozen block on numbed feet, looking for a warm grate, an alleyway, anyplace she could get out of the wind, away from the cold. When she finally woke, shivering and chilled, it was only to find that sometime during the night she'd kicked her comforter off the bed. All she had to do was pull it back up under her chin and she'd be warm again.

But it didn't work that way for the people who had no home.

It was cold in the van, too, as she and Tommy Raven made their rounds.

The ancient vehicle's heater was set on high, but the lukewarm air it pumped barely made a dent against the cold. Of course in the summer you couldn't get the stupid thing to shut off, but Ellie would gladly trade a sweltering summer's night for this cold. The metal walls of the van kept out the wind, but she could still see her breath. Frost fogged the edges of the window, crawling across the glass with dogged persistence.

"Tell me again why we're doing this," she said as she scraped her side window, creating a miniature snowfall that fell across her legs and the seat.

Tommy smiled. "I don't know about you, but I'm only in it to get rich and meet girls."

She arched an eyebrow and Tommy's smile widened.

"Or was that when I was thinking of starting up a rock band?" he said, returning his attention to the street ahead.

"I didn't know you were a musician. What instrument do you play?"

"I'm not. I don't. That's why the band never got off the ground and I'm driving this van tonight."

She punched him in the arm, but she laughed. In this kind of work you'd take the smallest sliver of humor and play it out. You needed it to help balance the way your heart broke a dozen times a night.

Tommy slowed down near the mouth of an alley, tires crunching on the hard snow that edged the pavement. Ellie almost didn't see the man, huddled up between stacks of newspaper that were waiting to be recycled. By the time Tommy stopped the van, the man had gotten to his feet and shuffled off, deeper into the alley. Ellie pulled her hat down so that the flannel side flaps covered her ears and got out. The blast of cold wind that hit her when she stepped onto the pavement almost made her lose her balance—the streets were like wind tunnels because of the tall office buildings rearing up on either side. She peered down the alley and saw that the man had already disappeared from view. Shrugging, she left a sandwich in a brown bag, a Styrofoam cup of coffee, and a blanket where he'd been sitting.

She knew the man would be back as soon as they drove off. The only reason he'd fled was because he was afraid they'd try to take him to a shelter. It was no use telling some of them that they'd only take them if they wanted to go. At this point they didn't trust anyone.

The van felt almost toasty when she was back inside.

"What do you think?" Tommy said. "You want to swing back to Bennett Street and see if that kid's changed her mind?"

Her name was Chrissy. Fifteen, shapeless in the old parka they'd given her a couple of nights ago, not even close to pretty or some pimp would have already turned her out. Ellie had talked to her a half-dozen times already, trying to get her into one of the programs that Angel administered from her Grasso Street storefront office, but with no luck.

"She won't have," Ellie said. "But I'm willing to give it another shot."

Tommy sighed. "She's a disaster waiting to happen."

Ellie nodded. If the weather didn't get her, some predator would. You didn't have to be pretty to be a victim.

They stopped on Palm Street where a covey of prostitutes, shivering as much from their need for a fix as from the cold, flagged them down for coffee and sandwiches. Then it was on to the Oxford Theater where they'd seen Chrissy panhandling earlier in the evening. When they rolled to a stop in front of the building they saw that the girl was no longer hanging around. That made sense. The theater crowd had gone home by now, taking with them the possibility of their handing out a bit of spare change. Ellie hoped Chrissy had found a place to spend the night, preferably someplace warm and safe, but what were the chances? More likely she was huddled on a hot air grate, too scared to close her eyes and sleep.

"Hang on," Ellie said as Tommy was about to pull away from the curb. "What's that?"

At first glance she'd thought it was only garbage, piled up in the snow outside the theater, but now she saw that there was a body lying alongside the green garbage bags. She couldn't tell the sex or age. All she knew was that it was too still.

"Maybe you better let me check it out," Tommy said, but she didn't pay any attention to him.

Before he could stop her, she had her door open and was out on the sidewalk, running to where the body lay. A man. Obviously a street veteran, so it was impossible to judge his age. He could have been anywhere from his early thirties to his late fifties.

She went down on one knee and put a hand to his throat. No pulse. That was when she saw the yellowish liquid dribbling from the side of his mouth. Oh, shit. He'd choked on his own vomit.

"Call 911!" she cried to Tommy.

Pulling off her gloves, she worked his mouth open and scooped the vomit out with her fingers. Her own stomach gave a lurch. The liquid was thick and slimy and clung to her fingers, but after three or four tries, she got most of it out. He still wasn't breathing. Wiping her hand clean, she reached in again, finger hooked this time, feeling for whatever was blocking his air passage. She couldn't find it.

A quick glance to the van told her Tommy was still on the phone.

She returned her attention to the man, opened his coat. Kneeling astride his legs, she placed the heel of one hand just above his navel, the other hand on top of it, and gave a half-dozen quick upward thrusts. This time when she swept his mouth with her finger, she found a wedge of some undefined spongy matter and managed to hook it out. When he still didn't begin breathing again, she started CPR.

First the chest compressions. After fifteen of them, she ventilated his lungs, gagging on the taste of his vomit. It was all she could do to not throw up herself. After two ventilations she went back to the chest compressions. Four cycles of this and she paused long enough to check for a pulse. Still nothing, so she continued with the CPR.

All she could taste, all she could smell, was his puke.

Don't even think about it, she told herself. Like it was possible not to.

The fourth time she ventilated his lungs, there was a gurgle deep in his throat, a faint rasp of breath. She paused, put two fingers against his carotid artery and checked his pulse again. Her hand was so cold, it was hard to tell. She put her cheek close to his mouth. Held her breath. Tried to ignore the sour taste in her own mouth. She felt a faint warmth on her cheek.

He was breathing.

She got off his legs and then Tommy was there to help her roll him into the recovery position—on his side, one leg pulled up.

"Here," Tommy said. "I've got some blankets."

She wanted to help cover the man up, but her own nausea was too much. Stumbling away, she threw up against the side of the building. Now the taste of vomit went all the way down her throat. She knew it was her own, but it still made her retch again. Nothing but a dry heave this time.

She leaned her head against the brick wall of the theater, weak, stomach still lurching.

"Try some of this," Tommy said.

He appeared at her side, put an arm around her shoulders to support her and offered her a cup of coffee. It was the only liquid they had in the van. All they carried was the few necessities to help the street people get through another night of bitter winter cold. Coffee and sandwiches. Blankets. Parkas, winter boots, mittens, scarves.

She took a sip of the coffee, gargled with it. Spit it out. Rinsed her mouth again. Tommy had cooled it down with a lot of milk, but because of the taste in her mouth, the milk seemed to have gone off. Her stomach gave another lurch. Tommy regarded her with concern.

"I . . ." She cleared her throat, spat. "I'm okay. How's he doing?"

Tommy returned to the homeless man, bundled up with blankets now.

"Still breathing," he said after checking the man's pulse. "How're *you* doing?"

Ellie tried to smile. "Well, they never tell you about this kind of thing when you take that CPR course, do they?"

They could hear an approaching siren now. Ellie pushed herself to her feet and went to reclaim her gloves. Setting the coffee down on the pavement, she thrust her hands into a snowbank, dried them on her jeans. She put on her gloves. Tossing the remainder of the coffee away, she stuffed the empty cup into the mouth of one of the garbage bags.

"Got any mouthwash?" she asked.

" 'Fraid not," Tommy said. "I must've left it at home with that love letter I got from Cindy Crawford this morning." He dug about in the pocket of his parka. "How about a mint?"

"You're a lifesaver."

"No, these are," he said and handed her a roll of peppermint Life Savers. Ellie smiled.

The ambulance arrived before the mint had a chance to completely dissolve in her mouth. Retreating to the van, they let the paramedics take over. They stood shoulder-to-shoulder, leaning against the side of the vehicle to watch as the medics lifted the man onto a stretcher, fitted him with an oxygen mask and IV, carried him back into the ambulance.

"My old man died like that," Tommy said. "So drunk he passed out on the pavement. Choked to death on his own puke."

"I didn't know that. I'm sorry."

"Don't be."

Ellie shot him a surprised look.

Tommy sighed. "I know how that sounds. It's just . . ." He looked away, but not before she saw the pain in his eyes.

Sometimes Ellie thought she was the only person in the world who'd had a normal childhood. Loving parents. A good home. They hadn't been rich, but they hadn't wanted for anything either. There'd been no drinking in the house. No fights. No one had tried to abuse her, either at home or anywhere else. She could only imagine what it would be like to grow up otherwise.

She knew that Tommy had gone through one of Angel's programs, but she'd never really considered what had driven him to the streets, what nightmare he'd had to endure before Angel could find and help him. Most of the people who volunteered for Angel Outreach and the other programs had come from abusive environments. The ones who stuck it out, who got past the pain and learned how to trust and care again, almost invariably wanted to give something back. To offer a helping hand the way it had been offered to them when it didn't seem like anybody could possibly care.

But they'd still had to go through some kind of hell in the first place.

"Ten years ago," Tommy said, "if that had been my old man, I'd have let him lie there and just walked away. But not now. I wouldn't have liked him any better, but I'd have done what you did."

Ellie didn't know what to say.

Tommy turned to look at her. "I guess we've all got our war stories."

Except she didn't. She'd hadn't thought of it before, but most of the people she volunteered with must think that she, too, carried some awful truth around inside her. That, just as they had, she'd been through the nightmare and managed to come through the other side well enough to be able—to *want*—to help others. But the only war stories she knew were from the people she tried to help. She had none of her own.

Before she could think of a way to try to explain this, a police cruiser pulled up. Tommy pushed away from the van.

"I'll deal with them," he said.

Ellie let him go. She watched him talk to the two uniformed officers when they got out of their cruiser. The ambulance pulled away, siren off, cherry lights still flashing. When it rounded a corner, she turned back to the van, but paused before getting in. Even in this severe cold, the incident had managed to gather a half-dozen onlookers. A couple of obviously homeless men stood near where she'd thrown up. The others probably lived in one of the buildings nearby, cheap apartment complexes that had long since seen better days.

Opening the side door of the van, she put a couple of sandwiches in the pocket of her parka, then poured two coffees. She took them over to the homeless men. They hesitated for a moment, looked from her face to the legend on the side of the van before accepting the coffees and sandwiches.

"Who was it?" one of the men asked.

"I didn't get his name," she told them.

The other man took a sip of his coffee. "I'll bet it was Howard. Stupid fuck'd sleep anywhere."

"Would you like a ride to a shelter?" Ellie asked.

"Come on, pretty lady," the second man said. "Do *we* look that stupid?"

No matter how cold it got, some of the homeless would never go to a shelter. They were afraid of what little they had being stolen, of something bad happening to them—like the possibility of freezing to death was a good thing, but what could you do? Some were so used to being outside, they couldn't sleep indoors anymore. Like feral alleycats, the close, heated confines of a shelter made them strike out in panic, attacking a worker, each other, sometimes trashing the place.

"Tell Angel thanks for the coffee and the grub," the first man told her.

They turned their backs and headed off down the block, shoulders hunched against the cold.

"I will," she said.

"It's a wonder they survive."

Ellie looked at the man who'd spoken. He was one of the onlookers she'd noticed earlier, a tall, dark-skinned man who towered over her own five-ten frame. His gray overcoat was almost as threadbare as those of the two homeless men, but it didn't have the same slept-in, ratty look. Like her, he was wearing a hunter's cap, the ear flaps pulled down, except his was real sheepskin; hers was only a quilted wool. His eyes were alert, his features knife-sharp and aged by the passage of time, not alcohol abuse and hard living. Even with the cold, his overcoat was unbuttoned, flapping in the wind. He wore no scarf.

"It scares me," she said. "We've already had four homeless people die of exposure this year."

"That you know of."

She gave him a sharp look, then sighed. "That we know of," she agreed.

There were places in the city where a body could easily remain undiscovered until the spring thaw. There'd been one last year in the Tombs, half-eaten by rats and wild dogs by the time someone stumbled over it. Her stomach went all queasy again, just thinking about it.

"Do you have any more of that coffee?" the man asked.

"Sure."

She tried to place his accent as she led the way back to the van, but couldn't. His voice had a husky quality—like someone unused to speaking, or uncomfortable with the language. She also got the impression that he was well-educated, though she couldn't have said why. But it would have been some time ago, she decided, when the overcoat was still new.

After drawing him a coffee from the urn, she started to fill a second cup for herself, then quickly changed her mind. She didn't much care for black coffee, but the thought of adding milk to it made her feel nauseous again.

"Here," the man said. "Have a nip of this."

He took a silver flask from the inside pocket of his jacket and held it out to her. Just what she needed with the way she was feeling—a shot of cheap whiskey. But the peppermint she'd been sucking on earlier had lost its effect and anything would be better than this sour taste in her mouth and throat.

"Thanks."

She took a sip, bracing herself, but the liquid went down smooth as silk, with the full body of a fine brandy. Not until it had settled in her stomach did she realize the kick it had. She gasped and her eyes began to tear. But a fluttering warmth spread through her and the sour taste was finally gone. The liqueur held a faint bouquet of honey and herbs, of a field of wildflowers. It was like drinking a piece of summer and for a moment she almost thought she could hear the buzz of bees, feel the heat of a hot summer's day.

"Wow," she said and peered into the mouth of the flask. She caught a glimpse of a light, yellowish-amber liquid. "What *is* this stuff?"

"Metheglin," the man told her. "A kind of Welsh whiskey made from hops and honey. Have some more," he added when she started to hand the flask back.

Ellie did, this time rolling the liquid around in her mouth before finally swallowing it. She looked down at the flask, noting the fine filigree worked into the metal before her eyes teared up again. She drew in a sharp breath, savoring the bite of the cold as it hit the roof of her mouth.

"So where would you find it in a liquor store?" she asked. "Under whiskeys or . . . you said it was made from hops. That's like beer, right?"

Except she'd never tasted either a whiskey or a beer that was this good.

The man shook his head. "Can't be bought, I'm afraid. A friend of mine makes it and gives me the odd bottle."

"Nice friend to have."

"All friends are good to have."

"Well, sure . . . I just meant . . ."

"I understand," he said as her voice trailed off. "Sometimes I am too literal for my own good."

Ellie handed him the flask and watched it vanish back under his coat. He took a sip of his coffee and smiled at her over the top of the brim. Amiable and not in the least threatening, but there was something odd about him all the same, something she couldn't quite put her finger on.

What *was* his story? She didn't think he was a street person, but he didn't really fit in this neighborhood either. It was something in how he stood, in the cut of his clothes—neither belonged in the cheap apartments to be found around here. His coat was obviously tailor-made—old and worn, it was true, but it hadn't come off a rack. It fit him too well. And that flask was quality silverwork, an antique, probably, and worth a small fortune. It wasn't something a street person would be carrying around.

But then you met all kinds on the street and who was to say what kind of bad luck had come his way? She'd served coffee to men who had been worth millions as well as to those who'd never had more than a few dollars to their name in their whole lives. Some were still proud; some pretended they'd chosen this life. Some had given up all pretense, or simply didn't care anymore. Which was he?

She was about to break one of Angel's cardinal rules and ask what had happened to put him on the street when Tommy joined them.

"The police want to ask you a couple of things," he said.

She gave him a questioning look.

"Nothing serious," he told her. "They just need a few more details to finish their report—if you're up for it."

"Sure."

She tossed a wave to the man and he gave her a grave nod in return. That was another thing, she thought as she walked away. He didn't act like a street person either. He didn't act like he even belonged in this century, though where that idea had come from, she couldn't say. But she'd met people like that before, men and women who seemed displaced in time. Or not to belong to any time. She remembered a boy in art school who'd been completely oblivious to the twentieth century. Walked everywhere, didn't watch TV, didn't even have a radio. He'd been amazed by the very idea of acrylic paints. And photocopying. And computers.

Only that wasn't really it either. Something about the man with the silver flask simply niggled at the back of her mind, the way a familiar face or forgotten name will. Not that she'd ever seen him before. It was just . . . something.

When she returned from the police cruiser, the stranger had left and there was only Tommy, sitting inside the van, waiting for her. She got in on the passenger's side and put her gloved hands up to the heat vent. Right now the vaguely warm air felt as strong as the heat put out by a woodstove. Somehow she'd forgotten all about the cold—at least she had until she'd walked from the police cruiser back to the van and the harsh winds made a point of reminding her with a fierceness that almost blew her off her feet again.

"Who was your friend?" Tommy asked.

Ellie shrugged. "He didn't say."

Tommy gave her an odd look, then shrugged.

"I haven't seen him around before," he said.

"Me, either. I'm not even all that sure he's a street person."

Tommy smiled. "Not everybody out at this time of night is."

"I know. It's just . . . he was strange."

Tommy raised his eyebrows.

"Have you ever heard of metheglin?" Ellie asked.

"Nope. What is it—some new kind of drug?"

Ellie shook her head. "No, it's more like a liqueur. He said it was Welsh, that it was made from honey and . . ."

Her voice trailed off as her gaze alit on a small business card lying on the dashboard in front of her. She took off a glove and picked it up. The card read:

MUSGRAVE WOOD

17 Handfast Road

"Where did this come from?" she asked, passing it over.

Tommy shook his head. "I've no idea."

"That man—was he in the van?"

"Not while I was here."

Tommy turned the card over in his hand. There was nothing on the reverse.

"Handfast Road," he said. "That's in the Beaches, isn't it? Up on the hill?"

"I think so."

"Where all the fat cats live."

Ellie nodded and took the card back. She pointed at the words "Musgrave Wood."

"So is that a person or a place?" she asked.

"I'd say person."

"But what kind of a given name is Musgrave?"

"Good point," Tommy said. "Maybe it's a business. Though I've got an aunt named Juniper Creek."

"Really?"

"Would I lie to you?"

"Yes."

Tommy's family seemed to include a veritable mob of aunts. They all had unusual names, dispensed folk wisdoms at the drop of a hat, and Ellie had never met a single one of them. Sometimes she suspected Tommy hadn't either. She looked at the card again.

"What's that little design?" she asked. "It seems familiar."

Tommy leaned over to have another look, then shrugged. "I don't know. Judging from the ribbonwork, I'd say it's something Celtic. I think I saw something like it on one of those Celtic harp albums Megan's playing all the time."

"You're right. And it's on more than one. I wonder if it means something."

"Sure it does. It's a secret code for 'Here there be Celtic harp music.' "

Ellie laughed. "Of course. What else?"

Then something else occurred to her.

"There's no phone number," she said. "Isn't that weird?"

Tommy smiled. "Anything is weird if you think about it long enough. Like why are our noses designed so that they'll drip right into our mouths?"

"Thank you for sharing that."

She flicked the edge of the card with a fingernail. The man she'd been talking to couldn't have put it on the dash, not with the doors and windows of the van closed the way they'd been. All the same, she was sure the card had come from him. He had to have opened the door and dropped it on the dash when Tommy was with the police and she was bringing coffee to the two homeless men. But that still didn't explain why he'd left it. Or what they were supposed to do with it.

She started to toss the card back where she'd found it, then stuck it in her pocket instead.

"Well," she said. She leaned back into her seat and buckled up her seatbelt. "It's still cold as hell out there and people need our help. The mystery of this card's just going to have to wait."

Tommy nodded. He put the van in gear, checked for traffic, then pulled away from the curb.

"Little mysteries," he said. "They're good for the soul."

"How so?"

"They keep us guessing."

"And that's a good thing?"

"Well, sure. Mysteries break the patterns we impose upon the world—or maybe let us see them more clearly for a change."

"One of your aunts tell you that?"

"I think it was Aunt Serendipity."

"Of course."

Ellie wasn't particularly fond of mysteries or puzzles herself. She always liked to know where she stood, how things fit. The fact that the universe wasn't always so obliging never stopped her from trying to keep everything in its place, lined up, just the way it was supposed to be.

"And speaking of mysteries," Tommy went on, "here's another one for you."

She turned to look at him.

"What's a quick way to tell if you're dealing with a transvestite or a real woman?"

Ellie shook her head. "I give up," she said, and waited for the punchline.

"You check for an Adam's apple," Tommy said.

"I don't get the joke."

"It's not a joke," Tommy told her. "That guy you were talking to . . ."

The niggling feeling she'd had earlier returned, then vanished with a snap of understanding.

"He didn't have one," she said.

Tommy nodded. "In fact, *he*'s a rather mannish *she*. I was surprised that you hadn't noticed."

"So why do you think she's walking around at this time of night, pretending to be a man?"

Tommy shrugged. "Why not?"

Ellie nodded slowly. Sure. Why not, indeed? On a one-to-ten scale of strangeness, it barely registered as a one. What a city this was.

2

WEDNESDAY MORNING, JANUARY 14

Hunter Cole stood at the cash in Gypsy Records. Leaning on the counter amid a clutter of invoices and record company catalogs, he stared out the big front window, only half-listening to the music playing on the store's sound system: a solo album by Karan Casey, the singer from Solas. He should have been enjoying the CD, but it could barely keep his attention today, little say engage it.

He couldn't fault the music; the trouble lay with him and nothing seemed to help. Not the music. And certainly not the weather.

Early this morning the latest cold snap had broken, but now it was snowing again. Big lazy flakes drifted by the display window, blurring the view he had of Williamson Street. For the way he was feeling, it should have been raining. A steady, depressing downpour—the kind of relentless precipitation that eventually overwhelmed even the most cheerful soul with its sheer volume and persistence. The snow was too postcard-pretty. It hid the ugliness, rounding off all the sharp edges until even a heartless behemoth like this city could seem to hold something good in it. But the softness, the prettiness . . . it was all a lie. Maybe you couldn't see them, but the sharp edges remained under the snow nevertheless, waiting to catch you unawares and cut you where it hurt.

Ria had still moved out. Four weeks and counting. He had a Christmas present for her, wrapped up and sitting on a shelf in his office at the back of the store, that he doubted he'd ever give to her now.

He was still in a rut—the same one he'd been in before he'd even thought of buying the store a few years ago—only now it ran deeper.

Buying the store. That had been a mistake.

Gypsy Records got its name from John Butler, a short barrel of a man without even a pretense of Romany blood running through his veins. Butler had begun his business out of the back of a hand-drawn cart that gypsied its way through the city's streets for years, always keeping just one step ahead of the municipal licensing board's agents. The store carried the usual best-sellers, but the lifeblood of its sales were more obscure titles—imports, and albums produced by independent record labels. They still carried vinyl, new and used, and they did brisk business with best-sellers, but most of their sales came from back-catalog CDs: country and folk, worldbeat, jazz, and whatever else you weren't likely to find in the chain stores.

Buying the store hadn't seemed like a mistake at first. Music was in his blood and he'd been working here for years. A true vinyl junkie, he'd always dreamed of opening his own place, so when John made him the offer that couldn't be refused, it had seemed like the best thing that could ever have happened to him. But on a day like this, when he faced slumping sales and his footsteps rang hollowly in an apartment he no longer shared with the person he'd been expecting to be with for the rest of his life, it all seemed so pathetic. He was thirty-eight years old and all he had to show for his life to date was a bank balance that edged precariously towards the red and a store that had become the proverbial millstone hanging round his neck.

Maybe he was only having a mid-life crisis. Though if that were the case, shouldn't he be out looking to buy a nice red sportscar? Not to mention finding some sweet young thing to drive around in it with him. He sighed. All he really wanted to do was dig a hole, crawl in, then pull the dirt in behind him.

He lifted his gaze from the clutter of invoices and looked for solace in the world that lay outside the display window. What he got was one of his staff materializing out of the falling snow—the diminutive and inimitable Miki Greer. He watched her approach the front door, a cigarette dangling from her lips. She spat the cigarette out and ground the butt under the heel of her Doc Marten before backing in through the door, holding a large Styrofoam cup of coffee in each hand. They'd agreed long ago that if she was going to keep going out for smoke breaks, she could at least make herself useful. So she made the runs to the bank, to the post office, to The Monkey Woman's Nest a few doors down for coffee and lunches.

"Hey, grumpy," she said as she put the cups on the counter.

She stepped back and shook herself like a terrier, spraying melted snow from her leather jacket and short-cropped hair. This week it was bleached an almost white blond.

"I'm not grumpy," Hunter told her. "I'm depressed. It's not the same."

"I'm sure. And you're welcome."

"Thanks."

She grinned. "But really. Grumpy, depressed—what's the difference?"

"Grumpy means I'd be snapping at everyone. Depressed means I just want to go slit my wrists or something."

"Cool. Am I in your will?"

Hunter shook his head.

"Then I'd think this whole thing through a little more carefully before you do anything that drastic."

"You're so sweet."

Miki nodded. "Many people say that."

She joined him behind the cash and stuffed her jacket under the counter. The black T-shirt she wore was missing its sleeves and sported a DIY slogan, carelessly applied with white paint: "Ani DiFranco Rules!" Surrounding the words were splatters of the same white paint, as though she'd flicked a loaded paintbrush at the shirt after scrawling her message. She perched on the stool Hunter wasn't using, popped open the lid on her coffee and took a sip. Hunter returned his gaze to the snowy view outside.

"I know it's hard," Miki said after a moment. "I mean, Ria leaving you and all. But you can't let it take over your life."

He turned to find her studying him, her bright green eyes thoughtful.

"What life?" he said.

"This life. You know, where you're a living, breathing human being in charge of your own destiny."

"How old are you, Miki?"

"Twenty-two, but what's that got to do with anything?"

Hunter could only sigh.

"Oh, please," Miki said. "Don't go all ancient on me."

"It's not. It's just you're . . ."

"What? Too young to fully appreciate the bummers of life? As if. I know all about heartbreak. Been there, done that." She plucked the fabric of her T-shirt. "Brought back the merchandise."

"I thought you liked DiFranco."

"I do," Miki said. "Stop being so literal."

"You're right. And I'm sorry."

"But I know what you're going through," she went on. "When the bad times come rolling in, it doesn't seem like anyone else could possibly understand. Or that they'll ever go away."

Hunter nodded. "That's exactly how I'm feeling."

"See? And I'm only twenty-two."

Hunter had to smile. It was hard not to be cheered up by one of Miki's pep talks. As her brother Donal had said to him once, she could make a stone laugh. But there was too much wearing him down these days and he couldn't hold onto that smile for more than a moment.

"It's not just Ria," he said, "though that's a big part of it."

"C'mon," Miki told him, immediately figuring out what else was bothering him. "It's still early in the year. Sales never start to pick up until the *turistas* hit town." She waved her hand around the store. "Besides, what's to buy? New product's not exactly flying in the door these days."

"And it wasn't exactly flying out over Christmas either, and those are the bills I'm still trying to pay."

"This is true. But everybody was down."

"Not this down," Hunter told her.

That gave her pause.

"How bad is it?" she asked.

Hunter shrugged. "I won't know till the end of the month. But I'm going to have to cut some hours."

"Is this your way of saying, maybe I should be considering a secondary career?"

"Not *your* hours," he told her. "It's just . . . nothing seems to be going right lately. Between Ria, the store, the weather . . ."

They both looked up as the front door opened and Titus Mealy came in, stamping the snow from his boots. A dour, mousy-haired man with the body shape of a stork, he was the store's shipper/receiver, an occupation that suited him well since it allowed him to spend the greater proportion of his time in the back room, packing and unboxing shipments, instead of out on the floor where he'd have to deal with customers. It wasn't that he was deliberately unfriendly—he could be quite charming on occasion—but for him to open up to you, first you had to pass some indecipherable Titus Mealy respect-meter test.

Most people didn't. But he had a regular contingent of pale-faced and soft-bodied misfits that came in to see him, usually buying up to a half-dozen CDs per visit, and he was a hard worker, so Hunter tended to leave him to his own devices.

"Now that's what I call perfect timing," Miki said.

Titus looked puzzled. "What's that supposed to mean?"

"We were just talking about things that bum us out."

"Ha, ha." He turned his attention to Hunter. "Any new shipments?"

Hunter shook his head.

"Then I guess I'll keep working on the returns."

He headed off towards the back room with the awkward gait of someone not entirely comfortable in his own body.

"See," Miki said. "Now that's grumpy. And probably depressed, too, though with him I'd say it was clinical."

"Are you ever going to stop ragging on him?" Hunter asked.

"I don't know. Do you think he'll ever learn any social graces?"

The phone rang before Hunter could reply. He picked up the receiver. "Hello. Gypsy Records."

"Do you have any Who bootlegs?" a high, nasally voice asked.

Hunter sighed and hung up the phone without replying.

"Who-boy?" Miki asked.

He nodded.

There were two daily occurrences they'd come to count on—if not look forward to. One was that the anonymous caller with what had to be a put-on voice would phone asking for Who bootlegs. He called at least once a day and had been doing it for years—not only to Gypsy Records, but to record stores all over town. The first time Who-boy phoned after the store got call display, they'd all crowded around the telephone to finally see who he was, or at least where he was calling from, but the liquid display had only read "Caller unknown."

The second thing was Donnie Dobson, a large, pink version of the Pillsbury dough boy in a polyester suit who came in and/or called the store on a daily basis looking for new country and easy-listening releases by female artists. But he at least bought music. Like Who-boy, Gypsy Records wasn't the only recipient of Donnie's interest, but since they went out of their way to bring in whatever album he was desperately looking for that particular week, he tended to give them most of his business.

For the longest time Hunter had no idea what Donnie did with everything he purchased—he couldn't possibly listen to it all, there was simply too much of it. Donnie had been doing this for years—long before Hunter got into the business, and Hunter had been working in music stores for almost twenty years now. But then one day Titus made an offhand remark about having been over to Donnie's house and how weird it was that he was still living with his mother. It was Titus who explained that Donnie listened to each new purchase once, then carefully put it away in one of the boxes that literally filled his mother's basement.

"But what were *you* doing over there?" Miki had wanted to know.

"I was looking for a Brenda Lee cut for this tape I was making," Titus had replied in a tone of voice that left one with the sense that it explained everything.

In a way, it did. He and Adam Snipe, Hunter's other full-time employee, were forever making compilation tapes, arranging and rearranging the order of the cuts with a single-minded focus that went far beyond obsession. They often seemed willing to go to almost any length to get exactly the right version of a song. "See," one of them would explain in the middle of yet another obscure song search, "I need something to put before this cut by Roger Miller and I figure it's got to be by Stealers Wheel because Gerry Rafferty went on to produce that version of 'Letter from America' by the Proclaimers and they covered 'King of the Road.' You see how it all connects?"

Hunter did, where most people wouldn't, but while he loved music, he liked to think he wasn't that obsessed by it. And neither were his other employees. Fiona Hale, the store's part-timer and resident Goth, all tall and pale, with lanky black hair and a chiaroscuro wardrobe, might love her Dead Can Dance and Cocteau Twins CDs, but she had a life beyond them. And as for Miki, well, she was Miki, and who could figure her out. She looked like a punk, played button accordion in a local Celtic band, and when it was her turn to choose what they'd play on the store's sound system, inevitably picked something by an old horn player like Bird, Coltrane, or Cannonball Adderly. Her musical enthusiasms were great, but then she had the same broad enthusiasm for anything that interested her. Sometimes it seemed that everything did.

"So Adam said you're going to let his band play in the store some Saturday," Miki said.

Hunter nodded. "Have you heard them? I've got this awful feeling I'm going to regret this."

"They're okay—kind of lounge music set to a reggae beat. Imagine 'The Girl from Ipanema' sung by Peter Tosh."

Hunter winced.

"No, really," Miki assured him. "It's fun. Except their horns are all sampled and that sucks." She cocked her head to look at him. "How come you've never had my band in to play?"

"You never asked."

"Adam says you offered them the gig."

"Adam's just trying to get a rise out of you."

Miki nodded slowly. "And wouldn't you know . . . it worked."

They fell silent, listening to the CD. Casey was singing now about a hare hunt in the low country of Creggan.

"So do you want to play here some Saturday?" Hunter asked when the song ended with a fade-out of a flute playing against the lilting rhythm of a bodhran.

"Nah. I wouldn't want to mix my store and band groupies. That'd be just too weird."

Hunter had to laugh. Both Miki and Fiona acquired small clusters of teenage boys and young businessmen on a regular basis, earnestly hovering around them in the store, buying their recommendations while working up the nerve to ask for a date. Fiona's were rather predictably Goth, but with Miki, anything seemed to go, from skateboarders and headbangers to lawyers in three-piece suits.

"There, you see?" Miki said. "If you can still find something to smile about, your life's not over yet."

"What do you do when you're depressed?" he asked.

Miki took a sip from her coffee. "Well," she drawled, "sometimes I do like in that Pam Tillis song and ask myself, 'What would Elvis do?' "

"And the rest of the time?"

"I imagine what it's like to be somebody else who doesn't have my problems. 'Course the downside of that is I have too good an imagination and end up obsessing over what I think could be depressing them. So we're talking way moody and not really a solution that works or anything."

"I never think of you as moody."

"I'm not—except when I'm in that kind of mood." She grinned. "Mostly I just play some tunes on my box and have a drink with a friend—at the same time, if I can arrange it. Works wonders."

"I think I'd need a whole orchestra and brewery, and even then I'm not so sure it would help."

Miki shook her head. "It's not the volume or quantity—it's the quality. And it's the being with a friend that helps the most."

"That makes sense."

"So instead of going home and brooding over Ria and store invoices after work, why don't you come out with me and have a little fun? There's a session at The Harp tonight, Caffrey's on tap, a lovely bottle of Jameson's behind the bar, bangers and mash on the grill."

Hunter started to shake his head. The last thing he needed right now was a pity date. But then he realized that wasn't what Miki was offering. She was just being there as a friend.

"Sure," he said. "Why not?"

Who knows? Maybe he'd actually feel better.

"Cool."

On the CD player, Casey was now singing a Yeats poem that someone had set to music. The front door opened and three customers came in, brushing snow off their coats and stamping their feet. The mat at the door was going to be soaked before the end of the day.

"Must be noon," Miki said.

She slid off her stool and walked out from behind the counter to see if she could give anyone a hand and all three men aimed themselves in her direction. Shaking his head, Hunter started to clear off the counter. When two more customers came in, one of them asking what was playing, he took the Casey CD off, made a mental note to order more copies, and put on something that they actually had in stock—a reissue of recordings Stan Getz had made for Verve back in the fifties.

Miki looked up from the worldbeat bins where she was talking up a recording by Violaine Corradi and gave him a thumbs-up.

3

Ellie made herself wait until she was well and truly awake before going over to the part of her loft that served as her studio. She sat at her kitchen table with a mug of coffee and had a bowl of granola while flipping through an old issue of *Utne Reader* that someone had passed along to her.

This issue's cover story was "Wild at Heart: How Pets Make Us Human." It made her wish, and not for the first time, that she had the sort of lifestyle that could accommodate a pet. The trouble was, she wasn't a cat person, and a dog needed way more attention than she would be able to give it at this point in her life. Between her work with Angel, private commissions, and the part-time graphic design work she did for the weekly arts paper *In the City*, she was already scrambling to find time for her own art, never mind take care of anything as dependent as a pup as well.

But one day . . .

She closed the magazine. Sometimes it felt as though her whole life revolved around things that might come into it one day instead of what was in it now.

Putting her dirty bowl in the sink, she poured herself another cup of coffee and walked across the room to where her current work-in-progress stood under a damp cloth. The sculpture was far enough under way that she could see a hint of the bust's features under the cloth—brow, cheekbones, nose, the rest lost in the drapes of the fabric. Viewing it like this, a vague, ghostly shape of a face under cloth, supported only by the length of broomstick she was using as an armature pole, it was hard, sometimes, to remember the weight of one of these busts. She could almost imagine it was floating there above the modeling stand, that it would take no more than a slight breeze to start it drifting away across the room.

The illusion only lasted until she removed the cloth and laid it aside. Now the still roughly sculpted head of gray clay was all density and weight, embracing gravity, and the wonder was that the armature pole could support it at all.

It was barely noon, though you wouldn't know it from how dark it was in the loft. The storm outside made it feel more like late afternoon and she had to put on a couple of lights to see properly. She pulled up a stool to the modeling stand, but before she could begin to work, the sound of the wind rattling a loose strip of metal on her fire escape distracted her, drawing her gaze to the window. She shook her head as she looked outside. The thaw over Christmas had lulled everyone into thinking that they were in for a mild winter for a change, but true to form, it had only been a joke. At least it wasn't freezing rain.

The fall of the snow was mesmerizing. She'd always wanted to find a way to capture its delicacy in clay, the drift and spin of the individual flakes as they fell, the random patterns they made, their flickering dance and the ever-changing contrast between light and dark, all conveniently framed by the window. But it was something she had to leave to the painters. The closest she'd ever come was an installation she'd done for a group show once where the viewer peered into a large, black box she'd constructed to see confetti being blown about by a strategic placement of a couple of small, battery-driven fans.

She'd painted tenements and alleys on the back and side walls of the box and placed a small sculpture of a homeless man, huddled under a rough blanket of newspapers, up against the painted buildings. Moody interior lighting completed the installation, and it had all worked out rather well—for what it said, as well as how it said it—only it wasn't clay. It wasn't a sculpture, but some odd hybrid, and the dancing confetti didn't come close to capturing the snow the way she'd wanted it to. Snow, such as was falling outside her window today, had both delicate presence and weight, a wonderful tension between the two that played them against each other.

She watched the storm a while longer, then finally turned back to her sculpture, thinking that at least the latest cold snap had broken. The street people would still have drifts of wet snow to deal with, but they would be spared the bitter cold of the past few nights for now.

The businessman whose commission she was working on wasn't available today, so she was stuck working from her sketches and the photographs she'd taken during earlier sittings. She collected them from the long worktable set against the back wall with its peanut gallery of drying busts, all looking at her. One, a self-portrait, her long hair pulled back into a loose bun at the nape of the neck, was almost dry enough to make its trip to the kiln. The others had all been hollowed out, but weren't nearly dry enough yet. Three were commissions of rather stodgy businessmen like the one she planned to work on today, the sort of portrait work that helped pay the bills. The last few were of friends—hopefully to be part of a show if she could ever get the money together to have them cast.

Returning to the modeling stand, she spread out her reference material and gave the bust a spray of water from a plastic plant mister. Then she began to work on the detailing, constantly referring to her sketches and photographs as she shaped the clay with her fingers and modeling tools.

When her doorbell rang, she sat up, startled to realize that three hours had simply slipped away unnoticed while she'd been working. She rolled her shoulder muscles and stretched her hands over her head before standing up. It didn't help much. Her back and shoulder muscles still felt far too tight. The doorbell rang again. Giving the bust another spray of water, she draped the damp cloth back over it. She wiped her hands on her jeans as she crossed the loft, adding new streaks of wet clay to the build-up of dried clay already there, stiffening the denim.

Opening the door, she found her friend Donal Greer standing in the hall-way, the shoulders of his wool pea jacket white with snow. He was a little shorter than her five-ten—the discrepancy evened out by the heels of his boots—and a few years older. At the moment, the snow on his full beard and long dark ponytail made him seem gray-haired and far older. As the snow melted, it dripped to the floor where his boots had already started a pair of puddles. He gave her such a mournful, woe-bedraggled look that she wanted to laugh.

"It's snowing," Donal told her The pronouncement was uttered in an Eeyore-like voice made stranger by the slightest burr of an Irish accent.

Most people didn't see through the moroseness he liked to affect. Ellie wasn't one of them, though it had taken her a while to catch on. They'd met at one of Jilly Coppercorn's parties, each of them having known Jilly for ages on their own, but never quite connecting with each other until that night. They'd talked straight through the party, all the way through the night until the dawn found them in the Dear Mouse Diner, still talking. From there it seemed inevitable that they'd become a couple, and they had for a while—even living together for a few months—but eventually they realized that they were much better suited as friends.

Donal gave a heavy sigh. "Truly snowing," he went on. "Great bloody mounds of the stuff are being dumped from the sky."

She smiled. "So I see. Come on in."

"I was beginning to think you weren't home," Donal added as he stepped inside. He looked over to the studio area. "I'm not interrupting anything, am I?"

"I needed to come up for air," Ellie said. "How'd you know I needed a break?"

Donal shrugged and toed off his boots, one by one. They immediately began to work at forming a new puddle around themselves.

"You know me," he said. "I know all and see all, like the wild-eyed Gaelic fortune-teller that I am. It's bloody depressing, I tell you. Takes all the mystery out of life."

Ellie rolled her shoulder muscles again. "I'd much prefer it if you'd sud-denly decide to become a masseur," she told him. "One who desperately needs someone to practice on."

"It'll never happen," he said, passing over a paper bag with grease stains on the bottom. "Mostly because it'd take far more energy than I could ever muster." He shed his pea jacket and dropped it against the wall by the door. "Instead, I've got these chocolate croissants and I was hoping to find someone to help me eat them. Would you have any coffee?"

Ellie glanced at her coffee maker and pulled a face. "Let me put on a fresh pot. That stuff's been sitting there all day now."

Donal followed her to the kitchen area, marked off from the rest of the loft by a kitchen table and chairs set up close to a large industrial steel sink, a long counter and the pair of old appliances that had come with the place: a bulky fridge and an equally stout stove, both dating back to the sixties. He settled in one of the chairs by the table while Ellie ground some fresh beans for the coffee maker.

"So I heard you were a bit of the hero last night," he said.

Ellie turned to look at him. "Who told you that?"

"Tommy. I ran into him at the Dear Mouse Diner when I was having breakfast this morning with Sophie and Jilly."

"God, what was he doing up at that time? We didn't get the van back to Angel's until six-thirty."

"I don't think he'd been to bed yet," Donal said.

Ellie shook her head. "We have *such* weird schedules. It's a wonder we can still function."

"And you're avoiding the subject. That was a good thing you did. Take the compliment, woman. We're all proud of you."

Ellie finished pouring water into the coffee maker. Turning it on, she joined Donal at the table.

"It was pretty yucky," she said. "I don't know what he'd choked on but it took me forever to get the taste of his vomit out of my mouth." She looked at the bag of croissants that he'd brought. "And doesn't that little thought do wonders for the appetite."

"Sorry I mentioned it."

"Don't be."

But she still wanted to go rinse her mouth out with mouthwash again.

"So your man's doing fine?" Donal asked.

Ellie nodded. "I called the hospital to check on him before I went to bed this morning." She paused, then added, "It's weird. When Angel had us all taking that CPR course, I didn't think I'd remember any of it. But when it was actually happening, it was like I went into automatic. I didn't even have to think about it."

Donal slipped into a broader Irish accent. It was easy for him to do, seeing how he'd been born and lived half his life over there. "Sure, and wouldn't that be the whole point of the course?"

"I guess."

Thinking about last night made Ellie remember the man who was actually a woman with her silver flask filled with Welsh whiskey.

"Have you ever tried metheglin?" she asked. "It's this—"

"Oh, I know what it is. Miki has a friend who makes it. Not quite Guinness, mind you, but it'll do. Bloody strong bit of the gargle. Sneaks up and gives you a kick like poteen."

Ellie nodded, remembering how the liquor had made her eyes tear last night.

"Where did you have it?" Donal asked.

The coffee was ready, so over steaming mugs and croissants, Ellie gave him a rundown of the previous night's events, finishing up with the woman she'd met while Tommy had been talking to the police.

"I would have thought she was a man, if it hadn't been for Tommy," she said.

"It's like one of those old ballads," Donal said. "You know, where your man finds out his cabin boy's really a woman. I wonder what she's hiding from?"

"Who knows? In this city, I'm not sure I even want to know."

Donal shook her head. "Jaysus, where's your sense of mystery? Maybe she's a deposed, foreign princess and all she has left of her former life is that silver flask. She'd be carrying herself with a tragic air, am I right?"

"Hardly."

"Fair enough. So she's learned to hide it well. To live with her disappointments. To put the past aside and get on with her life."

Ellie sighed. "You know, the way you and Jilly can carry on you'd think every street person is some charming eccentric, or basically a sweet and kind person who's only had a bit of bad luck. But it doesn't work that way. They need our sympathy, sure, and we should try to help them all we can, but some of them are mean-spirited and some of them are dangerous and some of them would be screwed up no matter where you found them. I don't think it helps anything to pretend differently."

"Yes, but—"

"I work with them almost every day and they're just people, Donal. More messed up than some of us, and certainly more unlucky. And if some of them choose to live the way they do, it's not because they have some romantic story hidden in their past. It's because they're kids whose home lives were so awful they prefer to live in the different kind of hell that's the streets. Or they're schizophrenics who can't get, or won't take, their medicine. They're alcoholics, or junkies, or on the run, or all of the above and then some. And the world they live in isn't safe. It's more dangerous than anything we can imagine. We go into it, but we can step back out whenever we want. They can't."

"I know," Donal said, his voice subdued.

Ellie sighed again, remembering that he'd suffered his own hard times, he and his sister Miki both, though they rarely spoke of those days. They hadn't gone through one of Angel's programs, but they'd still had to endure hunger and homelessness before they found a way out of the darkness.

"I'm sorry," she said. "I didn't mean to come off all high and mighty. It's just . . . it breaks my heart sometimes because there's so many of them and some of them are so young and we can't even come close to reaching them."

Donal reached across the table and gave Ellie's hand a squeeze.

"I know that, too," he said. "But I'm with Jilly on this one. We just like to see the magic in things, instead of focusing too much on the hurt of it all."

"When you're not pretending to be overcome by the doldrums."

"Pretending?"

"Pretending," Ellie said firmly. "And please. Magic?"

"Oh, not hocus-pocus, exactly. But you know, there's magic everywhere you turn, if you pay attention to it. Little miracles like your being in the right place at the right time to give that man CPR and save his life. Or the way some old rubbie can turn out to be the most gifted storyteller. You can sit there with him on a bundle of newspapers in some alley, but when he starts to tell a story, it takes you a million miles away. And some of the street people really are unusual and mysterious—I mean, what better place to hide than in plain sight, on the streets with all the rest of the invisible people?"

This was about the one subject on which Donal could enthuse for hours. Even talking about his art rarely did away with the long face and the Eeyore voice.

"You're beginning to sound like one of Tommy's aunts," she told him. "The mysterious and numerous Creek sisters."

Donal smiled. "Grand women, all."

"You've met them?"

"Sure," Donal said. "You haven't?"

"To tell you the truth, I wasn't sure they really existed."

"Well, I haven't met them all," Donal told her. "I mean, Tommy's mother has . . . what? Sixteen sisters? But they certainly exist. Let's see. I met Sunday one time on the rez when I went up to a powwow with Tommy and Jilly. And then Conception and Serendipity always come to the bake sale at St. Vincent's every spring. And Zulema's been doing work with Native kids through Angel for years." He paused and cocked his head. "What made you think they didn't exist?"

"I don't know," Ellie said, feeling a little embarrassed now. "Their names. The way Tommy talks about them like they're mythological figures."

"Up on the rez, everybody sees them that way. They call them the Aunts and they go to them for medicines and stories and that sort of thing. Bloody miracle workers, they are." He gave Ellie one of his rare grins. "And now that I think of it, Conception told me about a cure for sore muscles. I remember writing it down, but . . ." He pursed his lips, brow furrowing, then shook his head. "I can't remember where I put it. But if you asked Tommy, he could get it from her."

"Oh right. That'd be just what I need. He already passes along their little folk wisdoms at the drop of a hat."

Donal gave her a considering look. "Which, I'm guessing, is still the sort of thing that makes you uncomfortable."

"I'm as uncomfortable with it as you or Jilly are comfortable."

Donal shook his head. "Now that's extreme."

"But true."

On both sides, Ellie thought. She liked whimsy and magical things as much as the next person, but she kept it in perspective. One could read about it, or use it in one's art without believing it was real. Donal was bad enough with his teasing tales of the little people and all, but when it came to Jilly, well, sometimes it seemed that Jilly lived in an entirely different world than the one that Ellie and the rest of the world did—a world where the headlines from supermarket tabloids were tangible possibilities rather than outright fiction. It came out in her paintings, which depicted fairyland creatures wandering through urban cityscapes, as well as in her conversation. The latter required only the smallest opening and Jilly would be away with wild theories, supposed true-life anecdotes and the like.

There were times when Ellie found this sort of thing maddening, but it was also part of Jilly's charm, this fey streak she had and the ability to be so persuasive that, if it was late enough at night and you'd had enough glasses of wine, you could almost go along with her beliefs. You could almost accept that the world held not only what we all know it to hold, but also the fantastical tangents that people like Donal and Jilly almost seemed to draw into it, by their own absolute conviction, if nothing else.

"Okay," Ellie said. "Since you like mysteries, what do you make of this?"

She went over to where her parka was hanging and fetched the business card she'd found on the dash of the van last night. Donal took it from her, his eyes filled with curiosity until he'd read the few words on it. Then he placed it on the table and gave Ellie a puzzled look.

"It's a business card," he said.

"Duh. I know that. But what does it mean?"

Donal glanced down at the card, then back at her, obviously confused. "Could you explain the question again?"

"Is that a person's name, or the name of a business?" Ellie said. "And why isn't there a phone number?"

He shrugged. "Maybe it's like one of those Victorian calling cards that the Brits took around when they went visiting. Where did you get it?"

"I found it on the dash of the van last night—right after I met that strange woman."

"And you think she left it?"

Ellie nodded. "But why?"

"Maybe she wants you to call her."

"No phone number."

"Fair enough." Donal looked at the card again. " 'Handfast Road,' " he read. "That'd be up in the Beaches, I'm thinking, so it'll be all bloody straightlaced and la-di-da except for . . ." His face brightened. "Kellygnow. The artists' colony. Aren't they on Handfast Road?"

"Let me check."

Ellie found her telephone directory where it was half-hidden under a stack of art and design magazines and looked up Kellygnow.

"Here it is," she said. "The Kellygnow Artists' Community. 17 Handfast Road. There's even a number."

"There you go. Mystery solved. All you have to do is call up there and ask for Musgrave Wood."

"I suppose. Have you ever been up there?"

"A long time ago, and then it was just to a couple of parties that Jilly was invited to. But you know. It's not really our crowd."

Ellie nodded. Kellygnow had a close association with the university, whereas she and Donal and their friends were more connected to the Newford

School of Art, even though many of them had originally attended Butler U.
Ellie had never been up to Kellygnow herself. And except for *In the City*'s
mentioning who was taking up or leaving residence, she never really thought
much about it at all. It was just one more place in a very big city.

"So?" Donal said. "Are you going to call?"

Ellie shook her head. "What would I say?"

"Maybe there's a commission in it for you."

"I doubt that. If the name of the woman I met last night is Musgrave
Wood, and she does want to offer me a commission, don't you think she
would have said something when we were talking?"

But Donal wasn't going to be easily dissuaded. "Well, maybe they've got
an opening and want to know if you'd like to take up residence."

"As if."

Many of the most important and influential artists to come out of the
Newford fine arts scene had spent some time in residence at Kellygnow—
everyone from the late Vincent Rushkin, considered by many to be one of the
great twentieth-century masters, to the watercolorist Jane Connelly whose art
hung in galleries throughout the world. Ellie believed in her own work, but the
caliber of artists in residence at Kellygnow at any given time was in a different
class entirely.

"Then what *are* you going to do?" Donal asked.

"Nothing."

While she could see Donal's frustration, Ellie had no interest in following
up on anything so tenuous.

"But aren't you at least curious?" Donal asked. "I mean, Jaysus. It's like a
mysterious summons of some sort."

Still Ellie wouldn't be persuaded. "Of course I'm curious, but I don't like
mysteries."

Donal nodded. He got up and refilled their coffee mugs.

"It's your choice, of course," he said as he returned to the table and
spooned sugar into his coffee. He looked up, a sparkle in his eye. "But all the
same. It seems like such a waste of a good mystery."

"If someone up there really wants to contact me," Ellie told him, "my
number's in the book."

4

A wave of music, conversational noise, and hot, smoky air greeted Hunter
when he pushed open the oak and glass front door of The Harp and stepped
inside from the snowy street that evening. He looked around for a moment,
blinking in the haze, then saw Miki waving to him. She sat with her brother
Donal at a small table just at the edge of where a dozen or so musicians were
playing, the session led by a red-haired woman playing the uilleann pipes who
seemed familiar, but Hunter couldn't remember her name. The other instru-

mentation was mostly fiddles, flutes, and whistles, but there were also a pair of mandolins, a guitar, bodhráns, and the inevitable tenor banjo playing too loud above it all.

The Harp was in the Rosses, once the predominantly Irish part of town, north of the Market in Crowsea. The oldest Irish pub in Newford, it had been a Catholic stronghold, and meeting place for homesick emigrants and IRA sympathizers, but its partisan loyalties were no longer in evidence. As the make-up of the neighborhood took on a more international flavor and the clientele had come to encompass all nationalities, religious and political differences among the pub's Irish patrons had mostly been set aside in favor of the *craíc*—an Irish term that encompassed the shared enjoyment of good company, good drink, and good music. Even the musicians were no longer exclusively of Irish descent. As Hunter made his way to the table where Miki and Donal were sitting, he noted a black man playing the tin whistle, a Jewish woman on the guitar, a young Asian man on fiddle—all three playing with the sensibility of having just stepped off the plane from Ireland.

The popularity of Celtic music didn't surprise Hunter. There was something universal in its infectious dance tunes and mournful slow airs. He could hear echoes of it in everything from old timey and bluegrass to classical and the indigenous music of many other cultures. There was a purity in its cadences, a timelessness with which contemporary music couldn't compete. He sometimes thought that the difference between the two was like the difference between North America and Europe: The landscape of each was as old as the other, but it felt older in Europe where churches, castles, even a cottage, could easily be six or seven hundred years old. As far as Western culture was concerned, North America hadn't even existed until the last few hundred years and there were few pieces of architecture that could claim to be much more than a hundred years of age.

"You made it," Miki said as he squeezed through the last dense press of bodies and tables and sat down in the chair she'd been saving for him. She grinned at him, obviously pleased.

"I said I would, didn't I?"

"Yeah, but you've said it before."

Hunter nodded. But that was before Ria had dumped him. She'd never cared much for Celtic music or the noisy sessions in The Harp—perhaps that should have rung a warning bell, he thought now—so he'd stopped coming to them. "You go on ahead," she'd say when he'd suggest they drop by for a pint, but he never did. It didn't feel the same going out to them on his own, leaving her behind.

Don't go there, he told himself.

He was supposed to be trying to forget his problems, not brood on them. Yeah, right. But he could at least make an effort. So he turned to Miki's brother.

"How's it going?" he asked Donal.

The family resemblance wasn't pronounced between Miki and her brother, though that had more to do with the sorts of people they were than genetics. Where Miki was a cheerful punkette, Donal had the look of an old, serious hippie—nevermind that he couldn't have been much older than three and still living in Ireland during the Summer of Love. He was dark-haired and had a full beard, his long thick hair pulled back in a ponytail. His features were broader than Miki's, though he wasn't much taller than her. An often earnest gnome—or rather a leprechaun, perhaps—to her impish punk.

"I'm doing well," Donal replied. "Sorry to hear about you and Ria."

Hunter shrugged. So much for trying to forget, he thought.

Donal grimaced suddenly and Hunter realized that for all her innocent smile, Miki had given her brother a kick under the table.

"It's okay," he told them. "I can talk about it."

Miki shook her head. "Not tonight. Tonight we're not going to think about depressing things. Only fun things."

"What're you drinking?" Donal asked.

"Anything but Guinness," Hunter told him.

Donal shook his head and gave a deep, theatrical sigh.

"To think you can say that without a hint of guilt," he said mournfully.

He was up and out of his seat before Hunter could reply.

"Now I feel like I should apologize to him," he told Miki.

"Oh, don't let him guilt you out. The stuff's way overrated, anyway. Or at least what we get on this side of the Atlantic. Now the last time I was in Ireland . . ." She got a dreamy look on her face. "Sure," she said, affecting a brogue, "and didn't it have the flavor of the very nectar of life?"

"I'll have to try it if I ever get over myself."

"I think I lived on it the whole month."

"*You* probably could," Hunter said.

"Well, not Guinness alone. There was also the soda bread and jam. My gran's soda bread melts in your mouth like a scone."

She licked her lips at the memory and Hunter had to smile. He nodded towards the musicians. "How come you're not playing?"

He'd noticed her accordion case tucked under her chair.

She shrugged and lit a cigarette. "Because," she told him, eyes twinkling, "I plan to get feet-trippy drunk and have fun hanging with you instead."

"Go ahead and play a few tunes," he said. "I haven't heard your accordion in ages."

"Consider yourself lucky," Donal told him, returning to the table. He set a shot glass of whiskey and a pint of Smithwicks in front of Hunter and waved off Hunter's attempt to pay for them. "You wouldn't be so thrilled if every night you had to listen to a few hours of her teaching herself Coltrane solos on that box of hers."

Hunter raised his eyebrows. "Why don't you just learn to play the sax?" he asked.

"I don't have one," she said and stuck out her tongue at her brother.

Donal ignored her. "She probably doesn't even remember how to play a decent Irish reel on her box anymore."

Hunter took a sip from his pint, the foam moustaching around his lips.

"Go ahead," he said. He tapped his pint glass with his index finger. "Give me a chance to catch up to you."

She hesitated, obviously torn. "Well . . . maybe just one or two tunes, if you're sure you don't mind . . ."

"Really," Hunter said.

The piper had just started up "The Bucks of Oranmore"—a favorite of Miki's, Hunter remembered—and he knew she wouldn't be able to resist. Moments later she had the button accordion out and strapped on, her chair pulled closer to the musicians, and she was happily playing away with them. Hunter drank some more of his beer and tapped his foot in time to the music.

"Drives me mad," Donal said.

Hunter turned to look at him. "What does?"

"The punters," Donal explained. He indicated the noisy crowd with a wave of his hand. "They're so busy talking they don't hear a note, but you can bet that before they leave they'll be telling the players how grand the music was."

But that was the whole point of a session, Hunter thought. It wasn't for the audience. It was for the musicians, a chance to share tunes and play with each other. Unlike a concert, they were playing for themselves here. The audience could listen to the music or chat with their friends as they pleased.

"Oh, I know," Donal said. "It's not like a gig, but still. They're so bloody loud I wonder why they don't go someplace where they don't have to compete with the instruments to be able to hear themselves talk."

The crowd *was* loud tonight, Hunter thought. Or maybe it was just that he hadn't been here in such a while and wasn't used to it.

He tried a sip of his whiskey, chased its warm burn down his throat with a swallow of beer, and looked around the room. There were people two-deep at the bar, all the tables and booths were full, everyone talking and laughing and paying no attention to the music except for a group of men in one booth who seemed somewhat out of place from the rest of the crowd.

In some ways, things hadn't really changed since the days Hunter had been a regular patron of The Harp. There were the usual older men nursing their drinks, bohemian types up from Lower Crowsea, a gaggle of university students who appeared to be too young to be legally drinking, a handful of yuppies drawn by curiosity who'd probably leave after they finished their first round to be replaced by more of the same.

But there was something different about the men sitting in the booth. For one thing they were completely attentive to the music, dark gazes fixed on the musicians, no conversation passing between them at all. Their table was littered with pint glasses, mostly empty, though each had a Guinness he was working on in front of him. The lighting was no different where they sat, but shadows still seemed to pool in their booth. Or perhaps it was simply a darkness they carried with them—swarthy-skinned, black-haired, their dark suits shabby, shiny at the elbows, but clean.

Hunter nodded to them with his chin. "They're listening," he said.

Donal followed his gaze. He looked quickly away.

"The hard men," he said.

"What do you mean?"

Donal shrugged. "That's just what our da' used to call men like them. Moody, hard drinkers, always ready for a fight—though Thomas won't let this lot start trouble in here. It's because of their kind that the Irish still carry the stereotype of being nothing more than hard drinkers and quick-tempered fighters."

"They don't look Irish," Hunter said, thinking they were too dark-skinned.

"They're more Irish than Michelle or myself, and we were born there. They still speak the Gaelic—some of them can barely speak English."

"How do they get along over here?" Hunter asked.

"Who knows? But they've always got the money for their drinks and they're here every Tuesday night when Amy's hosting the session."

As soon as Donal said her name, Hunter realized why the red-haired woman on pipes had seemed so familiar when he'd first noticed her coming in. Amy Scanlon was something of a fixture on the Newford Celtic scene, playing with any number of bands over the years. Her musical partner Geordie was in the store at least once a week, always trying to convince them to open up and play this or that new release for him.

"Funny thing, though," Donal said. "They're never here the other nights, but let an impromptu session start up and they'll come drifting in within the half-hour. It's like the music calls to them and brings them in."

He touched Hunter's arm. Hunter's gaze had drifted back to the booth where the men were sitting. He returned his attention to his companion.

"Don't stare at them," Donal said. "They're quick to take offense. I should know. I did the same as you one night, kept looking at them, and later, on the way home, they were waiting for me, shouting in Gaelic."

"What happened?"

"What do you think happened? They thumped me something terrible and then went on their way."

"Didn't you call the cops?"

Donal shook his head. "That would just have made for more trouble. Men like that, they don't forget a wrong. Jaysus, I've seen enough of them back home. The pubs are full of them, brooding over their pints, remembering every hurt, imagined or real, that was ever done to them."

Hunter felt his gaze being pulled back to the men's booth, but he managed to overcome the impulse.

"Have they bothered you since?" he asked.

Donal laughed. "No. Now they think we're grand pals—always have a nod or a smile for me when they pass by."

There was a brief pause in the music and Miki turned in her chair to have a drink from her pint. She shot Hunter a happy smile.

"You doing all right?" she asked.

He nodded. "Donal was just telling me all about the hard men."

Miki's gaze flicked to the booth, returned.

"Oh, them," she said. "He tell you how they beat him up?"

"Mmhmm. But now they're friends."

Miki shook her head. "You can't be friends with their kind. You have to be one of them." She smiled at her brother. "But there are those they'll tolerate more than others."

"If you're willing to go through the initiation," Donal added.

"I think I'll pass," Hunter said.

"Good idea." She had another swallow of her beer. "I'm just going to sit in on a few more tunes. But let me know if Donal goes all morose on you."

"And you'll do what?" Donal asked.

"Cheer you up, ever so sweetly."

She turned her back and joined in as the tune the musicians were playing shifted into a high-energy version of "The Earl's Chair."

"Is she like that at work?" Donal asked.

Hunter nodded. "Relentlessly upbeat."

"You'd think she'd been taking lessons from Jilly," Donal said. He raised his glass. "God save us from the excessively cheerful."

They clinked their glasses together, finishing the beer in them. Hunter got up and bought the next round.

"She fancies you, you know," Donal said when Hunter returned to the table.

Hunter blinked. "Who? Miki?"

"Who else? The Queen of bloody Sheba?"

"Oh."

Hunter didn't know what to say. He'd never thought of her along those lines. But then he'd been comfortably in what he'd thought was a long-term relationship when he'd first really gotten to know her. Before that she was just this amazing little accordion wizard who'd sneak into the sessions when she was still too young to legally have a drink.

"Don't worry," Donal told him with a smile. "I'm not going to turn into some mad hard man to protect the honor of my little sister."

"Well, she's a bit young for me . . ." Hunter began.

"Ah, but she's an old soul."

Hunter shook his head. "So now what? Are you turning matchmaker?"

" 'Course not. I'm just looking out for the best for both of you. Don't tell her I've said a word or she'll have my bloody head."

"I won't," Hunter told him.

"Good man."

So far as Hunter was concerned, just the idea of it made everything feel far too complicated to think about, never mind talk about. But of course, now he couldn't *not* think about it.

"How's work going?" he asked to change the subject.

Donal sighed. "You know that new gallery down the street from your store?"

"*Le Grand Corbeau Bleu*," Hunter said with a nod. "I've seen they're hanging some of your work."

"And that's just lovely, except they've sold three pieces and I've yet to see a check from them. Now I'm as patient as the next man, their being a new business and all, but Jaysus, a man has to pay his own bills—do you know what I'm saying? It wouldn't be so bad if I thought they were trying to put me off, because then I could go in and shout and carry on and all. But they're so bloody earnest and broke . . ."

Donal left before either Hunter and Miki were ready to go. By twelve-thirty, the crowd had thinned considerably, though Hunter noted that the hard men were still in their booth. The music had changed now—not quite so frantic and showy. There were fewer musicians, the ones remaining being the better players. The music they drew from their instruments was as likely to be tender and heart-wrenchingly melancholy as up-tempo, the tunes all much more intricate and twisty than what they'd been playing earlier. Miki would have had no trouble keeping up, but she'd put her box back in its case and the two of them had moved to a bench near the fireplace, close to where the musicians were playing. It still left them out of the circle of players, but they were now near enough to be able to listen to the music without the distracting noise of the pub's remaining patrons.

They'd been sitting there for a while when Miki slipped her hand into the crook of his arm and gave him a contented smile. It seemed an entirely inno-cent gesture, but Hunter remembered what Donal had told him and an imme-diate awkwardness came over him. He could feel himself tense up and Miki was quick to pick up on the change.

"What's the matter?" she asked. She leaned closer to him, keeping her voice low.

"Nothing."

"Oh, right." She squeezed his arm. "The muscles of your arm feel so tight it's like you think you might catch a disease from me or something. So 'fess up already. What's the problem?"

"It's nothing, really. It's just . . ." Never mind what he'd promised Donal, Hunter decided. "Only Donal was saying . . ."

His voice trailed off but Miki shook her head and finished for him.

"That I have a crush on you."

Hunter nodded.

"Bloody hell. He's doing that all the time. It's his way at getting back at me for making his life miserable with what he calls my incessant practicing."

Hunter knew an immediate relief. It wasn't that he disliked Miki. Far from it. He simply wasn't ready for any more complications in his life at the moment. Not when the ache Ria had left in his heart was still so raw.

"So you don't . . ." Hunter began.

"I didn't say that."

He looked the question at her, but she only smiled.

"That's for me to know and you to find out," she said.

"But . . ."

"Shh. Listen. Isn't that a beautiful air?"

It took a moment for Hunter to switch gears and pay attention to what the musicians were playing. He didn't recognize the piece, but he loved the way one of the flute players interwove the sound of his instrument with that of Amy's pipes.

When the musicians began another piece, a complicated jig, Miki gave Hunter's arm another squeeze.

"About this business of who fancies who," she said. "Don't worry about it. Donal was only teasing you because he can be such a git and he wanted to get back at me."

"Sure . . ."

"And if I was teasing you, it's only because you can get way too serious."

She leaned back against the bench to listen to the music then, leaving Hunter to realize that she still hadn't really answered anything. To confuse matters even more, he found that, as though the whole conversation had been a catalyst to make him focus on her and see her in another light, now he *was* feeling an interest in her. The borderland between friendship and something more had suddenly gotten all hazy and undefined, and he wasn't quite sure where he stood in it anymore—or even where he wanted to stand.

The idea of being with Miki seemed to ease some of the hurt that Ria had left lodged inside him when she walked out of his life, but he couldn't tell if this new attraction to Miki was real, or had come about because he was feeling lost and on the rebound. Perhaps it was part of both because right now he was in a place where anybody, the first person he happened to meet, no doubt, could hold the road map he needed to lead him back to a place where it was possible to feel good again. And that wasn't exactly the most positive thing upon which to base a relationship.

Hunter stifled a sigh. Donal owed him big time for starting up this whole complication in the first place.

He glanced over his shoulder and found his gaze drawn to the booth where the hard men were sitting. One of them caught his gaze, his eyes narrowing, and Hunter quickly looked away.

He supposed there were worse things that could happen. He could have those hard men decide to beat the crap out of him. Or the store could go belly-up and he'd have to declare bankruptcy. Instead all he had was an ache in his heart and this forlorn sense of confusion.

Miki gave him a little poke in the side.

"You're doing it again," she said.

"What?"

"Thinking too much. Brooding. Trust me, I'm like a doctor. I know all about this sort of thing and it's really not good for you. Tell the little voice in your head to shut up. Have another drink and just listen to the music."

"Easier said than done."

Miki sighed. "I know. But it's worth trying because, what's your other option?"

"Just being depressed."

She gave him a smile. "Exactly. And where's the fun in that?"

"None at all," Hunter agreed.

He looked at her for a moment, wondering what it would be like to kiss her, to feel the press of her body against his, to wake in the morning and have her impish face on the pillow beside him, smiling that smile. He almost leaned in toward her to taste that smile, but the moment passed. He reached down and plucked his glass from the floor at his feet. Taking a sip, he leaned back on the bench and tried to concentrate on the music.

5

SATURDAY, JANUARY 17

The timer went off, but Bettina held her position. She knew from previous sessions when she'd posed for Lisette that the artist always needed that one more minute before Bettina could relax her pose and stretch cramped muscles.

"Just a moment more," Lisette said, right on cue.

"*Está bien,*" Bettina told her. "It's no problem."

She'd never known how hard an artist's model had to work until she'd become one herself. She soon discovered that the human body had never been designed to be held motionless for long stretches of time, protesting the abuse with cramps and aches where she'd never even known she had muscles. But she also enjoyed the meditative aspect of it, the way she could let her mind range free while she listened to the sounds the artist made at the easel. The scratch of pencil or charcoal on paper during the preliminary sketches and, later, on canvas. The scrape of the brush, loaded with pigment. The small, inadvertent sounds the artists made as they worked— everything from grunts and sighs and snatches of melodies to Lisette's habit of stepping back and sucking air in through her teeth as she studied the work.

Lisette Gascoigne was a tall woman, lean rather than slender, and fine-featured, with short black hair and eyes almost as dark as Bettina's. Not so much attractive as handsome. She was one of the artists who'd propositioned Bettina the first time they'd met—during Bettina's first week of living in Kellygnow. Bettina had been nervous about sitting for her later, but Lisette was all business once they were in her studio. Still, Bettina had to wonder why Lisette even required a model, never mind a nude one, unless it was that she simply liked to look at what she couldn't have while she worked. Lisette always had her pose in the nude, and the watercolor and pencil studies she did were absolutely wonderful, detailed realistic work that rivaled anything done by the great masters of portraiture and life drawing. Bettina had one that Lisette had given her taped up to the wall in her room, a loosely rendered figure study that she could never show to her mother even if her features were hidden behind the curtain of her dark hair.

But once Lisette took up her brush and began to fill the canvas, Bettina felt she might as well have been a handful of colored scarves, hanging over the back of the chair where she was sitting. The finished paintings were swirls of pigment—fascinating pieces for how the colors pushed against one another, but they bore no resemblance to anything even vaguely recognizable, never mind the human form.

Still Bettina wasn't one to complain. If posing for Lisette's abstracts were part of what allowed her to live at Kellygnow free of charge, then she was happy to do it.

"Good, good," Lisette said finally.

She stepped back to look at her canvas, whistling faintly as she drew the air in through her teeth. Bettina slipped on the silk kimono that one of the artists had given her on her first week and began a series of brief stretching exercises to get her circulation flowing once more. She looked out the window as she loosened up. It was sunny today, if cold. A new blanket of snow covered the lawn where *los lobos* had gathered last Sunday evening. The untouched drifts looked so inviting that she was tempted to take Chantal up on her offer to go cross-country skiing except that she'd promised Salvador she'd help him this afternoon. Earlier today a couple of loose cords of firewood had been delivered to the house and it all needed to be split, carried back to the wood-shed, and stacked.

After working out a final tight muscle in the nape of her neck, she came around to Lisette's side of the easel where she was surprised to find a rough likeness of herself looking out at her from the canvas.

Lisette smiled at her. "I *can* paint realistically," she said.

"I never . . . that is . . ."

Flustered, Bettina gathered the front of her kimono closer to her throat with one hand and let her words trail off.

"I know," Lisette told her. "You never said a thing. But I could tell by the look on your face every time you've come around to see what I've been painting."

Bettina shrugged. "I wondered . . ."

Lisette reached forward and brushed a lock of hair away from Bettina's brow. Bettina tensed, but the gesture was friendly, not flirtatious.

"I can see you in all the others," Lisette said. "But in this piece—" She indicated the painting on her easel. "I want others to see you, too." She smiled again. "It's early yet, but the likeness will come."

Some of the paintings from earlier sessions hung on the wall of the studio and Bettina turned to look at them. They were unframed, the paint on many of them still not quite dry. Their colors seemed to leap out from the canvas toward the viewer, barely tamed to Lisette's will, pigments laid on with thick brush strokes, complementaries pulsing against each other. Try though she might, Bettina could see nothing of herself in even one of them.

"What is it I'm missing when I look at them?" she asked.

"You're searching for form," Lisette said, "where I've painted only the impression of what the form clothes."

Bettina shook her head, still not getting it, but before she could speak, Lisette went on, saying, "How can I explain this better? You carry yourself with a languid grace, as though nothing matters, but one has only to look in your eyes to see that for you, everything matters. Under the skin, intense fires burn. Standing near you, I can almost feel the heat." She made a motion with her hand, encompassing the abstracts that hung on the wall. "These are about the fire. Now I want to clothe the fire with your skin."

Bettina glanced at Lisette, then turned back to regard the paintings in a new light. *Bueno*, she thought. This would teach her to make assumptions. Because now she understood. Lisette hadn't been simply playing with color. Instead, she saw *la brujería* and that was what she had been painting. Her abstracts were like small windows looking into *la época del mito*. They captured images of myth time, how the trace of it hung from Bettina's shoulders like a cloak, vibrant, but puzzling in all its mystery and confusion.

"I see it now," she said. She turned away from the paintings and smiled. "But we all carry that light inside ourselves. I'm not special."

"Perhaps," Lisette said. "Perhaps not. But in you it seems more intense. More tightly focused."

Bettina almost laughed, thinking what her *abuela* would have thought to hear this. The most-used phrase in her grandmother's vocabulary had been, *"¡Presta atención!"* It was always, "pay attention." *"¡Presta atención, chica!"* Because Bettina's mind had always been wandering, her attention captured by everything and anything and not always the task at hand. There was no place in the mysteries for a *soñadora*, a daydreamer. Only for true dreamers. "Remember this one small piece of advice," Abuela would say. "You must always be focused. You must see everything at once, as it is, or you will lose yourself in all the possibilities of what might be, and for you and I, who can so easily slip into *la época del mito*, that could take us a very great distance indeed. It could take us so far we might never return."

"You're amused," Lisette said, bringing Bettina back to the studio from that place where her memories had taken her.

Bettina nodded. "I was thinking of my grandmother. When I was young, her one complaint to me was always that I wasn't focused enough."

"Something you've outgrown, I assume."

"So it would seem," Bettina agreed, though she wasn't entirely sure. Sometimes she felt she was still too much the *soñadora*, not the true dreamer. Not serious enough. Though, she remembered, Abuela could be anything but serious, too. If the fancy happened to take her, she could readily play *la tonta loca*, the crazy fool.

Lisette walked back behind her easel and picked up a brush.

"Do you have time for one more twenty-minute session?" she asked.

"Sí," Bettina said.

But she paused as she passed the window, her gaze caught by a stranger she saw standing on the lawn by the tree line. Something in his stance reminded Bettina of that part of *la época del mito* where *el lobo* had taken her last weekend, of the priest she'd seen by the salmon pool whose existence *el lobo* had denied. The figure wore a dark overcoat with an old-fashioned cut and stood with his back to them, facing the forest.

Even from this distance Bettina could see how *la brujería* clung to him, like shadows to the branches of the trees beyond him. It was not a healer's magic, not quite witchcraft either, but something new to her. Potent and strange.

"Ah," Lisette said, joining her by the window. "The Recluse is back,"

"The who?"

Lisette shrugged. "I don't know her name, but she winters every year in the old cottage—you know, the original one that Hanson's supposed to have built and lived in. She usually moves in again around the end of November, the beginning of December."

Bettina remembered seeing smoke rising from its chimney the other night, but that hadn't struck her as odd. She'd thought that one of the writers was living in it.

"This is the first time I've seen her this year," Lisette went on. "I wonder where she spends her summers?"

Bettina turned to look at her. "You keep saying 'her' and 'she,' but . . . ?"

Lisette smiled. "Oh, I know she looks butch, but she's a woman, the same as you or me." Her smile broadened a little. "Well, probably more like me than you, if you know what I mean."

Bettina returned her gaze to the stranger who was walking along the tree line now, her face in profile. She still didn't look like a woman to Bettina. Not with her short-cropped hair and strong jaw, the man's gait and the masculine set to her features. Bettina thought of Kellygnow's housekeeper Nuala. She might dress as a man, but for her it seemed more a choice of style and a man's clothing could do nothing to disguise Nuala's womanly shape. This woman Lisette had referred to as the Recluse appeared to be deliberately confusing the issue.

And she still reminded Bettina of the priest by the salmon pool, though she wore no priest's collar today. *La brujería* had been strong then, too, but she had put that down as their being in myth time.

"Is she a writer or an artist?" Bettina asked.

Lisette shrugged. "I don't really know. She doesn't mix with the rest of us. Someone told me a couple of years ago that she's an old friend of the family— the Hansons, that is."

"I thought they were all dead and gone—that some foundation looked after all the business now."

"It does," Lisette said. "But that doesn't preclude special dispensation for certain individuals. Consider yourself. I don't think there's ever been a model in residence for as long as you've been—not that I'm complaining, mind you."

"And speaking of modeling," Bettina said.

Lisette nodded. "Yes. We should get back to it. I'm sure someone else has you booked for the afternoon."

Bettina shook her head. "Not today. I'm going to work with Salvador after lunch."

Lisette had been squeezing some paint onto her palette, but paused now. "Really?" she said.

"Mmhmm."

"Lord, you even have the look of one who relishes the idea."

"Oh, I do. I love physical labor. It helps center me."

Lisette smiled. "I'll take paint on my hands over dirt under my nails any day."

With that she went back to considering her palette. Bettina returned to the chair where she'd been posing. She lined up the chalk marks on the floor for her feet, on the arms of her chair for her hands, found the sightlines to get her head back in the right position once more.

"Move your head a little more to the left," Lisette said. "And bring your chin up just a touch. A little more. There. That's it."

Bettina and Salvador had most of the wood split when Nuala came out to join them. Normally they would have had it all split and stacked by the end of summer, before the first snow fell, but Nuala's intuition had told her that it was going to be a long winter so she had Salvador order in a couple of extra cords of seasoned wood just to be on the safe side.

Bettina was always comfortable in Salvador's company. He reminded her of the men on her mother's side of the family: strong and tall, darkly handsome, good-humored and generous of spirit. Now in his sixties, he was still straight-backed and strong, his hair and moustache a grizzled gray. And like her uncles, he was forever teasing her.

"Ah, *chica*," he said today, his breath frosting in the cold air. He leaned on the hardwood handle of his splitting maul and gave her a very serious look. "If only I had the courage, I'd leave my wife and run away with you."

Having been to dinner at his apartment on the East Side and seen first-hand how much he loved his wife Maria Elena, Bettina knew he wasn't being in the least bit serious. She might not have accepted his flirting so lightly if he'd been an Anglo, but he was too much like family for her to even consider taking offense. Instead she paused in her own work.

"Where would we go?" she asked.

"Mexico City."

"But you have relatives there. They would never accept me. They'd call me '*la adúltera*' or worse."

"Did I say Mexico City? I mean New Mexico. Santa Fe."

"Doesn't Maria Elena's cousin Dolores live there?"

"*¿Y bien?* We would not have to visit with her."

"But still she would gossip about us. We couldn't go anywhere without people talking."

"Then California."

"Too many earthquakes."

"Costa Rica."

"Too many monkeys."

And on it went. For every place he named, she had a reason why it wouldn't be suitable. When Nuala joined them, they switched to English and new topics, but as usual, Nuala contributed little to the conversation. Bettina wasn't offended. Last Saturday night's talk notwithstanding, it was simply Nuala's way. She wasn't being unfriendly; she was only being Nuala. Quiet, soft-spoken, but with that spark of *la brujería* smoldering deep in her eyes. Bettina hadn't exchanged more than a half-dozen words with her since Saturday.

While Salvador continued to split the remaining logs, Nuala and Bettina began to load the sled with split wood for the first of many trips to the woodshed where they would stack it. Despite the cold, the three of them were warm enough from their labor to be wearing only down vests over their shirts. The women made a half dozen trips to the shed before they started stacking the wood. This was the part that Bettina liked best, fitting the split logs together like uneven building blocks to make a stack along the back wall of the shed.

They worked in a companionable silence for a while, raising one stack to the roof of the shed before going on to start the second. Alone with Nuala, Bettina decided to see if she could draw her out again, reclaiming the ease with which conversation had grown up between them last weekend. She meant to find out what Nuala could tell her about the woman that Lisette had called the Recluse. Instead she found herself asking about *los lobos*.

"What are *an felsos*?" she said.

Nuala paused with an armload of wood and gave her a look that Bettina couldn't read.

"Where did you hear that term?" Nuala asked.

Something in her voice made Bettina hesitate.

"I can't remember," she said finally. "I just overheard it one day. It might have been a couple of the writers talking."

She had no idea why she'd lied, why it seemed important to keep secret her conversation with that one *lobo*. She needn't have tried.

"Or perhaps," Nuala said, "you heard it from a handsome, dark-haired man you met in the woods behind the house."

Bettina remembered the curtain in Nuala's room, how it had moved when she'd returned to the house from her meeting with *el lobo*, as though someone had been watching her from inside. Who else could it have been but Nuala?

"Perhaps," she admitted.

Nuala sighed. "I forget how young you are."

"I don't understand."

"When you are young," Nuala told her, "you are immortal. Nothing can harm you. You see dangers, but know that they can only harm others, not you."

"I don't think that way at all."

Nuala arched an eyebrow. "No? Then why do you spend time in the company of such a creature?"

"He doesn't seem dangerous."

"Let me tell you what *an felsos* means. It's from the old Cornish and translates to 'the cunning friends.' And they are indeed cunning, though rarely friends—at least to us. The term is used much in the way that faeries were referred to as 'the good neighbors.' Not because they were, but because such a reference was less likely to give offense."

"I thought you said they were Irish."

"They are. Irish, Breton, Cornish. The *genii loci* of the ancient *Gaeltacht*. In Ireland my people always referred to them as the Gentry."

Bettina frowned. *Genii loci* she understood. It was Latin; a *genius loci* was the guardian spirit or presiding deity of a place. But . . .

"*Gaeltacht?*" she asked.

"It's what we called the Irish-speaking districts back home," Nuala explained. "But I think of it as any home of the Gael—wherever the Celtic people gather and speak the old language, remember the old ways. Each of these places had a spirit, sometimes benevolent, sometimes not. More often they were neither good nor evil, they simply were—the third branch of the Celtic trinity, if you will."

"So these wolves that come to our yard," Bettina tried. "*En otro palabras*—in other words. They are evil?"

Nuala shook her head. "Not as you're using the word. Long ago, they followed the Irish emigrants to the New World, but this land already had its own guardian spirits. So there was no place for them. But here they remain all the same. They are homeless, unbound, and they neither feel nor think the way we do. When the Gentry gather in a pack they can be like a wild hunt, ravening and hungry for blood, but even on an individual basis, they're not to be trusted."

"Why not?"

Nuala shrugged. "Mostly, I think, because they are jealous of us—the way the dead are jealous of the living. We have what they can't have—we fit in, we have a relationship with our environment. We have homes. Most of us are comfortable in our own skins. They want this way we live. Some try to slip into our lives, pretending to be our friends, our family, our lovers, but never able to succeed because of their feral nature and their otherness. Some are only dangerous when we intrude into their lives, reminding them of what they can't have. Others actively seek us out as prey, tearing us open to see where we have hidden our souls."

"All are dangerous."

Bettina shivered. She remembered the sting of potential danger hanging in the air when she had walked with her wolf through *la época del mito*, but she was sure he meant her no harm. They had been alone. There were many things he could have done, or tried, but the worst he had done was speak in riddles.

Nuala laughed without humor.

"I can see it in your eyes," she said. "As I said earlier, youth considers itself immortal. You hear what I tell you. You understand the danger. But you are unable to conceive of it touching you."

"No," Bettina told her. "It's not that at all. *Por lo menos . . .*"

But Nuala wasn't listening to her. She turned her back and carried her armload of wood into the shed.

"You will see," she said over her shoulder. "In time, you will see. If you live so long."

Bettina started to follow, to argue further, then shook her head. She wasn't sure what the age difference was between Nuala and herself, but it was obviously enough for Nuala to consider her no more than a child, inexperienced and naïve. And just as obviously, Nuala was one of those adults who grouped young adults, teenagers, and children together in her mind and considered all of them to be deficient in common sense. Bettina had learned long ago that there was no use arguing with such a point of view. One could only carry on.

The housekeeper's attitude towards *el lobo* and his *compadres* irritated Bettina as well. Granted, she didn't entirely trust the wolf herself, but suspicion was not conviction. And when she considered how an outsider might view her father and the uncles from his side of the family, she was willing to give *los lobos* the benefit of the doubt. For now. She would be cautious, but then she was always cautious, Nuala's comments to the contrary.

She understood how *la época del mito* could be considered dangerous—it was mostly unknown territory, after all, no matter how often one crossed its borders. But she wasn't afraid of the unknown. She wasn't afraid of death, either. She didn't welcome its approach, she would struggle against it, but in her experience, those who feared death were those who believed it to be an ending instead of what it was: a change. A journey into the unknown much the same as the time one spent in *la época del mito*. The difference was, one did not normally return from the fields of death.

There were people who might disagree and point to ghosts as their proof, but ghosts were not spirits straying from *la tierra de los muertos*. They were those who had yet to move on from this world.

Eh, *bueno*. She would not let Nuala's prejudices sour the day. The crisp, cold air, so different from that of the dry Sonoran Desert she'd called home, filled her with a heady sense of well-being. It was all still so new to her. The winter, lying thick and deep all around them. The snowy fields. The wind and the cold. The locals could complain, but it made the blood sing in her veins and she refused to lose the feeling of being so alive.

When Nuala returned for another load, Bettina acted as though the conversation the housekeeper had walked away from had never occurred. Instead, she chatted happily about the windswept lawn and the snow piled deep in drifts, Chantal's offer to take her cross-country skiing and did Nuala think it would snow again tonight? Nuala gave her a considering look, eyes dark with *la brujería*, then shrugged, her gaze turning mild once more. As they continued to work, their differences fell silent between them, if not forgotten.

Later, Nuala went inside to begin dinner for the residents of Kellygnow. Salvador and Bettina finished stacking the rest of the wood, Salvador teasing her the whole time. He no longer wished to run away with her himself; instead, now he was trying to decide which of his nephews she should marry. Bettina laughed and shook her head at every suggestion he made. She followed him around to the side of the house where his old pickup truck was parked.

"*Vamos a mi casa*," Salvador said. "You can eat with us. You know Maria Elena—she always makes too much."

Bettina was tempted, but she shook her head. "I don't want to impose."

"Impose? How can you impose? You are like family."

Bettina had no plans, except to read for a while, perhaps go for a walk later. Then she remembered how walking on the grounds had turned out for her last Saturday night. She was in no hurry for a repeat visit with *el lobo*.

"*Entonces, gracias*," she said. "But only if you'll stop at the market on the way so I can bring something."

"What can you buy that Maria Elena hasn't already made?"

Bettina shrugged. "A salad. Some fruit for desert."

"*Bueno*. Only don't buy too much." Salvador patted his stomach, which was as flat as patio tile, and probably as hard. "I can't afford to put on any extra weight."

Bettina nodded solemnly. "I see what you mean."

Salvador gave her a shocked look. He put his hands on his stomach, and stood straighter than he normally did, if that was even possible.

"*¿Cómo?*" he asked. "What do you see?"

"*Nada*," she assured him. "Do I have time for a quick shower?"

When Salvador dropped her off at the house later that night, Bettina walked around back to the kitchen door, carrying the leftovers that Maria Elena had sent home with her. In one plastic margarine container was a leftover *chile relleno* and some refried beans. A smaller container held a serving of *albóndigas*—Maria Elena's famous meatball soup. She wanted to put them in the fridge on her way to her room and it was quicker to simply go around the house, coming in by way of the kitchen, than to navigate her way through the warren of halls from the front door.

The sky was clear and riddled with stars. Snow crunched underfoot and the wind blew cold air up under her parka, making her shiver. She paused by the door. With her breath frosting in the air, she looked to the woods, wondering if any of *los lobos* were nearby. She could sense neither man nor spirit. Studying the shadows between the trees, her gaze was drawn to the light that spilled from the windows of the Recluse's cottage, called to it as surely as the moths that fluttered against the screens in summer were drawn to the windows by the interior lights. Now that she had seen its inhabitant, it was impossible to ignore the witchy flavor her presence lent the building.

She should ask the woman if she had a brother, Bettina thought. A brother who was a priest.

Though what was more likely was that it had been the Recluse herself that Bettina had seen by the salmon pool. The Recluse, dressed as a priest. Or perhaps she'd only been wearing a collarless white shirt that had seemed like a priest's garb in the dark.

Pero, Bettina decided. The priest's identity wasn't the real question at the moment. She was more curious about what the priest had been doing in *la época del mito* in the first place, and why hadn't *el lobo* been able to see him. Or rather, why he'd pretended he hadn't seen him.

She turned back to the kitchen door.

It wasn't something she was ready to pursue at this time of night. It probably wasn't even any of her business, but it nagged at her all the same, the way mysteries always did. Because there was something in the way the priest had looked at her that night—if only in passing—before his gaze continued down to the pool where that enormous salmon lay sleeping . . . the creature that *el lobo* had called *an bradán*.

Perhaps she should have asked Nuala what *an bradán* meant, while the housekeeper had been willing to talk this afternoon.

Bettina shook her head. Oh, yes. *Bueno idea*. And receive yet another lecture. *No gracias*.

Nuala meant well, Bettina thought as she opened the door and stepped into the warm kitchen, but a mystery lay thick around her, too. Of course, that was none of Bettina's business either, though she'd never let that stop her before. Her sense of curiosity was too strong to let any puzzle remain unchallenged for too long.

"Ah, *chica, chica*," her *abuela* used to say. "If only you were as diligent with what I am trying to teach you as you are with your curiosity for everything else."

Bettina closed the door behind her and leaned for a moment with her back against its wooden panels. She could almost hear her grandmother's voice.

¡Presta atención!

Pay attention to this, to what is before you, not to every little whim and wonder the wind might blow your way.

"*Te echo de menos, abuela*," she said softly. "I miss you so very much."

6

Ellie wasn't exactly thrilled about having to spend Saturday morning with Henry Patterson, a businessman who'd commissioned a bust of himself from her as a gift to his wife, but she didn't see that she had much choice. Not if she wanted to keep him happy and collect her money. He was such a control freak—an exaggerated caricature of the sort of client she disliked the most. She supposed his type of person was useful in an office environment, get the job done and all that, though she certainly wouldn't want to be an employee in that office.

Here, in her studio, his abrasive manner went beyond simple irritation.

He needed to be involved in every step of the process, overseeing all the various aspects as if he knew the first thing about sculpture, which of course he didn't. The early stages when she was first building up a bust had been the worst. Yes, she'd told him. I need you here for this part of the process. I know there's no likeness yet, but these things take time. If you'll just be patient, I'm sure you'll be more than pleased with the final results.

But patience, apparently, wasn't one of Patterson's virtues, if he had any, which Ellie had come to doubt. By his fifth sitting she found herself wondering why he was still alive. He was in his late fifties—surely someone would have strangled him by now?

After every session, he'd go on at great lengths to critique what she'd done so far, showing a complete lack of understanding as to the basics of art in general, never mind sculpture. She could have learned to live with his ignorance except that it was coupled with a pretentiousness that was truly unbearable; it took all her willpower to simply bite her tongue and kowtow—verbally, if not literally. Somehow she put up with his inane and uninformed suggestions as to how she could do her job so much more expediently, so much more *professionally*, if she'd only do this, and perhaps that, and certainly this. Never mind that none of his suggestions would work, because, you see, he knew a thing or two about art, little lady—"Don't call me that," she'd tell him, for all the good it did—and on and on he'd go, *ad infinitum, ad nauseum*.

All she could do was try to get through the sitting. She'd maintain a stiff smile and fantasize about telling him exactly where he could shove said sculpture. And how she hoped it would hurt.

This morning's sitting was a complete and utter disaster. Bad enough that he hadn't had time to sit for her the past week so that she'd had to work from photographs. But when he stepped through the door of her studio and saw what she'd done so far, he had the nerve to immediately begin haranguing her about how she was deliberately making the portrait as unflattering as possible. It was almost funny coming as it did from someone like him, where ugly would be a compliment.

He was a hog of a man, puffed up with his self-importance, which translated physically into a grossly overweight specimen of dubious manhood squeezed into a suit that must have cost a fortune, but might as well have been made of sackcloth for all the good its classic lines did him. She couldn't believe he was complaining. Had he never looked in a mirror? She'd already made his nose smaller, tightened up the flapping jowls, and plied any number of other tricks to retain a likeness that would also be flattering.

"I'm sorry you feel that way," she said, keeping her temper in check with an effort, "but—"

"Don't you think for a moment that I don't know what you're doing here."

"If you'll calm down, we can—"

"You're mocking me, plain and simple. This, this . . . *thing*." He pointed a fat finger at the bust, face red, sweat beading on his brow. "I suppose you consider it to be some sort of artistic statement, a bohemian criticism of the corporate world—is that it? The creative individual standing firm against the fat cats of big business. But you listen to me, little lady. So far as I'm—"

"How many times do I have to tell you?" she broke in "Don't call me a 'little lady.' "

"Don't *you* interrupt—"

That was it, Ellie decided.

"Look," she said. "Just shut up."

He blinked, small pig eyes widening with surprise. His flushed face grew redder, jowls quivering with outrage.

What's the matter? Ellie thought. No one ever stood up to you before?

"If you're this bothered by how the sculpture's turning out," she went on before he could speak, "I'll simply return your deposit and we can call it quits. I'm sure we'll both live happier lives knowing that we'll never have to see each other again."

He shook his head. There was a cold look in his eyes now.

"And leave you with this mockery of a portrait?" he said. "And let you display it in some gallery for all the world to see and laugh over? I don't think so."

Like anyone she knew would even know who he was. Like they'd care. Like she'd take the time to finish it.

Ellie shrugged. "If you don't pay for it, you don't get it."

"I don't think so," he repeated. "I won't be leaving here without it."

"Jesus. Are you so cheap that you'll pull something like this just to get it for the hundred bucks you put down on deposit? It's not even finished yet."

"I will have my deposit from you," he told her in what she assumed was his boardroom voice. Cold, firm. No give. "And I will have that travesty of a sculpture, or you—" Now the chilly smile. "—little lady, can expect a visit from my lawyers."

"Oh," Ellie said. "Well, if you put it like that . . ."

She stepped over to the table and picked up her clay-cutting wire, a length of copper wire with short wooden dowels tied on either end. Pulling the wire taut between her hands, she laid it on top of the brow of the sculpture and with a quick downward jerk, sliced the face right off. The clay fell to the floor and she mashed it under her foot. Stepping back, she gave Patterson a sweet smile.

"Go ahead, fat man. Take it."

"You—"

"And then get your sorry ass out of my studio."

"My lawyers—"

"Send 'em by."

The cloud of rage that swept over his features was like nothing she'd seen before. The only thing that came close was the time that she and Tommy had been forced to hold down this raging schizophrenic in an alley off Norton Street, trying to keep him from hurting himself—and anybody else—while they waited for the ambulance to arrive.

Patterson took a step towards her, but she held up the clay-cutting wire, pulling it tight between her hands again.

"Don't even think of it," she told him, her own voice hard.

She watched him recover, watched him harness the red anger until it was only a burning coal in each of his piggy eyes.

"Now, that wasn't smart," he said. "You forget who I am, who I know. I can break you without even breathing hard. After today, the only commissions you'll get are from the scum on the street to whom you're so ready to lend a helping hand."

So he read the human interest section of the newspaper and had seen the piece on her and the homeless man she'd saved the other night. Big deal.

"Guess I'm due for a change," she said with more bravado than she felt.

"And you will hear from my lawyers."

"Can't wait. Here," she added as he started to turn for the door. She shoved the lump of clay that had been his face towards him with her foot. "You're forgetting something."

He looked down, but he was so in control of himself now that when his gaze rose back up to meet hers, there wasn't even a hint of rage left in his piggy eyes. His face was still flushed. Sweat still beaded his brow. But his features were calm, expressionless.

"Let me tell you something, little lady," he said, smiling as she gritted her teeth. "I *always* come out ahead."

Then he turned and left the studio, closing the door softly so that the lock engaged with only a very civilized click.

Ellie stared at the door for a long moment, then down at the now-unrecognizable face of her sculpture where it lay by her feet. Tossing the clay-cutting wire onto her worktable, she walked slowly over to her couch and sat down. The adrenaline rush that had propelled her through the last few minutes left her. She felt weak and a little dizzy, and her legs wouldn't stop shaking.

"Shit," she said softly. "Shit, shit, shit."

What had she been thinking? Yes, he was an officious little prick—make that an officious fat prick—but now what was she going to do? She'd have to return his deposit. She might even have to return the deposits of some of her other clients if he really had the kind of pull he claimed he had. And he probably did. Hadn't he gone on and on about sitting on the board of this and that company, how he owned this, was buying that. All the commissions she'd gotten to date had grown out of referrals. The last thing she needed right now was to have someone like Patterson bad-mouthing her to all and sundry. If her other commissions canceled out on her and also wanted their deposits back, she'd be in deep trouble.

Where would she find that kind of money? Everything she'd taken in had already been spent on supplies, rent, living expenses. And if she couldn't get any more commissions . . .

"Shit."

She looked across her studio at the line of portrait busts in various stages of completion on the back of her worktable. She felt like destroying them all, each and every one of them.

What was she doing anyway, taking all these commissions, doing work she didn't even care about in the first place? When she compared them to the busts farther along the table of Donal and Sophie and other friends, it was like seeing the difference between night and day. That one of Tommy—she couldn't wait to cast it. It was so individual, so Tommy. The commissioned portraits were all of a kind, almost interchangeable. Inoffensive and a little stiff, but safe. The ones of her friends, even the self-portrait, which she wasn't all that fond of, were infinitely more interesting. Varied. Full of life and expression.

Her legs had stopped trembling, but she still had a shaky feeling inside, a pressure behind her eyes.

No, she wasn't going to cry. She wouldn't give piggy-eyed Henry Patterson that satisfaction. But what *was* she going to do?

What she should do was another bust of him, this time staying relentlessly faithful to his likeness. Do him with those bloated features and the bulbous nose, the flapping jowls, little piggy eyes and all. Then when Patterson took her to court, she could wheel it out as "Exhibit A." She'd point at it, then at Patterson. "Your honor," she'd say. "Ladies and gentlemen of the jury. Is it still defamation when all I have done is copy what nature has already provided?"

Better yet, take a great big lump of clay and drop it on his head from, oh say, the top of one of those buildings he owned downtown. Hide out on the roof, thirty stories up from the street, and just let it go, bombs away.

Yeah, right, she thought. I don't think so.

She sighed and pushed herself up from the couch. What she really had to do was get out of here. She put on a pair of boots, collected her parka and knapsack, and left the studio to wander aimlessly through the wintered streets of Lower Crowsea. Anything to get in a better mood than this.

This being January in Newford, it wasn't warm, not even close, but she didn't mind so much today. The bite in the north wind helped clear her head, though after a while her forehead and temples got that feeling like an iced Slushie drunken too fast. She didn't have the streets to herself either. A winter's Saturday in the Market couldn't compete with a busy summer weekend, but the streets were still crowded. What always surprised her was how not even the frigid temperatures could keep the itinerant vendors from selling their wares, everything from fresh vegetables—imported, of course—cut flowers and various maple syrup products, to clothing, antiques, and a surprising diversity of arts and crafts.

The fast-food carts braving the weather were doing a booming trade with line-ups four or five people deep. There were even some buskers out, though the two she saw were standing over hot-air grates in front of the old Kellerman's Department Store. The long, brick building now housed a half-dozen smaller businesses, from a pawn shop on one end to a wonderful Italian grocery store on the other, with two restaurants, a gallery, and a used record store in between. One of the buskers was good—a Native fiddler playing those strange syncopated versions of Kickaha jigs and reels with their odd jumps where you felt a few notes were missing. The other was the inevitable folkie butchering Dylan and Crosby, Stills & Nash.

The shakiness that Ellie had suffered in the wake of her dispute with Patterson finally dissipated after a couple of hours of walking. All that remained was this sense of impending doom. The whole thing was so depressing. Not only the business with Patterson this morning, but how he might very well be able to scuttle what had developed into a fairly lucrative sideline for her. She'd worked hard to get the kind of commissions she was getting now and it wasn't fair that he might be able to take it all away, just like that, with a wave of his hand and the flapping of his jowls.

She caught herself staring at the icy pavement as she walked along, not even paying attention anymore to all the flurry of life bustling around her.

Enough, she told herself. This is just letting Patterson win.

She looked up to find herself back on Lee Street once more, just across the street from the Rusty Lion where she spied Donal sitting at a table by himself in a window booth. He was reading a newspaper, the remains of either a late breakfast or an early lunch on his table. Crossing over the street, she went into the restaurant and made her way through the tables to where he was sitting.

"Were you saving this seat for me?" she asked.

Donal lowered the paper to look at her. "Jaysus, Ellie. You look worse than I usually feel."

"Well, thank you for sharing that."

"Sorry," he said. "I didn't mean it like that." He folded his paper and set it aside on the padded seat beside him. "Sit down."

"Thanks."

Ellie sat down and signaled to the waiter. When she caught his eye, she pointed to Donal's coffee mug.

"I've had a lousy morning," she said, turning back to Donal.

"Welcome to my life. I'm still trying to air out from the deadly combination of Miki's cigarettes and accordion, both of which she has to experience in excess before going in to work. But today's worse, since she's got the day off to get together a last-minute gig for tonight. So it's going to be smoke and noise in the apartment, all bloody day."

"Why do you guys even live together?" Ellie asked.

"We're family."

Ellie shook her head. "Most siblings I know don't live together into their twenties. Not unless they're both living at home with their parents."

"And that'd be a whole other bottle of fish."

"Kettle," Ellie said.

"What?"

"It's 'kettle of fish.' "

The waiter came by with her coffee then and asked if she wanted to order. She was about to say no when she realized that all the walking she'd been doing earlier had left her with a real appetite.

"I guess I'll have the brunch special," she said.

After she went through the multitude of choices that ordering the special entailed—how did she want her eggs, toast or pancakes, bacon, sausage or ham, what sort of juice—she turned back to Donal.

"It's because of us, isn't it? I mean, your living with Miki now."

He shrugged. "I know. We should have taken it slower. I never should have given up my apartment. You don't have to say 'I told you so.' "

"I wasn't going to."

"It just seemed the right thing to do at the time," Donal said. "She needed someone to help with the rent when Judy moved out."

"Right."

"And now I've got my studio all set up."

"Of course."

Donal sighed. "I just forgot how annoying Miki can be." He gave Ellie a mournful look. "She's so relentlessly cheerful—especially in the morning. She makes Jilly seem positively dour."

Jilly was easily the most outgoing, cheerful person Ellie had ever met—until she'd been introduced to Miki—so it was difficult, if not impossible, for her to imagine anyone thinking of Jilly as dour.

"I like happy people," she said.

"Everybody does," Donal told her with his Eeyore voice. "And more power to them, I suppose."

Ellie knew that the real reason Donal had moved in with his sister was that he couldn't face living on his own again after they'd broken up. She still felt guilty about it sometimes. They'd only lived together for a few months when she realized that it wasn't going to work out. She knew that they could be great friends, but a more intimate relationship simply wasn't going to happen. She'd probably known it from the beginning. Donal had been the one who'd been in love, but it was she who'd let herself be persuaded that the friendship she felt for him was something more when she really should have known better.

Trying to explain it to him had made her feel terrible, but at least their break-up hadn't been acrimonious. They'd actually had been able to stay friends—were better friends for what they'd gone through, perhaps, though she also knew that he was still more than a little enamored with her. She kept hoping he'd fall in love again, with someone who could love him back as much as he deserved. It hadn't happened yet.

"But enough about you," Donal said. "Let's talk about me for a change."

Ellie smiled at him over the rim of her coffee mug.

"No, seriously," he said. "What made your morning lousy?"

She told him about Henry Patterson and had to force herself to calm down all over again, just repeating the story.

"So now it's your turn to say 'I told you so,' " she said when she finished up.

"Not a chance," Donal said. "Unlike you, I'm far too polite to rub it in. Except . . . well, I did tell you so."

Ellie nodded. "Don't I remember. 'Been there, done that, it doesn't work out in the long run,' " she quoted back at him.

"And it's hard work," Donal said. "It's one thing pleasing yourself, and then maybe selling what you've done. Quite another being so bloody subject to the vagaries of your clients' whims."

"I know," Ellie said. "And when you deal with someone like Patterson, you feel like all you've been doing is wasting your time."

"I used to feel like that," Donal told her. "But then I realized that I *was* getting paid to practice my craft. Not necessarily my own art, but at least I was learning what I could do with the tools at my disposal."

Ellie moved her coffee mug out of the way as the waiter approached with her breakfast.

"The thing is," Donal went on while she began to eat, "you'll meet some grand folks doing portrait and commissioned work, but some of the punters are so bad you just want to chuck it all and get an office job. Sounds like your man Patterson's one of those."

Ellie gave him a glum nod of agreement. She dipped a piece of toast in the yolk of her egg, but didn't lift it to her mouth.

"Do you think he'll really sic a lawyer on me?" she asked.

Donal shook his head. "It wouldn't be worth his while. The bloody lawyer'd cost him way more than your deposit. There'd be no profit in it and from what you say, Patterson would be one to want a profit."

"Except he could do it for meanness," Ellie said. She put the bite of toast in her mouth.

"There's that," Donal told her. "I don't know your man at all, but if he's got the connections he says he does, you could find your commissions in the business sector drying up."

"What can I do?"

"I've told you before. You need to do a show. It doesn't have to be a big deal, but you have to get your own work out there for the public to see. Build up a reputation in the real world, not with corporate punters like Patterson. You know, the kind of man who likes to think that even his shite smells lovely and will turn him a profit."

"But I've got nothing to show. And what would I live on while I was getting enough together *to* do a show?"

"Well . . ." Donal said.

He let the word hang there. Ellie waited a moment, then she realized what he was getting at.

"You think I should go up to Kellygnow," she said.

Donal nodded. "And find out what the mysterious Musgrave Wood has to offer."

"It might be nothing like you're thinking," Ellie told him. "With the caliber of artists that's usually in residence there, I doubt there'd be either a commission or a residency in the offing."

"I think you're selling yourself short."

"But still . . ."

Donal wouldn't let it go. "Until you follow up on it . . ."

"I won't know." Ellie sighed. "I hate this kind of thing. I'd have no idea what to say."

"If it'll make you feel any better, I'll come up with you."

"Really?"

He gave her one of his rare smiles. "Sure. And who knows? Maybe your man Wood—"

"Who's actually a woman."

"Maybe she'll offer me a gig, too."

Ellie laughed. "Maybe she will."

"So that's settled then. We'll run by Kellygnow first thing tomorrow."

Ellie immediately had a flutter of anxiety.

"I don't know," she said. "Maybe we should wait for a weekday."

"And maybe we should wait until *Riverdance* becomes a weekly sitcom—which for all I know, might actually happen, and I wonder, would your man Whelan be pleased with that? But we won't. You have to seize the cow by the horns."

"You mean 'bull.'"

He got a mischievous look in his eyes. "Strike while the peppers are hot."

Ellie didn't bother to correct him this time.

"All right, already" she said. "No more mangled phrases. We'll go tomorrow."

"That's grand. Maybe nothing'll come of it. But maybe you'll look back on this as one of those pivotal moments that changed your life."

"For the better," she said.

She was finished her meal now. Stacking her plate on top of Donal's, she pushed them both to the edge of the table and looked around for the waiter, wanting a refill on her coffee.

"Well, of course," Donal said. "I'm glad we got that settled."

She turned to look at him. "Now why can't I shake the feeling that I've just been manipulated into this?"

Donal would only offer her a look of perfect innocence in return.

"Admit it," she said. "You just wanted to satisfy your own curiosity about this Kellygnow business, didn't you?"

"I had nothing to do with your man Patterson going all mad on you."

"I didn't say you did. But I can tell by the tone of your voice that you're pleased with how this all turned out, all the same."

"What sort of tone of voice?"

"A satisfied one."

"Jaysus, Mary, and Joseph."

"And your accent gets stronger, too."

"Will you give it a rest, woman."

The waiter showed up at their table with a coffee pot just then, interrupting her attempt to get Donal to confess. She asked for some more coffee and her bill. Donal put his hand over the top of his cup when the waiter offered him a refill.

"Are you working for Angel tonight?" he asked when the waiter had left.

Ellie shook her head. "Tommy and I aren't on again until Monday. Why?"

"It's that gig of Miki's tonight. She's playing at the Crowsea Community Center—filling in for some band that was originally booked to play. We should go. There'll be music and Guinness and all the finer things in life."

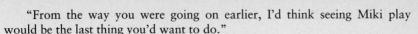

"From the way you were going on earlier, I'd think seeing Miki play would be the last thing you'd want to do."

Donal gave her a look of complete indignation.

"Jaysus, woman," he said. "She's my sister. And a bloody fine accordion player when she doesn't mess around with all that jazzy shite. It's my duty and pleasure to give her all the support I can."

"We are talking about you and Miki here, aren't we?"

"Unless the Queen of Sheeba's taken up playing the box."

Ellie gave up. "Okay. I'll go already."

"I don't know," Donal said, mournfully now. "Maybe you shouldn't. You might find it so dreadfully dull you'll barely be able to keep your eyes open. You could have the worst time ever and then you'll have to blame it all on me."

"What I should do," she said, holding up a fist between them, "is give you a good solid bang alongside your head."

Donal slid his chair back so that he was out of range. That rare smile of his lit up his face, and all she could do was laugh.

7

Miki had never understood the concept of stage fright. The only thing she liked better than playing her button accordion for its own sake was playing it in front of an audience. The larger the crowd, the better. It wasn't that she had a big ego, though she certainly had more than enough confidence in her instrumental ability and knew she could keep an audience entertained. Nor did she need the additional validation of applause. That wasn't the point of her love for playing music live. It was more that she didn't consider the music to be real until it had made the circuit from player to listener's ear and back again by way of the listener's reaction—a circle that could push the music up another notch every time it came around, building through a performance until sometimes when she came off stage, she'd be almost staggering, drunk on the music.

It didn't have to be a big audience—only one that gave the music a fair listen, and was willing to express how they felt about it.

So far as Miki was concerned, they had a grand audience at the Crowsea Community Center tonight. A dancing, foot-stomping, hand-clapping appreciative audience that was making the band work twice as hard since they'd started the set, just to keep the energy up. In short, the evening was unwinding exactly the way she liked it. She sat on a chair at one end of the line of four musicians that made up Jigabout, accordion bouncing on her knee, and was barely able to keep her seat she was having such fun, dancing on the spot, seated and all. Of course it helped to have musicians of this caliber to be playing with.

Jigabout was a pickup band, put together for tonight's gig when the Newford Traditional Music Society's featured act for the evening fell through earlier in the week. Miki had gotten the call from the society on Thursday evening and hastily put Jigabout together—not quite as difficult a prospect as might be imagined since all the musicians she'd rounded up had often played together.

The other members included Emma Jean Wright from Miki's regular band Fall Down Dancing on guitar. Unlike Miki, Emma Jean was a natural blonde, her corkscrew curls pulled back into a loose braid tonight. And she was tall—slender and wonderfully tall—a source of some envy to Miki, who got well and truly tired of her own diminutive size whenever something was out of her reach, which seemed far too often. Besides playing with Fall Down Dancing, Emma Jean doubled as a member of an all-female bluegrass group called the Oak Mountain Girls where she also played five-string banjo and provided vocals. She was one of the few guitarists Miki knew who could play as well in both styles, highlighting the proper accents of either a Celtic dance tune accompaniment or a flat-picked bluegrass breakdown as required.

Since the other members of Fall Down Dancing weren't available for tonight, Miki had fallen back on the Wednesday night sessions at The Harp to find a couple of other players, enlisting Amy Scanlon on pipes, whistle, and vocals, and Geordie Riddell on fiddle and flute. Amy and Geordie often played together as a duo and all four of them shared enough material in common that the big problem in putting together the sets they needed for this gig had been in what to leave out.

When they'd arrived at the community center for their sound-check, the society members had been carefully setting out rows of folding chairs in front of the stage. By now, halfway through their first set, the audience had folded most of those chairs back up against the walls and the seating area had been turned into a dance floor. There was even a kind of mosh pit to the right of the stage, right in front of where Miki was sitting, where various punky-looking kids, all piercings and tattoos, and baggy-clothed skateboarder types were pogoing and generally carrying on, not even trying to dance, but having a great time.

Miki knew that the way they carried on bugged some of the more staunch traditionalists. This sort of thing didn't show the proper respect to the music. But she didn't care. So long as they were having fun and not interfering with the others who were dancing, let them do what they wanted. Why, she thought with a laugh, if the fancy struck her, she might even have a go at crowd-surfing herself.

When the set of reels they were playing came to an end, Miki grinned at Amy, sitting at the other end of the stage with her pipes across her knees. The two of them had brought the tune to a close with exactly the same twiddly-dum-dee-dum flourish. A wave of applause and stamping feet rose up from the dance floor, drowning out the band's thank-yous. Looking down at the set list taped to the floor by her feet, Miki wished, and not for the first time, that she could bounce around the stage the way Geordie and Emma Jean could. But she and Amy were locked to their chairs by their instruments.

"Now," Geordie was saying into the microphone, "we're going to take you from County Clare, where that last set originated, all the way across the Irish Sea and up into the Shetland Isles for a set of tunes from the playing of

Tom Anderson. We'll start with a hornpipe he wrote for the pianist Violet Tulloch, then move on into a pair of reels. . . ."

The community center wasn't set up like a regular concert hall. The stage had some extra lighting on it, but the audience wasn't lost in the usual sea of darkness. Sitting where she was, Miki could actually see the audience. As Emma Jean started the hornpipe, fingerpicking the melody on her guitar, Miki studied the crowd, looking for familiar faces.

There was her brother Donal with Ellie—shame things hadn't worked out between them—and the rest of his Crowsea arts crowd, Jilly, Sophie, Wendy, and all. Here and there she spotted regular customers from the store—how had they even known she was playing this gig? The advertising had all been for the previously slated band with only small corrections running in the "What's On" sections of the papers on Friday and this morning. She recognized some Fall Down Dancing fans, then spied Hunter standing off to one side, near the back.

Amy had joined Emma Jean now, her whistle playing harmonies to Emma Jean's guitar lines. Hunter lifted a hand when he saw Miki looking at him.

Miki smiled, then looked down at her instrument and pretended to check the workings of her bellows. She could feel a flush coming on and hoped it wasn't noticeable from the audience—or at least not from where Hunter was standing.

Donal shouldn't have started in on teasing Hunter at the session the other night, and she shouldn't have kept it up, because things had been getting a little awkward at the store ever since. Where usually she and Hunter had such an easy rapport between them, now everything felt stilted. She kept catching him studying her, his face a mix of puzzlement and that look some of the regulars got when they were trying to build up the nerve to ask her out. By Friday it had been a relief to be able to have the excuse to take Saturday off to work on material for tonight's show.

The trouble was, she didn't know how she felt any more than Hunter knew how he did. For him the idea that she was interested in him would generate the simple relief that, okay, Ria had dumped him, but he wasn't a complete loser; other women still found him interesting. She could almost see him working out the difference between his pal Miki and the woman Miki he'd probably never really looked at all that closely before. Certainly not in this way. One thing you could say about Hunter: He was steadfast and true. The whole time he'd been living with Ria, Miki had never once got the sense that he was in the least bit interested in another woman.

For her own part, well, she'd been joking with Hunter at the session, taking it up where Donal had left it off, not at all serious, but it *had* been cozy, snuggled up beside him at the end there. She'd always looked at Hunter as a friend first, then her boss. Nothing else. Not because she didn't find him attractive, or charming. Or fun, when it came down to it—the past few weeks notwithstanding. Part of the reason she'd not even considered him as boyfriend material had been because, well, he was taken, wasn't he? And he was, what? Ten years older?

Except that gap in their ages didn't seem all that terribly wide—at least not anymore. When she was younger, yes, but now . . . And if they could get along as well as they did as friends, why should a closer relationship be any different? She'd always believed that lovers should be friends as well, because otherwise—

She looked up suddenly, realizing that the band had jumped into the reel that followed "Violet Tulloch's Hornpipe" and she'd missed her cue to come in with them. The audience wouldn't know, but Emma Jean was giving her a puzzled look. Miki shrugged an apology to her bandmate, then waited for the "B" part of the tune to come around. It'd sound better if she came in then— like it was part of the arrangement.

No more woolgathering, she told herself.

When the others came to the end of the "A" part's repeat, she was ready and joined in. Actually, she thought, that sounded pretty good. Gave the second part of the tune a nice little lift.

She made herself stop thinking of anything but the music then, concentrating instead on the wash of sound coming back from the monitors, letting it pull her back into that fey state she could fall into so readily when a great tune banged up against a great audience. It didn't take long before she was jigging in her seat once more, grinning wildly as she worked the bellows, the fingers of her right hand dancing up and down, and back and forth, between the two rows of melody buttons.

It wasn't until after the break, when they were playing their second set, that she noticed the line of tall, dark-haired men standing at the very back of the community center. Six, no, seven of them. She recognized them immediately from the sessions at The Harp. The hard men. Dressed in their dark broadcloth suits, cans of Guinness in hand. Appreciating the music, no doubt, though it was hard to tell from the guarded look in their eyes.

She hoped they weren't here to cause trouble.

Well, it wasn't her problem if they were. Jigabout had only been hired to play the music tonight, not deal with security as well.

The a cappella song that Amy and Emma Jean had been singing came to a conclusion. Next up was a set of Johnny Doherty reels that she and Geordie started off as a duet before the others came in. She looked away from the hard men and raised an eyebrow to Geordie.

"Anytime," he said.

She counted them in and they were off, fiddle and accordion playing the first tune on their own until Emma Jean joined them on guitar for the second time through. Miki cocked her head, smiling when Amy's pipe drones cut in at the beginning of the second tune. She loved the way they bottomed a tune with their bass hum. By the time Amy had joined them on her chanter, Miki had put the hard men right out of her mind.

8

"I don't get it," Ellie said to Donal.

They were standing on the edge of the dance floor, waiting in line to get a drink from the makeshift bar that the Newford Traditional Music Society had set up in the community center's kitchen. Donal had already wrinkled his nose earlier at the idea of Guinness in a can, though that hadn't stopped him from finishing one and probably planning to order another.

"Why hasn't Miki made an album yet?" Ellie went on. "For that matter, why isn't she off on tour somewhere instead of working at the record shop and only playing her music part-time?"

Donal shrugged. "I know why she hasn't recorded. She figures the tunes already exist on enough tapes and CDs by other artists and she doesn't see the point in recording one more version of them."

"But they'd be *her* versions."

"I know, I know. Only try telling her that. It's like trying to argue with a drunk—you'll get no sense out of her."

The man in front of them stepped away with his order and it was their turn.

"I'd like a Kilkenny Cream Ale, please," Ellie told the woman taking orders. She glanced at Donal. He offered up a weary sigh. "And a Guinness," she added.

She pushed his hand back into his jacket when he tried to pay.

"I feel like a kept man," he said.

"You should be so lucky."

After getting her change, she left a couple of quarters in the tip jar and they went and claimed a section of wall to lean against. From where they stood they had a good view of both stage and dance floor. Jigabout were in the middle of a set of Kerry polkas. Out on the dance floor, Jilly and the others they'd come with were doing impressions of mad Irish dervishes, combining spins and twirls with their own rather curious ideas of stepdancing. *Riverdance* it wasn't, but they were obviously having a great time.

"They're like bloody dancing machines," Donal said. "I don't know how they keep it up."

"You're just jealous because you don't have their stamina."

"I suppose that could be one theory," he said. He popped the tab on his can, pulling a face when he took a sip. "Thanks," he added, toasting her with the can, eyes mournful.

"Oh, at least pretend you're enjoying it."

"Never tasted better," he assured her. "At least from a can. . . ."

Ellie shook her head. "You're incorrigible." She had a sip of her own drink. "Anyway. So Miki won't record. But why won't she tour? I mean, listen to them."

"I know," Donal said. "Bloody magic, isn't it? And they don't even play together regularly."

Ellie nodded. "Exactly. Fall Down Dancing are even better."

"Or at least different."

"But easily as good."

"Easily."

"So why does she stick around here?"

"I don't know." Donal reached forward and tapped the shoulder of a man standing in front of them. "What do you say, Hunter?" he asked. "Is it true that the only reason Miki doesn't go off touring is because you've got her locked into some fairy-tale contract that she can only buy her way out of with her firstborn child?"

When Hunter turned around, Ellie recognized him from the record store. He was of medium height, an inch or so taller than Ellie herself, with green eyes and short brown hair. She'd always liked his features—there was so much character and kindness in them—but she'd never gotten up the nerve to ask him to pose for her. He smiled a hello to her, then frowned at Donal.

"I think I'm supposed to be irritated with you," he said.

He didn't really seem to be put out, Ellie decided, since the frown didn't reach his eyes.

"What for?" Donal wanted to know. "It's not about the other night, is it? Jaysus, can't you take a joke?" Turning to Ellie, he explained, "I was telling him at the session how much Miki fancies him."

"And does she?" Ellie asked.

"Who knows? I only said it for a bit of a laugh." He winked at Ellie before turning back to Hunter. "But I'm thinking someone took it seriously."

Hunter nodded. "See, I knew there was a reason."

"I'm the one who should be annoyed," Donal said. "After all, you gave your solemn word to keep it to yourself, only the next thing I know you've told Miki herself and who knows how many others." He glanced back at Ellie again, adding, "A word to the wise. Never trust your man here with a confidence."

"Don't mind him," Ellie told Hunter. "As I'm sure you know, he has no sense of propriety or manners."

"I'd resent that," Donal said, "except it's true."

"And he's surly, too," Ellie added.

"No, I draw the line at surly," Donal said. "Morose, yes. Even bitter. But I'm a bloody artist." He patted his pockets with his free hand. "And somewhere I've got the license to prove it. I'm allowed to be melancholy. Actually, if I read it right, I'm *supposed* to be melancholy."

"Oh, yes," Ellie said. "And he can also get very defensive."

"Do you think he has to work at?" Hunter asked.

She shrugged. "I hope not. Think how depressing it would be if it turned out he actually wanted to be the way he is."

"This is true."

"Right," Donal said. "I'm off to the loo. Will someone hold my drink?" He held the can of Guinness out, but pulled it back when Ellie reached for it. "Never mind," he said. "The mood you two are in, you'd probably drink it yourselves. Or give it away. Waste of a good drink, even if it does come in a can. . . ."

He wandered off to the men's restroom, his voice trailing along behind him. Ellie and Hunter looked at each other, then they both began to laugh.

"I think you owed him that," Ellie said.

Hunter nodded. "Of course it won't stop him from doing the same thing again, given half a chance."

"Of course."

Hunter took Donal's place by the wall, his shoulder next to hers, and the two of them listened to the band play through a set of jigs.

"What were you saying about Miki and touring?" he asked when the applause died down.

"I was just wondering why she doesn't. She's so good."

Hunter looked up at the stage where Miki had launched into an improbable story about the origin of some tune's name.

"You see," she was saying, " 'The Gravel Walk' is actually from China, not the Shetlands. The clue's in the misspelling of the title. It's supposed to be *w-o-k*, not *w-a-l-k*."

"All lies," Geordie put in.

"No," Miki assured the audience with a grin. "This is all true. I hope you're taking notes. Anyway . . ."

"I think she's got a phobia about traveling," Hunter said, returning his gaze to Ellie. "You know what it was like for her growing up, staying with relatives all up and down Ireland, and then emigrating here."

Ellie nodded. The same pattern had been repeated once the Greers had moved to North America, except they didn't have the same extended family to fall back upon here as there had been back home. Then Miki and Donal's mother had died giving birth to a stillborn girl and their father had taken to drinking worse than ever. He was rarely home, abusive when he was. Eventually he simply stopped working and was always home, always drunk. When they lost the last apartment they'd been living in, Miki and Donal had taken to living on the streets to escape Miki's being put into a foster home. Miki had been fourteen, Donal six years older.

"I never saw anyone so happy as Miki was when she got that apartment with Judy," Hunter was saying. "She was so proud of having her own place. Of having a home."

"I guess you've known them longer than I have," Ellie said.

"I suppose. I first met Miki when she was playing at one of The Harp's sessions. Thomas would turn a blind eye when she'd sneak into the pub. I mean, she was just this raggedy little girl—all bones and thick wild hair in those days. Too young to be able to order a drink, but lord could she play." His gaze drifted back to the stage where the band had begun another set of tunes. "I wish she would take the music further, too, but for all that she acts like such a free spirit, she's in serious nesting mode. The very idea of having to pack up and leave—if only for a short tour—terrifies her."

"It's a shame," Ellie said.

Hunter shrugged. "Well, yes and no. She's happy the way things are now, so why should she change? Besides, there's something to be said for playing music for the love of it, rather than it being merely the springboard towards fame and fortune."

"I guess you see a lot of that in your business."

"Lots of one-hit wonders," Hunter agreed. "That's why I admire musicians like them," he added, nodding towards the stage. "They haven't lost track of the music yet."

This was reminding Ellie of her own feelings this morning, weighing commissioned work and the steady money it promised against following her own muse and being broke.

"But can't you have both?" she said. "A career and still be true to your art?"

"Well, sure. But it only seems to work at a grassroots level. For every multi-platinum artist, there are any number of bands making far more interesting music that have trouble selling even two or three thousand copies of an album." He shrugged. "You can still make a living at it, but you have to be willing to do most of it on your own—all those things the labels and a good manager used to be able to do for you. Promotion, setting up the tours, even getting together the money you need for recording and then pressing your CDs."

Ellie supposed it was depressingly true for all the arts. The only thing that was different was the medium one picked to work in. Some chose music, some dance, some fine art . . .

Don't focus on it, she told herself. She'd come here tonight to get away from that kind of thinking, however true it might be.

"One of the things I like about this music," she said, to change the subject, "is how it appeals to such a diversity of people while still remaining true to itself." She looked out at the dancers. "Yuppies and punkers, rich and poor, old and young. There's a complete cross section of people out there on the dance floor—not to mention those who'd rather just listen. Like those guys standing at the back there. I mean, do they seem to be the sort of people you'd expect to like this music?" She laughed. "Though maybe 'like' is too strong a word. They don't seem to be having much of a good time—at least not nearly so much as the dancers."

Hunter glanced in the direction she indicated, then looked away.

"The hard men," he said.

Ellie nodded. "That's what Donal calls them. You see them in The Harp from time to time, and they never seem to be having any more fun there either. I wonder why they bother to come out."

"Donal says they beat him up one night."

"I remember. It was like some stupid macho initiation. First they beat him up, then they're all friendly with him the next time they see him. Or what passes for friendly with that bunch. It really makes you wonder about people, doesn't it?"

"I'm guessing that they must be carrying around a lot of anger," Hunter said.

"But that shouldn't be an excuse."

"I wasn't excusing them."

"I didn't think you were," Ellie told him. "I just get frustrated about that kind of thing. I see so much of that on the streets. You wonder how all those people who must once have been so full of hope grow so lost. And angry. Some take it out on themselves, some take it out on others."

Hunter turned to look at her. "That's right. You're involved with one of Angel's projects, aren't you?"

"Part-time. We're the ones that drive around in the vans at night."

"I don't know how you can do it. Where do you find the time?"

Ellie smiled at him. "Well, it does play havoc with my social life. It seems like half the time I can't date because we're out in the van and the other half I'm too tired to do anything but veg at home. It doesn't exactly make me scintillating company."

"Is that what happened with you and . . ."

Hunter's voice trailed off and he got an embarrassed look on his face.

"Me and Donal?" Ellie finished for him.

"Sorry. I didn't mean to pry."

"That's okay." Ellie looked out at the dancers again, not really seeing them, before she went on. "No, it wasn't that. It was more that I ended up realizing we'd make better friends." She returned her attention to Hunter. "Not that lovers shouldn't be friends as well. I never can understand why people don't concentrate on the friendship part of their relationship more than they do. There'd be a lot less divorces and breakups if they did."

"I think you're right. That's what got to me with Donal's teasing the other night. I started thinking about how Miki and I are such good friends, and how that seemed to automatically preclude us having any other sort of a relationship."

Ellie smiled. "So Donal was right. You do fancy her."

Hunter shook his head. "No. I keep finding myself looking at her and wondering about it, but I know it's not like that. What it really got me thinking about was how that lack of a solid friendship was what made my last relationship fall apart. After that big buzz that comes when you first connect, we just became a habit to each other. Turns out we weren't so good at the friendship part."

"You're talking about Ria?"

He looked surprised.

"We're a small crowd," Ellie said with a sympathetic smile. "And much prone to gossip."

"No kidding. I suppose Donal told you about it."

Ellie shook her head. "No, Jilly did."

"It *is* a small crowd, isn't it?"

"Pretty much. But don't worry," she added. "It's not like all the details are making the rounds."

"I guess I should be grateful for that."

Ellie smiled. "But it does feel weird when it's our own lives that become grist for the old gossip mill."

"Tell me about it. Imagine what it'd be like to be famous and to have to read about all your personal ups and downs in the tabloids."

"No thanks."

"But I haven't even asked you anything yet," a new voice said.

They both looked up to find Jilly standing in front of them, hands on her hips. Her cheeks were flushed, blue eyes sparkling, and a light sheen of perspiration dampened her brow. Loose strands of hair clung to her temples, having escaped from the bun she'd put up in a futile attempt to tame her usual unruly locks. Ellie didn't think she knew anyone who could cram so much energy into one petite package. Jilly had been dancing since the moment the group of them had arrived and didn't seem to be even remotely ready to stop. She grinned at the pair of them, her good humor so infectious that Ellie couldn't help but smile back.

"I know Donal can be a poop," Jilly said, "but I expected better from you, Ellie. This isn't a night to be wallflowering it—it's a night for silly feet and general hullabalooing. So come on." She took them both by the hand and gave them a tug towards the dance floor. "The band needs our warm bodies thrown about in mad jigging and reeling to keep them all revved up."

Ellie and Hunter looked at each other, then set their drinks against the wall and let her pull them to where the rest of their friends were dancing.

"Nice to see you out and about," Jilly said to Hunter.

Ellie had another smile as Hunter gamely tried to get into the swing of things.

"I hear you've been telling tales out of court," he said.

"Only the nicest ones," Jilly assured him. "Just to let everyone know that you're available once more. Wouldn't want you to get all lonely—or worse, all morose like himself."

"She means Donal," Ellie told him.

"I knew that."

9

After the show, Hunter stayed behind with Ellie and her friends to help put away the chairs and generally clean up the community center. It turned out that most of them were members of the Newford Traditional Music Society—no surprise there, Hunter thought, considering how much they seemed to like the music. The rest, like himself, were simply willing to pitch in and give a hand.

They were a much nicer group of people that he'd expected them to be, and that was a surprise. He'd met a number of them before, in the record store, or through Ria at various parties, gallery openings, and the like, but he'd never really interacted with them in the same way as he had tonight.

"You feel like an outsider," Ria would tell him when they got home after one of those soirées, "because you act like an outsider. You wouldn't feel nearly so uncomfortable if you took the time to get to know them."

Being the truth, it was hard to respond to. No one had ever made him feel out of place. In fact, they often went out of their way to make him feel welcome. But the problem was he *did* feel like an outsider. They were all such creative people, where he was lucky to be able to put together a window display that looked even halfway decent, never mind innovative. And if that wasn't intimidating enough, not only was it quickly apparent that they had wide-ranging interests—from the arts and literature, through the sciences, history, mythology, and current affairs—they were also able to discuss those same eclectic subjects with obvious ease and informed knowledge.

All he could enthuse about was music. He wasn't as badly introverted as Titus or Adam, but when he was among such outgoing people as this crowd, he usually felt as woefully lacking in the social graces as he knew his employees to be. It wasn't something that was very easy to explain to someone else, especially since it was so hard to admit it even to himself.

Ria never seemed to have the patience to listen through his stumbling attempts to articulate how her friends made him feel intimidated. Nor did she have much sympathy.

"If you want to be better informed about more things," she'd say, "get your nose out of those music magazines you're always reading and broaden your horizons a little more."

"I need to read those for my work," he'd explain.

"I know. Nobody's putting you down or thinks you're stupid. Can't you tell that they like you?"

But *I* feel stupid, he'd want to say.

He'd often wondered what it was that she saw in him. It hadn't been like that at first. When they first met, she'd been as scruffy as he still was, always happier in jeans and a T-shirt as opposed to what she had to wear to the office. She'd loved music, too—all sorts, in those days. But she'd changed—"I've grown, Hunter," was how she put it—and he hadn't. Or couldn't. Or, perhaps more truthfully, he didn't want to.

Music had become an intrinsic part of his life from the day he bought his first Dave Clark Five single. It wasn't a matter of performing himself—though that had been an ambition at one point—but simply to be involved with the music industry. To discover new sounds before anyone else did. To follow bands through their various lineups and solo efforts. He loved the buzz of getting a first listen to the new releases when the sales reps dropped off their promotional material. He loved introducing people to music they might never otherwise have tried.

But that was a kid's life, so far as Ria was concerned. Not a viable career for an adult.

She kept getting promotions, rising from a clerical position into management, dressing better, taking more care in her appearance, not simply at work, but at home as well. She took up painting with courses at the Newford School of Art, which was where she'd fallen in with Jilly and her crowd. She started talking about marriage and buying a home and starting a family. She was the one who'd talked him into buying the record store. "I thought the responsibility would be good for you," she'd said when the store became yet one more point of contention.

"It might have been," he'd told her, "if you'd cared about it as much as I do."

"You're not getting the point."

Only Hunter had. He just hadn't known what to do with it. They'd fallen into such a rut of bad habits and arguments that it wasn't until she left that he'd realized how much he still cared for her. But by then it was too late.

He almost hadn't come to the show tonight. Knowing that Jilly and the rest of them would be here tonight, he'd half-expected to see Ria as well. But of course Celtic music wasn't her thing anymore. If it ever had been. If it hadn't simply been one of those instances where one professed delight with a potential partner's tastes because everything had a rosy shine to it when a relationship began.

He didn't know what he'd have said to her if she had come tonight. They hadn't talked in weeks now. After she'd moved out he'd called her a couple of times at her parents' place where she'd been staying. Later, when she'd gotten a place of her own, leaving instructions with her parents that he wasn't to have her new phone number, he tried her at the office, but he only did that once because it was all too apparent there was nothing left to say.

"Get on with your life, Hunter," she'd told him that day. "That's all we can do now. Just get on with our lives."

What life? Hunter had wanted to ask her, because without her, there suddenly didn't seem to be any. But he'd only said goodbye and hung up. Took the Christmas present he'd bought her and stuck it away on a shelf in the back room of the store.

Leaning against the wall by the front door of the community center, he found himself thinking about all of that now. Maybe everything hadn't ended when Ria walked out the door. He just had to put some meaning back into his life, some import that didn't depend on anyone else for its worth. Easier said than done, he knew, but at least it was something to shoot for. And it sure beat the idea of wallowing in self-pity as he'd been doing for the past few weeks.

Donal and Ellie and a few of the others were going out to a coffee shop, now that the cleanup was done. When Miki asked if he was coming, he decided he might as well tag along. Not because Miki was going, because something might work out between them. And not even because of Ellie, who was gorgeous and smart and seemed to like him; he'd been in her company for most of the evening now and found that he'd quite enjoyed being there. He was going along with them for himself.

So he was waiting for the last of the musicians' gear to be packed away, errant scarves and jackets, parkas and snow boots to be tracked down, final swallows of beer to be finished before the cans went into the recycling bins in the kitchen.

Dancing tonight, he'd used more muscles than he remembered having. It had been a long time since he'd let himself relax enough to become one of what Jilly called the "mad, ballyhooing bohos" that she claimed the band needed to carry the music up to new heights. Polkas were obviously the general favorites—not the German beer garden variety, but the Irish ones that seemed to require twice the energy and steps of a reel. Or at least they did with this crew.

Tomorrow he'd definitely be feeling each and every one of those unused muscles. He knew, because he could already feel them aching. He appreciated this moment to catch his breath, to be alone for a few moments before he was plunged back into the pleasant maelstrom of their infectious camaraderie. When the door opened beside him, he barely registered the man who stepped through until he stood directly in front of him.

It was one of Donal's hard men.

Up close like this, Hunter decided the appellation was a good one. The man had intense eyes, cold and dark, and a slit of a mouth that one could easily imagine had never attempted a smile. His suit smelled of old cigarette smoke and something else Hunter couldn't quite identify. It wasn't until much later that he remembered the last time he'd experienced that odor. It had been at the zoo. A musky, wild dog scent that had hung around the wolves' enclosure.

"*An dealbhóir,*" the man said. His voice was thickly accented. "The sculptor."

The only sculptor here was Ellie, Hunter thought.

"What about her?" he asked.

"She's not for you," the man said, his dark gaze boring into Hunter. "Do you understand?"

Hunter shook his head. He was feeling somewhat nervous now, not to mention slightly tipsy and definitely out of his league.

"She has other work to do," the man told him.

Hunter swallowed thickly, cleared his throat. "And this is somehow your business—?"

The man gave him a quick, sucker punch to the kidneys. It happened so fast, Hunter never saw the blow. He gasped at the sudden pain and had to lean against the wall to stop from keeling right over. Hand on his side, he stared incredulously at his attacker.

"What—?"

"Careful now," the hard man said. "You don't want to fuck with us, you little shite." He grabbed a handful of hair and pulled Hunter's head up, bent his own dark face close. "Keep sniffing around her, and I'll have to have another little chat with you and it's my thought you'll be enjoying it even less than the one we've had tonight."

"But—"

The man jerked Hunter's hair. "Might we have an understanding now, do you think?"

"Hey!"

Hunter recognized Donal's voice, but it seemed to come from far away. Beside him, the hard man glanced over, then gripped Hunter by the shoulders and held him upright.

"Your man here seems to be feeling ill," the hard man told Donal. "Can't hold the drink."

He gave Hunter a little push in Donal's direction. While Donal was busy trying to keep Hunter from falling, the hard man did a quick fade out the door and was gone.

"Are you all right?" Donal asked.

Hunter nodded, feeling anything but. He straightened up, taking his weight from Donal's support, and backed up until he could lean against the table that stood by the door. Earlier, a couple of members of the Newford Traditional Music Society had been sitting behind it, collecting money and stamping the backs of people's hands once they'd paid. Now, in place of the cashbox and flyers describing the society's upcoming concerts, there were only a few jackets piled on the table, along with somebody's knapsack. Without the table to help hold up his weight, Hunter was sure he'd have fallen down.

Donal's gaze went to the door where the hard man had made his quick exit, then returned to Hunter.

"What happened?" he asked. "Are you really feeling sick?"

It was odd, Hunter found himself thinking. One could see far worse fights on a TV show or in a movie. But where in those choreographed brawls the participants were back on their feet in moments, all he felt like doing was curling up on the floor. He wasn't sure which was worse: the adrenaline crash, now that the moment of danger was past, or the sharp pain in his side.

"Was your man there giving you some trouble?" Donal said.

"He was . . . warning me away," Hunter finally managed. "From Ellie."

"From Ellie?"

Hunter nodded. "And then he . . . hit me."

Donal's gaze dropped to where Hunter was holding his side. He gave Hunter a sympathetic look.

"Jaysus and Mary," he said. "You're going to be pissing blood for a few days."

"Lovely."

"It could've been worse. The lot of them could have waited and jumped you outside."

Hunter nodded. Donal was right, though it didn't make him feel all that much better.

"What do you suppose he wanted with Ellie?" Donal asked.

"I have no idea." Hunter thought for a moment, playing the conversation back in his head. "He didn't exactly mention her by name—he just said 'the sculptor'—but I knew who he meant."

"There's a half-dozen sculptors here tonight," Donal told him.

"Maybe. Only I wasn't talking to any of them except for her."

Donal nodded, a frown furrowing his brow.

"Look," he said. "Do us a favor and don't mention this to Ellie, would you? There's no point in upsetting her until we know more."

"And how are we supposed to do that?"

"I don't know yet, but I'll think of something." Donal gave him a critical once-over. "You still up for the café?"

Hunter shook his head.

"I didn't think so," Donal said. "I'll make some excuses for you—might as well use the hard man's line and tell them you've come down with a lager flu."

"Whatever."

"And then I'll help you get home."

"I think I can manage to walk on my own."

Donal shook his head. "I wasn't planning on carrying you home, boyo. But I was thinking, maybe it'd be good for you to have some company, just in case somebody happened to be waiting for you to leave on your own. . . ."

Shit. Hunter hadn't even thought of that.

"Thanks," he said.

He stayed where he was, resting his weight on the table, while Donal went off to tell the others. Miki and Ellie returned with Donal, obviously worried, but Hunter managed to convince them that all he needed was a good night's sleep.

"Call me sometime," Ellie said. "When you're feeling better."

"I will."

"Do you want me to open up tomorrow?" Miki asked.

"No, I'm sure I'll be fine. Look, I'm sorry about all of this. I feel like an idiot."

"Oh, we've all partaken too much of the brew now and again," Miki said, giving her brother a mock-stern look.

Ellie nodded. "And dancing just makes it goes to your head all that much quicker."

Donal took Hunter's arm. "Right. Well, we're off. If I don't catch up with you at the café," he added to Miki, "I'll see you at home."

"I'll be waiting, breathless with anticipation."

Donal smiled. "You did good tonight," he told her. "Real magic."

He eased Hunter out the door, but not before Hunter caught the surprised look on Miki's face.

It was funny, Hunter thought, as they made their way down the street. Tonight was the first time he'd felt normal since Ria had left him. Or at least he had been feeling normal until the confrontation with the hard man. And then he remembered what Ellie had said, just before he'd left.

Call me some time.

Not the hard man's warning, nor the pain in his side, could stop him from smiling.

10

SUNDAY MORNING, JANUARY 18

Bettina had come outside to check the birdfeeders when the green Volkswagen minibus turned off Handfast Road into Kellygnow's driveway. She heard the *chug-chug* of its motor first, followed by the spin of the bus's wheels on the packed snow and ice that covered the asphalt. Hands in the pockets of her wool coat, she watched the odd little vehicle make it up the last of the slope and complete its approach to where she was standing, its apple-green panels standing out sharply against the snow-covered lawns on either side.

You didn't see many of those old minibuses in Newford, she thought as it coughed to a halt. Or even the old VW bugs. Not like at home. The bodies rusted out too quickly from all the salt they put on the roads up here.

She didn't recognize either the driver or his passenger, but that wasn't unusual. There were always new faces arriving at Kellygnow. The driver was a short Anglo—at least she assumed he was short since all that showed of him above the dashboard were a pair of dark eyes surrounded by a full beard and a mane of thick hair. There was something about him, a shadow clinging to him that told her he had either experienced great sorrows, or would cause them. Perhaps both would hold true. Bettina had already met too many people like him since she'd moved to this city.

His companion was much more interesting: an attractive woman about Bettina's age. She sat taller than the driver, her long dark hair spilling over the collar of her parka, her eyes bright with interest in her surroundings. In her, Bettina could sense *la brujería* flowing strong and pure. It came up out of her in a torrent, flooding her immediate surroundings.

Y bien, she thought. Wouldn't Lisette have a time painting *that* aura. One would have to be blind not to see it, to feel its pulse in the air, though curiously, the driver appeared oblivious. Perhaps he was merely used to it.

Bettina walked toward them when they disembarked.

"Hello," she said. "Can I help you?"

"Oh, I love your accent," the woman told her. "Is it Spanish?"

Bettina smiled. "Close enough. My name's Bettina," she added, holding out her hand.

"I'm Ellie Jones," the woman said.

Her handshake was firm, *la brujería* rising up from her fingers like a static charge, and yet, Bettina realized, the woman was as unaware of what she carried as her companion appeared to be. *Qué extraño.*

"And this is my friend Donal Greer."

Bettina dutifully shook hands with the driver. He smiled at her as though they were sharing a private joke, but the humor never reached his eyes. Bettina didn't get the joke, and wasn't particularly interested in pursuing what he meant by it, so she returned her attention to his companion.

"Can I help you find someone?" she asked.

Ellie hesitated, suddenly shy.

"Ah, go on," her companion said.

"It's just . . ." Ellie paused to clear her throat. "Is there someone named Musgrave Wood staying here at the moment?"

"The name is unfamiliar. . . ."

"Tall," Ellie went on. "Sixtyish and very striking—distinguished even. The last time I saw, um . . . him, he was wearing a dark, somewhat threadbare overcoat and a hunter's cap."

Bettina noted the hesitation before Ellie referred to a gender. There was only one person she could think who fit both that ambiguity and description.

"Perhaps you mean the Recluse," she said, regretting the words as soon as they were out. If this couple were friends of the odd woman staying in Hanson's old cottage, they might not take kindly to having her referred to in such a fashion.

Ellie and her companion exchanged glances.

"The . . . recluse?" Ellie repeated.

"I'm sorry," Bettina told her. "I didn't mean to be rude. Just because sometimes people keep to themselves, it doesn't mean . . . well, anything, ¿de acuerdo?"

But Ellie didn't appear to be at all upset by Bettina's slip of the tongue.

"The person we're looking for," she said, "could easily fit that sort of description."

"Y bien," Bettina said. "Let me take you around back to the cottage where your friend is staying."

She led the way along the side of the house to the rear, their footsteps crunching in the snow as they crossed the lawn. The sun was bright on the snow, awaking a pattern of blinding highlights on the open ground while deepening the subsequent shadows under the trees where the old Hanson cottage stood. As they neared the cottage, a pair of crows rose from the woods behind it, leaving in their wake an image of black wings touched with iridescent blue and the dwindling sound of their cawing.

"I've never been up here before," Ellie said. "It's so beautiful."

Bettina nodded. She liked this woman who spoke what came to mind and carried her own brujería sun inside her.

"I know," she said. "I feel so blessed to live here."

"Ah, yes," Donal said, tramping along at her side. His breath was forming frost in his beard. "What could be better than living the life of the rich and famous?"

"I'm neither rich nor famous," Bettina told him.

"No, but your benefactor is, or this place wouldn't exist, would it?"

"I suppose. . . ."

"Don't mind him," Ellie said. "He thinks being grumpy is charming and there's no point in trying to convince him otherwise, though Lord knows I've tried."

Bettina wasn't so sure it was as simple as that, but it was hardly her business. Shrugging, she led the way under the trees. The temperature immediately dropped when they stepped out of the sun and it took their eyes a few moments to adjust to the change in the light. This close to the cottage, Bettina could feel the presence of the Recluse's brujería, as potent and strange as it had been yesterday, but stronger now. She glanced at her companions. They gave no more indication of noticing it than they did the magic coursing through Ellie's own blood.

At the door of the cottage, Bettina rapped with a mitten-covered knuckle on the wooden panel. There was no immediate response so, after a moment, she rapped on it again, a little harder this time to make up for the muffling of the wool. She stepped back when she heard movement on the other side of the door. It was well she did. The door was flung open, banging on the log wall beside it, and then the Recluse was standing there, filling the doorway with her height. She regarded them each for a long moment, before her gaze settled on Ellie.

"So," she said. "You've finally come."

Bettina could readily appreciate the return of Ellie's shyness in the face of the Recluse's brusque manner.

"Um," Ellie began. "Did you leave . . ." She pulled off a mitten and dug into the pocket of her parka, producing a creased business card. "Did you leave this in the van for me?"

"Yes, yes," the Recluse told her, obviously impatient.

"So your name is Musgrave Wood?"

"It's as good as any."

Ellie cleared her throat. "Why did you—"

"Come inside," the woman said, stepping aside. "You're letting all the cold in."

Ellie went first. Before Donal could follow, the Recluse moved forward to block the door again. She reached for its inner handle and gave them each another considering look, her gaze lingering longer on Bettina.

"Go amuse yourselves," she finally said and pulled the door shut in their faces.

Bettina blinked in surprise, then turned to look at Donal.

"Jaysus," he said. "Your man's not exactly polite, is he?"

"She," Bettina told him.

"She?"

"She's a woman, not a man."

Donal gave a slow nod. "That's right. Ellie said something about that. But still. Bloody hell. It's cold out here."

Bettina had been looking at the cottage again. Now she returned her attention to him, noting the darkness in his eyes. She doubted it had all that much to do with the Recluse's rudeness.

Why are you so angry anyway? she wanted to ask, but instead she said, "Would you like to come back to the house for something to drink? Some cocoa or coffee?"

"You wouldn't have any Guinness, would you?"

She shook her head. "There might be a Corona."

He pulled a face. "Coffee'll do."

¡Por supuesto! Now she was stuck with him for who knew how long? May Santa Irene give her patience. Too long in Donal's company and she'd be pouring the coffee over his head. Whatever did his friend see in him?

"So speaking of yourself," Donal said as they walked back toward the house. "Would you be an artist or a writer?"

"Neither. I just model for some of the artists."

"Ah."

She gave him a sharp look.

"Gentle, now," he said. "I only meant that you'd be a delight to paint. There's so much character in your features."

¡Y qué! Bettina suppressed a sigh.

"I suppose you're an artist?" she asked.

He nodded. "It's the one thing I don't screw up."

Bettina stopped. She thought that was probably the first honest thing he'd said since he'd arrived.

Donal took another step before he realized she wasn't coming. Turning, he looked back at her.

"Why do you think that is?" she asked.

He regarded her for a long moment. "Jaysus, Mary, and Joseph. Don't you think it's a bit early in the day to be philosophizing? We don't even have a pint in us yet."

She nodded and started to walk again, leading him to the kitchen door. Just before they went in, he caught her arm. She looked pointedly down at his hand until he let go.

"Look," he said. "We're getting off on the wrong foot. I don't mean to be such a shite. It just happens. I don't even know what I'm saying 'till the words're out of my bloody mouth."

"You don't have to explain yourself."

"But I want to."

She waited.

"You're not making this easy," he went on. Before she could speak, he held up a hand. "I know, I know. There's no reason you should. It's just . . . I'm not much good with the social graces, you see, so I act like an eejit." He gave her a quick smile. She could tell he was trying, but the warmth still didn't quite reach his eyes. "When I'm painting, it's the only time I feel like I have . . . you know . . . any worth. . . ."

His voice trailed off. Bettina considered him for a moment. She could feel a fetish taking shape in her mind, how she would define him if he came to her for healing. She could see the stitches, knew the *milagro* she would choose. There would be paint pigment mixed in with the dirt. Cobalt blue, definitely. A touch of raw sienna.

"Perhaps," she said, "you should approach the rest of life as though you had a paintbrush in hand."

He looked at her for a long moment, then nodded. This time, when his lips twitched, the smile reached his eyes.

"That's good, you know," he said. "It's worth a try."

She shrugged, not entirely sure if he meant it.

"Go on inside," she told him, "and warm up. I'm just going to top up the birdfeeders and then I'll put on a pot of coffee for us."

"Let me help." When she hesitated, he added, "I'll keep my gob shut."

"Gob?"

"My mouth. I mean I'll be quiet."

"Bueno," she said. "We keep the seed in the shed out back."

True to his word, he held his peace, and surprisingly, the silence that fell between them as they measured out seed and filled the feeders wasn't uncomfortable.

Maybe he wasn't so bad after all. Bettina found herself thinking, but then she had to smile at herself. And maybe *el cuervo* could bleach its black wings and pass itself off as a dove. But it wasn't likely. Like a crow, this Donal Greer was no innocent. Let the smile reach his eyes. But beneath the kindly charm he presented to her now, a darkness remained. . . .

Y bien. It wasn't her problem.

11

The day wasn't unfolding at all the way Ellie had expected it would. Which, she decided, was becoming the story of her life, really. Just consider how well things had gone yesterday morning when Henry Patterson threw his control-freak hissy fit, ha-ha. Bloody hell, as Donal would say. She'd much prefer sailing through life on an even keel to the seesawing highs and lows that the weekend had produced so far, but what could you do? Unless you were Jilly or Miki—both of whom seemed to be gifted with the innate ability to spin some kind of gold out of the worst situation's straw—you simply had to take what was thrown at you and make the best of it.

And when you thought about, she really shouldn't complain. Take the good with the bad, as her mother would always say. Unlike the people she and Tommy saw most nights driving the Angel Outreach van, she at least had ups to compensate for the otherwise less-than-wonderful parts of her life.

Patterson had ruined yesterday morning, it was true, and he might well kill any potential she had to make a career as a portraitist of the city's business community, but she'd had a good time at the dance last night and it had been nice to get to know Hunter as more than a face behind the counter at the record store. And Hunter had seemed attracted to her as well, which was no small thing for a woman to whom the word "date" had simply come to mean the edible fruit of a palm tree. So he couldn't hold his liquor. So he'd had to go home early. That was no big deal. Considering how much Donal could put away—"I'm your man for the gargle," as he liked to put it—and how their relationship had gone, she wouldn't mind if the next man in her life was a complete teetotaler.

As for today's seesaw . . . Well, she'd had the pleasure of meeting Bettina, and wouldn't she make a great subject for a bust with her striking Latina features—those eyes, that hair—but then Donal had to start acting like such a little shit.

And now this.

Musgrave Wood, if that even was his/her name, was proving to be more cantankerous than Donal at his worst, and wasn't that saying something? The Old World charm Wood had conveyed when they'd met the other night wasn't even remotely in evidence today.

Ellie had been nervous enough about coming to Kellygnow in the first place, and she was of half a mind to simply walk right out of the cottage now, if this was what she could expect. But for all her dislike of mysteries and puzzles, curiosity had managed to get the better of her and she found herself staying. She supposed she'd been hanging around with Tommy too much lately. The next thing you knew she'd be driving up to the rez with him to ask the Aunts for advice.

"Would you like some tea?" her androgynous host asked.

Ellie glanced at the door Wood had so recently closed in Donal's face. She was surprised that he wasn't hammering on its panels.

"My friend," she began.

"Will be fine. No doubt they'll be waiting for you in the house." When Ellie didn't immediately respond, Wood added, "You've come this far. At least hear me out."

"I suppose. It's just . . ."

"First let me get the tea," Wood said. "Go on and take off your coat and sit. And don't worry about your boots. The floor's seen worse than a bit of snow in its time."

Ellie hesitated a moment longer before finally crossing the floor to where a pair of rustic wooden chairs stood at an equally roughly hewn table. Her boots shed melting snow with every step.

She'd often had a fantasy of moving into some little log cabin in the Kickaha Hills—the idea of it appealed to the same part of her that thought she liked camping. However the two times she'd actually gone camping, the discomforts had seemed to far outweigh the pleasanter aspects of those outings. But she thought she could live in a place like this.

The open-concept room was dominated by a rather large cast-iron woodstove. One corner of the floor space, the part where she was sitting, had been sectioned off as a kitchen area. The rest formed a combination sitting room and bedroom, furnished with a rather narrow four-poster brass bed that had a cedar chest at its foot, and a reading chair that was pulled up by the stove, a floor lamp standing behind it. The kitchen boasted a sink and counter, a hutch, fridge, and some cupboards under the counter. There was a row of books on a shelf near the bed, leather-bound, their titles indecipherable from where she was sitting, and a small curtained area in the far corner that was probably the bathroom, or a closet. Or both. It seemed wonderfully cozy, with the views from the windows looking out on only trees and lawn. One could almost think they were out in the hills somewhere, instead of the middle of the city.

Before Ellie sat down, she unzipped her parka, but kept it on, making it plain that she didn't expect to stay long. She glanced at her host. Wood gave no indication that she'd noticed, or understood, what was implied by Ellie's keeping her coat on, and busied herself at the woodstove. Pouring hot water from a kettle into a brown betty tea pot, she brought it and a pair of mugs over to the table where Ellie sat waiting.

"Milk? Sugar?" Wood asked.

"Both, please."

"Now then," Wood said, returning from the small old-fashioned refrigerator that hunched, murmuring to itself, beside the sleeker wooden kitchen hutch. "Where shall we start?"

She placed a sugar bowl and a carton of milk between them on the table and sat down across from Ellie, giving her an expectant look. Ellie was still holding the business card she'd found in the van the other night. Smoothing out its creases, she dropped the card onto the table beside the brown betty.

"Outside," she said. "When I asked you if this was your name, you were . . . evasive."

Wood nodded. "Yes, I was. I'm sorry. It's a bad habit."

"So is it? Your name, I mean."

"Why is it so important?"

Ellie shrugged. "I just like to know who I'm dealing with."

And what, she added to herself. She was sure, now, that Wood was a woman. A very mannish woman, though a woman nevertheless. But there was still something odd about her that had nothing to do with the blurring of genders.

Wood tapped the business card with a long finger and smiled. "I do answer to this," she said, "though it's not the name I was born to. It's a bit of a joke, really. Do you know what 'musgrave' means?"

Ellie shook her head.

" 'Grove full of mice.' "

All Ellie could do was give her a blank look.

"When I was a child," Wood explained, "the Kickaha lived closer to the lake than they do now. I used to be haunted by the ghosts of the dead mice that we had to kill—to keep them out of our dry goods, you understand. So the Indian children that I played with took to calling me Many Mice Wood—'Wood' is my actual surname. I related this story to a philologist friend of mine some time later and he promptly christened me Musgrave. Wood/grove—do you see? Full of mice."

"And all of this relates to . . . ?" Ellie asked.

"You wanted to know my name."

"Yes. Of course."

"I was born Sarah," Wood went on, "which was also my best friend's name in college. To lessen the confusion, I decided to rename myself." She tapped the card again. "To this. Of course Sarah—my friend Sarah—is long gone now and I've since reclaimed the name." Her gaze rose from the card. "Though Musgrave, I'll admit, still has a certain resonance for me that Sarah will never have, and I can't quite seem to let it go."

Since sitting at the table, Wood's manner had regained that Old World charm that Ellie remembered from the other night. The woman's moodiness was something else Wood shared with Donal, she realized. When the fancy struck him, he could switch as readily as Wood had between being cranky and wonderfully likable. Still, while that was true, and interesting on some level, it brought her no closer to understanding why Wood had left the card in the van than she'd been before coming up here to Kellygnow.

Opening the lid of the brown betty and peering inside, Wood pronounced the tea steeped and poured them each a cup. She drank hers black, pushing the sugar and milk over to Ellie's side of the table.

"So you used to see the ghosts of mice," Ellie found herself saying.

That was the sort of thing she expected from Jilly or Donal, not this rather formidable woman sitting across from her. Whimsical was not a word Ellie would have used to describe her.

"I still do," Wood informed her. "Mousy ghost, . . . and others, too."

I'm not going there, Ellie thought.

She stirred her tea and took a sip. Setting her mug down, she regarded her host.

"Why am I here, Ms. Wood?" she said. "Why did you leave your business card in our van the other night? And what did you mean with 'you've finally come' when you opened the door?"

"I have a proposition for you," Wood said. "A commission."

Don't let it have anything to do with ghosts, Ellie thought, of mice or otherwise.

"A commission," she repeated.

Wood nodded. "I would like you to cast a mask for me. You still do masks, don't you?"

"I haven't for years, but I can still do them." She paused, and gave her host a sharp look. "But how would you even know that? Actually, when it comes down to it, how did you know to approach me on the street the other night? And why didn't you ask me then?"

"My, you are full of questions, aren't you?"

"I think they're reasonable."

"Yes, well. Shall we take them one at a time then? I know your work because I make it my business to keep informed of such endeavors."

"But I haven't done masks in ages—and never to sell. The last ones I did were for a friend's play. And they weren't cast, either. They were papier-mâché."

"Nevertheless, masks you have cast." She smiled. "That rhymes, doesn't it?"

Ellie dutifully returned her smile.

"Now," Wood went on. "I hadn't planned to approach you on the street as I did—that was merely happy circumstance—though I certainly recognized you immediately. You have a—shall we say—quality that is unmistakable."

"What sort of quality?"

Wood regarded her for a long moment, then waved a hand dismissively. "And lastly, I didn't ask you then as you seemed somewhat otherwise occupied."

Ellie wanted to pursue this quality business, but realized that there probably wasn't much point. She remembered how earlier Wood had told her that evasiveness was a habit she had. Obviously she hadn't been lying about that.

"But you could have given me the card yourself," she said, "instead of leaving it on the dash like you did. You could have given me your phone number, or called me."

"Look around. I have no telephone."

"But . . ."

Ellie sighed. There didn't seem to be anything to be gained by pointing out that there were such things as payphones, or that the main house at Kellygnow had a phone. She knew that, since it was listed in the phone book.

"Okay," she said. "Never mind about the phone. What kind of a mask did you want to commission?"

And I hope I'm not going to regret getting involved in this, she added to herself.

"Perhaps it would be easier if I simply showed you," Wood said.

She rose from her chair and went to the chest at the foot of the bed where she took out a cloth bundle. When she brought it back to the table, Ellie saw that the soft cotton was merely being used as wrapping. Wood undid the leather thongs holding the pieces of cloth in place and folded them back to reveal two halves of a carved wooden Green Man mask.

Ellie had seen Green Men in numerous churches while traveling through England a few years ago—strange carved or stone faces that peered out from an entangling nest of twigs and leaves. She hadn't been much interested in the folklore behind them, but she'd loved the images themselves. This one was gorgeous. The wood was dark and polished—what sort, she couldn't say, but it had a beautiful grain. The carved leaves were life-size and remarkably life-like. The odd face they half-revealed was a strange cross between a gargoyle and a cherub, a fascinating mix that repelled Ellie as much as it appealed to her. The openings for the eyes were the most disturbing, she decided, though she couldn't say why.

The separation between the two halves was clean, as though the mask had broken along a meandering hairline crack, or perhaps a natural weakness in the wood. Ellie traced the edge of the crack with the tip of her finger, then ran her hand along a smooth wooden cheek until it was stopped by a spray of carved leaves.

"It's beautiful," she said, looking up at Wood.

Her host nodded.

"But it's made of wood," Ellie went on.

"Oak, actually."

"Whatever. The problem is, I don't work in wood."

"I realize that. I want you to make me a copy in metal."

"What sort or metal?" Ellie asked. "Like a bronze?"

"Something pure. No alloys. And nothing with iron."

Ellie gave a slow nod. "No iron," she repeated. An odd request, but what wasn't odd about this whole situation? She picked up one half of the mask and studied it for a moment. "I could make a cast directly from this, I think."

"No, it must be new," Wood told her. "You must start over from the beginning and redo it."

Was there any point in asking why? Ellie wondered as she set the piece back down on its cotton wrappings.

"I'm not asking for an exact copy," Wood said, "but rather for something that captures the spirit of the original. It's important that you have some leeway." She smiled, adding, "By which I mean that I expect you to use your artist's intuition in your rendering."

Ellie gave a slow nod. "It seems very old," she said.

"One might call it a family heirloom."

Not it was, but "one might call it." Ellie sighed. Why did some people have to make a mystery out of everything?

"How did it get broken?" she asked.

For a long moment Wood made no response.

"I'm not sure," she finally said. "The two halves have not been together for a very long time. There are stories as to how it came to be broken, the halves separated, but . . ." She shrugged. "There are always stories, aren't there? Suffice to say that I have been looking for them for many years now." She touched the right half. "This was recovered in England a decade or so ago, in a forest on the edge of Dartmoor."

"And the other?" Ellie asked when Wood fell silent.

"Was brought to me this summer. Friends tracked it down in Britanny, in the Forest of Paimpont—what was once called Broceliande."

She spoke as though the places she referred to should be instantly familiar, but they were mostly only words to Ellie. She'd heard of Dartmoor, of course. Britanny she thought was somewhere in France. But the others? They had the ring of storybook names to her.

Returning her attention to the broken mask, she found herself wondering what it had been used for. It didn't have the look of something that was simply decorative.

"I can offer you five thousand dollars," Wood said. "Plus expenses, of course."

Ellie blinked. "You're kidding."

Wood gave an apologetic shrug. "I'm afraid I'm on somewhat of a budget. I can't afford to pay you any more."

Ellie cleared her throat. It had suddenly gone all dry on her.

"No," she managed. "Five thousand dollars would be fine."

Like it wasn't a fortune. Five thousand dollars would go an awfully long way at the rate that she spent money.

"I'll, um, need to take the mask for reference," she added, trying to be businesslike about all of this when all she wanted to do was dance around the room.

"That's impossible."

"But—"

"Having so recently recovered the mask," Wood said, "I'm afraid that I'm too nervous about losing it again to allow it be taken very far from where I can keep an eye on it. I was thinking of having some studio space put aside for you in the house and that you could work on it there. Would that be suitable?"

Five thousand dollars *and* a residency in Kellygnow—if only for the duration of this commission? The residency alone was worth it, considering the gallery doors it would open for her.

"Yes," she said, managing to keep her voice level. "That would be fine."

Wood smiled. "Good. I'm glad that's settled. I'm sure you'll find everything you'll need to work with in the studio, but don't hesitate to ask if you require anything else."

"I, um, won't."

"Can you start tomorrow?"

Ellie nodded.

"Very well then."

When Wood stood up, Ellie scrambled to her feet as well.

"I'd like to apologize again for my bad humor when you first arrived," Wood said. "You caught me at a somewhat inopportune time." She gave Ellie a small smile. "In the middle of an old argument."

Ellie schooled her features to remain blank, but a warning buzz began to sound in the back of her head. Argument? she thought. With whom? There was no phone and the only door out of the building was the one she'd come in. Unless there was a back door behind the curtain in the far corner, which she doubted.

No, if her host had been having an argument, it had been with herself, and Ellie knew what that could mean from riding with Tommy in the Angel Outreach van. Hearing voices, arguing with them . . . when you put that together with sharp mood swings, you had the makings of a mental disturbance of some sort. It didn't mean the person was necessarily violent, but the potential was there, which was why Angel had her people work in pairs, with the women always having a male partner for more protection. Angel taught them that the people they had to deal with were usually not to blame for their condition—the chemical imbalance that was at the heart of most of these problems was simply a matter of genetic roulette. But that didn't make them any less dangerous. Or potentially so. Especially if they refused, as many did, to take their medication.

Are you taking yours? Ellie wondered, regarding Wood in a new light. Her gaze dropped down to the two halves of the broken mask. For that matter, could she take any of this seriously? The commission, the residency . . .

You're blowing this all out of proportion, she told herself. Musgrave Wood was simply an eccentric old woman with money to throw around, end of story. Don't pull a Tommy and look for the kind of deeper meaning that only the Aunts could unravel. But the warning buzz had never been wrong before and it wouldn't go away.

"Well," she said. "I'm glad you're feeling better now."

She kept her voice evenly modulated and held herself so that there was nothing threatening in how she stood. Smiled brightly.

Wood regarded her curiously for a moment, then shrugged.

"When you come tomorrow," she said, "go directly to the house and ask for Nuala. She'll see that you're looked after."

"Great," Ellie said. "And the mask . . . ?"

"Nuala will have it in keeping for you."

Ellie kept her smile in place. She knew it had to look phony, because it certainly felt phony, but she couldn't seem to stop herself. She was on automatic, following the rules that Angel had drilled into them during their training. Smile a lot. Keep your voice even. Never appear threatening.

"Until tomorrow, then," she said.

Wood gave her a slow, thoughtful nod, then walked with her to the door.

12

Musgrave stood with her hand against the door for a long moment before stepping over to the window. She watched Ellie walk across the snow-covered lawn towards the main house and marveled. So much *geasan,* housed all unknowingly in that mortal frame. It was as though an echo of the Northern Lights had been caught under her skin and was now escaping from her pores in pulsing waves.

I was like that once, Musgrave thought. *Not nearly so strong, of course, but at least I knew. Oh, I knew.*

There was the sound of movement behind her, a curtain moving, footsteps on the pine floor, but she didn't turn from the window until she heard the strike of a match on the wood surface of her table.

"I told you not to smoke in here," she said to the tall, dark-haired man lounging in the chair that Ellie had so recently quit.

The man regarded her, eyes dark, hand-rolled cigarette in his mouth, lit match in his hand. For a long moment their gazes held, then he smiled and shook out the match. He put the cigarette behind his ear, dropped the match on the table.

" 'Many Mice Wood?' " he asked.

She laughed and joined him at the table. There was still tea left in the brown betty. She poured them each a mug, giving him the one Ellie had been using. Since it hadn't been rinsed, a light film of milk rode to the top of the tea. The man didn't appear to notice, or if he did, care.

"Actually, it's a true story," she said.

"I'm sure it is."

He added milk and sugar to his tea and drank it down with relish. Setting the mug down, he picked up the two halves of the mask and held them up, looking at her overtop of them.

"Iron doesn't hurt us," he said.

"I know. But it doesn't conduct *geasan* well and . . ." She shrugged. "I thought it might set her thinking."

"She doesn't strike me as one overly interested in anything that can't be measured and weighed by some man in a white coat holding the same blinkered views of the world as she does."

"Don't start on that again," Musgrave told him. "She's an artist."

"She's human."

"She may not embrace the mysteries, but she still sees more than most do. That's the gift and curse of an artist. I agree it would be better if she realized she was working with truths, rather than stories, but consider what she has to offer."

It seemed that the argument Ellie's arrival had interrupted was about to begin again, but then her guest shrugged.

"The *geasan* runs strong," he conceded.

Musgrave nodded. After meeting the girl again today, she realized it was even stronger than she'd remembered. But that was the way of the *geasan*. It sidled and slipped, danced like shadows and light. Out of sight, out of mind. She'd given up wondering why a long time ago. If the mysteries were fathomable, they wouldn't be mysteries.

She took the mask halves from him. Placing them back on the cloth, she refolded it into a bundle and tied it closed with the leather thongs. Her guest took the cigarette from behind his ear and rolled it back and forth between his fingers.

"But she's a busy woman," he said after a moment. "Easily distracted."

"She'll do fine."

"Last night there was a man sniffing around her."

Musgrave sighed. "She's a young, attractive woman. What would you expect? Of course men would be interested in her. And what does it matter?"

"I don't like it."

"Why? Because it's not one of you Gentry doing the sniffing?"

He gave her a hard gaze, but she only laughed at him.

"Give it a rest," she told him. "And leave her alone. There's no need for you to keep watch over her anymore. Go get drunk and listen to that music you fancy so much."

"You don't understand."

"What? The drinking, or the music?"

He shrugged. "Either. It's hard, living as we do, and grows harder every year. The music takes us away. There's a promise in it, of all we never had."

Musgrave laid her hand upon the bundled mask. "When this is done, you will have whatever you want."

"Perhaps. If only she weren't human."

"We need her to make the mask," Musgrave said. "Not wear it."

He nodded, his dark eyes growing thoughtful.

"I don't trust the little bugger you have in mind for that job," he said, his voice soft. "I don't trust him at all."

"The trick is to use someone we can control."

"And if we can't?"

"Let me worry about him," she told him, with more confidence than she felt.

"It'll be on your head."

Didn't she know that, Musgrave thought.

"So you'll leave the girl alone until she's done her job?" she asked.

He gave another nod and rose to his feet. Musgrave remained at the table as he crossed the room and left the cabin. He had no word of parting for her and she kept her own peace. The lack of amenities between them didn't surprise her. They'd been uneasy allies from the first.

Outside the window, she saw him pause to light his cigarette, then slip off into the woods behind her cabin. A faint intuition prickled up the length of her spine.

Something was coming, she knew. She could taste it in the air, feel the weight of it in her bones. A change, certainly. Perhaps danger as well. But she couldn't place its source. It could come from the native spirits whose land the Gentry wished to claim for their own. It could come from the Gentry themselves. It could even come from a player who had yet to step onto the game board.

She thought of the young woman with the fierce aura of *geasan* that her body was unable to contain, thought of Ellie's innocence and the task they had set for her. Musgrave sighed.

No one was to be trusted. Not even herself.

13

The back door of the main house opened just as Ellie stepped up onto its low stone stoop. Bettina appeared in the doorway, a glimpse of the kitchen showing behind her. She smiled at Ellie's startled look.

"I saw you coming," she explained before Ellie could ask.

Stepping aside, she ushered Ellie in out of the cold.

I like this place, Ellie thought as she stepped inside. The kitchen was a big, comfortable room, warm and filled with the smell of baking bread and something savory—soup or stew, Ellie wasn't sure which. Whatever it was, it smelled delicious and made her stomach rumble. At a large wooden table by the window, Donal lifted a lazy arm in greeting. He had a bowl of soup in front of him, a thick chunk of bread beside it.

"We were just having some lunch," Bettina said. "Are you hungry?"

"Famished. But I don't want to impose."

"I've just invited you. *Por eso*, it's no imposition."

Regarding her, Ellie was struck again by the wonderful character in the other woman's features. Maybe there'd be time to capture them in a small sculpture, if Bettina would be willing to sit for her.

"Then, yes," Ellie said. "Thank you. It smells so good."

"Doesn't it? It's one of Nuala's soups—she's the housekeeper and cook here. Chantal says she must have gone to chef school."

"And graduated at the head of her class," Donal put in. He pointed at his bowl with a spoon. "This stuff is bloody poetry."

Ellie raised her eyebrows. Compliments from Donal? What was the world coming to?

"Can I meet her?" Ellie asked.

Bettina shook her head. "Not this afternoon."

She waved Ellie to the table as she spoke. Crossing to the stove, she filled a third bowl, cut a generous slice of the fresh-baked bread, and brought them back to the table with her. Ellie inhaled the steam from the soup when the bowl was put in front of her, breathing in a heady mixture of spices, herbs, and vegetables.

"Nuala's gone into town for the day," Bettina explained as she regained her own seat. "I don't think she'll be back before supper. Did you want to leave a message?"

Ellie shook her head. "No, I just thought it would be nice to meet her before tomorrow. It seems. . . ." She looked at Donal and grinned. "I'm going to be working here for a few weeks."

"Jaysus, Mary, and Joseph," Donal said. "Get away."

"No, it's true. Ms. Wood gave me a commission."

"What good news," Bettina told her. "That means we'll have the chance to get to know each other better."

Ellie returned the other woman's happy smile.

"So give," Donal said. "All the gory details."

"Well, it's a little odd, really. She wants me to cast a mask for her. A copy of a wooden one she already has that's broken . . ."

She gave a brief rundown of her visit with Musgrave Wood while they ate their soup. At first she was going to joke about the story behind the older woman's name and some of the other odd things that had come up in their conversation, but then found she couldn't. Wood had been so nice after the awkward way they'd started off that it felt as though it would be too much of a betrayal. In the end she didn't even mention the slightly schizoid aspect of Wood's personality, although that was something she meant to discuss with Bettina at the first opportune moment. While she was sure she'd blown it out of proportion, it wouldn't hurt to be certain.

"What's this 'green man' in the mask?" Bettina asked.

Ellie described the mask in more detail, adding, "All I really know about them is that they've got something to do with British folklore. I remember seeing them all over the place when I was backpacking in England a few years ago."

"Excuse me?" Donal put in. "Green Men belong to the Brits?"

"Well, don't they?"

"As if. Your man in the woods is just something else that they stole from the Celts."

"I didn't know they had Green Men in Ireland as well."

"The Celts didn't come from Ireland," Donal pointed out. "Ireland's only the last place we were driven into—before we sailed over here. But at one time we were all over Britain."

Ellie shrugged. "I don't know much about that sort of thing."

"Of course our Green Man wasn't some little gargoyle bugger looking out at you from a mess of twigs and vines, and he bloody well didn't have anything to do with churches. He was a man for the drink and the *craic*—a great big stag-horned man, fierce and wild. Not the kind of creature the churchmen could tame, I'll tell you that. I've heard him called Cernunnos, but only by scholars. The old folks didn't have a name for him, or if they did, they didn't use it. He was one of that pack of seasonal hero-king gods that your man Campbell liked to go on about." Donal grinned. "Liked to drink himself mad

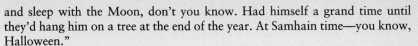

and sleep with the Moon, don't you know. Had himself a grand time until they'd hang him on a tree at the end of the year. At Samhain time—you know, Halloween."

"Whatever for?" Ellie asked.

Donal shrugged. "A way of closing the year, I suppose. They'd cut him down in his prime, at harvest time, but no worries. Every spring he'd return to give life to the crops. Beltane Eve—that was the big day when he'd be welcomed back, randy as a bloody goat and ready to party."

Trust Donal to know so much about this sort of a deity, Ellie thought.

"And this is a belief of the Irish?" Bettina asked.

Donal got an odd look at the question.

"Well, of some of the people I knew back home, and they were Gaeltacht Irish, so yeah, I suppose. But it's not like it was on everybody's mind or anything. There was a brother of my granddad—what would that make him to me?"

"A great-uncle?" Ellie tried.

"Whatever. Fergus was his name. He used to tell me these tales, that's all. He had all sorts of stories about how things were."

"Did he talk about the Gentry?" Bettina asked.

"Oh, sure. The original hard men." He gave her a curious look. "Where'd you hear that term?"

Bettina shrugged. "I can't remember."

Something about the overly casual way Bettina replied made Ellie think that she did remember, but she didn't want to say. Well, it was none of her business what Bettina wanted to keep to herself. Ellie turned back to Donal.

"You mean like those men who beat you up outside the pub that night?" she asked.

He hesitated for a moment. "Well, no. Language gets all tangled up on the Irish tongue—look at your man Joyce. Different words can mean the same thing; one word can mean different things—same as here, I suppose. So sometimes a hard man's a term of affection and sometimes it's meant literally, to describe the kind of man who likes to break heads for sport. Now these Gentry that Bettina was asking about, they were supernatural beings." He smiled when Ellie pulled a face. "Oh, yes, Ellie—your favorite sort of creature. Big bad fairies who were mean-tempered when you crossed them—and anything could be taken for an insult with that lot, if the stories are anything to go by."

"Fairies," Ellie repeated, putting a volume of feeling into the one word.

"Well, I don't mean your little bottom-of-the-garden variety, living in a flower, drinking dew out of an acorn cup and such shite. The Gentry were supposed to be our size or taller. Only more bad-tempered."

Ellie rolled her eyes, but when she looked over at Bettina hoping to find an ally, the other woman appeared to be quite intrigued.

"Why were they so bad-tempered?" Bettina wanted to know.

"Ah, you know how it is," Donal said. "It's like some people you meet—they always have a chip on their shoulder. The Gentry are like that, except instead of just giving you a bang on the ear when they're ticked off, they'll turn you into a lump of coal, or a bloody moth or something. Charming fellas, really."

Ellie could only shake her head. "I swear half this stuff he just makes up."

"It's true. I do. But not this half. I'm just repeating folklore."

Bettina looked as though she wanted to ask more about the Gentry. Instead, she smiled and offered them refills of the soup instead. Ellie and Donal both declined. There was some more small talk before Ellie bullied Donal out of his seat and into his coat. Left to his own devices, he'd sit there for the rest of the day, mooching meals and flirting with Bettina.

"I've got to get stuff ready for tomorrow," she explained.

"Of course," Bettina said. "Do you know where you'll be working?"

"No. Ms. Wood says that Nuala will show me tomorrow."

"I think you'll like it here."

"Jaysus," Donal said. "Who wouldn't? Grand food, grand company—"

"And grand fools," Ellie broke in. "Come on. We've taken up enough of Bettina's time."

"¿Y bien?" Bettina said. "It was my pleasure."

"I like her," Ellie said as they drove away.

Bettina had walked them out to the minibus and stood at the top of the driveway to watch them go. Looking out the back window, Ellie could still see her there, a small dark-haired figure, Kellygnow rearing up behind her out of the snow-covered lawns.

"Me, too," Donal said. He glanced in the rearview mirror before returning his gaze to the driveway. "And I think she fancies me."

Ellie laughed.

"Whatever gave you that idea?" she had to ask.

Donal shrugged. "A man just learns to read that kind of thing."

"Does he now?"

"Besides, did you not see her hanging on my every word?"

"I think she just likes fairy tales."

"Not like you."

Ellie smiled. "It's not that I don't like them. I just don't take them seriously. Between you and Jilly and Tommy's aunts . . . well, someone has to be sensible."

"Is that how you see it?"

She looked at him. "Why? How do you see it?"

"That you're afraid there really might be more to the world than you can see."

"Why would that frighten me?"

Donal shrugged. "I don't know. You tell me."

Ellie sighed and slouched in her seat. Maybe it was time she filled her life with some more normal people instead of all the half-mad artists and the like that currently inhabited it. The sort of people who'd see a mask as a mask, a folktale as just that—a story. Like Hunter Cole. *He* didn't strike her as the type to be looking for fairies under every bush.

"I don't know why I bother with you," she said.

"It's my Gaelic charm. The same as won Bettina's heart."

"You wish."

"Don't be harsh, Ellie. It doesn't suit you."

When he gave her one of those disarming smiles of his, she punched him in the shoulder.

"Hey, watch it. I'm driving."

"I'll drive you," she growled, but her heart wasn't in it.

Donal in a good mood was impossible to resist.

14

Playing CDs by singer-songwriters on the store's sound system was normally somewhat of a challenge for Hunter. If one of his employees didn't complain, as often as not at interminable length, then another did. Usually he simply didn't feel it was worth the argument. He was the boss, but he liked to keep matters on a somewhat democratic scale when he could, otherwise all you got were unhappy employees and that didn't sell records.

Except for "The Goddess" as she liked to call Ani DiFranco, Miki preferred instrumental music, or something sung in a language she couldn't understand, because she'd rather "make up my own stories as to what the songs're about." The members of the Goth bands that Fiona liked wrote their own material, but she didn't have much patience for what she considered the navel gazing of singer-songwriters. Hunter never had the heart to point out the irony of that notion. So far as he was concerned, Morrissey alone called up more angst in one song than most artists did in their whole body of work. As for Titus and Adam, their only criterion was how cool the artist in question was, which translated into who was playing on the album, or more importantly, who'd produced it.

So with the store to himself this morning, he was happily humming along with a limited-edition, six-track EP by Dar Williams that a friend had picked up for him at a concert in New England last fall. It had a solo, live version of "Are You Out There" on it, which was his touchstone for her work. He'd liked her first two albums, but it wasn't until *End of the Summer* came out last year, with the full-band version of the song on it, that he'd become completely enamored with her music.

The story of how an alternative, late-night radio show had changed the life of the song's protagonist struck a deep chord with him. He'd grown up in suburbia himself, in Woodforest Gardens north of the city, choking on all of those cookie-cutter houses with their perfect lawns, grotesquely manicured shrubberies, and insipid street names like Shady Lane. Tulip Crescent. Green-lawn Drive.

He used to feel himself getting swallowed up by the sheer banality of it all. The only thing had saved him were nightly broadcasts by a pirate radio station—Radio Fug Cue, they called themselves, and that in itself was a giggle, to hear over the air. No call letters. You simply twisted the dial across the band until you found their current broadcast frequency and out of your radio's speaker would spill an outrageous mix of hip music, opinionated reviews, and irreverent commentaries, all courtesy of Jack Thompson, aka Scatter Jack, the station's resident, and only, *DJ*.

Thompson was finally put out of business, which proved to be a windfall for the media when it was discovered that he was the son of a city councilor, Ray Thompson, a high-roller already involved in any number of other scandals, none of which actually went up before the courts. But Thompson's influence wasn't enough to keep his son out of jail.

Hunter met the younger Thompson years later, when Hunter had finally managed to escape the 'burbs himself, moving to the city's core and working in a secondhand record shop. Cool as he was, Hunter had still desperately wanted to find some way to thank Jack Thompson for how he believed Radio Fug Cue had literally saved him from white-collar oblivion, but by that point Thompson had co-opted with the enemy and become the program director for the worst of the local Lite Rock FM stations. Their tag line was "No metal, no rap, no crap."

Hunter hadn't even been able to shake Thompson's hand when they were introduced. He just couldn't do it, past debt notwithstanding.

But the Dar Williams song let him forget all of that, taking him back instead to those incredible nights when he'd sneak out of the house and lie out in the woods that still edged the housing development, transistor radio balanced on his chest, the world in his earphones taking him away from the ever-shrinking box that was his life. There, Scatter Jack had shown him all the possibilities that lay beyond the closed world of the perfect neighborhood he considered it was his misfortune to be growing up in.

Straightening up from the paperwork scattered across the counter, Hunter winced at the sudden pain in his side. There'd been no blood in his urine this morning, but he knew his kidney was swollen from the way it pressed up against his ribs. The whole area was bruised and sore, his back stiff. Every breath hurt unless it was shallow. He closed his eyes for a moment and the hard man's features leapt into his mind. The smell of him—tobacco smoke and something feral, a wild dog scent. The cold eyes. The flat voice.

You don't want to fuck with us, you little shite.

What had *that* been all about anyway?

The Dar Williams EP came to an end and for a long moment he let the silence hang. The store was empty. He'd only had three customers this morning and one had been returning a defective CD. Between the other two, they hadn't even put thirty dollars in the till. It made him wonder, and not for the first time, why he even bothered opening on Sundays, though of course he had to. Even if the customers weren't coming in, he had to be as available for business as the big chain stores were.

Hunter didn't really mind being in the store on a Sunday—especially not now, when his only other option was an empty apartment—but today it just made him feel depressed all over again. One of his staff had to go. There was just no way around it. That salary was just taking too big a chunk of his working capital.

This week he'd been cut off by one of his main distributors because he was late paying his bills. He knew he'd have it covered in a couple of weeks—hell, *they* knew it, too—but in the meantime, they'd cut him off and he could forget carrying any of their back catalog for a while. New releases he could get from Contact Distributors, a rack-jobber who serviced most of the smaller accounts in town, but that meant at least another dollar cost per unit. And since he couldn't raise his selling price and stay competitive, he'd be losing a dollar on every CD of theirs he sold. Which didn't help the money crunch he was feeling now.

This was the part of owning your own business that he'd dreaded the most. But someone had to go, and they'd all have to work longer hours, if he was going to keep his doors open. The question was who. It couldn't be Titus. With his lack of social skills and graces, how would he ever survive? Adam wasn't much better. Miki had seniority—next to him, she'd been working here the longest.

That left Fiona.

Sighing, he turned to take the EP out of the CD player, moving carefully when pain shot up from his side. A few moments later Dar Williams's sweet soprano was replaced by the high lonesome sound of Gillian Welch. Though Welch had grown up in California, you'd swear she'd just come down from the Appalachian Mountains by way of the Stanley Brothers to make this recording. He loved the raw, emotional narrative of the songs and her unadorned delivery. By the third cut he was in a bit of a better mood, the store's poor business and the pain in his side notwithstanding, and returned to finish up the last of his paperwork. It was only when the CD ended and he was back thinking about how he was going to tell Fiona that she was being laid off that his melancholy returned.

He considered his figures again, wondering if he could make it just a temporary thing. A few weeks, no more than a couple of months. Only until business started to pick up again with the warmer weather. He was still worrying at it when Miki came in a little later, wrinkling her nose at the Dan Bern CD he had playing on the store's sound system.

"Okay," she said as she offered Hunter one of the coffees she'd brought with her. "I realize that someone up there has decided that every generation needs its Bob Dylan, but really. Doesn't this guy sound like an *exact* clone to you?"

Hunter shook his head. "It's just a style of songwriting. You know, talking blues. Anecdotal."

"And it doesn't bother you, the way he's got Dylan down so well it might as well be Dylan? I mean, hello tribute city. Look at me, I'm pathetic."

"I don't hear it that way."

Miki raised her eyebrows. "Oh?"

"Besides," Hunter went on. "I hear he's really into Coltrane."

"Really?"

Hunter nodded, having no idea what Dan Bern's tastes in music really were. What he did know was Miki's inclination to forgive a great deal if your taste was what she considered to be good. Classic sax players were right up there at the top of the list.

"Oh, sure," he said. " 'Trane. Bird. Wayne Shorter. Lester Young."

"You're making this up."

"No, I'm sure I read it an interview somewhere."

Miki cocked her head, giving the CD another listen.

"Well, maybe he's not so bad," she said. "There is a kind of improvisational flavor to what he's doing, isn't there?"

Hunter managed to keep a straight face until she went to hang up her coat in the back room, only just wiping the grin from his face before she stepped back out into the store. Miki made her way slowly back to the front counter, straightening CD cases in their bins as she came.

"You're looking rather well," she said when she was standing on the other side of the counter. "Considering the state you were in last night."

"The—oh, right."

She leaned over the counter for a closer look. "You're not hungover at all, are you?"

"Quick recovery."

"Umhmm. Very quick. Now I'm wondering if you were even drunk in the first place."

"Very. Could barely stand up on my own."

"Which brings us to the question, why would you be pretending to be drunk?"

"Could barely see straight. Sick as a dog. Trust me on this one."

But Miki wasn't buying it. "You weren't just trying to avoid me, were you?"

"Of course not."

"Don't lie now. That'd hurt my feelings worse than if I thought you didn't fancy me."

"I'm not . . ." Hunter began, but he couldn't do it. This was Miki, after all. "It's just that Donal . . ." He broke off again.

"Oh, Christ. What did he tell you this time?"

"It's just . . ."

There didn't seem to be an out—not and be honest at the same time. So he told her all of it. Miki was quiet for a long moment when he was done. She regarded him thoughtfully from under long lashes.

"You and Ellie, eh?" she said finally. "I could see it."

"It's not like that."

"Not yet."

Hunter sighed, then gave her a slow nod. "Not yet," he conceded. "Maybe not at all. Who knows?"

"You're thinking I'm mad at you," she said.

Hunter shrugged.

"Don't be. I won't deny I was wondering a bit if things could go somewhere with us, but it was only wondering." She smiled. "Idle conjecture. The fleeting stuff of dreams."

"You are mad."

"Only at Donal. What was he thinking? First this business of trying to set us up in the pub the other night, and now this. You know he and Ellie used to be an item?"

Hunter nodded.

"He was quite desperate for her, but she didn't feel the same, which is why they broke up."

"So what are you saying? That all of this was planned?"

"Well, not the business at the pub. How could he even know you'd be meeting Ellie last night?"

Hunter laid a hand gingerly against his kidney. "And the hard man—"

Miki cut him off. "Donal's moody, and a tease, but he's not that mean. He'd never put someone up to that. But what's he driving at with this business of not telling Ellie?"

"He didn't tell me."

"And what would the hard men be wanting with Ellie?"

"He didn't tell me that either," Hunter said.

"Well, it can't be good. That lot aren't exactly renowned for their charity and goodwill towards others."

"Someone should tell Ellie."

Miki nodded. "But first I'll have a word with Donal. I'll ask him when I get home tonight and see what he's got to say for himself."

"Sure," Hunter said. "He must have had a good reason to want to keep it from her."

"He'd better. Or I'll give him such a rap across the head he won't see straight for at least a week. Ellie doesn't need this sort of thing, and neither do you."

"I forget how fierce you can be," Hunter said, laughing.

Miki gave him her most innocent look. "Why don't you come along after we close up tonight and be reminded?"

"Dinner afterwards at the Dear Mouse?"

"Done."

Miki took a swig of her coffee, then picked up the stack of inventory cards from beside the cash register and swaggered off to restock the items that had been sold yesterday.

"Stop smirking," she told Hunter who was hard put to stop from laughing at her antics. "I'm trying to be a manly man,"

"It's not working."

She rolled up the sleeve of her T-shirt and flexed her muscles. "How can you say that? Just look at these biceps."

Hunter dutifully admired them. "Donal will be shaking in his boots," he assured her.

"If he's involved in any of this, he'll be doing more than shaking. And that's a promise."

They closed the store a half-hour early. Along with freebie promotional copies of new releases—or better yet, pre-releases—making a judgment call about closing early was one of the few perks of actually owning the store. It hadn't been a hard one to make today. Except for a brief flurry of business in the midafternoon, they'd only had a half-dozen customers for the rest of the afternoon, and none at all for the last half-hour. Miki had wanted to hang a GONE FISHING sign in the door, just in case some diehard showed up at the door before the official closing time, but Hunter—using the power of ownership once again—vetoed that idea.

"Too frivolous," he explained.

Miki grinned. "As if. You need some frivolity in your life. An extra helping, in fact."

They took the subway across town to the market, and then walked the ten blocks or so up Lee Street to the Rosses and the apartment that Miki shared with her brother near the Kelly Street Bridge, going at a slow pace because of the steady ache in Hunter's side. It was still cold, and the temperature was dropping, but after being cooped up inside the store all day and then the crowded subway ride, they enjoyed being outside, never mind the chill.

"You've never been here before, have you?" Miki said as she ushered Hunter inside her building.

"Not since you and Judy had your house-warming."

"That's right. I forgot you'd come. But you didn't stay long."

Hunter nodded. "Ria got bored."

"I thought you said you were going to a gallery opening."

Hunter shrugged. "It sounded better than Ria being bored."

The building didn't look like much from the outside—just another ratty downtown brownstone—but once Hunter stepped into the foyer he realized that its tenants still took pride in the old war-horse. He'd forgotten how well maintained it was. There were still a few of these places left in the downtown area, buildings where the tenants refused to be intimidated by the steady exodus from the inner-city core and the subsequent arrival of those with less than a personal pride in keeping up the neighborhood. The tile floors of the foyer were clean, the walls freshly painted, all the overhead lights were in working order. The brass bank of mailboxes by the door was polished and gleaming.

"This place is in great shape," he said as they walked down the hall to Miki's ground-floor apartment.

"I know. Everyone puts the time in to keep it that way. Mind you, we do it for ourselves. The landlord couldn't give a shite."

"You'd think he'd be happy."

"I doubt he's ever set foot in this building," Miki said. She turned the key, unlocking the door. "Hey, Donal!" she called when the door was open. "Put on your trousers—we've company."

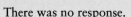

There was no response.

"I guess he's still out," Miki said.

Hunter followed her inside to find things no more familiar here than the foyer had been. No surprise, he supposed, considering how brief that earlier visit had been. The front hall was also part of the living room which boasted a pair of club chairs, an old stuffed sofa with a flower print that didn't quite match the Oriental rug under it, and a handmade shelf running along one wall that held Miki's stereo and a haphazard collection of vinyl albums, CDs, cassettes, books, and magazines.

From where they stood removing their boots and jackets, Hunter could see the kitchen at the end of the hall, and part of the dining room. The latter had been turned into a bedroom—Miki's, Hunter realized after a moment, noting a poster of John Coltrane and another advertising Italian-made Castagnari melodeons on the walls. Miki was always raving about their tone and the beautiful wood finishes on the Castagnaris, though she herself played a bright red Paolo Soprani that she'd had for ages, replacing her old Hohner that had wheezed more than offered up musical notes towards the end.

"You gave up your bedroom?" he asked as they walked past the dining room towards the kitchen.

Miki shrugged. "Donal needed the space for his studio. I didn't want him sleeping in the same room as all those noxious turps and the like. Bad enough he works with them."

"But it's your apartment," Hunter said. "It doesn't seem right that you don't even get your own space."

Miki glanced at him. "There were times when we didn't have anyplace to live and if it hadn't been for Donal, I'd have been taken in by social services and put into some foster home. I'd give up a lot more than a bit of personal space for him."

"You're right," Hunter said. "I wasn't thinking."

"I know he can be a right little shite, but he is my brother and he really does mean well."

On the other side of the hall they passed an open door which was obviously Donal's bedroom. Sparsely furnished, clothes draped everywhere. Miki paused at the closed door a little farther down the hall.

"Donal?" she called, rapping on the wood with a knuckle.

When there was no answer, she opened the door.

"Sometimes when he's really involved in his work," she told Hunter, "he doesn't even hear . . ."

Her voice trailed off.

"What is it?" Hunter asked.

He stepped around her and then he saw what had stolen away her voice. The room was dominated by a large canvas that had to be at least six foot by nine. Though obviously incomplete, the image caught in the paint was riveting. A naked man wearing a mask of leaves hung Christ-like from an enormous oak. His body was clothed in a nimbus of gold light that was picked up again in the leaves of his mask and the trunk of the tree behind him. Green blood poured from his mouth, the palms of his hands where they were nailed to the tree, and a gaping wound in his abdomen. No, Hunter realized as he stepped closer. Not blood. What poured out of the wounds was a liquid spill of finely detailed leaves and spiraling vines.

The rendering was so perfect that, at a first glance, you thought there really was a man hanging there. No wonder Miki had been so startled.

"Well, it's an amazing painting," Hunter said, "but I sure wouldn't want it hanging on my wall."

When Miki didn't respond, he turned to look at her. Her usually cheerful features were pulled into an unfamiliar scowl. Lurking in her eyes was an old sorrow that Hunter had never seen before.

"Oh, Donal," she said.

"What is it? What's the matter?"

She pointed at the painting. "That's the dying Summer King."

A feeling went pinpricking up Hunter's spine as she spoke. For a moment he found himself thinking of the hard men, of deep woods and the smell of cigarette smoke and wolves, of a sullen anger that ran so deep and wild that he could barely comprehend its surface, never mind empathize with its depth. Then the sensation faded.

He blinked and regarded the canvas again, trying to recapture what he'd just felt, but the immediacy was gone, leaving in its wake only a pale, ragged memory.

"The Summer King?" he asked.

Miki nodded. "Just look at the way he hangs there, a last gleam of goodness and light before the end of things."

"What do you mean? The end of what things?"

"The summer. The way we are . . . who we are . . ."

Hunter regarded her, confused by the depth of her concern.

"But it's just a painting," he said.

"For now," Miki said, her voice so soft he was unsure he'd heard her correctly until she said it again. "For now."

"Miki, what's so upsetting about—?"

But she didn't want to talk about it. Taking his arm, she steered him out of the room, firmly closing the door behind them. She gave him a bright smile.

"So," she said. "What was that you were saying earlier about dinner at the Dear Mouse Diner?"

Hunter wanted to know what it was about the painting that had so shaken her, but knew he had to let it go for now. Miki could be one of the most stubborn people he knew when she put her mind to it. When she was in headstrong mode, you might as well try arguing with a stone. So he let her change the subject, let her change the mood, and tried to go along with it. But where in the past few days an out-of-place sexual tension had lain uncomfortably between them, now there was something darker. Hunter had no idea what it was. All he knew was that he liked it even less.

15

Tommy Raven woke from a deep sleep to find his Aunt Sunday sitting patiently on the end of his bed, waiting for him to wake up. He got the sense that she'd been sitting there for hours. Knowing her, she probably had.

Like her sixteen sisters, Sunday Creek was a tall, big-boned woman with a broad, serene face and long crow-black hair, tamed today into a pair of braids that hung halfway to her waist. She was dressed for practicality rather than fashion: jeans, flannel shirt, a beaded deerskin vest. Had it been anyone else, Tommy would have wondered how she'd been able to get into his apartment and sit down here on his bed without waking him, but he'd spent the first fourteen years of his life growing up in a household that contained his mother and her sisters, and nothing they did or said surprised him anymore.

"Did I wake you?" she asked.

Her voice held the proper measure of concern, but laughter flickered in her dark eyes.

"I wasn't really sleeping," Tommy told her.

"Oh?"

"No, I was composing limericks. This one's for you: 'There once was an aunt of the cloth'—that's you, of course. A play on your name."

"Very clever."

" 'Who never was known to cough. Till one day a biscuit, got caught in her brisket, and the hack nearly took her head off.' "

"Brisket?"

"I needed the rhyme."

"You'd have been better off sleeping."

"That bad?"

"Worse. Do you have any tea?"

"Ah."

Tommy wasn't exactly a homebody. He lived off his welfare check, not because he was too lazy to hold down a regular nine-to-five, but because a regular job wouldn't let him do what he considered his real work. Welfare paid for his apartment, the meals he ate in diners and fast-food joints, gas for his pickup, but little else. Happily, the life he'd chosen didn't require much else. His apartment was utilitarian—though perhaps apartment was a misnomer. There was one small room that served as a combination bedroom and living area, furnished with a sofa bed that had only once been made up into a sofa since he'd moved in, and a wooden fruit crate turned on its side that held a selection of paperback books missing their front covers that he replenished as needed from the trash behind one of the bookstores on Williamson Street. There was a closet of a kitchen which he rarely used. There was an even smaller closet of a bathroom with a claustrophobic shower stall, a toilet, and sink crammed into the remaining space.

But he didn't need anything else. He'd made a promise to the Creator when Angel got him into detox the last time: Let me live through this and I'll dedicate my life to Beauty. That everyone had food in their stomach, shelter, knew a few words of kindness—that was his definition of Beauty. He believed in following what David Monogye, the elder of another tribe, had called humankind's original instructions.

"The original instructions of the Creator are universal and valid for all time," Monogye wrote in a letter to the United Nations. "The essence of these instructions is compassion for all life and love for all creation. We must realize that we do not live in a world of dead matter, but in a universe of living spirit. Let us open our eyes to the sacredness of Mother Earth, or our eyes will be opened for us."

When one considered the world in such light, Tommy thought, what need was there for personal property or a hierarchy of worthiness for those with whom he shared the Creator's gift of life? His only luxury was a pickup truck that his mother had given to him when he last got out of detox, and he only used it to get back and forth from the rez.

"There's no tea," he told his aunt. "Not much of anything, really."

"How about a kettle?" she asked.

He shrugged. "I've got a pot that holds water—and the left burner on the hot plate works. At least it did the last time I used it."

"Which was probably a month ago."

"Two weeks, actually. I had a hot date so I went all out and splurged on some gourmet TV dinners. We dined by moonlight."

His aunt's eyebrows rose.

"Okay. I was reheating a take-out soup."

Sunday reached into the pocket of her shirt and pulled out a pair of tea bags. All his life Tommy's aunts had had this ability to pull a needed thing from their pocket. Candy, gum, a smudgestick, herbs, charms.

"I'll go put the water on," she said. "Do you take your tea black?"

Tommy grinned. "Today I do."

She shook her head and got up from the bed.

"Get dressed," she told him. "We need to talk."

He waited until she'd stepped into the kitchen, then flung back his blanket. His clothes hung from the arm of the sofa bed. It only took him a few moments to put on jeans, T-shirt, a checked flannel shirt. Straightening the blankets on his bed, he went to stand in the doorway where he watched his aunt rinse out a couple of mugs. They hadn't been dirty, simply dusty from disuse.

"Aunt Sunday," he said after a moment. "Why are you here?"

"We're worried about you."

He didn't have to ask who she meant. "We" would encompass Sunday herself, his mother, and their fifteen other sisters, his aunts. He wondered, not for the first time, what it would have been like to have grown up in that household when they were young, all those gangly girls with their broad, happy faces; a pack of rambunctious and fey tomboys, by all accounts, running wild through the rez, touched by Mystery and Beauty. But they'd been grown women by the time he was born—the unhappy reminder of his mother's bad marriage, though no one ever said it in so many words.

"I chose this life," he told her. "I know I've never amounted to much, but what I'm doing now is a lot better than lying drunk in some alley."

Sunday turned from the sink to look at him. The humor that usually sparkled in her eyes had been replaced with an unfamiliar sadness.

"We've always been proud of you, Tommy," she said.

"Yeah, right."

He'd left home when he was fifteen, full of an anger he couldn't explain, torn between the traditionalists—best exemplified by his aunts, or by the Warrior's Society—and those who'd simply given up, the kids sniffing glue and gasoline in back of the community center when they couldn't score some booze or drugs, killing themselves slowly instead of the way the more desperate did: putting the barrel of a hunting rifle in their mouth, or taking a drop from the garage rafters with a rope around their necks. He'd just needed to get away. Away from the losers. Away from that house of women. Away from the sweat-lodge boys and the Indian Power champions.

So what did he do? He tracked down his father in the city and went to live with him. The first couple of weeks were great. Frank Raven welcomed his son into the seedy apartment he had in Lower Foxville, proudly introducing him to everyone as the long-lost son "the bitch" had stolen from him. But blood was true and a father's love always won out in the end, because here was his boy again, making a man's choice, the right choice, living with his father, where he belonged. There was a party every other night and no one said he was too young to join in. It was, "Welcome to civilization," and "Here, Tommy, have a brew," and "Fuck the elders; we'll make our own good times."

Then one night, without provocation, Frank beat the crap out of him in the middle of one of those parties and threw Tommy out on the street to fend for himself.

"You ever come back here again," Frank told his son, "and you're dead meat. Got it?"

Tommy lived on the streets then, too proud to go back to the rez with his tail between his legs, too scared to approach his father again. Frank's friends, when they saw Tommy, took to calling him Dead Meat after his father's parting words.

Life hadn't been easy after that. He turned to sleeping on the streets, panhandling, or turning tricks down at the Y. Some of the guys hanging in the changing rooms got real turned on by an Indian kid. They'd call him Chief, or Squaw Boy, slip him an extra few bucks if he'd use B-movie Indian dialogue. A year later he was in juvie hall where Angel bailed him out.

Angel. Her real name was Angelina Marceau and she looked like an angel—long dark hair falling in a waterfall of natural ringlets, heart-shaped face, the warmest eyes you could imagine. All she was missing were the wings. They called her the Grasso Street Angel, not because of her looks, but because of the way she helped people, especially kids and the homeless, out of a streetfront office on Grasso Street.

Like most of the men who knew Angel, Tommy was half in love with her from the first time they met. She'd organized an all-ages teen dance at the Crowsea Community Center which Tommy and a few of his street pals crashed, six of them, high as kites and drunk, floundering about on the dance floor, pushing kids around and having themselves a grand old time until suddenly Angel was standing there, staring them down. She didn't have to do anything. Just the look in her eyes shamed them into leaving.

But Tommy came back and helped clean up after the dance. He wouldn't talk to anyone—especially not Angel—but he wanted to be near her. There was something in her presence that soothed the constant anger that sometimes the drugs and alcohol dulled, sometimes they fed. To this day, he couldn't explain what it was. In those days he didn't even try.

He didn't turn over a new leaf after that night. A month later a brawl landed him in juvie where Angel bailed him out. She wasn't there to help him, but when she saw him slouched on a bench, she came over and sat down beside him.

"I remember you," she said. "You were at the dance last month."

Tommy stared at the floor, unwilling, unable to look at her.

"What are you in for?" she asked.

He shrugged. "Fighting."

"Did you start it?"

Tommy hesitated, then finally looked up at her, saw himself reflected in those warm, kind eyes of hers. He nodded.

She smiled. "Well, at least you're honest. You think it'll happen again?"

"Probably." That wasn't what he'd meant to say, but he couldn't seem to lie to her. "But I'll try not to."

She didn't say anything for a long moment, just studied him. It was weird, the way she looked at him. It wasn't judgmental, but it was definitely taking his measure. She made him think of his mother, he realized. His mother and the Aunts. They had that same way of looking at you that made you stop and think about what exactly it was you were trying to prove.

"I . . . I just get angry," he found himself saying. "I guess I'm always angry."

"What about?"

"Don't know."

She nodded. "Let me talk to the sergeant," she said. "I'll see if I can get the charges dropped."

Tommy had tried to do good after that. Angel got him into AA, found him a room in a boardinghouse, a job bagging groceries at a store on Grasso Street, just a couple of blocks away from her street-front office. He'd come into her office from time to time and help out, sweeping the floor, cleaning the windows. Mostly he'd listen to her talk, his own tongue stuck fast to the roof of his mouth so that he could only reply in monosyllables. Things were going well, but after a while he drifted back into the street life, why, he didn't know. But he started calling in sick at work, stopped going to AA meetings. He'd hang with the guys, drinking, fighting, boosting car stereos and the like. He

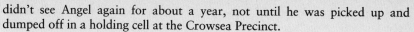

didn't see Angel again for about a year, not until he was picked up and dumped off in a holding cell at the Crowsea Precinct.

He was lucky. The only charges they had against him were vagrancy, and being drunk and disorderly in a public place. He didn't know how she found out, but when he looked up from the bunk in his cell the next morning, she was standing there on the other side of the bars.

"Hello, Tommy," she said. "How're you doing?"

He thought he'd die of shame. There was no recrimination in her voice, or in her eyes, no sense that she was disappointed in him. But seeing her there made him disappointed in himself.

"Not so good," he told her.

She stood up for him again. It was back to AA, another boardinghouse, another job—this time on the janitorial staff at a high school, cleaning up at nights when the place was empty. It was good to have something to do at night—it kept him from seeing the guys, falling back on his old ways. He could sleep through the day, work at night. Sometimes, when he finished up early, he'd go to the school library and read for a couple of hours.

The routine held until the day he found out that his father had died—drunk as usual. Frank had managed to choke to death on his own puke. One more loser brave, dead in an alleyway. Tommy didn't even think about what he was doing. He just walked into a bar and had himself a celebratory drink. Then he had some more. When the barman stopped serving him, he went to a liquor store and bought three mickeys of cheap whiskey.

When he came to a day-and-a-half later, he was lying in a nest of trash at the back of some alley. For all he knew it was the same one in which his father had died. He lay there for a long time, then finally stumbled to his feet. Hung over, sick to his stomach, reeling. He knew what he should do. Call his sponsor. Head for the nearest AA meeting. But what was the point? Like father, like son. It was in the genes, ran in the blood, and it was never going to go away. But at least when you were drunk, you couldn't think. Everything bad just blurred, was bearable.

So he went and bought himself another couple of bottles of oblivion.

When Angel found him in the drunk tank this time she had them open his cell so that she could sit beside him on his cot.

"I heard about your father," she said. "I'm sorry."

She still shamed him, but today he had a voice. This was territory he knew too well.

"I'm not." he said.

"Every death diminishes us."

He still couldn't look at her. "You sound like one of my aunts."

"I'll take that as a compliment."

That drew his gaze to her. "You know them?"

"I've met a few of them. Zulema helps me with some of the Native kids."

He nodded slowly. "So that's why I'm one of your pet projects."

He'd often wondered why none of his family had interfered with the mess he'd made of his life. In the first few months that he'd been on his own—and knowing his mother and her sisters—he'd constantly expected them to come drag him back to the rez. Now he knew why they hadn't had to bother. They'd just deputized Angel to stand in for them.

"Do you really believe that?" Angel asked.

He shrugged and returned to studying the floor.

"I didn't even know you two were related until a couple of weeks ago."

"I'm sure."

"Have I ever lied to you before?" Angel asked.

The unfamiliar edge in her voice pulled his gaze back to her.

"No," he said.

Angel smiled. "Okay. So long as we have that straight. I've talked to the judge and he says they'll drop charges if you'll voluntarily check into detox and then, once you're clean and back at work, you pay off the damages."

Tommy blinked. "Damages?"

"You don't remember?"

He shook his head.

As Angel started ticking off the items—plate glass window of a photography shop, glass and frames of photos on display—it began to come back to Tommy. One of the photos had been part of an advertisement for a photographic gallery show featuring the rez. He'd been stumbling by when the image of some fancy dancers at a powwow caught his eye. He'd picked up a garbage can and put it through the window, then to the soundtrack of the store's alarm, had systematically begun breaking each of the framed photos in the display.

"Why do you keep helping me?" he asked Angel.

She gave him a long serious look that made him want to flinch and look away, but he couldn't move his head.

"I believe in you," she said.

He thought of Angel saying those words to him in the drunk tank, how they'd actually pulled him out of the inexplicable anger and despair and set him on the road he walked today. It had been a long, hard struggle, but this time he'd stuck it out. He still had dreams about those days, but he savored the mornings when he woke up, knowing that was all they were. Dreams. The past.

He looked at his Aunt Sunday now, and made a sweeping motion with his hand.

"You're proud of this?" he asked.

She shook her head. Lifting her hand, she laid her palm against his chest.

"We're proud of this," she said. "The heart that beats in this man's chest. His generosity of spirit and strength of purpose. You have grown into a good man, Thomas Raven."

Tommy smiled. "Then why are you all so worried?"

"Ah . . ."

She took the pot from the hot plate and turned the heat off. Dropping the tea bags into the boiling water, she leaned against the kitchen counter and sighed.

This didn't bode well, Tommy thought. He couldn't think of a time when one of his aunts had been at a loss for words. They were never hesitant in offering an opinion, passing along a piece of advice, telling a learning story.

"It has to do with *manitou*," she said finally.

That was the last thing Tommy had expected to hear.

"*Manitou*," he repeated.

Sunday nodded. "Ours and theirs."

"Theirs?"

"The Europeans."

Now Tommy was really confused. "The Europeans have *manitou*?"

"Of course. What would you call the spirits that followed them here?"

"I never really thought about it."

He'd never thought that they might have even brought spirits with them, never mind what they might be called.

"They want our land," Sunday said.

"People always want our land."

"No, I mean the spirits. They mean to take the sacred places from our *manitou*."

Tommy's head filled with questions. Was such a thing even possible? All he knew about the spirits he'd learned through stories—stories that took place in some long ago, before the People had been forced to share their world with the Europeans. The stories had always been entertaining, but he'd never considered them to have much relevance to the present world.

"What does any of this have to do with me?" he asked.

Sunday gave him a reluctant shrug. "It's been *seen*. The details are less than clear, but you are involved."

"But *manitou* . . . you're talking campfire stories."

"Not true, nephew. The *manitou* are real. And they are dangerous."

Of course. In the stories, they were always dangerous. But true?

Tommy sighed. He loved his aunts, and trusted their instincts, heeded their advice. But this . . . it would have been funny if Sunday didn't seem to be taking it so seriously. And he still felt like laughing all the same. But then he made the fateful mistake of asking, "Who's seeing me in these stories?"

"Jack Whiteduck."

A great stillness entered Tommy and he felt like he needed to sit down.

There was a certain hierarchy on the rez. The chief and council were elected, but only with the approval of the Aunts—not his aunts, but the elders. On the rez there was no need to differentiate between the two. Everyone knew who you were talking about without the need to explain that you were referring to the elders, or the Creek sisters. In time, his aunts would be counted as elders, too, but that day was still in the future. For now, the Creek sisters answered to the elders, as did everyone on the rez. Everyone, that is, except for one man. Jack Whiteduck. The shaman. He answered to no one except the *manitou* and the Grandfather Thunders.

"This is . . . serious," Tommy said.

Sunday nodded. "I know. I'm sorry. I wish there was something more we could do besides pass on his warning."

"What am I supposed to do?" he asked. "Should I talk to him?"

Which was the last thing in the world he wanted to do. Like most of the people on the rez, Tommy had grown up in fearful awe of the old man. No one wanted to come to his attention because when you did, your life changed. For good or bad—it didn't really matter. Afterwards, you were a different person. The spirits knew your name. They could take you away, anytime.

A few moments ago, Tommy had been laughing about *manitou*. But now that he knew that Whiteduck was involved . . .

Sunday shook her head in response to his question. "Wait," she said. "If he wants to talk to you, he'll let you know. Just be careful, nephew."

She turned away, covering up her discomfort with the message she'd brought by fussing with the tea bags steeping in the pot, pouring their tea. She handed Tommy a mug, took the other for herself. Tommy cupped his hands around the china mug, feeling the tea heat the porcelain, but the warmth brought him no ease.

"I already feel changed," he said.

Sunday nodded sympathetically. "That's the way it starts."

And how does it end? he wanted to know, but he didn't ask the question aloud. He knew his aunt felt bad enough as it was, having had to tell him about Jack Whiteduck's vision. He took a steadying breath, sipped at the tea.

"So," he said after a moment. "How's my mother? Your sisters?"

Sunday gave him a grateful look. When they retreated to the other room to sit on the bed, she brought him up to date on all the gossip since he'd last been back home. It had only been a couple of weeks, but something was always happening on the rez. Events could run the gamut, from silly to tragic, but at least they were mundane, rooted in the real world rather than that of the spirits. Listening helped keep Tommy's panic at bay, but a supernatural dread had settled deep inside him now, along with the knowledge that his life was no longer his own.

Why did Jack Whiteduck have to see *him* in a vision?

16

SUNDAY NIGHT, JANUARY 18

Miki let herself into her apartment a little after eleven. Closing the door behind her, she shed her boots and hung her jacket on the doorknob of the closet. The apartment was quiet—Donal's absence reminding her of how angry she was with him all over again. She'd been able to forget for a while, comfortable in Hunter's company, enjoying the tasty, if somewhat basic fare at the Dear Mouse Diner.

He was quite the man, Hunter was. He'd always treated her well, right from the start, standing up for her when she was a bratty fifteen-year-old and trying to sneak into The Harp for the sessions, never talked down to her or tried to make her feel out of place or stupid. He'd stop and chat when he came upon her busking somewhere, take her out for a meal if he decided she was looking too skinny.

She'd played a battered-up old Hohner two-row in those days that was pure shite—not because of the brand, it was just such a sad old beast of a box. But she'd kept the reeds tuned, patched the tears in the bellows whenever a new one appeared, and it had treated her right, or as well as it could, all things considered. A bit like Hunter, really. Steady. No airs with either of them. She still had the Hohner sitting in a case at the back of her clothes cupboard— didn't have the heart to toss the poor old bugger out—and she still had Hunter as a friend.

Tonight was a perfect example. He hadn't pushed when he knew she wasn't up to talking about what had upset her. Instead he'd eased their conversation into silly, harmless discussions on new releases, odd customer encounters in—and out—of the store, and deliberations on just how weird their co-workers were. As usual, Titus had won out, hand over fist, but then how could he not? Adam was merely an arrested adolescent; one day he might actually grow up. But Titus . . . Titus was almost pathological.

But now they'd left the easy companionship of the restaurant behind, Hunter had gone off home after seeing her to her door, and all the bad feelings she'd left in the apartment—firmly shutting the door on them for the few hours she was gone—were back once more. Sighing, she went into the living room and slouched down on the couch. She left the lights dark, the sound system off, and waited.

Donal didn't get in until almost one, fumbling with his key in the lock, tripping over her boots when he got through the door, reeking of alcohol. She let him get his boots off and drop his parka on the floor. It wasn't until he went stumbling down the hall toward his bedroom that she called out his name.

"Jaysus," he said, banging back against the wall. "You gave me a right bloody start."

Miki said nothing for a moment. She had to concentrate on breathing evenly, to get her temper under control before she spoke.

"So what're you doing, sitting here in the dark?" Donal asked.

"Waiting for you."

There. That was good. Level tone. Breathing calm. Pulse still too fast.

Donal came into the room and dropped into one of the club chairs.

"Now isn't that sweet," he said. "Waiting up for her brother, she is. Why one would almost think she had no life of her—"

"Don't you dare start in with that shite," she told him.

So much for staying calm.

"That time of month then, is it?" he asked.

The thing many people didn't realize, mostly because of her size, was just how strong Miki was. It didn't take much—a good diet, plenty of the right kind of exercise. You didn't have to be big to be strong. Donal should have remembered, but he was too soused. He should have remembered her temper as well.

She shot out of the sofa, grabbed him by the scruff of his shirt, and hauled him out of his chair.

"Christ, woman!"

Instead of answering, she shoved him towards the hall. He went stumbling, arms flailing. As soon as he almost caught his balance, she shoved him again, continuing to keep him off balance until they reached the door of his studio. *Her* bedroom that she'd gone and given up like the bloody fool he'd played her for. At the door she gave him one final shove and he went tumbling. He grabbed at the nearest surface and brought a shower of paint tubes, rags, and brushes down upon himself as he fell.

She stood in the doorway, glaring at him. He made no effort to get up, but there was a royal anger in his eyes as well.

"So," he asked, the tone of his voice deceptively mild. "Have you lost your fucking mind?"

Miki knew that voice too well. It was the same one their father had used before he'd beat the shite out of one or the other of them. Sometimes both. It didn't scare her now. But it hurt, because the drunken brother lying on the ground was the same one who'd protected her from the worst of their father's rages, who'd looked out for her when they'd escaped the clutches of Social Services and went to live on the street.

"No," she said. "But it looks like you have."

Donal sat up. "What're you on about?"

She pointed at the canvas behind him. In the faint light that came in the window from the street lamps outside it looked even more realistic than it had earlier in the evening, as well as more disturbing.

"Oh, that."

"What's it about, Donal?"

He shrugged. "It's a bloody painting—what does it look like?"

"I'll tell you what it looks like," Miki said. "It looks like that shite Uncle Fergus was always on about. All that mad ugly talk about the Gentry and stringing up some poor sod who they'd treat like a king all summer, then nail up to a tree come Samhain for the luck of the community."

"Fergus would be our great-uncle, actually."

"And you know as well as I that his spew of meanness and spite, with its pretensions to Celtic Twilights and druids and Yeats and all, has no real basis in fact, mythical or historical—not the way he tells it. What he and his cronies spout is just some bloody hodgepodge stolen from a half-dozen different folklores that they've bent to their own liking."

Donal shook his head. "It's real."

"Oh, aye. In bits and pieces, each belonging to its own. But not the way they tell it. Their telling is just an excuse to nail up some bugger they don't like and fuck a few flower-draped handmaidens who're too scared of their stories about the Gentry and the like to tell them no."

"The Gentry are real," Donal told her.

"And my shite smells of roses."

"Who do you think the hard men are?"

An unhappy quietness settled over Miki. For a long moment she couldn't speak.

"Don't tell me you're spending time with the likes of them," she said finally.

"It's not a matter of choice," Donal said. "Once you've gained their attention, you're either with them or against them. You know what's said of them: There's no middle ground with the Gentry."

"Oh, Donal . . ."

"Don't you worry for me. They won't be hurting me."

No, just Hunter and whoever else came in their way. She'd been young when she'd had to sit there and listen to Fergus and his cronies go on with their hateful talk, voicing all their petty revenges and lusts with no thought of the children—her brother and herself—sitting there listening to them. But she hadn't bought into their rationalizations then, and she wasn't about to do so now.

"It's not you I'm worried about," she said. "It's those you plan to hurt."

"Jaysus, Mary, and Joseph. I haven't turned into some monster overnight."

Miki looked at the painting. On its own, it was a startling image, beautifully rendered, disturbing, but so were many of the images of Christ's crucifixions that hung in Catholic churches. She knew that. But Donal's painting spoke to her on a deeper level. It told her just how much her brother had listened to those mad ugly stories of their uncle, how different a man he really was from who she'd thought he was, to ally himself with men who would kill another for the luck it would give them, who would use fear and intimidation to take advantage of a susceptible young woman.

It was the symbol of it, that her brother could depict such hurt, that he could consider such hurt . . .

"Get that thing out of here," she told him. "And take yourself with it."

"Miki—"

"Go and live in the wilds with your Gentry. Bugger yourselves, for all I care. But don't be back here. And don't even consider hurting any of my friends again. They're under my protection—do you hear me? Go and tell your hard men that, and if they have a problem with that, they can come see me about it."

"It's not like you're thinking," Donal told her. "They're just looking for a home. For someplace they can call their own."

"And if it already belongs to someone else?"

Donal shook his head. "These aren't human men we're talking about. They'll take nothing from us."

"Then who will they be taking it from?"

"Jaysus, that's so like you. Why do you have to think anything'll be taken from anybody?"

"Because that's what their kind do, Donal. They take from others—and do you know why? Because it tastes sweeter to them when it's bathed in another's hurt. That's who you've allied yourself with."

"Now *you're* talking mad."

"Am I? Why don't you ask your hard men yourself? Better yet, why don't you stand in their way and see how well you remain friends."

"Miki . . ."

She shook her head. "It goes, and so do you."

Donal nodded slowly.

"Fine," he said.

The look in his eyes broke Miki's heart all over again. Standing up, he put his foot through the painting, then grabbed the torn edges of the canvas and tore it in half. The sound of the canvas ripping felt like pieces of Miki's soul being torn from her.

"There," he added. "That make you feel better?"

Miki took a deep, steadying breath. She faced his glare with a firmness she didn't feel.

"If only you could tear it out of yourself as easily," she said after a long moment.

"Jaysus woman. I was doing this for us."

"For *us*?"

"Who else?" Donal demanded. He softened his voice. "Do you never get tired of scrabbling for every penny?" he asked her. "Did you never want that one sweet chance to strike back at all those who spat and shat on us every chance *they* could?"

Miki shook her head. "That's not what it's about," she said. "And we both know it. It's you being himself—our father. Or Fergus. It's you being the big man."

"If you really believe that . . ."

"What else am I supposed to believe?" she asked. "If you want to be something, why don't you be a real man for once in your life? Admit that what you're doing is wrong. That the hard men are no more than a band of thugs who care only for themselves."

Donal gave her a grim look. He made a fist and smacked it against his breast.

"Here beats an Irish heart," he told her, the softness left his voice again. "I'll not bow down to any man—neither here nor at home."

"At home? Ireland's not our home and you and your hard men are no more Irish patriots than some IRA bomber, taking the war to the innocent."

"Fuck the IRA," Donal said. "And fuck the Provos, too. This is an older struggle."

Miki nodded. "Oh, aye. Between the mad and the sane."

He took a step to her, still the stranger, and once again she gave him a shove. But their argument had sobered him up some and this time he didn't lose his balance. For a moment, she thought he was going to strike her, but then he lowered his fist and sadly shook his head.

"You're blind, is all," he said. "I'll forgive you that."

When he moved forward, Miki stepped back into the hall, but he wasn't coming after her. He walked down the hall and picked up his parka from the floor.

"*You'll* forgive *me?*" Miki cried.

Donal nodded. He put on his boots. Taking out his key ring, he took off the key to the apartment door and tossed it onto the sofa.

"This is how you get a home," Miki told him, making a motion with her hand to take in the apartment. "You work for your money—earn it honestly. You pay your rent, or you buy a home. You fill it with things that mean something to you and you welcome your friends into it. It's not something you can simply take from a person."

"Oh, no? And those who took our home from us?"

"When you take a home, it's not a home anymore, is it?"

"It's whatever you make it to be," Donal told her.

Then he stepped out of the apartment, closing the door softly behind him.

Miki stared at the closed door. The enormity of what this argument had wrought settled inside her with a deep, sorrowful hurt. Her eyes filled with tears and she made no move to wipe them away as they ran down her cheeks. She made no sound either, as she wept.

Oh, Donal, she thought. Why did you have to listen to them?

She remembered overhearing someone in a pub once, the conversation coming around to the Troubles, saying how when the Irish get hurt, they stay hurt. It was true, too. Donal had never recovered from the pain of their childhood; why else would he have let the hard men take him in the way they had with all their shite of leaf-masked Summer Kings and the need for a home—not one made through love, but taken by pain.

No, Donal had never recovered. She had, but then she'd had Donal to look up at, to depend on. He'd had no one. She'd always thought his moroseness was only a kind of play; now she knew it was a true, deep melancholy that ran below everything he thought or did. She'd never really understood it until now. But now she knew just how he felt. Now it seemed that all the joy had been sucked out of the world and she couldn't imagine it ever returning again.

3

Chehthagi Mashath

Haz el bien y no veas a quien.
Do good and don't worry to whom.
—MEXICAN SAYING

SONORAN DESERT, SPRING, 1990

One Friday afternoon in early April, the year Bettina turned sixteen, her grandmother met her as she and Adelita were leaving school. Abuela pulled up at the curb in her dusty pickup and honked to get Bettina's attention. Beside her, Adelita rolled her eyes and stayed with their friends, but Bettina went running over to the truck. Standing on the running board, she leaned her forearms on the warm metal frame of window and poked her head into the cab.

"Abuela. What are you doing here?"

"We are going on a journey," her *abuela* told her.

Bettina grinned. "Adelita," she said, starting to turn. "Did you hear? We're—"

Abuela touched her arm, stopping her.

"Not your sister," she said. "Only you and me."

"But—"

"It's *Chehthagi Mashath*," Abuela explained. "The month of the green moon. And we are going on a pilgrimage to Rock Drawn in at the Middle."

Bettina's eyes went wide. "But will the O'odham let us?"

Lying west of the Tucson Mountains, the Baboquivari Mountains were a sacred place to the Tohono O'odham, for hidden at the base of the cliffs that formed the walls of Baboquivari Canyon was a cave that was considered a tribal shrine. This was where I'itoi Ki lived, the Coyote-like being responsible for bringing the Desert People into this world. The cave was an antechamber of an enormous labyrinth winding under the Baboquivaris—an image captured by O'odham basketweavers with the design of a small man standing at the beginning of a circular maze.

Because Baboquivari Peak towered over the cave and could be seen from almost every village on the Tohono O'odham reservation, it was considered the heart of the O'odham universe. The Desert People called it *Waw Kiwulik,* "Rock Drawn in at the Middle," referring to a long ago time when the granite obelisk was twice its present size. Wishing for more land, tribal elders had gone to I'itoi to ask him to move the mountains and make the valley bigger. He did so, toppling the upper half of the peak. The whole mountain range moved, widening Wamuli valley, but also angering Cloud Man who lived higher up in the mountains. Because of the people's greed, Cloud Man refused to supply water to the new land, so the O'odham were never able to cultivate that part of the valley.

"Ban Namkam is taking us," Abuela assured her. "And besides, we're all *Indios.*"

"Oh, I like Ban."

"*Sí,*" her *abuela* said, dryly. "That has always been rather obvious."

Bettina blushed. Lewis Manuel was the son of Abuela's friend Loleta, a handsome young O'odham that she'd first met at a saguaro fruit-picking camp last year. He was only six years older than her, but he might as well have been a hundred for all the attention he'd paid to her. Among his own people he was known as Ban Namkam—Coyote Meeter—because coyote was the animal he'd met in a vision while undergoing one of the four traditional degrees of manhood. Like most young men today, he probably wouldn't attain the fourth, since it consisted of killing an enemy tribesman.

"Does Mamá know we are going?" Bettina asked to take her grandmother's attention away from the dismal state of her love life.

"Of course," Abuela said. "I told her we are going to stay with Loleta for the weekend."

"But you said—"

Abuela shared a conspiratorial smile. "*Chica,*" she said. "You know how your *mamá* worries."

Yes, Mamá worried. And perhaps with good cause, Bettina thought.

Last year Abuela had taken her on another pilgrimage, down into Sonora, Mexico, to fulfil her *manda,* a secret vow she had made to San Francisco Xavier. They had walked from Nogales all the way to Magdalena, accompanied by dozens of other pilgrims. Each October, during the feast of St. Francis of Assisi, Desert People have made their pilgrimages to the reclining statue of St. Francis which is kept in the church of Magdalena de Kino, in Sonora. The confusion of feast days arose from the disorder that followed the replacement of the Jesuits by the Franciscans some two hundred years ago. The Desert People had been introduced to St. Francis Xavier by the Jesuits. When the Jesuits were expelled, they assumed that the St. Francis of Assisi the Franciscan priests spoke of was the same man.

Bettina had come expecting a fervent religious experience, and she hadn't been disappointed. The plaza surrounding the cathedral had been full of pilgrims, the new arrivals waiting in line outside the catafalque on which the statue of San Francisco rested in recline. They gathered around the child-sized statue, touching it, thanking him, offering up silent prayers, pinning *milagros* to his brown Franciscan habit. When her turn came, Bettina had found herself filling up with a great sense of serenity and mystery—more potent than anything she'd known under the desert skies.

This was before Abuela had taken her into *la época de mito*, when myth time still belonged to stories, rather than experience. That day Bettina felt more magic in the catafalque than she'd ever experienced before, and she realized her first difference with her grandmother. Yes, the desert was holy, but to her mind, the church, with its saints and the Virgin, was holier still. On their return to Tucson, she began to attend mass more regularly, which pleased Mamá to no end. Bettina had thought that Abuela would be upset, but her grandmother had merely smiled and said, "It doesn't matter where we find the Mystery, only that we do find her and bring her into our lives."

But for all the holiness in the cathedral, the fiesta was also a secular affair, an early Papago/Pima harvest festival to which the missionaries had merely attached some Christian motifs. When Bettina and her *abuela* stepped back into the sunlit plaza, it was to see a Yaqui deer dancer preparing to dance, the antlers of his stuffed deer-head mask bedecked with ribbons, rattles of dried cocoons tied to his ankles. From other plazas, and outside the small town, they could hear the rumble of the fiesta as several thousand people celebrated the Feast of St. Francis in their own way, lifting their voices in many languages against a backdrop of *mariachi* and *norteño* bands, merchants hawking their wares with amplified loudspeakers that were only a rumbling squawk against the cacophony of carnival rides.

Abuela had taken them first to where the herbal medicines were being sold, replenishing her own stock with herbs grown in wetter lands, necessary medicinal plants that she couldn't harvest herself in the desert. Then they walked by the booths selling trinkets, hardware, religious paraphernalia such as *milagros* and postcards of the saints, leather goods, and food. They bought gifts for those back home: cotton print scarves, postcards, a bottle of tequila for Bettina's father and his *peyoteros*. Bettina sampled the carnival rides; Abuela haggled with merchants. They admired the fresh produce stands, filled with corn, red chiles, striped squashes, and quinces, and feasted on stuffed chiles, fresh corn on the cob, and bowls of *calabacita*—boiled squash, chopped up and fried with onions, tomatoes, and asadero cheese. Abuela allowed Bettina a small glass of beer, and they finished their meal with barrel cactus candy and *alegrías*, cakes of popped amaranth seeds that, except for this fiesta, never reached farther north than Mexico City.

After night fell, they made their way to Calle Libertad, meeting up with friends from home in one of the open-air dance halls where a *mariachi* band blared tunes on a mix of brass instruments and violins. Bettina tried to stay awake, but by now she'd had a second beer and the mix of the unfamiliar alcohol and the long day finally took its toll. She fell asleep on a chair at the back of the hall. The last thing she remembered seeing was her grandmother happily dancing polkas with her friends.

When they returned home, Mamá had been furious, but Abuela, as usual, was unrepentant. Mamá hadn't spoken to Abuela for a week after that, filling the house with a dark silence that touched everyone. Bettina wasn't eager to repeat that part of the experience.

"Wouldn't it be better to tell her the truth?" she said to her grandmother.

Abuela shrugged. "¿Como? And when she forbids your going? We don't do this for her, *chica*. We do this for you. That you learn the old ways. That you are introduced to the spirits whose companionship and help you will need in the days to come. This is *curandera* business. You must trust to my judgment in this." She looked past Bettina's shoulder. "¡Hola! Adelita," she called as Adelita and the other girls approached. "Do you want to come with us to visit the Manuels?"

Adelita pulled a face. "I don't have to come, do I?"

"Of course not, *chica*," Abuela said.

"*Vamos a mi casa*," Gina, one of the girls accompanying Adelita, said.

"*Sí*," Abuela said. "Go with your friends. We will see you on Sunday night."

Bettina and her grandmother watched the girls saunter off down the dirt sidewalk that edged the road.

"You see?" Abuela said. "She doesn't even want to come."

"You didn't say anything about Rock Drawn in at the Middle," Bettina said.

Her *abuela* gave her an innocent look. "But we are going to visit the Manuels. As I told your mamá."

Bettina had to smile.

"And if we decide to take a drive later, perhaps a walk in the desert— would that be so wrong?"

Grinning now, Bettina got into the cab of the pickup.

"I've brought you some sensible clothes," her grandmother said as she pulled away from the curb. "For the desert. You can change into them on the way."

Ban Namkam appeared at his mother's house early the next morning, startling the Gambel's quail and doves into flight and a momentary silence. He stepped out of a pickup that was older, more battered, and even dustier than Abuela's, a tall and ocotillo lean man in faded jeans, a short-sleeved white shirt and well-worn cowboy boots. His long black hair was pulled back into a ponytail, his skin richly darkened by sun and genetics. When he smiled at Bettina, her pulse couldn't help but quicken. Compared to the boys at school Ban was all presence and bigger than life. But while he was as handsome as ever, he remained just as oblivious to Bettina's admiration now as he'd been the first time they'd met. When he casually ruffled her hair by way of greeting she could have bitten his hand.

Don't say it, she willed, but of course he did.

"I swear you get taller every time I see you," Ban told her.

Bettina could only grit her teeth. *No soy una niña,* she wanted to tell him. See, I have breasts and everything. But of course she didn't say a word, only hung her head and stared at her feet, feeling stupid and impossibly young. Then she caught her *abuela* grinning at her and that only made her more self-conscious.

Discreet questioning of Ban's mother the night before had allowed that, yes, he was still very much unattached. Unfortunately that was enough for Bettina to become the recipient of much gentle teasing on the part of both Loleta and Abuela for the remainder of the evening, not to mention this morning as well.

"Look, *nieta,*" Abuela said when they saw the dust of Ban's pickup approaching the house. "Here comes your boyfriend."

Bettina's warning glare had only made her *abuela* smile, but at least she said nothing now.

Truth was, Bettina wasn't sure she even liked him anymore anyway. At least so she tried to convince herself. Look at him. He was obviously too full of himself, too caught up with his own importance to even notice that she was quite grown up now, thank you. Yes, his uncle Wisag Namkam was a calendar-stick keeper, marking saguaro ribs with cuts and slashes to help him remember important events, his father Rupert a medicine man, but so what? A man should be judged by his own deeds, not by the importance of his family.

Bettina sighed. Except Ban's deeds did speak for themselves. He followed the traditional ways, but he was also working on a doctorate in botany at the University of Arizona. He was handsome, smart, kindhearted, loyal. She sighed again. And totally oblivious to her. It wasn't fair. Why couldn't she be more like Adelita? Her sister *always* had a boyfriend.

"Are you still in this world?"

Bettina blinked, then realized that her *abuela* was speaking to her.

"*Sí,*" she said quickly. "Where else would I be?"

Abuela gave Loleta a knowing look and they both rolled their eyes. Happily, Ban didn't notice. He was looking off into the distance where the Baboquivaris rose from the horizon, their tall and stately peaks towering high above the surrounding bajadas.

"I haven't been to the cave since Papá took me when I was a boy," he said, turning back to the others. "I hope I can remember how to find it once we reach the cliffs."

"Bettina will help you," his mother said. "I hear she has an affinity for lost places and causes."

Abuela snickered.

Ban looked from her to his mother, aware of undercurrents, but unsure of what they were.

"Why don't you ask Rupert?" Bettina said.

Ban shook his head. "He's out at the rainmaking camp till the end of the week. They're rebuilding the roundhouse for this August's ceremonies."

Bettina knew that. She'd just wanted to switch the focus of conversation to anything but herself. She gave her grandmother a pleading look.

"I'm sure Ban will find it just as easily as his father," Abuela said, relenting.

Loleta nodded. "Probably better, if the *peyoteros* are at the camp."

They drove to Ali Cukson—Little Tucson, a Papago village just a fraction of the size of the sprawling metropolis of Tucson some fifty miles away—and then up into the Baboquivari Mountains, a special permit on the dashboard of Ban's pickup since neither Abuela nor Bettina were tribal members. Above the white wake of dust stirred up by their wheels flew turkey vultures and Harris hawks. Coyotes watched them from the ridges, roadrunners darted across the road in front of them, and a bobcat was startled into immobility by the unfamiliar presence of the truck before it faded away into the brush.

At the end of their road they came to a canyon that held an abandoned stone cabin with a flood-water field, the latter overgrown now with mesquite, catclaw, creekside desert olives, and wild chile bushes. Ban parked the pickup and they stepped out to stare up at the cliffs rising hundreds of feet above them. Bettina hoped for a glimpse of a coatimundi, the raccoonlike animal that Ban had told her could sometimes be found here. This canyon, he told her, was one of the few places in the States where it could be found—it and the five-striped sparrow. But neither made an appearance today. There was only a crested caracara, floating high up on a thermal, long-necked and long-tailed against the bright blue of the desert sky.

Shouldering backpacks, they started up the canyon on a narrow trail leading through the dense undergrowth, flushing quail, startling the Mexican jays and phainopeplas. Further up the canyon they walked among the Mexican blue oak, mulberry, and enormous jojoba that prospered here in the more humid narrows. They passed by puddles of standing water in the otherwise dry wash, continuing to follow it until a white-necked raven flew by with a laughing cry. Ban watched its flight for a long moment.

"A guide?" Abuela said.

Ban smiled and nodded, then led them away from the creekbed, up a steep slope, leaving the shade behind.

It was hotter out in the sun, walking along the exposed slope. The bajada here was all thorn and spine as they wound their way between ocotillo, cholla, prickly pear, barrel, and saguaro cacti. But if the way grew harder, the view became ever more spectacular. They could follow the paths of all the drainages that led down from the western slopes to empty into Wamuli wash. To the east, the sharp peak of Rock Drawn in at the Middle rose to its awesome height.

They rested there for a while, drinking from their canteens, rendered silent by the panorama—even Abuela, who almost always had something to say.

Finally they turned their backs on the view and climbed the last stretch to the cliffs. When they reached the thornier scrub at their base, they were a thousand feet above the desert floor, with the cliffs rising up behind them another thousand feet.

This part of their trip had been simple, if arduous, but finding I'itoi's cave was another matter entirely. They spent a half-hour searching, finding only small overhangs and caves—nothing like what I'itoi's cave should be.

"You *have* been here before?" Abuela asked Ban when they finally took a break.

He nodded. "But only that one time with Papá and he led us right to the cave. I thought I'd have no trouble finding it, but everything seems different today . . ." He shrugged.

"*Y bien,*" Abuela said. "I've not come this far to give up now."

Bettina's heart sank. What had been an adventure this morning had lost much of its luster by now. She was hot and tired, scratched, and more than a little frustrated that the entrance to the cave remained so elusive. Usually a foray into the desert with her *abuela* was a much more relaxed affair—rambles rather than such formidable treks. For the past half-hour she'd been more than ready to head back down the forty-five-degree slope to where they planned to camp in the canyon.

The white-necked raven they'd seen earlier flew by once more, still laughing—at them, Bettina decided—but its presence made Ban smile.

"I remember something," he said. "There were white streaks on the cliffs and my father led us past them."

They turned back, following the base of the cliffs, more eastward this time, in the direction of Rock Drawn in at the Middle. They found the streaks, stark against the darker rock, but dusk fell and it seemed they had to give up. Finally, Bettina thought, but then she caught the flash of the sun's last rays on a crevice in the rock, just the other side of a large jojoba bush.

"There," she said, pointing.

The sun dropped out of sight, but Ban had marked the spot. In the deepening twilight they made their way to the tall slit in the rock. It began at waist height so they had to step up to it, then awkwardly squeeze sideways through the narrow opening.

"Wait," Ban said once they were inside.

Bettina could hear him rustling about in his backpack. He struck a match, lighting a candle, and her eyes went wide with delight. The candlelight pushed the darkness back from the opening of the cave where they stood, illuminating a tangle of offerings that hung from the ceiling above them: rosary beads, ribbons, chains with *milagros* and rings wound into their links, shoelaces, belts, scarves. On the floor were small statues of terra-cotta and unfired clay—oddly proportioned toads, lizards, dogs, birds—jars of saguaro cactus syrup and preserved jams, a single shoe, dried bunches of marigolds, the red flowers of desert honeysuckles, and pink fairy clusters. In little niches in the walls people had stuck bullets and shotgun cartridges, cigarettes, chewing gum and hard

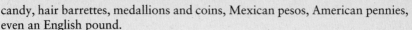

candy, hair barrettes, medallions and coins, Mexican pesos, American pennies, even an English pound.

The offerings reminded Bettina of a story one of the O'odham elders had told late one night around a campfire during the saguaro fruit harvest. "When you visit I'itoi," he said, "you have to leave him something, whatever you have—a cigarette, a coin, a bracelet." Then he told of a group who had visited the cave once. One of them was a Protestant priest who wouldn't leave anything because what harm could come to him, a priest? When it was time to go, he turned around, following the voices of his companions. But the darkness deepened and the cave mouth shrank and shrank until it was far too small for him to climb back through.

"Leave him something, Father!" his companions called.

But still he hesitated. The opening kept shrinking until finally he took his hymn book out of his pocket and laid it on the floor of the cave. A strong gust of air blew him towards the tiny hole of daylight and the next thing he knew, he was tumbling out into the scrub where his companions were anxiously awaiting him.

She'd repeated that story to Ban and her grandmother on the hike up the canyon.

"I remember that," Ban said. "Only it was a nun in the version I heard and she left behind her rosary."

Bettina reached into her own pocket, looking for what she would leave. All she had was some smooth pebbles she'd picked up on their climb and a piece of candy. She doubted I'itoi would need any more stones, no matter how pretty they were with their turquoise and quartz veining, so it would have to be the candy. She hoped it would be enough.

It was hard to judge the size of the cave. As their eyes grew accustomed to the poor light, they were able to see about twenty feet ahead of where they stood, but the cave obviously went farther than that. Bettina thought of the spiraling designs of the O'odham basketweavers, how they were said to twin a much larger spiral that lay here under the Baboquivaris. She pictured its corkscrew shape, the slow coils tunneling through the rocks below her feet. In her mind, the spiral went on forever, as though she stood on the edge of a door leading into Abuela's *época del mito*, with I'itoi's lair at once only a step away and immeasurably distant.

Though the air was musky and cool, she felt a sudden flush of heat. The weight of the cliffs above pressed down on her. The slight draft that came from deeper in the cave felt like I'itoi's breath on her face. I'itoi breathing. I'itoi the Creator.

She had to put a hand out against the wall for balance, suddenly dizzy. The darkness spun and fell away. She closed her eyes and slid down to her knees.

"Abuela!" she heard herself cry, her voice coming to her as if from a far distance.

But when she knelt, it was on rough gravel and sand, not the floor of the cave, and an impossibly bright light flared red-orange against her eyelids. Opening her eyes, she blinked at the sudden, stark sunlight. She was no longer in the cave, but out on the scrub slopes of the bajada, a great-aunt of a saguaro rearing tall above her, signaling some slow semaphore to her relatives on a distant slope.

Bettina's pulse quickened with panic. What had happened to the night? Where was the cave? Where were Ban and her *abuela*?

Then she realized what must have happened and she grew more anxious still. Somehow she had crossed over into myth time, alone, without Abuela to help her back to the world she'd inadvertently left behind. She could be any-when. In the ancient past when the Anasazi were first building their cliff-side dwelling, north, in slickrock country, or in some unimaginable future when human beings no longer walked the world at all.

She might never find her way back home. Everyone said *la época del mito* was a dangerous place to visit—especially for the inexperienced. Even her father, one of the few times he'd talked to her of what he called men's business, had told her he never traveled into the mysteries on his own. He went in the company of his *peyoteros* with Mescal to show them the way and then bring them back home when their visiting was done.

"Abuela," she called, her voice no more than a hoarse whisper, her throat tight and dry with fear. "Papá."

She wanted to be brave, but courage fled, the harder she tried to grasp it. Turning, she searched for the opening of the cave once more, but the sun glared on the towering cliffs, washing away detail in a sheen of shimmering heat waves and light. Nothing looked quite the same anyway. The coloring of the rocks. The feel of the slope underfoot. The intense blue of the sky.

The vegetation was different, too—some of the saguaro were taller than she remembered, others smaller. The prickly pear grew in changed patterns. There were no jojoba bushes close to the cliff itself.

"Por favor," she said, meaning to address the spirits of this place, to beg their indulgence and ask for guidance, but then she heard something odd.

She sat up straighter, head cocked to listen. The sound she heard was singing, a singing that seemed to be a mix of high-pitched children's voices and coyote yips. It came from just over the next rise where a flush of prickly pear clustered at the base of another tall saguaro, the same piece of nonsensical verse repeated over and over with an innocent exuberance that pulled a smile from her tight lips:

> No somos los lobos
> no somos los perros
> somos los cadejos
> cadejos verdaderos

Fearful still, but too curious now to be cautious, she clambered up the slope to peek over the other side of the ridge. Her smile broadened into a delighted grin and all fear fell away when she saw the improbable singers.

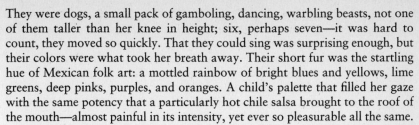

They were dogs, a small pack of gamboling, dancing, warbling beasts, not one of them taller than her knee in height; six, perhaps seven—it was hard to count, they moved so quickly. That they could sing was surprising enough, but their colors were what took her breath away. Their short fur was the startling hue of Mexican folk art: a mottled rainbow of bright blues and yellows, lime greens, deep pinks, purples, and oranges. A child's palette that filled her gaze with the same potency that a particularly hot chile salsa brought to the roof of the mouth—almost painful in its intensity, yet ever so pleasurable all the same.

What would such fur feel like? she couldn't help but wonder. Soft, or stiff like a terrier's?

Because there was something of a bull terrier in the shape of their heads, long and rounded like a bullet. But they weren't quite as barrel-chested. Looking more closely, she saw that instead of a dog's paws, they had the feet of goats. The sound of their little hooves on the rocks as they danced added a counterpoint rhythm to their song.

Clickity-clackity-click.

We are not wolves, we are not dogs.

Clickity-click.

We are *cadejos*.

Clackity-click.

Cadejos, truly.

Clickity-clackity . . .

She started to stand, wanting to go down, to join them and make a joyful noise. To be a *cadeja* to their *cadejos*, whatever a *cadejo* might be. It didn't really matter. She could be happy to paint her skin a dozen bright colors and dance in the sun with them.

"I wouldn't go down there," a voice said.

Startled, she slipped a few steps back down her side of the slope and turned to see a roadrunner lolling on a nearby rock. She looked around, but there was no one nearby who could have spoken unless it was an invisible spirit.

She shivered at the thought and returned her attention to the roadrunner. It was lying with its back to the sun, tail dropped, wings spread wide, the speckled feathers lifted on its back and crest to expose a "solar panel" of jet black underfeathers and skin. Bettina had seen them do this before, absorbing heat from the sun, but usually this was only in the winter when their body temperature dropped overnight. The birds used the sun's energy to warm themselves up, rather than increasing their metabolic rate the way hummingbirds or poorwills might, reducing their caloric needs by as much as forty percent—the equivalent to her skipping breakfast or lunch. In the winter, when food was in short supply for the birds, it was an efficient way to heat their bodies.

She shook her head. Why was she thinking such things? She wasn't in school, or learning lessons while out hiking with her *abuela*.

She looked again past the sunning roadrunner, out over the rough scrub of the bajada. Singing dogs were one thing—especially when they seemed so full of fun—but she wasn't sure she was really prepared for invisible spirits.

"*¿Quién habló?*" she asked, pitching her voice low so that it wouldn't carry to the strange dogs cavorting on the other side of the ridge. Who spoke?

The roadrunner cleared its throat.

"Are you always this rude?" it asked when it saw it had her attention.

Bettina regarded the bird for a long moment. The dogs should have prepared her for this. This was *la época del mito*, after all. The place where, according to Abuela, what passed as folktales in their world were no more than matter-of-fact occurrences.

"*Perdona,*" she said finally. I'm sorry.

"I should think so. What would your grandmother say?"

"My grandmother?"

"*¡Claro!* Everyone in this place has heard of her: Dorotea Muñoz—*la curandera de pequeños misteriós.*"

"How do you know her?"

"Let's say we have shared certain . . . intimacies."

Bettina's eyes widened. "But you . . . you're a bird."

"Is that what you see?"

As Bettina began to nod, the roadrunner folded up its short, rounded wings and rose onto its feet. A heat wave traveled the length of its speckled black and white plummage, heightening the greenish iridescent cast the feathers already held. Bettina found her gaze caught by the bright blue around its eyes where the heat wave shimmered the strongest. The intensity of those blue feathers brought a return of the vertigo she'd suffered in I'itoi's cave and she had to close her eyes for a moment. When she opened them again, the roadrunner was gone.

A small, dark-skinned man sat in its place.

"*¡Dios mío!*" Bettina managed to squeeze from a suddenly dry mouth.

In any other circumstance, she would have given him no more than a passing glance. He was short in stature, certainly shorter than herself, but otherwise he could have been any middle-aged O'odham on the rez. Scuffed cowboy boots, worn blue jeans, white cotton shirt, baseball cap. But his eyes were almost black, with bird-bright highlights and circles of blue shadow, his face long and lean, especially his nose. There was a roadrunner speckling of black and white in his dark brown hair, and he carried enough weight around his waist to give him the body shape of a bird.

"Where did you come from?" Bettina asked, though she already knew.

The man smiled. "Where did any of us come from?"

"That's not an answer."

"Perhaps not. But I believe the most important questions only lead to more questions."

"Now you sound like *mi abuela.*" Bettina said.

"A fine woman. You must give her my regards."

"Who shall I say is sending them?"

"Tadai."

"You mean Tadai Namkam? *¿Cómo un apodo?*"

"No, not a nickname. Just Tadai, nothing more . . ."

Bettina shook her head. *Tadai* was simply the O'odham word for road-runner. It was as if Bettina were to call herself *Chehia*. Girl. Then she found herself wondering if her present experience was like Ban's meeting with the coyote that had given him his tribal name. Perhaps now *she'd* be called Tadai Namkam. It was all very confusing. But one thing her fifteen-year-old wisdom told her:

"That's not a regular name," she told him.

"And yet it's the only one I have," Tadai said.

Bettina gave him a considering look. *"¿Es verdad?"*

"Más o menos." More or less.

Aha. But she decided not to press him on it. She was more interested in the singing dogs.

"Why did you warn me away from the dogs?" she asked, hoping to get a straightforward answer for a change.

"Not dogs," Tadai said. *"Cadejos.* Weren't you listening to their song?"

Which had now stopped, Bettina realized. She hoped her conversation with Tadai hadn't driven them away. She tried to listen for some sound on the other side of the ridge. A click of goatish hooves on stone. A murmur of song. There was nothing.

"They seemed like such fun," she said, not even trying to hide her disappointment.

Tadai nodded. "But they are dangerous. *Cadejos* are the children of volcanoes. How can they not be dangerous with such powerful entities as parents?"

"I've never heard of them before."

"In your world they are invisible . . . and mostly forgotten."

"But *why* are they dangerous?"

"Bien. For one thing, they are doorways and can pull you between worlds."

"Is that how I got here? Did the *cadejos* bring me?"

Tadai gave her a tired look. "Either that, or you were sent here by someone weary of your endless questions."

"Now who's being rude?"

"Me perdona. But you are a most conversational child."

Again the child business.

"I'm almost sixteen."

"Ah." As though that explained everything.

"In the old days I'd be married now, with children."

Tadai shook his head. "Children having children. What a sad world you come from."

Bettina decided she had listened long enough to this sort of talk. It was bad enough that Ban ignored her, without complete strangers voicing their opinions on how young she was. She stood up and with great dignity carefully brushed the dirt from her jeans.

"Where are you going?" Tadai asked as she started up the slope.

"Home," she told him without turning. "If you haven't scared them off with all your talking, I'm going to ask *los cadejos* to send me home."

"But—"

Bettina paused to look back at him. "You're the one who said that they're doorways between worlds."

Tadai scrambled to catch up to her.

"*Sí,*" he said. "But you don't necessarily get to choose *which* world they will send you into."

Bettina wasn't interested in listening to him anymore. She quickly gained the top of the ridge and was half walking, half sliding down its far slope before Tadai could stop her. The *cadejos* were below, sprawled out in repose like a pack of javelinas.

"*¡Por favor!*" she called to them. "Send me back home."

They rose in a wave of color, yipping and laughing, blue and green and bright pink tails wagging, and surrounded her as she came the rest of the way down the slope, arms pinwheeling to keep her balance.

"*¿Dónde está tu casa?*" one of them cried. Where is your home?

"*¡Tu casa, tu casa, tu casa!*" the others took up.

"*¡Qué suerte! Tienes una casa.*" How lucky. You have a home.

"*¡Tu casa, tu casa, tu casa!*"

"*Somos los homeless.*"

"*No tenemos casa.*"

"*Verdaderos, verdaderos.*"

"*¡Somos los cadejos!*"

They ran around and around her as they yipped and barked and made a bewildering noise. Bettina grew dizzy as she turned around herself, trying to focus on one of them long enough to make herself understood. But the *cadejos* danced around her like so many spinning carousel animals, with her at their hub, unable to move, while they were always in motion, Catherine-wheeling finally into a blur of color and sound.

"Bettina!" she heard Tadai call.

She tried to see where he was, but there were always *cadejos* in front of her, yapping, chattering, laughing. The vertigo rose up again, a huge dark swell of it, and this time she didn't fight it. At least it would take her away from the blur of motion and their voices. Except the dogs leapt up at her now, not attacking, not even playing, but jumping at her all the same, little cloven hooves scattering dirt behind them, and into her chest they went, swallowed into her skin, and she could still hear their voices as she tumbled towards unconsciousness, only now they were echoing inside her head.

As everything went black, Tadai reached the place where she'd been standing.

"And sometimes they make *you* into a doorway," he said, but he was alone on the bajada now, Bettina and *cadejos,* both gone.

Bettina's spirit rose up from the darkness to find a hundred faces peering down at her, all of them spinning and turning like the carousel of *cadejos* had earlier. But slowly they resolved into two faces, Ban's and her grandmother's.

"*Chica, chica,*" Abuela said. "You've made us so worried. I thought my heart would stop when you disappeared the way you did."

Ban put his arm around her shoulders and helped her sit up when she couldn't quite manage it on her own. The sudden movement made her head spin once more, but the vertigo quickly ebbed. Candlelight filled her sight, flickering on the offerings stuck into the cave's wall niches and hanging from its roof. When she saw them she realized that they were still in I'itoi's cave. So it had all been a strange dream. Except . . .

"I . . . I disappeared . . . ?"

"*Sí,*" Ban said. "One moment you were here, the next you were gone."

"I thought it was a dream . . ."

"What did you see?" her *abuela* asked.

Bettina didn't answer for a long moment. She felt surprisingly clear-headed and was enjoying the sensation of being so close to Ban. See? she wanted to say to him. Does this feel like a child you hold in your arms?

"Bettina?" Abuela said.

Bettina sighed and looked at her grandmother.

"I met Tadai," she said.

"A roadrunner?"

"No. Yes. At first. Then he became a man. He said he knew you, Abuela. That you had been lovers."

Abuela's eyebrows rose. "Did he now."

Bettina could feel herself blushing. "Well, he said you had shared intimacies."

"I see."

"And that I should give you his regards."

"Very thoughtful of him."

"*Do* you know him?"

Her grandmother smiled. "I know a rather short, shape-shifting *curandero* whose imagination often gets the better of him. Did he . . . harm you in any way?"

Bettina shook her head. "Why didn't you come for me?" she asked. "I called to you."

"I know," Abuela said. "I heard you. But, *chica, la época del mito,* it is a large place with many layers of time and myth laid one upon the other. It could have taken me weeks to find you. I thought it better to wait a few minutes first, to see if you could return on your own."

"A few minutes?"

Ban laughed. "Time moves to its own rhythm in that place," he said. "Half a day there can be but a minute here. You were gone no more than a few moments."

"I felt like it was at least an hour. . . ."

"It is a confusing place," Ban agreed, "especially at first. But come, let's get you outside. You'll feel better under the open sky."

He and Abuela started to help her out through the cave opening, but she made them wait until she could dig into her pocket and leave behind a piece of candy for I'itoi. Outside, the night lay dark upon the bajada, a hundred thousand stars peering down on them from the clear sky overhead. But there was no moon. And Ban was right. She did feel better now that she was out of the cave. More herself. More inside her own skin.

"We'll camp here tonight," Ban said, "and make our descent in the morning."

"*Sí,*" Abuela said. "Tonight you will rest."

"But I'm feeling much better."

"*Bueno.* Still, humor your old grandmother. Tell us, what else did you see?"

So while her grandmother and Ban readied the camp, Bettina sat on a blanket and related the whole of her adventure, from when she first heard *los cadejos* singing, to when they leapt into her chest and brought her back to I'itoi's cave.

"*Cadejitos,*" Ban murmured thoughtfully.

Bettina corrected him. "*Cadejos.* That's what they called themselves."

They had been small and cute, but somehow the diminutive felt disrespectful.

Ban smiled. "Still, I've never heard of such creatures."

"I have," Abuela said. "In Guatemala. But I know little more about them than what Tadai told you."

As they continued to talk, Ban brought out the food Loleta had sent along with them. He didn't build a campfire, but rather took a small Coleman stove from his pack on which he heated the beans and shredded meat that his mother had cooked earlier. Garnishing them with diced tomato and cilantro, he rolled them up in soft tortillas. Bettina liked watching his hands move, shadowy shapes in the faint glow cast by the stove. He rolled two tortillas for each of them which they washed down with cups of one of Abuela's herbal teas.

Though insisting she wasn't at all tired, at Abuela's request, Bettina lay down after they'd eaten. She shifted about until the jut of her hip and shoulder settled into the small depressions Ban had shown her to dig. It was more comfortable than she'd thought it would be, lying there with a blanket pulled around her against the chill of the desert night. She heard Ban settle down as well, but her grandmother sat up, a small shadow against the starred sky, saguaro uncles and aunts rising up on the slope behind her.

"Did you know this would happen to me, Abuela?" she asked.

She couldn't see her move, but she could feel her grandmother's gaze find her.

"I brought you here to introduce you to *los pequeños misterios,*" Abuela said after a moment. "The spirits you must come to know for your *medicina* to be potent. But I had not thought they would take you away. I always meant to accompany you on your first visit to that other realm."

"So these *cadejos,*" Bettina said. "They're to be my guardian spirits?"

Her *abuela* made a *tching* noise in the back of her throat. "*¿Quién sabe?* They are a mystery to me."

"But—"

"Sleep now, *chica*. We will speak of this again in the morning. Tonight you need your rest."

Bettina thought it would be impossible to sleep, but when she laid her head down once more, weariness rose up like a swell of dark clouds.

"*Ahorita,*" she heard a small *cadejo* voice whisper deep in her mind, just before she fell asleep. "*Tenemos una casa.*"

Now we have a home . . .

Bettina woke in the hours before dawn, uncertain as to what had roused her. From where she lay she could see Ban still sleeping. He lay with his hands folded on his lower chest, face to the stars. Somewhere in the distance, one of his namesakes yipped at the moonless sky, joined moments later by a *compadre* on another hill. Abuela had left her place under the saguaro and her blanket was still folded beside her pack, but that didn't surprise Bettina. Her grandmother often wandered abroad at night—in the desert, in *la época del mito*, wherever *los pequeños misterios* took her. Bettina would have been more surprised to see Abuela sleeping on her blanket as one would expect from a normal person. She was half-convinced that her grandmother never slept.

It was while she was turning onto her other side that she realized what had woken her. First she smelled the cigarette smoke. Sitting up, she looked around to see the tall, lean shape of her father sitting on his haunches a half-dozen feet from where she lay.

"Papá?" she said, whispering so as not to disturb Ban.

"I am here, *chiquita.*"

He stubbed out his cigarette on a stone and stowed it away in his pocket before coming closer. When he sat down beside her, Bettina snuggled against him. He smelled as he always did, of cigarettes and feathers, of the dry desert after a rain.

"I came as quick as I could," he told her. "I would have woken you, but you were sleeping so peacefully." He cupped her chin in his hand and looked into her face. "You are unharmed?"

"*Sí*, Papá. But I was frightened at first."

"How was it your *abuela* allowed you to travel so far on your own?"

"It was an accident," Bettina said, and then she told him how it had happened, who she had met on the other side.

Her father had always been a good listener. Bettina had often watched him with other people, saw how he focused all his attention on them when they spoke. She knew he wasn't the sort to wish he was somewhere else, or be thinking of what he would say when the other speaker was done the way she sometimes found herself doing—especially with some of Adelita's friends. Anyone in her father's company had his complete and undivided attention which, she'd also noticed, many found to be unnerving.

But she didn't. She held close to this rare moment of intimacy with him. It wasn't that he neglected them, but that he was an anachronism and his life moved to a different current from that which pulled his family. Though he remained close to them, he could not live as they did, always walking on cement and carpets. He needed the earth underfoot. He needed to hunt for his food in the desert, instead of in a store; to go into the wild places where his *Indio* blood called him. He had never been in a car. He had never used a telephone. He saw no reason to change a way of life that had already endured for thousands of years.

"You don't own a home," he would say. "You only visit in it for a while." Though of course Mamá, raising a family, disagreed.

"These new tribes that have come to this land," he would say, "they have no understanding of the desert, the mountains, the wild places and the spirits living in it. They have their politics, but we have the rituals. They have religion, but we live *with* the spirits. They live in a world without harmony, without mystery."

Bettina had often wondered what had brought them together, her *Indio* father and her mostly Mexican mother. Her *abuela*, her mother's mother, seemed closer kin to her father than Mamá did. But this was not something she would ever ask either of them. And they seemed content in their own way, only arguing when it seemed the girls grew too wild. Then Papá would walk off into the desert for longer than usual and Abuela would make his arguments for him. Since her grandmother had come to live with them, her father spent more and more time with his *peyoteros* in the desert.

"Papá," Bettina said when she finished relating her tale. "I think they're still inside me. *Los cadejos*. I can feel them . . . shifting sometimes, against my bones. Or I hear a faint echo of their voices in my head."

He regarded her for a long moment, dark gaze seeming to look under her skin, into her spirit, before he gave her a slow nod.

"I don't think they mean you harm," he said. "*Pero*, if you are worried, you must ask your *abuela* to take you to the shrine of the *inocente*. Do you know the place I mean?"

Bettina nodded. It was north of where they lived, along the river, a crude shrine built from old adobe bricks with only the vague memory of an image in their center. On every ledge and protruding space of the shrine stood the stubs of burned-down candles, a lava flow of wax drippings that almost covered the bricks in places. A man had killed his son in this place, the story went, killed him for simply talking to his beautiful second wife, not recognizing his victim as his own son until it was too late. That innocent ghost was said to be able to chase away unwanted spirits, to take care of those who had been wronged as he was.

"Go there," Bettina's father told her. "Light a candle for the *inocente* and pray."

"I will, Papá."

He ruffled her hair. "I have heard of these *cadejos*, you know. When I lived in Sonora, the elders still had stories of them. There were two: *la cadejo*

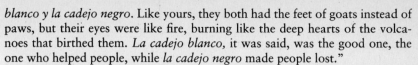

blanco y la cadejo negro. Like yours, they both had the feet of goats instead of paws, but their eyes were like fire, burning like the deep hearts of the volcanoes that birthed them. *La cadejo blanco,* it was said, was the good one, the one who helped people, while *la cadejo negro* made people lost."

"Truly?" Bettina asked.

"*Verdaderos.* In those days, many people would say they had seen them, and one of the elders once told me that *la cadejo negro* was the good one really."

"And they said only that? There was only a white and a black one in those stories?"

Her father shrugged. "You know how stories are now—there is no one way to tell them anymore. This had already begun before I came to Sonora." He smiled, teeth flashing in the dark. "I have never heard of your brightly colored volcano dogs. But there are so many things we have never heard of, you and I, and yet they are true, eh?"

Bettina nodded.

"Still there have always been stories of *los perros misteriosos* among our people. A dog is never simply what we think we see. He keeps us safe from the wolf and coyote, but deep in *su corazón* he *is* a wolf, a coyote. He is the one that can walk between the worlds, who leads us in the end to Mictlan."

Bettina shivered at the mention of the land of the dead. It could seem too close on a night so dark, with her father telling his spooky stories.

Her father smiled at her reaction. He lowered his voice dramatically "Only the dog may go into the underworld and return. He leads us there, but he can also lead us into the other worlds, just as your *cadejos.* He is descended from the clown dog of the old gods, as you know, fickle and unpredictable."

Bettina remembered that story from another night of storytelling.

"*La Maravilla,*" she said.

"*Sí.* When he comes for us, we know we have no choice. We must follow where he leads."

"Now I'm scared," Bettina said. "Did *los cadejos* come to take me back to Mictlan?"

"No, no, *chiquita.* But all dogs are spirits. They carry potent *brujería,* so we must always be careful in our dealings with them. Death is the gift we offer to the world in thanks for the life it has given to us, but no one should seek it out."

"All dogs?"

Her father shrugged. "You will know them when you see them, *los perros misteriosos.* And remember, they bring the little deaths, too: sleep, dreams, change, the step from this world into *la época del mito.* You don't need to be afraid of them, but you should respect them."

"I will try, Papá."

"And go to the shrine with your *abuela.* If she can't take you, I will."

Bettina nodded, then stifled a yawn, tired once more.

"I must go," her father said. "Do you want to come home with me?"

They were so different, her *mamá* and *papá*. Mamá would never even ask such a question. But she loved them both, he for his mystery, she for the home she made in their house, in their kitchen, in her heart.

"No, Papá," she said. For then he would have to forsake his hawk's flight to walk her home. "Thank you for coming."

"You are my blood, *chiquita*. How could I do less?"

He kissed her on the brow, then stood. So tall, Bettina thought. He and all her *Indio* uncles. She heard him strike a match, light his cigarette.

"I love you, Papá," she said.

"*Te amo también,*" he told her, but she was already asleep. "I will look in on you in the morning."

There were hawks in the sky when Bettina woke the next morning, a half-dozen of them, dark against the dawn clouds. *Brujo* spirits, riding the high thermals.

"*Tu papá y sus peyoteros,*" Abuela said. "You called to him as you did to me—when you were in *la época del mito.*"

Bettina nodded, remembering—that and something else.

"He was here last night," she said. "*Mi papá.*"

Abuela nodded. "I was out walking among the uncles and aunts and saw him on my return, hawk wings lifting him into the early dawn."

"He told me to ask you to take me to the shrine of the *inocente.*"

"Because of *los cadejos.*"

Bettina nodded.

"It is a good thought." Abuela paused for a moment. "But I have been thinking, too. Had they meant you harm, they would not have brought you back to us as they did. I believe they are your *medicina* guides."

"But Papá said—"

"We will go to the shrine and burn a candle," Abuela assured her. "If they mean you ill, the spirit of the *inocente* will drive them from you. But if they are your friends, the spirit will know and he will leave them untouched."

When they returned home that evening, Bettina went to evening mass with her mother. She wanted to talk to Mamá about her experience in I'itoi's cave, how Papá had come to her, crossing the Tucsons and the desert on his hawk wings, but it was a conversation she couldn't even begin. So she sat beside her mother, listening to the priest with her hands folded on her lap, and went up to the rail for communion. Afterwards, she waited with her mother by the confession booth, but when her turn came, she could no more speak to the priest about it than she could to her mother.

Was that a sin? she wondered as she confessed to arguing with her sister and a half dozen other small transgressions. Would God understand?

She wasn't sure that he would, but she knew the Virgin did. Throughout the service Bettina's gaze had been drawn, as it invariably was, to the Virgin's statue with its blue and white robes, her serene presence. The Virgin had lived in a desert, too. Surely she had been aware of the small *misteriosos*, before the miracle birth of her Son.

Later she did tell Adelita.

"I saw Papá today," she said as they lolled on a bench they had made in the backyard by placing a found board on matching stacks of adobe bricks. "Out in the desert."

There were no flowers in their small garden—only herbs and vegetables and the cacti that had been there before their house had been built. Neither Mamá nor Abuela understood the concept of watering plants that one could not eat. It was one of the few things on which they agreed.

"He and *nuestros tíos*," she added.

"They aren't really our uncles," Adelita said.

"I know that. But I like them all the same."

Adelita said nothing. She scuffed at the dirt with her toe, a little put out because Mamá wouldn't let her go off with her friends this evening.

"They were in their hawk shapes," Bettina said.

That made Adelita laugh. "You can be such a little child."

"I am not."

"Then why do you still believe in *los cuentos de hadas*?"

"It's not a fairy tale."

Adelita gave a practiced adult shrug.

"You weren't always this way," Bettina said.

"No," her sister agreed. "But I grew up. One day you will, too."

"I will never grow up if growing up means no longer seeing the truth."

"Then they will lock you away with all the other *locos*."

Early Monday morning, when the dawn was still pinking the sky and long before Bettina had to be at school, Abuela walked with her along the river-bank to the shrine of the *inocente*. They walked quietly but still startled up coveys of Gambel's quail and doves. When a roadrunner crossed the path ahead of them, Bettina stopped, her pulse quickening.

"It is only what it seems," her *abuela* told her. "A bird, nothing more."

Bettina gave a little nervous laugh.

"I knew that," she said.

Her grandmother said nothing.

The riverbed they walked along was mostly a dry wash now, damp in places from the spring rains, the only water puddled in the bed's lowest depressions. Mesquite and palo verde grew along the river's banks, sometimes hanging over the path where they walked. On the other side of the path patches of Mexican poppies the color of marigolds and purple blue lupines clustered around cholla skeletons.

The sun rose over the peaks of the Rincon Mountains just as they reached the shrine. The white wax covering the adobe bricks gleamed in its light, high-lighted by the small *milagros* and other metal offerings that were caught in its flow. Bouquets of drying flowers lay around the base of the shrine, tied together with ribbons and strings. Photos, curling and sun-bleached, lay among them. While Abuela lit a single candle and placed it on the shrine, Bettina knelt on the ground. All the wax on the shrine made it look as though it was melting back into the earth, she thought. There was little bird sound, little sound at all. Closing her eyes, she prayed, asking the spirit of the shrine to cast out the *cadejos* if they meant her harm.

When the candle was lit, Abuela sat beside her and they remained so for some time. After a while Bettina opened her eyes, blinking a little in the light. She let her gaze travel over the shrine, then to the vegetation beyond it. Prickly pear and the mesquite. A few saguaro, one tipped at such an angle that it would surely topple over this year. The palo verde trees. A barrel cactus growing under them with a large yellow blossom growing from its thorny top.

"Do you see him?" she asked her grandmother. "*¿El inocente?*"

"No. But I feel his presence. Can you?"

"I feel something . . ."

Her *abuela* nodded. "And *los cadejos?*"

Bettina thought for a moment before answering.

"You know when someone is laughing, but making no sound?" she said. "They're like that inside me. Like a tickle, or a happy thought."

"Does their presence frighten you?"

Bettina shook her head. "But it's a funny feeling, to have little mysteries living inside you like this."

"We all carry mysteries," Abuela told her. "Some are merely less hidden than others." She looked out across the dry wash of the river, past the mesquite to the mountains beyond. "The next time you visit *la época del mito*," she added, "you will not travel alone. I should have taken you a long time ago, but I was waiting . . ."

Her voice trailed off.

"For what?" Bettina asked.

"For when the time felt right."

Bettina sighed. Sometimes it seemed as though her entire life was simply made up of waiting.

"When do you think Ban will realize that I'm a woman?" she asked.

Abuela smiled. "When you become a woman. You are still a girl, Bettina. *Mi chiquita*. Don't be in such a hurry to grow up. Age will come to you soon enough. Never fear. There will be many boys in your life, many men. And much mystery, too. That is the way it is with women such as us with the *brujería* in our blood. But only the mystery stays with us."

"All I want is a boyfriend. Like Ban. He'd be perfect."

"*Sí*. And what does Ban want?"

Bettina shrugged. "I don't know. I never asked him."

"Perhaps he is ready for a wife and children. Are *you* ready to be a mother?"

"I don't know. Maybe. Do you think I should talk to him?"

"I think you should wait. The world is large with possibilities for those with patience."

"But sometimes you have to do something," Bettina said. "You can't always just wait for things to come to you."

"Of course not. That is where the wisdom comes in."

"What wisdom?"

The wisdom you got from growing older, Bettina supposed, feeling like she was walking around and around in circles.

"The wisdom I share with you," Abuela said.

Bettina studied the shrine for a long moment. She thought about how frightened she'd been in *la época del mito*, but how exciting it had been, too. Her life had changed this weekend, she realized. Now she had the children of volcanoes living inside her and she'd talked to a man who could change his shape. She almost laughed. Talked to a man who could change his shape? *¿Y qué tiene?* Her Papá flew the desert skies on a hawk's wings.

She turned to look at her grandmother, thinking of all the wisdom Abuela had to offer her if she could only be patient.

"I can wait for that," she said.

4

Masks

Our job is to be an awake people . . . utterly
conscious, to attend to the world.
—NATIVE AMERICAN BELIEF

1

Ellie checked her watch again. Almost nine and Donal still hadn't shown up to give her a ride as promised. Nor was he answering his phone. It figured. Knowing him as long as she had, and having lived with him for part of that time, she knew exactly how untogether he could be about the simplest thing. But this was really pushing it.

It had been over an hour now while she sat with her parka close at hand, a packed suitcase and a box of art materials on the floor by the door, waiting for something, she began to realize, that wasn't going to happen. Still, she allowed Donal another fifteen minutes before giving up and calling Tommy's apartment. A woman answered the phone, startling Ellie. Tommy never had anyone over at his apartment, never mind a woman.

"Who's this?" she found herself asking before it occurred to her how rude the question might seem.

"Sunday."

"You're kidding. As in his *Aunt* Sunday?"

The woman on the other end of the line laughed and Ellie realized that now she'd compounded rudeness with stupidity.

"I'm sorry," she said, "it's just . . ." I didn't believe any of you really existed, she'd been about to say, which would have only made things worse.

"You'll be Ellie," the other woman said.

"How could you know—"

"I'm psychic."

She'd have to be, Ellie thought.

Sunday laughed again, a throaty, pleasing sound that woke a smile on Ellie's lips.

"Don't take me so seriously," Sunday said. "The truth is, except for his family, I think you're the only woman in Tommy's life."

"That's not true," Ellie said. "He knows any number of women."

"Really?" Sunday replied. "Are you keeping secrets from your aunt?" she added, her voice growing fainter as she took the receiver away from her mouth. "I've just been told that you're a regular Casanova."

"Give me that," Ellie heard Tommy say.

"What have you been telling your aunts about me?" Ellie asked when Tommy came on the line.

"Don't you start," Tommy growled, but there was no real anger in his voice.

"Easy does it, Romeo."

Tommy sighed. "So what's up, Ellie?"

"I was going to ask you for a ride up to Kellygnow, but now that I know you have a guest—"

"It's okay. She was just leaving—weren't you?" he added, obviously to his aunt. "What time do you have to be there?" he asked Ellie.

"There's no rush."

"I'll be over in ten minutes or so."

"But—"

She was too late. "Catch you," Tommy said and the line went dead.

Ellie slowly hung up the receiver on her end and went to sit by the window where she could see the street outside her front door. She felt a little guilty for imposing on Tommy like this. He so rarely did normal things like visit with his family.

Just before Tommy arrived, she saw a dark sedan pull up in front of her building. The man who stepped out of it was plain-looking, with light brown hair and a business suit on under his open overcoat, but he had an official air about him that she'd come to recognize through working with Angel. Not a cop, but someone in the law enforcement community. Maybe a private detective or a process server. She wondered who he was coming to see in her building, then Tommy's pickup pulled in behind the sedan and she turned away from the window to put on her parka and gather her things.

She had just locked her door behind her and was picking up the box with her art materials when the man she'd seen come into the building topped the stairs and walked towards her.

"Ms. Jones?" he asked. "Ms. Ellie Jones?"

Oh shit, Ellie thought, managing to keep her features schooled. What does some official type like this want with me? But then she remembered the threat Henry Patterson had delivered when he left her studio on Saturday morning and realized he hadn't been bluffing. He really was going to take her to court.

"I'm afraid not," she lied, giving what had to be a process server a sweet smile. "Ellie left for Florida yesterday. I'm just looking after her place until she gets back."

The man gave her a suspicious look, but what could he do? It wasn't like he was a cop with any real authority.

"When will that be?" he asked.

"Late spring. Can I take a message?"

"No, I'd rather talk to her in person."

"Well, you'll have to wait then. Say, can you give me a hand with that suitcase?"

"Well, I don't—"

"This is great," Ellie said, heading off with the box, acting like he'd already agreed to help. "You're saving me a lot of time. When I agreed to put this stuff into storage for Ellie, I had no idea there'd be so much of it, you know?"

She paused at the top of the stairs. The process server gave her a considering look, then picked up her suitcase and followed her down to the street where they met Tommy coming in.

"Tommy!" Ellie said. "You're on time for a change. And here I went and got this nice man to help me carry Ellie's stuff all the way downstairs. Why did you say you wanted to see her again?" she added, turning to the process server.

"I didn't. It's . . ." He looked from her to Tommy, then set the suitcase down. "It's not that important. If you're talking to her, tell her I was by."

"And who do I say the message is from?"

"It's really not that important," he repeated, almost mumbling now as he pushed past Tommy and beat a retreat to his car.

"What was that all about?" Tommy asked as they watched him drive away.

"I'm pretty sure he was a process server."

"Well, he was some bureaucratic lowlife, that's for sure. What did he want with you?"

"He never said, but I'm guessing the commission I blew off on Saturday really is going to press charges."

"That sucks. How'd you managed to convince this guy you weren't, well, who you are?"

"I don't know. He even caught me coming out of my studio, but I just told him I was apartment-sitting and that 'Ellie' had left for Florida and wouldn't be back until the spring."

Tommy grinned. "I didn't know you were such a good bullshitter. I'm going to have to be more careful around you."

"Oh, please."

Tommy picked up the suitcase the process server had abandoned. "Come on," he said. "I want you to meet one of those aunts of mine who don't exist."

"Oh, god. You didn't tell her that, did you?"

"No. But I could."

Ellie's heart sank, but Tommy behaved himself and the nervousness she was feeling faded almost as soon as they reached the pickup and she slid onto the seat beside Sunday Creek. Instead of the mysterious old wise woman Ellie had been picturing, all seriousness and pithy sayings and omens, Sunday was a cheerfully good-natured woman who looked a great deal younger than the forty-some years of age she had to be if she was one of Tommy's aunts. Even sitting she was tall, a serene, broad-faced woman with lustrous black hair. And she had a wicked sense of humor. The whole way out on the drive to Kellygnow she had Ellie giggling with her stories of the rez and the characters that made up her immediate circle of friends and family.

It wasn't until they pulled up in front of the big house at the top of the hill that was their destination and Ellie was about to get out of the car, that Sunday grew serious. She caught hold of Ellie's arm and regarded her gravely.

"You will watch out for Tommy, won't you?" she asked.

Ellie gave her a puzzled look.

"Don't start, Sunday," Tommy said.

His aunt ignored him. "I ask you because we can't always watch over him, what with his living down here in the city so far from home as he does, but you're close to him, and I know you care for him as much as we do."

Ellie glanced past Sunday to where Tommy was offering up a "What can you do?" look, but it barely registered. Instead she was thinking how Sunday was right. She did care for Tommy. It wasn't something she'd ever really stopped and thought about much, but he was like a big brother to her—a big brother she wanted to shake some sense into every once in a while because he could be doing so much more with his life than he was. But that didn't stop her from caring for him.

"He doesn't listen to me," she said, returning her gaze to Sunday.

"That's not news," Sunday said. "He doesn't listen to anybody."

"Hello?" Tommy broke in. "I'm here, too. You don't have to talk about me like I've stepped out of the cab."

"The trouble is," Sunday went on as though he hadn't spoken, "this turn of the wheel's taking us into a dangerous time, especially for Tommy, and it would help set our minds at ease to know you were using your medicine to protect him."

"My what?" Ellie said.

"You're talking to the wrong person," Tommy told his aunt. "Ellie doesn't know *mamàndà-gashkitòwin ondji pate* and thinks they're pretty much both the same thing. Magic from smoke," he added in English for Ellie's benefit.

Sunday's dark, serious gaze remained fixed on Ellie.

"Is this true?" she asked. "With the medicine as potent as it is?"

A strange prickling sensation went up Ellie's spine, but she remained silent, not knowing what to say. The conversation had taken such an odd and unexpected turn that the ability to use language momentarily fled.

"You really don't know, do you?" Sunday said after a long moment. "You have no idea how strong the Maker's gift runs in you."

She was talking about magic, Ellie realized. Talking about it, but not like Donal or Jilly did, as though it was some mysterious, distant thing. Sunday spoke of it as though it was an everyday part of life, the way she might discuss someone's health, or the weather.

Ellie cleared her throat. "I'm sorry," she said, "but I don't really believe in that sort of thing."

"Ah."

Just that. No attempt to convince her otherwise. No cataloguing of extraordinary, mysterious occurrences followed with a "So explain that, then," as Donal would do. None of Jilly's sad, sympathetic looks, conveying an unspoken but no less understood "You're missing so much."

"It's just not anything I can relate to," Ellie went on.

"Of course."

"I mean, it's not real."

Sunday smiled. "There's no need to explain. But will you do this for me? Think positive thoughts of Tommy from time to time. Concentrate on his continued well-being."

"But . . ."

"Trust me," Sunday said. "It will be of great help."

"Okay. I . . ."

Ellie glanced at Tommy, caught him grinning.

"It was so nice to finally meet you," Sunday said.

Ellie returned her gaze to Tommy's aunt, certain now that she'd been the butt of some obscure joke, but Sunday's features were guileless, friendly. The curious prickle she'd felt earlier grew stronger, rising up from the base of her spine and spreading out along the roadmap of her nerves. It was a disconcerting, though not altogether unpleasant sensation.

"Um, me, too," Ellie said. "I mean, it was good to meet you as well."

"And thank you for humoring me in this."

"Sure. Well, I should go."

Sunday clasped one of Ellie's hands between her own.

"Keep your strength," she said. "And walk in Beauty."

Whatever that meant. But Ellie nodded.

"You, too," she said.

She slipped out of the cab, boots crunching in the snow when she stepped over to the bed of the pickup to get her box of art supplies.

"What was all that about?" Ellie asked as Tommy helped her with her suitcase to the front door.

"Aunt business," he said. "Weren't you expecting something like that—if they even turned out to be real?"

"I'd whack you," she told him, "only my hands are full."

"Don't worry," Tommy said. "My family lives in another world from this one. You'd probably have to be born into it to see what they see."

"And do you see what they see?"

Tommy nodded, serious for a moment. "I guess," he said finally. "When I don't try to pretend that none of it's real. Why do you think I stay away from the rez? The world's complicated enough as it is without bringing the world of the spirits into the equation as well."

That spine tingle grew stronger again, as though trying to tell her something. Tell her what? That everything she thought she knew about the world was a lie? As if. That was Donal talking.

Tommy put her suitcase down on the steps.

"Are you going to be okay?" he asked.

Ellie nodded.

"Do you need a ride home tonight?"

"No, but we're on for the van run tonight, aren't we? Would you mind picking me up here?"

"No problem. It should be a fun night. The weather forecast's calling for freezing rain."

"Lovely."

"Don't worry. I'm putting my studded tires on the truck this afternoon so we'll use it if the driving gets too bad. It may not be legal off the rez, but we won't get stuck. And if the weather's so bad that if we do need them, nobody's going to hassle us."

"Okay. Tell your aunt I'll think good thoughts your way."

Tommy laughed and headed back to the pickup.

Ellie waited until he got back in the cab. Tommy and his aunt waved to her and she waved back, then Tommy was backing up, the pickup pulling away. Ellie returned her attention to the house. When she rang the bell, a tall, red-haired woman answered and welcomed her in. Ellie hesitated a moment. She turned to look at where the pickup was making its way back down the steep, icy incline, brake lights flashing red against the snow as Tommy tapped them to slow their descent. The weird prickling still whispered along the length of her spinal column, but fainter now, fading.

Her life, Ellie decided, had gotten much too complicated lately. Thankfully she had this project of Musgrave Wood's to immerse herself in. With any luck, working on the mask would allow her to forget about everything: the potential lawsuits and strange buzzy feelings, the curious utterances of Tommy's aunt and all.

2

Miki was trying to learn a Ben Webster solo when the knock came at her door. Staring at a section of Donal's painting that she'd torn from the ruined canvas, she ignored whoever it was, just as she had the phone that seemed to ring every five minutes, and continued to play. The only thing that was keeping her sane at the moment was immersing herself in an impossible task such as this: trying to recapture Webster's sweet tone on her button accordion. It kept coming up too Irish, like an air, instead of a sax solo. The problem, she knew, were the instruments, free reed versus blown reed. It was like banging in a nail with a rock. It'd work, but a hammer was so much better for the job.

The knock came again.

"Go away," she told whoever it was.

She started over at the beginning of the solo, one Webster had done when sitting in with the Art Tatum Group. Cole Porter's "Night and Day." Closing her eyes, she let Tatum's piano roll through her head. She kept time with her foot. Tap, tap, tap. Felt the swing of the music. And now she'd come in, fingers spidering across the buttons. Getting the notes wasn't the problem. But that tone was going to elude her forever.

"Come on, Miki," she heard Hunter say through the door. "Open up. I know you're in there."

Well, duh. That was so obvious, he lost points for saying it. But she stopped playing and leaned her arms on top of her instrument.

"I'm too sick to come to the door," she told him.

"Bullshit."

What was Hunter doing here anyway? He was supposed to be at the store. So was she, of course, Monday morning bright and early, nine-thirty through to three or so unless it got really busy, except, hello world. Her life had ended. She had the best of reasons for wanting to be on her own, considering how well she'd handled things with Donal last night. What was Hunter's excuse?

"Miki?"

Sighing, she slid the strap of her accordion from her shoulder and went to stand beside the door.

"Who's watching things at the shop?" she asked.

"Fiona."

"I thought you were letting her go today."

There was a long silence from the other side of the door.

"I couldn't do it," he said finally.

Miki undid the lock and swung the door open.

"Wimp," she told him, more out of habit than with any feeling. Her heart simply wasn't into teasing him today.

Hunter came in and toed off his wet boots.

"How could I do it?" he said. "The store feels like a family—"

"It's as dysfunctional as one at least."

"And letting her go would be like you kicking Donal out of your apartment. It just wouldn't feel right."

Miki felt as though she'd been hit in the stomach—but of course Hunter couldn't know. It was an innocent remark, nothing more.

She turned and led the way back into what had once been the dining room. Once she threw out all of Donal's stuff, she supposed she could reclaim her bedroom and this could be the dining room again. Or she could hang herself from the light fixture and then Donal and his Gentry freaks could turn the whole place into a wolfish den.

God, now she was beginning to sound like some of Fiona's little Goth friends, the ones who thought death and suicide were so cool.

"You're just too soft," she told Hunter, trying to keep her voice light.

"That's not quite how my accountant's going to put it."

"But it is why we all love you so much."

She sat down on the end of her bed and lit a cigarette, waving Hunter to a chair. He slumped into it, adjusting the seat cushion where it sagged.

"You're not helping," he told her.

"Sorry."

"So, really—what gives?"

She shrugged. "I just felt like a time-out."

"Right. You never blow off anything." He glanced around the room. "Is your phone working? I tried calling, but there was no answer."

"So that was you."

"Miki, you know you can . . ."

His voice trailed off. Miki saw where he was looking. Why'd she have to go and leave that lying around?

Hunter picked up the torn piece of canvas. It was most of the Green Man's head, the paint smeared in one corner where it hadn't quite dried yet. Miki still had a smudge of green on her jeans where she'd wiped off her fingers. It had looked like blood, weird green blood, the kind that would come from the veins of a tree man.

"That's part of Donal's painting, isn't it?" Hunter said. "What happened?"

Miki wouldn't look at the piece of canvas in his hands. She'd had her fill of looking at it.

"Miki?"

"Nothing happened," she said. "Donal came home in a snit and trashed it, end of story."

"But after all the work he must have put into it . . ."

Miki shrugged. "It was supposed to be him, you know. Like a self-portrait. I didn't realize it until I got up this morning. You can see it in the eyes."

Hunter looked, but it was plain he couldn't find what she had.

"But why would he—"

"Trash it, or paint the damn thing in the first place?" Miki broke in, her voice sounding oddly calm to her ears. "That's easy enough. He put his foot through it so he wouldn't have to drag it around with him when he left last night."

She was aware of the worried look Hunter was giving her, but she couldn't seem to stop.

"And he painted it because he thinks they're going to make him the Summer King, the stupid little shite."

"The summer king?"

"Umm. Only say it capitalized— the way Pooh bear would."

"You're losing me here," Hunter told her.

Miki sighed and butted out her cigarette in an overflowing ashtray. "Donal's got himself mixed up with what he thinks are the Gentry—you know those hard men that were after you the other night?"

"Yes, but what do they have to do with anything?"

"It's a long, tedious story. Sure you wouldn't rather go for a beer instead?"

"It's not even noon."

"Well, I could go for one, except I'm fresh out. You can't keep beer in this place—not with Donal around. But I suppose that'll change now."

"He's going on the wagon?"

Miki laughed, wincing at the bitter edge she could hear, the complete lack of humor.

"As if," she said. "No, I threw him out last night."

"You—"

"That's right. Out on his ear."

"Because he was drinking . . . ?"

Hunter didn't try to hide his confusion. What would be so unusual in Donal drinking?

"No," Miki said. "Because of the painting."

"The painting."

She could see that he was trying to understand, but not making any headway. She didn't blame him. It made no sense, considering how close they'd always been, she and Donal, the two of them against the rest of the world.

"Because of what it means," she told Hunter. "Because he's bought into all this old, hurtful shite and I don't want to see where it takes him. Maybe I can't stop him but I'll be damned if I'll watch him do this to himself."

"You've totally lost me," Hunter said. "You're going to have to start at the beginning."

Miki gave a slow nod. "How about we at least do it over a cup of tea?"

"Sounds good. Do you want to have it here, or go out for it?"

"I think pretty much anywhere but here would feel better."

3

Bettina found herself dreaming about *los cadejos*—something that hadn't happened in almost seven years, not since the night her grandmother had walked out into the desert during a thunderstorm and never come back. The little pack of raucous dogs came to her while she was wandering through the winter Newford streets, a burst of rainbow colors, yipping and yapping some silly song, gamboling all around her, goat hooves clacking where the pavement was bare. She wasn't sure how long they went traipsing through the streets together, but after a while *los cadejos* drifted away, leaving only the echo of one of their nonsensical songs behind, and then it was her *abuela* walking with her, arm-in-arm on one side, the Virgin Mary on the other—completely improbable, *claro*, but this was a dream, and wasn't anything possible in a dream? Or at least one didn't think to question the improbabilities while dreaming.

Just before Bettina woke up, the three of them were sitting on a patio outside a Lower Crowsea restaurant in a snowstorm, trying to get a waiter's attention. *La Virgen* had been particularly testy, constantly repeating, "All I would like is sòme mineral water. Is that so much to ask? One small bottle of mineral water. You would think I was asking for the blood of my Son."

Bettina woke to a terrible guilt, feeling as though she should go to confession for even dreaming such a thing about the Virgin. But after seven months of living in this city, she still hadn't found a church to attend. Truth was, she hadn't tried very hard. She *had* looked, especially when she first arrived, but she didn't feel at home in any of the ones close to Kellygnow—there were too many *gente rica*, rich people, for her to feel comfortable—and Our Lady of Assumption on the East Side, where Salvadore and Maria Elena went, was too far away, though Salvadore had offered to pick her up whenever she wished to go.

Pero, she and her faith were no longer as close as once they'd been. She wasn't sure if it was her fault, or that of the church, but she hadn't been attending mass regularly even before she'd left home to come here. She couldn't remember when she'd last been to confession. The only tangible result so far was Mamá's exaggerated disappointment.

Bettina sighed. Sitting up, sleep still thick in her eyes, she regarded the John Early statue of *la Virgen* that stood in her room. There was no recrimination in her eyes, but then the Virgin never accused.

"Perdona," Bettina apologized. "I know you have unlimited patience and would never be so rude."

The house seemed quiet as she washed up and got dressed, as though everyone in residence was either out this morning, or sleeping late, but when she reached the kitchen, Nuala was there as usual, pouring Bettina a mug of coffee as soon as Bettina came in through the door. There was guilt in this, too, for Bettina, having someone see to her needs the way Nuala did. While she could understand the housekeeper looking after the others—the artists and writers—she was uncomfortable when Nuala's efficient administrations included her. Meals, laundry, coffee, and tea. "You are a guest in this house," Nuala explained to her. *Sí* but not one of any great importance.

Sometimes Bettina felt everyone was far too generous to her.

"A package came for you this morning," Nuala said.

Bettina smiled her thanks for the coffee and carried the steaming mug over to the table where the package waited for her, brown paper, wrapped in twine, with an Arizona postmark.

Mamá, she thought until she saw that the return address was La Gata Verde in Tubac. Adelita's store. She opened the package to find a cardboard box. Inside was a letter lying on top of tissue paper. It read:

> Mi estimada Bettina,
>   It was rude of me to speak the way I did last night—I am writing this on Monday morning, I wonder when you will receive it? Before the weekend, I hope, but only if I get it into the mail today.
>   You know I'm not one to analyze my feelings—certainly not the way Suzanna does. She watches way too much Oprah, so far as

I'm concerned. But I do know there are hidden reasons for why we do and say the things we do, and I have thought much on why I am so unforgiving when we speak of Abuela and things mystical. The truth is, mi hermana, I am jealous. It seemed to me that Abuela always had more time for you. I know this was because you never tired of her stories and desert treks as I did, but logic doesn't always enter into how we feel, does it?

Earlier this morning I went down the street to La Paloma to look at their chimeneas to use in back of the house for those times I can't get Chuy to build a campfire. There I found these little wooden dogs. They reminded me of the stories you used to tell me about the children of a volcano that you said had come to live inside your chest—do you remember? What was it that you called them?

I hope you will accept them as a small apology for my impatience with la brujería. I will try harder in the future.

Chuy and Janette send their love—the painting is hers. ¿Está bonito, no está él? I swear I don't push her, but I can't keep her away from my art supplies and she's fascinated with the prints Suzanna runs off her lithography press. Perhaps she will be an artist, too.

Mama asked me to include a little something from her, I have no idea what it is.

Call me soon. Te echo de menos, hermanita.

love
Adelita

Bettina smiled as she set the letter aside. That was Adelita, her writing, as always, a mix of stiff phrases and casual conversation. She was never as comfortable putting words on paper as she was putting images. Bettina pulled the box closer. Funny that she would dream of *los cadejos* on the same day that this package came. She hadn't even thought of them in years.

Unfolding the tissue paper, the first thing she saw was Janette's painting: a small watercolor of a lizard, poking its head up through a cluster of Mexican poppies. Although the subjects were accurately rendered, Janette had been more liberal in her color choices. The flowers of the poppies were the brilliant gold-yellow they should be, but their stems and leaves ran a gamut of light pink through to rich purples. The lizard was a dark, deep blue with yellow markings, the ground a lighter blue, while what could be seen of the sky was an almost iridescent rose color, as though it had been formed from an endless cloud of fairy dusters. In the bottom right-hand corner Janette had carefully printed out her name in neat block letters.

The whole thing reminded Bettina of a desert sunset. Homesickness thickened in her throat and made her chest feel too tight. It wasn't so much the desert she was missing as Janette's growing up, day by day, so far away from where Bettina was making her home. Living here, Bettina was missing it all.

"That's lovely," Nuala said, coming over to the table to look at the painting.

"My niece painted it for me."

"She seems to have as much talent as her mother."

Bettina nodded. With the painting removed from the top of the package, she could see a small bundled piece of cotton cloth that had been tied closed with a piece of twine. She picked it up. Through the cloth she could feel what seemed to be beads. A necklace, perhaps, she thought, but undoing the knot in the twine, she folded the corners of the cloth back to find a rosary.

This could only be from Mamá.

While her first thought was that it was yet another attempt of Mamá to play on her guilt, when Bettina studied the rosary more closely, she realized it was anything but. The beads were made from various sacred beans and seeds that had been collected in the desert, the crucifix carved from dried cholla spines. Combined they evoked two potent *brujeríos*: that of the Virgin, and that of the desert. This was something Abuela might have given her, or Papá. To have it come from her mother felt . . . confusing, she supposed.

Looking up, she found Nuala's gaze riveted upon the rosary as well. The older woman reached out a hand, fingers brushing the air above the threaded beans and seeds.

"This is very powerful," she said.

"It's from my mother."

"She is a wise woman."

For a moment Bettina thought how incongruous the idea was. Of all of them, Mamá would have the least to do with Abuela's medicines and *brujería*, or Papá's *Indios* mysteries. But then she considered how Mamá had kept them all together, fed and clothed them, tended to their bodies and their spirits.

"*Sí,*" she said, nodding slowly. She closed her hand around the rosary and felt it grow warm between her palm and fingers, felt it tingle against her skin the way the air did before a thunderstorm. "In her own way, she is very wise."

She carefully stowed the rosary in the pocket of her vest and returned to the package, taking out Adelita's gift. Nuala chuckled as Bettina set the small wooden dog carvings on the table by her coffee mug. There were five in all, Mexican folk art dogs painted in a rainbow palette of pinks, blues, lime greens, and bright yellows. Two stood on their hind legs, one seemed to be trying to sniff its own genitals, the remaining two were posed like coyotes made for the *turistas,* snouts pointing at the sky.

Truly *los cadejos,* Bettina thought.

"What fun," Nuala said. "Your niece could have painted them."

Bettina smiled. The freedom of color was similar, though the carvings were much more garish, almost fluorescent.

"They were born in a volcano," she said.

Nuala gave her a puzzled look.

Bettina smiled. "Once upon a time," she said, laying the palm of her hand between her breasts, "they lived inside me."

The good humor left Nuala's features.

"Think of this," she said. "What do you call a wolf that pretends to be your friend?"

Bettina shrugged. "*No lo sé*—I don't know."

"A dog."

"I don't understand what you mean," Bettina said.

But she remembered something her father had told her once, about dogs and wolves.

A dog is never simply what we think we see. He keeps us safe from the wolf and coyote, but deep in his heart, he is *a wolf, a coyote. He is the one that . . .*

"They walk between the worlds," Bettina said.

Nuala nodded. "And *between* is an ancient and potent piece of magic. It always has been, in all its shapes and guises. From the bridge that spans the gorge, or connects one side of the river with the other, to that moment that lies between waking and sleeping. From the gray mystery that lies at the junction of night and day to those twilight places where mingle and meet all the languages and cultures of the world, all the stories and landscapes and arts."

Bettina nodded, the memory of her father's voice growing stronger in her mind.

All dogs are spirits. They carry potent brujería *so we must always be careful in our dealings with them.*

"And in those places," Nuala said, "you will always find him waiting: the dog, the wolf, the fox, the coyote. In some guise or other. And no matter what he promises you, death is the secret he keeps hidden in his eyes. In the end, there is always death, and it isn't his."

Bettina shivered. But her father had spoken of that as well.

Remember, they bring the little deaths, too: sleep, dreams, change, the step from this world into la época del mito. *You don't need to be afraid of them, but you should respect them.*

Bettina touched one of the colorful carvings that she'd placed on the table before her.

"I'm not afraid of them," she said.

"No," Nuala told her. "The innocent never are."

Bettina frowned, but Nuala was already turning away, back to the counter where she had been chopping vegetables for a stew. Gathering up the carvings, Bettina returned the colorful dogs to their box, along with Janette's painting and her sister's letter. She stood up from the table, the box in one hand, her coffee in the other.

"What?" Nuala asked, the steady rhythm of her chopping falling silent for a moment, speaking now as though their earlier conversation had been about nothing more profound than the weather. "Won't you have some breakfast?"

"*No, gracias,*" Bettina said and returned to her room where she set out *los cadejos* around the base of *la Virgen*.

She regarded them thoughtfully, sitting on the end of her bed, finishing her coffee. If death was the secret in a dog's eyes—and Bettina knew that Nuala had really been speaking about *los lobos*—then what was the secret in Nuala's eyes?

Setting the empty mug down on the floor, she took the rosary Mamá had sent from the pocket of her vest. She fingered the beads, saying a decade of Hail Marys before she even realized what she was doing. A smile touched her lips when she was done. It had been a while, but the comfort she'd once gained from the simple act could still affect her. She started to lay the rosary at the base of the statue, making room for it among the carvings, but then replaced it in the pocket of her vest.

It was time to go. She was supposed to sit for Chantal this morning. But first she made the sign of the cross before the statue, lowering her gaze respectfully. She would have to phone Mamá and thank her for the rosary.

Chantal de Vega had a studio on the ground floor, on the other side of the house from Lisette's. She was a sculptor, a tall, square-shouldered woman with a long blonde braid, a healthy ruddy complexion, and a penchant for loose-fitting clothes. Bettina always thought of her as an incarnation of Gaia, a statuesque earth mother, larger than life and generous to a fault. She had the easy good nature that Bettina remembered from her father's amicable, if somewhat laconic, *Indios* cousins, and the most beautiful hands, large and strong, capable of easily lifting fifty-pound bags of clay, or pulling the finest detail from a sculpture. Bettina didn't think she'd ever seen her in a bad mood and today was no exception, although she was apparently packing up her studio when Bettina arrived for her sitting.

"*¿Y bien?*" Bettina said, her unhappiness plain in her voice. "What are you doing?"

Chantal gave her a cheerful smile. "Got handed my walking papers this morning."

"But how can that be possible? You've only been here a few months."

And of all Kellygnow's residents, Chantal would be the last person to be asked to leave because she didn't get along or fit in.

Chantal shrugged. "Well, it's sooner than I thought it'd be, but it's not like it's some big surprise or anything. Everybody who comes here knows it has to end sooner or later."

Bettina crossed the room to where Chantal stood, filling a line of cardboard boxes with the materials she'd brought to outfit the studio last autumn. She knew that this residency had meant a lot to Chantal, allowing her a comfort zone to explore a new direction with her art.

"I loved what I was doing," she'd explained to Bettina once. "But I needed something more. Don't get me wrong, I'm not one of those people who draw a strict boundary line between craft and fine art, but I'd been a potter for too long, and frankly, I'd been too successful at it as well. I was always in that enviable position—at least from a business point of view—of getting more orders than I could fill. It's pretty amazing in this day and age to work at something like I was doing and have to turn away commissions.

"But for all that I love making art you can use—you know, teapots and mugs and vases and bowls and the like—I've always wanted to do more fine art. More sculpture. Not just a piece here and there where I could fit in the time, but to really devote myself to doing it full time. The trouble is, it was a real struggle turning my back on the cash flow just to find the time to see if I could do it. If I even really *wanted* to do it. That's what Kellygnow's giving me. The opportunity to find out who I want to be."

"And will you give up your pottery if you find you do like being a sculptor more?" Bettina had asked.

"Lord, no," Chantal told her. "I couldn't ever give up the feel of the clay between my hands when it's turning on the wheel. I just don't want to *have* to do it." She grinned. "I want the luxury of doing whatever I damn well feel like doing and have somebody out there willing to pay me for the results."

Now what was she going to do? Bettina thought.

"It's a little early to say," Chantal replied when Bettina asked. "I still have some money in the bank, but you know how quick that can disappear in the real world. Except for what I've got here, most of my stuff's in storage. Truth is, I'm tempted to put it all in storage and just take off for a while."

"It doesn't seem fair," Bettina said.

"Well, I won't deny that I wish I could have finished that piece I was doing of you."

"Just tell me when you've set up a new studio and I'll come sit for you."

Chantal smiled. "You're okay, Bettina. I appreciate that."

"*De nada*. Don't worry about it." She sat down on the windowsill, feet dangling. "But I still don't understand why they want you to leave."

"That's simple. They need the space for someone else."

"I wonder who."

With perfect timing, Nuala appeared in the doorway carrying a suitcase in one hand, a small bundle wrapped in cloth in the other. Entering the room behind her with a cardboard box in her arms was the woman Bettina had met yesterday. Ellie Jones. Various art supplies poked out of the top of the box she was carrying, sculpting tools, books, sketchpads.

¡Mierda! Bettina thought. This was all her fault. If she hadn't helped Ellie out yesterday, Chantal wouldn't have lost her residency.

"Hello," Nuala said, greeting them, her voice mild, guileless. "Lovely morning, isn't it?" She set down the suitcase and placed the cloth bundle on a nearby table. Turning to Ellie, she added, "I'll leave you all to get acquainted then, shall I? You remember where I said your bedroom will be?"

"Yes. Only—"

But Nuala was already out the door, as suddenly as though she'd been carried away on a sudden gust of wind, and an awkward silence rose up to fill the space she'd left behind.

4

"They're like fallen angels," Miki said.

She held her tea mug cupped between her palms, as though needing the porcelain's warmth to get her through this. Hunter nodded encouragingly when she fell silent. He'd considered taking her to Kathryn's Café, out on Battersfield Road, but she hadn't been up for either a long trek in this cold weather, or for taking public transport, so they'd settled on Rose & Al's Diner, just around the corner from her apartment. The atmosphere wasn't as warm and relaxing as Kathryn's, but it had its own charm, being an odd hybrid of an English tearoom and an old-fashioned all-night diner, complete with booths, a curving counter and padded stools, chrome and red jukebox in the corner.

The couple who ran it were from Somerset, England, and couldn't make a decent cup of coffee if their life depended on it, but they served their tea by the pot, baked their own biscuits and crumpets, and it was one of the only places in Newford that served real Devon cream. Some places offered all-day breakfasts; at Rose & Al's you could get an English tea with scones, jam, and that Devon cream, from opening until closing.

"These . . . uh, Gentry," Hunter said, prompting Miki when she didn't continue. "You say they're like fallen angels."

She nodded. Shaking a cigarette free from her pack, she lit it and exhaled a stream of blue-gray smoke away from their table.

"Think of them as—what's that Latin term?" It took her a moment before she found it. *"Genii loci."*

Hunter gave her a blank look.

"You know," she went on. "Spirits normally tied to some specific place. A valley, a well, a grove of trees. These—the ones I'm talking about—are ones who've strayed too far from their normal haunts. Without that connection to their native soil, they've all gone a little mad—the way the angels who sided with Lucifer did when they lost their connection to heaven."

"Okay."

Miki gave him a sad smile. "Christ, I know how this all sounds, and I don't half believe it myself. But that's not the point. They believe it, and so, apparently, does Donal."

"But what exactly is it that they believe?"

Miki sighed and took a sip of her tea. Hunter had already finished his first cup and was working on his second. Eleven o'clock on a Monday morning, they pretty much had the place to themselves. Which was probably a good thing, considering where this conversation was going.

"What *don't* they believe?" Miki said. "I listened to so much of this shite when we were staying with my Uncle Fergus that all I have to do is think about it and I can hear his bloody voice ranting away in my head. God's truth, at the time it all sounded like adolescent boys deciding what they'd do if they ruled the world. You know, take a bit of this Roman lore, some of that Druidic ritual, a dash of Wagner and Yeats, mix it all together so that it works—in your own mind at any rate. I can't recite all the details, in all their bloody confusion, but basically it boils down to a belief system that conveniently incorporates whatever they might find appealing or useful from a number of different folk traditions. Most of it comes from sources that have their origin in folklore from the British Isles and the Continent—myths, granny tales, fairy stories—but it becomes unrecognizable in their hands."

"Such as?"

Miki stubbed out her cigarette and lit another. "Well, this business with the Summer King, for one. It's an old belief, the idea that the ruler of a land is directly tied into its well-being. He sows his seed in the spring, lives high and mighty through the summer as the crop grows tall and green, then comes the harvest and he's cut down with the rest of the yield, sleeping in his grave through the winter only to rise up again the following spring. But in the hands of Fergus and his lot it comes along with all sorts of made-up garbage that, in the end, lets them simply string up some poor, daft bugger—to give them personal luck and power, forget the welfare of the land, if such things ever did work."

"You mean they kill him?"

Miki nodded. "Which makes for a Summer Fool, rather than a King, I'd think. Of course the poor sod never knows the truth until it's too bloody late. And you can bet there's no rising from the dead involved either. That dumb bugger's dead and he's not coming back."

"How do you know all this stuff?"

"That's the laugh, isn't it? From my da', the old drunkard. But I'll give him this much: Even he turned his back on Uncle Fergus and his cronies. 'A man can find enough ways to hurt himself on his own,' I heard him tell Fergus once, 'without turning to the likes of your hard men and their ugly magics.' "

Hunter shifted in his seat.

"Makes you uncomfortable?" Miki asked. "Calling it magic, I mean."

"No, it's just this bruise on my side. Doesn't matter what position I'm in, it just starts to ache after I've sat still for too long."

"That's something else Donal owes us."

"You don't think he had anything to do with it, do you?"

Miki shrugged. "I don't know him anymore, so I can't say."

Her voice was casual, but Hunter could see how much it pained her to say it.

"So why do you call it magic?" he asked. "You don't believe in that kind of thing, do you?"

"If you'd asked me yesterday, I'd have said no. But right now?" Her gaze took on a distant look and for a moment Hunter thought he'd lost her again. But then she took another drag from her cigarette and focused on him once more. "Right now, I don't know anymore."

Hunter decided it was time to get back to her brother and what had started her off on this morbid line of thought which was so out of character for her.

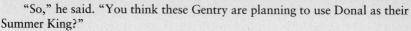

"So," he said. "You think these Gentry are planning to use Donal as their Summer King?"

"I know it," Miki told him. "Why else would he paint his own face behind the Green Man's mask?"

"But he knows the same stories you do."

Miki nodded. "Except it's like my cigs," she said, holding up the cigarette she was smoking. "I know they're going to kill me, but somehow I can't believe that it'll actually happen to me. Don't ask me how it happened, but it seems Donal's got himself convinced that he and the Gentry are working for the same cause: taking back a piece of the world for themselves because, well, the bloody world owes them, doesn't it? It's so pathetic, but I shouldn't be surprised. It would take an Irishman to buy into such a cobblework of shite and pledge himself to their cause."

"What does being Irish have to do with it?" Hunter asked.

"It's that you'd have to be either drunk or mad, and we're too good at both."

"But—"

"Well, Ireland's a peculiar place, isn't it?" Miki said. "It seems to breed loyalties that grow all out of proportion to reality or common sense. Back home, a feud is as real today as it was a few hundred years ago. It doesn't matter that all the original participants are long dead and gone. The descendants will continue with the hostilities until there's no one left, on one side or the other."

She lit another cigarette from the smoldering butt she'd been working on before adding, "It must be something in the air, or that comes up from the land itself."

All Hunter could do was think of the former Yugoslavian Republic, or Rwanda, or any of the how many other places in the world where intolerance was the norm, genocide the solution.

"I think it's an unfortunate part of human nature," he said.

"Maybe so, but it also seems particularly Irish to me. What are we known for?"

"Before or after *Riverdance*?"

"Ha, ha. No, I'm serious." She held up a hand and ticked them off. "Drinking, fighting, melancholy . . . and overwrought songs and novels concerning the three. It's bloody pathetic, but you know, it's not such a bloody lie, either. Christ knows I like a drink myself, and I'm just as liable to give someone a whack to settle a difference as talk it out."

"I think you're generalizing."

"Well, of course I'm generalizing. But the thing with generalizing is that it holds a certain grain of truth, overall. Look at the peace process Blair's negotiating. Everybody's going, hurrah, but if you think Northern Ireland's not still a bloody powderkeg waiting the tiniest spark to set it off, then I've got a bridge to sell you."

There was nothing Hunter could add to that.

"Anyway," Miki went on, "what seems to be happening here is, one, the

Gentry plan to use Donal as their Summer King, and two, something to do with that—maybe the power they'll accrue—is going to let them take the land here from its own *genii loci*."

"That's presupposing any of this is real," Hunter said. "Summer Kings. Magical powers. Even the *genii loci*."

Maybe especially them, he added to himself.

Miki nodded. She butted out her cigarette into the ashtray and for once didn't immediately light another.

"I *know* it sounds mad. But there's something else besides us in the world, don't you think? And if there is, who's to say what it'll be like? You've seen the Gentry. They're not just creepy, there's something *more* to them."

Hunter put the palm of his hand against his side.

"Being nasty doesn't also make them supernatural," he said.

"But where do they live? How do they live? All they do is speak bloody Gaelic, so how do they get by?"

"They spoke to me in English," Hunter said. "With a thick accent, I'll grant you, but it was still English."

"Fine. But that doesn't change the *otherness* of them."

"And I still say—"

"I know, I know. But ever since I listened to Donal go on about them last night, I've had a bad feeling that all this shite Fergus and my da' talked about could be real."

"So we need to rescue Donal from them."

"I don't think that can be done," Miki told him. "You know Donal. That moroseness of his isn't all an act. If he thinks he sees a way out, a way to get even with the world, he'd take it. And he's so bloody stubborn."

"Unlike you."

That won him a faint smile.

"I'm only stubborn when I'm right," she said.

"And you're always right."

The smile grew a little. "As good as," she said, before it went away again.

"So what is it you want to do?" Hunter asked.

"It's not a want so much as a need."

Hunter nodded encouragingly.

"I don't want to see them take what isn't theirs from those who were here before them."

"But that's how it works," Hunter said. "Isn't history one long summation of conquests and the like? The Celts didn't originate in Ireland—they took it away from someone else."

"That doesn't make it right."

"No. But . . . well, why wait until now? What happened when these Gentry showed up with the original conquering Celts?"

"Well, my da' had something to say about that, too—when he was sober, or at least not so drunk that he could still talk. See, the *genii loci* preside over a particular place. When the landowners change, those original spirits remain. It's only how they're perceived that changes. They're the same spirits, but they wear different names, different shapes. But for some reason, when the famine and all the troubles drove our people out of Ireland to cross the Atlantic, some of these originally localized spirits made the journey as well. The Europeans were able to displace the original inhabitants of this land, but it appears the Gentry weren't as successful with the local spirits. Or so my da' said.

"They've been able to claim the cities for their own, but I'd guess it's only because the local spirits aren't interested in streets and buildings. The Gentry have spent so much time walking among us, that a forest of concrete and steel buildings doesn't trouble them the way they would spirits more in tune with their natural environment. But now . . ."

"Now they want it all," Hunter said.

"And they think that calling up the Glasduine will give it to them."

"The what?"

"Glasduine. It's an old name for a Green Man."

"And he's this Summer King you were talking about earlier?"

Miki shrugged. "According to folklore and tradition, they're not the same, though if you follow the threads you can see where they meet from time to time in figures such as Robin Hood. But it doesn't matter to the Gentry. When I think back to all the things Uncle Fergus attributed to them, it was just one big borrowed mess that'd take either a scholar or a madman to decipher."

She fell silent again and this time Hunter didn't know what to say. None of what she was telling him made much sense in the view he'd always held of the world. And, just supposing it was real, why get involved in a struggle that was so far out of their league? If the local spirits were half as powerful as the Gentry were supposed to be . . .

He put his hand against his side again. There was nothing supernatural about his pain—nor in how he'd gotten it. But the hard man who'd hit him definitely fit in with Miki's description of them being mean-spirited.

"Aw, Christ," Miki said suddenly. She drank off the remainder of her cold tea, stuck her cigarettes in her pocket and stood up. "I feel like a bloody fool, going on like this. It's just Donal's got me going and I can't tell up from down anymore. Last night, it was like seeing himself again—my da', in all his drunken, stupid glory."

Hunter stood up as she started to put on her coat.

Miki shook her head. "I half expected him to take a swing at me, but I guess he knows I wouldn't even begin to stand for that sort of shite."

"Let me walk you home," Hunter said.

"Yeah, I don't suppose I'd be much use around the shop today."

"It's not that."

She put her hand on his arm. "I know. Thanks for putting up with me."

"I've heard worse."

"Oh, please. I'd like to know from who."

"I meant in terms of going through a bad time," Hunter said.

Miki cocked her head. "You're not going to go all sage and wise on me now, are you?"

She almost sounded like her old self.

"I doubt I could pull off either," he told her.

"Yeah, you'd at least need white hair and a beard. But you've got a deep enough voice . . ."

They paid their bill and walked back through the cold streets to her apartment with Miki cracking jokes along the way. Hunter wasn't fooled by her sudden change of mood. It was just her way of dealing with . . . well, everything, he supposed. From when he first met her as a kid, busking, living on the street, she'd always been as cheerful as Donal was morose. He'd just never stopped to think about what that cheerfulness might be hiding.

By the time they were climbing the stairs onto the porch of her building she seemed completely like her old self, though Hunter didn't think he'd look at her in quite the same way again. Not with what he knew now.

"So you see," she was saying as she opened the front door into the foyer, "it's probably better this way. I don't doubt I was getting on Donal's nerves as much as he was getting on . . ."

Her voice trailed off and it took Hunter a moment to realize what was the matter. Then the smell hit him, a thick musty reek of wet animal fur and urine and worse. He stepped past Miki, breathing through his mouth, and looked around. The foyer was as spotless as ever.

"Where's it coming from?" he said.

He turned to look at Miki, but she made no reply. She stood frozen by the door, a stricken expression on her face. And then he knew, just as she did, unable to explain how, he just knew. He took the keys from her fingers and crossed the foyer to her door, unlocked it, pushed it open, almost gagging as an enormous wave of the horrible stench came rolling out into the foyer.

He'd been prepared for bad, but this was far worse than his imagination had been able to call up. It looked like a storm, no, like a hurricane had torn through the apartment. The furniture was all overturned or smashed, upholstery shredded. CDs, books, magazines torn apart and thrown about as though spun in a tornado. Feces were smeared on the walls, where the drywall hadn't been kicked in. Urine dripped in long streaks among the smears, puddled on the floors.

Christ, Hunter thought, gagging on the horrible reek. What had they done? Robbed a sewage plant?

All that remained untouched were the windows—to keep the stench locked in, he realized. But nothing else was in one piece. Even some of the baseboards and molding had been torn up and broken.

Then he saw her accordion, the Paolo Soprani, torn in two at the bellows, the keyboards on either side smashed in, bass and treble reeds broken and scattered around the ruins of the instrument that lay in a pool of urine. And just to make sure the message of hate and disdain was absolutely understood, someone had taken a huge dump right on the shattered remains of the instrument. Even if it could be repaired, who would want to?

Hunter turned around, tried to stop Miki from coming in and seeing what had been done, but she pushed by him. For a long moment she stood there, staring at the ruin of her apartment, her gaze finally resting on what had been done to her accordion.

"You see what I mean?" she said in a tight, hard voice.

She was so angry that the awful stench didn't even seem to register, but it was all Hunter could do to keep down his tea.

"I'm surprised they didn't just level the whole building with a bomb," she went on, toeing the remains of her accordion with her boot. "This was to cut me right to the heart."

"We'll buy you a new one," Hunter said.

"And get the money from where? A store that's going under? Get real."

Hunter shook his head. "Doesn't matter." He knew how inadequate this was, how the loss of her accordion was, perhaps, the least of her worries, but he seemed to be stuck focusing on it, like a needle caught in the groove of a vinyl record. "We'll figure out some way to raise the money."

All Miki did was look at him. The unfamiliar mix of sorrow and rage that warred across her features turned her into a stranger, though he'd seen that face before on newscasts, on the faces of victims when they looked at the remains of their homes and families. In Belfast. In Oklahoma City. In Sarajevo. It wasn't the look of one who'd survived a natural disaster, but that of one left standing in the aftermath of some horror for which a human being was responsible.

There were those you'd see, numbed by shock, or with tears blinding them, streaming down their cheeks. Huddled in small groups, or standing alone, staring, stunned, miserable in their loss, empathetic towards those whose loved ones had died so that some megalomaniac could make an obscene point.

Then there were those whose faces plainly said, someone must pay for this. Who stood stiffly, their backs straight, fists clenched.

"Now do you see what shites they are?" Miki said, her voice as unfamiliar as her expression, low, dangerous. "Do you see why we should ally ourselves with anyone who stands against them?"

Hunter felt a twinge in his side, not a real pain, for he hadn't moved. It was the memory of the pain. Of when the hard man hit him. Of the threat of what he'd do to Hunter if he had to come back.

Hunter shook his head. "They're too dangerous," he told her. "Too powerful."

"Exactly. And we're on their shit list, so what we have to do is ally ourselves with those who are just as powerful."

"Spirits," Hunter said slowly.

Miki nodded.

"Local spirits. Magical beings."

She nodded again.

"How would we even find them?" Hunter asked, adding to himself, that's saying they even exist.

"I don't know. But there'll be a way. Someone will know them, how to contact them."

It was so preposterous, such a long shot, Hunter had no trouble agreeing. It wasn't that he didn't crave a bit of his own revenge—for how the hard man had made him feel with that sucker punch, for what they'd done to Miki's place; it was just that, if Miki was right, if the hard men were everything she said they were, then they were way out of his league.

"We should call the police," he said.

Miki shook her head. "I can't stay in here."

"I meant from a neighbor's apartment."

"I just can't, Hunter. The longer I'm here, the more I want to kill somebody."

"Okay. But—"

"And we can't call the police anyway."

"Are you crazy?"

"No. But it'd make them crazy." She looked at him, that stranger's light in her eyes, a smoldering dark anger. "I want them to think they've won. They've beaten me and I'm running with my tail between my legs."

Nobody'd ever think that, Hunter thought, but he wasn't up for the argument.

"Then let's get back to the store," he said. "You can stay at my place, but we'll have to get you some stuff. Clothes, toiletries . . ."

Miki gave him a distracted nod before stepping over the mess that had been her accordion. She held her scarf to her face to cut back on the stench. Hunter followed her lead, breathing through his mouth into his own scarf as he trailed her through the apartment, assessing the damage. She stopped at her clothes cupboard, an old pine armoire that she'd bought in a junk shop and refinished into something both useful and attractive. It lay on its side, door kicked in, old planks that had withstood who knew how many years of normal wear and tear finally undone by a hard man's boot. Her clothes were shredded and soaked with urine—How could anyone piss this much? Hunter wondered—but at the back of the armoire they could make out the corner of a black box that seemed unscathed.

Miki kicked the sodden clothes out of the way, then gingerly lifted the box out.

"Well, they left me this," she said.

"What is it?"

"My old Hohner."

Pulling a face when she had to touch it some more, she laid the box on its side and undid the clasps, lifted the lid. The accordion sat inside, unharmed. Wiping her hands on her jeans, she pulled the instrument out, cradling it as though it were a child.

"Now we can go," she said, standing up once more.

Hunter thought of telling her that they could wash down the outside of the case, but then realized that no matter how clean they got it, she'd still smell the stink of urine, still feel a dampness in the leather that covered the wooden case.

"Is there anything else you want to take?" he asked.

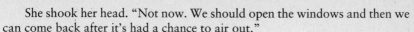

She shook her head. "Not now. We should open the windows and then we can come back after it's had a chance to air out."

Hunter didn't think this stench would ever air out, but he went and opened all the windows, then walked with her back to the store. He'd never breathed air that tasted as clean and crisp as it did once they were outside on the street once more. He turned to Miki to remark on it, then saw her still cradling the child that was her accordion, still with that dark anger in her eyes. They walked back to the store in silence.

5

Talk about your awkward moments, Ellie thought.

She gave a quick look down the hall, but the housekeeper who'd met her at the door and brought her here had abandoned her and was already out of sight. Reluctantly, Ellie turned back into the studio to where the two women were waiting. She remembered Bettina from yesterday, but the tall blonde woman was a stranger. Obviously, from the looks of this studio, she was a sculptor. And also obviously, from all the boxes in various stages of being packed, she was being kicked out of her work space so that Ellie could take it over.

"Well, this is a little embarrassing," Ellie said.

"Don't fret it," the blonde woman said.

"Yes, but—"

"It's all right, really. My name's Chantal and this is—"

"Bettina. We met yesterday."

"Truly," Bettina said, turning to the blonde. "I had no idea."

But Chantal only laughed. "Come in, come in," she told Ellie. Shaking her head, she added, "I'd swear. From the pair of you, you'd think the world was ending."

Well, yours is, Ellie thought. At least insofar as Kellygnow was concerned.

But she set down the box she was holding and came over to the other side of the room where they were. Lined up along the worktable behind the women were a fascinating array of sculptures waiting to be packed, mostly teapots and bowls that were outrageous in their proportions and completely impractical, but nevertheless lovely and whimsical. They listed, one towards the other, frozen dancers with inspired glazes that appeared to have been applied in a dream state. There were also a few more traditional busts, beautifully rendered, including a work-in-progress draped with a damp cloth and so remained a mystery in terms of its subject. Ellie doubted she would have known the model anyway.

"I love your work," she told Chantal.

"Thanks. It's something new for me."

Which was what Kellygnow was all about, Ellie thought. A place where you could try out new things, where you could experiment without having to worry about your overhead. And now she was taking that away from Chantal.

"This isn't exactly what I had in mind when I agreed to take this commission," she said.

"What commission is that?" Chantal asked.

Ellie couldn't figure her out. Chantal seemed genuinely interested and not in the least bit upset about losing her studio here.

"Look, this isn't right," she said. "I feel terrible. If I'd known they were booting somebody out to make space for me, I would've told them to just forget it."

Chantal waved a dismissive hand. "Oh, enough worrying about it already. I'm not upset about it, so why should anybody else be? Honestly. I've had a wonderful stay here and now it's someone else's turn. It's not such a big deal and I think it's a great opportunity for you . . ." She glanced at Ellie, raising her eyebrows in a question.

"Ellie Jones."

"Oh, Jilly's raved to me about your work, but I've never had the chance to see any of it myself. Did you bring any finished pieces with you?"

Ellie blinked in surprise. Was there no end to this woman's generosity?

"No," she said. "I didn't really think to . . ."

"Well, maybe some other time. Anyway, like I was saying, a residency here is a great opportunity for you, so let's not spoil it with feeling awkward or carrying around bad feelings. Kellygnow is a place where the Muses live side-by-side with us—which I think is a blessing one doesn't get to experience very often. Don't you think it'd be pretty small-minded of us to get all petty and catty with each other in an environment such as we've been provided with here?"

"Well . . . yes," Ellie said. "Except you're the one who's getting the short end of the stick."

"Except I'm not unhappy, so why should anyone else be?"

Ellie shook her head. "Wow. Are you for real?"

"She is very much so," Bettina said.

Ellie pulled a chair out from under a table and turned it around, sitting down with her arms leaning on the backrest.

"This is a pretty big room," she said. "I don't know what kind of space you need to work in, but I could do with half or even less."

Chantal smiled. "You see?" she said to Bettina. "Things work out." Then she returned her attention to Ellie. "We can ask and see what they say. But can you work with someone else in the room?"

"Are you kidding? I'd love it. I'm way tired of being shut away by myself in my own studio. I lived with another artist for a while and it was great working together—at least until our relationship went on the rocks and we spent more time arguing about things than doing art."

Chantal laid a hand over her heart. "Avowedly heterosexual in this corner," she said.

Ellie had to laugh. "Yeah, me, too."

"So tell us about the commission that got you into Kellygnow," Chantal said.

"It has to do with this mask," Ellie said and she got up to show it to them. The two women had completely different reactions to the mask. Chantal regarded it much the way Ellie had when she first saw it yesterday, enamored with the beauty of its lines and marveling at the skill it had taken to render it so perfectly in wood. She immediately picked up one of the broken halves and ran her fingers across the mask's smooth contour cheek, up into the braiding of carved leaves.

"This was planed by hand," she said, her fingers returning to the cheek. "Can you imagine how hard it would be to get it this smooth without a lathe and sandpaper?"

When she went to hand it to Bettina, the smaller woman frowned and shook her head. She appeared, not exactly frightened, but certainly wary of it.

Chantal smiled. "It won't bite," she said.

"It is very old," was all Bettina would say.

Ellie nodded. "I wonder how old? Ms. Wood gave me the impression it's completely ancient, but how long does wood stay in such excellent condition?"

"Don't ask me," Chantal said. "I work with clay."

"Anyway," Ellie went on, "I'm supposed to make a copy of it in clay for a casting."

"What will you cast it in?"

"I don't know yet," Ellie said. "My only instructions were that there's to be no iron in the metal I end up choosing."

"Weird."

"Mmm." Ellie's gaze drifted to where Chantal's busts stood alongside her more whimsical work. "I wonder why they didn't just ask you to do it?"

"Beats me."

"Because of your *brujería*," Bettina told Ellie.

As Ellie turned to her that strange buzzing that Tommy's Aunt Sunday had woken in her whispered up her spine again.

"My what?" she said.

"Your magic. It is very potent. As is this mask. To make a new one as potent as the old needs a person such as you—someone with a powerful spirit as well as the necessary artistic skills."

Twice in one day was just too weird. Like Sunday, Bettina stated it completely matter-of-factly, none of this glib, trying-to-impress, New Age, aren't-we-spooky-and-wise-stuff here, which only made Ellie feel all the more uncomfortable with it. What was happening anyway? Did she have "I'm gullible, tease me about mysterious stuff" written on her forehead or something? But before she could get too caught up in the strange coincidence of it, Chantal gave one of her merry laughs.

"Bet you didn't know we have our own resident wise woman," she said. "Seriously. It's kind of eerie the way Bettina can pick up on stuff no one else notices. And she makes these charms that really work."

"Um, no offense," Ellie said, "but I don't really buy into that kind of thing."

"You can be a friend of Jilly's and say that?"

"I think Jilly has enough belief for the both of us and then some."

Chantal smiled. "Yes. But don't you *want* to believe?"

"Not really."

"We'll just have to win her over," Chantal said to Bettina.

The dark-haired woman shook her head. "The spirits do not require anyone's belief to exist. They were there at the beginning of the world and they will still be here, long after we are gone. Whether or not we believe in them is irrelevant."

"She can be way more fun than this," Chantal assured Ellie.

The twinkle in her eye made it plain she was teasing, but Bettina seemed to take it seriously.

"*Me pasa,*" she said. "I'm sorry. I was being rude."

"No," Ellie told her. "I'm the one who should be apologizing."

"Oh, please," Chantal said. "Enough with the 'I'm sorrys' already. The one of you's worse than the other."

Ellie and Bettina exchanged self-conscious smiles.

I like her, Ellie thought, talk of spirits and magic notwithstanding. And if she could put up with the way Jilly and Donal carried on about the strange and mysterious at times, then she could do it with Bettina as well.

She turned to Chantal and said, "Maybe we should go find Nuala and see where Kellygnow stands on shared studios."

"Are you certain this is what you want?" Nuala asked Ellie when they caught up with her in an upstairs hallway.

Ellie thought it was a little odd that the housekeeper seemed to be making a point of only asking her, but she nodded. Nuala regarded her for a long moment, as though giving Ellie one more chance to reconsider.

"Very well," she said. "I will speak to the executors about it. I'm sure they'll agree when they learn this is your wish."

"And in the meantime . . . ?" Ellie asked.

"Enjoy each other's company," Nuala told her.

They waited until they were around a corner and out of Nuala's sight before giving each other high-fives, smiling and laughing like a trio of schoolgirls on an unexpected holiday. Ellie didn't know why she was so giddy. Part of it was simple relief that she wasn't going to be responsible for Chantal's getting sent away. But mostly it was the unexpectedness of making new friends in a place where she hadn't really anticipated she'd fit in at all. Truth was, she'd half-expected to be found out as a fraud and turned away from the front door before she'd even gotten a chance to step inside. Because, really. The caliber of artists who'd been in residence here was way out of her league.

"I am so happy," Bettina said, linking arms with them as they continued down the hall. "My old friend and my new both get to stay."

"Actually," Chantal told Ellie, "it's just that she's really vain and didn't want me out of here until I finished the bust of her that I'm working on."

Bettina blushed, but she smiled when Ellie laughed.

For once, Ellie thought, things were going her way.

When they reached the stairs, they went down single-file. Halfway down, Ellie paused at a side window. She'd been distracted at first by a group of figures on the lawn, a group of men, Natives, she guessed from their dark skin and black braided hair, standing in a loose circle, smoking and looking up at the house—right at her, it felt like. Then she realized that they were only wearing thin white shirts and broadcloth suits, some of them not even bothering with their jackets. She leaned closer to the window. And standing barefoot in the snow.

"What is it?" Chantal asked from a few steps lower down.

"There's these guys out there," Ellie replied. "It's like they think it's summer."

When Chantal and Bettina joined her at the window, the sculptor gave Ellie an odd look.

"What guys?" she said.

"Ha, ha."

"No, seriously," Chantal told her. "I don't see anything except for an empty lawn, covered in snow."

Ellie turned to look at her and was shocked to realize that the other woman wasn't simply teasing her.

"Chantal can't see them," Bettina said.

Ellie slowly turned to face her. "What do you mean?"

"Dark-haired, dark-skinned men," Bettina said. "Dressed in dark suits and white shirts. Barefoot. Smoking. Staring up at us."

Ellie nodded along with the description. "Exactly."

"I don't see anything," Chantal repeated.

"Your sight isn't strong enough," Bettina said.

Ellie shook her head. "Hang on here. Are you trying to tell me—"

"They stand in *la época del mito*," Bettina told her. "The spiritworld. That is why you can see them and Chantal can't."

"No. That isn't possible."

"Everyone carries magic in them," Bettina said. "But to be able to use it, one must be either trained in its use, or have a high natural ability."

"But . . . I've never seen things before. Things that aren't there, I mean."

Except they were. Dark eyes watching her from below, cigarette smoke wreathing about their heads.

"Then something has woken it in you," Bettina said.

"Tell me you're just putting me on," Ellie said to Chantal. "This is all some kind of initiation prank, right?"

Chantal continued to stare out the window, but she shook her head.

"I swear to you," she said. "I don't see anything. I wish I did."

Ellie turned away from the window and leaned against the wall. That eerie sensation of something moving up her spine had returned and her chest was tight, as though her bones were shrinking.

"I don't want this," she said.

Bettina laid a steadying hand on her arm. "Unless you specifically seek it out, the spiritworld makes those choices for you. It's better to accept its interest in you as best you can, for fighting it only adds to the stress you feel. Come," she added. "Let's go back to the studio. I'll make you a tea that will calm you down."

"More . . ." Ellie had to clear her throat. "More magic?"

Bettina shook her head. "No. A simple herbal remedy, nothing more."

"Okay," Ellie said and let the smaller woman lead her away.

"Can you make me one that'll let me see this stuff?" Chantal asked from behind them.

Ellie didn't know if Bettina had put some enchantment on the herbs and the boiling water she used to make her tea, or if it was simply the natural properties of the ingredients, but the tea did calm her down. The soothing liquid couldn't erase the memory of what she had seen, nor the unfamiliar sensations it had woken in her—a kind of floating in her nerve ends, a sharpening of her vision, a clarity in her thinking. But it laid a thin gauze between the immediacy of the idea of magic, the anxiety it had woken in her, and her normal self.

After a while she was actually able to take her suitcase up to her room and unpack, then rejoin the other women in the studio. There she set up her side of the studio and worked on some preliminary sketches for Musgrave Wood's mask while Bettina sat for Chantal on the other side of the room.

She was a little jealous of Chantal having Bettina as a model and kept glancing in their direction. It wasn't simply that Bettina was so beautiful, though she certainly was. No wonder Donal had been smitten with her. But there was more to her than that. She had great character in her still-youthful features and something else as well. Some undefinable charisma that made it impossible to *not* want to make a rendering of her.

In the end, Ellie found herself filling a half-dozen pages of her sketchbook with surreptitious drawings of the pair, Bettina on her stool, Chantal at the modeling stand, her large fingers pulling the most delicate details from the bust. She didn't think Ms. Wood would mind. After all, there had to be a settling-in period, didn't there, and she had already come up with some great ideas for the mask.

The one thing she did, Bettina's tea notwithstanding, was keep her gaze away from the windows in the studio. They looked out onto the rear lawns where she'd seen the strange group of men and she wasn't taking any chances. Perhaps it was childish—pathetic, really, for a grown woman to expect that if she couldn't see something, then it wasn't there—but she couldn't help herself. From the way Bettina had spoken earlier, if she did look, she might find a whole other world waiting for her out there, and Ellie truly wasn't prepared for anything but the simple winter landscape that rationality told her had to be on the other side of the window's panes.

6

"Oh, man," Fiona said when she heard about what had happened to Miki's apartment. "That really sucks. What is wrong with people, anyway?"

She sat perched beside the cash register on the front counter of Gypsy Records in full Goth mode: long straight hair, lace blouse, calf-length skirt and leather bodice, all black and contrasting sharply against her porcelain skin. Here and there silver jewelry twinkled about her person like stars viewed through a layer of dark clouds. Rings, bracelets, earrings, an eyebrow ring, choker.

"Many of them," Miki said from where she was slouched on a chair behind the counter, "are simply shite."

"Yeah, really. I wonder who you pissed off."

Miki only shrugged.

"Because a friend of mine—remember Andrea? She's sort of gangly, with long black hair and a slinky wardrobe."

"Fiona, that describes most of your friends—male and female."

"Yeah, well. When the people in her building found out she was a pagan, there was this big fuss about having a Satanist living in the building, you know, conducting unspeakable rituals and all that crap, as if. But before it all died down, someone broke into her place and trashed it, wrote Biblical quotations all over the walls and stuff."

"It's not exactly the same thing."

"No, but it just goes to show you. Nobody had anything personally against her, there were just people who didn't like who she was on principal, and even then they didn't have a clue."

"And the point is?"

"The point is, I don't know. Maybe somebody really hates Celtic music or accordions or something. It could be a clue."

Miki had to smile at that.

"Anyway," Fiona said. "Do you want some help cleaning up?"

Miki shook her head. "I'm never going back there."

"But all your stuff . . ."

"Is ruined," Hunter put in as he passed by the cash filing CDs. He paused to lean against a browser. "It's like somebody emptied out the vats of a piss factory in her place."

Fiona grimaced. "Well, thank you for that lovely image."

Hunter shrugged and went back to filing CDs.

"It's true," Miki said. "They didn't miss anything except for my old Hohner. I swear, they must've had bladders the size of hot air balloons."

"You're grossing me out."

"This from a woman who enjoys Marilyn Manson."

"It's not the same."

Miki nodded. "No, I don't suppose it is."

Hunter tuned them out as they got into a discussion of Goth versus Metal and where various artists fit in. Humming along with the Sam Bush CD that was playing on the store's sound system, he went to the front of the store and started rearranging the new release display to accommodate the latest set of Verve reissues that had come in that morning. He didn't know what made him look up and out at the street, but when he did, he found himself face-to-face with one of the hard men standing outside the store, smirking at him. When the man saw he had Hunter's attention, he took a hand out of the pocket of his trench coat, did a Michael Jackson crotch grab, and sauntered off.

Hunter stood there for a long moment trying to fight down the sudden rage that had flared in him, Oscar Peterson and Bill Evans CDs forgotten in his hand. It was hard to let the adrenaline rush go, because fear had been as much a part of what had called it up as anger. When he finally felt calm enough to trust his voice, he turned slowly to see if Miki had noticed the hard man, too, but she and Fiona were still arguing musical classifications. He found a place on the rack for the CDs he was holding, then returned to the counter.

"Fiona," he said, breaking into their conversation. "You know a lot of these New Age types, right?"

She looked confused. "What, you mean like John Tesh and Yanni fans?"

"No, not music. The other kind of New Age. Healing crystals and Tarot cards and that kind of stuff."

"I guess. Why? You planning on consulting an oracle to find out when business is going to pick up?"

She grinned at him and turned to Miki to share the joke, but Hunter could tell Miki knew where he was going with this and she only managed a half-hearted smile for Fiona. He wondered if her nostrils had filled with the memory smell of that rank urine back at her apartment the way his just had.

"I was wondering if you knew anybody into Native American spirituality," he said.

"You mean like for real?"

Hunter nodded.

"Well, Jessica goes up to the rez all the time—"

"You know her," Miki put in, obviously unable to pass up the opportunity to tease, even in her present mood. "Kind of gangly, with long black hair and a slinky wardrobe."

Fiona punched her in the arm.

"Like it's not true," Miki said.

"What about Jessica?" Hunter asked.

"Well, her boyfriend's father leads a lot of the sweats and he's really into the old ways of doing things."

"Any chance I could talk to either of them?"

"I suppose, but neither of them's easy to get hold of. They live back in the bush, without a phone. You might be better off with one of the Creek sisters."

"Who are they?"

"Oh, I know them," Miki said. "Or a couple of them, at least. Verity and

Zulema. They often help out at those benefit concerts for street people that I play at every year."

"Interesting names," Hunter said. "Are they Natives?"

Fiona nodded. "There's like twelve or thirteen of them and everybody up on the rez treats them with deference."

"So how do I get hold of one of them?"

"I don't know," Fiona said. "I'll call Jessica when she gets home tonight. I can't call her at work because they're not allowed to get personal calls there."

Hunter gave a thoughtful nod. "Maybe I should start thinking about that."

Fiona gave him a whack on the arm at the same time as Miki threw a section of the newspaper at him.

At closing time Fiona asked Miki if she wanted to stay over at her apartment.

"Depends," Miki said. "Are you planning any Satanic rituals?"

"Only if you're still a virgin, as if."

"And you won't expect me to dye my hair black?"

"No, but you will have to wear something black and slinky and listen to at least a couple of hours of All About Eve."

"You still listen to them?"

"Hey, at least the people who write the music I like are still alive."

Hunter just shook his head. He couldn't see the pair of them surviving the night, if they kept this kind of thing up.

"You'll be okay?" he asked Miki.

She nodded.

"Then I'm going to let you lock up."

"Do you want me to do up the deposit?" she asked.

"We made enough for a deposit?"

"Well . . ."

"Leave it till tomorrow," Hunter said. "And good luck. Both of you."

"What, you don't think we can get along?" Fiona asked.

Hunter gave them an innocent look. "No, I think you get along famously." He paused for a moment, inserting one of Fiona's "as ifs" to himself. "I meant good luck getting home. Crappy weather and all."

His excuse wasn't that far off the mark. Over the afternoon, the skies had gone from dismal gray to what it was doing now: letting fall a steady drizzle of freezing rain. The streets and pavement were already slick with ice. Buildings, traffic and street lights all sported long dripping icicles. The traffic was bumper to bumper on Williamson and in the past couple of hours he'd seen more than one pedestrian almost take a fall. Near the bus stops, clumps of wet commuters huddled under the closest awnings, ignoring the way the canvas drooped alarmingly under the growing weight of the ice. Or maybe they no longer cared, just wanting to get home as quickly and as dry as possible, given the circumstances.

He put on his coat, not relishing having to go out and join the misery.

"Call me if you get a number for one of those Creek sisters, would you?" he said to Fiona. "If I'm not in, just leave a message on my machine."

"Yessir, boss."

"It wasn't an order."

"Nosir."

Hunter sighed as the pair of them giggled. The phone rang, and that, too, for no reason Hunter could discern, struck them as funny. Miki was still snickering when she picked up the receiver.

"No," he heard her say. "We still don't have any Who bootlegs."

Putting up his collar and wishing he had a hat, he left them in the store and immediately lost his footing on the icy pavement, only just saving himself from a fall by grabbing onto the side of the store's front window. He refused to look back inside at their grinning faces. Instead, he shuffled off like the rest of the pedestrians, sliding his feet along the ice instead of lifting them, feeling like one more drone, inching his way down the assembly line.

By the time he got a few blocks away, his hair was plastered to his head with a thick coating of wet ice and his legs were aching from his awkward gait. If it were just ice, or just rain, it wouldn't have been so bad. But the ice on the pavement was also covered with puddles which made the footing even more treacherous. You literally couldn't do anything more than shuffle along.

He hated the winter, he decided. Or maybe just this winter, where it seemed that everything that could go wrong, had. And then some. He didn't bother wasting his breath cursing how things had turned out. What was the point? But the miserable weather was putting him in the perfect mood for what he planned to do this evening.

7

Donal woke fully dressed on an unfamiliar bed, with a foul taste in his mouth and a pounding in his head. Sitting up made his stomach do a small flip. He waited a long moment, dully curious as to whether or not he was going to have to throw up, but the nausea went away. If only the headache would. Reaching under his pillow, he pulled out a mickey bottle of whiskey. About a half-inch of golden liquid sloshed in the bottom—what the old man used to call a cure in the morning. He downed it, grimacing at the bitter taste.

Jaysus. Jameson's it wasn't. It was barely a step above rubbing alcohol, insofar as taste was concerned. But it was eighty-proof and he could already feel the pounding in his head begin to recede a little.

Swinging his boots to the floor, he clomped across the uneven floorboards to what he hoped was a toilet. It wasn't until he'd relieved himself and come back into the main room that he sat down on the edge of the bed and took a good look around, orienting himself. A hotel room, obviously, with the blinds drawn and next to no light coming in. Not exactly four-star. Not exactly a half-star, truth be told. The whole room seemed to sag—ceiling, furniture, the bed, the floor. Old and tired and worn out. But cheap, no doubt. He couldn't remember checking in, but considering the state he must have been in, that was no surprise. He had so little memory of the latter part of the night, he'd probably blacked out before he'd passed out.

He picked up the mickey bottle and tilted it so that the last few errant drops could fall onto his tongue. Where had he gotten it? Most of the previous night really was a blur. He remembered leaving Miki's apartment after she'd had her little snit, and really, what was her problem? You'd think she'd be happy that a Greer might do well for a change. Besides drinking and arguing, that was.

He turned the bottle over in his hands. There was no label on it, but why should there be? The bars had all been closed, so he'd come down to Palm Street, wandering aimlessly around the Combat Zone until he'd found a small after-hours bar down at the end of some alley. He'd had a few drinks there he was sure, then finally wandered off with this bottle of the barman's homemade poteen, though it hardly deserved so poetic a designation.

Back home, poteen was the water of life. Kicked like hell once it got down, to be sure, but it was smooth on the going down. Or at least smoother than this rotgut the barman had foisted off on him. Jaysus, but wasn't it foul. Mind you, he wouldn't say no to another bottle of it right now.

He set the empty bottle down on the night table beside an old digital alarm clock radio with an LCD display so tired the time was barely visible. He leaned a little closer. Just past eight. There was something he was supposed to be doing by eight, he realized, but he was damned if he could remember what.

Go somewhere. Do something. With someone. Not Miki, he decided, bless her hard little heart. Cold as one of the Gentry, she was last night.

Then it came to him. It was Ellie. He'd promised to drive her up to Kellygnow this morning. Well, he'd be a little late, and she'd be a little ticked off, but surely she was used to it by now. Had he ever been on time for anything? Not likely. Ah, and what was the rush? That's what he always asked. What was the rush? Jaysus, stop and appreciate things a little bit for a change, even if all you had to appreciate was that your life was shite.

Oh, don't go all maudlin, he told himself. Things were looking up. Ellie was starting on the mask today, and between it and the Gentry backing him, he'd soon be looking back on days like these and fall down on his arse laughing that he'd taken it all so bloody seriously.

Pity he had to share the mask's power with the Gentry though. He was taking all the risks, not them. Bloody mask could cook his brains into a stew if it wasn't done just right. 'Course they were all vague about the details, them and herself, that strange old dyke who'd slammed the door in his face yesterday, pretending she didn't know him. Should've been a bloody actress, that one.

But Donal didn't need their help. He had it all sussed out on his own. Because he knew how to pay attention, didn't he? He hadn't been like Miki, sitting there with her hands over her ears when Uncle Fergus and his cronies were going on back home. Nor falling down drunk like the old man. He'd paid attention to the tales those bitter old men told, sorted the wheat from the chaff in their spill of story.

It took intent. It took a man capable of putting everything aside and concentrating his will on what was needed. The new mask was merely a focus—powerful enough in its own way, especially when created by someone with the *geasan* the Gentry claimed Ellie carried, but hardly the almighty talisman they made it out to be. If that was the case, any fool could pick it up and call on its power. No, it required a man such as himself. Focused, determined. Someone who didn't much bloody care about anything except getting exactly what *he* wanted for a change.

Of course it helped that he'd been as intimate as he had with the woman who was making it, left his seed in her and you couldn't get much more bloody intimate than that, could you? Even the old dyke up in Kellygnow had to admit he was the best man for the job and you could just tell she was aching to slap that mask up onto her own face. But it needed a man to wear it and wield it, which she wasn't, for all her dressing butch and pretending to be male. It needed a man, a mortal man, and that left the Gentry fretting, too, but sod them all. This was his turn to be on the top of the wheel and no one was going to take that away from him. Not Miki's misguided conscience, nor the needs of the Gentry and that old dyke they'd kept alive well past her time. What use did they see in her anyway, exiled for two-thirds of the year in the Gentry's otherworld for every few months she could live in this one?

Well, he thought, who really gave a shite?

He pushed himself up from the bed and tucked his rumpled shirttails into his pants. He'd better go pick up Ellie or the mask would never get made. He wondered where he'd left the van. Had to be somewhere nearby.

He didn't bother closing the door when he stepped out into the shabby hall beyond his room. Humming a bit of reel, he followed the path that had been worn into the carpet by a few thousand other feet heading for the same stairwell as he was now. He stopped when he realized it was some tune of Miki's. Ah, Miki. She wouldn't be so high and mighty once he was wearing the mask. Once she saw the world give him his due, she'd be begging for a taste of the same.

Maybe he'd share, maybe he wouldn't. It all depended on how repentant she was when she got down on her knees and asked him.

But they'd all listen to him. Miki and Ellie and that soft-spoken Spanish woman up at old Kellygnow who wanted him, he could tell. They'd be singing his praises and mooning about, looking for a bit of his kindness then.

He reached the lobby. The fat woman at the check-in desk looked up from her fashion magazine and gave him a once-over before returning to the depictions of that vastly better life that the waif models were living in its glossy pages.

No, Donal thought. I didn't steal any of your towels. Jaysus, I wouldn't want to *touch* the bloody things.

He continued to the exit. It wasn't until he'd pushed through the dirty glass doors and stepped onto the street outside that he realized it wasn't eight in the bloody morning. It was eight at night and pissing down rain. Freezing rain.

"You see what I mean about everything being shite," he muttered.

A businessman passing by shot him a quick look, then hurried on his way.

"The hookers are over on Palm!" Donal shouted after him. If they were stupid enough to be out in this foul weather. Of course, their pimps and whatever jones rode around in their guts weren't about to let them take the night off, regardless.

The man ducked his head, slipped on the icy sidewalk, and only just caught his balance before continuing on his way.

Donal looked away. He sighed, the man already forgotten. Ellie was going to be livid and that wasn't good. Part of what made him important to the Gentry was the closeness of his relationship to her. Lose that and the Gentry could try to cut him out and find someone else to wear the mask, and that wouldn't bloody do at all.

Not that he gave one silver shite what they thought or did. As soon as the mask was his, they'd be the first to go. But until he had it, it had to be, yes, mister scary elf lord this and, of course, mister scary elf lord that. Bloody punters.

So first thing on the agenda: Make nice with Ellie.

As he got ready to leave the shelter of the hotel's awning, the heavy canvas sagging about him, he caught a glimpse of himself reflected in the glass door of the hotel. Jaysus, didn't he look the sight. Before heading out to see Ellie he'd better take a run by Miki's and get some clean clothes. With any luck, she'd have climbed down from that high horse of hers by now and would let him in long enough to have a shower and change. And if his luck really held, she wouldn't be at home at all.

He hunched his collar up against the freezing rain.

Stop for a pint on the way? he wondered as he stepped out from under the hotel's awning. Better not, though lord knew he could do with a drink. Maybe Miki'd have some beer in the fridge.

He took a brisk step, another, and then did the same comical lunge for balance that the man passing him earlier had done, only just managing to stay on his feet.

Jaysus, Mary, and Joseph. What a foul night.

8

After dinner, Bettina walked with Ellie to the front door where the sculptor planned to wait for her ride. Neither had been outside since the morning and while they'd been aware of the nasty turn in the weather, they hadn't really paid much attention to how much freezing rain had actually fallen. When Ellie opened the door to see if Tommy had arrived yet, Bettina gave a small gasp of pleasure.

"What is it?" Ellie asked.

Bettina made a motion with her hand, encompassing the whole of the outdoors.

"Es muy bello," she said.

And it was beautiful. The lights from the house awoke a thousand high-lights on the ice-slicked trees and other vegetation. The longer grass and bushes at the edges of the property were stiff and beginning to droop, as were the boughs of the trees as the weight of the ice built up, but the reflected lights shimmered and sparkled in the ice, turning everything they saw into a magical fairyland.

"Beautiful," Ellie agreed. "But treacherous, too."

Bettina only shrugged. She'd had so little experience with ice and snow before coming to Newford that every new aspect of winter delighted her. Sleet and snow. The cold, the frost. Bone-chilling winds and sun so bright on the snow that it blinded you. Blizzards. An ice storm such as this. Perhaps in a year or two, if she was still living in this city, she'd grow as tired and blasé with winter as most of the natives seemed to be, but somehow she doubted it. She knew snow, but it rarely lasted out the day in the saguaro forests where she'd grown up. And something like this . . . could one ever become indifferent to such marvelous beauty?

But she could also understand the danger presented by the ice-slicked roads and tree limbs growing too heavy under the steadily increasing weight of the ice. As if to punctuate that realization, there came a sharp crack from the woods behind the house, followed by the crash of a falling limb and a muffled sound like breaking glass that Bettina realized was the ice fragments rattling against each other in the wake of the fallen bough.

"If this doesn't let up soon," Ellie said, "that's going to become an all too-familiar sound."

Bettina nodded. And they wouldn't simply be falling in the woods. Trees and boughs would come toppling down onto houses, across streets, taking down power lines . . .

She turned to her companion. "Do you really think you should go out on a night such as this?"

"I have to," Ellie told her. "It's at times like this when the street people need us the most."

"But—"

"You should come out with us sometime," Ellie went on. "Maybe you could use your magic to help them."

Bettina gave her a considering glance. She could tell that Ellie had surprised herself in saying that, was perhaps even a little embarrassed by it, considering her vehement denials to the subject earlier. Eh, *bueno*. Bettina didn't blame the sculptor. Anything could be disconcerting, if you weren't familiar with it. Something like *la brujería* would be even more so, since to someone like Ellie, it went against all she'd been taught and had experienced in the world to date. It wasn't as though she had grown up with a *curandera* for a grandmother, or spent her whole life as Bettina had, with one foot in this world, one foot in the other.

"*La brujería,*" she said, "only helps those who want to be helped, Ellie."

"Don't you have to believe as well?"

Bettina shook her head. "Does the sun require our belief before it can rise or set?"

"No, I suppose not."

Bettina laughed. "Don't look so glum. What's happening to you doesn't have to be a bad thing."

Before Ellie could reply, they heard the approach of an engine on the driveway, then saw the vehicle's headbeams. A few moments later, the Angel Outreach van made its way up the last part of incline, tires slipping as they sought traction.

"Here's my ride," Ellie said, no doubt relieved at the timely rescue.

Bettina nodded. "*Cuidado,*" she said. "Be careful."

"I will."

Bettina watched Ellie pick her way carefully across the icy driveway to where the van waited. Reaching the vehicle, the sculptor got in, waving before she closed the door behind her. Bettina returned the gesture. She waited until the van had made its slow way back down the sharp incline of the driveway before turning to go back inside, but once she'd closed the door on the wet night, she felt uncharacteristically restless. It was nothing she could put her finger on, only a disconnected feeling that had her wandering from one common room to another until she finally found herself in the kitchen. There she stood by the window and looked outside at the freezing rain, her gaze settling on the uninvited visitors who had gathered on the ice-covered lawns.

How could they be here again, on such a night . . . ?

She put on her coat and boots and went outside to where the wet night was waiting for her. The wet night and *los lobos.*

Once outside, she paused for a long moment by the back door of the kitchen, sheltered from the freezing rain by its overhang, and watched the dark-haired men. They didn't sit tonight, standing in their rough circle instead, still smoking their cigarettes, gazes still on the house. Not all of them at once, but there was always at least one of them regarding the building.

Basta, she thought. Enough. She only had so much patience.

She pushed herself away from the door and started towards them, losing her balance in the process. Her boots slipped out from under her on the slick ice and she flailed her arms. She was falling, she would have fallen, except strong hands caught her from behind and held her upright. As she turned, her rescuer keeping a grip on her arms so that she wouldn't lose her balance again, she found herself facing one of the wolves. Which one? She couldn't tell at first. They were all too much alike. And when she glanced at where they'd been standing, there was no sign of them at all. The others had all slipped away and only this wolf remained, holding her arms the way one held a child just beginning to walk.

Despite herself, her pulse quickened when she realized he was the same one who had approached her the other night.

"Can you stand on your own?" *el lobo* asked her.

He let her go as he spoke and Bettina had to do an awkward shuffle to stay upright.

"Who are you?" she demanded when she finally had her balance. "What do you want from me?"

"Not even a thanks?"

"*Perdona.* I am grateful for your help."

Her hair was rapidly getting plastered against her head—a cold and decidedly uncomfortable sensation. *El lobo*, she noticed, wasn't even damp. Nor had the others been. Of course. They were only partly in this world, enough to see and be seen, but not enough to be affected by the inclement weather. She concentrated for a moment and sidled into that in-between place herself. The relief from the freezing rain was immediate, though she still had a chill and her hair continued to drip icy water down the back of her neck.

"But you have questions," *el lobo* said, smiling.

He began to walk across the lawn to where the woods began. Bettina couldn't help but return the smile. She fell in step beside him, neither of them touched by the sleet, their footing steady in that in-between place.

"*Claro,*" she said when they reached the first trees. Of course. There were always questions.

El lobo nodded. "You asked what was wanted from you. They," he nodded to where the other wolves had been, "want nothing. Their concern is with the sculptor."

"They," Bettina thought. He says "they." Why not "we?"

"Do you mean Ellie?" she asked.

Again he nodded. "If that is her name."

"But you've been out here long before she arrived."

"There is another in that house with whom they have unfinished business."

Once more it was "they." But he didn't have to identify Nuala by name for Bettina to know who he meant.

"What business?" she asked.

He shrugged. "That is between them. My interest is with you."

Bettina schooled her features to show nothing of how he'd made her blood quicken. She considered all of Nuala's warnings. Was this the moment when he would try to drag her off into the woods? She would have a surprise for him, if he tried. She was stronger than she looked, and not afraid to use that strength. But perhaps he'd come with gentler courting in mind.

"Do you have a name?" she asked, pretending a calm she didn't feel.

"You may call me Scathmadra."

Not, "My name is Scathmadra." Only that she could call him by it, this *apodo* of his, and he would answer, but it would have no hold over him as would his true name. And what sort of a nickname was Scathmadra? A *felsos* name. A Gentry's name.

"*Bueno,*" Bettina said. "And what is it you want from me?"

"Your help."

Bettina studied him for a moment, surprised. Was this who had called her up out of the desert, this wolf of a spirit who wouldn't even share with her his true name?

"And yet you are the enemy," she said.

His eyebrows rose in a question.

"I have been warned against you."

"Who . . . ?" he began, then nodded. "Of course. The housekeeper. What did she say about us?"

Now he included himself with the others, Bettina noted.

"Only that you mean me no good. *¿Y bien?*"

"I cannot speak for the others," he told her, "but for myself . . . you could be putting yourself in danger if you agree to help me."

"Danger from whom?"

"The others."

Bettina smiled humorlessly. "And yet you are one of them."

"No," he corrected. "I am part of them, but no more one of them than you are one of your father's *peyoteros.*"

"What do you know of my father?"

"That we share a kinship, no matter how distant."

He spoke the truth. Bettina couldn't explain it any more than she could this unfamiliar attraction she felt towards him. It wasn't that he was so handsome. She had met handsome men before.

"No one in my family has ever been to Ireland," she said.

"Are you sure?"

She had to shake her head.

"I've never been there either," he said.

"But . . ."

"And neither have the wolves. They were born and bred here, but they are no more native to the land than are those who sired them. And if anything, their hunger for the land is stronger than that of their parents. All they've ever had to claim for their own are the cities—and those they have to share with mankind. Outside of the cities, others hold sway. Your people."

"My . . . ?"

Bettina didn't try to hide her confusion.

"*Peyoteros,* like your uncles."

He meant shaman, she realized, rather than the peyote men in particular.

"And other, older spirits," he went on. "Like your father."

"My father was a man."

"Was he?"

Bettina didn't have to close her eyes to picture the hawks, soaring above the desert.

"Not all of your uncles needed a ceremony to change their shape," *el lobo* went on. "And your father never did."

Bettina had always suspected as much. It explained the claim the desert had on him. Why her *mamá* was so patient with his absences. You didn't tame a wild creature; you only shared his company.

"How do *you* know him?" she asked.

"I didn't know him. I only know of him. I . . ."

He hesitated.

"*Bueno,*" Bettina told him. "If you want my help, then you must be honest with me."

He waited a heartbeat longer, then nodded in agreement.

"Few in this present day and age ask for truth as payment," he said.

"I didn't say it was payment."

He smiled, rakish again for a brief moment. "No, but it will be. You will see."

"*¿Y bien?* I see only a wolf in man's skin who loves the sound of his own voice too much—especially when he talks in riddles. It may amuse you, but it annoys me."

"I apologize."

Bettina refused to let him win her over so easily.

"Tell me this truth of yours."

"Did your father or grandmother—"

How do you know my *abuela* as well? she wanted to ask, but she made herself listen to him, to hold her questions and let him finish.

"—ever speak to you of shadow people?"

Bettina regarded him for a long moment, remembering a conversation she'd had with Abuela on one of their desert rambles. "You must be careful," she'd said, "of all the parts of yourself that you discard. It might make you feel good and strong, denying hatred and anger and whatever other base emotions you manage to set aside, but remember this: they can take on a life of their own. And the stronger, the more potent your *brujería*, the stronger this shadow self will be. Better to hold these things inside, to accept that you can feel such things the same as any other does, rather than deny them. Hold them fast, bind them in some hidden place inside you where they can harm no one but you can still guard them. Freed, there is the chance that they will become an enemy, one strong enough that few can easily dispel."

"She called them *sombritas*," she said. "*Las pequeñas sombras*—little shadows."

El lobo nodded. "As good a name for them as any." He fell silent, gaze turned inward to some distant memory, Bettina thought, before blinking back to the present. "I was a *sombrita*," he told her. "I was all the discarded pieces of the one who leads these displaced Gentry, a tattered and fraying bundle of hope and kindness and whatever else he wouldn't keep in that black heart of his."

"But *sombritas* have no real substance," Bettina said, interrupting despite herself. "They are little more than uncertain ghosts or . . . or . . ."

"*An aisling,*" he said, his voice gone soft. "A dream."

"I suppose . . ."

"And they can take on substance," he went on. "Surely your grandmother told you that as well?"

Bettina nodded. "She said they could be dangerous."

El lobo gave her a feral grin. "She spoke truly. I *am* dangerous."

Bettina swallowed thickly, but managed to stay her ground.

"So you are his shadow?" she asked. "The one who leads the pack."

"Indeed."

"What is his name?"

"We don't have names," *el lobo* told her, "except for those you give us. We have no need for names amongst ourselves, no more than a true wolf has need for a name. We know who we are."

So he hadn't been keeping his name from her, she thought. She refused to consider why this should please her.

"*¿Y bien?*" she said. "How does this explain your kinship—" To me, she almost said. "—to my father?"

"While what you call *sombritas* have no substance of their own, they can acquire substance."

"I know this."

El lobo nodded.

Bettina felt uneasy now. What he said was true, but Abuela had told her that the way the shadow people gained substance was by acquiring the bodies of the recently dead.

She frowned at him. "What is it that you're saying?"

"I harmed no one," he assured her. "But I found one dying, a spirit of this land. Before he passed on, I asked him for his body and he gave it to me."

"His body . . . ?"

"The shell he would leave behind. I made this of it." *El lobo* touched his chest. "This shape I wear."

"From this you claim kinship?" she said. What he suggested seemed preposterous.

He nodded. "We are blood kin through this body. Distant, it is true, but still kin. And *an felsos* can claim kinship to my spirit. So I have a foot in each of their worlds, the same way we stand in between time and timelessness in this place." He hesitated a moment, then added, "I spoke the truth when I said that helping me could be dangerous for you. I have no idea how much control the pack leader has over me. It is possible he can influence me, make me do things I would not do of my own free will."

Bettina shook her head. "*¿Cómo?* Why would I help you in the first place?"

"Because the Gentry mean to kill the native spirits of this place and if you won't accept kinship to me, you can't deny it to them. Would you have your kin die, when you might have been able to prevent their deaths?"

But Bettina was still shaking her head. Abuela had warned her more than once, don't get involved in the affairs of the spiritworld. Only trouble and sorrow came when one chose sides in any struggle involving the inhabitants of *la época del mito*. One had only to see how it had turned out for her *abuela* to know the truth of that. Except, how could she not choose sides? And even if she did nothing . . . wasn't the simple act of standing aside and refusing to be involved no different from choosing a side?

"No lo sé," she said.

And she *didn't* know. It was all so confusing. She knew too little, but she knew too much as well. And then there was the messenger to consider, this handsome *lobo* with his sweet tongue and impossible origin. That a *sombrita* could acquire its own body, its own independent life, in such a manner, was true. But this kinship he spoke of? She wished Papá or her grandmother were here to advise her, but they had both disappeared into the desert many years ago, the one on a hawk's wings, the other by walking into a thunderstorm.

"It is difficult to kill a spirit," she said finally.

"Tell that to the one who owned this body before me."

"The Gentry killed him?"

El lobo shook his head. "The changing world killed him. He didn't retreat quickly enough and died when the concrete was poured, when he could no longer breathe clean air and his waterways were poisoned."

"Yet his body serves you well enough."

"An felsos aren't troubled by a proximity to man and his cities and I have that of the Gentry in me."

Bettina nodded. She had heard of such spirits. They grew up from the underbelly of a city where mean-spiritedness was the fashion, unkindness the rule. Cities weren't evil, by and of themselves, but there was something about their darkest corners, their most hidden byways, that nourished such bitter fruit. Like called to like, which explained ethnic neighborhoods as much as it did creatures such as these wolfish Gentry.

"What was their plan?" she asked her companion.

"I don't know the details, but it has something to do with an artifact."

An immense stillness settled inside Bettina. *Claro.* That explained what she had felt when Ellie brought out that ancient wooden mask in the studio earlier today. She hadn't sensed evil about it so much as power, an enormous potential. And shadows clung to that power, a pattern of darkness discoloring the wood, like a sudden foul odor on a clean clear spring morning in the desert when you stumbled upon some dead rotting thing lying amidst the wildflowers. A poisoned coyote. A discarded tangle of rattlesnakes, killed for their rattles.

What she'd sensed had been the touch of the Gentry, unrecognized until this moment.

"You know something," el lobo said. "I can see it on your face."

She knew next to nothing, but more than he, apparently. The Gentry meant to use Ellie and the mask. They were both potent, but unfocused. Brought together as they had been, what might be created?

"I don't know enough," she told him.

"But . . ."

Shaking his head, he let his voice trail off. Neither spoke for a long moment. Bettina watched the freezing rain as it continued to fall, coating the trees and lawn around Kellygnow with thickening layers of ice.

"Will you help them?" *el lobo* asked finally. "If not for my sake, then at least for theirs? Will you help your kin?"

"I must think on this," she said.

He nodded. "I see."

"I didn't say I wouldn't."

"And didn't say you would."

Bettina sighed. "Consider what you've been telling me—how it must sound."

"Are you truly so distrustful of dogs?" he asked.

Dogs, wolves, coyotes . . .

"Why shouldn't I be?" she responded.

He shrugged. "Because I can hear them singing in you."

Before she could reply, he stepped away, deeper into *la época del mito* and she was alone in the place between the worlds, still untouched by the freezing rain that fell so constant around her. Listening to the tree boughs crack and tumble down in the woods around her, she was no longer so enchanted by the weather. *El lobo* had helped bring about her change of mood, with his dire warnings and parting words.

That was three times in one day, she thought. The dream. The figurines that Adelita had sent. And now this. *Los cadejos*. Lost for so many years.

"I don't hear them singing," she said softly, but no one was there to hear. "I don't hear them at all anymore."

Not since Abuela went away.

She would have had a hard time returning to the house, but she stayed in that half-world, the place between, until she was by the kitchen door again. There she stepped fully out of *la época del mito* and immediately the slick ice underfoot had her grabbing for the doorknob before her legs went out from under her and she took a spill. She managed to get back inside without mishap, removing her boots, hanging her coat on a peg by the door. Her hair was still wet from when she'd first gone out and she made an attempt to dry it with a dish towel before going to the bathroom to find one more substantial.

Returning to her room, her gaze came to rest on the little figurines that Adelita had sent her. She fingered the rosary still in the pocket of her vest and remembered that she'd wanted to call Mamá this evening. It was too late now. She would do it in the morning. For now she had questions that only one person in Kellygnow might be able to answer.

She walked down a long hall until she reached the door of Nuala's room. Since there was still light coming out from under the door, she went ahead and knocked on its wooden panels. If Nuala was surprised to see her, it didn't show in her features. Bettina came straight to the point, asking Nuala if she knew what *"Scathmadra"* meant.

Nuala offered her a humorless smile. "Is that the name he gave you? Oh, he's a sly wolf, that one. 'Scath' means 'shadow,' but it can also mean 'shelter' or 'bashfulness.' " She gave Bettina a look that was at once thoughtful and mocking. "So," she went on. "Has this innocent wild thing managed to set your heart at ease with his honeyed tongue and gentle naming?"

Bettina refused to be baited.

"And madra?" she asked.

"Dog."

Bettina mulled that over. Shadow-dog. Or shadow of the dog?

"I have no advice for you tonight," Nuala added. "I see no point, when you won't listen to it anyway."

Bettina shrugged. "You'd be surprised," she said.

"I hope so."

Bettina wanted to ask more, about the enmity between Nuala and the wolves, what it was that had set them against each other, but she managed to still her curiosity.

"Good night, Nuala," was all she said. "I hope you sleep well."

Nuala gave a tired nod. "Dreamless would be a gift."

"I could make you a tea."

She watched the older woman hesitate, but then give another nod.

"Thank you," Nuala said. "That would be kind of you."

9

Hunter was in a wretched mood by the time he finally reached Miki's street. He carried a bag of cleaning supplies that he'd bought at a hardware store along the way, and it only seemed to make it harder to maintain his equilibrium on the icy streets. Between the weather, which showed no sign of letting up, and the bad temper of just about everybody that was out in it, there wasn't any respite. The only good thing was that his side didn't hurt as much anymore. There were still twinges when he moved too suddenly, or stretched in the wrong way, but otherwise he was almost back to normal. Enough so that he felt up to the unpleasant task of cleaning Miki's apartment. He wasn't sure that he'd actually be able to make the place habitable again, or if Miki'd want to live there even if he could, but he wanted to at least give it a shot.

As he got closer to the apartment, he kept an eye out for those tall, dark-haired Gentry, but there was no sign of them. There was no sign of anyone, except for a small figure farther down the block, shoulders hunched against the weather, chin against his or her chest. Other than that, the street was deserted—all the sane people were inside, dry and warm. Hunter decided he was going to give this other lost soul a cheerful hello when they came abreast, a small thumbing of the nose against the general malaise that had gripped the city, but when they both reached Miki's steps, he realized who it was out on the wet streets with him tonight and his temper flared.

He had this sudden urge to smash Donal in the face—an alien feeling since

Hunter had never been prone to violence, not even in daydreams, though lord knows, some of his customers could stand to have some sense shaken into them. Or to be sharply rapped on the top of their head with the flat side of a CD jewel case. Be that as it may, his free hand clenched into a tight fist, and it was all he could do not to take a swing at him.

"Christ, you've got your nerve coming back here," he said.

Donal lifted his head, water streaming from his face, hair turned into an ice helmet the same as Hunter's.

"Yeah, well, hello to you, too, boyo," he said. "Weather making you a little testy?"

Hunter could only shake his head. "After what you did to Miki . . ."

"Oh, Jaysus. What's she told you? We had a little tiff, is all. That's what family's for, isn't it? Gives you someone to argue with, built in, as it were."

"And trashing her apartment was just sibling hijinks?"

Donal's eyes narrowed. "What are you on about?"

"And I suppose pissing over everything she owned and kicking apart her accordion, that was just in good fun, too."

"Maybe you'd better start explaining yourself," Donal told him.

There was an unfamiliar hardness in his voice, a dark light in his eyes that reminded Hunter of Miki when she'd first seen what had been done to her apartment.

"Why don't I just show you," Hunter said.

Doubt had begun to grow in Hunter, but it wasn't until he saw Donal's genuine shock and anger at the awful state of the apartment that he was sure Donal hadn't had anything to do with it. It was that, or he was a damn fine actor, Academy Award material, no question. At this point, Hunter simply didn't know anymore.

"I'll kill those fuckers," Donal said in a dark cold voice.

He started to turn away, but Hunter caught his arm.

"Don't go off half-cocked," he began.

Donal pulled out of his grip. "This doesn't concern you anymore," he said.

"But those Gentry—"

"Ah, so Miki's been talking, has she? Strolling with you down memory lane to visit all those places she thought she'd hidden away for good in that pretty little head of hers."

Hunter sighed. "Look, they're too powerful for us—"

"You forget something," Donal said, cutting him off.

"What's that?"

"Maybe the Gentry are more powerful than us, but they're not fucking immortal—not so long as they're wearing skin and bones. Big or small. Human or faerie. Everything can die."

Donal held Hunter's gaze for a long moment before he stalked away, a small, bedraggled and sodden figure crossing the foyer and pushing out through the front door. Hunter followed him to the stoop. Small though he was, Donal walked with a straight back and a firm step, as though his anger was large and strong enough to negate the slippery ice underfoot. But it was only that one of the city sidewalk cleaners had been by while they were inside, scattering a mix of sand and salt onto the ice. With the way the sleet continued to fall, the sure footing would last another ten minutes or so at best.

Hunter watched Donal until he reached the far end of the block. He'd been so taken aback by the man's parting comment that he simply stood there in the rain, blinking like a fool. He half-considered going after Donal, calling him back, but in the end he simply let him go.

Like Miki, Donal could be too stubborn for reason. Let Donal handle things the way he wanted, Hunter decided. He would stick to his own plan. Try to clean the place up. Talk to one of these Creek sisters. One thing at a time. Though that, he thought, as he stepped into the apartment and the full reek of the place hit him again, might be easier said than done. Wouldn't you know it. Even faerie piss had to be bigger than life and more potent than that of mere mortals.

The windows he'd left open earlier in the day had helped some, but the stench was still overpowering. Hunter pulled a small plastic bag out of his pocket. Inside was a handkerchief, dabbed with sweet-smelling oil, some sort of peach/apple mixture. He tied it around his face and it helped a bit more, though with his luck, some neighbor would think he was a burglar wearing this thing and call the police and the next thing he'd know, he'd be down at the Crowsea Precinct, trying to explain what he was doing in this fouled apartment. Hell, they'd probably think he was responsible. Still, what could he do? He had to deal with the stench and this was the best he could come up with, though even with the perfumed handkerchief the reek of the urine and feces was enough to make him gag. Maybe he should have brought along a clothespin instead.

He decided to start in the kitchen and took his bag of cleaning supplies back there with him. Rescuing a large metal pail from one corner, he banged out its dents as best as he could with a heavy ladle, then filled it with hot water. He stirred in an industrial-level cleanser that was heavy on the ammonia, pulled on a pair of rubber gloves and got to work with a sponge. There was a secret ingredient to any cleanup, his mother used to say, and that was good, old-fashioned elbow grease. Well, she'd be proud of him tonight.

Funny, he thought as he scrubbed the linoleum, how things had turned out. The last people he'd have thought to be at odds with each other were Miki and Donal. Granted, Donal had given a good show of knowing nothing about the apartment being trashed, but Hunter wasn't sure what to believe anymore. If you could have faerie lords like the Gentry wandering about with their skinhead attitude and bladders the size of hot air balloons, then maybe anything was possible.

He had to laugh at himself. Twelve hours ago he would have had a hard time believing in ghosts, or even precognitive hunches, but now here he was considering a whole shadowy otherworld peopled with creatures from folklore and legend, mean-tempered Gentry, doomed Summer Kings and all. Still, with all those stories . . . was it really such a huge leap of faith to accept that maybe they'd grown up around some kernel of truth? Mythic barnacles attaching themselves to the bones of somewhat plausible events until they took on their current legendary status.

Well, yes, he thought. It was. But here he was, allowing the possibility all the same. Or at least beginning to accept that these Gentry were more than ordinary. Still, you'd think if you were a magical being you'd do more with your life than these losers apparently did. Drink Guinness, listen to music, rough up somebody every now and again, trash an apartment, piss on your handiwork. Mind you, for some people, that might be considered living large. Unfortunately, the world did take all kinds.

He began to make good progress, carrying on a conversation with himself in his head, for lack of anything else to listen to. Drudge work like this always went better with good music—some Motown would definitely go down well right about now—but Miki's system was a bust, literally, and he hadn't thought to bring a boombox, or even his Walkman, along with him. He supposed he could try singing himself, but even he hated the sound of his own voice, raised in song. He was okay singing *along* with a recording, if you cranked the sound way up, and he could certainly be enthusiastic, but talented he wasn't.

Whenever one arm got sore, he used the other. Look at me, he thought. The amazing ambidextrous cleaning man. He was even getting used to the awful reek—or maybe his efforts were actually beginning to make a dent in the stench.

"Toilets of the Gentry," he muttered to himself as he dumped a pail of fouled water into the toilet and filled it up again. "Coming soon to a theater near you. Experience the horrors of faerie piss in widescreen, stink-o-vision. If you dare."

He added a generous ration of cleanser to the hot water and got back to his task, amusing himself by casting the movie in his head. A blond Christina Ricci to play Miki, he decided. Did Ricci have a brother with the same witchy eyes who could be Donal? *Buffy*'s Joss Whedon to write the screenplay, definitely. Or maybe Kevin Williamson. Either way they'd all sound smarter and a little more hip than they really were. At least he would. Who to play himself? He'd pick someone like Brad Pitt, but with his luck he'd get Pee-Wee Herman.

He was so caught up with the work and the stream-of-consciousness soliloquy running through his head that he didn't realize someone else had come into the apartment until he heard the harsh, heavily accented voice speak to him from the kitchen doorway.

"You just don't learn, do you?"

A twinge of phantom pain grabbed his side as Hunter looked up to see one of the hard men standing there. He had long enough to register that the newcomer wasn't even wet—had he been hiding in the apartment all this time?— before the man started forward.

Hunter surprised himself. He should have been scared. He was scared. He was almost wetting himself. But more than that he was angry. For the second time that night, the first response that came to mind was violence.

He half-rose at the hard man's approach, bringing up the pail of hot water and cleanser as he did. The hard man was so sure of himself that Hunter's response took him by surprise. Hunter had a good momentum going by the time the pail sped by the hands, raised in defense too late. The pail struck the man in the head, showering dirty, ammonia-sharp water all over the kitchen. His eyes went wide with shock, and he stumbled back.

Hunter hit him again with the pail, only half-full now, and the hard man went down, cracking his head on the side of the counter as he fell.

"Oh, fuck," Hunter said.

He stared down at the still body splayed out on the linoleum and had trouble swallowing. Blood leaked from a gash on the side of the man's head. Ordinary red blood, turning pink where it ran into a puddle of water.

"Wh—why couldn't you just leave me alone?" he said.

The hard man made no response. Was he dead?

Hunter swallowed, his throat feeling thicker than ever. He was scared and his pulse was hammering, but the worst of it was, it had felt good to strike back as he had. He was horrified to see the slack figure sprawled on the floor at his feet, unconscious, maybe even dead, and he'd put the man there. But an immense satisfaction rose up in him all the same, swamping the already confused mess of emotion running through him.

He'd never done anything like this before.

The pail dropped from his hand and went clattering across the linoleum. He gave the doorway a quick glance. Were there more of them out there? He cocked his head to listen, but heard nothing, only the rattle of the ice storm outside. His gaze crawled back to the man on the floor, half-expecting from Miki's stories for the body to dissolve into dust or go up in smoke or something. But it simply lay there, still, unmoving.

Nervously, he gave the man's leg a push with the end of his boot.

Still no response. Hunter wasn't even sure if the man was breathing.

Self-defense, he thought. If I killed him, it was in self-defense.

If he's dead . . .

His stomach lurched at the thought.

That was bad enough. But what if he wasn't? What was going to happen when he came around? Or when his buddies found out what had happened to him?

Hunter backed away until he was brought up short by the kitchen counter.

Whatever way you looked at it, he was screwed. If this was just a man, then he was going to have to do a lot of explaining to the police. He was going to have to live with the fact that he'd killed a man. And if the hard man *was* some kind of supernatural creature, then basically, Hunter was a dead man, too, because he had no illusions as to what the Gentry would do to him when they caught up with him. If they'd sucker punch him simply for dancing with Ellie . . .

He stared at the body, trying to see if it was breathing, not sure which he hoped for more—that the hard man was, or wasn't dead. After that one contact, boot against limp leg, he didn't have the courage to go any closer again. Too many horror movies and thrillers were running through his mind, images of the seemingly dead body suddenly sitting up and grabbing him as he bent near, the way the dead did in all those movies.

Face up to it, he told himself. Call 911 and let the cops deal with it.

But then he heard Donal's voice in his head, what he'd said back in The Harp the other night when Hunter had asked him if he'd called the police when the Gentry had beaten him up.

That would have just made for more trouble. Men like that, they don't forget a wrong. Jaysus, I've seen enough of them back home. The pubs are full of them, brooding over their pints, remembering every hurt, imagined or real, that was ever done to them.

And then Miki: *Back home, a feud is as real today as it was a hundred years ago. It doesn't matter that all the original participants are long dead and gone. The descendants will continue with the hostilities until there's no one left, on one side or the other.*

In the end, he simply grabbed his coat and fled, still wearing the handkerchief over his face and the pair of bright yellow rubber gloves he'd put on when all that was ahead of him was to clean out Miki's fouled apartment. He ran, or tried to run, skidding and sliding on the ice-slicked pavement, soaked to the skin in minutes, both by the sleet and the falls he took that sprawled him into puddles of icy slush.

10

Ellie couldn't remember a night as foul as this one. There just didn't seem to be any end to the constant rain. It was so deceptive, falling as water, hardening immediately into ice upon contact. The weight on the trees had to be unbelievable. Everywhere she looked, tree boughs were sagging, snapping off. They drove by cedar hedges that were bent almost in two, lilacs that had simply collapsed under the ice. The hardwoods were standing up better, but even they were getting a battered, war-torn look as they lost their smaller limbs. On the side streets, the ice-slicked pavement was carpeted with fallen branches and Ellie counted at least three cars and a couple of porches with boughs lying across their roofs. But so far the power lines were up. For how long, it was impossible to say, if the freezing rain continued. From the way the lines sagged, she wasn't sure if they'd snap under the weight of the ice, or if a tree would take them down.

Tommy had the heater going full-blast in the van, but considering how inefficient it was at the best of times, they had to get out every few blocks to scrape off the latest build-up of ice. Angel had sprung for new tires for the van at the beginning of the winter, but they weren't studded like the ones Tommy had put on his truck and didn't help much for either traction or quick stops. All they could do was inch along the streets at a slow crawl. But at least they were moving. Everywhere they went, they saw abandoned vehicles, few of them properly parked. Most rested at odd angles to the sides of the streets, many up on curbs.

The city still had power, but according to the radio, hydro lines were going down in the outlying regions, blacking out whole communities. And this was only day one. The weather forecasts predicted that the ice storm was just settling in and might be with them for the better part of a week. Ellie couldn't imagine what the city would be like after another few hours of this, never mind a week.

As it was, she and Tommy pretty much had the streets to themselves. Regular citizens had completely deserted the city by the end of the work day. With everything closed up, there was nothing to keep them downtown. The van drove past block after block of darkened marquees and signage, all of them shut. The clubs. Restaurants. Cineplexes. Concert halls. Restaurants. Theaters.

And it wasn't simply the legal trade and its customers. With their johns driven away by the weather, the Palm Street hookers had either called it a night or taken their business inside. The homeless—runaways, derelicts, bag ladies and all—had managed to find someplace to go as well, though the shelters weren't overcrowded. Where had they gone? Holed up in Tombs squats, Ellie supposed. Abandoned tenements and old factories that would at least keep the sleet from them. Some of them had probably made their way down into Old Town, that part of the city that had dropped underground during the big quake and was now claimed by the skells and other unwanted. You couldn't have gotten her to go down there on a dare.

Most people were going to be able to make do for one day. But what were they going to do if the storm dragged on throughout the week as predicted?

Wait until we start getting power blackouts, she thought.

Out in the country, most people had the option to heat with wood. Here, few had what might soon be considered a basic necessity rather than a luxury. The community centers would become makeshift shelters for all those good upstanding citizens who never thought they'd have to rely on the kindness of strangers to survive. Tommy had seen it happen before, out by the rez, and predicted it could easily happen here. Every winter, he told Ellie, there'd be at least one major storm that shut down this or that small town. Hazard. Champion. Even Tyler, the county seat.

But nothing like this. He'd never heard of anything like this.

With their regular clientele absent, Ellie and Tommy found themselves doling out hot coffee to the increasing number of rescue crews that were out on the streets tonight. Police. City workers. Ambulance drivers. Hydro repairmen. The pair were warned more than once to get off the streets for their own safety, but not even the police were prepared to enforce their advice as they munched on sandwiches and drank coffee provided from the back of the Angel Outreach van. With most of the all-night convenience stores and restaurants closed for business, there was nowhere else for them to go.

It was so eerie. Ellie had never seen the streets so quiet.

"How're we doing for supplies?" she asked Tommy after she got back inside from yet another bout of scraping down the windshield.

He shrugged. "Maybe one urn of coffee left and half the sandwiches, but the doughnuts and cookies are all gone. We should probably get back to Grasso Street and stock up while we can."

He pulled away from the curb, the rear of the van fishtailing, though he'd barely touched the gas pedal with his foot.

"And maybe switch over to my truck while we're at it," he added.

"I wonder if this is what your Aunt Sunday was talking about," Ellie said.

Tommy shot her a puzzled look.

"You know, the dangerous times I'm supposed to protect you from."

"What? Poor driving conditions?"

"The storm's a little more serious than that."

"It is," he said, keeping his gaze on the street. "She was talking about something else."

Ellie waited a moment, but he didn't elaborate.

"So what was it?" she asked.

"Things you don't want to know about." He gave her a quick smile. "All that mysterious stuff that drives you crazy when Jilly talks about it."

"Try me," she said.

"Come on, Ellie."

"No, seriously. After the weird day I've had, it'll probably make sense."

Now Tommy looked concerned. "What happened to you? It's that house, isn't it? I've never trusted the place. It just feels all wrong up there."

"Now you tell me."

He shrugged. "And you were going to listen?"

"Probably not," she admitted. "But I'm listening now."

"First tell me what you were talking about."

Ellie sighed. Did she really want to get into this? She still remembered Tommy's parting shot this morning.

My family lives in another world from this one.

Meaning, he'd explained, the world of spirits. And Tommy was right. It wasn't something she'd ever felt comfortable talking about with any seriousness. There were enough wonderful and strange things in the real world to capture her attention without needing to venture into some New Age fairyland. As if.

But wasn't that what she'd seen from the window of Kellygnow? Bettina had given it some Spanish name, but it translated into the same thing. The spiritworld. And those men in their broadcloth suits and bare feet had been spirits, she'd said. The reason she could see them and Chantal couldn't was because she had some kind of magic in her.

Feeling stupid, even though she knew he wouldn't make fun of her, Ellie related her morning to Tommy—how it turned out that Bettina was supposed to be a witch or something; describing the odd men in the garden, why it was supposed to be that she could see them.

"What kind of thing would wake up magic in a person?" she asked. "I mean, here I've gone through my whole life, perfectly normal—"

Tommy snorted.

"Okay. Non-supernaturally inclined. So how come this is happening to me? Why now?"

Tommy shook his head. "How would I know?"

"I thought Native beliefs included that kind of thing."

"Right," Tommy said, smiling. "Like Indians are all one universal tribe. It's not like being Catholic, or a Buddhist, you know. There are hundreds of different tribes on this continent, each with their own language and culture and beliefs. What's sacred to one group, might be a joke to another."

"But at that powwow you took me to—"

"Powwows are a culture unto themselves," Tommy told her. "They're a mishmash of everything Indian. The name's borrowed from the Chickasaw. And what do you get at them? Mohawks doing Sioux sun dances. Crees weaving Navajo blankets. Kickaha frying up buffalo burgers. You can't go to a powwow without smelling sweetgrass, seeing Haida, salmon and raven imagery, grass dancing, Hopi beadwork—doesn't matter what part of the country it's in. Remember Chief Morningstar in his big feathered headdress?"

Ellie nodded.

"Not a part of Kickaha culture. But it sure looks cool, right? And how about those dream-catchers? They're a good-luck charm of the Lakota, but they're like the symbol of Indian spirituality now, aren't they? Everybody's making and selling them. The damn things drive me crazy."

"You've got one hanging from the mirror in your truck."

"You bet," Tommy said. "It's better than the Club. Indian kids aren't going to boost my pickup because the dream-catcher tells them I'm a blood, too."

"I thought you liked powwows," Ellie said.

"I do. But I like going because it's fun and I get to see a lot of old friends that I wouldn't see otherwise. Not because it's some kind of pan-Indian evangelical meeting hall."

He broke off as they rounded a corner to see some hydro workers removing a tree limb that was dragging down an already overextended power line. Pulling over, he and Ellie got out of the van to hand out a round of coffees and sandwiches to the grateful men. Returning to the van, Tommy took his turn at scraping down the windshield and then they continued on to Angel's Grasso Street office.

"See," Tommy said, taking up where the conversation had left off, "for most Indians there's no mystical mumbo jumbo in our spiritualism, and that's probably our strongest common ground. What our teachings instruct us to do is to live our lives with truth and honesty and respect. Or as the Aunts say, 'Our job is to be an awake people, utterly conscious, to attend to the world.' That lies at the heart of the teachings of most tribes. It's in the details that we differ, but those differences are what give each tribe its individual identity."

"Protestant, Catholic, Baptist."

"Exactly." He smiled. "If they were tribes."

"But you and your aunts," Ellie said. "You all believe in more than that, don't you?"

"More how?"

"That . . . these spirits. The spiritworld. That it's real."

Tommy nodded. "Oh, it's real, all right. But we don't have a particular claim on it. I think it's like Jilly says. The spirits are out there, but how they appear to us depends on what we bring to them. A shaman might see Old Man Coyote, a priest might see an angel. You might see one of those junkyard faeries that Jilly puts in her paintings."

"Except," Ellie said, "Bettina described those men in the garden exactly the way I was seeing them."

"Hey, I'm no expert. I keep telling you that."

He fell silent and pulled over so that Ellie could scrape down the windshield once more.

"If you want to know about magic," he said when she climbed back in, "you should talk to one of my aunts."

"Well, Sunday seemed nice . . ."

Tommy laughed. "Meaning she wasn't this weird old woman who looked like she was going to turn you into a moth or a toad."

Ellie punched his shoulder.

"Hey," he said. "Don't damage the merchandise."

"I know, I know," Ellie said. "Hearts would break everywhere in the world of the supermodels where you are king."

"I'm like a drug dealer," Tommy told her. "They just can't resist what I have to offer."

"Bountiful humility, for one."

Tommy shook his head. "No. I sneak them pork chops."

Ellie went to punch him again, but then out of the corner of her eye she caught movement on the street.

"Look out!" she cried at the same time as Tommy eased on the brakes.

A man had burst out onto the street from between a couple of parked cars, the whites of his eyes reflecting weirdly in the van's headlights. Ellie had long enough to see he was wearing a handkerchief tied across his face like a bandit's mask and bright yellow rubber kitchen gloves, before he slipped on the icy street and went down right in front of the van.

"Oh shit," Tommy muttered.

He braked and the van's rear end began to fishtail, sliding on the ice before it came to a stop that left it standing broadside in the middle of the street.

"Did we hit him?" Ellie asked as she fumbled with her seatbelt. "I didn't feel us hit him."

But Tommy was already out the driver's door and didn't answer.

11

Hunter was about four blocks from Miki's apartment and breathing hard when he realized he was being followed. The first he knew of it was a pinprick sensation in the nape of his neck, an animal-level warning that resonated up through the levels of his consciousness until it finally registered in the reasoning part of his mind. He turned, sliding on the wet ice underfoot until he was brought up short by a parked car. He caught hold of the car as best he could, rubber gloves finding a grip on the ice sheath that covered the vehicle. He used the hood of the car to support his weight and looked back the way he'd come.

Nothing.

But he knew something was out there. The wet hairs at the back of his neck were still raised like hackles.

He pushed away from the car and continued down the sidewalk, shuffling along rather than lifting his feet since it was easier to keep his balance that way. The freezing rain continued to fall, but it didn't make that much difference anymore. He was already soaked through and through by the sleet and doubted he could get much wetter. He'd been out in it too long, taken too many falls in icy puddles since he'd fled the apartment.

The apartment. Forget the stink, at least it had been warm. He didn't feel like he could remember warm and dry anymore. The apartment seemed like hours ago, though he knew it was only minutes. His teeth chattered. Movement, already hampered by the unsteady footing, was made more difficult still with his wet heavy clothes weighing him down.

When he neared a lamppost, he caught hold of its slick metal pole and swung around. This time he caught a glimpse of something moving low to the ground, a dark, quick-moving shape that darted out of sight behind a parked car.

A dog? Something on all fours, at any rate. Too fast, and not enough body mass to be a man.

He waited, but whatever it was didn't show itself. Nor did he see any others. But he knew it was there, just as he knew it wasn't alone. Just as visual confirmation wasn't needed to tell him who it was, no matter what shape it might be wearing at this particular moment. Everything had changed for him. In the long minutes since the hard man had first appeared in the doorway of Miki's kitchen, he'd been jerked out of his familiar world into some nightmare country. He was stumbling through unknown territory where nothing was the way it should be. Whatever doubts he'd had when Miki was telling her story had all vanished now.

He knew her fairy-tale Gentry were real. Pretending they weren't didn't fly for the animal senses that lay just under what he realized now was only a façade of rationality. The animal inside him was alert, alert and terrified.

The Gentry were real and they were after him, it was as simple as that. What was to stop them from taking some kind of animal shape? Who was going to notice a stray dog, or even a pack of them? With this weather people had more pressing concerns on their mind.

Wiping the water from his eyes, he stared at the place where he'd seen the dog vanish.

He thought he knew why it was hiding. It was probably a scout, waiting for the others to catch up before they took him on as a pack. They'd be cautious, thinking he was dangerous, knowing that he'd already killed one of them. What they didn't know was that it had been no more than blind, dumb luck. That he was such a terrified mess they could knock him over with the flick of a finger. He was about as likely to hurt another one of them as the original Clash line-up was to launch a new tour.

He set off again, using the parked cars for support as he skidded and slid his way down the sidewalk. The place where the hard man had sucker-punched him the other night was aching again. His chest was tight, his breathing too fast and shallow. Turning suddenly, he caught sight of two low, quick shapes, slipping out of sight, sensed others.

Christ, they could move fast. What were they waiting for?

He pushed himself off the car he was holding onto, sliding to the next one, a fancy black Cherokee jeep, encrusted in ice. He thought his heart would stop when a mechanical voice commanded him to, "Step back from the car."

He reeled away from the vehicle, flailing his arms for balance.

Car alarm, he thought as he went down in another puddle. That's all. Just a stupid car alarm.

He crawled back to the Cherokee on his hands and knees and slapped the side of the jeep, ignored the car's warning, banged against the metal until the warnings were done and the Klaxon wail of the alarm started up. He thought his eardrums would burst, but the pain was worth it. Surely the sound would draw some attention to him.

Look out the window, he willed the vehicle's owner. Dial 911, for God's sake. Can't you see I'm trying to steal your car?

He banged on the door again, denting the metal.

I even look the part, he realized, with this handkerchief tied across his face.

He'd forgotten all about it. Playing Good Samaritan and trying to clean up Miki's apartment didn't feel like hours ago anymore, but a lifetime. He started to pull the cloth away from his face, then caught a glimpse of movement back down the street he'd just come down. Those low slinking shapes, darting from the doorways of stores to the parked cars and back again, getting closer with every dash. And then he saw one of the hard men come around the far corner, walking on the sidewalk as though it were bare pavement, not covered with a slick coating of ice.

His sudden appearance seemed to be a signal. The other Gentry rose up from behind the cars, stepped out of the doorways, men now as well, dark haired and dark-eyed, the tails of their trench coats slapping against their legs as they fell in step with the first one. None of them had trouble with the icy footing. They didn't even seem to be wet.

Hunter wasn't surprised. Why should the foul weather prove any sort of impediment to them?

The car alarm was making him deaf but he still heard the sound of a car engine above it. He turned to see its approaching lights. A van. He hauled himself to his feet and, using the hood of the jeep as a springboard, propelled himself out from between the vehicles. The van's headlights caught him as he staggered out into the middle of the street. Then his legs went out from under him. He fell into yet another puddle and came up spluttering in time to see the van skidding on the ice, sliding right at him. He stared wide-eyed, waiting for the impact, but the vehicle slewed to one side, finally stopping with the front fender rearing directly over him.

He couldn't hear the van's doors opening over the wail of the car alarm, but he saw the vehicle shift on its springs as whoever was inside disembarked.

Oh, Christ, he thought. The Gentry. Don't let them hurt these people.

He sat up and smacked his head on the fender, fell back into the puddle. The next thing he knew there was someone bending over him. Dark-haired, dark-eyed. He waited for the killing blow, but it didn't come. He had long enough to recognize the Native American features of one of his customers before the face was suddenly jerked away.

Too late, Hunter realized. The Gentry had them now.

He was hauled up out of the puddle and onto his feet, the hard man holding him upright effortlessly. Hunter saw the man who'd stopped to help him lying on the street, the breath knocked out of him. As he watched, one of the Gentry smashed the window of the Cherokee with his elbow and reached inside, ripping something out of the jeep. He straightened up from the vehicle with a fistful of wires in his hand. The car alarm stopped and the ensuing silence seemed deafening.

He shouldn't have been able to do that, Hunter found himself thinking. Who breaks a car window with his elbow?

Goddamn fairy-tale hardcases, that was who.

"I warned you, you pathetic little shite," the leader of the Gentry said.

But before he could hit Hunter, another voice spoke. A woman's voice. It was familiar, but so out of context that Hunter couldn't place it.

"Don't you hurt him."

Yeah, Hunter thought. That's really going to stop these guys.

But the hard man let him go. Hunter started to fall, caught himself on the grill of the van.

"You," the hard man said, looking to where the woman was standing.

Hunter looked as well.

"Ellie?" he asked.

She gave him a confused look until he remembered the handkerchief tied across his face. He tugged it down.

"Hunter?" she said.

12

What in God's name was going on? Ellie thought as the man by the hood of the van pulled down his handkerchief and she recognized Hunter. She recognized the men chasing him as well. They were Donal's hard men. But give them long hair, she realized, and they'd be exactly like the group she'd seen on the lawn behind Kellygnow earlier today. Bettina's spirit men. The only difference was they weren't barefoot now and they were wearing trench coats over those dark suits of theirs. But the rain didn't seem to bother them any more than the cold. Maybe they only wore boots and overcoats when they were out on the streets so that they would fit in better. Except that didn't explain how their hair got longer and shorter.

She had a moment's hysterical thought. So what? Did people in the spirit-world go around in wigs or something? What was *that* all about?

"Are you certain this is your wish?" the man who'd been holding Hunter asked her in response to her telling him to leave Hunter alone.

All Ellie could do was stare at him. An unsettling sensation of déjà vu worried through her. She could hear Nuala's voice in her head, what the housekeeper had said when they'd gone to her to ask if she and Chantal could share the studio.

Are you certain this is what you want?

Who *were* these people? Why was what she wanted so important to them?

But though her head was brimming with questions, she had enough of her wits about her to nod in response.

"Yes," she said. Her voice came out as a croak. They were so scary-looking, these men, spirits, whatever they were. She cleared her throat before adding, "I'm sure."

The hard man gave her a feral grin and turned away to where Tommy was sitting up, one hand rubbing the back of his head where he must have hit it. She replayed the moment when the man had basically tossed Tommy out of the way and shivered, finally beginning to believe that there was something more than human about these guys.

"All . . . all of us," she managed.

"Oh, aye," the man said. "And is the whole fucking world under your protection?"

"I . . . I . . ."

He walked past Tommy, stopping by the black jeep with the broken window. He bent down and hooked the fingers of one hand under the running board. In one sudden movement he lifted the vehicle and heaved it onto its side.

Ellie winced at the sound of the crash, her eyes wide with shock. The small gibbering voice of panic that had been hiding in the back of her head reared in mindless fear and it was all she could do to just stand there and at least pretend to be strong.

"Fair enough," the man said, still grinning. There was no humor in his eyes. "But remember to fulfill your side of the bargain or I'll hunt the lot of you down and gut you like the little shites you are."

Bargain? Ellie thought. What bargain?

But she knew enough to keep her mouth shut and simply nod her head.

The hard man held her gaze for a long moment. Ellie could feel her knees turning to water. Then he finally gave a brusque nod to his companions and turned away. As silently as they'd come, untouched by the weather and unencumbered by the unsteady footing, the men went back the way they'd come.

Ellie collapsed against the side of the van, holding onto the mirror for support.

"Somebody want to tell me what the hell that was all about?"

She glanced over at Tommy to see he was now standing. His hair and shoulders had acquired a thin sheath of ice and his face was dripping. She was getting soaked herself, standing out here in the freezing rain, but he'd landed in a puddle and was far wetter than she was.

"I don't know," she told him. Her gaze drifted to the far end of the street where the men were just turning the corner. "Those are Donal's hard men, but they could be twins to the guys I saw at Kellygnow."

"M-m-miki says they're called the Gentry," Hunter put in.

They both turned to look at him. He was like a wet rat, utterly drenched and shivering, and somewhat ludicrous with the bright yellow rubber gloves he was wearing.

"What's with the get-up?" Tommy asked him. "You given up selling CDs for some new career as a janitor?"

"C-c-can we take this inside?" Hunter said. "I'm fr-fr-freezing."

Ellie nodded. She slid open the side door and they all piled in. Too cold and miserable to be shy, Hunter stripped off his sodden clothes and put on dry pants, socks, a shirt, and a sweater that he picked out of the spare clothes they kept in the back for the homeless. When he was dressed, he wrapped himself up with a couple of blankets. It made him look like a derelict—a weird derelict with those rubber gloves. Ellie watched him try to deal with the gloves, but his hands were too numbed from the cold. She helped him peel them off, then handed him a coffee. He cupped his hands around the Styrofoam cup, spilling hot coffee onto fingers, but he didn't seem to feel the liquid.

Ellie and Tommy used a couple of other blankets to dry themselves off and helped themselves to coffee as well.

"Th-th-thanks," Hunter said finally. "For everything. For all of this. I mean it. But especially for getting those guys off my back." He took a sip of the coffee, sloshing more down his chin than he got in his mouth. "How did you do that anyway?"

"Yeah, Ellie," Tommy said. "What gives? That one guy was talking about some bargain."

"I don't know," she told them. "I've seen them in The Harp whenever there's a session on, but I've never talked to them. They're the ones who beat Donal up awhile back, remember?"

Tommy nodded.

"But the weirdest thing is, give them long hair and they could be the men I saw this morning at Kellygnow, hanging around in the backyard, some of them just in shirtsleeves. Like the cold couldn't touch them." She turned to Hunter. "What did you call them?"

"Ge-gentry. They're some kind of . . ."

His voice trailed off and he got an embarrassed look on his face.

"Spirits," Tommy put in.

Hunter gave him a grateful look and nodded. He took another long swallow of coffee, this time drinking more than he spilled. The hot liquid seemed to be helping, since he wasn't shivering so much and his teeth had finally stopped chattering.

"They trashed Miki's place earlier this morning," he went on. "I went out there tonight and thought I'd try to clean things up for her, but then one of those guys showed up and . . . and . . ."

He had such an anguished look on his face that Ellie reached over and laid a comforting hand on his arm.

"I think I killed him," Hunter finished.

"Oh, man," Tommy said. "No wonder they're so pissed off at you."

"They haven't liked me from the start," Hunter said. "Ever since—" His gaze went to Ellie. "—that night at the community center when I met you and one of them warned me to stay away from you."

"What?"

Hunter nodded. "I know. It didn't make any sense to me either. Donal said he'd figure out what they wanted—what was going on, you know?—but that was before he went all weird."

"All weird how?" Ellie asked.

Hunter told them then. About the painting Donal had been working on, Donal and Miki's fight, how she'd thrown him out of the apartment after he'd destroyed his canvas, all the weird things she'd told him, what had happened to her apartment, meeting Donal just before the hard man showed up. It was a long convoluted story that complicated things more than it explained, so far as Ellie was concerned. The more Hunter talked, the more she shook her head in disbelief. None of this made any sense.

"Has the whole world gone insane?" she asked when he was done.

"Is that a rhetorical question," Tommy asked, "or did you really want an answer?"

"You've got an answer?"

He nodded. "The world's like it always was. You're just seeing it differently."

"Oh, great."

"So what do you think the hard man was talking about?" Hunter asked. "With this bargain, I mean."

Ellie thought she knew at least that much, though it didn't explain things any better.

"You said the figure in the painting was wearing a mask?" she asked.

Hunter nodded. "Miki called it a Green Man's mask. It looks like it's made of leaves and vines and stuff."

"I know what it looks like," Ellie said. "That's what my commission from Musgrave Wood is. To make a new version of this old wooden mask they have."

"So that's the bargain," Tommy said.

She nodded. "Looks like it, doesn't it?"

"So now what do we do?" Hunter asked.

"There's going to be hell to pay if I make this mask, isn't there?"

"And hell to pay if you don't," Tommy put in.

"Thank you for that."

"Come on, Ellie. I'm not trying to—"

"I know, I know," she said. "But I'm just so confused about all of this . . ."

She stared out the front windshield, not that there was anything to see. They had the van's engine still running, but a coat of ice was already thickening on the glass. Angel really needed to get some new vehicles.

"We need help," she said. "Expert help."

"Fiona," Hunter offered. "One of the women who works for me. She was telling me about these Creek sisters . . ."

He broke off as Tommy began to laugh.

"What's so funny?" he asked.

"They're his aunts," Ellie explained.

"That's what Fiona called them. The Aunts."

"I mean they're literally his aunts."

Hunter gave Tommy a considering look. "But Fiona made it sound like they were these, I don't know, supernatural wise women or something."

"What can I say?" Tommy told him.

"Maybe we *should* talk to them," Ellie said. "I can't believe what I just said," she added in a mutter.

Tommy was kind and made no comment. Nodding, he took out the cell phone and punched in a number. After a few moments, he hit the "End" button and punched in another number, repeating the process a few more times.

"Looks like the phone lines are down on the rez," he said.

"Then we're going to have to drive out there," Ellie said.

Tommy shook his head. "With this rain? I don't think so. The roads are going to be a mess. I doubt the highway's even open. We'll have to wait until the weather clears."

"That might not be until the end of the week," Ellie said. "I don't know if we can wait that long. I'm supposed to be working on this mask, but now we know I can't because who knows what sort of horrible thing those guys'll do with it. So what's going to happen when they figure out I'm stalling?"

No one wanted to put it into words. They'd all seen the hard man lift the jeep like it was no heavier than a cardboard cut-out and flip it over on its side.

"Thing is," Tommy said. "If they're so tough, how come just whacking one with a pail of water was enough to kill him?"

"I don't know," Hunter told him. "I don't even know for sure that he is dead."

"But still."

Hunter nodded. "And remember what Donal said before he left me: Everything can die. When it comes to these Gentry, I figure he should know."

"After what you've told us," Tommy said, "I don't know if I'd trust him on anything."

Reluctantly, Ellie had to agree. She supposed the most depressing thing about all of this was that she wasn't particularly surprised by what Hunter had told them. There had always been something about Donal that had made her keep a certain distance between them. It was why she hadn't been able to reciprocate his love, why even as a friend, his moroseness could sometimes be wearying. It was one thing to tell yourself it was only a mannerism—which is what it had always seemed to her, part of the angsty, Irish-expatriate artist image he liked to project—but when it went on as relentlessly as it did . . . She hadn't been able to live with it. And now this.

The mask had been pulled away and who would have guessed what had really been lying there under the façade?

"We're getting off the topic here," she said. "Let's concentrate on getting out to the rez to see Tommy's aunts."

"You're sure you want to do this?" Tommy asked. "If we get stranded halfway there, slide off the road in some godforsaken part of the mountains . . ." He shook his head. "The cops have probably already closed off the highway."

"You think?"

He shrugged. "If not yet, then soon."

"So let's get out on the road before they do."

13

After dinner, Miki pulled one of the dining-room chairs over to the window that overlooked the street below Fiona's apartment and sat there for the rest of the evening. She watched the sleet come down outside, cradling her old Hohner on her lap. Occasionally she fingered a tune on its keyboard, but since she didn't work the bellows, the only sound she made was that of the buttons being pressed and released, a series of soft, almost inaudible, hollow clicks. Mostly she smoked her cigarettes and stared out the window. Fiona tried striking up a conversation from time to time, but Miki simply couldn't muster the energy. The events of last night and this morning, and then having worked to put on a good face about it through the day, had left her too drained.

"It's not you," she told Fiona. "Honestly. You've been great. But I've run out of steam, you know?"

"If you want to go to bed . . . ?"

Miki shook her head. "No, I'll just sit here for a while."

And try not to feel so bloody depressed. But it was hard, and Fiona's apartment didn't help.

Fiona had carried the Goth obsession of her wardrobe over into her interior decorating scheme. Between the promo posters of Morrissey, The Cure, Dead Can Dance, Rhea's Obsession, and the like, and the somber minimalism of the furnishings—really, who put up solid black curtains?—it would be hard to feel cheerful in this room in the best of circumstances. All the furnishings were black, what little of them there were. Entertainment unit holding the stereo and TV. Wooden IKEA couch and chairs that Fiona had repainted, recovering the cushions with black fabric. Coffee table, lamp, and a small bookcase. The chairs and dining-room table in the part of the room where Miki was sitting. Only the mantel was cluttered, draped with black and red lace and holding a fake human skull, an obviously beloved collection of Anne Rice novels, and what looked like two hundred candles. It was enough to make Miki want to slit her wrists.

She didn't blame Fiona. Her co-worker was actually a very sweet woman for all her fixation with the dark and gloomy. She'd cooked a great stir-fry for dinner, kept up a cheerful conversation from when they'd first left the store through when they sat down to dinner, and even put on an Enya CD after the meal, making some comment about how it bridged the gap between Celtic and Goth. Miki didn't have the heart to tell her that the cloying harmonies and sameness of the disc put her nerves on edge. She'd have preferred some early 'Trane or Lester Young. A remastered Bird reissue or Wayne Shorter's new CD. Anything with an edge. She'd even have settled for one of Fiona's Goth bands, if there actually existed any recordings among them where the tempo changed from one cut to another.

She half-listened to Fiona making some phone calls. One to her friend Andrea, commiserating on the closing of the club where she was supposed to start working that night. Another to Jessica, tracking down a telephone number for the Creek sisters. Passing that information on to Hunter's answering machine since it seemed he was still out. God, what could he be finding to do on a night as miserable as this?

"What are you looking at?" Fiona asked as she pushed the "End" button on her phone and laid it on the floor by her feet.

Miki turned from the window and shrugged. "Nothing."

Though that wasn't true, she realized as she turned back to her vigil. The real reason she was keeping watch was that at any moment she expected to see the Gentry come ambling down the street. The slippery footing wouldn't bother them and the rain would simply run off their trench coats, if they even bothered to wear them. They'd come stomping up the stairs to Fiona's place and trash it just as they had hers. But first they'd vent their anger on Fiona and her.

"Whoever wrecked your place isn't going to find you here," Fiona said.

Miki turned to look at her again, a little embarrassed that she was being so transparent.

"Is what's going on inside my head that obvious?" she asked.

Fiona shook her head. "You wouldn't be normal if you weren't worried about that. How would they even know to look for you here?"

"These aren't your run-of-the-mill, intolerant assholes," Miki said. "Finding someone who's trying to hide anywhere in this city is the least of their abilities."

"This have anything to do with why Hunter wants to contact a Native elder?"

"Pretty much."

Fiona pulled her feet up onto her chair and wrapped her arms around them, looking at Miki over the tops of her knees.

"No offense," she said, "but neither you nor Hunter seem much inclined to the spiritual."

Miki wanted to laugh. Spiritual was the last word she would have used to describe the Gentry. They were so wired into base, earthly concerns that the only thing spiritual about them was their love for Guinness and whiskey. Not quite the spirits Fiona had in mind.

"I guess," she said. "I can't really speak for Hunter, but the only experiences I've ever had with things not quite of this world have been shite."

Fiona regarded her for a long moment.

"You mean your place got trashed by bad spirits?" she finally asked. "Like some kind of, what? Poltergeists?"

"Oh, no," Miki told her. "The Gentry have physical presence. Too bloody much of it, as far as I'm concerned."

"The Gentry?"

Miki sighed. "It's a long story," she said. "But to give you the short version, I had a big fight with Donal last night because he was acting like a stupid little self-centered shite—"

"Or, in other words, he was being himself."

Miki raised an eyebrow.

"Well, really," Fiona said. "I mean, I'm sorry, he being your brother and all, but he's never exactly made himself easy to like, has he? At least not for us. What does he call everyone who doesn't quite match up to his obviously high standards?"

"Punters?"

"Exactly. Sometimes all he has to do is walk into the store and it's all I can do to not give him a good smack across the head."

Miki was so used to the way Donal could be that she never really thought all that much about how negatively other people might view him. She supposed it was because she'd always gotten to see the other side of him, the protective older brother capable of great generosity. Gone now. Lost to her in a welter of Gentry lies and promises.

"He's not all bad," she said, surprised that she could still defend him after the past twenty-four hours.

"Neither's getting sick with a really bad cold—I mean, you do get the time off work—but still, who wants one?"

"Anyway," Miki went on. "We had this fight and that brought me to the attention of these friends of his who ended up trashing my place."

"Nice friends."

Miki nodded. "But what makes it complicated is . . . well, they're not exactly human."

"Say what?"

"I know, I know. It sounds ridiculous."

"Well, that depends," Fiona said. "Do you mean not human as in they're such nasty pieces of work we don't want to claim them as part of the human race, or are you talking *X-Files*?"

Miki never watched the show, but you couldn't have any awareness of contemporary pop culture and not know something about it by now.

"I don't know," she said. "Does *The X-Files* deal with *genii loci*? We're talking immortal earth spirits here, bad-tempered ones with a mean streak a mile wide who can change shape and pull your arms and legs off if they happen to get pissed off with you."

Fiona gave her a considering look. "You mean for real?"

Miki nodded.

"You're supposed to tell me you're kidding now," Fiona said.

"I'm serious."

"And that's what's scaring me," Fiona said. "I mean, I like getting spooked as much as the next person. A little Anne Rice. Checking out *Scream* and stuff like that. But then I always have the comfort of knowing that when I close the book, or leave the theater, I'm back in the real world."

"I'm not going to be able to do that."

"You've actually *seen* these guys?"

"I've been on the periphery of them all my life," Miki told her. "I guess I was just lucky that I didn't catch their attention until now."

"And your brother's connection is?"

"He thinks they're going to make him immortal, too. That they'll give him the power to pay back every wrong that's ever been done to him, imagined or real, and nobody'll be able to call him on it because he'll be this supernatural hard man then, too. Just like them. One of the Gentry."

"Why do you keep calling them that?"

Miki shrugged. "That's just the way everybody referred to them when I was growing up. Calling them by their real names is supposed to be bad luck— puts their attention on you and you don't want that because they'll turn you into a newt or something."

"Oh, boy."

"I know," Miki said. "It's a lot to swallow. I'm surprised you haven't laughed me out of the room by now."

Fiona gave her a funny look. "I guess," she said after a moment, "it's because no matter how rational we think we are, we always suspect that there's more out there than we can see. It's like the old boogieman under the bed, as if—right? I know he's not there, not really, but I still don't sleep with a foot or a hand hanging over the edge of the bed."

"But it's just me telling you about it," Miki said. "You don't have any proof that any of it's true."

"No. But I've worked with you for a long time now and the Miki I've always known isn't the same as the Miki who came into the store with Hunter this morning. I knew *something* really weird and serious had happened to you and it wasn't just your apartment getting trashed. You've been through a lot of shit and that kind of thing would only piss you off."

"I was pissed off."

"Yeah, but you were scared, too."

Miki nodded. That was true. It was still true.

"And I guess I'm kind of primed for this sort of thing," Fiona went on. She waved her hand in the general direction of her Anne Rice books and the skull on her mantle. "For it to be, you know, more than just make-believe."

They fell silent then. Miki returned her attention to the wet streets outside. The last CD they'd been playing had finished, but Fiona didn't get up to put on a new one.

"So do you really think they're going to come after you?" Fiona asked. "That they could track you down here?"

"I don't know. They're probably not even thinking about me anymore. I'm no threat to them and they made their point in my apartment this morning."

"Except you hold grudges, too, don't you?"

Miki shrugged.

"And if they don't know it, Donal will." Fiona shook her head. "I know he's a self-centered little shit, but I can't believe he'd take sides against you."

"Yeah. That . . . hurts."

More than she could possibly put into words.

"So maybe we should do something," Fiona said. "Protect ourselves."

"How?"

"I don't know. We could call the number Jessica gave me for the Creek woman and ask her advice."

"I suppose."

"Or barricade the door. Or—"

At that moment the power died and they both jumped with fright. A sudden stillness settled over the dark apartment. All the normal murmurings of fridges and clocks and the like were gone. And because of the weather, the streets outside echoed that strange oppressive quiet.

"Do . . . do you think they had anything to do with this?" Fiona said.

"No, it's just the weather," Miki told her, hoping she was right. "Look. They still have power across the street. I guess they're on a different part of the grid."

"Why doesn't this comfort me?"

Miki laid her accordion on the floor and stood up.

"Come on," she said. "Let's light some of those candles of yours."

"And make sure the front door is locked."

Miki hesitated a moment, head cocked to listen, sure for a moment that she heard Gentry boots on the stairs coming up to Fiona's apartment.

"And make sure the door's locked," she agreed.

14

It was almost midnight before Donal finally made it up to Kellygnow. He never did find his van and it took forever to flag down a cab, mostly because there were none out on the street by the time he left Hunter at Miki's apartment. Who could blame them? The weather was worse than foul and there were no fares to be had anyway. The whole city was shutting down. Donal trudged past closed restaurants, convenience stores, clubs, theaters, diners. The only people he met were city and hydro workers. The only vehicles belonged to police and other emergency services, so there were no rides to be had. He was happy to keep his distance from the former and wouldn't have presumed on the latter.

But a cab eventually stopped for him. The driver was off duty, on his way home and heading west anyway. He took pity on Donal, driving him across town and over the river at Lakeside Drive, before finally letting him out at the bottom of Handfast Road. Donal tried to pay for the ride, but the cabbie shook his head.

"Do somebody else a good turn," he said.

"Thanks, mate," he told the cabbie. "I will."

Maybe stick a blade in the guts of one of the Gentry. Rip the smug smirking grin from a hard man's gob as he felt his life turning to shite and bleeding away on him. That'd make for a good turn wouldn't it?

"Drive carefully," he added as he shut the cab door.

He stood in the freezing rain and watched as the vehicle pulled a one-eighty, piece of cake on the icy street, and headed back across the river. Donal was impressed. You had to be a damn fine driver to pull a trick like that in these conditions. When the cab's taillights finally blinked out behind the hump in the road that rose up in the middle of the bridge, he started up Handfast. And got nowhere.

The road proved impassable. It was so steep and slick with ice that he couldn't get a foothold. Eventually, he went by the back way, up through the backyards of the big expensive estates, breaking the thick crust of ice on top of the snow with each step. It was just as wet and miserable as being on the street, but Jaysus, at least he had traction. For the first time since he'd left the hotel where he'd woken up earlier this evening, he felt as though he was actually in full command of his own limbs, instead of simply trying to keep his balance. Still, the going was slow.

The night was full of sound as he went. He kept hearing the sharp crack of tree limbs breaking, the thumps of the branches falling, the tinkle like breaking glass as the smaller twigs and bits of broken ice went skittering across the crusted ice.

Halfway up he saw the huge limb of a Manitoba maple split from the main tree trunk and come crashing down on the side of a house, stoving in the roof, walls, windows. The house's security system kicked in and a shrill alarm began to bleat.

Donal paused, wondering if he should see if anyone needed help, but then shook his head and continued on. The fat buggers in these houses thought they shat roses. Let them have a little taste of real hardship. Do 'em bloody good.

The alarm followed him up the hill, until it was suddenly turned off. He glanced back, but the place was out of sight by now. His gaze moved on to take in what he could see of the city through the winter-bare trees. The carpet of lights he'd been expecting was present, but there were patches here and there where areas were blacked out. Power failures. As he watched, another section, a few dozen blocks, winked out, just like that.

Jaysus, what a bloody night. It was like magic, more power to it. The whole world feeling a bit of his own misery. Inconvenienced, are you? Power failed and you can't run out and spend your cash? Well, sod you. Sod on the lot of you.

He was grinning as he finally made it up through the trees behind Kellygnow, soaked to the skin and shivering, legs aching from the hard trek of breaking through the ice crust with each step.

"In a good mood, are we?" a voice asked him from out of the darkness.

"Why not?" he replied. "It's a fucking beautiful night."

One of the Gentry stepped out from the trees, a smile flickering on his lips.

"You're the hard little shite, aren't you?" he said.

"Maybe. But not as hard as you lot."

"Don't you forget that, boyo."

All Donal wanted to do was grab him and start pounding his Gentry head against the nearest tree, but that would serve no purpose except to allow him to vent his anger. There was no percentage in it. Nothing to be gained. Donal could be patient. Time enough to deal with them when he had the mask. Until then, they were simply walking dead men, so far as he was concerned. But powerful enough in their own way. No need to test their mettle.

So he put on a friendly mask, the one he always wore around the Gentry, a little hard, a lot wary. They liked it that he stood up for himself, but they liked to think they scared him, too. He could accommodate them. He'd always been good with masks, but then most people were. Who showed their true face, their true feelings, anymore? The Green Man mask would simply be one more, though more potent to be sure. When he had that, all the other masks could be thrown away.

For now he squinted at the hard man. He was looking for something you wouldn't know was there unless you knew to keep an eye out for it. The heavy sleet continued to pound down on him while the hard man was unaffected and Donal knew why. It was because he stood between, in that uncertain and shifting place that separated this world from faerie. It wasn't a place Donal could find on his own, but with the hard man there, he could mark its boundaries. He slid a foot forward, concentrated on not looking straight at it, coming to it sideways, and then he was there, too, watching the rain, rather than feeling it, sensing the cold, but untouched by it.

He wiped the water from his face, raked his fingers through beard and hair to break up and dislodge the ice that had crusted on it. That was better.

"What're you up to tonight, boyo?" the hard man asked him.

"I've come to see Ellie, but I got a little delayed by the weather."

"She's gone. Drove off in that van."

With Tommy, Donal thought, translating the shorthand. So they'd actually gone off to make their rounds in the Angel Outreach minivan. Well, good luck to them in this weather. Considering what he'd seen on the way over, the only people they'd be serving up toddies and treats to would be police and repairmen.

"She'll be back," Donal said.

The hard man shrugged. "Maybe, maybe not. There's been a problem."

Donal turned to look at him.

"Your man in the music store," the hard man said.

"Hunter?"

"That's a good name for him, considering."

"Considering what?"

"How he's up and murdered one of us."

Donal's eyes widened slightly, the mask almost slipping. Jaysus, he thought. Good on you, Hunter. I didn't think you had it in you. But you'd better run far and fast now because you've gone and signed your own bloody death warrant, don't think for a moment you haven't.

"So what have you done with him?" he asked.

"Nothing. He's under her protection."

"Her?"

"*An dealbhóir*. The sculptor."

"Ah."

None of this made sense. What was Ellie doing with Hunter when she was supposed to be out in the van with Tommy? And then there was Hunter himself, killing one of the Gentry. Jaysus, Mary, and Joseph. How was *that* possible? A few days ago Hunter had been incapacitated by a simple sucker punch, and now he was killing Gentry?

"So now what will you do?" Donal asked the hard man.

He shrugged. "We're thinking on it."

They were cunning, these hard men, capable of putting together plots of Machiavellian complexity, but not particularly bright, for all that. The thinking could take a long time, so maybe Hunter had a chance. If he traveled fast and far enough.

"Well, I'm off," the hard man told him. "There's a thought *an dealbhóir* might be reconsidering her bargain."

That made Donal snap to attention.

"She wouldn't," he assured the man.

Jaysus, she'd better not, or he'd be left without a bargain himself.

"Then why's she heading north?" the hard man asked. "Into the mountains where the enemy lives?"

"There's some reasonable explanation."

The hard man shrugged. "I suppose we'll find out. The others are already on their way. We'll follow and see who she meets, and if it goes badly . . ." He ran a finger across his throat. "We can find another."

"You won't have to."

The hard man gave another shrug. "We can be patient."

"But to be so close."

"Aye, there's the rub. You ask me, we've been listening too much to the

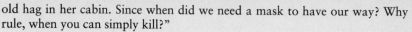

old hag in her cabin. Since when did we need a mask to have our way? Why rule, when you can simply kill?"

"Because there's so many of them. A Green Man can run them off the land like lemmings over a cliff."

The hard man spat. "I don't like it."

As he started to walk away, Donal called after him: "Do you mind if I hang about awhile? Stay dry while I'm waiting for Ellie to come back?"

He knew they didn't like anyone messing about in their territory and if this between wasn't, then what was?

"Might be a long wait," the hard man told him. "And what happened to the fucking beautiful night you were telling me about?"

"Lost its charm with your cheery news."

The hard man laughed. "Do what you want. But watch out for the shadow. The little shite's been sniffing around again tonight."

Donal had yet to fully understand what the shadow was, and why the Gentry didn't simply get rid of him if he bothered them so.

"I'll be careful," he said.

"Like I give a fuck," the hard man told him.

Donal watched him slip away under the trees until he was lost from sight. The smile on his face disappeared and he turned back to look at the house. It wasn't quick he wanted them to die, but slow. Let them remember every cold word and disdainful smirk they'd given him.

He slid down, back against a tree, and sat on the ground, dry here, in the between, tufts of dried grass cushioning his rear.

Don't mess this up one me, Ellie, he thought.

He'd wait here until morning, then go round by the house whether she was back or not. Worm his way inside, look around. That Spanish woman fancied him, no matter what Ellie thought. She'd be his ticket.

Because he had his own ideas about how necessary a new mask was. The old one had belonged to a hundred Kings in the Wood in its time, bestowing a Green Man's mantle on them all. Who was to say it wasn't potent enough for one more change on its own, just as it was? The Gentry couldn't know. It needed a mortal man to work its enchantment, and they were anything but.

Still, they could die by a mortal's hand. Hunter had proved that much. Truth was, he hadn't been so sure, for all his brave words to Hunter.

He shook his head, still surprised. Jaysus. Hunter killing a man. Who'd have thought he'd find the balls?

Been hanging around with me too much, he thought with a grin. A little bit of courage had to have worn off on him.

15

Once Tommy agreed to drive up to the rez, Ellie didn't want to waste any time, decision made, let's do it. But it wasn't that simple. For one thing, the van would never make it, not unless they had it towed up there by some treaded behemoth like a front-end loader. So after they cleared off the windshield yet again, Tommy drove them back to Grasso Street where they could swap the van for his pickup. While he and Hunter transferred what they needed from the van to Tommy's truck—more warm clothes, blankets, candles, and the like, which the residents of the rez might be needing about now—she went inside to replenish their supplies and check in with Angel.

The office was deserted, but there was a note from Angel on the desk addressed to all of the volunteers saying that they should call it a night.

"Okay, it's a night," Ellie muttered as she continued to read.

Angel herself was working with a couple of the local churches, prepping basements and meeting halls for shelters in case they were needed and anyone was welcome to come down and help out, but the streets had become too treacherous for them to keep the vans out tonight.

Ellie felt a little guilty that they were taking off and abandoning Angel like this, but she didn't see that they had any other choice. There were times when your personal life took over and if this didn't count as one of them, then what did? Thank god she didn't have to explain things to Angel—where would she even have begun? Considering how little patience Angel had for Jilly's stories, it would have been a tough sell.

Happily, all she had to do was scrawl a note at the bottom of Angel's, letting her know that they'd brought the van back and were safe. She chewed on the end of the pen for a moment, wondering if she should add that they were going up to the rez, then decided that it would only give Angel something to worry about. And what if the Gentry came by and read it? That'd be all they'd need, to have those guys realize that she was backing out of whatever deal they thought she'd made with them. Better the three of them just lost themselves up on the rez and hope that Tommy's aunts could sort something out for them.

That made her stop and think. How easy was it to hide from creatures such as the Gentry? They seemed to have their own, and fairly effective, ways of finding people if tonight was any indication. Still, why make things any easier for them?

She refilled a couple of their coffee urns, packed some paper bags with sandwiches, doughnuts, and muffins, and headed back out behind the office where Tommy and Hunter were waiting for her.

"What did Angel say?" Tommy asked as she climbed in the passenger's side of the pickup.

Hunter got in after her and closed the door.

"She wasn't there," Ellie said. "They're off getting some of the churches ready in case they're needed for shelters."

Tommy nodded. "Smart. That's Angel—always thinking ahead."

He put the truck in gear and pulled out. The rear end fishtailed a little, but not nearly as badly as the van had. Tommy shot his passengers a grin.

"Let's hear it for studded tires and four-wheel drive," he said.

. . .

The trip out of town was slow, but uneventful. There were power lines down now, with blocks of darkened buildings and the occasional unpassable street as a result. Work crews were everywhere, hydro as well as city, cutting branches, dealing with the live wires, clearing streets of debris. And still the freezing rain came down, only a drizzle at this point, but no less dangerous for that. It wasn't until they reached the north end of the city, where Williamson Street turns into Highway 5, that they were waved over to the side of the road by a police officer. He left his car and approached the truck, his slicker glistening with rain and ice.

"Is the highway closed off?" Tommy asked the officer when he reached the window.

"No, but I'll bet it will be soon. Where are you heading?"

"Up to the rez."

"Bad night for it." He peered closer. "Hey, you're one of Angel's people." Tommy nodded.

"You, too," the officer said to Ellie. "I saw your picture in the paper last week."

Ellie smiled. "You're not going to ask for an autograph are you?"

"You got anything dry to write on?"

She shook her head and the officer laughed.

"Well, I'm supposed to be warning people off the highway, but . . ." He stepped back, took in the illegal tires. "I guess if it's important . . ."

"It is."

"You got a radio in case you go off the road?"

"CB and cell phone."

"Well, you might as well go through. Take it slow, and—what'd you say your name was, son?"

"Tommy Raven."

"No, shit? My name's Tommy, too. Tommy Flanagan—like the piano player, though I can't play an instrument to save my life."

"Join the club."

The officer stepped back from the truck. "Remember, slow and easy. And Tommy? I don't want to see those tires when you get back to town."

"Consider it done."

"I will. Give Angel my best."

Tommy waited until the officer had returned to his cruiser before putting the truck in gear and pulling out. He beeped his horn as he passed the cruiser and Flanagan gave them a wave, then they were on the highway, heading north.

Flanagan hadn't been exaggerating about the condition of the highway. If anything, it was worse than he'd let on and it took all Tommy's attention to keep them on the road and moving forward. On the plus side, there was no other traffic to contend with, which made the treacherous driving conditions a little less dangerous. But at this rate, the hour-and-a-half drive was going to take them twice the time.

Ellie sighed. "It feels like it's never going to let up."

"Just pray the temperature doesn't drop," Tommy said, "or we'll be in deep shit."

Ellie nodded. If it did, all the water and slush would freeze up solid and most roads would become completely impassable. Not to mention the problems it'd cause in all those places that had lost their power. Burst water pipes. No heat. Nothing to cook on.

"Christ, I should've thought of this sooner," Hunter suddenly said. "Can I use your phone?"

"Sure," Tommy said. "Who're you calling?"

Hunter picked the cell phone up from the dash and punched in Fiona's number.

"Miki," he said as he waited for the connection to go through. "I should tell her about what happened at her apartment. That guy might have come by because the Gentry knew I was there, but what if he was looking for her? She could still be in danger."

Ellie only half-listened to his side of the conversation until she heard him talking about the mask.

"I don't think you should be telling her that," she said.

"Hang on a sec'," Hunter told Miki. He put his hand over the mouthpiece and looked at Ellie. "Why not?"

"Well, she's Donal's sister . . ."

"Didn't you hear what they did to her apartment?"

"I guess. It's just, we thought we knew Donal and look where that got us."

"This is different. I've known Miki forever. I'd trust her with my life."

"Like we trusted Donal?"

Hunter gave her a sympathetic look. "I never did," he said.

Of course not, Ellie realized. Most people took him at face value. To them he was just this morose man whose basic moods were cranky and bitter. She should have done the same.

Hunter finished his conversation and pressed the "End" button.

"I'm sorry," he said. "I didn't mean to make you feel worse than you're probably already feeling."

"It's okay," she assured him. "I need these reality checks to remind me of how things really are."

Tommy chuckled.

"What?" she said.

He shrugged. "Nothing. It's just funny hearing you talk about how things really are when they're so far from anything you'd even talk about before."

"Ha, ha," she said. She slumped in her seat, but her seatbelt made the position too uncomfortable. "Did I mention how I was hoping you'd keep bringing up these thinly veiled I-told-you-sos?" she asked as she straightened up once more.

She looked at Tommy, but it was Hunter who replied.

"Look at that," he said, pointing alongside the road on his side of the truck.

"What is it?" Tommy asked, not wanting to take his attention from the highway.

"A dog," Ellie said. "Pacing us."

"There's more than one," Hunter said. "I can see a couple more a little farther back."

Ellie nodded. "And they're on the other side of the road, too. They don't seem to be having any trouble keeping their balance on the ice . . ."

She and Hunter exchanged worried glances.

"Oh, shit," she said. "It's the Gentry, isn't it?"

"Don't weird out," Tommy told her.

"No, no. Of course not. Let's not think about how that guy just flipped over a car like it was made of cardboard."

"She's got a point," Hunter said.

"How many of them are there?" Tommy asked.

"It's hard to tell. Six or seven."

"And all they're doing is pacing us?"

"So far," Ellie said. "Maybe they're just waiting for a really desolate stretch of road."

"They've had plenty of that," Tommy said. "My guess is they want to know where we're going. Look," he added, shooting Ellie a quick glance. "If they'd wanted to hurt us, they could have jumped us back in the city."

"Except now they know we're taking off on them. Reneging on this stupid bargain I didn't even know I was making."

"They can't know that for sure," Tommy said. "Which is why they're following us."

"Not anymore," Hunter said. "They're falling back."

Ellie twisted in her seat to see for herself. It was true. The dogs now stood across the middle of the road, motionless, staring at them, growing smaller as the pickup continued to pull away from them.

"I don't get it," she said. "Why are they giving up all of a sudden?"

Hunter pointed out the window. At first Ellie didn't know what he meant. But then she saw them, too. Strange figures standing in amongst the ice-coated trees. They were driving slow enough that she could pick out details but they didn't quite register. Tall naked men, dark against the snow, swallowed by the trees where the shadows lay deeper. Their dark skin glistened, like statues coated by a fine sheen of frozen rain. Their hair hung in long braids, or matted dreadlocks; it was hard to tell. The headlights of the pickup flashed on small objects that had been woven into their twisted hair.

"My god," she said in a low voice. "They've got horns."

"Antlers," Tommy corrected.

There was something strained about his voice, but Ellie didn't pick up on it immediately.

"They're just headdresses of some sort, right?" she said.

When she looked at him for confirmation, he was shaking his head. She slumped in her seat.

"More spirits," she said.

Tommy nodded. "You got it."

"How come all of a sudden we're all seeing these things . . . and seeing them everywhere?"

"Aunt Nancy says that once you get a glimpse into *manidò-akì*—the spiritworld—you're always open to it."

"And these would be?"

"I'm guessing they're the *manitou*," Tommy told her. "The ones that belong here."

She looked at him, finally registering the odd catch in his voice.

"You've never seen them before, either, have you?" she said.

Tommy didn't answer. He didn't have to. The wonder in his eyes said it all.

5

Los Días de Muertos

Caras vemos, coazones no sabemos.
Faces we see, hearts we know not.
—SPANISH PROVERB

At the end of October, when Anglo children were preparing for Halloween, the San Miguel household readied itself for *el Festival de Communión con los Muertos*, more commonly known as *los Días de Muertos*, the Days of the Dead.

Mamá would pack the family into Abuela's pickup and they would go to stay with her brother's family in Nogales on the Mexican side of the border. Papá would come, too, walking into the desert to find his own way south from Tucson. Mamá would pretend ignorance as to how he traveled, but Abuela and Bettina knew. Bettina would watch the skies the whole drive down to the border, looking for hawks. She knew better than to talk to her sister about it. Adelita remained forever embarrassed by a father who had never ridden in any sort of vehicle powered by an internal combustion engine, who wouldn't even sleep under a roof if the floor underfoot wasn't dirt.

They left home early on October 27th, reaching Tío Raphael's house outside of Nogales in plenty of time to help hang water and bread outside as offerings for the spirits of those with no survivors to greet them and no home to visit—meager offerings, perhaps, but at least the visiting souls found something. On October 28th more food and drink were placed outside the house, this time for spirits of those who died by accident, murder, or other violent means. On the night of the 31st, when Anglo children went trick-or-treating door to door, the spirits of dead children came to visit, staying no later than midday of November 1st when the church bells began to ring to welcome the adult spirits, the Faithful Dead.

This was the time that the family formally greeted the most recently deceased adult, acknowledging through him or her all of their ancestors. In Tío Raphael's home, the candles and copal incense were burned for Gerardo Muñoz, Mamá's oldest brother. Afterwards, Tío Raphael led the family to the homes of his neighbors who had lost a family member during the past year. Food was offered to these spirits as well, but also treasured belongings from times past. A familiar guitar. A holy image. A favorite brand of cigarettes. A bottle of soda. Anything to make the visiting spirits feel at home.

The days were busy, as there was always something to do, some errand to run. A child to comfort, a baby to hold. Sauces needed stirring, nuts had to be ground, fruits sliced. There was always someone being fed, someone hurrying to the market for more peppers or squash, tortillas being heated and spread with chile sauce, a baby bottle being refilled. With each passing day the altar for Tío Gerardo filled with added fruit and candies, flowers, a bottle of tequila, a hot mug of *atole,* pink and blue colored *pan de muerto,* fresh from the bakery.

At sundown of the 1st, everyone went to the public cemetery for the all-night vigil of communication with the dead.

They came by the thousands. Outside the Panteon Nacional, the traffic was bumper to bumper, with countless others arriving on foot, climbing down from the hills above, walking along the dirt road in groups of three and four and more. Inside the cemetery it was impossible not to step on a grave. There were people everywhere, of all ages. They sat on the stones or drew up chairs, stood in clusters. All the graves had been repaired, the area about them swept and cleaned, the stones bedecked with new coats of paint. Tombs, gravestones, slabs, crosses.

It wasn't quiet. There was talking and laughter and gossip, recorded music from radios and cassette players, live music from the small *mariachi* bands who strolled through the crowds playing for a fee. Commerce was everywhere, with vendors selling flowers, balloons, blankets, food and drink, calling from their booths, even using loudspeakers. Many brought their own food as the San Miguel and Muñoz families did. Spicy *mole,* corn-wrapped *tamales,* tortillas, autumn fruits, *pan de muerto,* sugar skulls.

The graves were covered with carpets of colorful marigolds, baby's breath, and purple cockscomb. Copal incense burned, filling the air with its pungent scent. Candles were lit and placed on the gravestones, one for each lost soul, until by midnight the acres of graves in the Panteon Nacional were filled with thousands of candles flickering in the windy autumn darkness. It was at once an eerie and a magical sight. Wrapped in blankets as the night cooled, the crowd thinned, but many stayed through dawn and into the following day.

By the evening of the 2nd, the party was over. The ghosts returned to the world of the dead, encouraged to leave by masked mummers whose job it was to scare away any of the stubborn spirits who tried to linger too long.

"They are brave behind their masks," Papá remarked one year.

"*Claro,*" Tío Raphael told him. "*Los espíritus* can't see their true faces."

"*Aquí estamos,*" Mamá put in. "*Encuéntrenos si puedes.*" We are here . . . find us if you can.

Tío Raphael tried to hand him a skeleton mask but Papá smiled and shook his head.

"At this point in my life," he said, "it would take more than a mask to make me invisible."

There was a moment of uncomfortable silence until Abuela said, "Then perhaps you should bathe more often."

"*Sí,*" Papá told her with a grin. "I could put on a dress and wear perfume as well."

The tension broke with laughter and the moment was forgotten, but it reminded Bettina once again of how differently they saw the world from the others. Abuela, her *papá*, she herself. The others left offerings for the dead, spoke to them, but Bettina could see them, from the sad little dead children on the night of the 31st, to the crowds of ghosts who gathered in the cemetery two days later.

This year was no different. When they had their picnic on Gerardo's grave, candles dripping wax onto the newly painted gravestone, Gerardo's spirit was there, smiling conspiratorially at her as he inhaled the odors of the food and drink they had brought, breathed deep the incense and the scent of the candles. He was already gone when the family began to pack up to leave.

Abuela remained behind when the others left, ostensibly to clean up the mess they had left and commune a little longer with the dead. This was the third year that Bettina stayed to help her. There was little to pick up, and no family spirits left to commune with, but that wasn't why they stayed. It was to do what the mummers in their skeleton masks did, scaring away the stubborn spirits, but Abuela was so much more effective at the task. She sent them on with affection and reasoning.

While Bettina finished gathering their trash, Abuela knelt by her son's gravestone and laid a kiss on the white-washed stone.

"*Vaya manso, mi muerto dulce,*" she said, bidding farewell to Gerardo's ghost, then she rose to her feet.

"You loved him very much," Bettina said.

Her *abuela* smiled. "*Sí.* I love all my children. *Soy madre.* How could I not?"

"Even Mamá?" Bettina asked slyly, knowing how much they argued.

"Perhaps especially her," Abuela said. "She is my only daughter."

"Tío Gerardo was the oldest, wasn't he?"

Bettina had known Tío Gerardo when he was alive, but only briefly. He'd died when she was very young and the memory of those long-ago days was dusty and veiled with cobwebs. She knew him better as a ghost.

"The oldest in this family," Abuela said.

Bettina frowned. "What do you mean?"

"I had another family before. A husband and two beautiful boys."

"What happened to them?"

"Mexican soldiers killed them. They killed everyone in our village. They thought we were Apache."

Bettina frowned. When had the Mexican army fought the Apache? She tried to recall the history lessons in school that she never really paid much attention to.

"But that must have been . . ."

"A very long time ago, sí. I am much older than I look, nieta. I escaped only because I was in the bajada when they came, gathering medicines. When I returned to our village . . ." She looked out across the Panteon Nacional, away to the mountains, her dark eyes unreadable. "I had many graves to dig that day."

"That's so horrible."

Abuela nodded. "It was a terrible time."

"Do you ever . . ." Bettina hesitated, then went on. "At this time of year, do you ever want to go back . . . to be there for when their spirits return . . ."

Abuela touched a hand to Bettina's cheek. "I go every year," she said. She moved her hand and laid it between her breasts. "Here. In my heart."

"Next year I will burn candles for them," Bettina said.

"They would like that," Abuela told her. "But now, come, chica. We have work to do."

They were not alone in their task. Other curanderas walked in the immense acreage of the Panteon Nacional as they did, following a winding path through the graves, pausing wherever a spirit still lingered.

"Es el hora de ir, mi encantó uno," they would say. It is time to go, my loved one.

And they would wait until the spirit understood and drifted away, then move on themselves. It was close to dusk when Abuela and Bettina started back for the gates of the cemetery. As they drew near to Tío Gerardo's grave once more, Bettina spotted a little black dog with a white patch over his left eye, sitting on the grave. It was looking at them, expectant, tongue lolling.

"Look," Bettina said. "What a funny-looking dog, with that patch on his eye."

She turned to find Abuela standing still, regarding the dog with an expression Bettina had never seen before, a strange mix of sadness, surprise, and fear. That last emotion woke a shiver up Bettina's spine. She had never seen her grandmother show fear of anything.

"What is it, Abuela?" she asked, her voice hushed.

"His name is Pedrito," Abuela replied. "He was my dog when I was a little girl."

Bettina couldn't imagine her abuela as a little girl. Then she realized what Abuela had just said. If the dog had been hers when she was a little girl . . .

"You mean he looks like your Pedrito," she said.

Because that dog on Tío Gerardo's grave was no spirit animal, no ghost. It was a living, breathing creature, of that she was sure.

"No," Abuela said. "It is him. I would know him anywhere. We were inseparable for years. He went away when I was only a little younger than you are now."

"Went away. You mean he died?"

Bettina couldn't take her gaze from the dog. He reminded her a little of her *cadejos*, without their outrageous coloring and goat's feet. But he had their lolling smile and obvious good nature.

"No, he didn't die," Abuela said. "He simply ran off one day and we never saw him again."

As if that had been his cue, the dog jumped to his feet. He barked at them, once, twice, a third time, then scampered off through the graves until he was lost to their view.

"What . . . what does it mean, Abuela?" Bettina asked. "You seemed almost frightened . . ."

Abuela smiled. "Frightened? Of Pedrito? ¡No probable! But seeing him there on Gerardo's grave certainly startled me."

"Papá says we must be careful of dogs," Bettina said. As she spoke, she could feel *los cadejos* stir inside her. "That they can open doors into other worlds."

"*Sí,*" Abuela agreed. "But they can close them as well."

"What do you mean?"

"Nothing. Come, we should join the others. Your *mamá* will be thinking that we have wandered off into the mountains."

Bettina let herself be led out of the Panteon Nacional, back to her *tío's* house. Once they were outside the cemetery, she kept an eye out for the little black dog with the white patch over his eye, but he didn't make a reappearance. By the time she did see him again, it was too late to undo the damage he had done.

SONORAN DESERT, NOVEMBER / DECEMBER

The next night, Bettina was home in her own bed. Tomorrow was Sunday and she'd promised Mamá that she would go with her to early mass, so she hadn't stayed up as late as she normally did. But it was now close to midnight and she still couldn't sleep. She wasn't sure why, since she was tired enough. Perhaps it was having stayed up so late the past few nights in Nogales, or the stirring of *los cadejos* who sometimes woke an inexplicable restlessness in her. Perhaps it was only the change in the air pressure. The skies had been heavily overcast all day, the air thick with the promise of a thunderstorm that had yet to come. So far it remained on the horizon, lightning flickering above the mountains accompanied by the faint rumble of distant thunder. Occasionally, the clouds above released a scattering of fat raindrops that were quickly absorbed into the ground. So far, that was all.

After a while she got up and sat by the window, looking out at the darkness that lay beyond the spill of their yard light. As she watched, another splatter of rain ran across the yard, spitting up dust as it hit the ground and was then swallowed by the thirsty dirt. The grumbling thunder sounded closer.

She was about to return to her bed when she saw movement at that place where the darkness of the desert came up to meet the farthest spread of the yard light's illumination. She leaned closer, expecting to see a coyote, hunting cats, perhaps, or a scavenging javelina. But it was the dog who stepped into the light and sat down in the dust. The little black dog with the white patch over his eye that she'd last seen by Tío Gerardo's grave. He was ignoring the raindrops, all of his attention focused on their house.

Bien, she thought. This time I will have a closer look at you.

But before she could dress and leave her room, her *abuela* came walking around the side of the house. The dog waited for her as she approached him, his head cocked to one side, pink tongue hanging from the side of his mouth.

Bettina sat still. An uncomfortable feeling of guilt rose in her, as though she'd planned to sit here and spy on her grandmother, but she couldn't turn away now. The dog bounced to his feet as Abuela drew near to him, then bounded away into the darkness. Abuela appeared to hesitate for a moment, then followed him out into the desert.

Where was she going, following that dog? It seemed so strange, especially remembering that unfamiliar trace of fear in Abuela's features when they'd first come upon the little dog in the Panteon Nacional.

At her window, Bettina pressed closer to the glass. It was no use. Beyond the range of the yard light, the darkness was simply too profound. The glass fogged a little from her breath. Suddenly lightning flashed close by, illuminating the yard and the desert beyond. She had a glimpse of tall saguaro, clusters of prickly pear and cholla, her *abuela*'s back, some distance from the house now, then the light was gone. She jumped as a thunderclap boomed directly overhead, pulse quickening.

The rain followed almost immediately, great sheets of it that came down so hard that even the backyard was no longer visible. It was as she finally turned from the window that the sensation came to her, as abruptly as the flick of a light switch. One moment she was aware of her *abuela*'s presence in the world, the connection that stretched between them, a thousand colored threads of experience and memory all twisted together into the braid that was their relationship. Then it was gone. Cut clean and sudden as though it had never existed. Abuela was no longer in the world. No longer in *la época del mito*. No longer in anyplace that Bettina knew.

The loss tore a hole in her heart that she could not imagine filling again, a bottomless shaft that seemed to put a lie to everything that was good—kindness, hope, love—leaving only an unfamiliar despair.

She couldn't sleep for the rest of the night, hoping she was wrong, knowing she was not. All she could do was sit at the window and stare out into the rain, searching, waiting for the familiar connection to her grandmother to return. But it never did.

The next day, no one could help her. Papá had gone off into the desert with his *peyoteros* as soon as the family had returned from Nogales and everyone else appeared to have an enchantment clinging to them, an onion-skin layer of false memories, thin but impenetrable, that left her frustrated and confused. When she asked after Abuela, Mamá and Adelita looked surprised, spoke of the trip she'd been planning, how she wouldn't be returning for some time. They spoke as though this was old news, as though Abuela had left on this trip a long time ago.

Abuela's friends were no help either. In town, in the desert, in *la época del mito*, the enchantment held true. She hitched a ride out to the Manuels with Juan Vicandi, one of Adelita's older friends who owned a car, but Loleta and Ban seemed as surprised by her questions and offered no new answers to them. The gossips in the market, who could easily devote an hour to someone's change of hair color, were remarkably incurious. In the desert she spent hours tracking down prickly-spined cholla spirits and the calm, slow-speaking saguaro aunts and uncles, she spoke to jackrabbits and phainopepla and Coyote Woman, and learned no more. Deep in *la época del mito*, she found Tadai one afternoon, sunning himself on a flat red rock, and he told the same tale.

It was not that Abuela had never existed, only that she had gone away, had been gone for some time now, and no one was worried or even curious. It wasn't until Papá finally returned she was told another tale. She walked out into the desert with him the evening he came home, comforted by his presence, the smell of his cigarettes, the clasp of his hand around her own. They sat on a rock above a dry wash as she finished her story. From where they sat they could look down on the winding path the wash had taken, the bed still damp from the recent rains. They could hear quail murmuring under the palo verde and mesquite, and the breeze brought them a brief, pungent scent of javelina, here, then gone. In the west, the sunset cast a sliver of orange and pink across the lightly clouded sky.

"*Este perrito,*" he said when she was done. "She said it was her pet when she was a child?"

Bettina nodded. "He was with her for years until he ran away."

Papá grew sorrowful. "*Era el payaso perro de los dioses viejos,*" he said. It was the clown dog of the old gods.

Bettina grew cold. She shook her head, refusing to believe. It couldn't be. But she remembered the stories both Abuela and Papá had told her about *la Maravilla*, how it returned for its master or mistress to show them the way to Mictlan, the land of the dead. Tears welled in her eyes. How had she not connected the stories with the arrival of her *abuela*'s childhood pet and her subsequent disappearance?

"But . . . but why?" she said. "Abuela wasn't sick or . . . or anything . . ."

She couldn't continue.

Papá laid his arm around her shoulders. "There comes a time when each and every one of us must journey on. I know this is no comfort to you now, *chiquita*, but it is the way of things."

Bettina buried her face in his shoulder. For a long time, all she could do was sob. Papá held her close, stroking her hair. He murmured comforting words, but he might as well have been speaking Chinese, for all she could understand or take consolation from them. Finally she was able to sit up. She blew her nose on a crumpled tissue Papá pulled from his pocket and gave to her. Red-eyed, she stared out across the darkening desert. In the distance a coyote yipped and she knew a moment's dark anger for it and all its canine clan.

"If she . . . if she is dead," she finally said, "where is her body? Why does everyone act as if she's only gone away on a trip somewhere?"

Papá rolled a cigarette and lit it before answering. The smoke he exhaled soon disappeared in the dark air.

"*Su abuela,*" he said. "Dorotea Muñoz. She was never like other people. You know this. She traveled to other places, spoke to those that the rest of the world can only imagine. We know this to be true, for you and I, we walk in those same worlds. We know the spirits firsthand."

He glanced at Bettina and she nodded.

"This is a wonderful thing to be able to do," he went on, "but it can be dangerous as well. The spirits are, how do you say . . . *inconstante.*"

"Fickle."

"*Sí. Muy* fickle. And easy to offend. Approach them with respect and they will mostly treat you well. But interfere in their business and they have no patience with you. Their anger is as legendary as their kindness."

"What did she do to make them angry?"

Papá shrugged. "You know your *abuela.* She was never one to allow an injustice to go unchallenged and among the spirits—as it is with us—life is not always fair. What she did . . . this is not something she would speak of, any more than she would speak of her life before marrying your grandfather."

"She told me about it yesterday."

Papá nodded, as though that explained something. "What I do know," he continued, "is that she aligned herself with one spirit which set her at odds with another." He took a final puff from his cigarette and ground it out on the stone they sat upon, pocketing the butt. "It is best not to interfere in the business of spirits—your *abuela* told you that?"

"*Sí.*"

"It is a lesson she learned with more difficulty."

They sat for a time in silence, watching the last of the light leak from the western sky.

"So for that," Bettina said finally. "They just took her away?"

"That," Papá replied. "It is such a small word and can hold so much. Who can tell what enemies she made by interfering in their business? What bargain she struck that she might come safely away once more? *Caras vemos, coazónes no sabemos.*"

Bettina sighed. It was true. One could only guess at what another was thinking or feeling. It was impossible to know.

"I miss her," she said.

Papá put his arm around her again. "*Sí,*" he told her. "I know you do."

"Is there nothing we can do to help her?"

He shook his head. "We must abide by her decision. She went of her own choice? No one forced her?"

"She only followed the little dog, out into the storm."

"Then we have no choice but to respect her choice."

"And mourn."

He nodded. "And mourn. But surely, *chiquita*, with all you have seen and done, you know that departing this life is but the beginning of a new journey."

"But not for us. Not for those who are left behind."

"It seems very final now," he agreed. "Now you must mourn. Light a candle for her and pray for her soul."

It was with great effort that Bettina didn't begin to weep again. She was afraid that if she did this time, she might never stop.

"What—what will we tell the others?" she finally managed to ask.

"Nothing. Whether the enchantment is one she left behind, or that of the spirits, who are we to interfere with it?"

"But why are we untouched by it?"

"You were closer to her than any other," he said. "Some things not even enchantment can take away."

"And you?" she asked.

Papá shrugged. "I am not easily enchanted, by man or spirit."

Who are you truly? Bettina wanted to ask him. Or perhaps the question should be, what are you? Man, hawk, desert spirit. *Curandero*, shaman, *peyotero*. Which, or all? But in the end, she realized, it didn't really matter. He was her *papá* and that was enough.

She leaned closer to him, wishing it was as easy to call Abuela back from where the little dog had led her as it was to be comforted by her *papá*'s embrace.

But she could not spend her life attached to Papá like some Siamese twin. They had each their separate lives. Being able to share the loss of her *abuela* with him helped some, but her sadness remained a gaping hole that nothing seemed to fill. When he went back into the desert, this time to stay, though she did not know that until much later, she tried to carry on with her own life. A life without Abuela who was gone now forever, but who would never be forgotten. She lit a candle in church and another at the shrine of the *inocente*. She skipped school every day and walked out in the desert, repeating Abuela's lessons to herself so that she wouldn't forget them. One day she packed some clothes and went to stay with Rupert and Loleta Manuel, to complete her education in herbal and desert lore.

Mamá would not, could not understand, why she needed to do this. They argued until finally Bettina simply had to walk away. It was months before they spoke again, for Mamá had a formidable way with silence, wielding it like a weapon.

Life with the Manuels was different from how it was at home. Loleta treated her as an adult, spoke to her as an equal, but Bettina also had to shoulder far more responsibility than she did living with her own family. Often it was she alone who set the meals on the table for Loleta and Rupert and what guests they might have visiting that day. She gathered wood for the fire, shared the cleaning, the washing, the preparing of ointments and *amuletos,* learned when to ask assistance of *los santos* and when of the spirits, when to massage an ill, when to treat it with medicine.

But she had freedom, too. Early mornings, afternoons, and sometimes late at night, she walked in the desert surrounding the Manuels' home.

One day Ban came over for dinner and she was surprised to discover that she was no longer interested in whether he viewed her as a woman or a girl. The realization made her feel both relieved and sad. She helped clean up after dinner and sat with the family for a little while before finally making some excuse and escaping out into the night. She wore a sweater against the coolness and went up into the hills, winding through the scrub and cacti until she came to a favorite sitting spot on the stone lip of an arroyo. Far below, mesquites, willows, and cottonwoods clustered along the length of a dry wash. Closer, a few handbreadths from where her feet dangled, petroglyphs had been cut into the gray-brown stone. I'itoi's spiral. What looked like hand prints. Stylized lizards and frogs. Small patch patterns such as could be seen on pottery. Wiggly lines that might be winding rivers or snakes.

It was amazing, Bettina thought every time she saw these ancient markings, that they could last so long. That made her wonder if the occasional spray-painted graffiti she stumbled across would also be here for the next thousand years. She had to smile. Who was to say that the petroglyphs weren't the ancient people's graffiti?

She heard Ban approaching long before he reached her, sensed his *brujería* moving through the scrub. She nodded to him when he sat down on the stone beside her. He hung his long legs over the edge beside hers, toes pointing at the wash below. Somewhere close by she heard an owl hoot. Moments later, they heard the sound of its wings as it passed by overhead, so close that Bettina felt she could have lifted her hand and brushed its wings with her fingers.

Ban pulled an apple out of his pocket and offered it to her. Bettina polished it on her sweater, felt the smoothness of the apple's skin where her gaze saw only a dark round shape in her hand.

"*Gracias,*" she said and bit into it. The sweet juice ran from the corners of her mouth. "Mmm. *Está bueno.*"

Smiling, he reached back into his pocket and took out another for himself.

"I was in the spiritworld today," he said after they'd been munching on their apples for a while. "I went to meet with my namesake, but instead I had a conversation with the spirit of a fairy duster." He hesitated before adding, "Have you met them yet?"

Bettina nodded. Like the flower whose shape they wore, they had a delicate appearance, hair like a pink mist of curls, sweet bony features, eyes slightly too large for their features. She regarded Ban, wondering what it was that had brought him out into the desert to sit with her, what it was that he didn't want to tell her.

"What did you speak of?" she asked.

"*Su abuela.* She . . ." He gave her a pained look. "She is not coming back."

Bettina could feel the tears press against the back of her eyes. Two months now, but the pain was still as constant as her breathing.

"I know," she said, her voice tight.

"This trip she undertook . . ."

"It was no trip. Not like you or I would take—that we, or anybody, is ever ready to take. She followed the clown dog."

"You're sure?"

"I saw them go."

"But you never said anything."

"What could I say?" Bettina asked. "Everybody except for Papá and I were under *un encantamiento.*"

Ban gave a slow nod. "*Sí.* It *was* an enchantment. I was held fast in it as much as anyone else, until the fairy duster told me as much. When she spoke, I could feel the veil lift from my eyes. It was like that time when we were looking for I'itoi's cave. Until you pointed it out, none of us could see the entrance, though it was there in front of us all the time."

"What do you see now?" Bettina asked.

Ban looked away, into the darkness that lay on the far side of the arroyo.

"Sadness," he said. "Yours, mine. My mother and father's when they learn what I have just told you."

"It doesn't go away," Bettina told him.

"How could it?" Ban said. "She filled our lives."

Was that the reason behind the enchantment? Bettina wondered. Had the spirits meant it as a kindness so that Abuela's departure would not leave them all feeling so bereft?

"This spirit you met . . . did she say why Abuela was taken?"

"It was to ransom her daughter—your mother. Long ago, before either you or Adelita were born. One of *los santos* came to bear the child's spirit away, but your *abuela* would not allow it. She made a bargain with Death, who laid his protection upon the child and kept *los santos* from taking her."

So that explained Abuela's distrust of the church, though not Mamá's devotion.

"Because of that, her life was forfeit to him," Ban went on. "*A la Muerte.*

Not then. Not for many years, as it turned out. But when he called, she would have to come, willingly and alive."

"Why alive?"

"Of what use is a dead *curandera*? Dead, she is only a spirit such as the rest of us will one day be."

"But what would Death need with a healer?"

"Who can say what illnesses they might suffer, even in Mictlan."

Bettina nodded. She considered what she'd been told.

"It was for *la brujería*," she said finally. "That is why Abuela made her bargain. That *la brujería* pass through Mamá to Adelita and me." She shook her head. "It was not worth her life."

"No?" Ban said. "Not when she knew, as we all know, that one day we must die anyway? Who would not have their death mean something?"

"But she's not dead. She went alive into Mictlan."

"*Sí*. But dead or alive when entering, no one returns from *la Muerte's* realm."

"Except for *los Días de Muertos*," Bettina said.

Ban nodded. "When the spirits of the dead visit, not the spirits of the living."

Now Bettina truly understood the bargain her *abuela* had made. When all the other dead returned to their graves and places of death, her *abuela* would not be able to join them, would not see how she was honored and remembered herself. Bettina would never see her again, alive or as a spirit.

"Papá thought she had come between rival spirits," she said after a moment.

"It seems to me that she did."

"I suppose. I never thought of *los santos* in such a way. As spirits, I mean."

"The saints and martyrs . . . none of them are alive anymore. What else can they be?"

"*Es verdad.*"

Bettina sighed and shook her head. It made no sense.

"*Los santos*. The desert spirits," she said. "What would any of them want with a newborn child?"

"Its purity. This is not a new thing. Yours *papá's* ancestors used to offer virgins to the gods."

Bettina had come to realize that her *papá* was much older than those ancient peoples all of them had considered to be his ancestors, but she made no mention of that now.

"Was the world ever sane?" she said.

"Do not be so hard on your *abuela*," Ban said. "It could not have been for *la brujería* alone that she made this bargain."

"What other reason was there?"

"The love she had for her newborn daughter. Would you have denied your *mamá* her chance at life?"

Bettina felt sick at the thought. "*¡Mi dios!* Of course not."

The moon had risen while they spoke, transforming the surrounding desert into a magical landscape that Bettina only half noticed. In the moonlight, the distance between this world and *la época del mito* seemed nonexistent. The far-off cries of coyotes, the hooting of owls, the snuffling of javalenas down in the arroyo, mingled with the voices of the spiritworld. Saguaro aunts and uncles. The spirits of cholla and prickly pear, mesquite, and desert broom.

"I wonder why the fairy duster spoke to you and not to me," she said. "I thought I had asked them all. Surely it would have known my need."

Ban shrugged. "I respect the spirits," he said, "but I don't understand them."

"*Sí.* Who truly does?"

"What will you do now?" Ban asked.

"Become the person who would best make Abuela proud," she replied without hesitation. "I will learn all I can and become a good *curandera*. I will gather what power the spirits will allow me and use it to benefit whoever asks for my help."

"Power is not something you want," Ban told her.

She gave him a puzzled look. "*¿Porqué no?*"

"Because whenever one person has it, someone else doesn't. There is only so much to go around. Power is an ugly thing, like a man hitting a woman or a child. You want to ask the spirits for luck."

He used the word in a context Bettina wasn't sure she understood.

"What do you mean by luck?" she asked.

"Unlike power, luck is sweet. Like a kiss, or a hug."

Bettina gave a slow nod. She remembered Abuela often speaking of luck, but she had simply assumed her grandmother was referring to *la brujería*. Now she understood. Luck was a gift, a loan, something one held only to pass on.

"Who taught you that?" she asked. "Your spirit namesake?"

"No. It was Rupert."

Bettina smiled. "We are lucky to have such wise *papás*."

"*Sí.*"

They sat a while longer, absorbing the night and the quiet companionship they were able to share with each other. After a time, Bettina turned to look at Ban, studying his features in the moonlight.

"Did you ever want to make love to me?" she said.

She couldn't believe she was asking him that. From Ban's astonished expression, she supposed that he couldn't either.

"No," he said, shaking his head. "You are like a little sister to me. What makes you ask such a thing?"

"I . . . I was just wondering. I had the biggest crush on you for the longest time."

"This was something you wanted? That we be . . . lovers?"

She nodded. "But not anymore."

She could tell the conversation was making him uncomfortable, but she could sense he was flattered as well. And curious.

"What changed?" he asked.

She had to look away.

"I have only a hole in me where once I kept the ability to love," she said. "I feel only emptiness inside."

He put his arm around her shoulders, but it was a brother's arm, to comfort her, nothing more.

"And your *cadejos*?" he asked.

"I am not so fond of dogs anymore," she told him.

"You sent them away?"

"I didn't have to. They know how I feel about spirit dogs now. They must be gone for I haven't felt them stir since the night Abuela walked into the storm."

She searched for them as she leaned against him, but there was nothing. No stirring deep inside her chest. No distant inner voices that were part child's cry, part coyote yip. She didn't miss them. The loss of her *abuela* overshadowed everything that had to do with feelings, everything warm and kind that might lie in her heart.

6

Ice

The fates lead him who will; him who won't they drag.
—OLD ROMAN SAYING

1

TUESDAY MORNING, JANUARY 20

Ellie realized that she hadn't really known what to expect when they finally drove into the rez. Not teepees, of course, or even log cabins, but she'd thought it would be more rustic, more indigenous, than what it was: basically a combination of an old suburban housing tract gone to decay, ramshackle unfinished buildings, and a trailer park. Except for a few fancier homes that stood out because of their obvious quality, it was all double-wides and bungalows and aluminum siding, where the walls weren't simply uncovered Black Joe or Styrofoam board insulation.

"You're getting a good view of the place," Tommy said. "It almost looks pretty tonight."

Really? Ellie thought. But she supposed he was right. The ice storm had lent its magical sheen to the scene, a cascade of shimmering sparkles highlighted by the pickup's head-beams. Theirs was the only strong light. They'd passed downed power and phone lines a few miles back on the highway. With the power out, the only illumination coming from the buildings was the dim glow cast by candles, oil lamps, and fireplaces. While it looked romantic, the reality would be anything but. Especially if the temperature dropped and water pipes started to freeze and burst. When she mentioned this to her companions, Tommy told them about the young daughter of a friend of his who, during a power failure last year, said to her mother, "Mommy, let's go home and watch TV by candlelight."

Ellie and Hunter laughed with him—a little more than the joke was worth, but by this point, they needed all the laughs they could get. The dashboard clock read 4:35 A.M. All three of them were punchy from the tension of the long drive. The longer they were on the highway, the more treacherous the driving conditions had gotten. Ellie was surprised that they'd actually made it to the rez without running off the road.

"Looking at the houses," Tommy added, "you can tell who had the good crops this year."

"How so?" Hunter asked.

"Anyplace that doesn't look like it's about to fall in on itself, the people did well."

"What do they grow?" Ellie asked.

Tommy laughed. "In these hills, what do you think? Kickaha Gold."

"You mean marijuana?"

"I don't mean corn."

"How do they get away with it?"

"Well, the cops send in choppers, but there's a lot of wild land out there and they don't find everything. This is kind of a new thing for the rez, actually. I mean people always grew a little dope, but not on the scale they do now. See, there used to be this hillbilly Mafia that lived up in Freakwater Hollow. The Morgans. They pretty much had all the major-league bootlegging and dope fields sewn up until back in the mid-eighties when the whole clan got wiped out. But before that happened, you just didn't step on their turf."

"What happened to them?" Hunter asked.

Tommy shrugged. "There's different stories. Some said they got into a feud with some competitors. My aunts say they got on the wrong side of one of the *manitou*. The facts, at least according to the newspapers, is that this black guy got pissed off with them and cleaned them out, all on his own, if you can believe it. Went up with some army ordnance weaponry and took them all down, then just stood there waiting for the cops to show up and take him away. He got the death penalty and was executed back in '84 or '85, I guess."

"I think I remember reading about that," Hunter said.

"Yeah, it was a big deal at the time. The Morgans weren't particularly well liked or anything—we're talking serious white trash, here—but he must've killed around forty of them, and nobody wants that kind of guy running around."

"Why did your aunts think he was a spirit?" Ellie asked.

"Think about it. There's forty or so well-armed and mean-tempered Morgans up there, and he's this one guy. Those kind of odds only work out in a Bruce Willis movie." He gave Ellie a grin. "Or spirit tales."

"I still don't see why the elders let this go on," she said. "When you think of all the problems with addiction there already are on the rez . . ."

"Nobody sells their crops here," Tommy told her. "It all goes out to the big cities. Hell, nobody here could afford to buy it except for the other grow-ers, anyway, and why would they buy it? But personally, I don't get all turned around about smoking a little dope. Kids here'll do anything to get high. I'm not promoting it or anything, but I'd rather see them smoking dope than sniff-ing glue or gasoline or becoming an alkie like yours truly."

"I suppose. But if it starts them on the road to harder drugs—"

"Oh, that's such bullshit," Tommy said. "What turns people into junkies and alkies is an addictive personality. Hell, most of us have a bent towards an addiction of some sort or another, we're just not all as extreme. But when you combine a seriously addictive personality with the hopelessness of the poverty most of these kids grow up in, smoking a little dope barely enters into the equation."

"I guess I got lucky," Hunter put in. "I'm just addicted to music."

"Amen, brother."

"It seems so simplistic," Ellie said. "When you put it like that."

"I guess. But it's a funny old world, isn't it? Who knows what'll set any one of us off on the road better not traveled. In a perfect world the kids wouldn't need to get high just to get through a day, but it's not a perfect world. We all know that firsthand."

This was about as good an opening as Ellie thought she'd get to talk to Tommy about how she didn't have a troubled past like everybody else work-ing with Angel, but she wasn't comfortable bringing it up with Hunter in the cab. Then the opportunity was gone.

"Okay, we're coming up on my Aunt Nancy's place," Tommy said. "A word of warning. She fits the scary wise woman profile better than any of her sisters."

"Oh great," Ellie said.

"Don't worry. She won't be mean, or get all aggressive or anything. She's just kind of . . . formidable. But she's also got the most knowledge for the sorts of things we want to ask about because she draws on more than one tradition."

"How's that?" Hunter asked.

"She had a different father from the other aunts. He was a descendant of one of the freed slaves who came to the hills after the Civil War."

"I don't understand why she has such a normal name," Ellie said. She turned to Hunter, adding, "All the aunts I've heard about so far have names like 'Conception' and 'Serendipity.' "

"I don't know," Tommy said. "Maybe her father gave it to her."

"What happened to him?"

"He had a fatal run-in with those Morgans I was telling you about earlier."

He pulled into a laneway as he spoke, the pickup slewing sideways on the ice. Only the sharp incline of the land leading down to the house saved them from going into the ditch.

"I don't know if we're going to get back out of here," Tommy said as they slid toward an old black Dodge Sedan.

He managed to stop the pickup before it kissed the Dodge's bumper. For a moment they sat in their vehicle, looking at the house. It was a long bungalow that appeared to have been built in pieces, each added to the next when the inhabitants decided they needed more room. Sections had aluminum siding, others some kind of cheap wood paneling. The part of the building closest to the laneway was all Black Joe, peeling in places. Candlelight flickered dimly from one of the windows. Smoke billowed up from a stovepipe chimney that rose out of what appeared to be the oldest part of the house. Parked behind the Dodge was a Chevy pickup and a small Datsun that seemed to be held together by its rust.

"I take it her crop wasn't that great this year," Hunter said.

"Aunt Nancy doesn't do much fieldwork these days."

Ellie shot him a surprised look. "You mean she used to grow marijuana?"

Tommy laughed. "Hardly. But she did spend over half the year in the bush, running a trapline in the winter, harvesting medicines, that kind of thing. Now she just makes day trips. She's in her sixties—still lively, but she says her bones don't appreciate sleeping on dirt anymore."

He opened his door and stepped cautiously out onto the icy lane.

"Watch it," he warned them. "It's slippery."

They made a comical sight, working their way to the front door, hanging onto each other as their feet kept threatening to slip out from under them. Ellie kept an eye out for the antlered men they'd seen earlier, standing half-hidden in the trees alongside the highway, but she couldn't see anything out of the ordinary. Only the ice, so thick now that the cedars were bent almost in two, great arcs of encrusted limbs that touched the ground in places. They hadn't seen the *manitou* since the pack of dogs had given up their chase earlier in the night. One moment the antlered men had been there, mysterious shapes standing guard against the intrusion of the Gentry, the next there were only the trees with nothing lying between them but ice-covered snow drifts.

Tommy knocked on the door, then opened it and ushered them into a warm, dark hall. There was a smoky smell in the air, mixed with other less easily defined odors. Sage, Ellie guessed. And maybe cedar.

"Smudgesticks," Tommy said, as though reading her mind. "Whenever I smell that mix of sage, cedar, and sweetgrass, I know I'm home."

Following his example, they hung their jackets on pegs, removed their boots, then followed him into a candlelit room where three women were waiting for them. Ellie recognized Sunday and nodded hello. Tommy introduced the others as Zulema and Nancy.

It wasn't hard to peg Zulema as Sunday's sister. She was a little taller, face not quite so broad, but the family resemblance was there. There was also a familiarity that she hadn't sensed with Sunday.

"I feel like I've seen you before," Ellie said as they were introduced.

"Probably at one of Angel's benefits. Verity and I help out with them every year."

Ellie nodded. "And around the office, too." She turned to Tommy. "How come you never introduced me before?"

Tommy shrugged. "Didn't think of it."

More likely, Ellie thought, he'd just wanted to keep her off-balance, quoting them the way he did, but making her feel that they didn't really exist. Tommy could drag a joke out way longer than anyone she knew.

Aunt Nancy sat in a rocker by the woodstove. Her features were Native, but with less family resemblance than the other two women shared. Her skin was dark, like coffee with just a dash of milk, and she had the blackest eyes Ellie had ever seen. They appeared to be all pupil, or at least the irises were so dark it made little difference. Though she was obviously much older than either of her sisters, Tommy's description of formidable had been an apt one.

The shadows hung thick on the wall behind the old woman and for a moment they seemed to take on the shape of an enormous spider reaching out towards where Ellie, Hunter, and Tommy were standing. Ellie stifled a gasp and started to take a step backwards, but then one of the candles flickered, the shadows moved, and the spider was gone. The *impression* of a spider, Ellie told herself as Tommy and Hunter looked at her curiously.

Aunt Nancy gave her a toothy smile, then turned to Sunday.

"You had that much right," she said. "Lots of medicine in this one. I'm not surprised the dog boys chose her."

"I'm sorry?" Ellie said.

Aunt Nancy returned her attention to her. "Don't be. You can't be responsible for what others want from you."

"No. That is, what did you mean about medicine and . . . dog boys?"

But she had a good idea without needing to be told. The medicine was what Sunday and Bettina had been talking about, some kind of magic that they insisted she had. The dog boys could only be these Gentry who thought she'd made some kind of bargain with them.

A flicker of humor touched Aunt Nancy's dark eyes. "You don't really need to be told, do you?"

"No," Ellie said slowly. "I guess not."

"Well, I could use a translation," Hunter said.

Aunt Nancy's gaze settled on him.

"I smell blood on you," she said.

"He had a run-in with one of the Gentry," Tommy said.

"Is that what those-who-came are calling themselves these days?" Aunt Nancy asked. "I hope you made him suffer."

"Aunt Nancy's not so enamored with these Irish *manitou*," Tommy explained to the others. "Not to mention the Irish themselves."

The older woman frowned at Tommy. "They didn't make any friends by bringing the dog boys over on their ships."

"You can't blame the Gael for these Gentry," Sunday said. "It's not like we don't have our own monsters."

Zulema nodded. "Windigo. Mishipeshu."

Aunt Nancy continued to frown, but nodded in grudging assent. Then she added, "Although our spirits don't go looking to make trouble."

"Oh, that's right," Zulema said. "I forgot. We're all such innocents, we Kickaha and our *manitou*."

It seemed to be an old argument. There was a moment of uncomfortable silence broken only by the crackle of the fire in the woodstove, then Sunday stood up.

"Sit," she told Ellie and her companions. "Make yourself comfortable and I'll put on some tea. Then you can tell us what brought you."

Over tea and homemade corn biscuits, they related everything that happened to them so far. Most of the telling was left up to Ellie, though Hunter filled her story in with his own experiences and what he'd learned from Miki. Towards the end, Ellie kept having to stifle yawns. The combination of the herb tea, the long night's drive, and the smoky warmth of the room was making her drowsy.

"We can help you," Sunday said when Ellie finally finished up.

Aunt Nancy nodded in agreement. "The first thing we need to do is get that mask away from the dog boys. Spirits we can protect you from—for a time, anyway—but the creature that mask would call up is deep, old trouble."

"I didn't think Green Men were evil," Hunter said. "At least not from the little I know about them."

"They're not," Zulema said. "They simply are, neither good or bad. But they'll take direction from whoever wears the mask. If a good man were to call that old spirit up, no one would have to worry. The thing is, good men don't reach for that kind of power in the first place."

"But if someone like Donal were to put it on . . ." Ellie said.

"From what you've been telling us, we could have a monster on our hands."

Aunt Nancy stood up and stretched. "But first we need to get some rest. I've seen you yawning, girl," she added as Ellie began to shake her head. "You'll be no good for anything, asleep on your feet."

"I doubt the highway's even passable now anyway," Tommy said.

Ellie looked around the room, searching for an ally. "But . . ."

"Those-who-came can't do anything until you've fixed up the mask for them," Aunt Nancy said. "Isn't that what you said?"

"I don't know for sure . . ."

"And they won't come looking for you here. Trust us in this. Get some sleep. If the weather doesn't let up, there are other ways to get to the city, but right now all the dog boys'll be able to do is sit around and sniff each other's asses."

"If you say so," Ellie said.

Her tired eyes went wide as the shape of that giant spider seemed to grow out of the shadows behind Aunt Nancy's chair once more.

"Don't worry," the older woman said. "I know a thing or two about spirits."

Ellie swallowed dryly and let herself be led away to a bedroom. She thought she'd lie staring at the ceiling for hours, but she was out as soon as her head hit the pillow.

2

Miki woke with one side of her face resting on a soft shoulder, the other feeling a little numb from the cold. She and Fiona had fallen asleep on the couch, the comforter from Fiona's bed pulled up around their chins. Sitting up now, she felt Fiona stir awake beside her.

"This sucks," Fiona mumbled.

Miki nodded. It was cold enough in the apartment that they could see their own breath.

"The power's still off," she said.

"Figures. I could kill for a cup of coffee."

Miki pushed aside the comforter and walked over to the window, hugging herself to stop from shivering. On the couch, Fiona gathered the comforter closer about herself.

"Anything out there?" she asked.

Miki shook her head. "Just the rain."

"So we made it through the night." When Miki turned to look at her, Fiona added, "I don't suppose these Gentry hole up during the day like vampires are supposed to?"

"Not that I've ever heard."

"Great. As if. So now what we do?"

"We could go by the store and see if it's got power," Miki said.

"But we wouldn't open for business?"

Miki smiled. "Only idiots would be out today if they didn't have to be. I'm betting the whole city's shut down, so who would we sell anything to?"

"At least we'd be warm."

"We could bring a kettle," Miki said, "and the makings for coffee."

Fiona threw back the comforter and stood up. "You just said the magic words."

It turned out they weren't the only idiots braving the weather this morning, though there certainly weren't many people out and about. The downtown streets were like a skating rink, all except for a few of the major thoroughfares like Williamson and Lee that the city work crews kept plowing and salting on a regular, rotating basis, but there was little traffic even on them. Most of the businesses they passed were closed—confirming Miki's feelings. So they wouldn't bother to open Gypsy Records either. She and Fiona would just get warm, have a coffee, and listen to some sounds while they waited for the weather to break.

It took them forever to get to the store, slipping and sliding, wishing for the skates neither of them even owned as they shuffled along like a pair of old ladies. When they finally arrived, not only were they still cold, but they were wet as well from the steady drizzle of freezing rain. They found some fellow idiots waiting for them outside the store: Adam and Titus, huddled up against the front door where they had a little bit of protection from the rain. They nursed cardboard cups of take-out coffee that smelled like heaven when Miki caught a whiff.

"Hey, it's about time you showed up," Adam said. He pushed the wet mop of his normally spiky hair away from his eyes. "We should have been open, like, a half-hour ago."

He was wearing his leather vintage motorcycle jacket as usual, which always amused Miki since the closest he'd ever been to owning a two-wheeled vehicle was a bicycle. Jeans and sneakers, with the inevitable T-shirt under the jacket, completed his wardrobe, all of which added up to his being as cold and wet as they were, though his discomfort was from a fashion choice. Not that he chose to be miserable; he just had to look cool. Bedraggled, dripping icy water, sniffling from a running nose, didn't really cut it as cool so far as Miki was concerned. But then she doubted that she or Fiona looked any more charming. She wondered if he or Titus had been shivering in a cold apartment all night the way they had.

"Open for who?" Miki asked.

He had to think about that for a moment. "For the principle of it," he said.

Fiona laughed. "As if."

"So why are you here?" Titus asked.

"The power went off just before midnight," Miki said, "and we've been freezing ever since."

Adam waved a hand towards the store. "Well, there's light and heat inside. All we need is a key."

"Which I have."

"I'm going for coffee," Fiona said. "The Monkey Woman's open, right?"

Adam held up his cup and nodded. "I don't think Ernestina's ever been closed for anything."

"That's true," Fiona said. "I'm so glad we don't have to go the instant coffee route. You want anything, Miki?"

"Coffee, toasted fried egg sandwich, and a pack of smokes."

She handed over a couple of bills to pay for her share, then produced her store key and opened the door. While Fiona set off for the Monkey Woman's Nest, the rest of them trooped inside the store.

"I'll get the alarm," Titus said.

Miki nodded. She shut the door and smiled. It was dry. It was warm. Breakfast was on its way. And to her surprise, she was even happy to have found Adam and Titus waiting on the stoop of the door. Would wonders never cease?

"What are you grinning about?" Adam asked.

"Small pleasures," she told him.

She walked by him and went behind the counter. Switching on the sound system, she put on a CD by the Specials, one of Adam's favorite Ska groups.

"You're not feeling well, are you?" he said as the infectious music woke on the sound system.

Miki took off the knapsack she'd borrowed from Fiona to carry her Hohner, the kettle, and makings for coffee, carefully setting it in a corner where no one would step on it.

"Life's shite, and then you die," she said.

"Your point being?"

"I find that unacceptable, so I've decided to have a more positive outlook on everything."

Adam shook his head and started for the back room. Before he reached the door, Titus popped his head out.

"So should we keep working on the returns?" he asked.

"Can if you want," Miki told him. "I'm not expecting any shipments or customers myself, so I'm just going to curl up with a magazine and enjoy the warmth, bugger the idea of business."

Titus gave her a confused look.

"She's gone all warm and hopeful," Adam told him. "It's the new Miki. Apparently aliens have stolen the old one away."

"Oh," Titus said.

He gave her another look, considering this time.

"Well, that's all right, then," he said and disappeared back into his shipping-receiving lair.

Later Miki was sitting by herself at the counter, flipping through an issue of the British music magazine *Mojo*. Coltrane was on the CD player, but no one was complaining—though perhaps the fact that they were all hiding out in the back room was some sort of statement as to what they actually thought of the album. Their loss. She wasn't going to let it spoil her hard-earned good mood. She'd had her breakfast and a coffee, and she was finally warm enough to consider standing out by the front door to have a cigarette.

"Is it true?"

She started at Adam's voice. She hadn't heard him come out from the back.

"Is what true?" she asked.

"What Fiona was saying, about how some goblins trashed your apartment."

Miki shook her head. "They weren't goblins."

"Then what were they?"

Miki sighed. She really didn't have the strength to go through it all over again.

"I'm not making fun of you," Adam told her. "I'm just curious. I mean, it's a weird story."

"Very," she agreed.

"So what were they like? You've got Fiona all freaked about them."

"They're just these . . ."

Movement by the window caught Miki's attention, pulling her gaze away from Adam's face. When her head turned, his own gaze followed hers. Miki's heart sank, good mood fled like the pathetic lie it had been. For there they were, the original bad pennies, standing in a line in front of the store window. The Gentry in all their mean-spirited glory. Miki swallowed, her throat feeling thick.

"That . . . that's them?" Adam asked.

"Yeah."

"They look like something out of a bad spaghetti Western with those dusters."

They're not funny, Miki wanted to say, but one of the Gentry kicked the door, and there was no more time for talk. The door swung open, crashing against a rack of CDs that Miki had thought of moving all morning because they seemed to be too close to the door. The rack tumbled over, spitting CDs all over the floor.

"Hey!" Adam said as the Gentry came sauntering in.

Miki grabbed his arm when he moved towards them and pulled him back. "Don't," she told him.

The Gentry filled the room with their presence, laying a heaviness on the air, a promise of violence that made it hard to breathe. There were savage lights in their eyes and they smelled like wolves.

"So she was very specific," one of the hard men said in a thickly accented voice. He seemed to be the leader. "Your sculptor, that is. Very specific about who was under her protection and who wasn't. Funny thing, though. She didn't say anything about you lot. Makes you bloody wonder, doesn't it? Here you go, thinking you're all friends, and then she just abandons you like the shite you are."

"What . . . what the hell's he talking about?" Adam said.

"Blood for blood," the hard man said.

"Nobody here's hurt you," Miki told him.

"But he did," the hard man said. "Your man who owns this place. And he's under her protection."

He was talking about Ellie, Miki realized, clueing in to the sculptor reference, but otherwise she didn't know what he was on about with this protection business. Still, she knew who'd been hurt. Hunter had told her last night about the dead Gentry he'd left in her apartment, how the others had chased him through the streets until he'd managed to run into Tommy and Ellie.

"So that leaves you lot to pay," one of the other hard men said.

"Miki . . . ?" Adam began.

He turned, looking to her for direction. But she had nothing to say. What could she say? Her own fear had already banished any bravado she might have been able to muster. Yesterday's red anger at what they'd done to her apartment was somebody else's memory, somebody else's raw emotion. All she could do was hold onto the edge of the counter and pray for some miracle that wasn't going to come.

3

Kellygnow, like the other estates on the hill, had lost its power and phone services overnight, but Bettina had already been asleep when the lines went down. She didn't know anything about it until she woke to a cold room the next morning and suspected the worst. Shivering, she dressed and made her way down to the kitchen where she found Nuala and a number of the other residents gathered around the big cast-iron stove that stood in one corner of the room. Bettina had never seen the stove lit before. She hadn't even known it actually worked. But she was glad of it now. The warmth of the kitchen was like a welcoming embrace as she came in from the cold hall.

"What happened?" she asked Chantal.

"The lines are all down. Penny was just listening to her Walkman and they say we might not get our power back for three or four days."

Bettina glanced at the small, blonde writer Chantal had mentioned, then turned her attention to the window.

"And it's still raining," she said.

Chantal nodded. "Which is only making things worse. They get a line back up on one part of a block, only to have the weight of the ice bring a tree down across it again a little farther down the street."

"Half the city's blacked out," Penny said, lifting one of her earphones away from ear. "And most of the outlying regions. You know that line of big hydro towers that you can see from Highway 14? They came toppling down this morning, one after the other, falling like dominoes. And the worst thing is the weather office is calling for the freezing rain to continue through to the end of the week."

"When a cold front'll probably move in," someone else offered, "and then we'll really be screwed."

Nuala appeared at Bettina's elbow, offering her a cup of coffee and a plate with a fresh blueberry muffin on it. Bettina smiled her thanks and accepted them gratefully.

"This is serious," she said.

"Very much so," the housekeeper replied. "We have a generator to keep the freezer going and the pipes from freezing if the temperature should drop, and we can heat many of the rooms with their fireplaces, but others in the city aren't going to be so well prepared."

"We'll have to help them."

"We will do what we can," Nuala agreed. "But first we need to take a head count to make sure everyone here is accounted for. Has anyone seen Franklin or Ellie?"

There was a general shaking of heads, with one person asking, "Who's Ellie?"

Bettina shook her head. "I just got up."

"How about James?" Nuala asked.

"I don't think Ellie came back last night," Chantal said. "We were going to share a room, remember, but she wasn't back by the time I went to sleep and her bed hasn't been slept in."

"If she was out last night," Lisette said, "she'd never make it back up Handfast Road again. It's got to be a skating rink, except—" She tilted her hand at a forty-five-degree angle. "It won't exactly be flat."

"Are the phones working?" Bettina asked.

Nuala shook her head.

Bettina sighed. "I hope Salvador and his family are all right."

"I'm sure they're fine," Nuala said.

Taking charge, Nuala divided them up then, sending them off in pairs to go through the house for the head count. Bettina and Chantal were given the cottage detail. Chantal gave Bettina a look of mock horror and mouthed the words "the Recluse."

Qué suerte, Bettina thought, remembering the unfriendly woman from the other day. How lucky for them.

But she was curious to go outside.

They put on coats and boots and headed out the door, where Bettina found last night's wonderland transformed into this morning's dismal prospect. Water dripped everywhere, as though the world had come down with a bad cold overnight and woke with a runny nose. Everything was depressingly gray. Even the evergreens, coated as they were with ice and drooping, had been leached of most of their color. There were puddles the size of small ponds in the lower parts of the lawn and at least an inch of water lay on top of the ice at the bottom of the stairs and along the walk. The smaller trees were bent almost in two, the boughs of the larger ones dipped alarmingly. Everywhere she looked there was a clutter of fallen branches.

"God, what a miserable day," Chantal said, the gloomy view penetrating even her usual good humor, if only for a moment. "Still it could be worse."

"It can always be worse," Bettina agreed.

"Yeah. We could be mailmen, or meter-readers. Imagine having to make rounds on a day like this. Though maybe it'd be considered a, what? A rain day, I guess, and they'd get the day off, so actually it would be good to be a mailman today."

Bettina laughed. "I don't think Nuala will give us a rain day," she said and started down the stairs.

Her feet went out from under her as soon as she stepped on the ice at the bottom of the stairs. She grabbed for Chantal and they both would have gone down if Chantal hadn't managed to catch hold of the end of the banister and steady them. They grinned at each other.

"Well, now," Chantal said. "If they start considering synchronized falling for the Olympics, we'd be a shoo-in."

Bettina thought of simply taking Chantal into the between where they'd have neither ice nor rain to contend with, but she knew it wouldn't be a good idea. Most people found the sensation of that place between this world and *la época del mito* as disorienting as *la época del mito* itself.

"You're knocking on the Recluse's door," Chantal said as they edged their way toward the lawn where at least they could break the crust of ice on top of the snow and get some steadier footing.

"No, no," Bettina told her. "It'll have to be you."

"I don't want her snapping at me the way she did with you the other day."

"Your smile will win her over."

"Oh, right."

They reached the snow and Bettina immediately felt better with the surer footing. They started across the lawn towards the cottages, only stopping when a man's voice hailed them.

"Bettina! Wait up there!"

Turning, they found a wet Donal slogging across the lawn towards them. Bettina regarded him suspiciously. He was wet, but not as wet as he should be. It was more as if he'd been hiding in one of the sheds, waiting to make his presence known.

"Do you know him?" Chantal asked as they waited for him to join them.

"He's Ellie's friend."

"Jaysus, Mary, and Joseph," Donal said as he reached them. "Can you believe this shite for weather? I'm Donal," he added, offering his hand to Chantal.

Bettina introduced Chantal, then asked, "What brings you up here?"

"I'm looking for Ellie. Is she inside?"

"She never came back last night."

"Bloody hell."

"How'd you get here?" Chantal asked.

"I feel like I swam, and uphill to boot. My van got bogged down in a puddle the size of a lake over by Battersfield and I came the rest of the way on foot. The roads are pure shite, sheets of ice from one side to the other. So what're you lot up to?"

There was the smell of the wolf about him, Bettina found herself thinking.

"We're just checking to make sure everyone's okay in the cabins," Chantal said.

"You mind if I go in the big house and dry off?" Donal asked.

Bettina thought that perhaps she did. She'd been uneasy with him the first time they'd met. Today she didn't trust him at all, though she couldn't have said why. But they couldn't simply send him away, not in this weather.

"Sure," Chantal told him, obviously unaware of the signals Bettina was receiving. "Go in through the kitchen door. If no one's there, help yourself to some coffee. We won't be long."

"Brilliant. I'll see you inside when you get back."

Bettina stood where she was, watching him go, until Chantal touched her arm.

"Earth to Bettina."

She turned to look at her friend. "*Perdona.* It's just . . . he worries me, that man."

Chantal's gaze went past Bettina, following Donal as he reached the kitchen door and went inside.

"Is this magic worry or everyday worry?" she asked.

"I can't tell," Bettina said. "It's only a feeling."

Chantal's gaze returned to Bettina. "What do you know about him?"

Bettina shrugged. "Nothing. Just that he's a friend of Ellie's."

Chantal considered that for a moment.

"Well," she said finally. "Nuala won't let him get out of line. And we won't be long. Unless you want to keep arguing about who's going to knock on the Recluse's door."

"We'll save her for last," Bettina said. "Besides, there's smoke coming from her chimney. I'm sure she's okay."

"At least the place isn't made of gingerbread," Chantal said as they walked by, their footsteps crunching in the snow.

Bettina gave her a confused look.

"You know," Chantal said. "As in Hansel and Gretel, wicked witches eating innocent passersby."

"Oh, the fairy tale."

"Well, yes. Jeez, where did you grow up?"

"In the desert."

Chantal ducked under a low-hanging branch that was twice its usual diameter with the thick sheath of ice coating it.

"I knew that," she said.

"I learned different stories," Bettina told her as she ducked under the branch as well.

A twig caught in her hair. When she pulled free, dozens of little shards of ice fell around her, tinkling on the ice-encrusted snow.

"Is it always like this in the winter?" she asked as she caught up to Chantal.

"Pretty much. I mean, we always get some freezing rain, but I can't remember it ever being this bad before. Something else we can blame on El Niño, I suppose."

"Since we won't take responsibility for it ourselves."

Chantal nodded thoughtfully. "That's true."

They'd reached the first of the cabins. Chantal rapped on the door with a mittened knuckle.

"Anybody home?" she called.

4

Perfect, Donal thought as he slipped into the kitchen. He paused a moment to get his bearings, then crossed the floor to where a door opened out into a hallway. The sculptors' studios were all on the ground floor, he remembered from when he'd come up for a couple of parties with Jilly, though that was years ago. Still, he doubted things had changed much. He stopped again in the main hall, undecided, then he heard footsteps approaching. Turning, he saw a short blonde woman wearing a Walkman.

"Hello, there," he said.

This moment's mask was warm and friendly, projecting all harmlessness and charm. He had every right to be here. No, he was *expected* to be here.

The woman pulled the earphones from her head. "Hello. Are you looking for something?"

"I just need to know where the sculptors' studios are."

"Down that hall," she told him, pointing. "Follow the right turn, then it's the next three or four doors on your right."

"You're a dear," Donal said, letting his accent grow a little stronger. He turned up the wattage on his smile. "Ta."

She returned his smile, and then he was off again, ambling, no hurry, no worry, until he turned a corner and quickened his pace. He counted doors, opening the third. He took a quick look, definitely a sculptor's studio, but he didn't recognize anything that belonged to Ellie and there was no mask. He tried the next room. Bingo. There it was, lying on what must be Ellie's worktable as though it were no more than some curious knickknack.

He glanced down either side of the hallway, saw he was still alone, and slipped into the room, closing the door behind him. There was no lock, but he didn't need any more time than it would take to slip the two halves of the mask into one of the oversize pockets of his coat. Crossing over to the worktable, he studied Ellie's sketches. There were more of Bettina and the woman he'd seen her with outside than there were of the mask, but enough that he could see where she was planning to go with it.

No doubt about it, it would be a beauty. But it wasn't necessary. All that was needed was a little glue and what was already here would do admirably— he was sure of it. Never mind the Gentry's convoluted plans. They were only complicating matters. The mask was here, the two pieces so long separated finally brought together again. Jaysus, wasn't that magic enough?

He could feel the power pulsing in the wood when he picked the pieces up and fit them together. The join was almost seamless. He hesitated, smoothing the wood with his thumbs, but couldn't resist fitting the mask up against his face, carefully holding the two pieces together. For a moment there was nothing, only the odd view of the room as seen through the eye slits and a deep, woody smell—mulch and black dirt and old rotting wood all swirling together into a heady brew. But then he could feel the mask settling against his face, embracing his features as though it was no longer wood, but something more pliable like cloth, fitting itself to the contours of his face.

Spooked, he started to pull it off. The bloody thing wouldn't budge. What the . . . ?

He didn't panic until the burning began. It felt like the mask was metal, hot from the forge, pressed against his face, searing his skin. The pain dropped him to his knees. He scrabbled at the mask with his fingers, trying to find the edges, but there was no longer any differentiation between the mask and his body. The edges of the mask had grown into his skin. He dug harder, fingernails burrowing into what felt like bark and pulpy plant tissue. His hair and beard were thick vines now, sprouting tendrils and splays of leaves. He could feel his body swelling, pressing against his shirt and coat until the cloth split along the length of his spine.

The pain spread everywhere, burning deep into his chest, his groin, his limbs. He pressed his head against the floor, fell over onto his side, still clawing at the mask.

Sweet Jaysus . . .

He could hear a distant wailing and realized it was his own voice, a desperate, wretched sound that rang only in his head because his jaws were locked shut, more wood than flesh and bone.

He found himself remembering a bad acid trip he'd taken once. His last one. No sooner had he dropped the tab, than he knew it was all going wrong and there was not a thing he could do until the drug had worked its way through his system.

"What did you do?" a friend asked him.

"I just let go," he'd replied. "I just lay there in the middle of the bloody floor and let it take me away. Eight hours, gone out of my life, just like that. And that's why it's Guinness, and only the gargle, for me now."

And that's what he did now. He stopped struggling and let the monstrous beast fill him. It allowed the pain to go away. It allowed him to go away. Where his spirit had been, there was now only the raw emotion that had fueled so much of his life. The anger. The rage. The pent-up fury. The railing against the unfairness of the world when it came to how it treated Donal Greer.

5

Ellie woke suddenly out of a dead sleep. She bolted upright, pulse racing, confused, wondering where she was, why she was still wearing her clothes, what had woken her. Then she felt it again, a sensation like fabric tearing, except the fabric was a piece of the world and she was feeling it through the threads that connected her to it. It was as if someone was tearing away a piece of her.

She put her hands to her head and pressed against her temples, as though the pressure would restore her equilibrium the way it could sometimes ease a headache. It helped, but only a little. At least she was able to orient herself. She was in a back bedroom in the house of one of Tommy's aunts, a room where the warmth from the stove didn't reach. She was wearing all her clothes because it was so damned cold with all the power lines down and she'd been too tired to get undressed anyway.

But this thing that had woken her, this lost and desperate feeling . . .

Then the door of the bedroom opened and a tall woman stood there, the shadow of an enormous spider rearing up behind her. Aunt Nancy, Ellie thought and she shivered. For this time the impression of the spider didn't slip away.

"You said it was broken," Aunt Nancy said. There was a grim darkness in her voice. "You said it was broken and you hadn't even started to make a new one."

"But . . . it's true . . ."

"Then how do you explain this?"

This? Ellie thought. But then it came again, that tearing sensation, and she knew.

"I can feel it," she said. "It's like something's tearing."

The older woman said nothing.

"I swear," Ellie told her. "I had nothing to do with whatever's going on. Not that I know of, anyway."

"Yet the world has a hole torn in it and the Great Wheel falters."

"Why?" Ellie asked. "What is it?"

Aunt Nancy regarded her from the doorway for a long moment. The shadowy spider grew wide and tall, spilling into the room.

Please don't let it touch me, Ellie thought.

She held her breath, waiting, arms wrapped around her knees to stop herself from shaking, until slowly it faded away.

"Something terrible has been born," Aunt Nancy said in a quieter voice.

"This has to do with the mask?"

The older woman nodded. "Someone has put it on and woken a sleeping monster."

"But it was broken. Right in two. I saw it. I held the pieces in my own hands."

"That doesn't seem to have made much difference."

"But who did it?" Ellie asked. "Who put it on?"

And if it was so dangerous, why would they be so stupid?

"It must have been your friend," Aunt Nancy said. "The Irishman."

"Donal?"

When Aunt Nancy nodded, Ellie slumped, her hands falling to the bed. Of course. Donal could be that stupid. Hadn't Hunter told them about the painting and what Miki had said, how Donal thought the power of the mask would allow him to get some sort of payback for all the wrongs that had been done to him, imagined and real.

"So now what do we do?" she asked.

"We find him and we stop him."

"And you know how to do this?"

For a moment she thought Aunt Nancy was going to get all pissed-off again, but then the older woman slowly shook her head.

"No," she said. "But there are things we can try."

When Aunt Nancy turned and left the doorway, the room seemed to brighten, as though some of the shadows had followed after her. Ellie tried not to think of that huge spider presence she kept seeing behind Aunt Nancy. She didn't need this, any of this, the magic and the scariness and the way her whole life seemed to be slowly dissolving into one that belonged to a stranger.

The problem was, no one was listening to her. No one was coming up to her and saying, it's okay, we'll take it from here. Instead it was just more and deeper weirdness every time she turned around.

She waited a long heartbeat. No one was calling her, but she knew they were waiting for her all the same.

I don't have anything except for inexperience and disbelief, she wanted to tell them, but that didn't cut it anymore. Not with all she'd seen. Not with *manitou* and the powerful Gentry and the spider shadow and this thing inside her, this tearing sensation like an open wound.

Deal with it, she told herself.

Yeah, right.

Slowly she lowered her feet to the floor and got up to follow Aunt Nancy out into the main room of the house.

6

It was mostly the writers who took up residence in the cabins behind Kellygnow. Bettina wasn't sure why. Perhaps they felt solitude a closer companion, here under the trees, than it could be in the house itself. Except Penny Angelis stayed in one of the cabins and she seemed to spend most of her time in the house, hanging out in the kitchen, gossiping with the various artists in their studios, writing in the library, so what did that say? That people were different, Bettina supposed.

She and Chantal passed by Penny's cabin without bothering to check it since the blonde writer was already accounted for, and moved on to the last of the small outbuildings. It stood on the edge of the property, just before the land took its sudden plunge to the city's streets far below in a tumbling waterfall of granite, hemlocks, and cedar.

"This is August's cabin, isn't it?" Chantal said as they drew near.

Bettina nodded. "Though I haven't seen him for a couple of weeks."

"That's not saying much."

It was true. August Walker wasn't the most sociable of Kellygnow's residents, but sociability wasn't exactly a prerequisite. Only talent was. The one slim volume of his work that Bettina had read was astonishing. Tender, wry, lyric, warm. Not one adjective that would have suited the author himself. He was almost as much of a recluse as the mysterious Musgrave Wood.

"It's funny," she said, thinking of how she'd kept returning to passages in August's book, simply to savor their beauty. "You'd never think, from reading him, that he could be so—"

She was unable to finish. A nova flare of white light exploded between her temples and she dropped to her knees as though she'd been physically struck. Chantal immediately crouched in the snow beside her, her knees crunching through the icy crust. She put her arms around Bettina's shoulders, her gaze darting nervously about.

"Bettina!" she cried. "What is it? What happened?"

Bettina allowed her to help her sit up. For a moment she couldn't speak.

All she could do was look at the house while the intense pain in her head slowly faded to a dull ache.

"Something old and dangerous has been called into the world," she finally said.

"What are you talking about?"

"In the house," Bettina said. "Someone has torn through the fabric of the world . . ."

Someone? Her pulse quickened. Not someone. Donal Greer. So eager to get out of the wet and cold when he had barely seemed to be touched by the weather. Of course. He'd been waiting in the between for an opportunity to get inside the house and commandeer the mask.

"Interesting, isn't it?" a voice said.

Bettina looked away from the house to find her wolf leaning against the trunk of a tree, his own gaze fixed on Kellygnow. His pose was as languid as ever, but his dark eyes glinted with tension.

"Who're you?" Chantal asked, obviously disconcerted at his sudden appearance.

"*Está bien,*" Bettina said. She rose slowly to her feet, grateful for Chantal's arm to keep her steady. "It's okay. He's a friend . . . I think."

"You never answered my question from last night," *el lobe* said.

"I haven't had time to think about it with all the trouble this storm has brought."

"And now it's too late. They have their monster."

Bettina shook her head. "This is different. Ellie never finished the mask."

"Then what was screaming inside my head a few moments ago?" *el lobo* asked.

"A man named Donal Greer."

"I know him. He's a puppy. Desperate to run with the pack, but he lacks the *geasan* to be more than a hanger-on."

By *geasan* Bettina intuited he meant *brujería*. Though he might have meant *cojones*.

"*Quizá, quizá, no,*" she said. "But all the same he was able to wake some old forest spirit with nothing more than his will and that broken mask."

El lobo returned his gaze to the house once more.

"I see," he said softly.

"Well, I don't," Chantal said. "Is anyone going to tell me what's going on?"

"Where to begin?" Bettina said. "We've stumbled into what my *papá* once warned me against, and in no uncertain terms: a struggle between the spirits that has spilled out of *la época del mito* into this world of ours."

"And this *época de* whatever would be what?"

"The spiritworld."

"Of course." Chantal looked from Bettina to *el lobo.* "And you're the good guys, right?"

Bettina shook her head. "I don't even want to be involved, but . . . *so que va.* Here I am in the middle of it all the same."

"And tall dark here?" Chantal asked.

She left "handsome" unsaid, but *el lobo* stood straighter and smiled all the same.

"He is . . . related to those on one side of the struggle."

"Oh, well put," *el lobo* said. "I am Scathmadra," he added, bowing slightly to Chantal and offering her his hand. "At your service."

Chantal shook his hand and introduced herself.

"I know what your name means," Bettina told him. "Surely you can come up with something better?"

"Than the truth?" he said.

"I am so far out of my depth here," Chantal began, "that I don't even—"

She broke off as they heard a great crash from the direction of the house. It was the sound of masonry collapsing, breaking glass, stone blocks tumbling against each other. They turned as one toward Kellygnow.

"*¿Qué . . . ?*" Bettina said.

She'd thought for a moment that one of the towering oaks had come down upon the house, but she soon saw it was something worse. A great, ragged gap had been pounded out in a portion of the wall facing them. Through it came such a creature that even Bettina, in all she had experienced in her travels through *la época del mito,* had never seen the like of before.

It was tall and broad-shouldered with a man's shape, but the proportions were not quite right and its skin seemed more like rough bark than human flesh. The mask Bettina remembered from Ellie's worktable was now a face, fluid, mobile, dark-eyed. Its scraggly hair and beard were a thick tangle of vines. Branches sprouted from its temples like a stag's antlers. A cloak of bark and leaves and tangled vines fell from its shoulders. Caught up in the folds of the cloak and pushing up out of the creature's barklike skin were feathers and bits of fur, moss, fungi, and other less recognizable things.

The creature moved awkwardly, as though uncomfortable in, or unused to its body. For a long moment none of them could speak. They watched it lumber into the woods, its gait growing more graceful with each step. By the time it was lost from their sight, it was moving soundlessly, slipping between the trees like a whisper.

"*Madre de Dios,*" Bettina murmured finally.

"Indeed," *el lobo* said. "The Glasduine is woken and won't this keep the pack busy. There will be no war between them and the local spirits now."

Bettina gave him a questioning look.

"Think of it," he told her. "The pack was to be the creature's master. Now they will be the hunted."

"Why would it go after them?"

El lobo shook his head, as though he was dealing with a child.

"Do you think the Glasduine wouldn't *know* what they had planned for it?" he said. "How they would profane its mystery and glory?"

"*Sí,*" Bettina agreed. "If it was only that great spirit on its own. But Donal called it up. His desires will set its emotional balance."

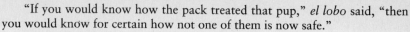

"If you would know how the pack treated that pup," *el lobo* said, "then you would know for certain how not one of them is now safe."

"*Sí, pero todavía . . .*"

But *el lobo* was already gone, stepping into *la época del mito*. Bettina heard Chantal gasp beside her. Of course. To her friend it would seem as though the wolf had simply disappeared. She gave Chantal a sympathetic look.

"It can't be easy," she said. "So many marvels, all at once."

Chantal gave a slow nod. "Remember when I was saying I'd like to be able to see the stuff you do? Well, I take it back—okay?"

"It's too late for that."

"I kind of thought you'd say something like that." She took a deep breath and slowly let it out. "Okay. I'm going to deal with it. One step at a time—if I get to choose the pace at all."

"This is new to me as well," Bettina said. "I can't promise anything."

"So what do we do now?"

Bettina pulled her gaze away from where the creature had disappeared to look back at the house.

"We should make sure no one was hurt," she said.

Chantal nodded and fell into step beside her.

"You know what it looked like?" she said after a moment. "That thing that came out of the house? Like those Green Men from British folklore. You see the image all over the place in England, in churches and the like."

"Donal said something about that."

Donal had said a lot, Bettina remembered, that morning when he and Ellie had first come to the house. Much of it, in retrospect, unpleasant. He'd subscribed such hedonistic and shallow impulses to the Glasduine he remembered from his own childhood stories. If those were what he was using to focus its spirit, the creature would indeed be a monster.

"But I don't remember those Green Men being thought of as evil," Chantal went on. "They were more like primal forest spirits. Jack-in-the-Green. Robin Hood. Even Shakespeare's Puck. More like a trickster than something nasty."

"Old spirits such as they dwell too far away from the world now," Bettina said. "They live deep in the spiritworld, deeper than most travelers can access. To be able to return, they need a vessel to hold their spirit and that's usually a man or a woman. The trouble is, the vessel brings his or her own influences into what has been called forth."

"I don't understand."

"When you bring something like that into the world," Bettina explained, "it takes on your characteristics. If you're kind, it will be a benevolent spirit. But if you are mean-spirited . . ."

"Oh, I get it," Chantal said. "And this Donal guy, he's . . . ?"

"Very troubled," Bettina told her. "I saw a lot of unhappiness and darkness in him. There was goodness as well, but it was a servant to the shadows, not its master."

She put up a hand suddenly and brought Chantal to a stop.

"What . . . ?"

Bettina put a finger to Chantal's lips. "Wait," she said, her voice pitched soft.

Ahead of them they saw the Recluse leave her cabin and stare across the back lawn to where the hole gaped in the side of the house. She began to walk over to it, but then Nuala stepped out of the gap and clambered across the rubble. Nuala met the Recluse halfway across the lawn where an animated argument ensued.

"I'm going to do something that will feel odd to you," Bettina said, still whispering, "but I need to get closer to them to hear what they're saying and I don't have time to explain."

Before Chantal could question her, she pulled the other woman with her into the between, deep enough inside so that they wouldn't be easily remarked by anyone who might look their way, but not so far that they would miss what was being said.

Chantal leaned against her. "I think I feel sick to my stomach."

"I'm sorry," Bettina said.

She would have left Chantal behind, but she was afraid of the creature circling back through the woods and coming upon the sculptor.

"It will pass," she assured Chantal.

"Not quick enough to suit me," Chantal grumbled.

Her face had gone pale and perspiration beaded on her brow.

"Truly," Bettina said. "I'm sorry."

Chantal tried to smile. "What did I tell you about apologizing all the time?"

Eh, *bien*, Bettina thought. She would make it up to her friend, that was a promise. But for now she took Chantal's hand and led her closer to where Nuala and Musgrave Wood were arguing. The freezing rain had plastered the women's hair to their faces, a rain that Bettina and Chantal no longer felt in the between.

"—wake such a thing inside?" Nuala was saying. She was angrier than Bettina had ever seen her, her *brujería* flashing in her eyes. "Someone could have been killed."

"This wasn't what we had planned when—"

But Nuala wasn't listening. "I thought I'd made it clear. Kellygnow is under my protection and I will not have you playing the Morgana within her walls."

"Don't you dare take that tone with me," Musgrave told her, standing taller, glaring at the other woman. "You forget who I am. You are here only on my sufferance."

Nuala shook her head.

"And if it wasn't for me," Musgrave went on, "the Gentry would have taken you down from that high horse of yours a very long ago."

Nuala laughed, but without humor. "Is that what they told you?"

"I know what I know."

"Then mark this, woman. I have always been what you only pretend to be."

"Don't you—"

"And," Nuala went on, "I have what they don't. I have a home; they have only the wilds."

When she said that, Bettina was reminded of her first encounter with her *cadejos*, those rainbow dogs who had been silent for so long, silent because she'd turned away and refused to listen to them after the death dog had stolen her *abuela* away. They, too, had spoken so longingly of a home, had been so grateful to find it in her. She felt a sudden shame to have denied them for so long, for she knew what Nuala was saying was true. All spirits yearned for a home. To be grounded in one place, to have a safe haven waiting for them no matter how far their wanderings might take them.

She wanted to listen for her *cadejos* right now, to call to them, but she couldn't concentrate with the argument going on in front of her.

Musgrave was shaking her head. "You don't have any power . . ."

Nuala's laughter darkened. "Power? Power is for little boys such as those wolves you run with. It's a hurtful thing—have you not understood that yet?"

"You can say that, being what you are. Death has no hold on you."

"Oh, no, Sarah," Nuala said.

Her voice had taken on a sympathetic tone. Bettina and Chantal exchanged glances, the same question rising in both of them. Sarah?

"That's another Gentry lie," Nuala went on. "We can die as readily as a human. Perhaps not by illness or age, but by accident and murder, certainly. The difference is, not all of us fear dying."

"Says the immortal," Musgrave said, bitter. "Death doesn't wait for you around every corner. It doesn't require you to make bargains with the wolves simply to maintain your health."

Nuala shook her head. "No," she said. "So says one who lives in harmony with life, who knows that it is defined by its limitations. Who sees death not as the closing of a door, but the opening of one."

"I can't believe you," Musgrave told her.

"I know. That is why I live in your house, why I have the home, while you live in the wilds with the wolves."

"I have no choice."

"There is always choice," Nuala told her. But she seemed to be growing tired of the argument, and her tone grew less sympathetic. "And here is one you will not forget again: in future, choose to keep your games out of the house, or truly, you will understand what suffering can be."

"You—"

"Listen to me," Nuala told her, her voice hard now. "I am older than those wolves you run with and I am patient, but my patience has limits. Leave me and the house in peace. Do not involve the residents in your games. Ignore my request again and I will wake the salmon and you will finally understand what change means."

Musgrave took a quick step back from the other woman.

"What?" Nuala said. "Do you think I haven't seen you sniffing around his pool, your little mind whirring as you try to see a way to steal his wisdom without risking his waking?"

Musgrave turned abruptly and stalked back to her cabin. Her route took her within a few feet of where Bettina and Chantal were standing in the between, but she took no notice of them.

"They really can't see us, can they?" Chantal whispered to Bettina.

"Or hear us. Are you feeling better now?"

Chantal nodded. "Do you understand any of what they're talking about?"

"Not everything," Bettina told her. "But it has cleared up some things that were puzzling me. Unfortunately, none of it helps in dealing with this creature Donal has pulled into the world."

She paused suddenly, realizing that while Musgrave had been oblivious to their presence, Nuala had not been so easily fooled. Of course she wouldn't be, if all she'd told the Recluse was true. Sighing, Bettina took Chantal by the hand again and stepped back into the world, back into the winter with its wet snow underfoot, the chill in the air and the freezing rain.

"I didn't take you for a spy," Nuala said.

"I'm not," Bettina said, dropping her gaze. "I mean, I'm not usually. I'm just pulled by curiosity into places I shouldn't necessarily be."

"I know," Nuala told her.

Bettina looked at her. "You do?"

Nuala's laugh had all the warmth that her humor with Musgrave had lacked.

"Not the details," she said. "Only that you have a good heart. And that is often enough—if you are also willing to do more than think kindly of others, but help them as well."

"You know that I—"

"Whisht," Nuala said. "I'm not angry. In truth, it's good to not have to hide who I am from at least a few."

"You're like a brownie or a hob," Chantal said. "Aren't you? Keeping everything shipshape, but you'd have to leave if people knew who you were and showed their appreciation."

Nuala smiled. "Something like that."

"How do you know all this?" Bettina asked Chantal.

"I told you before," Chantal said. "I grew up on fairy tales."

When this was all over, Bettina planned to go the library and catch up. For now there was too much else to do, though she couldn't resist trying to satisfy another small puzzle if she could.

"That woman," Bettina asked Nuala. "You called her Sarah, but I thought her name was Musgrave."

"She owns them both, but Sarah was the earlier of the two."

"Sarah Wood?"

Nuala shook her head. "Sarah Hanson. The woman who originally had Kellygnow built as an artist's retreat."

"But she's . . ."

"Long dead?" Nuala finished for her. "So she would be. But she struck a bargain with the wolves. By spending much of each year in the spiritworld, her life has been extended. Have you not noticed that humans who spend much time there don't age as other people do?"

So that was how Abuela could have lived what seemed like more than one lifetime.

Nuala turned her attention to Chantal now.

"How much do you know?" she asked the sculptor.

Chantal sighed. "Way too much."

Nuala nodded. "So it seems at first. Come," she added. "We have work to do at the house. We will speak more of this later."

"But the Glasduine . . ." Bettina began.

"Is hunting wolves," Nuala told her. "And that's not such a bad thing, is it?"

That depends, Bettina thought, worried for her own wolf. But she kept it to herself.

7

There wasn't going to be a miracle, Miki realized. The hard men were going to have their way just like they always did. They'd trash the place. They'd beat her and everybody else up, maybe worse, and there was nothing they could do to stop them. Because these weren't human bullies. They were living remnants of what had been waiting for us in the darkness since time primordial, ready to pounce and tear as soon as we left the cave, the hearth, the safe haven. They were spite and cruelty given human shape, but there was nothing human about them.

As though to emphasize the point, one of the Gentry standing near the front racks straight-armed the new release display and sent it crashing to the ground. CDs flew in all directions. A few landed near him and he crushed their jewel cases under the heel of his boot.

"You owe us," the leader told her, grinning.

His thick accent woke a flood of memories in Miki. Dimly lit pubs, the smell of cigarettes and beer, Fergus and his cronies, their faces flushed with Guinness and spite as dark as fresh peat.

"And these," another of the Gentry said, crushing more jewel cases underfoot, "aren't enough."

The leader nodded. "We need blood."

Their sheer, ignorant callousness was what put Miki in motion. She was still desperately afraid, but she was more angry. As one of the Gentry moved toward the counter, she picked up the stool she'd been sitting on and flung it at him. If Hunter could stand up to them, she thought, then so could she.

"You stupid little bint," the leader said.

He moved now. When Adam tried to block his way, he grabbed Adam by the shirt and flung him across the room. Adam landed badly, falling against the CD bins, before tumbling to the floor with his face twisting in pain. That crash brought the others from the back room. Miki saw Fiona come out first, followed by Titus, who took one look at what was going on and darted back out of sight.

Get out of here, too, Miki wanted to shout at Fiona. Before they see you. But there was no time for warnings. She was too busy looking after herself.

Another of the Gentry had leapt up onto the counter. Miki saw only two choices. Bolt for the open space beyond the counter and have him jump on her back, or take the offensive. She didn't even have to think about it. As the hard man swung a boot at her, she grabbed his leg and pulled it out from under him. He fell awkwardly, his spine hitting the cash register. He slid off it onto the counter, pushing magazines and the phone onto the floor by Miki's feet. But he was kicking out as he fell and one foot connected. The blow sent her staggering back, knocking the CD player and all the promo CDs off the shelf behind her. She fell on top of them, scrambled to get back on her feet, but then the leader was standing over her. He gave her a kick that caught her in the shoulder and threw her back onto the slippery pile of CDs. Her eyes flooded with tears of pain.

That's it, then, she thought, feeling oddly distanced and calm for all that her pulse was drumming in overtime. The next kick would take her in the head. If she was lucky, she'd wake up in hospital. If she wasn't . . .

But the attack broke off as suddenly as it began. As one, the hard men lifted their heads to stand like statues, some dark ache flaring in their eyes, twisting grimaces from their lips. Their heads all turned to look out the window. Miki had no idea what they were seeing, what was going on. There was only the rain out there, the empty streets. Still, she took the opportunity to crabwalk backwards, out of range of the leader's boots. When she neared the man she'd toppled from the counter, she grabbed the phone and smashed it down on his head, then looked at the leader, ready to throw it at him. But he was still preoccupied with whatever it was that he sensed or saw outside.

When the Gentry started for the door, leaving their fallen comrade behind, Miki slowly rose to her feet, steadying her balance by holding onto the edge of the counter. She watched them step out into the rain, one by one, trench coats flapping against their legs. The leader was the last to leave. He turned to look at her from the doorway, an unreadable, confusing expression in his eyes. But there was nothing confusing about the threat he left her with.

"We'll be back," he told Miki. "We have unfinished business, you and I." Then he was gone as well.

This made no sense at all.

She stared at the door, sure they'd come sauntering back any moment to finish what they'd begun, laughing at the joke, at the false hope their departure might have woken, but the only thing coming in through the open door were splatters of freezing rain and a growing puddle. Catching movement from the corner of her eye, she turned to see Titus stepping warily out of the back room with a baseball bat in hand.

That was unexpected as well. Diffident Titus going all fierce? Next Fiona would go surfer-blonde.

She moved her arm, working her shoulder muscle. It didn't hurt as much as she expected, though she knew she'd have bruises for souvenirs—there and on her torso. Her gaze dropped to the hard man lying still at her feet. He didn't move when she toed him. Perhaps she'd killed him.

Serve him right, she thought as she stepped over his limp form and joined the others. Fiona was kneeling beside Adam, pushing the hair from his eyes.

"What happened to them?" she asked, looking up at Miki. "What made them go?"

"I have no idea," Miki said.

Adam tried to move. He moaned, scowling at the pain the movement brought. His face was so white it was like typing paper.

"We need to get him to the hospital," Fiona said.

Miki nodded, not really listening. She was still filled with fury at how the hard men had come in, so ready to hurt them, and for what? To prove they could. That was all. To prove they could.

She looked at the bat in Titus's hand.

"You've just jumped way up in my estimation," she told him as she took the bat from his hand and headed for the door.

"Miki," Fiona said. "We really have to get Adam some help."

But Miki wasn't listening at all now. She stepped out into the rain and saw the Gentry making their way down the street, walking in a group, about to turn off onto a cross street and head west.

"Hey, shite for brains!" she called after them.

The group paused. The leader's gaze was like molten fire but Miki was too angry herself to care. She waved the bat at them.

"Why leave so soon?" she asked them. "You aren't afraid of me, are you, you sorry pissants?"

For a moment the features of a wolf were superimposed over the leader's features turning him into some morphing combination of beast and man. He bared his teeth and Miki could hear the growl in her chest from where she was standing. But she stood her ground.

"Don't like it when your victim fights back, do you?" she said.

The hard man turned to the nearest hydro pole and lashed out with his foot. The crack of the wood snapping rang like a clap of thunder up the length of the street, then the pole came tumbling down, ripping phone and power lines apart as it did. Miki could feel the ground shake underfoot when the pole hit the ground. Live wires flashed sparks and flared, sending up showers of electrical discharges as they whipped in the air. The lights went out in the buildings all along the street.

Grinning, the leader of the Gentry made a gun with his forefinger and thumb and fired it at her. Then he turned and the pack loped off, out of sight.

Miki stared numbly at the damage that had been done.

Brilliant, she told herself, her anger fled. Really sodding brilliant. The leader of the Gentry had been right. She *was* a stupid little bint. She couldn't leave well-enough alone. No, she had to play the hero and now look where it had gotten them. No power, no heat. No phone service.

She turned slowly back into the dark store. When her gaze settled on the others, her guilt became more pronounced. Never mind the power and heat. Adam needed hospital care and how were they going to get him there now? She wasn't sure if an ambulance could get through the mess that was out there on the streets, but they certainly couldn't get him there on their own.

She tossed the bat away, wincing at the startled faces of her friends as it clattered against a display rack.

In her own way, she was no better than Donal, she realized. She hadn't stopped to think how any of this might affect anyone else; she'd simply let her temper get the better of her again.

And she'd always been like this. You don't really grow up no matter how old you get. But what was perhaps a little cute in a child, the frown surrounded by ringlets, the little stamping foot, wasn't so endearing in a woman. Christ, all she had to do was think of Donal's sour puss.

She got away with it because she was usually so relentlessly cheery, but that was still no excuse. All she had to do was look at Adam, ribs cracked surely, maybe some other more serious internal injuries, to know how wrong it was. Because when you only looked out for yourself, other people suffered. It was like the fucking Provos and IRA with their bombs and guns and endless retributions. The civilians were invariably the ones to suffer. The bystanders. It was so pathetic. *She* was pathetic. And not very proud of herself at all.

But she couldn't wallow. Adam was seriously hurt, Titus and Fiona were standing around clueless. Someone had to take charge. She could beat herself up when this was all over.

"Come on," she told Titus. "Let's see if we can rig up something to carry him on."

"I, uh, don't think we should move him," Titus said. "You're not supposed to move people with a back or neck injury, are you?"

Fiona nodded. "I think he's right."

Oh, well done, Miki, she told herself. You've made a brilliant mess of this, haven't you just?

"Okay," she said. "New plan. See what you can find to keep Adam warm. I'll go for help."

Fiona gave her a worried look.

"Are you sure it's safe?" she asked.

Probably not, Miki thought. But did it matter? It had to be done.

"I'll be fine," she said.

Before anyone could argue, she put on her coat and headed for the door. Just before she stepped outside, she thought about that look the leader of the Gentry had given her. The memory was enough to make her retrieve the baseball bat from where she'd thrown it in the corner and take it with her.

8

Hunter had hoped that the storm would let up by morning. But even if it didn't, he'd thought that at least they'd be somewhere warm and safe. There might be warring spirits out there in the freezing rain, but here, inside, they had a wood-stove, food, protection from both the elements and the Gentry. There were worse places they could've ended up than this calm in the eye of the storm.

Wrong, he realized when he woke up.

Tired as he'd been, it had still taken him forever to get to sleep last night, lying awake in a borrowed sleeping bag near the woodstove, every sound mag-nified in his imagination to be one made by a hard man, breaking in. He felt as though he'd just gotten to sleep, but here it was, morning already, and the household humming in a bustle of ordered chaos.

Getting up from his sleeping bag, he joined Tommy where the other man was sitting on the couch. Hunter tried to clear the cobwebs from his head, but without much luck. He didn't see either Aunt Nancy or Ellie around. There were only Tommy's other two aunts, standing on the far side of the room, having what appeared to be an urgent conversation. Hunter couldn't under-stand what they were saying since they were speaking in what he assumed was Kickaha.

"What's going on?" he asked Tommy.

Tommy shrugged. "Everybody got some kind telepathic bad news except for you and me."

"I don't get it."

"Be grateful for life's small gifts."

"No, I mean—"

"I know," Tommy said. "I was joking. Or maybe not. This is all new to me, too."

"But I thought you grew up with this stuff . . . the magic and spirits and everything."

"Only with the stories," Tommy said. "Not the reality of it."

"So it *is* real . . . ?"

Hunter had been hoping that last night's experiences had only been part of some complicated and confusing dream—never mind that he'd woken up here on the rez.

"Oh, yeah," Tommy said. "And isn't that a kicker?"

Hunter nodded slowly. To put it mildly. Because that meant he'd really killed one of the hard men last night. He, who'd never even stood up to school bullies except once in junior high when he'd gotten a black eye and bruised ribs for his trouble. Now he was a murderer. That it had been self-defense didn't seem like much of an excuse when a man lay dead because of what he'd done. It was one thing in the movies, a vicarious thrill, rooting for the villain to get his comeuppance. But the movies didn't tell you about the sick and empty feeling he had inside him right now. They didn't tell you how to deal with it.

"Are you okay?" Tommy asked.

Hunter nodded.

"Because—no offense—you look like hell."

"I just didn't sleep all that well," Hunter told him.

Tommy looked as if he wanted more of an explanation than that, but just then Zulema stepped away from where she'd been talking with Sunday and gave the pair of them an expectant look.

"Come on," she said. "You haven't even got your coats on."

"And we're going where?" Tommy asked.

"The city. Haven't you been paying attention?"

Tommy shook his head, obviously feeling as confused as Hunter himself felt.

"I hate to burst your bubble," he said, "but we barely made it here in one piece last night. There's no way we're driving—or even walking—anywhere today. Not with that rain." "

"Don't argue," Zulema told him. "We need you to drive."

"But . . ."

Something flickered in her eyes and Tommy quickly rose to his feet. Zulema nodded, then headed for the hallway. Tommy rolled his eyes at Hunter.

"We're not even going to get out of their driveway," Tommy told him. "Not unless we're all pushing. And then all that's going to happen is we're going to go into some ditch maybe two yards down the road."

Hunter was slower to rise to his feet.

"I don't think you have to come," Tommy added. "Except you could help us get out of the driveway—if you feel up to it, I mean."

"I'm not bailing now," Hunter told him.

"But if you're feeling sick . . ."

"It's not that kind of sick," Hunter said.

Something changed in Tommy's eyes.

"It's that guy," he said. "In Miki's apartment."

Hunter nodded.

"I'm not going to say he had it coming to him," Tommy told him. "Even if he did. But that's not what this is about, is it?"

"No. It's just . . . I just . . . killed him."

"First time?"

"God, what do you think?" Then Hunter gave Tommy a closer look. "Why? Have you?"

Tommy shook his head. "I've come close. And there was a time I wouldn't have lost any sleep over it. But no. I guess the aunts drummed the message too firmly in my head: All life's precious." He laid a hand on Hunter's arm. "But you know, the man you killed, he had a lot of the responsibility for what happened to him. It's not like you went out looking to hurt someone the way he did. What he forgot was, what you put out comes back to you."

"I don't know . . ."

"Look, you have to shoulder some of the responsibility, too," Tommy said. "No question. But you also have to cut yourself some slack. You didn't ask to step into a war zone. He had to know the risks, though a guy like that, he was going to think he's immortal anyway."

"They *are* immortal. Isn't that what your aunts said?"

"Good point. Doesn't change a thing, though, except you'd think he'd have gotten some smarts over the years."

"Tommy!" one of the aunts called from the hallway. Hunter couldn't see which one.

"We're on it!" Tommy called back. He turned back to Hunter. "But seriously, you want a break, take it, because things aren't going to get any less dangerous from here on out."

Hunter shook his head. "It's hard to explain, but I have to see it through."

"I understand."

No, you don't, Hunter thought. Because it wasn't just sticking with them to see this thing through. There was also the way Ria had been after him to get out of, and stay out of the safe cocoon of his life. This wasn't exactly what she'd meant, or the way he'd planned it, but he couldn't back out now. That was too much like giving up—not only this, but everything.

"But just let me add this," Tommy said. "Once things get hairy . . . if you're with us, we're going to be depending on you. So if you are going to bail, now's the time to do it."

Thanks, Hunter thought. Put the pressure on. But he refused to bow to it.

"I thought you said we weren't even going to get out of the driveway," he said.

Tommy grinned. "There's that. But then you don't know my aunts. If they think we're going somewhere, we probably are."

As they walked towards the hall they met up with Ellie and Tommy's Aunt Nancy. Ellie looked the way Hunter felt, washed out and exhausted, but there was also a lost, anguished look in her eyes.

"Did you feel it?" she asked. "It was like someone tore out a piece of my heart."

Hunter shook his head.

"Only you superhero magic types got to feel it," Tommy told her.

Ellie gave him an exasperated look, but then she shook her head. Smiling, she punched him in the shoulder.

"Thanks," she said. "I needed that."

"What? The punch or the compliment?"

"There was a compliment?"

Tommy put a finger to his lips and nodded in the direction of the waiting aunts with an exaggerated look of alarm. Shaking her head again, Ellie continued down the hall. Tommy and Hunter followed behind.

Outside it was worse than Tommy had predicted. The driveway was like polished glass, the highway beyond one smooth sheet of ice. All around them, the fields were littered with broken branches and trees bent almost in half. And the rain continued to fall without respite from the thick gray cloud cover above. Tommy stepped gingerly out from under the porch's overhang and immediately lost his balance. Before he could fall, Aunt Nancy seemed to almost pluck him from the air and bring him back to steadier footing.

Hunter and Ellie exchanged glances. Like the Gentry, Aunt Nancy was a lot stronger than she looked.

"I told you," Tommy said. "We're not going anywhere."

"You've lived in the city too long," Aunt Nancy told him.

She directed them all to hold hands.

Now what? Hunter wondered. Were they going to have a prayer circle?

But no words were spoken. Instead, the ground seemed to shift underfoot and an unaccountable nausea rose up in his stomach.

Should have taken the time to have some breakfast, he thought. He couldn't remember the last time he'd had something to eat. That was all this was, though it felt more like motion sickness. When he glanced at Ellie, she seemed to feel it as well, maybe worse than he did. She leaned against him, stifling a burp. He let go of Zulema's hand and put his arm around Ellie's shoulder to steady her. She gave him a weak smile in return.

"What's happening?" he asked.

Tommy appeared to be feeling a little queasy as well. Only the aunts seemed unaffected.

"We have stepped into a place between our world and that of the *manitou*," Sunday explained. "It can make you feel a little sick to your stomach until you get used to being here."

Hunter shook his head. "But . . . why are we here?"

Wherever here was, because except for the nausea, nothing seemed to have changed at all.

"In this place we aren't affected by the climate in either world."

When Hunter still looked confused, Sunday pointed to where Aunt Nancy and Zulema were confidently walking across the sheet of ice that covered the driveway.

"Come on," Sunday said. "Let's not keep them waiting."

Reluctantly, he followed the older woman out onto the ice, his arm still around Ellie's shoulders to give her support. Ahead of them they saw Tommy gingerly step onto the ice. He took one step, another, then turned to grin at them.

"This is unbelievable," he said. "Look."

He did a little dance step on the ice, as surefooted as though it was dirt underfoot. But Hunter was no longer so surprised, because he and Ellie were out on the ice now as well. It was a little disconcerting, knowing the ice was there but not slipping on it, like going down a stopped escalator, only this was easier to adjust to.

"Can you do this number on the truck?" Tommy was asking Aunt Nancy.

She nodded and laid her hand on the bed of the vehicle. Zulema tossed some blankets into the back, then she and Aunt Nancy got into the cab with Tommy, leaving Sunday, Hunter, and Ellie to clamber up into the bed.

"Is it passing?" Sunday asked as they settled on the blankets. "The queasiness?"

"Not really," Hunter said.

Ellie shook her head.

Sunday dug into a pocket and offered them each what looked like a small round cookie.

"Here," she said. "These will help."

Hunter shook his head. "No, thanks."

The thought of eating anything right now made his stomach do a slow flip.

"What is it?" Ellie asked. "Some kind of magic?"

Sunday smiled. "Hardly. Mostly oatmeal, sugar, and flour, with some herbs to help the nausea. Anise, cinnamon. Peppermint."

Tommy started the engine. Putting the pickup into gear, he started cautiously up the incline, but he needn't have bothered. The tires had no trouble finding traction. The vehicle's motion quickened the nausea Hunter and Ellie were feeling.

"I'll have one," Ellie said, taking the cookie from Sunday.

"Me, too," Hunter said.

The mix of licorice with cinnamon and peppermint made for an odd flavor, but it left an oddly refreshing taste in his mouth. And better yet, worked almost immediately on his queasiness. By the time they were a mile or so down the road, the nausea had completely fled and he found himself actually enjoying this odd drive. He could see the rain, but it didn't touch them. He could see the ice, but the pickup stayed on the road as though the tires were rolling across dry asphalt.

"This is really weird," he said.

Sunday nodded. "It's not how we normally use the between, but it is proving helpful today."

"Now all we have to do is figure out how to deal with this thing Donal called up," Ellie said. "The Glasduine."

"What are we going to do with it?" Hunter asked.

Whatever *it* was. He wasn't that worried himself about some forest spirit Donal might have called up with an old mask—not when there were the hard men still to deal with. The last time they'd been protected because they wanted some service from Ellie. Now all bets were off, which made the Gentry seem to be a much more immediate concern.

"We'll have to see when we get there," Sunday said. "Hopefully we can banish it deeper into *manidò-akì* where it won't be able to hurt anyone, though how we'll manage that with a creature as strong as this, I have no idea."

"But Aunt Nancy knows what to do," Ellie said. "Right?"

Sunday shrugged. "Nancy tends to play everything by ear."

"Great."

Ellie settled back on her share of the blankets and leaned against Hunter. He hesitated a moment, then put his arm around her shoulders again.

"I'm glad you're here," she said.

"Circumstances notwithstanding," Hunter told her, "I'm glad to be here."

They rode for a while in silence, listening to the hum of the engine. The freezing rain continued to fall everywhere except on them. Hunter let his gaze travel to the side of the road. The roadside vegetation was decimated by its burden of ice, weeds all flattened, trees bent over at alarming angles where the branches hadn't simply snapped off.

He was about to turn away when he caught movement in between the decimated trees. His breath went still and he stiffened when he recognized the shapes for what they were.

"*Manitou,*" Sunday said, turning to see what had captured his attention. "Don't worry. They won't harm us."

Ellie pressed closer to him. Hunter knew just what she was feeling. Until he'd experienced the presence of the Gentry, and later the native *manitou,* he hadn't really known the meaning of awe. But then that begged the question . . .

"I don't understand," he said. "They look so powerful—they are powerful," he corrected himself, remembering how the leader of the Gentry had so effortlessly turned a car over onto its side back in the city. "How could I possibly have killed one just by banging him on the side of the head with a pail of water?"

"Spirits become susceptible when they take physical form," Sunday explained. "They retain a supernatural strength, but are no longer impervious to pain or death."

"But why would they do it?"

She gave another one of her easy shrugs. "To fully experience life, I suppose. Without a physical form, they can't experience the tactile. I have traveled in spirit form and can tell you that even your sight and hearing have more presence in a physical body. Everything is more fully rounded, more rooted in this world where our physical senses rule. Think of how you feel a bass drum resonating in your chest at the same time as you hear it."

Hunter nodded slowly. It was like the difference between a recording and a live concert, he decided. We made do with recordings, but nothing could take the place of actually being there at the performance. Seen like that, he could easily understand what would make spirits take on physical form. Especially the Gentry, considering their love of music and Guinness.

But then the memory of what he'd done to the hard man in Miki's apartment came crushing down on him again. The life taken.

He could feel the tightness swell up in his chest once more and forced himself to breathe normally.

"Are you okay?" Ellie asked, giving him a worried look.

Hunter shook his head. "Not really. But I'm working on it."

9

Under Nuala's direction, the current residents of Kellygnow had gathered up boards and other scrap wood from the basement and outbuildings, using it to erect a makeshift wall in the sculpting studio where the creature had broken through the side of the house. They could have easily closed off the door to the studio—which they did anyway once they were done with the wall—but Bettina understood Nuala's rationale behind the manual task. It was a way to get the residents' minds off the impossibility of what had occurred. Only a few of them had actually caught a glimpse of what Donal had become, but their descriptions of it, along with the wreckage the Glasduine had left behind, was enough to put everyone in a high state of agitation.

It didn't help that their power and phone lines were down. The only news available from the outside world was what they could get from Penny's battery-operated radio. According to the most recent reports, the city was on the verge of being declared a disaster zone with the mayor having already called in the army to help with evacuating seniors and the disabled from their homes, removing dangerous power lines, and guarding against looters.

"Looters?" Bettina had repeated, incredulously, when Penny passed along that last piece of information.

"Hey, the city's shut down," one of the other residents replied. "For some people that's an open invitation to help themselves."

"Isn't that the sorry truth," Chantal said.

None of the residents had to stay in Kellygnow. While its steep driveway and the streets beyond were too treacherous to chance, they could still leave the way Donal had claimed he'd come, down through the backyards where they could break a trail through the ice-covered snow to gain firmer footing. But where would they go? They were better off than most. Here at least they had the woodstove for heat, food, and water, and each other's company.

When someone suggested they see if any of their neighbors needed help, Nuala nodded in agreement.

"I'll go," Chantal said. "I really need to be doing something . . ."

Her voice trailed off and she looked at Bettina, who understood all too well what her friend was going through. The storm on its own was stressful enough; everything else Chantal had experienced today would only have added to her need to immerse herself in some mundane, useful task. Something that would allow her to understand that while there was more to the world than she'd ever realized, the world she did know was still carrying on with the business of living.

"I'll come with you," Bettina said.

"I'd rather you didn't," Nuala told her.

"*Pero—*"

"We have things to discuss, you and I," Nuala said, pitching her voice low so as not to carry beyond where the three of them were standing.

She needn't have worried about being overheard. The other residents were already too busy making their own plans to pay any attention. Now that the house had been secured against the elements, their charitable impulses had risen to the fore. They were all eager to get outside and assay the damage to the area, lending a hand where it might be needed.

"It's okay," Chantal said. "There's plenty of us to do what needs to be done. You go on and deal with, you know, the stuff you deal with."

Her smile was a little too bright, Bettina thought, but she didn't argue with her friend. Chantal needed to be grounded more than any of the others.

Bettina only wished she'd realized sooner how badly the experiences of the morning had affected Chantal. She would have prepared a soothing tea for the sculptor had she thought of it, but her own mind wasn't as clear as it could be either.

"*Cuidado,*" she told her friend. "Be careful."

Chantal nodded and went to join the others, leaving Bettina standing with Nuala.

"*Bien,*" she said to the housekeeper. "What would you have me do?"

Nuala waited while the residents put on jackets and boots and trooped out of the house before she replied.

"I'm not sure," she said then. "Is there anything in the lore of your people that can help us deal with this creature? Something that might tell us how it can be slain?"

"I won't knowingly cause harm to any of God's creatures," Bettina said, her voice firm.

Nuala smiled. "God?"

"Who do you think made the world? Who else peopled it? Even the spirits are here because He gave them the gift of life."

"Perhaps God is a woman," Nuala said, her amusement still apparent.

"*No estoy así seguro de eso,*" Bettina replied. She wasn't so sure of that. "It seems too much a man's world for that to be true."

"What if I told you it wasn't always so?"

Bettina shrugged. "I wouldn't know. But at least He gave us the Virgin to intercede on our behalf." She smiled herself as a thought came to her. "Perhaps it is the same in God's house as it is down here. The man thinks he runs the household, but the woman actually does."

"You are such an innocent."

Bettina frowned. This again.

"Don't mistake my youth or peaceful intentions for ignorance," she said. "I am a *curandera*. Something summoned me to this place for my healing talents—not as a warrior."

"And if your life, or the lives of your friends, depend upon battle, what will you do then?"

"She will have me to fight for her," a new voice said.

Bettina turned to find that her wolf had joined them in the kitchen. So intent had she and Nuala been upon their conversation that neither had heard his approach. Bettina nodded a greeting to him, but Nuala was furious.

"You!" she said, eyes dark with anger. "You dare enter this house—"

She took a step towards him, stopping only when Bettina moved to block her path.

"He is my guest," she said. "And he is not what he seems."

She hoped it was true. She needed it to be true.

"He is one of them," Nuala said, her voice as cold as the ice that blanketed the landscape outside, "and you presume too much to protect him under this roof."

Bettina straightened her shoulders and wouldn't budge.

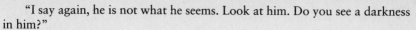

"I say again, he is not what he seems. Look at him. Do you see a darkness in him?"

"I see shadows."

"But he is not like the others," Bettina insisted.

Nuala narrowed her eyes, studying him. *El lobo,* for his part, lounged against the door jamb, regarding the pair of them with mild amusement.

"I see what you mean," Nuala said finally. Her voice admitted defeat, but her wariness didn't lessen. "He is, indeed, something else again."

"I think I prefer your other friend's description," *el lobo* said to Bettina. Bettina had to laugh.

"She called him 'tall, dark,' " she told Nuala.

"Inferring the handsome, of course," Nuala said.

El lobo grinned. "Of course."

"Well, you're no more shy than the Gentry," Nuala said, "but at least you have a sense of humor that doesn't depend on another's misfortune."

"I am everything they are not," *el lobo* told her.

"Are you now."

El lobo shrugged. "You would know best."

Bettina turned to the housekeeper when Nuala made no reply. She could taste some undercurrent running through their conversation—merely its presence, not what it augured. All she could be certain of was that it had something to do with the ongoing enmity between Nuala and the wolves.

"What does he mean by that?" she asked. "That you would know best?"

"Better you ask him," Nuala replied.

But one look at *el lobo* told Bettina he would be no more forthcoming than the housekeeper.

"And you call *me* childish," she said.

That woke a laugh from her wolf and another frown from Nuala. But then the housekeeper sighed.

"You are right," she said. "I shouldn't measure you by my own experiences. Just because I was foolish when I was your age, does not mean the mistakes I made apply to how you choose to live your life."

"I'm impressed," *el lobo* said. "It's almost an apology."

"But not an explanation," Bettina said.

"The history that lies between the Gentry and me is too long a story," Nuala told her, "and not relevant to our present situation."

El lobo nodded in agreement. "We have more pressing business anyway," he told Bettina. "It's time we were going."

Bettina gave him a puzzled look.

"Because your fierce friend's right," he explained. "We can't leave the Glasduine to wreak havoc out in the world as it surely will."

"But what can we do?"

"If you can't heal it, then I'll have to kill it."

She shivered, unsure if his breezy confidence was feigned or sincere. How he would even do such a thing was beyond her. If Nuala was at a loss, what could he, a *sombrito,* hope to accomplish?

"And it's we who must go," he added, "because—what shall I call you?" His gaze turned to Nuala, the laughter still flickering in his eyes. "My aunt?"

Nuala glared at him. "You could lose that tongue if it keeps wagging that way."

"Our brave housekeeper, then," *el lobo* said, ignoring her threat. "You see, she can't, or at least won't, leave her charge."

Bettina gave him another puzzled look. What was it with spirit folk that had them make everything a secret and a riddle?

"Kellygnow," he said. "This house. She would sooner die than forsake it now. Am I not right?"

Nuala gave him a reluctant nod.

Bettina recalled the recent argument between Nuala and the Recluse.

"Because it is your home?" she asked, wondering again at the need spirits seemed to have to claim a place as their own.

"Because it is my responsibility," Nuala said.

"Which among us," *el lobo* added, "amounts to much the same thing. After all, spirits of a place need a place. Without it, they become like certain wolves we won't mention."

"You would not understand such a thing," Nuala told him.

"That is where you are gravely mistaken," he replied. "My stake in this is higher than yours. My flesh is borrowed. Were I to shirk my own responsibility, this gift of a body I wear could well be reclaimed, leaving me nothing more than a shadow again."

Nuala regarded him for a long moment, then slowly nodded her understanding.

Bettina shook her head. "But the one who gave you this . . . your body. You told me he was dead."

"I didn't only accept his body," *el lobo* said. "I also accepted the responsibilities he once held when I took on his flesh. There are higher powers than us in the world and they are very specific in dealing with those who renege on their promises—at least among beings such as Nuala and I. Now come. We must go. Every moment we stand here, the masked one grows that much stronger."

Nuala nodded. "Go. But only mark where the Glasduine bides for now, what it appears the creature means to do. I will consider other strategies until your return. Between the three of us, we will find a solution to this."

El lobo grinned. "You have to love a woman so sure of herself."

Nuala stiffened.

Dios dame fuerza, Bettina thought. Her wolf seemed to thrive on rubbing everyone the wrong way.

"That's not helping," she told him.

"Perhaps not. But it's in my nature."

"Then you should consider changing that part of it," she said.

Before he could reply, she crossed the kitchen and took down her coat from the pegs by the door. She put on a pair of boots, nodded to Nuala, then stepped out into the rain, quickly moving into the between so that she wouldn't get wet again. Her hair had only just dried from her last outing. *El lobo* joined her before she was on the lawn, that infuriating smile still flirting in his eyes.

"I don't know why I trust you," she said as they walked toward the woods.

"Your heart knows I mean you no harm."

"Perhaps. And yet . . ."

El lobo smiled. "Your heart has played you false before."

"Has anyone ever told you that you talk too much?" she asked.

"Never. But I rarely have the opportunity for conversation. Perhaps I overcompensate when the opportunity does arise."

"And is that almost an apology from you?" she asked.

"Almost."

He moved ahead to where the creature had broken a trail through the undergrowth, pausing when the spoor disappeared. Where at first the creature had simply forced its way through the trees and brush, at this point it seemed to have suddenly acquired the ability to move across the terrain without disturbing even a twig.

"We watched it go," Bettina said. "When it first came out of the house, it was ungainly, as though unused to its body."

"I remember that feeling."

Bettina glanced at him. She couldn't imagine what that must have felt like.

"But step by step," she added, "it gained confidence until, by the time it was out of our sight, its passage was silent."

"Or it walked elsewhere," *el lobo* said.

"You think it crossed over?"

His nostrils flared. "I can't catch his scent, not here, nor in the world we've just quit."

While he considered the direction the Glasduine would have taken, Bettina studied him.

"You don't have a plan at all, do you?" she said finally.

He shook his head. "But I know we must do something."

"What made you change your mind about helping with the creature?" she asked.

"I never said I wouldn't help. Only that I'd enjoy seeing it deal with the Gentry. I have as much unfinished business with them as either Nuala or your friend Donal."

"He's not my friend."

El lobo shrugged. "The pup, then."

They stood silent for a long moment, listening to the sound of dripping that came from all around them.

"If the Glasduine's gone into the otherworld," Bettina finally said, "we might never find it. Unless your nose is as sharp as your tongue."

He smiled. "Alas, I can't make that claim. But you have the means to find him."

"I?"

"Not you, precisely, but the dogs I can hear singing in you."

Bettina regarded him steadily. "I hear nothing. *Los cadejos* are long gone."

"Or you have simply turned your back on them."

That cut too close to home, for she'd done exactly that. When *la Maravilla* led her *abuela* away into the desert, when no one and nothing could help her find Abuela again, she had turned her back on the whole of the canine clan as it related to *la época del mito*, utterly and completely until this wolf had pushed himself into her life.

"They would be of great help to us at the moment," he said.

Bettina shook her head. "I don't trust them."

"You don't trust me either."

"That's different. You . . ."

"I, what?" he asked when her voice trailed off.

You are too handsome to ignore, she'd wanted to say. Too charming not to want to trust.

"How can I hear them again?" she asked instead. "How can I call them up?"

El lobo shook his head. "I don't know."

"But you hear them."

"I do, only—"

"So you must call them up for me. You will, won't you?"

She couldn't understand his reluctance until he explained, "If they do prove untrustworthy, you will blame it on me."

"Perhaps. But I will try not to."

He smiled. "What if I told you it requires a kiss?"

"Does it?"

He shook his head. "No. But I've wanted to find an excuse to kiss you since the first time I saw you."

A flush rose up Bettina's neck and spread to her cheeks.

"We . . . the Glasduine," she said, stumbling over her words. "We are upon a serious undertaking."

"I am serious, too. Perhaps if we kissed once, I wouldn't be so distracted from the task at hand."

Bettina remembered all the warnings Nuala had given her. A kiss now, then it was off into the woods with her jeans pulled down about her ankles. Her *abuela* had been full of warnings, too, of getting too close to beings who had originated in *la época del mito*. Relationships with the spirits were always doomed to failure, Abuela would say—speaking from the voice of experience, Bettina assumed, since she knew that her grandmother had dallied more than once with such beings.

She didn't doubt the danger, of either being pulled off into the woods or having her heart broken, but somehow it didn't matter. Not with *el lobo*'s handsome features so close to her own, his breath on her face, sweet as a summer garden. Not with the loneliness that rose in her, so many months away from home, so many longer with no close confidant. No lover.

So she lifted her face to his and their lips met. His arms went around her, drawing her close, enfolding her with warmth and a gentle strength, and time stopped. When they finally drew apart, she was breathless. But so was he.

"Ah," he said, adding after a moment, "Now I have no choice but to prove myself worthy so that you will trust me."

"I—"

He laid a finger across her lips. "Not yet. Say nothing. Let there only be hope between us until the task is done."

He took her hand then and led her deeper into *la época del mito*.

"For the moment," he added with a grin, "we have singing dogs to find."

This time Bettina thought she could actually hear them. Distant, but for the first time in years, clearly audible. Their voices were no longer simply a memory.

10

After her argument with Nuala, Musgrave returned to her cottage in a foul mood. She slammed the door and stood staring about herself. The place was as much a prison as a haven. She could never be away from it for too long because it was only on this estate that she had access to the otherworld. She wasn't like the Gentry, or as Ellie could be, able to cross over wherever and whenever she so desired. Because of her weak *geasan*, she had only the access gate here that the Gentry had provided for her, a space between two trees that, when she spoke a certain charmed word, allowed her to cross over. And she needed to cross over, for it was only by spending the better part of the year in the otherworld that she was able to prolong her life as she had.

All that had been supposed to change with the mask. The Glasduine they planned to call up with it would have given the Gentry power over the local *manitou*, but it would also have given her immortality and enough *geasan* to be a player rather than a pawn in the world of spirits and magic.

Now Donal Greer had stolen that opportunity from her and she was back to where she had started before she'd used her wealth and influence to track down the pieces of the mask. The difference was, she was older. So much older. Her youth had been stolen from her. Damn Greer. *He* had stolen it from her.

By the time she heard the Gentry outside her door, her anger towards Nuala and Donal both had grown into a smoldering rage. She opened the door only to find that the wolves had bypassed her cabin and were walking deeper into the woods. When she called after them, the one in the rear turned to look at her, but then moved on with the others.

Their forms flickered, half in this world, half in the other, until they suddenly disappeared from sight. Cursing, Musgrave closed the door to her cabin and hurried to her own gate into the otherworld. Speaking the charm the Gentry had given her, she stepped through the trees into that other place. She turned slowly, listening. She saw her cottage where it stood under the trees, beleafed now, winter fled in this place. Here the small building was the only man-made structure on the hill. There was no city below, no road leading up from congested streets to the quiet of the hilltop, no estates scattered like an uneven quilt pattern on the slopes rising up to what bore the name of Kellygnow in the world she'd just quit.

Her gaze moved on, finally settling on the pool where Father Salmon slept. There she saw the Gentry, gathered around its rough stone wall, smoking cigarettes as they stared into the dark, still water. There was no pleasure in the leader's face when he looked up at her approach. Turning away, he reached into the water and stroked the scaled back of the sleeping fish.

A thrill of anticipation and fear went up Musgrave's spine at the thought that the salmon might wake. It would bring great change, but perhaps now, with all their plans in shambles, a change might be welcome. They would be transformed, but into what? Musgrave wondered if will was enough on its own to guide the change. If so, she had will and to spare, and she knew exactly what she would become.

"Was he brought here, do you think?" the leader of the Gentry said, speaking around the cigarette that dangled from his lips. "Or did he come on his own?"

"I think it's like the First Forest," she replied, crouching beside him so she could look into the water. "All forests are a reflection of it, but they are all a path back to it as well."

The leader nodded. "Which would make this pool connected to where he sleeps at the beginning of time."

"So it would seem."

"Yet I can feel him under my hand. I could wake him." He looked at her. "Yet one more mystery, eh?"

"I suppose . . ."

He straightened up and wiped his hand dry on his trousers. Turning, he sat on the stones that lipped the pool. He took a final drag from his cigarette, then flicked the butt away. Around him, the other wolves lounged. They gave the appearance of being half-asleep, uninterested in anything, but Musgrave knew they followed every word, every motion.

"It's all gone to shite, these plans of ours," the leader said.

Musgrave sat back on her heels. "We can blame Nuala for that."

"How so?"

"She should have kept better guard of the mask."

The leader shook his head. "She was never a part of this. How would she have known to guard it?"

Musgrave didn't really hear his words—she heard the sound of them, but not their meaning.

"I think she did it on purpose," she said, still seething at how the housekeeper had spoken to her. She straightened her back and gave the leader a stern look. "She is no longer under my protection. You and the others . . . you can do with her what you will."

For a long moment there was only silence, then the wolves began to snicker. The leader laughed out loud.

"She was under *your* protection?"

" 'Was' being the operative word," Musgrave said. "She was useful, I'll admit, and could possibly remain so if she were able to mind her own business, but I won't have my employees speak to me with the disrespect she did earlier today."

"Gave you a dressing-down, did she?"

"What do you find so amusing?"

The leader smiled. "That Nuala would need protection, for one thing. How small is your brain, woman?"

"I don't understand. The enmity between you. . . ."

"Oh, there's no love lost, I'll grant you that, but even if we could harm her, we wouldn't."

Musgrave began to get an uneasy feeling. What did he mean by even if they *could* harm her?

"Why not?" she asked.

"Because she has the right to feel as she does for us. I'm surprised that with all your study and research you never unearthed the story."

Musgrave's uneasiness grew. There was a dangerous look in the leader's eyes, a sense of anticipation that rose from the other Gentry.

"Will you tell me?" she said.

"Why not? It's old business. Here's the way I know it. Back in the homeland, some randy old godling grabbed himself a lovely maiden, stole her from her sacred wood and dragged her into the deeper forest where he and his mates had their way with her for a month or so. Do you want the details?"

Musgrave shook her head.

The leader smiled and lit another cigarette. "Well, they finally grew tired of the game and tossed her away. Trouble is, they left her with child—not a single birth, as a human might have, but a litter.

"She fled her homeland and came here, stealing passage on one of the famine ships. Deep in the forests of this new land, hiding from both men and the native spirits on whose lands she encroached, she gave birth to her litter. She did her best with her unruly pack, raising them from pups to young men. But every time she looked upon them, she was put in mind of their sires, and finally she could bear the memories no more. So she left them to fend for themselves and went wandering.

"Does any of this sound familiar yet?"

Musgrave shook her head, though she could guess where the story was going. "I don't know what hardships she faced," the leader went on, "though loneliness must have been one. Loss of place another. But finally she found a haven and though she didn't call for us, blood calls to blood, and we came anyway."

"She's your mother," Musgrave said.

"And a loving woman, too, don't you think?"

Musgrave ignored the comment. "So you've never even been to Ireland."

"Ah, well as close as. We've visited by way of the otherworld, but there's not much room there for the likes of us. It's got its own hard men and patience isn't one of their virtues either—though marking and protecting their own territory certainly is."

Musgrave nodded, her thoughts turning back to Nuala and her relationship with the wolves.

"So," she said. "The animosity you feel towards Nuala comes from her having abandoned you."

The leader of the Gentry laughed. "Not at all. We got along fine. We had the city, she had her house on the hill, and if sometimes we sniffed around her woods, we kept our distance and took care not to disturb her charge."

"So what happened?"

"You woke ambition in us."

"I?"

"Oh, don't play the innocent shite. All your talk of gaining power and wresting land from the native spirits, of being more than men so we deserved whatever we could take and hold—what did you think that woke in us?"

"But—"

Again that mocking laugh. "Don't worry. We've no regrets. But you can see how our mam might not be too pleased to see us turning out like the father."

Musgrave nodded. "She set her own sights too low."

"Perhaps. But we set ours too high."

"No, we can still salvage something out of this. Ellie can still make the copy of the mask, infuse it with her untapped *geasan* . . ."

Her voice trailed off as the leader shook his head.

"We're done now," he said. "If we're not gone soon, the pup will be after us in all his buggering glory. We mean to be long gone before he begins his hunt."

He stood up, took a drag from his cigarette, then dropped the butt into the pool.

"I'd look to your own skin," he added. "The pup won't be any more enamored with you."

Musgrave held her breath, but the cigarette butt only hissed and went out. Father Salmon didn't stir.

"Wait," she said, standing up as well.

When the leader began to turn away, she caught him by the arm. A growl rose in his chest and he pulled free.

"You can't leave," she said. "Where will you go?"

"West. I hear there's great *craíc* on the coast."

"But you can't leave me here on my own. If you can't stand up to the creature, what can I do?"

He shrugged. "Grow old. Die."

Again turned, and again she caught his arm.

"We can still make the new mask work," she said.

This time the leader didn't pull his arm away. Instead, he put his hands on either side of her face.

"You know what I won't miss?" he said.

Her voice felt trapped in the back of her throat and his grip was too firm for her to shake her head. But he didn't seem to require an answer.

"Your endless schemes and prattling," he told her.

Then he snapped her neck and let her go. She went limp, dead before her body could crumple to the ground. The leader looked down at her for a long moment, then spat on her body and turned away.

"In future," he told his companions, "remind me never to listen to the advice of women."

The others laughed, then followed him in a pack as he led them west, their path wandering in and out of the spirit world to throw off the scent they left behind.

11

It was only about twenty blocks to the hospital, but Miki wasn't all that sure she'd actually make it. They were long blocks, and the streets and sidewalks had grown even more treacherous than they were earlier when she and Fiona had made their way to the store. It was impossible to walk normally. She had to feel her way along the sides of buildings to keep her balance, sliding one foot gingerly in front of the other. Crossing streets was a nightmare. The rain continued to fall, shifting between sheets of actual hard rain and the insistent freezing drizzle that clung to whatever it landed upon, so there was about an inch of water lying on top of the ice. When she crossed a street, she shuffled her way over the slippery surface like a very unsteady tightrope walker, arms held out from her side. The baseball bat had long been relegated to being stuck through her belt around back.

She had the streets entirely to herself. There were no pedestrians at all, which was an eerie enough feeling. The only cars she saw had been abandoned, many of them at odd angles to the sidewalks. Twice she went through intersections where there'd been an obvious accident, the cars involved having been simply pushed to the sides of the streets and left there. She assumed that the salt trucks had been by—this was downtown, after all—but you wouldn't know it from the unsteady footing.

She really should have ice skates, she thought again. Then she could just whip up to the hospital in no time at all. Though how the ambulance would get to the store with these road conditions was another question entirely. Maybe they could put a gurney on runners and skating interns could push it to the store and back again.

She could have wept with relief when she turned a corner and saw an army vehicle inching its way down the street in her direction. Now there was the way to travel. Everyone should have one of these Bisons, a twelve-ton, eight-wheeled armored personnel carrier. With one hand on the corner of the building, she waved frantically at the vehicle. Soldiers riding on top waved back and the Bison made its way across and down the street to where she waited for it.

Who'd have thought the day would come when she'd be happy to see the army? But then, this wasn't Ireland, and these soldiers weren't British.

"Do you need some help, Miss?" one of the soldiers called down to her when the Bison came to a stop by her corner.

Miss? Miki thought. Now weren't they a polite lot. A sarcastic retort rose in her mind, but she sensibly kept it in check and merely explained her problem, giving them the address of the store. She mentioned the attack, describing the Gentry merely as looters. Lord knew what they'd make of the dead one she'd left behind the counter. Maybe they wouldn't even notice it until she could get someone to help her remove it.

"Let me give you a hand up," the soldier said, "and you can ride back with us."

Miki was tempted. She'd had enough of the cold and rain to last her a lifetime, but the walk had also given her time to think—about the mess she'd made of things back at the store, about how badly she'd misjudged Donal and how extreme he had gotten, but mostly about the Gentry and where they might be going. She'd seen them heading west. What lay west but Kellygnow, where Hunter told her that the Gentry had set Ellie to some task. Kellygnow, where Donal had been all too eager to have Ellie take on some commission. It took no genius to realize that the two, task and commission, were one and the same.

She knew Ellie was safe with Hunter and Tommy up on the rez, but she still had to go to Kellygnow herself. There was unfinished business with Donal, and perhaps the Gentry as well, though she now had her murderous intentions well in check. It was more that she needed to give Donal one more chance, to see if she couldn't talk him out of this madness.

"You go on," she told the soldier. "I've got to head 'round to my mum's place and see how she's doing with the weather."

The soldier gave her a doubtful look.

"No, really. I'll be fine."

Finally he nodded. "Try to keep off the streets once you get there. If you fall and break your leg, you could be lying in the slush for hours before someone finds you."

"I'll be careful," she promised him.

She stood by the corner, leaning against the building and watching them go, before turning west herself.

You really, really are a stupid bint, she told herself. What could she possibly do once she got to Kellygnow? Even if Donal was there, why would he listen to her now? But she had to try. Not for Donal as he was now, but for the Donal he'd been. The older brother who'd always looked out for her, the two of them alone against the great big, uncaring world.

It was easy to understand Donal's rage in that context. But those days were long past now. There was nothing to be gained by dwelling on them.

They were bad, sure, but except for their da', no one had actively been trying to hurt them, and even he'd have to be drunk first before he raised a hand. The rest of the world had merely offered them indifference. That wasn't something you paid back. It was something you had to get over and simply carry on with your life.

Somehow she had to get that through to Donal before he did something that he'd forever regret.

12

All Donal had left were regrets.

The last thing he'd expected when the Glasduine rose from the floor of the sculpting studio was that he wouldn't rise with it. That he wouldn't stand tall and be in control of the new shape his body had taken. But all he could do was lie on his side, huddled on the wooden floor with his knees drawn up to his chin, and watch as the creature lumbered to its feet. Crossing the room, it stopped by the windows, staring out the glass panes at the ice-covered trees on the far side of the lawn while Donal lay curled up on the floor, a frail shadow of who he'd been, no more substantial than a ghost.

It took him a long moment to realize what had happened: The Glasduine had taken all his strongest emotions, using them as the fuel it required to manifest in this world. What was left behind were only the parts the creature couldn't use. Donal was now like the Other, that lone wolf who dogged the Gentry, a shadow made up of the discarded portions of the hard men's leader who had gained a more substantial existence by acquiring the body of a deceased native spirit. Musgrave, in a rare expansive mood, had explained it to him one day when he asked about the straggler who always seemed to be hovering on the periphery of the pack's enterprises. The leader of the Gentry himself refused to acknowledge the Other's existence, giving Donal a cuff across the back of his head the one time he'd asked who that was, so often following them.

This separation between himself and the Glasduine . . . it wasn't how it was supposed to be, how Musgrave and the Gentry had promised it would turn out. Either the hard men and the hag in the cottage had lied to him—a distinct bloody possibility—or he'd changed the rules himself by using the old broken mask. Perhaps control could only have been his with the mask Ellie was supposed to make, a new one, imbedded with her potent *geasan,* and lacking any previous history.

Though that would have probably turned to shite as well. The Greer luck, after all, was rarely good. But this . . . this was unacceptable. Was there even a chance that he could regain some semblance of a physical self? Perhaps he could appropriate some recently deceased body the way the Other had. But he knew that wouldn't be enough. Even with the intensity of his emotions stolen from him, he burned with a need. He wanted his own body back, his own passions. He was supposed to be standing there in all his power and glory, Lord

King Shite of all the Green Wood, not huddled here on the floor like some pathetic worm.

He sat up slowly and was immediately disoriented as the trivial motion sent his bodiless form floating up towards the ceiling. Flailing his limbs didn't provide any sort of control and panic reared in him. He forced himself to be calm. To think. He let himself turn in a wobbly circle while he considered what exactly had set him drifting up in the first place. He hadn't moved the way he'd normally do in a physical body. He'd simply *thought* of sitting up and that had set him floating.

He willed himself to stop turning like some bloody balloon and was instantly rewarded with success.

That was more like it. Being able to move like this could almost make up for not having a body, though being unable to drink in this form was definitely shite. Jaysus, but he had a thirst.

One thing at a time, he told himself.

He directed himself towards the Glasduine just as the creature crashed its way through the windows, taking down huge chunks of the stone walls with it as it pushed its way out onto the lawn.

Now that was subtle, Donal thought, the great big stupid git. Tell the whole bloody world you're here, why don't you? Though he supposed the Glasduine wouldn't care. After all, what could hurt it? Nothing in this world, that was sure.

It didn't slip on the ice outside—either it was too heavy of foot and deliberate in its movement or, more likely, too grounded, too much a part of the heartbeat of the world to be inconvenienced by ice and slush.

As it lumbered across the lawn, he willed himself to its side, sticking to one of its enormous shoulders like a burr on a wolf's pelt. Contact made the Glasduine aware of him, but it also opened the creature up to him and his mind filled with the roil and burn of its thoughts.

No! he thought, breaking away to float in the Glasduine's wake. I never wanted any of that.

But even as he denied it, he knew the images he'd seen were based on the endless fantasies he'd carried around in his head. Of revenge for a life of hurt. Of a final payback to all the shites who'd done him wrong. Of wallowing in oceans of Guinness with any woman he bloody well fancied to be had for the bedding.

Inside the Glasduine's mind, Donal had seen it viewing itself awash in blood and gore, creating some huge fresco on the side of a building with body parts and organs, blood, and the tears of the dead and the dying while the sky rained whiskey and Guinness. Some mad reel played dissonantly against the sound of a storm and all around the Glasduine's feet lay naked women, broken and weeping, discarded now that the creature was done with them. Donal had recognized familiar faces in amongst those of strangers. Ellie and Bettina and—

Jaysus, Mary, and Joseph.

Miki.

If he'd had a body, Donal would have lost the contents of his stomach at

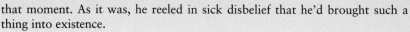
that moment. As it was, he reeled in sick disbelief that he'd brought such a thing into existence.

Where was the wonder, the calm power, the majesty of the Green Wood captured in human form? Not in this monster.

His gaze followed the Glasduine as it lumbered on through the woods, its passage quieting as it grew more assured with its new physical form.

I never wanted any of that, he thought. I only wanted my due, for the world to play me fair for once. Not that. Never that.

But it didn't matter what he'd wanted before he picked up the mask, or what he wanted now. Regrets never solved anything. The Glasduine was born, brought into this world by his own small-minded arrogance, and it was up to him to set things right before the monster ravaged the world. If even one innocent was harmed, Donal knew he was damned forever.

But sweet Jaysus, where did he even begin to stop it?

Contacting that foul mind again was the last thing he wanted, but he knew he had no choice. He had to confront the Glasduine. So he followed after, steeling himself for what was to come. It would not be an easy struggle, he knew. The chances were bloody good that he wouldn't survive it either. But that didn't matter so much anymore. He didn't matter at all. Only that the Glasduine was stopped.

Because perhaps the worst thing of all was that the Glasduine had also discarded parts of itself when it was born and these lay inside Donal's spirit now, dormant, sleeping, never to waken. They were all the things the Glasduine could have been. Prosperity for the natural world. A presence in the wild that would rekindle the awe and wonder that mankind had once held for the forests and hills that had lain unclaimed and untamed beyond their farm lots and city walls. An old magic that Donal had quenched with the raw torrent of his angers and hatred.

Fergus and his cronies had lied, Donal realized. The Gentry, that hag in her cabin. All of them. What the Glasduine should have been wasn't some chess piece to be moved about on a gaming board. It was an echo of the life spirit itself, of all that was good in the world. If it was to be reawoken, it would be to bring an echo of that grace back into the world. But just as he'd allowed rage to corrupt himself, he had corrupted that old magic. Others might have lied to him, but he had actually called it up and fed it with his despair and rage. He was the serpent in the garden and he had no one to blame but himself.

He could see the Glasduine ahead of him again, moving silent as a ghost through the trees, each of them covered with a frozen sheath of ice. The creature didn't dislodge a single icicle or twig as it moved. Neither did Donal, though he would have given much to be able to do so. He'd rather turn back the clock, he'd rather be stumbling around in these frozen woods in his own body, risking hypothermia, with the Glasduine never woken. But wishes were shite.

He launched himself at the Glasduine, not clinging to its shoulder this time, but plunging deep into the morass that was its mind. And there they fought for control of Donal's transformed body. The Glasduine had the advantage of the greater strength, but Donal had the stubbornness of a Gael. The more he was beaten and pushed away, the harder he clung, the deeper he burrowed into the miasma of the Glasduine's mind.

Time lost any meaning. They might have struggled for only moments; they might have struggled to the edge of forever. Battered and numbed, Donal held firm, but he knew it was a losing battle. He simply didn't have the strength. Unlike the Glasduine, he had no mystical reserves to call upon. He had only himself, and a weakened, subdued version of himself at that. He knew it was only a matter of time before the Glasduine dealt with him and the carnage would begin.

But then, just as he was losing all hope, he caught a flicker of motion from the corner of the Glasduine's eye, saw with its vision shadow shapes flitting through the ice-bedecked trees. They were a long way off, more in the between, or even the otherworld, than the world of the here and now, but he marked them, recognized them, saw a use for them.

There, he told the Glasduine, directing the creature's attention in their direction. *There is the true enemy.*

It had acquired his most powerful emotions and one of strongest among them was the resentment and hatred he'd felt towards the Gentry for the way they treated him like such a useless little shite. He wasn't sure that the Glasduine would understand or care at this point, but it grunted when it recognized the shapes. With a roar, it set off in pursuit. Donal clung to the Glasduine's mind, egging it on.

Finally there was a use for the buggers, he thought as the Gentry fled.

He just hoped they'd lead the Glasduine long and deep into the otherworld, so far that it might never find a way back to this world where he'd so stupidly called it up.

13

They returned to the city in only a fraction of the time it had taken Tommy to drive them up to the rez the night before. Driving smoothly through the between, unencumbered by either the weather or poor driving conditions, they were soon coming down from the mountains and approaching the outskirts proper.

"Look," Hunter said, his voice reflecting the awe he was obviously feeling. "There they go."

Ellie leaned on the side of the truck bed and watched the *manitou* step away, moving deeper in amongst the ice-covered trees. They faded like deer or wolves, seen for a moment along the highway, then gone, but she knew they were so much more. An ache woke in her heart when they were gone.

What if I never see them again? she wondered.

Sunday touched her arm.

"You will," she said, as though Ellie had spoken the words aloud. At Ellie's surprised look, the older woman added with a smile, "You look just the way I felt the first time I saw them—like your best friend had disappeared. But don't worry. Part of their mystery is that once you become aware of them, you will always be able to see them again."

"I like the way you put that," Hunter said. "They did feel like friends. A little scarier than the people I normally hang out with, mind you, but there was definitely some deep connection thing happening here."

Ellie nodded, wondering if she'd be able to hold enough of them in her mind to sculpt them, though she had no idea how she would even begin to bring them to life. So much of them lay between the lines of what one saw. But if she could capture even a fraction of the feelings they'd woken in her, she'd have accomplished some remarkable work indeed.

Tommy pulled over to the side of the road then and she had to hold onto the side of the truck bed for balance. Looking in through the back window of the cab, she could see him arguing with Aunt Nancy. She rapped on the window and Tommy slid it open.

"What's the problem?" she asked.

"Aunt Nancy wants us to drive straight up to Kellygnow."

"But wasn't that the plan?"

Tommy nodded. "Except we're in the big wide world now. What's going to happen when people see us cruising by, easy as you please, making time the way we are on roads that nobody else can use?"

"I don't really see the problem."

"Maybe not now. But some cop sees us, he's going to wonder, take down my plate number, and then, when this is all over, I'm going to have to answer questions I don't have answers for. I'm supposed to tell them about the between?"

"Why don't we go by the *manidò-akì?*" Sunday said.

"If you can find me a road in the otherworld, I'm game," Tommy told her. "But this is no all-terrain vehicle. I'm guessing we'll get about the length of a meadow."

"What we need," Zulema said from where she sat between Aunt Nancy and Tommy, "is for Nancy to put a charm on the truck, but—" She glanced to her right. "Someone considers that a waste of her juju."

"Who cares what white people think?" Aunt Nancy asked. She glanced back at Ellie and Hunter and added, "No offense."

"Tommy has to live here," Sunday said. "I think we should respect his wishes."

"No, Tommy *chose* to live here."

"Hey, Tommy's sitting in the cab with you," Tommy said, "and he's getting real tired of being referred to in the third person."

"That's the problem with these Raven boys," Aunt Nancy said. "Can't seem to get them into mischief when you want to; can't get them out when you don't."

"Please?" Zulema asked.

Aunt Nancy gave a heavy sigh. "Oh, fine. Put an old woman out."

She opened the passenger door and stepped onto the side of the road, moving with exaggerated stiffness. Once she was outside, she gave a theatrical stretch, then went around to the four corners of the pickup. Muttering to herself, she took pinches of some powder out of a small buckskin bag and sprinkled it on the end of each bumper.

"Is she always like that?" Ellie whispered once Aunt Nancy was back in the cab.

"Only when she doesn't get her own way," Sunday replied, also in a whisper.

"I heard that," Aunt Nancy said through the window. Then she turned to Tommy. "Well? What are you waiting for, Raven boy? Drive."

"Um . . ."

"Don't worry. No one will see us. Or they will, but they'll see something they're expecting to see, not precisely us."

"It's okay," Zulema said.

So Tommy started up the truck and on they went again.

The city, once they were driving through it, was a disaster zone. Ellie felt as though they were in some end-of-the-world movie. The ice was a slick carpet covering everything. Trees and telephone poles littered the sides of the road; buildings were all dark. There were next to no people. There were no other vehicles, except for those that had been abandoned at curbs and medians, though once they got closer to the city core they saw hydro trucks and various army vehicles.

No one gave them a second glance, but Tommy got off Williamson as soon as he could anyway. He drove toward the Beaches by back streets, crossing the river at the Kelly Street Bridge, then taking River Road through the Butler University campus to where it met up with Lakeside Drive. If anything, the storm damage was worse once they got to the Beaches. Or perhaps it only seemed worse, since no one had been working on clearing the streets of fallen trees and utility poles so they were strewn where they'd fallen—across porches and houses, crushing vehicles, blocking parts of the street. Twice they had to turn around and find an alternate route, but eventually they reached Handfast Road and began the long climb up to Kellygnow.

Ellie stared around herself in shock. There was so much damage from the ice storm. She glanced at Hunter.

"You wouldn't think that something as simple as freezing rain could create such a disaster zone, would you?"

"Depends on how much of the stuff you get," Hunter replied.

Ellie nodded, still stunned at the chaos that surrounded them.

When they finally reached Kellygnow, Aunt Nancy directed Tommy to drive by the house, crossing the lawn and then in between the trees. She had him park by the Recluse's cabin and everybody scrambled out. Aunt Nancy turned to Zulema.

"Ellie and I will go on alone from here," she said. "See if you can find where the creature crossed over, then use its spoor to lay a doubling-back charm that will return it to the spiritworld whenever it tries to cross over here. You remember how to do that?"

Both Zulema and Sunday nodded, but Ellie was sure she hadn't heard right.

"You want *me* to go with you?" she said.

"Of course. Who else? You wanted to help, didn't you?"

"Well, yes. But why me? I don't know anything."

Aunt Nancy's dark gaze settled on her.

"I need you," she said, "because your medicine is stronger than any I have seen outside of the spiritworld. Between the two of us . . . you have the medicine and I know how to use it. If we're lucky, that will be enough. And no," she added, turning to Tommy. "You're not coming. Remember what White-duck said."

"He didn't say I was in any real danger," Tommy said. "Only that I would be involved."

"He didn't need to say you were in danger. Just telling us you were involved was specific enough. Why else would he have bothered?"

"Since when do you listen to him?" Tommy asked.

"I have the utmost respect for Jack Whiteduck," Aunt Nancy said in a deferential tone of voice that even Ellie could tell was insincere. "Especially when he's right."

"They don't usually get along?" Ellie asked Sunday.

The other woman shrugged. "He doesn't much care for the Creeks."

"Why not?"

"Women's magic versus men's. He has a problem with it. We don't."

"And," Aunt Nancy put in, showing that she was listening to their conversation as well, "we aren't so foolish as to ignore his wisdom when it's sound. Are we, nephew?"

"Okay," Tommy said. "I'll stay already. But I don't like it."

Hunter cleared his throat. "But I'm coming," he said.

"You?" Aunt Nancy turned her gaze on him, but Hunter didn't flinch. "What do you have to offer?"

"I . . ."

"Don't forget, he killed one of the wolves," Tommy put in.

"Um, that's right," Hunter said. "And . . . well, Mr. Whiteduck . . ."

Aunt Nancy smiled. "Mr. Whiteduck. Oh, he'd like that."

"He didn't have any warnings about me, did he?"

"He doesn't even know you," Ellie said, but Aunt Nancy was already nodding.

"True enough," she said. "We could use a warrior to watch our backs." When she turned back to the truck to get a small backpack she'd left there, Ellie touched Hunter's arm.

"You don't have to do this," she said.

"And you do?"

"That's different. Somehow I managed to get involved and I can't back out now."

"Me, too," Hunter told her.

"Remember what I said about seeing this through," Tommy said.

"I won't let anybody down," Hunter said.

Tommy regarded him for a long moment, then nodded.

"I'm glad you're going," he said. "Aunt Nancy doesn't always remember the frailties of human flesh. With two of you going, you'll keep her honest. Pace yourself, no matter how she tries to shame you otherwise. Don't forget, she's lived her whole life in the bush. She can wear out half the Warrior's society lodge when she gets going."

He broke off when he saw Aunt Nancy looking at him.

"You Raven boys," she said, shaking her head. "I don't know where you get your sass."

"Probably from our side of the family," Sunday said.

Aunt Nancy shook her head, but she was smiling. "Come on, then," she told Hunter and Ellie.

Hunter fell in step with her, but Ellie paused beside Tommy for a moment.

"Look," she said. "I've been wanting to tell you this for a while. I don't know why it's important, but it just is. I guess it's because I'm always feeling guilty about it."

"Oh-oh. You're not going to tell me you've been badmouthing me to my supermodel girlfriends, are you?"

She punched his arm. "No. It's just . . . I want you to know that I don't have the same background as you or anybody else that works with Angel. I don't come from a broken home or any kind of a tragedy."

"I already knew that," Tommy said.

"You did? How?"

He shrugged. "It's just something you know as a survivor."

"It made me feel like such a phony. But I just wanted to help."

"Ellie," he said. "Don't you see? That only makes the time you put in that more precious. I mean for the rest of us, it's payback. A way for us to say thanks to Angel for how she helped us by helping others." He grinned. "But you. Not only are you a superhero, but you're a saint as well."

"Great. Now I'm a saint."

"Seriously," Tommy said. "You've nothing to feel guilty about. Go and fight the forest monsters with a clear conscience."

"Right."

"And, Ellie?"

She turned back to look at him.

"Be careful, okay?"

"I will," she said.

Then Aunt Nancy took her and Hunter by the hand. With her leading the way, they passed through the far border of the between and stepped into another world entirely.

14

Tommy hated feeling so useless. Once Aunt Nancy took Ellie and Hunter away into the spiritworld there was nothing for him to do but sit on the front bumper of the pickup and watch his other two aunts wandering about between the ice-covered trees, casting for spoor like a pair of blue tick hounds.

Funny how your world changes, he thought.

A day ago, the most he had to worry about was whether or not he was doing as much as he could to help Angel's clients. Were they reaching everyone? How could they raise more money? What other sources could they hit for food and coffee, clothing and blankets? Could he convince the garage on Perry Street to give the van yet one more free tune-up?

Now he was sitting—literally—on the edge of the *manidò-aki*, the spiritworld, hidden in some between place that separated the world of the *manitou* from the one he knew. He was untouched by the freezing rain that continued to drizzle onto the trees all around them, and everything was different. *Manitou* had stepped out of campfire stories into the real world. Some magical forest monster was running amok. Nice, normal Ellie turned out to be carrying some sort of deep well of medicine. And his aunts really did have the spooky powers everybody on the rez had always attributed to them.

That was the real kicker. Maybe if he hadn't come to the city, looking to count coup in a whiskey bottle, he could have been learning some of this stuff from them. He could be out there with Ellie and Aunt Nancy right now, hunting down this spirit monster, doing something, instead of sitting here twiddling his thumbs. The stoic Indian bit had never been something he could pull off; he just didn't have the patience. Not like his aunts, who could sit there for hours waiting for whomever had come to them to explain what it was they wanted.

But back then he'd been as interested in shamanism as he'd been in the traditionalism of the Warrior Society, which was not at all. He'd been, and still was, all for Indian rights, but he saw them as something one had to look for in the future, not in the past. In the end, he'd gone looking for them in a bottle. By the time he finally surfaced to some level of rationality once more, he didn't see himself as an Indian so much as a survivor. Which was why he was sitting here, on the sidelines. If he'd had some knowledge, some experience with all this weird stuff, then Whiteduck probably wouldn't have given his aunts the warning he had, or if Whiteduck still had, Tommy's aunts would have ignored it because they'd have known that he could handle himself.

At least Hunter had gone with them. Tommy loved Nancy as much as he did any of his other aunts, but he didn't entirely trust her. It wasn't that she was prone to meanness, so much as that she used whatever was at hand to deal with a problem. If she happened to need Ellie's medicine, she was as likely to take it all. Though what Hunter would actually do if that situation arose . . .

Hell, Tommy thought. Hunter *had* killed one of the Gentry, hadn't he? So he just had to trust that, if Hunter had to, he would find a way to deal with Aunt Nancy as well.

Tommy looked up when he heard his aunts returning to the pickup where he was waiting for them.

"Any luck?" he asked.

They shook their heads.

"The spoor is everywhere," Zulema said. "It's like a berry dye dissolving in water. It starts out distinctly enough, but give it enough time and your whole bucket takes on the color."

Sunday nodded.

"Which means?" Tommy asked.

"That we can't contain the creature in the spiritworld," Zulema said. "Anytime it wants to come back here, all it has to do is step across."

"And it will come back," Sunday said.

"Oh, yes," Zulema agreed. "Out there it's a little fish in a big pond. But here . . . here it can have anything it wants."

"But if it's taken on physical form, it can be hurt," Tommy said. "Right? Like the Gentry."

His aunts exchanged a glance.

"This is something older and far more dangerous than the simple spirits of a place," Sunday said.

"Then what's Nancy going to do with it?" Tommy asked.

"I'm guessing she'll try to use its own strength against it," Zulema said.

"Which is easier to do in the spiritworld," Sunday added.

Zulema nodded. "*And* if its path back here is cut off."

"But you can't get a fix on where it went through?" Tommy asked.

"It's too powerful," Sunday explained. "Everything reverberates with its presence."

Tommy looked from one to the other. "So Ellie and the others . . . they're on their own? Without any backup?"

"I'm afraid so," Zulema said.

"Great."

"We're not giving up," Sunday told him. She looked to her sister. "Maybe we can go back to where the creature was first called into the world and work our way out from that point."

"It's worth a try," Zulema said. When Tommy got up, she added, "You might as well stay here—you know, in case the others come back and need something."

"Sure," Tommy said.

Right, he thought as he watched them go back towards Kellygnow. Stay here in case the others needed something, translated into keeping out of the way.

Sighing, he opened the door of the cab. He paused as he started to get in, gaze alighting on a crushed cigarette butt that somebody had left on the floor. Picking it up, he looked out toward the trees where his aunts had been searching earlier. After a moment, he leaned into the cab and opened the glove compartment. He took out the matches that he kept there with a couple of candles—emergency heating in case he ever broke down on some back road—

and walked around the front of the pickup to where a piece of granite pushed up by the roots of one of the big oaks, protected from most of the freezing rain by the trees' drooping boughs.

He split open the cigarette butt and made a little pile of the leftover tobacco on the rock, then lit it with a match. Sitting on his heels, he watched the tendril of smoke rise and returned his gaze to the trees.

"Grandfather Thunders," he said. He had to stop, clear his throat. "Look, I'm not exactly the best example of my people, but I never meant any disrespect, you know. And I'm not asking anything for myself, here, just so's we understand. But if you could see your way clear to making sure Ellie makes it through this in one piece, I'd be really grateful."

The tobacco was mostly ash now, smoldering on the rock.

"I know this offering's pretty puny," he went on, "but as soon as I can get to a store, I'll get you a whole pouch of the stuff. And I'll have the Aunts teach me how to offer it up to you properly, okay?"

He watched the last of the tobacco burn. The thin thread of smoke finally died. He waited a while longer, almost expecting some response, now that he knew that all the campfire stories were true. But there was nothing. He had to laugh at himself as he stood up. Like the *manitou* were suddenly going to come at his beck and call. He'd probably wet himself if one of them actually did show up. But maybe what he'd done would make a difference.

"If you hear me," he said, "I just want to say, you know, thanks. For listening, I mean."

He waited a while longer, then returned to his seat on the front bumper. The hardest thing about being useless, he realized, was knowing that you were. And there was not a damn thing you could do about it.

Christ, he could really use a drink. And that was something he hadn't felt this strongly in a long time.

He was seriously considering going into Kellygnow himself to see if he could cadge one from somebody when he heard a sound, far off in the distance. He lifted his head, waiting for it to be repeated, but it didn't come again.

Okay, he thought. It's raining. Big storm. Maybe it wasn't so surprising. But it was also the middle of winter, and how often did you hear thunder in the winter?

"Thank you," he said. "Really, I mean it."

He was still grinning when his aunts returned from Kellygnow with a tall red-headed woman in tow.

7

En el Bosque del Corazón

El que con lobos anda a aullar se enseña.
He who keeps company with wolves learns to howl.
—MEXICAN-AMERICAN SAYING

1

Wasn't that just like a man, Bettina thought as she followed her wolf into *la época del mito.* Where did they learn to keep everything in its own box the way they did? She knew the kiss had meant as much to him as it had to her, yet he was able to put everything aside and carry on with the task at hand as though nothing had happened between them. Which was what they *should* do, she knew. What they must do. But it still made the promise woken from that kiss seem of so much less consequence than she hoped it was.

El lobo looked back at her when they'd crossed over.

"What's the matter?" he asked.

"Nothing," she said. "No *importa.*"

"When a woman says, 'nothing,' " he said, "she means, 'everything.' "

"You shouldn't generalize."

A flicker of amusement woke in his eyes. "Or I should at least encompass more with my generalizations. Perhaps I should have referred to most people instead."

Bettina sighed. "My grandmother and Nuala both warned me about keeping company with wolves. *El que con lobos anda a aullar se enseña,* Abuela would say."

"He who keeps company with wolves learns to howl," *el lobo* translated.

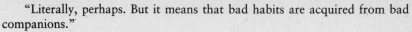

"Literally, perhaps. But it means that bad habits are acquired from bad companions."

"And what bad habits have you acquired from me?"

"None," Bettina said. "So far."

"I like the literal meaning better."

"*Sí.* But you would."

He nodded, serious now. "Though perhaps not for the reason you think. Sometimes it's better to cut yourself free from what you know and . . ." He shrugged. "Howl is as good a word as any. To let loose the constrictions that normally bind your actions and run wild for a time."

"Only we can't, can we? We have a duty."

"Ah, so that's what this is about."

Bettina shook her head. "No, I understand that we must first deal with the task at hand. But you seem to put the . . . other business away so easily."

"Would you rather I bed you right now, here among the ferns and leaves?"

Sí, Bettina found herself thinking even as she shook her head again. It was bluntly put—deliberately so, she didn't doubt, to get a rise out of her—but the thought of it appealed to her all the same, though only if *he* felt what she was feeling . . .

"I don't know what to think," she said. "It's all very confusing."

"I know," he told her. "Don't doubt that I am any less confused."

"Truly?"

He nodded.

"That makes it easier for me," she said.

He shook his head, but then offered her his hand. "Come," he said, and led her in the direction of the pool where, in this world, an ancient salmon lay sleeping. The forest was different by day, still mysterious with the cathedralling trees rearing above them as they walked, but it felt more welcoming than it had when she'd been here the other night, also in the company of her wolf. The ice storm had vanished, left behind with the winter they'd escaped. Here it felt like late autumn, the air rich with a musky scent of dark earth and secrets. Bettina had almost forgotten why they'd come until they neared the pool and saw the Recluse lying on the grass by its low stone wall. *El lobo* glanced at the body.

"It seems they've had a falling-out," he said, then meant to continue on his way.

Bettina pulled him to a stop. Letting go of his hand, she knelt by the still form. She could tell by the angle of the neck that it was hopeless, but she still felt for a pulse, still called up the healing spirit in her heart and asked for help from the spiritworld to diagnose what might be used to help the hurt woman.

"*Bendígame, Virgen. Bendígame, santos, Bendígame, espíritus,*" she murmured. "*Deme la fuerza a ayudar esta pobre alma.*"

The blessing rose in her but it was too late. The woman's death wound was far too grievous, and here in *la época del mito,* spirits were quick to leave their bodies and travel on.

"You're wasting your time."

Bettina looked up to *el lobo*, a little disappointed that he would be so callous of one so recently slain.

"I had to try," she said.

"But why? She is the cause of all our troubles."

"What do you mean?"

He sighed and crouched beside her, sitting on his ankles. She felt a pang of memory when she looked at him. So her father had sat, he and his *peyoteros*, talking long into the night, smoking their cigarettes. Men unused to chairs, who could find no use for man-made conveniences.

"Until she came along," *el lobo* said, "the Gentry were no different from Nuala. Content to roam the city, to have a den in the wild acres behind Kellygnow. They didn't need to take anything from the native spirits—they had all they wanted already: a den they could call their own, pubs for drink and the *craíc*, the music. It was she who woke ambition in them, woke the evil we all carry in us, fanned it with admiring words and false promises."

"You said you didn't know about the mask."

"I didn't. But I still knew there was something, some artifact they sought after, and would, as we've seen, eventually find. And all the while the Gentry, their baser instincts awoken, simply grew worse. It was she who encouraged them to be more territorial. To be harder of heart and mean-spirited. To take what they wished, for it was owed to them."

"Why would she do such a thing?" Bettina asked.

El lobo shrugged. "To keep them from thinking too much, I suppose. From seeing how she led them about by their noses."

Bettina looked down at the dead woman.

"What did she get from it?" she asked.

"A longer life. The Gentry showed her a way into the spiritworld, where she spent most of the year."

Bettina nodded. Time moved differently here and didn't rest so heavily on the body.

"And for power, of course," *el lobo* added.

"Power."

"She meant to use the Glasduine as much as the Gentry did. I don't doubt she chose both who would wear the mask and who would repair it."

"Ellie was supposed to make a new one," Bettina said. "A copy, but infused with her own spirit and creative impulses."

"To infuse it with her own considerable, if untapped, power, you mean."

Bettina nodded. It was all so depressing.

"The Recluse should have asked for luck," she said, remembering a conversation she'd had with Ban, years ago now.

"How so?"

"Luck is sweet. A gift, a loan. When you have made your use of it, it goes on, undiminished. Power is finite and when one has it, it means another doesn't."

El lobo nodded with understanding.

"And now look at her," Bettina said. "For all the heartache and pain she caused, she has earned nothing but the death that was always waiting for her. What an evil woman."

"Or a fool."

Bettina gave her wolf a questioning look.

"There's often not a great deal of difference between the two," he said.

He rose easily from his crouch. Turning, he offered Bettina his hand and lifted her to her feet. They paused at the pool, looking down at the sleeping salmon. *El lobo* plucked a cigarette butt from the water and carefully placed it on the stone wall among the other offerings.

"We should go," he said.

Bettina nodded. But having seen the dead woman made her question once more her own involvement in this hunt.

"*¿Y bien?*" she said. "I don't even know why I'm here."

"To right a wrong."

"Is that it? I felt the pull of these forests, I left my beloved desert, and for this? To try to heal some monster that will no doubt need to be killed anyway?"

"I don't think you were called to try to heal any monster," *el lobo* said. "How could you have been? It didn't even exist until today."

"Then who have I been called to heal? You?"

"I think you are here to heal yourself."

She shook her head. "*No seas tonto.* I don't need healing."

"No? Perhaps I'm not so crazy. You've been here for months, but to what use have you put your studies beyond some simple charms? Calling on the spirits to help the Gentry's pet human is the closest you've come to being a true *curandera* since you arrived."

"I have been waiting . . ."

"Yes, to be healed."

Bettina frowned at him. He could be so infuriating.

"Healed?" she demanded. "Of what?"

"Shall I make a list of all that troubles you?" her wolf asked.

"Please do."

He counted the items off on his fingers. "There is the question of your faith, how the spirits confuse your feelings towards the church and cause a rift with your mother. There is your grandmother's abrupt disappearance from your life. Your sister's denial of the spiritworld and how she belittles your grandmother's teachings. The guilt you feel for sending *los cadejos* away after promising them a true home. The confusion of having a father who lives in the desert as a hawk, forgetting he was ever a man. The loneliness that comes from how you long for love, but believe no man will understand you, and no spirit will keep faith. Shall I go on?"

She was too shocked to be angry. "Who are you? How can you know all of this?"

"I am who I have said I am."

Bettina shook her head. "You know too much about me."

"I'm a good listener," *el lobo* said.

"Those are things I've not spoken of with anyone. And certainly not here."

He nodded. "I didn't hear it from you. I listened to the gossip of the spiritworld. When you first came, I asked after you, and the stories came to me. Of you, your *abuela*, your parents."

"Why would they speak of me? What could they hope to gain?"

El lobo laughed. "They would gain nothing. It's simply the nature of spirits to gossip. Surely you've seen by now that they're worse than humans? If you don't want to be gossiped about, you must ask them specifically not to." He shrugged. "But even then they will still talk, couching their stories in riddles and half-truths."

"Is there anything you *don't* know about me?" she asked.

"Everything."

"You can say that after the list you've just recited."

"Those are things that are spoken of about you," he said. "One can infer a great deal from such, but not what matters most. I don't know how you truly feel. What your hopes and dreams might be. I have listened to the spirits speak of you; I have yet to hear you speak."

Bettina turned from the pool with its sleeping salmon and walked away, under the trees. *El lobo* fell in step beside her, quiet now. His gaze, when she glanced his way, held only concern; the teasing humor fled.

"It's all true," she said after a while. "*Más o menos.* I did not specifically send *los cadejos* away, but I have not made them welcome since the night Abuela followed the clown dog into the desert. And my beliefs, Abuela's teachings. While it's true they have caused a rift between my mother and sister and myself, I have reconciled my faith with my knowledge of the spirits." She looked at him again. "I see room for all in God's world. Perhaps we do not all practice the charity we should to each other, but surely He does."

"I know nothing of your god," *el lobo* said.

"Why would you?"

"But I would like to understand this hold he has on his followers."

She nodded. "*Ése está extraño,*" she said. "The first night you took me to the salmon's pool, I saw the Recluse there, but she seemed like a mission priest to me. You told me you saw no one."

"I told you I saw no man."

"Ah. But why would you keep her a secret from me?"

"Because you weren't involved," he said. "If you weren't a part of what she and the Gentry were up to, why draw you into it?"

They'd walked farther now than Bettina had ever been in this part of *la época del mito.* By now, in the world where Kellygnow stood, their way would have taken them through the neighboring estates. Here, there was only the wild wood, ancient and tall, the immense trees untouched by the lumbermen who had founded so much of Newford.

"I hadn't known about my father," she said. "That he had forgotten he was a man. I thought he had abandoned us—out of love," she added. "That he thought it would hurt us to grow old while he remained forever unchanged."

"Only he can say."

She nodded. "When this is done, I will find him and ask him."

El lobo hesitated, then said, "It's not always wise to question the motives of an old spirit such as he."

"Are you warning me against asking you too many questions?" she asked with a smile.

The humor returned to his eyes. "I am hardly an old spirit. To tell you the truth, I'm not entirely certain what I am."

"But still I will ask him," Bettina said. "He may be an old spirit, but he is still my *papá*."

"This is true."

"*¿Y bien?* And as for love—do any of us trust or understand it?"

"I don't understand it," her wolf told her. "I can only feel it."

"Do you trust it?"

"If you mean, do I trust the feeling? Then certainly. Do I feel it will be returned . . ." He shook his head. "I have no idea. Do you seek it?"

"Everyone looks for love," she said. "But I have learned not to make my happiness depend upon it. My *abuela* would say that even in a relationship, one must be happy with oneself as an individual, or what do you have to offer the other?"

"I would have liked to have met your grandmother. You still miss her, don't you?"

"*Sí,*" Bettina said. "I think of her every day."

She gave him a wan smile and they walked on in silence for a time. The forest remained unchanged, the tall trees rearing skyward to their impossible heights, the footing even, mostly moss and a carpet of autumn leaves with little undergrowth to impede their way. It was not a forest they could have found in the world they'd left behind.

"I thought we would have come across some sign of the creature by now," *el lobo* said finally. "Or at least heard about its passage. But the trees are silent to my ears and the gossips are most noticeable by their absence."

Bettina nodded. This aspect of *la época del mito* was completely unfamiliar to her, so she had been following her wolf's lead. Now she glanced at him.

"You were going to show me how to call up *los cadejos,*" she said.

The thought of their return filled her with mixed emotions. She'd realized ever since her dream and Adelita's gift the other morning just how much she missed them. She was anxious as well. How would they react to her contact after such a long silence?

"I was," *el lobo* said. "I will. But I was hoping to find the creature's trail before we needed to do so."

So he was nervous, too. That didn't bode well. What wasn't he telling her now?

"Why was that?" she asked, striving to sound calmer than she felt.

He shrugged. "Because there is always a danger in coming to the attention of old powerful spirits."

He left so much unsaid, Bettina thought, but she understood exactly what he meant, his reservations obviously mirroring her own. She stopped and turned to him.

"Even if we didn't need their help," she said, "this is something I must do. I have not treated them fairly. I must make amends for my broken promise."

El lobo nodded.

"*Y así,*" Bettina said. "So how do we do this?"

El lobo shook his head. "Not we, but you. You must welcome them back to you. But we must do it in some place that is familiar and dear to you both or else they might choose not to hear you."

"The desert is too far from here," Bettina said. "We don't have the time to make such a trip."

El lobo gave her that maddening smile of his. "Surely your grandmother taught you that the spiritworld can be whatever you need it to be?"

"No," she replied. "We ran out of time before she could tell me so many things."

"Most clothe it in a landscape with which they're familiar, or one that they expect to find, as we did when we crossed over. We were in the eastern woodlands when we left your world, so that is how we see the spiritworld now, or at least an idealized version of those forests. But it doesn't have to be so. The spiritworld can be anywhere we need it to be."

"I see . . . I think. But that doesn't explain how we can change where we are now into the desert."

"That's somewhat more complicated," *el lobo* admitted. "It would be easier if your *croí baile* was in the desert."

As had happened the first time she and her wolf had met in *la época del mito*, not all the Gaelic words he used were automatically translated by the spiritworld's enchantment.

"My what?" she asked.

"The home of your heart. That one place where you feel truly and completely at home. Each of us has one, though not everyone cherishes it as they should. We carry an echo of it with us. Here." He laid a hand on his chest. "It comes with us wherever we go—no matter how far we travel from the physical location."

Bettina nodded. "I have heard of that. Abuela called it *el bosque del corazón*. The forest we carry with us in our heart."

"When you are here, in the spiritworld, you are always but one step away from that place. The actual location, I mean."

Bettina's eyes lit up. "So that's why she called it *el bosque del corazón*."

"What do you mean?"

"Abuela would often make these pronouncements, but before you could ask her what she meant, she had already gone on to something else. It never made sense to me that she would call it a forest, but now with what you've told me, I understand."

"I still don't follow you," her wolf said.

"You know the story of the First Forest—how all forests are an echo of it and reach back to it?"

"Of course."

"Then don't you see? This is our own version of it—*we* connect to our heart home just as all forests echo back to the First Forest."

El lobo smiled. "Good. So you understand. And does the forest in your heart echo back to the desert?"

"I have never considered it. But it must. That's the only place I am ever truly happy."

"Then that is where you must bring us," he said.

For a long moment Bettina could only look at him. Everything he said made perfect sense, but it still left her feeling dizzy. She had never looked inside herself for her own *bosque del corazón*, so how could she bring them to the place it echoed? And never having attempted such a task before, who was to say where they might end up? She was not exactly the most focused individual when it came to journeying through *la época del mito*. As easily distracted as she could be in myth time, anything could happen to them.

"I can't," she said. "I don't even know where to begin."

"Look inside yourself," *el lobo* told her. "Call that place up in your mind, clearly and truly."

"And then?" Bettina asked, unable to keep the doubt from her voice.

"Hold it in your mind like a waking dream and will us to be there. Your father's blood will ensure that we will journey true."

"My father's blood."

El lobo smiled. "Have you studied your grandmother's teachings so diligently that you've forgotten your father's lineage? You have the blood of shapeshifters and shaman running in your veins—the oldest and truest *geasan*."

"I . . ." She hesitated, then knew she had to admit it to him. "I'm not the most assured of travelers in *la época del mito*."

"I say again, your father's blood will see us through. Tell me, have you ever been harmed in the spiritworld?"

She shook her head.

"I would wager that your father's blood keeps you safe. Any you meet here would recognize that old blood of his that you carry. I wouldn't doubt it's what first called *los cadejos* to you."

"You make it sound so simple."

"It is simple. Especially here, in the spiritworld. We are the ones who make such things complicated."

"Now you sound like Abuela."

"Just try," he said, his voice gentle.

Bettina truly didn't know where to begin. The desert was the forest she carried in her heart, a seeming contradiction in terms unless one knew the Sonoran. But what part of it? She understood from what her wolf was saying that she must focus on a particular aspect of it, but she'd walked so much of it, alone or in the company of her *abuela* and Adelita, with Ban and his mother and her own father. What one place could her *bosque del corazón* echo? The desert was large and she loved it all. And complicating matters was how she'd always wandered in and out of *la época del mito* when she did go out hiking.

But then she remembered another gift that had arrived the morning she'd been reminded so strongly of *los cadejos*. She reached into the pocket of her vest and drew out the rosary that her mamá had sent along in Adelita's package. Though undoubtedly Mamá hadn't meant it to be used for such a purpose, it was exactly what Bettina knew she could use to focus.

Her wolf regarded the rosary with interest.

"Where did you get that?" he asked.

"My *mamá* sent it to me."

He reached out with a hesitant finger to touch it.

"This is a potent *geasan*," he said as he let his hand fall back to his side. "Your mother has *Indio* blood, too?"

Bettina nodded.

"I didn't think the *geasan* of old spirits and the church could join in such a fashion," he said. "She must be a remarkable woman."

Bettina hadn't even considered that her mother might have made this herself. How could she have known how to do it, to combine the mysteries of church and desert like this? Who would have guided her hand? No one in the church, that was certain, but when had her mother even believed in the spirits of the desert, little say let one of them instruct her in anything?

But, "She is," was all she told her wolf.

She held the rosary in both hands.

"*Virgen bendita*," she said, closing her eyes. "*Espíritus de los lugares ocultos salvajes*. Help me find this place I seek. *Lo imploro*."

When the image came slipping into her mind it was like greeting an old, long-lost friend. Of course, she thought. How could she not have remembered this place on her own? It was the crest of low-backed rise that stood in a part of *la época del mito* a few miles from her mother's house, a secret place guarded by saguaro aunts and uncles that looked down into a dry wash. In the human world, one could see the Baboquivari Mountains in the distance, rising tall and rugged on the western horizon. In *la época del mito*, those same mountains shone with an inner light, the mystery of I'itoi Ki rising up from Rock Drawn at the Middle in a spiraling column of multicolored hues, reaching for the heavens. It was as though the most amazing desert sunset had been captured in *cadejos* . . .

How often had she and Abuela walked there, camped there, talked long into the night and through the day in that place? She had been there with her father, too, on more than one occasion.

There, she thought, gathering her will and focusing it on that image in her mind. That is where we must go.

There was no sensation of transition. She only heard her wolf say something softly in Gaelic that roughly translated to "Oh my," and then the cool autumn glade was gone and she had bright sunlight bathing her face. She could smell the desert, felt the shifting dirt underfoot, heard the quail and doves in the mesquite that grew down in the wash.

She opened her eyes, the rosary still held fast in her hands, her face turned to the sky. The first thing she saw was a red-tailed hawk, coasting on its broad wings as it rode the air currents high overhead.

"Papá," she said.

But it was only a bird, not an old spirit in the shape of a hawk, his human form lying forgotten under his feathers. She knew a moment's sadness, then put the old ache aside. It was too hard to hold onto it at this moment. She drew a deep breath, tasting again the familiar air. It was enough to lift her spirits once more. She turned to her wolf, astonishment and delight dancing in her eyes.

"Well done," he said. "If this is the forest of your heart, then you are well-favored, indeed. Only . . . where are the trees? Or did your grandmother only mean this to be a forest in a figurative sense?"

Bettina laughed and pointed to the tall saguaro.

"What do you think those are?" she asked.

"Very tall cacti."

She nodded. "A forest of aunts and uncles."

El lobo smiled at her infectious pleasure.

"You see?" he said. "Your father's blood runs true."

Bettina turned slowly around, drinking in the sounds and smells and sights. Not until this very moment did she realize just how much she had missed it. Truly, the desert was in her blood and she would not be whole living anywhere else.

That thought made her look at her wolf and recall what he'd said earlier, how perhaps it had been to heal herself that she'd sensed this mysterious call drawing her to Kellygnow. Sometimes one needed distance to appreciate what one had, lying close at hand. So perhaps it was true. Because she had long forgotten how it was to be so grounded as she felt at this moment. This is how it had been for her before everything had changed. Before *la Muerte* had sent the clown dog for Abuela. Before Papá had forgotten his human form. Before she had turned her back on the promise she had made to *los cadejos*.

Those old sadnesses rose up to nibble at her joy. She could do nothing for Abuela and if her father slept in a hawk's thoughts, it would do no harm for him to sleep so a little longer. But the broken promise . . .

"To call *los cadejos* to me," she asked her wolf. "Is it the same as how I brought us here? I must hold the thought of them in my heart and mind and will them to return?"

He nodded. "All but the willing part. It might be better if you simply asked."

"*Por supuesto*," she said. Of course.

And if they would not come?

She shook her head and told herself not to think like that. She looked down at the rosary she still held and put it back in the pocket of her vest, unsure of how *los cadejos* would react to it. Besides, she didn't need it to help her focus. The memory of their happy voices and rainbow colors was too immediate for her to need any sort of talisman.

She closed her eyes and let the memories rise up.

"*Perdona*," she whispered. "Forgive me. It was unfair of me to turn away from you as I did."

She listened for the sound of their voices, the high-pitched merry yelps.

"Come back. *Por favor*. Tell me how I may make amends."

She could feel her wolf's sudden tension at her side and knew what troubled him. One did not lightly put oneself in debt to old spirits such as these. But she didn't care. The broken promise was an enormous weight that she hadn't recognized she was carrying until *el lobo* had spoken of it earlier. She was at fault, so it was up to her to atone.

"I will do whatever you ask," she said, "so long as it harms no other living thing."

She reached out into the desert and deep into her heart, searching for the rainbow dogs, but could find no trace of them.

"*Perdona*," she said again. "*Por favor, mis amigos los espíritus*. Do not abandon me as I abandoned you."

She feared her wolf was wrong. That not even calling to them in this place would be enough.

Their aid in tracking down the Glasduine no longer mattered to her. At this moment it was of far greater importance that she make her peace with them, that she be forgiven her broken promise and given another chance to do right by them.

But if they didn't come.

If they refused to hear her apology—

"Bettina," her wolf said softly.

She opened her eyes to look at him and he nodded higher up the hill where a cluster of prickly pear were gathered like a skirt around the base of a towering, many-armed saguaro. The Baboquivari Mountains rose up behind the giant cactus, the rainbow lights that were the mystery of I'itoi Ki spiraling up from the cave hidden in their heart. Then she saw that an echo of the spiral's rainbow colors was reflected on the ground at the base of the saguaro.

No, she realized. It wasn't an echo of that light.

There were goat-footed, barrel-chested dogs standing there among the prickly pear, the bright shock of their pelts even more vibrant than the spiral rising in the sky behind them.

Los cadejos had answered her call.

Her heart filled with a sudden happiness that just as quickly drained away. For there was no welcome for her in their small dark eyes. There was no emotion to be read at all.

"There is more . . . luck gathered here," he said, "than I have ever seen in one place before."

Luck, Bettina thought. *Sí*. Or perhaps it was something darker.

The dogs moved towards them, fanning out in a half-circle, their cloven hooves clicking on the stones underfoot. Their happy voices were silent. The laughter she remembered in their eyes had turned to thoughtful consideration. Their gazes judged.

Bettina shivered. Perhaps what was gathered here was power.

2

Miki didn't think she'd ever been more miserable than when she was slogging through this wretched weather. By the time she reached Battersfield Road her wet clothes made her feel as though she'd doubled her weight and her boots squished unpleasantly with every step she took. Her nose was running and she could already feel the telltale tickle at the back of her throat of a cold coming on. With her luck, she'd end up with pneumonia.

Bloody Donal.

What were the chances she'd even be able to get anything through that thick skull of his? Her new vow to watch her temper notwithstanding, if he was standing in front of her right now, she'd be hard-pressed not to pull the baseball bat out of the back of her belt and give him a good whack with it.

She had the streets to herself except for the maintenance crews desperately trying to restore power to the city's core and the occasional army vehicle. The city and hydro workers were too busy to pay any attention to her, but the soldiers kept trying to be helpful. The third time one of the eight-wheeled Bisons stopped near her, the sergeant insisted that she accompany them to a shelter.

"Is the city under martial law?" she asked.

"It's officially been declared a disaster zone."

"You didn't answer my question."

The sergeant sighed. "No. But be reasonable, miss. At least let us give you a lift to your mother's house."

The bit with her mother's house was starting to wear thin, Miki realized. Next time one of the Bisons stopped for her, she'd have to think up something better. But it was too late to change her story in this instance.

"Right," she said. "And as soon as you've got me on board, you'll head off to one of these shelters."

The sergeant shook his head. "I promise you we won't. First we'll pick up your mother."

Oh, great. The mother who didn't exist. She couldn't have them drive her anywhere—certainly not to Kellygnow. Donal would go mad to see her pull up in the company of this lot. And since she had no mother waiting for her, there was nowhere else she could have them take her. With the way her luck was running, once they found out she was lying to them, they'd probably arrest her as a potential looter.

"I don't know how to put this politely," she said finally as the sergeant waited patiently for her response, "so why don't you just sod off and make yourself useful with someone who wants your help. Would that be too much to ask?"

With that she marched off as resolutely as she could, feet squishing in her boots as she slid her way along the ice. The fine hairs at the nape of her neck prickled with uneasy tension. She expected them to come after her at any moment, and then what would she do? Defend herself with her trusty baseball bat? Oh, that would be so effective.

But no one followed and a few moments later she heard the vehicle move off.

Amazing. Her good luck was holding. If you could call slopping through this mess good luck.

She continued along Battersfield Road, inching her way along the side of the street where the footing was marginally less treacherous than the glare ice of the sidewalk. Five minutes later she heard another vehicle coming up behind her. Bloody hell. She didn't know if she had the strength for yet another confrontation. She was so damned wet and cold and tired that the soldiers could just pick her up by the scruff of her neck like some bedraggled kitten and there wouldn't be a thing she could do about it. But when she turned, it was to see a battered old pickup truck approaching her at a crawl. The driver was dark-haired with a thick moustache, Spanish, or maybe Lebanese. It was hard to tell at this distance. He gave a little honk of his horn, then the truck started to slew into the curb as he braked.

Miki had to jump back as the vehicle came sliding towards her. She made the pavement, but immediately lost her balance and would have fallen if there hadn't been a NO PARKING sign there for her to grab onto. Meanwhile the pickup had come to a halt and the driver had opened his door. Standing on the running board, he looked over the top of the cab at her, plainly concerned.

"Are you hurt?" he called.

Miki straightened up. Spanish, she decided from his accent.

"No," she told him. "I'm fine." Adding, "Now go away," under her breath.

He seemed friendly enough, but he also looked very strong and capable, and really, what was *he* doing out here? He could be one of the looters, for all she knew, what with that truck and all. Lots of room in the bed for all sorts of things.

"Let me give you a lift," he said.

"It's okay," she said. "Really."

"I can take you as far as Handfast Road."

He *was* a looter, she thought. Because there was no way anyone from the Beaches would be driving such a scruffy old truck. But he didn't look mean, and she was so bloody wet and tired, and he was going right to Handfast, and what was he going to get from her anyway? There was nothing to loot except a baseball bat and she was sure she didn't exactly look the picture of enticement and allure, no matter how hard-up he might be. She was more like some half-drowned alley cat.

"Okay," she said, sliding her way over to the pickup. "Thanks."

When she got in, he turned up the heat then reached behind the seat and pulled out a colorful Mexican blanket which he handed to her.

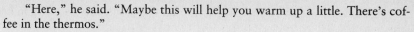

"Here," he said. "Maybe this will help you warm up a little. There's coffee in the thermos."

Oh, lord. Coffee. Warmth.

She hesitated a moment, then took the blanket and wrapped it around herself.

"How come you're being so nice to me?" she asked.

He gave her a surprised look.

"I don't mean to be rude or anything," she went on, "but it just seems a little weird. It's not like you know me or anything."

"Wouldn't it be a better world if we all looked out for each other?"

"Well, yeah," Miki replied. "Except it'd also mean that we were on Mars or something."

He gave her a thin smile. Putting the pickup into gear, he started it on its forward crawl once more.

"I think this storm is a good thing," he said. "It reminds us that we don't have to live in a faceless city, where we are all strangers. We are a collection of communities. To get by, we need to count on each other."

"Until someone stabs you in the back."

"I live over on the East Side," he told her.

Miki nodded to show she was listening, though she didn't understand the context of what he was telling her. There was a regular barrio there in amongst the projects, separate from, yet a part of the cheap housing the city had put up for those in need of shelter. The buildings had all been filled up and fallen into disrepair almost before they'd been erected.

"Today," her Good Samaritan went on, "I saw known drug dealers and gang members helping neighborhood widows clear ice from their roofs, pick up groceries, move their families to the shelters when they lost their power."

"And the point being?"

He shrugged. "We are working together for a change. I find myself wishing this community spirit was something that would last beyond the storm."

Miki nodded. She helped herself to a Kleenex tissue from the box on the dash, then poured herself a cup of the coffee. All she needed now was a cigarette.

"So why are you going to the Beaches?" she asked.

"I work on one of the Estates," he said. "At a place called Kellygnow. Their phone is out and I'm worried about how they are doing. I would not have come but Maria Elena—my wife—could see how I was worrying, so after I took her to stay with a neighbor who still has electricity, she told me to go." He glanced at Miki. "I would not have left her otherwise."

Miki felt about two inches tall.

"I thought you were a looter," she said.

"Why? Because I'm Latino?"

"God, no. Because of the truck. I mean, can you see the rich hoity-toits up there driving something like this?"

"And now?" he asked.

"I feel like a bloody eejit."

He smiled and took a hand from the wheel, offering it to her. "I am Salvador Flores."

"Miki Greer," she said, shaking.

"Should that not be Minnie?"

"What . . . ? Oh, right. Ha ha. Big Disney fan, then?"

"So where are you going?" he asked.

"Same place as you—Kellygnow."

"I've not seen you there before."

"I've never been there before," she told him. "But I think my brother's gone up there to cause some trouble and I want to stop him before he does."

Salvador frowned. "Trouble? What sort of trouble?"

"I wish I knew. He's fallen in with a rough crowd. Do you know anything about the Gentry?"

He shook his head. When Miki went on to describe the hard men, he added, "I've seen no one like that on the grounds."

"Then maybe I'm wrong. Maybe they're not at Kellygnow."

"I hope they're not. We don't need more trouble. The weather's enough."

"Nobody needs trouble," Miki said.

She sunk lower in her seat and finished off her coffee. She was warmer, but that only made her wet clothes that much more clammy and uncomfortable. Her throat was feeling worse by the minute.

"You are not a happy woman," Salvador said after a few moments.

Wet and bedraggled as she was, who would be? But she knew that wasn't what he meant.

"There hasn't been a lot of good going on in my life these days," she said. "Too many disappointments, I guess."

"Because of your brother?"

Miki shook her head. "Not really. I'm more disappointed in myself."

"That's not so good," Salvador said. "In the end, all you have is yourself."

And when that's shite? Miki wondered. Great. That made her feel just bloody wonderful. But he was right. If you couldn't like yourself, how could you expect anybody else to like you?

"Do you mind if I have a smoke?" she asked.

He shook his head. "But we've arrived."

She looked up through the windshield as he pulled over towards the curb. The pickup slid to a stop against the sidewalk. Salvador shifted into neutral and put on the hand brake.

"Or at least we've come as far as the truck will take us."

No kidding, Miki thought. Handfast Road was one solid sheet of ice going up the hill. There was no way the pickup could make it up that slippery grade. She didn't think anyone could even walk up it.

"Perhaps you should stay in the truck," he added. "There's plenty of gas and you can warm up while you wait."

"No," Miki told him. "This is something I've got to do."

Salvador shrugged. Reaching behind the seat again, he pulled out a yellow rain slicker to match the one he was wearing.

"Put this on," he said. "It's Maria Elena's, but she won't mind."

"Thanks." .

He waited for her on the pavement while she struggled to put the rain slicker on. Outside she lost her balance, but he plucked her up as she was falling and set her on her feet. He was strong, she thought.

"We can't use the road," he said, nodding towards it with his chin.

Miki took in the ice-slick slope of the street once more and sighed. Lighting a cigarette, she let him lead the way around behind the houses where they crunched a path through the crust of snow that covered the lawns in back.

3

After all he'd experienced in the past twenty-four hours, Hunter felt he shouldn't have been surprised by anything at this point. He'd already learned the hard way that the world held far more in its familiar boundaries than he could ever have imagined. It was all so astonishing, from the mean-spirited threat of the Gentry to the quiet awe of the native *manitou*, never mind the business of avoiding the ice storm by moving through some between place where the foul weather couldn't touch them. But nothing could have prepared him for that moment when they stepped from winter into autumn.

The otherworld forest reared about them like some fairy-tale wood. There was nothing New World about it. Any time Hunter had been in the bush around Newford it was all undergrowth, the spaces between the trees choked with new growth, fallen trees, weeds, saplings, brambles. This forest was like something out of the Brothers Grimm. The trees were the size of redwoods, rearing up to impossible heights, except they were oaks and ashes, chestnuts and beech, trees that had no business being this big. The ground between them was covered with ferns and a carpet of moss and fallen leaves that was springy and soft underfoot.

"So there really is a wood beyond the world," Ellie said, her voice holding the same astonishment and awe he was feeling.

He turned to look at her. "What do you mean?"

"It's just this book I read when I was a teenager. I fell in love with the art of the Pre-Raphaelities, so I thought I'd try one of William Morris's novels."

"I thought he designed furniture and wallpaper patterns and that kind of stuff."

She nodded. "He did. He also painted and drew, had his own printing press and designed books, wrote essays and poetry, and still found the time to invent the fantasy novel while he was at it."

"How very interesting," Aunt Nancy said. "And how will this help us with the Glasduine?"

They both started, having forgotten her presence. Hunter turned to face the older woman's frowning features.

"Look," he said, surprising himself that he could talk back so firmly to her. "We're just trying to put this into some kind of perspective, okay? I know it's all old business for you, but we're feeling kind of cut off from anything that makes any sense. So if we grab a few moments of just normal conversation, it's not because we don't care. It's because we're trying to connect, if only for a moment, to something that actually does make some sense."

Aunt Nancy regarded him with a long considering look, then smiled. For some reason, Hunter wasn't particularly put at ease by that smile.

"You'll do," she said. "Take your moment. I have some business of my own to attend to."

She walked a little way from them and sat down on the roots of one of the giant oaks, her backpack between her legs as she rummaged around in it. For all her talk about being an old woman, not to mention the fact that she looked her sixty-plus years, she moved with an easy grace that Hunter had only ever seen in dancers and gymnasts.

"Can you see it?" Ellie whispered to him.

"See what?"

"It's like her shadow's got a mind of its own—and it doesn't even have her shape. It looks more like this huge spider."

"Oh, man . . ."

He didn't see it, but he could all too easily imagine it. Somehow he knew that he was never going to be able to trust anything anymore, that what he actually saw was ever all that was there.

"What's she doing now?" Ellie asked.

Hunter shook his head. He had no idea.

As they watched, Aunt Nancy used the side of one boot to clear a flat patch of ground by her feet. Then she took a small pouch from her backpack and shook a handful of what looked like bird bones into the palm of her hand. Setting the pouch aside, she cupped her hands around the bones and gave them a brisk shake before dropping them onto the dirt.

"Hmm," she said.

Hunter and Ellie approached her. Hunter could see nothing in the pattern of the bones, but Ellie seemed entranced.

"They're so full of light," she said.

Aunt Nancy nodded. "I've had them for a long time. Things people like us use a lot tend to store medicine like a battery."

"What are they?" Hunter asked. "Something like an oracle?"

She gave him a grin. "Something like that."

"So what do you see in them?"

"More questions than answers," she replied. She swept the bones up and replaced them in their pouch. "I was hoping to get a fix on the Glasduine, but it's too new-born. Doesn't have much scent. Doesn't really leave a trail. And it's not using its medicine, so I can't track it by that either. What little it has used is just kind of spreading out like a mist and soaking into everything."

Looking up at them, she added, "But the interesting thing is, we're not the only ones out here looking for it."

"The Gentry," Ellie said.

Aunt Nancy shook her head. "Nope, I caught a trace of them, but they've lit a shuck for the territories, so far as I can tell. Finally gave up on trying to take what wasn't theirs, I'm guessing, and they've headed somewhere else where the pickings might be easier. West, it seems, though compass directions aren't as reliable here as back home."

"Then who?" Hunter asked.

"Can't tell for sure. There's two of them—full of medicine, but nobody I know. Everybody's got a kind of signature, you know, the way the medicine runs in them, how they use it, if they use it. So what's strange is, one of this pair reminds me of a spirit guide I met back when I was a girl. Hadn't seen him for a time and then I heard he died some years back."

"And the other?"

"That one's got First People medicine, real strong, but not any kind I know."

"You mean Native American?" Ellie asked.

"No. Older than that."

Hunter and Ellie exchanged glances. Hunter couldn't shake the impression that this new complication had Aunt Nancy feeling nervous, and if she was feeling nervous, how were he and Ellie supposed to feel?

"So is this good or bad news?" he asked.

Aunt Nancy shrugged. Standing up, she brushed bark and moss from her jeans, then swung her pack onto her back.

"Hard to tell," she said. "The good news is that while we can't track the Glasduine, we can follow them. Kind of like tracking the coyote that's hunting the rabbit we're really after."

"And the bad news?" Ellie asked.

"We don't know what the coyote wants."

"So . . . are they dangerous?" Hunter asked.

"Let's put it this way," Aunt Nancy replied. "They're powerful. And everything you meet in the spiritworld has the potential of being dangerous. But there's no point in worrying over any of it right now. We've got a ways to go before we run into them. I know a few shortcuts, but nothing like they seem to know."

Ellie and Hunter fell in step behind her as she set off. The awe that Hunter had felt when they'd crossed over into the spiritworld had shifted into nervousness. Every tree trunk, he realized, could hide some danger. Some *big* danger, because these weren't exactly shrubs. Then he had to laugh.

"What's so funny?" Ellie asked.

He shook his head. "It's not really funny, ha ha. I was just thinking of how Ria was on at me about getting out of the ruts of my life."

"So?"

"Well, look at where we are, what we're doing. I mean how far could I have gotten from the way things were than where we are now?"

"Point," Ellie said. "But at least we're not alone."

"Like I said before we crossed over," he told her. "I'm in for the duration."

She offered him her hand. "I'm glad you came."

"Well, you know, this is the weirdest date I've ever been on."

"We're on a date?"

"I'd like to think so," he said. "Helps make it seem more normal. I mean, first dates are always a little awkward, don't you think?"

She leaned closer and kissed his cheek.

"You're an idiot," she told him.

"But an idiot on a date."

She smiled. "Definitely a date. But what'll we do for a second one?"

"I was thinking of a trip to the moon."

She gave him a whack on the shoulder with her free hand, but she laughed and squeezed his fingers at the same time.

Hunter wanted to keep it light. That way it wouldn't feel as weird as it was. It would stop him from brooding about what he'd done already, what he might have to do when they caught up with this thing they were chasing. He glanced ahead to catch Aunt Nancy giving them a look. Her eyes were so dark, her features stoic; she was impossible to read. He thought she might say something again about how they should be taking things seriously, but then she smiled. Turning her head forward again, she continued to lead them on.

4

"So," *el lobo* said. "Do you think they remember that you're supposed to be friends?"

"*No lo sé,*" Bettina told him. I don't know.

Because it was impossible to say. These *cadejos* weren't the whimsical creatures she'd taken to heart all those years ago. In their place had come strangers to answer her call, dark-eyed, aloof, and dangerous. They neither spoke nor sang and that silence frightened Bettina more than anything. There was no happy dancing, little cloven hooves keeping time as they clicked and clacked on the stones. No childlike songs. These *cadejos* approached on stiff legs, the hackles of their brightly coloured fur lifted at the back of their necks and down along their spine.

"But can we blame them for their anger?" she added. "Perhaps I was never such a good friend to them. Does a true friend shut you out of their life the way I did with them?"

"I suppose not," her wolf said.

He moved closer to her, standing in such a way that should the dogs attack, he could easily step forward to protect her. But Bettina put a hand on his shoulder and gently moved him to one side.

"We're not here to fight," she said. "But to ask forgiveness." She turned her attention back to the little rainbow dogs. "*¿Me perdona?*" she asked of them. Will you forgive me?

Still they remained silent, dark gazes watching them with the singular intent of hunters. She saw there were seven of them. *Qué extraño.* How odd, she thought, that she should be able to number them like this. They'd never stayed still for long enough before for her to get an accurate count, always dancing, gamboling, never all of them quite in her line of sight at the same time. Now they sat in a half-circle, the colors of their pelts making a peculiar, furry rainbow against the desert soil—like one that had been drawn by a child who had her own idea as to how the bands of colors should be ordered.

"You know I meant you no harm," she said. "But my sorrow was so great. When the clown dog came and led Abuela away . . ."

"*No somos la Maravilla,*" one of them finally said.

Its voice gave away nothing of what it was feeling, but at least they had spoken, Bettina thought. At least they were willing to communicate. She knelt on the ground to bring herself closer to the level of their heads. Beside her, *el lobo* followed suit, sitting on his heels.

"I know, I know," Bettina said. "Of course you're not. But I felt betrayed by spirit dogs."

"*Se traicionamos.*" We were betrayed.

"*Sí.* I understand that now."

She waited for them to go on, but they fell back to their silent watching.

"What can I do to make amends?" Bettina asked.

Still they gave back silence.

"*Por favor,*" she said. "*Lo imploro. Hable a mí.*" Speak to me.

Finally one of them blinked.

"Why should we trust you?" it asked.

"You only want us to kill monsters," another said.

"You think we are monsters."

"*No somos monstruos.*"

"*Somos los cadejos.*"

"*Infeliz.*" Unhappy.

"*No deseado.*" Unwanted.

"*Los homeless.*"

Bettina thought her heart would break. They were still so serious and grave, so unlike the happy creatures she'd known. She could hear the pain in their voices and to know that she was the one who had put that pain there, that she had stolen away their joy, was almost too much for her to bear.

"I can't make you trust me," she said. "How could I? I can only ask you to give me another chance to prove myself true."

Los cadejos looked at each other, as though communicating silently.

"We see you are sincere," one of them finally said.

"Or think you are sincere."

"So we are willing to forgive you."

"But there is a cost."

Bettina refused to look at her wolf. She knew what he was thinking, but it didn't matter.

"What will be the cost?" she asked.

"You must give up that which you hold most dear."

"For as long as you gave us up."

"By this you will earn our trust."

Bettina looked at them for a long moment, then slowly shook her head.

"I can't do it again," she said.

Los cadejos cocked their heads.

"*¿Qué significa?*" one of them asked.

"Don't you see?" she told them. "During all that time . . . Abuela, Papa, you . . . all were lost to me. How can you ask me to do so again?"

"We were part of what you held dearest?"

"*Sí.*"

"Then why did you abandon us?"

"I did not know I was doing so until you were gone. And then . . . then . . . you must understand. The coming of the clown dog marked the beginning of all my losses. It made me angry and afraid of spirit dogs."

"I can vouch for that," her wolf said.

Los cadejos looked his way.

"Please," Bettina said to him. "This is between us." She returned her attention to the half-circle of rainbow-colored dogs that sat before her. "I was wrong. But I did not send you away. You left on your own. What I did wrong was not calling you back to me until now."

"We must think on this," one of *los cadejos* said after they had all looked at each other again.

"*Gracias.*"

"We promise nothing."

"I understand."

"We are not here to hunt monsters for you."

"*Sí,*" Bettina said. "I understand. I do not ask this of you."

The little dogs rose then and returned the way they'd come, disappearing among the prickly pear. Bettina sighed. Then why are you here? she had wanted to ask them. Why did you ever choose me in the first place? Surely they could make a home for themselves anywhere.

"Well, that was productive," *el lobo* said.

Bettina turned to look at him, disappointed.

"How could I ask anything of them but forgiveness?" she said.

He shrugged. "You said it yourself. You didn't send them away. Your only crime was in not calling them back to you when they left."

"It seems to me more complicated than that."

"Perhaps. But now we're back where we started. There's a monster loose and we have no way to find it. Unless . . ." He gave Bettina a thoughtful look.

"Unless what?" she asked, certain she wasn't going to like whatever it was.

"You call the Glasduine to us," he said. "The way you called the little dogs."

"I have nothing in common with that monster."

"No. But you knew the pup."

"Barely."

"And," her wolf went on, "if he had even an ounce of manhood in him, he would have found you attractive."

Bettina blushed. "Oh, please . . ."

"But don't you see? It's a connection. I'll wager that if you call to it, the Glasduine will come."

"And then?" she asked.

"We will deal with it as we must."

He sounded far more confident than he could be, Bettina thought. But she knew they had no other choice than to try. It was that, or abandon the chase and then whatever harm the Glasduine did, they would have to accept some responsibility for it, since they hadn't tried to stop it.

"*Bien,*" she said. "But not here. I won't have it come to this place—not now that I know what it is and have so recently found it."

"Agreed," *el lobo* said. He rose smoothly to his feet and offered her a hand up. "Where did you have in mind?"

Bettina dusted the dirt from her knees. She raised her gaze to the sky, wishing her *papá* was there, that she could ask his advice. But she already knew what he would say: Don't get involved in any struggle between spirits. See where it led your *abuela.*

"Somewhere out of the view of those sacred mountains," she said.

El lobo nodded. He glanced up the hill to where *los cadejos* had disappeared.

"And the little dogs?" he asked.

"They will find us when they're ready."

He nodded again. Neither of them said what lay unspoken between them: If there was anything left of them to find after they had confronted the Glasduine.

They made their way down to the dry wash and walked along the smooth sand under the mesquite trees, backtracking the course the water took rushing down from the higher ground during the rainy seasons. After a while, the wash brought them to a long, meandering arroyo that cut deeply into the hills. Scrambling around boulders, they moved steadily uphill, the sides of the arroyo rising just as constantly on either side of them until eventually they reached a place where the peaks of the Baboquivari Mountains could no longer be seen. Bettina finally stopped by the long, ribbed remains of a saguaro that had toppled over many years ago. It was obviously a place where others had stopped in some long-ago time for many of the stones on either side of the gorge held marks that the previous visitors carved onto their surfaces.

"This will do," Bettina said.

El lobo nodded. He wandered over to the side of the gorge and traced a spiraling pictograph with his finger before joining her by the fallen saguaro.

"Have you been here before?" he asked.

She shook her head. "But I've been in places like it outside of *la época del mito.*"

"I have not," he told her. "It's all rather . . . remarkable. There seems to be so much space and the sky has such weight I almost find it hard to breathe."

Bettina smiled. "It's just the opposite for me," she said. "Here I feel light-footed and my heart swells to fill the space around me. Your forests make me feel claustrophobic."

"But it's easier to avoid prying eyes in my forests. And here everything is so . . . prickly."

"It's easy enough to find privacy here if you want it," she told him. "The difference is it has more to do with stillness and distance."

"You will have to show me . . . when this is done."

"*Sí*. When this is done."

She chose a broad, flat stone near the dead saguaro and sat cross-legged upon it. From her pocket she took the rosary her mother had sent her. Her wolf gave it a dubious look.

"Do you think that will help with a spirit as old as this?" he said.

"It's not for the Glasduine," Bettina told him. "It's for me. To remind me that I have my own ancient spirits looking out for me."

El lobo regarded the small cross. "The Glasduine was already ancient when the man they hung on that cross was born."

"Perhaps," Bettina said. "But who made spirits such as the Glasduine? Who called it and all the world into being? Is He not more ancient still?"

"I have heard a different story as to how the world came into being."

Bettina shrugged.

"And you trust this God?" her wolf asked. "I've heard he doesn't think so highly of women."

"I'll admit I've had my difficulties with that as well," Bettina said. "But when I pray, it's not to the Father or the Son, but to *la Novia del Desierto*. The Mother who was a bride of the desert before she was a bride of the church."

El lobo regarded her for a long moment, then nodded. "As things stand, I wouldn't turn my back on anyone who might be able to help us. I'd welcome the devil himself if I thought he could give us a hand."

"Don't even joke about such a thing," Bettina said and quickly made the sign of the cross.

"Who said I was joking?"

"Please . . ."

"I'm sorry," he told her, when he saw that she was genuinely upset. "But you know, one religion's demons can be another's gods."

"*Sí*," Bettina said.

She knew that. She had only to look at herself, at how she was brought up with the curious mix of folklore and Christianity, to understand the contradictions that could mingle, jostling elbow to elbow in one's belief systems.

"But I think," she went on, "that we have only ourselves to look to for strength in what we undertake today."

Her wolf nodded. They both knew the dangers of what they were about to attempt. *De verdad*, Bettina doubted they'd be able to either heal or destroy this creature she was about to call up. But they had to make the attempt.

"I've had a thought," *el lobo* said, as though reading her mind. "About the Glasduine."

Bettina raised her eyebrows in a question.

"It came to me," he said, "from this business of *croí baile* we spoke of earlier. What you call *el bosque del corazón*."

"What of it?"

"Well, the Glasduine must have one as well—don't you think? Its own heart home."

"I wouldn't know."

"But it stands to reason. All spirits must have one."

"*¿Y así?*"

"Well," her wolf said. "If it turns out that you can't heal it, and I can't kill it, perhaps we can trap it in its *croí baile*. Lock it in there so that the only thing it can hurt is itself."

"It would be a terrible place," Bettina said. "Wouldn't it? If the Glasduine was created out of Donal's basest instincts . . ."

"It would probably not be good," he agreed.

"And Donal? Do we trap him in there with it?"

"There is always a price to be paid," *el lobo* said. "The pup knew the danger when he played with the mask."

Did he? Bettina wondered. But she knew her wolf was right. If Donal needed to be sacrificed for the greater good of ending the Glasduine's menace, she could make no argument against it.

"*Es verdad,*" she said. It's the truth. "Now prepare yourself."

Her wolf shook the tension out of his hands and rolled his shoulders.

"I'm ready," he said.

At least one of them was, Bettina thought.

Running her finger along the seeds of the rosary her mother had sent her, she closed her eyes and sent out the summoning call. Not asking this time, as she had with *los cadejos*, but demanding. Firmly, with a strength she didn't truly feel.

5

Aunt Nancy lifted her head. "Did you hear that?" she asked.

Ellie swallowed, and gave a slow nod. She realized that it had been floating there on the periphery of her senses for some time now, only drifting into her awareness at this moment, when the call had suddenly grown so much stronger. It was an eerie sound, audible only inside her head. She recognized it as a summons, but while it made her skin prickle, she knew it wasn't directed at her. When she glanced at Hunter, she saw that even he had heard the silent call. The unnatural intrusion into his mind had drained his features of much of their color.

"What . . . what is it?" he asked.

"That pair we're following," Aunt Nancy said. "They're calling the Glasduine to them. Come, we must hurry."

If Ellie had ever taken a stranger journey, it was only in her dreams. Truth

was, all of this felt like dream—from first seeing the men smoking their cigarettes in Kellygnow's backyard to this increasingly disconcerting expedition.
Stepping across from the Newford ice storm into a fairy-tale autumn wood
had been unsettling, though not altogether unpleasant, but the subsequent
journey was leaving her feeling more and more disoriented with each chunk of
distance they put behind them. Because nothing stayed the same.

One moment they were in the fairy-tale wood, then they were walking
across arctic tundra, the horizon stretching impossibly far on all sides with no
sign anywhere of the forest they'd just quit. They moved from marshlands
where they had to pick their route with care, every lifted step making a sucking sound as they pulled their feet from the wet ground, to arid badlands
where the dry air seemed to pull all the moisture out of their skin and the air
tasted like dust. A dip in the ground took them into a lush, sleepy valley where
willows clustered along the banks of a slow-moving river and herds of grazing
deer barely raised their heads at their passage, then they turned a bend to find
mountains as tall as the Rockies rearing up all around them, the ground underfoot turned to shale and loose stones.

The seasons changed, too, running through spring and summer, autumn
and winter, following no particular order. Sometimes the climate changed
with the landscape, sometimes it abruptly shifted while the landscape
remained the same. They went from carrying their winter jackets under their
arms, to bundling up and wishing they had down parkas.

What was most disconcerting was that these transitions between the various landscapes and climates were subtle. There was no abrupt change like that
first cross-over; you simply became aware that you were somewhere else, or
that the pleasant summer's day had suddenly acquired a wind with a winter's
bite. The seamless flow from one to another was what made the journey feel so
dreamlike in particular. Where else but in a dream could one experience such
a phenomenon?

"So," Ellie said at one point. "Is it always so confusing here? How do you
even know where we're going?"

Because unless all of these pocket worlds were laid out in some set pattern,
she had no idea how anyone could navigate so easily among them.

Aunt Nancy shrugged. "*Manidò-aki* is what we make it."

"*We're* doing this?"

"Not just the three of us, but all people. Everyone carries a piece of the
spiritworld in them, and that fragment is echoed in our hearts—we call it our
abinàs-odey. One's heart place. What we are traveling through here is an area
that is thick with them, a quilt pattern that overlays the spiritworld, little
pockets of many people's *abinàs-odey*."

"Can anybody just—" Ellie searched for the word. "Connect with their
heart place? I mean, travel there?"

"Most people do so only in their dreams."

"And it's always like this?" Hunter asked. "Some lonesome place out in
the wilderness?"

"Oh, no. You can find whole cities created out of the crazy-quilt pattern of several thousand *abinàs-odey*. Cities, towns, villages, but also more solitary places of habitation like a single farm, or a hunt camp."

"Mine would definitely be a city place," Hunter said. "All this wild country kind of spooks me."

They were traveling at the moment through a landscape of rugged red hills, the predominant vegetation being scrub brush and clumps of dry, browning grasses. The sun was just starting its climb up from the horizon and the air was chill enough for them to see their breath.

"I like it," Ellie said. "Especially places like this, where it feels like all the excess has been stripped away and you can see the real heart and bones underneath."

"I prefer the woodlands of the Kickaha Mountains," Aunt Nancy said. "There's something comforting about the close press of the trees when you move through those forests. You can't take a step without touching something and it feels to me like the land itself is welcoming me with the scrape of a twig, the brush of a leaf. Like a mother, tousling the hair of her child as she runs by."

"I like that, too," Ellie said. "And I like the way you put it. It's not what . . ."

Her voice trailed off as she realized what she'd been about to say.

"What you expected from some old bush woman?" Aunt Nancy finished for her.

"No. Well, maybe a little bit."

What had happened was that the simple poetry of how Aunt Nancy had described walking in the woods around her home had made Ellie reconsider the image she was carrying of the older woman. She wasn't just this brusque, kind of scary old medicine woman.

Aunt Nancy shot her a grin, as though aware of what Ellie was thinking.

"There's a lot we don't know about each other," the old woman said. "Which is why it's always better to walk up to any new experience without any preconceptions."

Ellie nodded. "I should know that. I'm sorry."

But Aunt Nancy's grin only grew wider. "Hell, girl. Don't be sorry. I cultivate that image. I can't tell you how much wasted time it's saved me, not having to get all warm and cuddly with people who just want a piece of my medicine but otherwise wouldn't give me the time of day. I figure if I make it a little tough on them, maybe they'll take the time to think of some way they can deal with their problems on their own, instead of always looking for a quick medicine fix."

They reached the crest of one of those tall-backed red hills. The sun was higher and the hills just seemed to go on forever. The summons for the Glasduine grew more urgent for a moment, then faded again, as though the force of its call was being swept back and forth across the spiritworld and they were no longer directly in its range.

"Trouble is," Aunt Nancy went on, "is you get into the habit of being who you're pretending to be. That's the problem with masks. The reason they're so seductive is because they're so easy to put on. And that's also the reason you should always take care of who you go walking with in the spirit-world because this is a place where masks don't fit the same as they do on the side of the borders where we normally live. The seams and cracks start to show and whoever you're here with could come away knowing more about you than you're comfortable having them know." She smiled at the pair of them. "You find yourself rambling on too much, the way I'm doing right now."

"But we're interested in all of this," Ellie said. "Really we are."

Hunter nodded in agreement.

"Or you're good at sucking up," Aunt Nancy told them.

It's no good, Ellie thought. We can see through you now. But rather than follow that train of thought, she wanted to know more about how things worked, here in the spiritworld.

"So all these pieces of people's dreams," she said. "Is that what makes up the spiritworld?"

Aunt Nancy shook her head. "Every single being, animal or human or otherwise, owns a little piece of *manidò-aki*. Yet if you put them all together, they make up but the smallest fraction of what can be found here. It stretches as far and wide as the imagination allows it to—not our imagination, but that which belongs to the land itself."

"You're saying it's sentient?"

"I don't know about that. It's not like I've ever had a conversation with it." She bent down and picked up a handful of the dry red dirt, letting it sift through her fingers back onto the ground. "But you just have to touch it to know there's more going on here than dirt we're walking on. If you listen close enough, you can hear a heartbeat. That's what we do when we drum, you know. We're talking to the heartbeat of *manidò-aki*—the spiritworld."

The summoning call swept over them again, louder and stronger than it had been yet. Aunt Nancy straightened up. Her nostrils flared as though she was trying to catch a scent.

"We're close now," she said. She gave them each a considering look. "Where do you think it's coming from?"

"Lower down," Ellie replied immediately, not knowing how she knew.

Aunt Nancy nodded. "That's what I'm thinking, too. Maybe one or two *abinàs-odey* away. Don't worry," she added at the puzzled look on Ellie's face. "It's just your medicine waking up inside you."

She descended the slope, picking her way along a narrow path that took them to the lip of a steep gorge. There another path let them wind their way to the bottom of the gorge. The land changed around them as they went down, changing from badlands to desert. The scrub became cacti and desert brush. The temperature rose a half-dozen degrees. When Ellie looked up, she saw that the sun was at high noon.

Approaching a turn in the gorge, Aunt Nancy suddenly dropped behind a jumble of boulders. Ellie and Hunter followed suit. Neither spoke, knowing how far their voices could carry in the clear air. When the summoning call swept over them again, it was so close and immediate that Ellie could feel the reverberation of it in her chest like a deep bass note.

She crept close to where Aunt Nancy crouched and peered over the boulders. What she saw held her motionless. The last thing she'd expected was to see anybody she knew in this place. But there they were, further down the slope of the gorge, Bettina and one of the dark-haired Gentry that she'd first seen in Kellygnow's backyard. Bettina was obviously generating the summoning call. She sat cross-legged on a broad-flat stone, eyes closed in concentration. Her companion was studying the heights of the gorge on either side, looking slowly from one to the other.

"It's Bettina," Ellie whispered, unable to believe that she was seeing her new friend here, in this place.

But Aunt Nancy only had eyes for Bettina's handsome, dark-skinned companion.

"With one of those-who-came," she said. "A dog boy. What did you say they called themselves now? The Gentlemen?"

"Gentry," Ellie said.

They all ducked out of sight as Bettina's companion looked in their direction. Aunt Nancy put her back to the boulders and sat down.

"One of those," she said. "Only different, somehow."

Hunter looked from Ellie to Aunt Nancy.

"You actually *know* these people?" he asked.

"Bettina lives at Kellygnow," Ellie explained. "She's . . . Chantal, one of the other women I met there, said she was kind of a, I guess you'd say, witch."

"She's a skinwalker," Aunt Nancy said.

Hunter glanced at her. "Say what?"

"She has very old blood—older than that of the creature we're looking for."

"So is that good or bad?"

"You need to ask that question when we find her in the company of a dog boy?"

"But you said he was different . . ."

Aunt Nancy gave a slow nod. "He's gone and stolen the body of one of our *manitou*. That's what I recognized earlier. His name was Shishòdewe. Walks-at-the-Edge-of-the-Forest."

"Um . . ."

Aunt Nancy looked to Hunter.

"Why would he steal a body?" Hunter asked. "Wouldn't he have one of his own?"

"Why do those-who-came do any of the things that they do? For the sake of greed. For the sake of power."

Ellie didn't want to think ill of Bettina, but it really didn't look very good, finding her here in the company of one of the Gentry, calling to the Glasduine the way she was.

"What do we do?" she asked.

Aunt Nancy seemed to slump into herself, becoming suddenly smaller, older, more frail.

"Truly, I don't know," she said. "If we stop them before they bring the

Glasduine here, we lose our chance at the monster. If we wait until it comes, we will have the three of them standing against us."

"Maybe more," Hunter put in, his voice gloomy. "I've never seen those Gentry on their own. There's probably more of them around."

Ellie began to worriedly inspect the surrounding landscape.

"I don't sense anyone else close by," Aunt Nancy said.

Ellie returned her attention to the older woman.

"Can't you use all this . . . this magic that's supposed to be in me to do something?"

"I don't trust myself to make the right decision," Aunt Nancy said.

"How can you say that? You're the medicine woman. You're supposed to know everything."

"The trick to being a good leader is to be decisive and to appear to know everything. But seeing what was done to Shishòdewe and knowing that what they are calling here is a hundred times more powerful . . ." Aunt Nancy shook her head. "I suddenly feel like an old woman, way out of her depth."

"No," Ellie said. "You can't bail out now. You're the one who knows how to use whatever this is I've got inside me. I can't do it by myself."

As they were speaking, Hunter had eased back up to peer over the boulders. He leaned on one of the stones and looked down.

"Something's happening down there," he said.

But before either of the women could reply, their heads were filled with a towering, raging voice that knocked them to the ground. Above them, Hunter slumped forward, his head falling onto his forearms. Where his companions were only momentarily incapacitated, the sheer power of that intruding roar had rendered him unconscious.

6

Miki stood out on the lawn with Salvador and the others, acutely aware of the freezing rain that was now drying on the slicker Salvador had lent her. She stared at where they'd been told that the Glasduine had simply bulled its way through the window of the studio, taking down a good part of the wall in the process. She tried to imagine the size and strength the creature had to be to do this sort of damage, and couldn't even begin to. But she had a clear enough picture of what it would look like. All she had to do was think of Donal's painting, that hybrid beast that had made up its central image, part human, part tree. Except, notwithstanding her experiences with the Gentry, never mind this between place in which she and Salvador now found themselves, how could such a thing even be real?

"You're *sure* it wasn't a bomb?" she said.

Kellygnow's housekeeper shook her head. "Oh, we're very sure of that."

"Bloody hell."

Salvador nodded slowly at her side. *"Madre de Dios,"* he muttered. "I'm gone only a day and look at this."

When she and Salvador had come around to the back of the house it was to find the red-haired housekeeper Nuala having an animated discussion with three Natives: two women she didn't know and this guy named Tommy who came into the record store from time to time. The weird thing was, the bloody foul weather didn't appear to affect any of them. They weren't wet or cold or anyway near as miserable as she was feeling. It was like they were standing on the other side of a window, looking in at the freezing drizzle from someplace else. Which is exactly what it turned out to be when they drew her and Salvador into what one of them described as the between.

Salvador made the sign of the cross at the transition. Miki just wanted to throw up, and probably would have, except Tommy gave her and Salvador each a spice cookie that took their nausea completely away.

"Does this work for a hangover?" she asked.

"Probably," Tommy told her.

The Native women turned out to be a couple of his aunts, Sunday and Zulema. They were friendly enough, and Tommy had recognized her right away, giving her a big smile as soon as they approached, but Nuala's reaction had been a seriously antagonistic frown, as though her and Salvador's presence here was just one more complication that she didn't need. Miki was glad it was Salvador who worked here instead of her; if Hunter treated her like this back at the store, she'd quit. Or whack him across the back of the head to smarten him up. She couldn't do that here, of course. And then, when the housekeeper found out that Miki was Donal's sister, the cold front had really moved in. Surprisingly, it was Salvador who immediately came to her defense, for all that he barely knew her.

"Do not be so quick to judge," he told Nuala. "She came all this way, in this weather, to help you. It's not her fault she is too late to stop her brother."

Miki thought the housekeeper was going to bite off his head, she gave Salvador such a hard stare, but then the woman sighed.

"You're right," she told Salvador, then turned to Miki. "I'm sorry. This hasn't been the best of days."

Miki nodded. "So where did the creature go?"

"Into the spiritworld," one of Tommy's aunts said. It took Miki a moment to remember her name. Sunday.

"And Donal . . . ?"

"He is the Glasduine's host," Nuala said.

Miki had known this, but she'd needed to hear someone say it all the same. But even hearing it said, the words hanging there in the air between them, it was simply too big for her to process. Donal was really gone. Swallowed into some pathetic piece of half-baked mythology that shouldn't have been able to exist in the first place. How could her Uncle Fergus and his loser cronies have been right? Why would any supernatural being listen to the likes of them, or Donal for that matter?

"What about the Gentry?" she asked, more to distract herself than because she actually wanted to know. "The last time I saw them I was sure they were headed this way."

The housekeeper's gaze clouded for a long moment before she finally replied. "Happily, they at least have been absent."

"You must let us into the room where the Glasduine was called forth," the other aunt, Zulema, said. She was obviously continuing the argument that Miki and Salvador's arrival had interrupted. "Unless we can track it to where it crossed over, we won't be able to block its return from the spiritworld."

"An admirable objective," Nuala said, "but there will be no more magics called up inside Kellygnow. There has already been enough damage done."

"You don't understand. If we don't—"

"No, I understand all too well," Nuala told her. "This house is under my charge and I will not allow it to be used as a battleground."

"There will be no battles fought inside its walls," Sunday assured her.

"And you can guarantee this?"

"I—"

"Because I am no stranger to enchantment," Nuala said. "You must know as well as I do that every time a spell is cast, it leaves a door ajar to the spiritworld. Those rifts can linger open for weeks, even months. I will not have Kellygnow riddled with the remnants of your spells and enchantments."

"Why don't you do it from outside the window where the Glasduine broke through?" Tommy asked. "Wouldn't that be close enough?"

His aunts looked to Nuala.

"Will you allow us that much?" Zulema asked.

The housekeeper hesitated.

"Don't forget," Sunday added. "If we don't block the Glasduine's return to this world, who's to say that, when the creature does come back, it won't smash in a few more of your precious walls? Are you capable of standing up to it by yourself?"

"She will not be alone," Salvador said. "There will be no more smashing of walls while I am here."

If determination alone could stop the Glasduine, Miki thought, it would be hard pressed to get past the combination of Salvador and the housekeeper.

But Nuala gave up. She put a hand on the gardener's arm.

"They're right," she said. "There's no way we could hope to stop the Glasduine on our own. Go ahead," she added to Tommy's aunts. "Only, please. Try to be careful with what you call up."

"Thank you," Sunday said.

Zulema nodded. "You could help us. Your own medicine runs strong and by helping us, you would be there to keep watch and sweep away any residue my sister and I might miss."

"I don't know . . ."

"We don't plan any sort of complicated ceremony," Sunday assured her. "More a mild form of divination. We only want to call up a memory of the Glasduine's passage so that we can then track it to where it crossed over."

Nuala remained reluctant, but gave in. "Very well. I will help you."

"It would be better if we had a drum," Zulema said. "Do you have one in the house? We didn't think to bring one."

"A drum," Nuala repeated.

"It will make it easier to connect to the world's heartbeat," Sunday explained. "So the *manitou* will hear us."

Nuala nodded in understanding. "I don't have one," she said. "But I do have something else that would work."

She left them to go into the house. Tommy's aunts stepped through the rubble to get closer to the wall, with Salvador trailing along behind. Miki took the time to light a cigarette, then she turned to Tommy.

"So do you do a lot of this in your spare time?" she asked.

"Yeah, right. This is as new to me as it is to you."

"Hey, I could be some big-time sorceress. How would you know?"

He only smiled and shook his head. "And that's why you work in a record store."

"It could be my secret identity."

"Could be," Tommy agreed. "Just like I've got a harem of supermodels waiting for me at home for when we're done here."

Miki sighed. "Bloody hell. Can you believe we're actually here, taking any of this seriously?"

"It's probably a little easier for me," Tommy said. "I mean, these are my aunts, after all. The thing is, I just always thought it was stories, all this talk of *manidò-akì* and *manitou*."

"Yeah, I had my own fill of fairy tales when I was growing up."

They fell silent when Nuala returned. She carried a small brassy-looking dish about the size of a salad bowl that Miki recognized from having seen a bunch of them in a shop on Lee Street specializing in jewelry and clothing imported from the Far East. Their stock also included all kinds of incense and soaps, statues and knickknacks, bamboo flutes, meditation mats, but it was the Tibetan singing bowls like the one Nuala was carrying that had really captured Miki's fancy. The store's stock had ranged from those tiny enough to hold in the palm of your hand to one so big it would take a couple of husky men to simply lift it.

The shopkeeper had talked about the seven different metals that were used in the casting of the bowls, showed her the wooden stick shaped like a pestle that was used to play it, and then demonstrated how the bowls were used. First he tapped the stick against the side of the bowl, waking a clear, bell-like sound that seemed to ring for ages. But what had really sold Miki on them was when he rubbed the stick around the lip of the bowl. It was like the way you could get a musical note using a wet finger on the rim of a wineglass, but the sound he woke from the bowl was like the voice of the earth itself, a low, thrumming sound that felt as though it was coming up from the center of the world to resonate deep in her chest and belly.

She would have bought one then and there, but if she was to have one, she'd want one of the big ones, and they were selling for a few hundred dollars, which she couldn't possibly afford at the time.

"What's with the Tibetan bowl? Tommy asked Nuala, obviously recognizing the instrument as well. "I thought you were Irish."

"Should we all be defined by only one facet of who we are?" she replied. "Would you prefer to only be known as an Indian? Or the driver of one of Angel's vans? As an abused child? As a recovered alcoholic? Or aren't you all these things and more?"

Tommy flushed. "How do you know all this?"

"How can she not?" Sunday said, laying a hand on his shoulder. She gave Nuala a small, respectful bow. "I see now that you are a *manitou* yourself. Far from home, perhaps, but no less venerable because of that."

Nuala gave a dismissive wave with her hand. "I'm only a housekeeper."

"And I am an only child," Sunday replied.

Nuala sighed. "We are all who we are, none of us more important than the other."

But Tommy's eyes had gone wide. Miki knew exactly how he was feeling because she was still stumbling over Sunday describing the housekeeper as belonging to the spiritworld.

"Wait a sec'," she said. "Do you mean—"

"We don't have time for this," Zulema said, interrupting.

Nuala nodded. She sat down on a piece of the wall. With the bowl on her lap, she began to caress its perimeter with the stick. Within moments the circular motion woke up a deep, resonant drone that seemed far out of proportion for the size of the bowl. Sunday and Zulema sat on their heels in front of Nuala so that the three of them made up the points of a triangle. Miki and the others stood back, watching.

Sunday took smudgesticks out of her pocket and gave one to her sister. When they lit them, the sweet smell of cedar and sage filled the air. Miki shook her head. Anyone looking at them would think they were getting soaked by the freezing rain that continued to fall a heartbeat away from wherever it was that they were standing, but here they were, untouched by the weather and dry enough to be burning smudgesticks.

Sunday and Zulema began to chant, their voices rising and falling in twinned cadences that played against the thrumming drone that came from the bowl. Nuala remained silent, but her eyes were closed in concentration.

"What're they saying?" Miki whispered to Tommy.

"I don't know exactly. Calling on the spirits to help, I'm guessing."

"We're not going to see them, are we?" Miki asked. "I mean, they're not going to actually show up or anything, right?"

Salvador leaned close to catch Tommy's answer, a worried look in his features.

"I don't think so . . ."

"*Todo está loco,*" Salvador muttered.

Miki didn't really know any Spanish, but it wasn't hard to figure out what he'd said. Things *were* crazy.

"No kidding," she said.

And then the strangeness factor got cranked up yet another notch.

The chanting suddenly broke off. The hum of the bowl took longer to fade, although Nuala had removed the stick from its rim long moments before.

Turning back to look at the wall of the house, Miki and the others were just in time to see a flood of light come spilling through the makeshift wooden barrier that had been built over the hole the Glasduine had made when escaping. It was a dazzling display made up of a thousand different shades of green, veined with blue and gold and amber bands, all of it shimmering and shifting. The light hung there by the wall, a throbbing glow that swelled with each rhythmic pulse until it suddenly sped off across the lawn, disappearing into the trees. In its wake it left behind a pathway of that same green and gold light that undulated from the wall of the house to where it ran into the woods. It was like a ribbon touched by a constant breeze, four feet across. A path of light in which colors glimmered and flared, echoing the heartbeats of those watching.

The three women backed away from it until they were standing near Miki and the others.

"This isn't right," Zulema said.

Sunday nodded, turning to Nuala. "Believe me. This is nothing we called up."

"I know," the housekeeper said, her voice tired. "It's easy to see now that it was there all along—invisible until we allowed it to manifest itself. I knew we should have left well enough alone."

"But what *is* it?" Miki wanted to know.

She walked up closer to it. The pulsing of the colors woke an odd yearning inside her. They put her in mind of childhood days when she was able to escape the pubs and kitchens where her uncle held court, and her father drank himself senseless. The smell of peat came to her. The rich greens of hills.

"It has something to do with the Glasduine," Nuala said. "I can feel its presence in that light."

Miki glanced at her before returning her gaze to the mesmerizing ribbon of light.

"But the Glasduine's evil," she said. "Isn't that what you told us? This doesn't feel evil at all."

"No," Nuala agreed. "It simply is."

Sunday nodded. "This is the thread connecting the Glasduine to the place from which it was drawn."

"You mean like some kind of spiritual umbilical cord?" Tommy asked.

"Pretty much," Zulema told him.

"It almost looks like you could pick it up," Miki said. "Like . . . like the fabric they use in those installations that people have done where they run some piece of cloth that's hundreds and hundreds of yards long over the side of a building, or across a lawn like this. I wonder what it feels like."

"Don't!" Nuala and Sunday said simultaneously.

But they were too late. Miki had already stooped down to touch the pulsing ribbon. Her hands went into the light and she was immediately pulled onto it and carried away, tumbling head over heels along the length of the path that the Glasduine had taken after bursting through the wall.

"Oh, shit!" Tommy cried.

He ran forward to try and grab her legs before it took her too far away. Zulema moved to block his way, but she miscalculated and only succeeded in knocking him off-balance. His arms pinwheeled for balance before he fell onto the ribbon as well. The light carried him off, as quickly and smoothly as it had Miki, and then they were both gone.

"We must—" Sunday began.

"Do nothing," Zulema said, her voice heavy with the loss they were both feeling. "Except finish the task Nancy left us. We'll follow the path to where it crosses over and close this world to the creature."

"But . . ."

"I know. We should have realized that Whiteduck's prophecies always have a way of fulfilling themselves, no matter how we try to forestall them."

"But Miki," Salvador said, staring helplessly at the pulsing ribbon. "And your nephew. What will become of them?"

"We must protect this world from the creature's return," Zulema told him. "That is our first priority."

The Creek sisters left the two of them standing there by the house and followed the ribbon of light into the woods, their backs stooped as though they carried a great weight.

Salvador turned to Nuala. "*¿Y bien?*" he said. "They said you have some power over the spirits. Won't you help them?"

Nuala shook her head. "I can't. I have no power except for that which lets me protect this house in my charge." She glanced at where the creature had broken through from the sculpting studio. "And you see how effective I have been."

She collected her singing bowl from where she'd left it, then walked back towards the kitchen door.

"*Mayo ellos vaya con Dios,*" Salvador said in a low voice.

He made the sign of the cross, then slowly followed the housekeeper inside.

7

At some point, the Gentry simply refused to run anymore.

What passed for hours in the world they'd left behind was a hunt of long days and nights in the spiritworld. The Gentry ran as wolves through an ever-changing landscape, deeper and deeper into the spiritworld, the Glasduine following relentlessly on their heels. They managed to keep ahead of the creature, but it pressed them so close that they could get no respite, not even a moment's rest. No matter what tricks or wiles they brought into play, the Glasduine saw through them all. In the end it came to a test of endurance and finally the Gentry turned on their pursuer, determined to make a stand while they still had the strength to fight.

What they had wasn't enough, Donal realized as the Glasduine finally came face to face with its quarry. What they had would never have been enough. They were a primal force, but the Glasduine was a part of the very source from which the Gentry drew their strengths.

Most recently, the chase had led through a territory of high mountains and deep canyons, with the Gentry loping along ridgebacks, scrambling up slopes of loose rock fragments and boulders, the Glasduine following in their wake as though they were joined, their minds linked, their fates inexorably tied to each other. The Gentry made their stand at the flank of a towering butte where two canyons met in a V. They were to await the leader's signal, attacking as a group, rather than individuals. But when the Glasduine came upon them, one of the wolves couldn't wait.

He lunged for the Glasduine's throat only to be plucked from the air and torn to pieces. Sickened, Donal tried to turn the Glasduine away from attacking the rest, but with that first kill, he couldn't pretend to be in control any longer. While he might have set the Glasduine on the trail of the wolves, the creature had taken up the chase only because it had its own score to settle with them.

For a long moment the Gentry stood motionless, staring at the remains of their comrade that lay scattered upon the stones around the Glasduine. It was only when they attacked, coming at the creature from all sides in a snarling rush, that Donal realized that they, too, knew they had no hope to bring their pursuer down. They attacked as they did so that they would die fighting, as the hard men they were, rather than be hunted down like rodents.

The battle was short, though the Gentry fought like devils. The leader was the last to die. He met the Glasduine's gaze without flinching, a half-smile playing on his lips, blood dripping from a half-dozen wounds, his companions torn apart, transformed by the Glasduine into nothing more than chunks of bleeding flesh.

"Ah, you're hard," he said. He spat on the stones at his feet, a spew of red. "I'll give you that. But I've this much bloody consolation. You're corrupted now and there's no going back for you. All it took was killing the first of us and you're just as bloody damned as I am."

Donal couldn't tell if the Gentry's leader was talking to him or the Glasduine. It didn't matter. Either way it was true.

"So fuck off away with yourself," the leader managed to get out before he made his final charge and the creature tore him apart.

For a time the Glasduine went away into itself then, its mind going somewhere Donal couldn't follow. He drifted out of its body, still linked, but no longer housed in the flesh. He floated in the still air, slowly turning in a circle, still the ghost. He would always be a ghost now. There would be no return to how things had been.

Now what? he thought.

He'd managed to turn the Glasduine away from those he loved, from the world he'd imperiled, but what was to stop it from returning? They were deep in the spiritworld, so deep he knew it would take him forever and a day to find his way back, if he even could. But that was him. He was nothing. The Glasduine might be able to return in the blink of an eye. And once there it would—

His mind went still when he saw that the Glasduine had returned from whatever place its attention had drifted to. Its head was cocked, listening. And then Donal heard it, too. The summons. An insistent call that demanded to be heard and answered. Like the Glasduine, he recognized its source. He knew the Glasduine was so powerful that this summoning call had no power over it, but because of who it was that called, it would answer. For its own corrupt reasons.

No, he thought. You can't—

But he had no more control of the Glasduine now than he had ever had.

As it allowed itself to be drawn to the source of the summoning call, there was only time for Donal to will himself back into the Glasduine's flesh and ride along in the creature's body to where it would execute its next act of horror.

8

Bettina hadn't actually expected the summoning to work. Unlike her wolf, she didn't believe that she had any true connection to either the Glasduine or Donal, nor did she consider herself to have the necessary *brujería* the spell would require. But there was so much at stake that she had to make the attempt.

So she sent out her summoning call with a pretense of strength she didn't feel. Sent it out with power when all she truly held were small parcels of luck. Her *brujería* was a healing magic, augmented by her father's blood, perhaps, but mostly entwined with her knowledge of a *curandera*'s art. She knew herbs and the use of medicines from what her *abuela* and Loleta Manuel had taught her. She had her relationship with *los santos* and the spirits. She could infuse charms and *milagros* with the push those who accepted them needed to accomplish what they could have done on their own, if they only had the necessary self-confidence to do so.

These weren't powerful spells. They were only small magics that depended more on paying attention to how the world worked, to recognizing the pattern all things had to one other and helping to make connections between them when those connections were severed, or too tangled to be of practical use. They were a *curandera*'s magic, not a *bruja*'s, and she was sure that they would no more help her summon the Glasduine than they could raise the dead.

But it did respond.

The Glasduine arrived in the canyon like a dervishing wind, with a suddenness and force that knocked her and her wolf off their feet. That wind sent up a cloud of dust and tore apart the remains of the fallen saguaro, spraying its broken ribs about them like bullets. It was only because they were sprawled on the dirt at the time that neither of them was hit by one of the wooden projectiles.

"Sweet Bridget," *el lobo* said, his voice holding the same shock that Bettina was feeling. "How could we be so naïve as to think we could stop such a creature by ourselves?"

Bettina had no words to reply. Through the settling dust, she stared in horror at the towering monstrosity. It seemed to be as much tree as human, a man-shaped fusion of bark and branch and corded roots from which sprouted an untidy snarl of twigs and leaves, feathers and bits of matted fur. But the barklike skin was supple and the Glasduine moved with an easy, panther's grace. Its face was the wooden mask she remembered from the sculpting studio in Kellygnow, only now the features were mobile, snarling, eyes dark with a cunning rage. The rough tangle of vines and leaves that trailed from its shoulders and made up its hair and beard moved of their own accord, coiling and writhing like a nest of disturbed snakes.

The only movement in the canyon were those vines. Neither Bettina nor her wolf felt able to get up from where they'd been thrown. The sheer weight of the Glasduine's presence paralyzed them. They could see that they wouldn't be its first victim. The creature had blood splattered on the bark of its limbs and torso—stark against the green leafing and barklike skin. Fresh blood, from the wet glisten of it.

For a long moment the Glasduine seemed content to simply hold onto its anticipation, devouring Bettina with its dark gaze. When it finally took a step toward her, she scrambled to her feet. Before she could dodge, a long powerful arm reached out to snatch her, fingers with a grip like a vise closing on her shoulder.

"No!" she cried, but the sound came out as the shriek of a hawk.

The Glasduine's touch woke something inside her—a long frenzied wail that shifted the bones under her skin, an ache rising deep up from the marrow of her soul. It brought her father's blood bubbling up through her veins and she was wracked with an indescribable pain, as though every muscle she had was spasming, her skin tearing, her bones grinding against each other. Her mother's rosary dropped from her hand. Feathers burst out over her skin, her face pulled into a sharp, narrower shape, and she was suddenly only a fraction of her normal size, slipping free from the rough fingers that had trapped her.

The Glasduine tightened its grip, but not quickly enough to stop the hawk Bettina had become from rising up, panicked, frantically beating the air with her wings. She might have escaped then, but she was too unfamiliar with this new form, floundering where her father would have easily risen up into the sky. The Glasduine's other fist whipped around and struck her a glancing blow that sent her tumbling head over heels through the air, down into the dirt. Barely conscious, stunned as much from her own transformation as from the blow, she could only lie there and watch the Glasduine move towards her.

But her wolf was quicker.

He had transformed, too, from a handsome wolf of a man into a true wolf, though unlike Bettina's change, his was of his own will, practiced and smooth. He darted ahead of the Glasduine and snatched her up with a bite that was firm enough to hold her, but didn't break the skin. The Glasduine roared as *el lobo* took off, racing down the canyon with his small feathered burden. No fool, he. One look at the creature was all he'd needed to know that they couldn't possibly stand up to it. Their only hope was to flee.

He ran as only *an felsos* could run, blindingly swift, like wind, like lightning, weaving around boulders and other obstructions when he couldn't simply clear them with a bound.

But the Glasduine was as quick, perhaps quicker. It kept up easily. Too easily. Glancing back over his shoulder, *el lobo* despaired. That first burst of distance he'd managed to put between them and the Glasduine was steadily being eaten away and the damned thing was almost on his heels.

9

Ellie wasn't as quick to recover as Aunt Nancy, but she still managed to get to the top of the rocks where Hunter had collapsed in time to see Bettina and her companion's transformations, the Glasduine's attack, the fleeing wolf with the hawk in its mouth, the monster hot on its trail. She put a palm against her temple, pressing hard in a futile attempt to relieve some of the pain that had lodged behind her brow.

"*That's* what we're supposed to be stopping?" she said to Aunt Nancy, staring at where the Glasduine had disappeared around a bend in the canyon. "Are you completely insane?"

"There's no one else," Aunt Nancy said.

"Like hell there isn't. There must be something stronger than us that can try to deal with it."

Aunt Nancy gave her one of those discomforting grins that did nothing to put Ellie at her ease.

"You have no idea how strong we are, girl," she said.

"That's right," Ellie told her. "I have no idea about *anything* that's been going on since I was first stupid enough to show up at Kellygnow." She took another look at the now-empty canyon. "I guess Bettina and her friend were playing out of their league, too."

"I think I misjudged their intentions."

"What? You saw them call up the Glasduine."

Aunt Nancy nodded. "Except it seems to me that they summoned it for the same reason we've been chasing it."

Well, that was one small comfort, Ellie thought. She'd hated the awful feeling that she'd so misjudged her new friend. Although even if Bettina *was* trying to stop the Glasduine, what was she doing in the company of one of the Gentry? For all the things Ellie didn't know she was at least sure of this: the hard men weren't their friends.

"Now come," Aunt Nancy said. "We have no time to lose."

"What about Hunter?" Ellie said, turning to where he lay.

He didn't seem to be physically hurt. He'd saved himself from cracking his

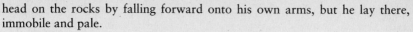

head on the rocks by falling forward onto his own arms, but he lay there, immobile and pale.

"We'll have to come back for him," Aunt Nancy said.

Ellie couldn't believe what she was hearing.

"You don't get it, do you?" she said. "If we try going up against that thing we just saw, we're not coming back at all."

"Then Hunter will be on his own."

Ellie shook her head. "No, this is way too far off the map of anything I can deal with."

"You said you would help."

"Yeah, but help with what? Killing ourselves?"

Aunt Nancy sucked in a breath between her teeth. Before Ellie knew what she was doing, the older woman grabbed her by the arm and slung her over a bony shoulder. Ellie had to put her arms around Aunt Nancy's neck to keep from falling back down the slope behind them. Once she had her balance, she tried to slip off Aunt Nancy's back, but then the body under her changed.

The transformation was as sudden as that of Bettina's companion, but rather than man to wolf, it was woman to spider. A gibbering panic began to howl in the pit of Ellie's stomach. The change was impossible enough—never mind how she'd just seen Bettina and her companion shift their shapes—but to add to Ellie's terror, the spider Aunt Nancy had become stood as tall as a horse. It was as if she had become that enormous shadow Ellie had seen looming behind Aunt Nancy. A fantastically oversized wolf spider, and here she was, clinging to its back.

She started to loosen her grip—she no longer cared how far she fell down the slope behind them—but the spider suddenly launched itself forward, leaping over the rocks and scuttling down the far side with a blinding speed.

"Ohmygod, ohmygod, ohmygod!" Ellie cried.

But she had no choice but to tighten her grip around the spider's neck, her own torso and legs splayed out along the breadth of its thick-furred back. It was that or fall off and crack her skull. Her skin shrank in on itself, she was so repulsed at the contact, so frightened by the terrible speed as those eight, many-jointed legs carried them down the canyon.

Quiet, a voice she recognized as Aunt Nancy's said in her head. *The god you call upon won't answer you here, but if you call loud enough, something else may. And trust me, girl. You wouldn't like what that might be. Not everyone you meet here is as nice as I am.*

Please, let me be dreaming, Ellie prayed. Just let me wake up.

Gather your courage. It was Aunt Nancy's voice, ringing in her head again.

Trembling, Ellie could only tighten her grip.

"I'm too scared to be brave," she mumbled into the thick fur under her face.

It was softer than she might have expected, like a cat's rather than a boar's.

Here in manidò-akì *our medicines are strong,* Aunt Nancy told her. *Trust in it. Trust in yourself. We may not be as strong as that* panàbe, *so we will have to be that much more clever.*

"You've got a plan?"

I am working on one.

Ellie went back to her prayers.

10

Hunter regained consciousness just in time to see what he thought was a giant spider scuttling off down the canyon—with Ellie clinging to its back. He rubbed his eyes and looked again. The apparition was gone. Just some leftover weirdness from whatever it was that had knocked him out, he decided.

He didn't feel as bad as he thought he should after having passed out. The only other time he'd fainted like that was one night when he'd accidentally taken too many prescription painkillers. He remembered standing at the sink one moment, the next he was coming out of some strange dream to a whirligig of faces that spun around above him for a long moment until they'd finally settled into Ria's features. He'd been so weak he'd barely been able to stand, and when Ria finally got him to his feet, he'd wished she hadn't, because it only made him feel sicker.

Right now he only had the fading residue of a headache and felt a little weak-kneed. That was about it.

He shifted his position, and turned to look back down the slope where Ellie and Aunt Nancy had been just moments ago. They were gone.

How long had he been unconscious, anyway? And why would they just leave him here? Though maybe they hadn't. Maybe something had taken them away.

The image of Ellie riding that giant spider popped into his head again.

Yeah, right.

He made his way back down the slope and looked around, softly calling their names. There didn't seem to be any sign of a struggle, but he wasn't exactly Daniel Boone. Give him a trashed apartment in the city and he could figure out that something bad happened. Out here, everything just looked the same. There could be a thousand clues staring him in the face and he wouldn't recognize one of them.

After calling some more, he made his way around the jumble of boulders, down to where Bettina and her friend had been earlier.

Again Ellie and the spider popped into his mind.

Okay, he thought. Let's pretend that she rode away on a spider. So where was Aunt Nancy?

That was when he remembered something Ellie had told him about this big shadow spider she kept seeing behind Aunt Nancy.

He shook his head. No way. He didn't care how deep they'd stumbled into Neverneverland, people didn't turn into giant spiders. The truth was, he must have been unconscious for a lot longer than he'd thought. No surprise there. You couldn't trust the way time moved here—not the way they'd been traveling through landscapes and climates like turning the pages of an encyclopedia. Ellie and Aunt Nancy were somewhere ahead of him. For whatever reason, they'd had to go on without him, that was all. He'd find out why once he caught up with them again.

When he reached the area where Bettina and the hard man had been earlier, he realized there was something different. It took him a moment to remember. Right by this flat stone where Bettina had been sitting, there'd been the huge fallen trunk of one of those tall cacti. It was gone now. All that remained was dirt and sand, swirled into a spiral pattern and overlaid with seriously large footprints.

He put his own foot inside one of the footprints. There was enough room for him to put both feet in there.

Okay, this was creepy.

Then he saw the bits of wood scattered all around. It was as though the fallen cactus had exploded.

What exactly had happened here?

He started to move back to the where the dirt had been swept into a spiral, pausing to pick up what looked like a necklace made of seeds. No, it was a rosary, he realized, when he saw the small, roughly carved cross. Who had this belonged to? With it dangling from his fingers, he returned his attention to the spiral, hastily stepping back when a greenish-gold light began to glow in the center of it.

This couldn't be good, he thought as he took a few more steps back.

He jumped when a flood of the light suddenly flowed out of the ground. It pooled for a moment in the spiral, then flowed off down the canyon, rippling like a wide ribbon in a breeze. He stared at it, this river of unnatural light, trying to figure out what it was.

There's an explanation for this, too, he told himself. Somewhere. Nothing that would make sense to him, probably, but to somebody. Everything was eventually labeled and put in a box. In the meantime, would somebody please wake him up.

That was when he saw Miki come bubbling up out of the ground and go tumbling down the ribbon of light. Before he could come to terms with the shock of her sudden appearance, Tommy came up next. He called out to them, but neither of them seemed able to hear or see him.

Oh, man, he thought. There's got to be way too many mind-altering drugs in the air of this place.

He stood watching as the light carried his friends down the canyon, watched until a bend in the landscape took them out of his sight, the two of them bobbing like driftwood, Miki's blonde hair contrasting sharply with Tommy's black.

Who's next? he wondered. He wouldn't have been surprised to see Titus or Adam go sailing by next.

The ribbon was following the same route his hallucination of Ellie and the giant spider had gone. If they *had* been a hallucination. He looked down at the ribbon. Because if this could be real . . .

He found himself wanting to touch it, but knew that would be just stupid. Instead, he set off at a trot, the rosary still dangling from his fingers as he followed the stream of light to wherever it had taken his friends.

11

It didn't take long for *el lobo* to realize that they weren't going to outrun the Glasduine. He ran at full tilt and the creature only continued to gain ground. It was like trying to outrun the wind. The Glasduine would be on them in moments and he had no idea what they could do to escape.

If Bettina had any experience with this hawk shape of hers, it would have been different. Then she could at least evade the creature's grasp by taking to the sky. The Glasduine was an earthbound spirit, its existence still entwined with the root voice of the world, for all that it was an aberration to the heart of the grace from which it had been drawn. It would be unable to chase her if she followed the wind roads. But the skies were closed to them. Bettina's hawk wings were too new to her and he was tied to the ground, like the Glasduine, so he was denied escaping by air as well. That only left turning to confront the Glasduine—as sure a form of suicide as slitting their own throats, though far more painful. Judging by the blood splattered on the creature, its prey did not die easily.

As they came around another curve of the canyon and raced down a straight stretch, the decision was taken out of his hands. The Glasduine drew near enough to take a swipe at him. The thick bark tips of its fingers brushed against his hindquarters, just enough to make him lose his balance. He went down, the hawk knocked from his mouth. She rolled across the dirt in a tangle of panicked flapping wings and then the change came over her again. By the time she landed up against the red dirt at the base of the canyon wall, it was Bettina who lay there, coughing in the dust she had churned up with her fall.

He didn't fare much better. He kept his shape, but went tumbling, tail over head, bouncing off a boulder before he could scramble to his feet. He ignored the pain in his side where he'd hit the boulder and rose snarling to face the Glasduine, but it was already out of range.

The Glasduine overshot both of them. Turning quicker than should have been possible for its bulk, it went for Bettina, its strange mask-like features twisted into a grin.

El lobo howled his frustration. He called to any power that would listen, promised anything, if she would only be spared.

As if in response, a stream of green-gold light came pouring down the canyon, following the path they'd just taken themselves. *El lobo* recognized the ancient mystery of that ribbon of light as it shot straight for the Glasduine, stopping it dead in its tracks before it could reach Bettina, but he didn't understand its presence here, at this time. There was no reason that the powers that

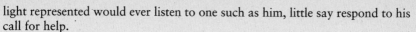

light represented would ever listen to one such as him, little say respond to his call for help.

A moment later he saw two figures in the light, bobbing like corks in a fast-moving stream. A small, blonde-haired woman came first. The Glasduine stood in her path, swaying and unbalanced. She hit feet-first, knocking it off its feet before she bounced from its broad back and went sprawling onto the dirt beyond it. The Glasduine was just recovering from her impact when the second figure, this time a dark-haired man, smashed it with a full body check, knocking the creature down again.

El lobo considered going for the Glasduine's throat while it was down, but he hesitated a moment too long and the opportunity was gone.

The Glasduine rose in a fury. The man who'd knocked it down the second time tried to scrabble out of its reach, but the Glasduine struck him across the back, cutting through cloth to the flesh below. The man was thrown a dozen feet or more, landing on the far side of the canyon where he lay as he'd fallen, limbs splayed, blood welling up from his wounds.

No, *el lobo* thought. How can the light allow this?

But then he realized what that light was—not a green and golden echo of the world's grace, come to answer his cry for help, but rather a ribboning tether of memory, like the thread that connected a spirit to its body when it traveled outside of its flesh. It was a display of the route the Glasduine had taken to get here, but to the Glasduine, it also served as a reminder of the place from which it had been drawn. That was why the Glasduine had been stopped so suddenly in its tracks when the tether of light manifested. The light was pure grace—an unpleasant and discomforting remembrance to a creature that was now the antithesis of the ancient mysteries that light represented.

El lobo gave over considering the light when the Glasduine returned its attention to Bettina. He lunged across the dirt to put himself between the two, calling out again to anything that might hear him and lend them aid.

You can have my life if you wish, he promised, only spare hers.

12

Ellie clung to Aunt Nancy's spider back as she sped down the canyon, scuttling over the stones with a surefooted grace that Ellie might have admired if she wasn't feeling so disoriented and scared. At one point, the spider eschewed a slower, more roundabout passage by securing a dragline and dropping them down a thirty-foot drop with a stomach-lurching motion. Just as they reached the bottom, Ellie caught a flow of motion from the corner of her eye. Something green, touched with gold. The spider saw it, too, and paused in its flight.

They watched the ribbon flow by.

I smell my sisters' involvement in this, Aunt Nancy's voice said in Ellie's head.

As soon as she spoke, Ellie heard faint echoes of powwow chanting and a low thrumming drone, here one moment, then gone again.

"What—?" she began.

The question died in her throat as she saw Miki come bobbing by, riding the stream of light as though it was a watery current. What on earth was she doing here? But then this wasn't earth, was it? That was all part and parcel of the problem. This was the world where nothing made sense, landscapes changed at the drop of a hat, old Native women turned into spiders . . .

When would the improbabilities stop?

But they had nothing to do with that, Aunt Nancy added, plainly puzzled.

A moment later, a dark-haired figure shot by, also riding the green-gold stream. For one hysterical moment Ellie thought it had to be Elvis, but then his passing features registered.

"Tommy . . . ?"

Aunt Nancy made an inarticulate sound. Her head turned, gaze fixing on her passenger. Ellie was held in spellbound horror by the grotesque features. It was the eyes that got to her the worst. Four small ones looking slightly down from the face and a little to each side. On top of these, two larger ones looking directly at her. Lastly, another pair, on top of the head, looking up. Each and every one of them, for all their silvery alien sheen, recognizably Aunt Nancy's.

Someone will suffer for this, the voice in Ellie's head said.

The grimness of its tone turned Ellie's blood to water.

Enough, she thought. This is where I get off.

But before she could slide down, Aunt Nancy sprang into motion and Ellie had to cling once more to the furry back. If anything, they went even faster down the canyon, chasing the bobbing forms of Miki and Tommy around one curve, another, before they abruptly came to the end of the chase.

They saw Bettina, crouched in the dirt and coughing. Her wolf companion charging the Glasduine, getting batted away as though he was nothing more dangerous than a stuffed toy. Miki lying sprawled on the ground on the far side of the creature. And Tommy . . . Tommy lying so still, his back torn open and bleeding.

Now I will have further loan of your medicine. Aunt Nancy said in a voice that would brook no argument. *The battle is at hand.*

"But . . . I don't know . . ."

It's simple. Keep a grip on my back and give me permission.

"But how—"

Just say it.

Ellie couldn't look away from Tommy's body. She cleared her throat.

"Do it," she said.

She clung tighter as the spider leapt for the Glasduine.

13

Bettina didn't see Miki and Tommy's arrival on the ribbon of light. Disoriented by the abrupt transition from hawk shape back into her own body, she lay on the ground for a long moment before finally sitting up. She coughed, choking, her throat and nose filled with dust. When her blurred vision cleared enough it was only to see the Glasduine coming for her, her wolf batted help-lessly aside as he tried to protect her. In her mind she heard *el lobo*'s cry for help, ringing out through the otherworld with an urgency that made her own earlier summoning call seem to have been no more compelling than a whis-pered request. She heard that cry for help, and then the promise he made to whoever might answer.

You can have my life if you wish. Only spare hers.

¡Es un trato! came an immediate response. It is a bargain.

No, she wanted to cry, even with the Glasduine upon her. I won't let you give your life for mine.

The Glasduine hoisted her up, rough bark fingers digging into her shoul-ders as it lifted her from the ground. Though she struggled, the effort was futile. The creature's grip was immovable. It shook her with a fierce grin dis-torting its features and held her high, as though she was some prize that all the world must see it had acquired. But it had only the one moment of triumph before Bettina's rescue was at hand, the rescue for which her wolf had traded his life.

A monstrous wolf spider leapt seemingly out of nowhere and bore the Glasduine to the ground, jaws closing on its shoulder. Once again Bettina was thrown clear, this time rolling across the dirt towards her wolf. She rose into a crouch and stared aghast at the struggle as the two monsters fought, her gaze widening in surprise when she realized there was a woman clinging to the spi-der's back.

She jumped when a hand touched her shoulder. Turning, she found her wolf tottering in human form, his features drawn with pain. She drew him down beside her, only just supporting his weight until he was able to kneel on the ground beside her.

"It . . . it's the sculptor . . ." he said, his gaze on the struggling figures.

Ellie? It couldn't be.

But when the Glasduine gave the spider a sudden shake, making her scrab-ble for balance, Bettina got a different view of the pair and she saw that her wolf was right.

She shook her head. "But if Ellie brought this spider," she said, "then who answered your call?"

"They spoke Spanish," he reminded her.

"They . . . ?"

She realized what he meant as soon as the word left her mouth. The reply had been made up of many voices, speaking in unison. So she wasn't surprised by their arrival, a line of brightly colored *cadejos* on the heights above the canyon. They came down the steep sides, finding passage along almost invisi-ble ridges and trails, goat hooves scrambling in the loose rocks. When they reached the bottom of the canyon, they paid no attention to Bettina and her wolf. Launching themselves at the battling monsters, they broke the pair apart and herded them to separate sides of the canyon with all the assurance and skill of a pack of border collies.

The spider let them back her up against the canyon wall where she shifted from spider shape to that of an old Native woman who promptly collapsed into Ellie's arms. The Glasduine wasn't nearly so acquiescent. Snarling, it struck out at the closest of the little dogs. It might as well have struck the side of the mountain for all the good the blow did. The *cadejo* was unmoved, unhurt. The Glasduine narrowed its eyes, studying its attackers. It feinted toward one of the little dogs, grabbed at another.

But *los cadejos* were quicker. One of them darted in and tore the creature's arm from its torso. Dragging it across the dirt, the *cadejo* worried at the still moving limb as though it was a bone. Another of the little dogs charged forward, knocking the creature to the ground. Two more leapt for its throat.

"*¡Para!*" Bettina cried. Stop. "Don't harm it."

"Are you mad?" her wolf asked.

She ignored him. "Your bargain must be with me," she told *los cadejos*. "I won't have another die for my sake."

"What does it matter who makes the bargain?" *el lobo* said. "We need the monster dead."

But Bettina had the little dogs' attention. The Glasduine took the opportunity to try to break free, but they kept it pinned to the ground, small immovable weights that snapped at it every time it moved. A sappy green blood seeped from where it had lost its arm, but it didn't seem greatly affected by the loss of blood, or the limb itself.

"It matters to me," Bettina said. "*¿Y bien?*" she asked *los cadejos*. "Is the bargain between you and me?"

She wondered if descendants were always doomed to repeat the mistake of earlier generations, for here she was, putting herself in the middle of a struggle between spirits—just as her *abuela* had done to her own great loss so many years before. But she refused to let her wolf pay the price. It was because of her that *los cadejos* were here in the first place. Any pacts to be made with them would be hers and hers alone.

"We already have a bargain," one of *los cadejos* told her.

She shook her head. "We have a debt. This will only put me more deeply in it."

The little dogs had one of their moments of silent communication before the foremost nodded.

"We will kill it for you," it said, agreeing. "Not for your wolf."

"Is that how it must be?" Bettina asked. "Can it only end with the Glasduine's death?"

"Once woken, *un monstruo* such as this cannot be sent back to its place of origin. Even with its *vida en hilodela*"—the little dog nodded with its chin to the ribbon of light that was still connected to the creature—"to show the way."

"So we let it go or we kill it," Bettina said.

She was unhappy with either choice. With the Glasduine's rampage momentarily contained, she felt they had the breathing space to consider other

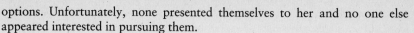

options. Unfortunately, none presented themselves to her and no one else appeared interested in pursuing them.

"Why are we even discussing this?" her wolf asked. "We have no choice but to kill it."

Bettina sighed. She knew he wasn't being so much bloodthirsty as pragmatic. The Glasduine was simply too powerful. If *los cadejos* hadn't answered *el lobo*'s summons, it was likely they'd all be dead by now and then who knew how many others would be imperiled? *Pero* . . .

"There is a third option," a new voice said.

Bettina turned to see that a stranger had approached while they were talking. He was an unimposing man, not a great deal older than she was. New to *la época del mito*, she judged, by the nervous glances he kept giving *los cadejos* and the Glasduine they guarded.

"Who are you?" she asked.

"I'm Hunter."

For one moment she thought he'd meant he *was* a hunter, that he was here to deal with the Glasduine. Then she realized it was only his name.

"*Y bien,*" she said. "And I am Bettina."

He held out the rosary her mother had sent her. Bettina hadn't even realized that she'd dropped it.

"Is this yours?" he asked.

She nodded, accepting it with a nod of thanks.

"What can you tell us of this third choice?" she asked.

"Well, I'm no expert . . ."

14

When Hunter finally caught up with the others his first thought was that he'd stumbled into some otherworldly circus. It was the colored dogs more than the grotesque creature that gave him this impression. The dogs seemed so . . . frivolous. At least they did until he realized that they were all that was keeping the creature contained.

As he approached, he listened to the conversation and a thought occurred to him which was what led him to speak up. Normally, he'd have been just as happy to keep in the background, out of the way of everybody else who were undoubtedly far more competent to deal with the situation. But like the woman who'd introduced herself as Bettina, he was unhappy with the idea that violence was the only solution. The death of the hard man he'd killed in Miki's apartment still haunted him.

"It's just," he said, "from all I've been told about these kinds of beings, they're not evil of and by themselves, are they?"

"It makes little difference at this point," muttered the man who knelt beside Bettina. He looked far too much like the Gentry for Hunter's comfort.

"Let him speak," Bettina said.

Hunter nodded his thanks. "They're supposed to be some kind of fertility symbol—part of that whole hero-king business. They bring in the spring, bless the fields for seeding. All the things we need for the world to pull out of winter and get back to the pursuit of growth and recovery."

"*Sí.* This I have been told as well."

"So that potential must still be inside it. Kind of like yin and yang. It has two sides, destructive and creative."

"The Glasduine has as many sides as the personality of he who calls it up," Bettina's companion said.

"But what if you bypass that personality? You know, go directly to the heart of the creature and bring up its inherent goodness."

"I knew there was a reason we brought that boy along," Aunt Nancy said.

Hunter glanced her way. The older woman was kneeling beside Tommy now, directing Ellie who was pressing his wounds with the bottom half of her shirt to stem the blood loss. Aunt Nancy seemed frailer than Hunter remembered. Her features drawn, shoulders stooped. But her eyes still had their fire and the grin she gave him made him feel good and nervous at the same time. He gave her a nod, then returned his attention to Bettina. She was shaking her head and Hunter couldn't tell if she was disagreeing or confused.

"How can we do this?" she asked.

"I don't know," he had to admit.

Bettina turned to the dogs. "Can you do this thing?" she asked them.

There was a general shaking of heads among the brightly colored dogs.

"That we cannot do."

"We are born in the fire."

"The dance of our flames can make you laugh."

"Or ponder."

"We can burn you to ash."

"We can open doors for you."

"We can open doors in you."

"But they all lead to what is."

"Not what might be."

"Or might have been."

Hunter was only momentarily taken aback when the dogs began to speak, talking in a chorus. But given what he'd been through during the past forty-eight hours or so, he didn't think there was much left to surprise him. Until he realized they were speaking in Spanish, but he still understood them. He waited a moment to make sure the dogs were done and no one else had anything to add, then cleared his throat.

"The Glasduine was called up by a mask, wasn't it?" he said when Bettina had turned back to him.

Understanding began to dawn in her eyes.

"So we need to make a new mask," Hunter went on, "to undo what was done before."

"Is that even possible?" Bettina asked.

Hunter realized that she wasn't asking him directly

"If it was made by someone with powerful *geasan*," the man who looked like one of the Gentry said.

That brought Ellie into the conversation.

"I guess that means me," she said, looking up from where she worked.

Under Aunt Nancy's direction, she'd taken a water bottle and a packet of dried, powdered comfrey roots. Cleaning the long narrow wounds on Tommy's back with the water, she then applied a liberal dose of the rootstock. Tommy remained unconscious throughout the procedure, which didn't bode well so far as Hunter was concerned. He remembered Tommy's aunts talking about this warning they'd gotten from some shaman back at the rez. They'd tried so hard to keep him out of the line of fire, but here he was anyway, the shaman's predictions coming true.

"Well, you know," Ellie went on. "I'm supposed to have all this magic floating around inside in me—"

"Oh, you do, girl," Aunt Nancy said. "Trust me on that. You've got medicine like nobody's business. I've never shifted over to a spider that size before. You've got to know it was all your doing."

Ellie shrugged. "And I'm the one who was supposed to make the mask in the first place."

"This wouldn't be a copy," Bettina told her.

"I know. I don't much care to do copies anyway."

"But you think you can do it?"

"I can make a mask," Ellie said. "And I can make it be positive—you know, uplifting to look at and . . . well, feel, I guess. But put magic into it?" She gave another shrug. "Someone's got to show me how."

"There's nothing to show," Aunt Nancy told her. "What do you think the creative impulse is but a piece of magic?"

"I never thought of it like that. I just think of it as a way of people expressing themselves."

The older woman nodded. "Sure. But it also holds echoes of the place that stick and leaf monster came from in the first place. Some people have a closer connection to it than others. People like you."

"So what? Is that supposed to make me more creative or something? I don't think so."

"No, it makes what you do more powerful."

"Do we have time to go back to Kellygnow for her to make the mask?" Bettina asked.

"We can't hold the monster here forever," one of the little dogs told her.

"It grows stronger every minute."

"Its *vida en hilodela* feeds it with strength."

"Is there some way we can cut it off from that source?" Bettina asked.

The little dog shook its head. "That would not be wise."

"We speak of ancient powers here."

"Older even than us."

"You would not want them to be angry with you."

"But we only want to stop the Glasduine from causing any more harm," Bettina said. "Surely they would understand."

"They do not see the world as you do," the little dog told her.

"They would not understand."

"They would see only that you impede the flow."

"I don't have to go back to Kellygnow," Ellie said, "if we can find clay around here." She looked at Aunt Nancy, then Bettina's companion. "The clay doesn't have to be fired, or even dried, does it?"

"It only needs to be true," the dark-haired man told her.

Aunt Nancy nodded. "And that is something you already know how to do."

"Okay," Ellie said. "Then let's get to it."

15

Hunter and Ellie accepted complete responsibility for making the mask, Ellie to do the actual hand-building of it, Hunter the grunt work of fetching and carrying.

First they had to break up the red clay they found lower down in the canyon, bringing it back with them using jackets as makeshift sacks. For the water she needed to make the clay pliable enough to work with, one of *los cadejos* showed them to a small seep still lower down in the canyon. It took Hunter a dozen or so trips to get enough water since they only had Aunt Nancy's water bottle to carry it in. As it was, the resulting mixture was far coarser than what Ellie was accustomed to, though it was still workable for hand-building. It wasn't as though she would be using the clay on a wheel or was going to fire the mask when it was done.

While they worked on the mask, Bettina tended to Tommy. With her mother's rosary wrapped around the fingers of one hand, she called on the spirits and *los santos* to help her diagnose what was needed to help him.

"I will have to gather medicines," she told Aunt Nancy when she had the information she needed. She turned to *los cadejos*. "Will you let me do this?"

"We have a bargain," one of the dogs replied.

"We are not your masters."

"You may go where you will."

Leaving Aunt Nancy to watch over her nephew, Bettina went searching for the plants she needed. Her wolf accompanied her, insisting he'd only been bruised in his brief encounter with the Glasduine. Bettina was grateful for the company, only worried that he might hold her back. But like so many of the spirits she had met in *la época del mito*, he was resilient and quick to heal.

While they were gone, Aunt Nancy cradled Tommy's head on her lap as he drifted in and out of consciousness. She burned smudgesticks, thrusting them on end into the dirt beside them, and crooned old healing songs into his ear. The smoke rose skyward in pungent trails, speaking her need to the

Grandfather Thunders. She trusted in Bettina's abilities, but she also wanted the *manitou* of Tommy's own people to be aware of his situation and lend what aid they might.

"He is a good man," she would say when she paused in her singing. "A strong warrior. He works with those who need help most, but today he needs your help."

Tommy's wounds were extensive and the only reason he wasn't feeling the pain of them at those points when he did regain consciousness was because of something Bettina had done as soon as she had come to help him, manipulating pressure points so that the pain was diverted before it could reach the nerve bundles in his mind. After one of Aunt Nancy's prayers to the *manitou*, he opened his eyes to look up at her.

"Who are you talking to, Aunt?" he asked.

She took comfort in the clearness of his gaze.

"The grandfathers," she told him. "I'm asking them to look in on you."

He regarded her for a long moment, then smiled.

"So that's why I keep hearing this drumming," he murmured before he drifted away again.

Los cadejos watched the doings of the humans with great interest, small dark gazes following every movement with all the single-minded curiosity of ordinary dogs. They were most interested in Miki, smelling in her the blood kinship she bore to the Glasduine. Miki hadn't spoken to anyone since she'd arrived except to tell Hunter she was fine when he'd asked after her. All she had done was sit cross-legged in the dirt, as close to the creature as the little dogs would let her, smoking cigarettes and staring at the monster her brother had become.

But one by one *los cadejos* had to turn their attention to the Glasduine. As they had warned Bettina, the creature continued to grow more powerful. It didn't yet strain their abilities, but as time progressed it required more and more of their concentration to keep it contained.

16

"What can I do now?" Hunter asked.

They'd spent the last half-hour working on the red clay, finally getting it into a consistency that satisfied Ellie. Hunter had gone to refill the water bottle. When he returned, Ellie was in the exact same position she'd been in before he'd left, hands palm-down on the clay, fingers spread out, a small frown furrowing her brow as she looked off into some distance that only she could see. She blinked when he spoke and gave him a brief smile.

"Nothing," she said. "I need to be alone."

Hunter nodded and began to turn away, pausing when she added, "That sounded harsher than I meant it. It's just that I have to concentrate."

"It's okay. I understand. There's a lot riding on this."

Thanks for reminding me, Ellie thought, but she only gave him another quick smile then returned her attention to the task at hand. She knew he hadn't said that to add to the pressure she was feeling, but it hadn't helped.

She watched him go, walking over to where Miki sat. When he put a hand on Miki's shoulder, she looked up and Ellie felt her heart would break. She'd never seen Miki looking so disconsolate. The worst of it was, no matter what the outcome of what they were trying to do today, Miki had still lost her brother. And she'd still lost her friend.

Oh, Donal, Ellie thought. How could you do this to us? How could you have become such a stranger? Or had they ever really known him at all?

It was so depressing. She knew she shouldn't be dwelling on it because it would only make her task that much harder—how do you create positive art when you feel like shit?—but it was impossible not to.

Donal's gloomy moodiness had driven her as crazy as it had everybody else, but she'd always believed that it was more a schtick than something based in reality, as though he'd decided that the way to set himself apart from all the other artists struggling to make a name for themselves was to become the Eeyore of the art world, gloomy, but almost good-humored about it. Half the time he'd actually pulled it off. They'd even been able to joke about it. But now . . . now she didn't know anymore. Now it seemed that under the act had been a real darkness, a streak of cruelty and meanness that she still found difficult to reconcile with the Donal she'd always known. But she knew Miki wouldn't lie about something like that.

Her gaze drifted from where Hunter was comforting Miki to the creature itself, guarded by Bettina's brightly colored, fierce little dogs. Was Donal still somewhere inside that Glasduine, or had his spirit already traveled on?

Stop it, she told herself. Just stop it right now. Concentrate on what you're supposed to be doing.

It was easier said than done, but she made the effort once more, laying her hands on the clay, feeling its texture, cool and damp, the smoothness pocked with tiny pieces of grit. A *tabula rasa* waiting for her to pull shape and sense out of its raw state. She searched for the spirit of the clay, listening for it, feeling for it, and considered her options.

At first she turned to her memories of the sketches of the original mask she'd done the other day, the changes she'd envisioned, the decorative leaf-work she'd planned to enhance the feel of the forest in it. Twinings of ivy, clusters of nuts, a bark-like texture in place. But that no longer worked for her. Anything to do with such forests just reminded her of Kellygnow and Donal, and started the spiral down to depression once more. She needed something entirely new.

Her gaze lifted to the giant cacti that grew here and there along the sides of the canyon and stood guard on the top edges, like Indian scouts. She would begin with them, she decided.

She rolled the clay out on the flat stone Hunter had found for her, working it until she had a flat circle perhaps a half-inch thick on the stone. Regarding it for a long moment, she wet it down, then went over to the side of the canyon, climbing up the loose stone and dirt to where the closest of the saguaro was growing. She ran her fingers along the smooth surface in between the spines that grew along the edges of its ribs. The top of this giant which reared some twenty feet above her was different from all the others she'd seen, sporting a gnarled, fan-shaped comblike shape that was almost five feet wide. It looked awkward and strange and startlingly beautiful, all at the same time.

These cacti already made her smile because of the way their arms appeared to be waving hello to her, wherever she looked. They gave off an inherent sense of calm and well-being, like kings and queens of the desert. The crown of this one only enhanced its regal air. That was what she'd aim for, she decided, half-sliding, half-stepping back down the uneven surface of the slope. She'd make the mask to mimic this stately crown with its spiraling, almost Pre-Raphaelite pattern of rib spines. She couldn't think of anything that reminded her less of the forests north of Newford, of dark-haired Gentry wolves and Donal.

With the decision made, she was able to work quickly, concentrating on the overall impression, forgoing unnecessary detail. She wasn't making a true representation here. She was creating a feeling, an impression, a connection to all the good things that the saguaro seemed to stand for: the warmth, sunshine, growth and growing, their royal heights and whimsical arms. But most of all, their great spirit.

By the time she had something that satisfied her, she was surprised to find that hours had gone by. She sat up straight, stretching out her back, and looked around. Bettina had returned, obviously successful in her hunt, for Tommy appeared to be sleeping peacefully, his head still resting on his aunt's lap. Bettina sat close by them, her hands resting on Tommy's chest as though in benediction. Her wolf sat a few yards away, eyes closed, resting.

Looking the other way, she found Hunter still comforting Miki. He had his arm around her shoulder and she leaned against him, looking smaller and more frail than Ellie had ever seen her. Past them, the Glasduine appeared to be docile, until she realized that all seven of the little, brightly colored dogs were keeping it in place. The arm that one of them had torn off lay abandoned. Ellie shivered when she saw that it was still twitching.

"I'm done," she said, turning back to Bettina, since Bettina seemed to have taken on the responsibility of leadership. Even Aunt Nancy deferred to her.

Bettina looked up, her eyes hollow, her features drawn with weariness. But she managed a smile.

"*Está bueno*," she said. "*Los cadejos* are beginning to have trouble keeping the Glasduine restrained."

She stood up, stretching as Ellie had. Aunt Nancy caught her arm before she could walk over to where the sculptor sat with the finished mask.

"You are a true healer," the older woman said. "You know this, don't you? You don't need the plants and herbs to do your work for you. The medicine lies inside you, in your hands, in your heart."

Bettina gave a slow nod. She had felt it herself when she'd worked on

Tommy, realized for the first time that the *brujería* was rising up from inside her, rather than coming from the plants she'd been able to gather. She glanced at her wolf. She wondered if this was part of what he'd meant about her needing to heal herself—a greater understanding of who she was.

"I'm in your debt," Aunt Nancy said, "for what you have done here for my nephew."

Bettina nodded, too tired to argue that helping someone as she had just done with Tommy, had nothing to do with debts or payments. It was what a healer did. She gave Aunt Nancy a distracted smile, then joined Ellie, her wolf trailing along behind her. They looked down on the mask. Ellie felt too close to the piece to be able to judge it herself. She hoped she'd managed to capture the essence of the giant cactus in the clay. With the Glasduine growing steadily more powerful, they were only going to get the one chance, so it had to be right.

"Oh, you've done a marvelous job," Bettina said. "I can feel the blessing of the aunts and uncles in your work here today."

Her wolf nodded. "The *geasan* is potent. It makes me smile simply to look upon it."

"*Sí,*" Bettina said. "But there is mystery there as well. An old *brujería* that makes the heart quicken."

"You mean the magic?" Ellie said. "Because I'll tell you the truth, I didn't know if that was happening or not. It didn't feel any different from any other sculpture I've worked on—except I did this one a lot more quickly."

"Then all your work holds magic," Bettina told her.

Ellie thought of all those commissions of businessmen she'd done, culminating in the half-finished bust of Henry Patterson she'd destroyed and would probably still be sued over.

"I wouldn't go that far," she said. Before they could discuss it further, she added, "So now what do we do? Who wears the mask?"

"We put it on the Glasduine," Bettina said. "And hope the mask is able to reach back into the grace and draw forth what is needed to counteract the creature's evil."

"We're really grasping straws here, aren't we?" Ellie said.

Bettina shook her head. "My heart tells me this is what we must do. It tells me there will be a price to be paid as well, but not what that price will be."

Her wolf sighed. "There is never an end to it . . . once you begin bargaining with the spirits."

"Yet there will be an end to the Glasduine," Bettina said. "And that is all that must concern us now."

"But if it doesn't work . . ." Ellie began.

"Then *los cadejos* will have to kill it."

Ellie still had her doubts, as they probably all did. The biggest danger so far as she could see was that the mask would work, it would draw more magic into the Glasduine, except it wouldn't change it. It would only make it stronger, so strong that not even these fierce little dogs of Bettina's would be able to deal with it. But she couldn't bring herself to speak that fear aloud.

She cleared her throat. "Okay," she said. "Well, I guess there's no point in waiting to do it."

Carefully, she worked the mask free from the stone and carried it over to the Glasduine on the palms of her hands. She almost dropped it when the Glasduine lunged at her. The creature was only just contained by the little dogs. Her heart drummed wildly and for a moment she didn't think she'd be able to go through with it. What if it all went wrong? It would be on her head, then. All the damage and deaths the Glasduine caused if they weren't able to stop it here.

Los cadejos leapt at the Glasduine, bearing it to the ground. They pinned its thrashing limbs, its torso. One of them sank its teeth into the creature's hair, holding the head down.

"Do you want me to finish?" Bettina asked. Her voice was gentle, with no recrimination in it.

Yes, Ellie thought, but she shook her head.

Walking forward, she circled around to where the one little dog held the Glasduine's head still. The monster bucked, its body twisting this way and that, but the dogs were still able to hold it in place. For now.

Swallowing thickly, Ellie hurried forward to get this done. She searched the Glasduine's features as she approached, looking for some trace of Donal in them, in the eyes, anywhere. There was nothing.

"Here goes," she said.

She dropped to her knees. Leaning forward she pressed the wet clay mask into place.

The Glasduine howled.

It burst free from the grip of *los cadejos,* scattering them. Whipping its head back and forth, it tried to dislodge the mask but only succeeded in striking Ellie a bruising blow that tumbled her to the ground. *Los cadejos* recovered quickly and nipped at the Glasduine as it stood, but it paid them no mind. Now it was the immovable force and nothing they could do would budge it. With its one hand, the Glasduine tore at the clay, but it was fused to its skin as surely as the wooden mask had fused to Donal's face in Kellygnow.

Arching its neck, the creature turned its face skyward and howled again, a sound so fierce and loud it had a physical presence. *Los cadejos* were scattered by it. The humans were sent to their knees, hands clasped over their ears.

Tears of pain streamed from Ellie's eyes. Through their blur, she saw the Glasduine whipping its head from left to right, its howl of pain growing louder and stronger. She pressed her hands as tightly as she could over her ears. And then her gaze caught movement. She looked at the ribbon of green-gold light that connected the Glasduine to its place of origin. The light appeared to be bubbling, roiling and twisting, throwing off sparks.

"Oh, shit," she said, the words drowned out by the Glasduine's bellowing cries.

It was definitely time for Plan B, but *los cadejos* couldn't get near the Glasduine now. Whenever they charged the creature, no matter from what direction they made their approach, they were batted aside as though they were no more than toy dogs.

They had screwed up big-time, she realized, and now they were going to pay.

17

Why didn't they simply kill it? Donal had wondered when the strange little dogs first rendered the Glasduine helpless. That's what he would have done, put the bloody bugger down, quick and fast, no regrets. Then its only victims would have been the Gentry and his own grand bloody self, and they'd brought it on themselves, so there'd be no great loss.

Truth was, Donal was ready to go on. Better or worse, at least there was a chance to start over again with a clean slate in whatever place came next. Given a choice, he'd choose the unknown over the shite he already knew.

But when he realized what Bettina and the others were hoping to do, he found himself agreeing it was worth the effort. If they really could turn the creature around, then perhaps something good could still come from all of this. Maybe someone with a bigger and better heart than his own could awaken the Glasduine's true potential, turn the monster into an avatar of joy and spiritual growth. Christ knew, the world could use something like that about now.

With the Glasduine immobilized by the dogs, he felt free to drift from its body. Guilt reared strongly in him when he hovered near Tommy, but it was far worse when he looked to Ellie and Miki. Caught up in making a new mask, Ellie, at least, was able to focus on the task at hand instead of dwelling on his betrayal of them. But Miki . . . oh, Miki. She always wore her heart on her sleeve, and right now he could see it broken and bleeding. If he was given only one wish, one chance, it would be to make it up to her. How could he have done this to his own bloody sister? It was worse than anything their da' had done—he at least could claim the doubtful immunity of having been blind bloody drunk every time he'd taken after them.

Donal had no such excuse.

That's what had to hurt the worst, he realized, as he drew near to his sister. That he, the one who'd always protected her, could have become this monster.

When had he changed? she'd be thinking. How much of their life together had been a lie?

He reached towards her, trying to brush away a tear that crept down her cheek, but his incorporeal fingers sank into her flesh. He pulled back with a start and fled. For the rest of the time that Ellie worked on the mask, he floated up near the top of the canyon, so busy hating himself that he almost missed the moment when the mask was done and Ellie was fitting it onto the struggling monster's face.

Quick as a thought, he darted back down, reentering the Glasduine just as the wet clay of the mask settled onto its features.

The agony he shared with the Glasduine made his own experience of first calling the creature up back in Kellygnow seem no worse than if he'd stubbed his toe.

It's grown so strong, he realized. While he was off playing the bloody martyr, so busy feeling sorry for himself, hating himself, the Glasduine had been quietly building up strength. And now that gathered strength was feeding back against the mask, intensifying the pain as the Glasduine struggled against the magics Ellie had managed to call up.

The raw, acid burn of it was nothing a human could bear.

His own wailing shriek merged with the Glasduine's howl as the creature broke free from the little dogs and tore one-handedly at the mask. He shared its agony for one long moment, then thrust himself out of the Glasduine's body with such force that he went tumbling and spinning down the canyon. Stunned, he could only watch as the Glasduine fought off the little dogs, scrabbling and ripping at the mask. He saw the ribbon of light, how it began to change, the colors bubbling and boiling. The change began where the light connected to the Glasduine, then went coursing away, following the ribbon back to its source.

Jaysus, Mary, and Joseph, Donal thought. The Glasduine was so foul, its evil grown so powerful, that it was overcoming both the purity of the light as well as the enchantment snared in Ellie's mask.

He stared as the ribbon of light began to discolor, feeling sick and disoriented.

Why hadn't her mask worked? When he'd used the other one it had easily pulled everything that was ugly out of him to give the Glasduine purpose and shape.

And then he knew.

There was nothing pure or good in the Glasduine. It had only Donal's ugliness, his meanness and spite and hatred, blown up into enormous proportions. There was nothing good left for Ellie's mask to call up. Everything else, every potential for goodness, had been shed when the creature had been born.

Sweet Mother of God, he prayed as he sent himself back into the creature. Let there be enough decency left in me for her mask to work. I don't ask it for me, but for Miki and Ellie and every other good soul that this monster will hurt if it's not stopped here and now.

It was like plunging himself into a fire.

The raw agony of his pain made him reach out, wanting to connect with the parts of himself that he'd used to bring the Glasduine to life. To strike back at the cause of the pain. Because it hurt too much to try to do good. What he felt was all the pain and shite of his life gathered into one, unending moment that threatened to burn him forever.

But he forced himself beyond it. He made himself look at Miki and that helped. Not to ease the pain, but to divorce himself from all the dark and ugly emotions he'd used to create the Glasduine. He made himself think of good things, good times. Of those moments when he'd made a positive difference in the world, instead of shitting on it. Like every time he'd protected Miki from their da'. Those were the parts of himself he offered up to the enchantment of Ellie's mask.

But it felt like a losing battle.

Deep in his mind he became aware of a pinpoint of pure light, that he was falling toward it. Into it.

The real irony, he thought, was that even if he had managed to turn the day, no one would have known. They'd still carry the memories of what a little, mean-spirited pissant he'd been.

The light was suddenly huge, enveloping him.

I would've liked one wee drink before I went, he thought. I'd like to have heard Miki squeeze one more tune out of that old box of hers . . .

Then the light swallowed him and he was gone.

18

Bettina stared in growing horror as the Glasduine batted away her *cadejos*. She could feel the creature growing stronger, rather than weakening. She saw its power flood out into its *vida en hilodela*, fouling the purity of the greens and golds until the ribbon boiled and foamed. The light lost its intensity. It became discolored and spent as it sped back to its source while the Glasduine stood taller than it had before. Something was sprouting from where *los cadejos* had torn off its arm, a bristle of twigs and buds that quickened and grew as she watched.

"We blew it," Ellie said. She stood so close the words were like a breath in Bettina's ear.

Though Bettina shook her head, she couldn't even convince herself. Her *cadejos* continued to rush at the Glasduine but it was much stronger than the little dogs now and it was all they could do to keep it backed up against the wall of the canyon. Ellie's clay mask was still attached to the creature's face, the features mobile now, the good humor and warmth of the saguaro that Ellie had infused into it distorted and changing.

What had gone wrong? Bettina had been so sure that they'd found a creative solution rather than a destructive one. That they could heal the Glasduine, turn it from the awful path it had stumbled upon when Donal first called it up. But the healing hadn't taken. Instead the Glasduine's dark nature had swallowed the *brujería* of the mask, spoiling it like a cancerous growth as it rampaged through a once-healthy body.

For some things it seemed there was no healing. That realization made the world feel like a smaller place, raising walls where once the view had been unending. Except . . .

Bettina looked down at her hands.

She'd learned today of the healing gift she'd been given. But such healing required the laying on of hands. And strength. More strength than she had, certainly, but she wasn't alone here.

"No," her wolf said as she turned to Ellie.

Oh, he was quick, that one, Bettina thought. He could read her like a tracker read signs.

But she shook off his grip.

"Ellie," she said. "Will you lend me your *brujería* as you did Aunt Nancy?"

"Bettina, please," her wolf tried.

Los cadejos chorused their own protests.

"No good will come of this," they cried.

"The monster is too strong."

"You can only flee."

"We will hold it back as long as we can."

"But go now."

"*¡Pronto! ¡Pronto!*"

"We must flee."

"Do what you must," she told them. "And so will I. Ellie?" she asked again.

The sculptor gave her a slow nod.

"I understand your fear," Bettina told her. "I'm scared, too."

"No, no, no!" *los cadejos* cried.

"You risk your life."

"You risk your wings."

"You risk our home."

Bettina ignored them. She looked to Aunt Nancy.

"I'm not in the kind of league that can handle this sort of thing," the older woman said, nodding at the monster with her chin, "but you've got my support. If I can do anything . . ."

"Only say the word," *el lobo* told her.

"You've changed your mind?" Bettina asked.

He shook his head. "Not about our chances. But I was never going to walk away and leave you to face this on your own."

"Count me in, too," Hunter said. He stood with his arm around Miki whose gaze remained locked on the Glasduine. "Don't know what use I can be, but . . ."

Miki finally looked away, turning her anguished gaze to Bettina.

"Just finish it," she said.

"You can all help," Bettina told them. "Pray for us. Lend us your hopes and strengths."

Aunt Nancy nodded. She crossed her arms, making an X of them upon her chest. The shadow of a spider rose up behind her, inclining its head to the shadow of a hawk that lifted its strong features behind Bettina in response to the spider's appearance.

Anansi, the hawk said, its voice ringing in all their minds. *You are far from home.*

The spider shook its head. *Not I*, it replied. *I am but an echo of my father's presence.*

As am I, the hawk replied.

"Àngwàizin," Aunt Nancy said.

Bettina smiled. Yes, she thought. That was what was needed here. Luck, not power. The borrowed, not the owned. And the reminder that not all the spirits of *la época del mito* stood against them—only this one, and even it was not to blame for the horror it had become.

She reached forward and took Ellie's hands.

"Hold my shoulders," she said.

She gave Ellie's fingers a squeeze, then let go and turned around. Ellie hesitated for a moment, then placed her hands on Bettina's shoulders and fell in step behind her as Bettina approached the monster.

The Glasduine was twice as large now, barely contained by the wearied *cadejos*, a towering monstrosity that seemed only mildly affected by the pain that had so ravaged it earlier. Its lost arm had partially grown back. Glittering eyes focused their gaze on the two women. The kind smile Ellie had worked into the red clay of the mask twisted into a grin.

At Bettina's approach, *los cadejos* finally broke from the Glasduine. One by one, they circled the two women, flowing like quicksilver, a shimmering rainbow of colored fur. Then, as they had so many years ago in another part of *la época del mito*, on the slopes below the Baboquivari Mountains, they entered her, vanishing into her torso like ghosts. Spirit dogs, adding their strengths to hers.

Bettina knew a surreal calmness. Her father had told her about it once, how it could come to you when you were in enemy territory and all the odds were against you. You told yourself, I won't get out of this alive. I am already dead and there is nothing to be gained by worrying over the exact details, the how and when of it happening.

She held the rosary her mother had sent her in one hand, the strand of desert seeds wrapped round and round her palm, the carved cross hanging free. She called on the spirits of the desert, on the saints and the Virgin, to help her with this healing.

The Glasduine grinned hugely. It opened its arms to embrace them, the one arm stunted, the other long, a supple branch. Then lifting from between its legs came a third appendage, knobbed and swollen.

"Oh god, oh god," Ellie moaned.

The sculptor gripped Bettina's shoulders too tightly, hands shaking.

But neither the proximity of the Glasduine nor her companion's fear were able to pierce the calm that had come over Bettina. Part of this was a gift from *los cadejos*, she realized, given to her so that she could face the creature unencumbered by fear, clear-headed, her entire being focused and sure.

Bettina drew on Ellie's *brujería* and felt the warm pulse of it flow into her. She heard the supportive chants of *los cadejos* echoing deep inside her. The spirits of the desert drew close, the living presence of the aunts and uncles; of coyote, mesquite, and marigold; of cholla, lizard, and mountain lion; of turtle, poppy, and javalina. A hawk's wings unfolded inside her chest. The soothing voice of St. Martin de Porres, the patron of paranormal powers, seemed to join her own as she sent a silent prayer to the Virgin.

Ave Maria
gratia plena
Dominus tecum
Benedicta tu in mulieribus
et benedictus fructus ventris tui Jesus
Sancta Maria,
Mater Dei
ora pro nobis peccatoribus
nunc et in hora mortis nostrae
Amen

She spoke the last word aloud and the Glasduine laughed, a harsh booming sound that echoed up and down the canyon. Bettina merely gave the creature a serene smile in response. Beyond fear or anxiety now, she was strong with Ellie's *brujería* and her faith, bolstered by the support of those gathered here to help her and a host of invisible spirits. She stepped into the Glasduine's open arms and laid her hands upon its chest, pushed through the tangle of vines and leaves to the bark beneath that served as skin.

The Glasduine's laughter died, cut off as though severed by a knife.

Their gazes locked, Bettina's and the Glasduine's. The healing *brujería* mixed with that of Ellie's mask and the creature's own. White light flared, deep inside them and burst out through the pores of their skin like a hundred thousand laser slivers, blinding those that watched. The Glasduine's *vida en hilodela* was immediately made pure.

But there was a price. Their blood turned to lava, hot and burning. Every nerve end screamed. Wailing filled the air, harsh and keening, both their voices howling their pain. The Glasduine bucked and Ellie lost her grip on Bettina's shoulders. She went stumbling, blinded and moaning, before she fell into the dirt. But Bettina dug her fingers into the vegetative matter of the Glasduine's chest and held fast. She repeated another "Hail Mary." The Glasduine grew again, a sudden spurt that took Bettina's feet from under her. She kept her grip, hanging from the Glasduine's chest, forcing herself to ignore the pain, to concentrate on the task that had put her here.

Under the blinding light she could feel the darkness of the creature rising up once more, swelling like a maggot-ridden corpse. She caught the tattered wisps of the *brujería* born in Ellie's mask, and holding onto them like a handful of threads, she plunged an arrow of her spirit into the morass, searching for some part of Donal that the Glasduine hadn't already swallowed and taken into itself.

She had to navigate through the flood of the creature's hatreds and lusts, experience the gruesome deaths of the Gentry, delve deeper and deeper until she felt she could go no further and was ready to give up.

But finally, there it was.

A tiny, warm kernel of Donal's goodness, hard-shelled like a seed, protecting itself from the awful stew in which it floated.

Bettina focused the arrow of her spirit until it was so small and sharp it could pierce the kernel and enter it. Before the darkness could rush in after her, she connected the tattered threads of the mask's *burjería* to it, then sealed the opening she'd made and enclosed the whole of it, kernel and connecting threads, in a protective sheath. She waited only long enough to see that the kernel was beginning to swell, then retreated, her stamina spent.

She allowed the Glasduine to expel the arrow of her spirit. It returned to her with a shock, withered and trembling. Loosening the numbed grip of her fingers, she let the Glasduine fling her away. She hit the ground hard, went tumbling over the loose stones and dirt. Her fingers, the palms of her hand were raw, the skin burned away. There was nothing left of the rosary her mother had sent her. She could barely lift her head, but she did. She couldn't look away.

The Glasduine had fallen to its knees. Illumination still flared from its pores, laser-thin and bright, a thousand blinding lines of white light. It was still howling, but the sound was different. Almost fearful.

Grow, Bettina told the seed she'd found in the Glasduine's darkness. Be strong.

She said another "Hail Mary."

She couldn't bring her hands together—even the movement of air across the raw wounds was agony. With an effort, she managed to dampen the worst of the pain. Her gaze remained locked on the Glasduine.

The shafts of light began to swell, to join. The Glasduine's upper torso drooped. By the time it had bowed its head, pressing its face into the dirt, all the shafts of light had joined into one tall pillar that rose up from the arch of the creature's back. Colors swelled up from the bottom of the pillar, the familiar greens and golds of the creature's *vida en hilodela*. A moment later and the light had swallowed the Glasduine whole.

Bettina and the others couldn't look away.

Something became visible in that light. They were being given a glimpse, as though through a stained-glass window, of enormous trees, giants that dwarfed the cliffs around them. Impossible behemoths that rose and rose up into the sky.

"Forever trees," Bettina heard her wolf whisper. "In the long ago."

By that she knew they were looking in on the First World, the source from which the Glasduine had been drawn. She drank in the sight, leaning closer when she saw a woman walking under those trees.

Bettina wasn't sure who the others saw—she sensed that each of them recognized her in their own way—but she saw a dusky madonna, modestly clad in blue and white robes, and knew it was Our Lady of Guadalupe, the Virgin as first seen in a vision by Juan Diego at the chief shrine of Tonantzín on Tepeyac Hill, centuries ago. Those trees were far from Cuautlalpan in Mexico, but *La Novia del Desierto*'s presence felt as natural in that ancient forest as it did in the Sonóran.

The woman lifted her head and looked their way. She smiled and Bettina's heart grew glad in a way it hadn't since her *abuela* had followed the clown dog into the storm. Then the vision was gone.

But the marvels continued.

The pillar of light dwindled until it pooled around the fallen body of the Glasduine. Bettina held her breath, watching the liquid light pulse. Then something moved in the center of the pool. For a moment Bettina thought it was the salmon from the pool behind Kellygnow, but then a saguaro rose up, swallowing the body of the creature as it grew.

By the time it stopped growing, it towered fifty feet into the desert sky, two tons of cactus, enormous by any standards, though dwarfed in Bettina's mind by her brief glimpse of the incredible heights of the forever trees.

The giant stood there for a long moment, gleaming in the sunlight, gleaming with its own inner light. Then one of its arms dropped off. Another. And it fell apart as quickly as it had grown, the green waxy skin browning, rotting. In no time at all the only thing that remained were the saguaro's ribs, the lower halves still standing tall, their upper halves drooping like the spokes of an umbrella. Caught in the middle, with ribs thrusting up from its chest, was a small body.

Donal, Bettina realized at the same time as Miki ran forward. Miki wept, trying to break off the saguaro ribs. Hunter joined her, pulled her away.

"Let me try," he said.

He lowered her to the ground and with *el lobo*'s help began the grisly task of breaking the brittle ribs so that they could free Donal's body. Miki remained where Hunter had left her, tears streaming down her cheeks.

Bettina glanced at Ellie. The sculptor's eyes were wet with her own tears when she turned to Bettina.

"What . . . what happened?" she asked.

"Neither Donal nor the creature lived a good life," Bettina said. "So the shape would not hold for them. There is an old *Indios* saying. If you live a good life, you come back as saguaro; you become one of the aunts and uncles. Live a bad life, and you come back as a human." She hesitated for a moment, then added, "You chose well for your mask."

"Yeah, like I knew what I was doing."

Bettina shrugged. "Your heart and your hands . . . your *brujería* knew."

Ellie slowly stood up.

"So . . . we won, I guess."

Bettina nodded.

"So why do I feel like shit?"

"Because we are just people," Aunt Nancy said, joining them. "Because the world isn't black and white and it cuts us so deeply when those we love—those we think are good people—do bad things. It's hard to celebrate a victory that has come about through the death of one we loved."

Ellie gave a slow nod. "I still can't believe Donal had it in him."

"There was goodness, too," Bettina said. "In the end, that's what saved us."

"It just seems like such a senseless waste."

"*Sí.*"

"Let me see your hands," Aunt Nancy said to Bettina.

Ellie went pale at the sight of them.

"Oh, my god," she said. "Your hands . . ."

"They will heal."

"I have a small jar of bunchberry/cattail paste in my pack," Aunt Nancy said. "Let me get it."

"Thank you."

"Can't you, you know, heal it with magic?" Ellie asked.

"I have been working on it," Bettina told her, "but such healing never works as well on yourself. Mostly I'm concentrating on dampening the pain and retaining my hands' mobility."

Aunt Nancy returned and with a touch as gentle as the brush of a butterfly wing, she applied a thinned mixture of the paste to Bettina's hands. The bunchberry immediately cooled the burns, penetrating deep under them to relieve the pain. The cattail helped to numb the worst of it.

"There's always a price," Aunt Nancy said.

Bettina nodded. She thought of *los cadejos*. They hadn't even named theirs yet.

"Some pay in coin more dear than others," she said.

She looked at the slope of Miki's back as she continued to weep, silent now. Then past her to where Hunter and her wolf were freeing Donal's body.

"My sympathies lie with the living," Aunt Nancy said. "And the innocent."

"You're tougher than I am," Bettina told her.

Aunt Nancy shook her head. "No, I'm just older. I've seen that much more of the hurt we do to each other."

19

It took them over an hour to free Donal's body from the wreckage of the dead saguaro. Without *el lobo*'s exceptional strength, it would have taken them much longer, for the saguaro ribs that pierced the body were resilient and hard to break. It was a grisly, unhappy task, but they finally pulled the body free and were able to lay it out on the flat stone where Ellie had worked on the mask. Hunter fetched more water and Miki carefully washed Donal's face and hands. Her tears were gone, but Bettina could see that the heartbreak remained.

Later, they sat in a half-circle around the body, all except for Tommy, who was propped up against another stone close at hand, cushioned on a thin mattress of dried grasses that Ellie and Hunter had gathered lower down in the canyon. He had to lay on his side because of the long furrows the Glasduine had torn across his back. Bettina had worked on them again, ignoring her own pain when she had to lay her hands directly onto the wounds. All that remained now of the furrows were thick, red welts that were still very tender. While Tommy tried to remain alert and follow their conversations, he kept drifting in and out of consciousness. But at least when he closed his eyes now, it was because he was sleeping.

Aunt Nancy lit a smudgestick and set it on the stone by Donal's head.

"I always thought I was the strong one," Miki said after a moment, rocking back on her heels.

She reached out and brushed the hair back from Donal's brow. When she sat back again, Ellie put her arm around her shoulders.

"But I see now," Miki went on, "that a lot of that was Donal looking out for me that let me be strong. For so many years, he kept all the bad things in the world at bay."

"He wasn't an evil person," Bettina said. "Misguided, yes, but—"

"Oh, please," Miki told her. "He was a bloody, self-centered bastard. Look at what he did. We could all be dead." Her voice went quieter. "But he was still my brother."

"What he did was wrong," Bettina agreed, "but in the end, he allowed us to banish the creature."

Miki shook her head. "I don't know that it makes up for it. I always knew he was bitter, but I never knew he was carrying such venom around inside him."

"None of us did," Ellie said.

"But we should have. We should have paid more attention to all those tirades of his. We should have gotten him help."

Ellie shook her head. "Even if we'd known, he wouldn't have let us."

"But we still could have tried."

Ellie sighed. "You're right. We should have tried."

"I don't excuse your brother," Aunt Nancy said after they'd all fallen silent, "but consider this. If all the darkness each of us carries within us, all our angers and unhappiness and bad moments were pulled out of us and given shape, we would all create monsters."

"But it's not something we'd do on purpose," Miki said.

"I doubt he meant for it to turn out as it did," Aunt Nancy told her.

Later still, *el lobo* carried the body up to a small cave he'd found set high above the water line for when the floods came. The trail leading up to it was better suited for goats, but except for Tommy, they all made the trek up. They sealed the opening with boulders and rocks, everyone pitching in. When they were done, Ellie took a sharp rock and scratched a picture on the face of the stone above the cave. It looked like a rough cartoon of a donkey or a horse to Bettina.

"What's that?" she asked.

"It's Eeyore," Ellie said, her eyes welling with tears.

"What's an ee-yore?"

Miki began to cry again when Ellie explained.

Bettina wasn't strong enough to attempt to guide them all out by the direct route she and her wolf had taken to get here, and no one was up to the long trek it would take otherwise, so they made a rough camp out of the canyon, higher up on the west side. *El lobo* carried Tommy up while Ellie, Hunter, and Miki scavenged wood to fuel their fire. They came back with lengths of mesquite and ironwood and they soon had a small fire to hold back the night. For food they had to share a few biscuits and some beef jerky that Aunt Nancy pulled out of her seemingly bottomless backpack, along with a packet of tea.

"It's the first thing you learn when you go into the bush," she said. "You never go without provisions."

She also had a small tin cup in there which they all shared for the tea.

There was little conversation. One by one, they turned in until only Aunt Nancy, Bettina, and her wolf remained awake. They let the fire die down. A three-quarter moon rose after a time, its appearance welcomed by a chorus of coyotes, yipping in the distance. The moonlight let them see the towering heights of the Baboquivari Mountains, far to the west.

"It's a beautiful night," Aunt Nancy said. "If you'd like to go for a walk, I can watch over things here."

Bettina smiled at the older woman's subtlety. She liked Aunt Nancy, with her mix of toughness and kindness, and the mysteries lying so thick around her. If Bettina looked at her a certain way, she could see Aunt Nancy's spider shadow, that echo of the shape she'd been wearing when she first attacked the Glasduine. And then, recalling the spider, Bettina felt a whisper of wings stretching in her own chest.

She remembered how those shadows had spoken to each other just before the final assault on the creature, known each other. That was another mystery Bettina would like to explore further, but now was not the time. She was too drained from the ordeal, distracted by the constant burn of the pain in her hands and the presence of her wolf, sitting so close to her that she could feel his body warmth.

"A walk would be nice," she said, rising to her feet.

El lobo hesitated, until she smiled at him, then he rose, too.

They walked along the lip of the canyon, easily marking their path, for they both had keen night sight, the one because of her *brujería,* the other because of his own otherworldly heritage. Bettina wanted to hold her wolf's hand, but even that much pressure on her palms would be too much. So she slipped her arm into the crook of his.

There was much still unsaid between them, but for now they allowed an affectionate silence and each other's company to suffice. The desert night stirred around them, crowded with spirits, tranquil and resonant. After awhile

Bettina had to sit down. Her heart was full, but her energy level was lower than she could ever remember it being before.

"*Y bien,*" Bettina said. "This was an awkward and unpleasant way to come back home, but I'm still glad to be here."

"I would like to know it better," her wolf said, "but . . ."

His voice trailed off.

"I'm not going back," Bettina said, her voice soft. "Not to stay. Only to collect my things."

Her wolf couldn't look at her. His gaze went off, into the desert night.

"And I can't stay here with you," he said finally. "This body . . ."

"Gives you responsibilities back in the Kickaha Mountains. I know."

She knew he was bound by the promise he'd made to the *manitou* who had given him the body he now wore.

"What will become of us?" *el lobo* asked.

Bettina sighed. Could there even be an "us"? So much lay between them, differences that could push them ever further apart. But there was as much to draw them together, if they were willing to work at spanning the distances.

"*No lo sé,*" she said. She really didn't know.

"Sometimes it seems that the whole of our lives are bound to the debts we owe to others."

Bettina nodded. "But what kind of life would it be to always live alone?"

"An unhappy one."

"*Sí.*"

"So we accept our debts and obligations." He paused a heartbeat, then asked, "And *los cadejos*. Have they spoken more of the bargain you made with them?"

Bettina shook her head. "No. But I can feel them inside me, distant and weary. And something else. The sensation of wings unfolding in my chest."

Just speaking of it woke a flutter in her chest, a rustle of feathers that only she could hear.

"You never knew?" her wolf asked.

"*No seas tonto.* That I was so much like Papá that I could take to the skies as a hawk, just as he and his *peyoteros* do? How could I have known? This is something else I must come to terms with."

"But it doesn't frighten you?"

"*Claro.* But only a little."

"Wise, lucky, *and* brave."

Bettina smiled. "I never felt brave."

"Bravery is acting in spite of your fears."

"I suppose." She hesitated a moment, she added, "The Gentry are dead—the Glasduine killed them."

Just saying it aloud made her shiver again, knowing all too well how they had died. But she left it at that and he didn't ask for more details. Having seen what the Glasduine was capable of, he would know that they had died hard.

"I thought as much," her wolf said. "And I can't deny that I wondered if I would survive their death."

"How could you not? You are your own being now."

"I don't always feel that way," he told her. "Mostly I feel as though everything I am is merely made up of the borrowed and discarded parts of others."

He spoke matter-of-factly, without a trace of self-pity, but it made Bettina's heart go out to him.

"It must be strange," she said. "But, even those of us with less extraordinary origins—aren't we all pieces of those who came before us? We carry the bloodlines of our ancestors and we form our beliefs from what we learn from others as much as from what we experience ourselves. What is important is who we become—despite our origins as much as because of them."

"You see? Yet another wise response."

"I would punch you," she told him, "except it would hurt me more."

Her wolf made a sympathetic sound and put his arm around her shoulders. She leaned gratefully against him, savoring the comfort of his body's warmth, the strength that the muscled arm represented.

"Have I earned my kiss yet, do you think?" he asked.

"*Por lo menos,*" Bettina said. "Many times over."

She lifted her head and their lips met. When they finally came up for air, her wolf sighed.

"What will we do with ourselves?" he whispered.

"Shh," Bettina told him.

Before he could speak, she kissed him again.

20

WEDNESDAY AFTERNOON, JANUARY 21

They returned to the wet misery of Newford and the ice storm on the following day. *El lobo,* supporting Tommy for the short trek back, walked beside Bettina, the others following in a ragged line behind. When they finally crossed back over from *la época del mito,* they found Sunday and Zulema waiting for them in the woods behind Kellygnow. The Creek sisters were eager to depart, wasting little time in packing Tommy into the bed of the pickup, fussing over him with auntly concern. They offered lifts to whoever wished to come with them, which Hunter, Ellie, and Miki accepted.

Before the pickup pulled away, Aunt Nancy approached Bettina and her wolf. She knelt for a moment, reaching into her seemingly bottomless backpack to take out two small items. Her sisters remained near the pickup, neither friendly nor unfriendly, studying Bettina and her wolf with measuring gazes, but the others drew near as Aunt Nancy spoke.

"You will always find honor and welcome at our fires," she told Bettina and her wolf, offering them the gifts she held. "Both of you."

She gave them small sacks—squares of red cloth, closed with a twist and tied with a leather thong. From the smell of tobacco and sweetgrass that rose from hers, Bettina knew Aunt Nancy was honoring them with this. She held hers lightly in the open palm of her hand so that even its small weight and touch wouldn't chafe her tender skin. Her hands were healing, but even with her *brujería*, it was a slow process.

"I was angry at first," Aunt Nancy said to *el lobo*, "when I knew Shishòdewe was dead and you were walking around in his body. But it's plain to me now that you could have had nothing to do with his death. I know that you will honor his gift to you and remain true to his obligations."

El lobo lifted the red sack to his lips and kissed it before placing it the pocket of his jacket. He inclined his head to her but said nothing.

Bettina winced as the cloth of her jeans rubbed against her hand, but she reached into her pocket all the same, hoping for and finding one of the *milagros* she used for her *amuletos*. She always seemed to have one or another in her pocket, absently tucked away in the process of making the charms. She looked at the one she'd found before she gave it to Aunt Nancy and smiled.

"Back home," she said, "we pin these to the robes of *los santos* when we ask for their intercession. If I was seeking their help, this would represent the burns on my hands, but *por ahora* . . . I'd like to think it represents the helping hand we offered each other."

The *milagro* was in the shape of a small silver hand.

"I will weave it into a beadwork collar," Aunt Nancy told her, "and whenever I wear it, I will remember you and what we did."

Bettina nodded. As Aunt Nancy turned away, Bettina looked over to the pickup to see Tommy waving at her from the litter of blankets on which he lay in the bed of the truck. Bettina waved back. When she returned her attention to the others once more, Hunter and Miki murmured their goodbyes, then retreated to the pickup where they climbed into the back with Tommy. But Ellie came over and gave them each a hug.

"Are you going to be okay?" she asked Bettina.

"Of course," she said. "Will you?"

"I don't know. With all that's happened . . . it's a lot to digest."

"You don't have to use the *brujería*," Bettina told her. "Except as you always have—in your art."

"I suppose. But it makes you think. Why do I have it? Where did it come from? Am I a sculptor because of it?"

Bettina shook her head. "*Brujería* doesn't make you need to create; it only makes what you create that much more true."

"Do you think I should do more with it? I mean, something like what you're doing . . . being a healer and all."

"You must do what's in your heart."

"I don't know what's in my heart anymore."

"Kindness," Bettina assured her. "Faith in others. Hope. All the things you already bring to those you help with Angel's programs."

"But maybe I can do more with it."

"*Quizá, quizá no,*" Bettina replied. "Time will tell. But one thing . . ."

"Yes?"

"Promise me you'll be careful with whatever future commissions you accept."

Ellie smiled and gave her another hug. "That I can promise you."

Salvador and Nuala came out of the house when Bettina and her wolf emerged from the woods and followed the pickup out onto the lawn. They stood together to watch the vehicle drive away, the pickup moving effortlessly across the slick ice and slush that made the lane so treacherous.

"How is that possible?" Salvador murmured.

"The same way you've been kept dry and warm," *el lobo* told him. "By stepping in between this world and the one beyond."

Salvador made the sign of the cross.

"*No esté nervioso,*" Bettina told him. Don't be nervous. "Nothing here will harm you now."

Salvador nodded and gave her an unhappy look.

"Have you always been a part of . . . all of this?" he asked her.

"*Sí.* But I didn't lie to you. I simply never spoke of it."

"*No, por supuesto que no . . .*"

She could see the unspoken word in his eyes, for all that he tried to hide it. *Bruja.* Witch.

His hand twitched because he would not allow himself to insult her by making the sign of the cross to her face. It saddened her that such a simple word could make her friend fearful of her. The small charms she'd made were one thing—even Maria Elena had asked for one. But witchcraft . . .

She remembered how occasionally children back home, daring each other until one braver than the rest would call out to her *abuela*—

¡Bruja! ¡Bruja! ¡Bruja!

—before they would all run away, shrieking with laughter and fright.

"No," she said, responding to the unspoken epithet she saw now in Salvador's eyes. "There is no need for you to be wary of me."

"I mean no disrespect . . ."

"Salvador, *por favor*. I am who I have always been. It's true I have *brujería* in my blood, but I am a *curandera*. I don't harm; I heal."

He said nothing for a long moment. Then he swallowed, gaze darting momentarily to *el lobo* before returning to settle on her.

"When this is over," he said, waving a hand to indicate the ice storm. "You and . . . and your friend. You will come to dinner at my home?"

"Oh, Salvador," she cried.

She gave him a hug, careful to keep her hands in the air. He was stiff for only a moment before he enfolded her in his arms.

"I am going away," she told him as she finally stepped back. "But I will return so that we can be your guests."

He smiled and went off content, leaving only Nuala for them still to speak with, but when they turned to her, they found the housekeeper was already gone. Bettina sighed. She was still only one step away from exhaustion, but she wanted to finish this now. To pack up her things and be gone. The marvels of winter no longer held any charm for her. The dreary endless rain weighed on her spirit in a way that the frost and snow never had. She was tired of the cold, tired of the horizons being so close.

The house seemed empty as they went to her room. Where was everyone?

They paused in the sculpting studio where Donal had called up the Glasduine and stood there awhile in the doorway. The memory of what had been done here lay heavy in the room, a palatable presence of twisting shadows that made Bettina shiver. She turned away and led her wolf to the hidden alcove that was her bedroom.

El lobo helped her gather her things, being the hands she could not use herself at the moment. There was not a great deal to pack. She left most of the books, taking only her clothing and the artwork she'd been given, which she meant to leave with Adelita.

"What of these?" *el lobo* asked.

He indicated the colorful carved dogs her sister had sent. They still stood ranged around the feet of the Virgin. She nodded and he stowed them away in her suitcase.

Finally they went down to the kitchen. Nuala was sitting there, alone, staring out at the miserable night. *El lobo* set Bettina's suitcase and backpack down by the back door. Bettina stood in the doorway through which they'd entered, waiting for the housekeeper to acknowledge their presence, but *el lobo* approached Nuala first. When he was a few steps away, Nuala looked up and *el lobo* went down on one knee in front of her.

"Lady," he said. "I hope you won't think ill of the one who brings you the bad news."

"What bad news?"

"*An felsos* . . . they didn't survive."

Nuala's lip twitched. "What makes you think I care?" she asked

"Lady, I know they were your sons."

"And you?" she said. "I suppose you now expect to take their place."

"I would not presume." He hesitated a moment, then added. "And I was never like them."

Her steady gaze lay on him. "No, you are all the parts they discarded—isn't that the tale you tell?"

He shook his head. "I do not tell tales."

Bettina hated seeing her wolf be like this. With all she'd learned recently, she felt Nuala deserved no one's respect, least of all his. She walked to his side, laid a hand carefully on his shoulder.

"They were your *children*," she told the housekeeper.

"I didn't ask for them," Nuala replied. "And look how they turned out—the spitting image of their sire."

"Because you abandoned them."

"Do you really think so? You know nothing of the true nature of these wolves."

"I know that everyone, human or spirit, can become the being you expect them to be. If they had been mine, I would never have abandoned them."

"I would do it again," Nuala said.

"I'm sorry for you."

Nuala shook her head. "Come speak to me of this again when you've experienced rape and exile from all you hold dear."

Bettina turned away. Her wolf joined her and gathered up her belongings.

"Did your grandmother never teach you about the dangers of consorting with wolves?" Nuala called after her.

"Yes," Bettina told her. She looked back and met the housekeeper's gaze. "She also taught me about forgiveness."

She stepped outside with her wolf and he closed the door behind them before the housekeeper could respond.

"I would have liked to have said goodbye to some of the others," Bettina said as they crossed the lawn, walking back towards the woods.

"You'll be back," her wolf said. When she made no comment, he added, "Won't you?"

Bettina nodded. *"Más pronto o más tarde."* Sooner or later.

She glanced at her companion, but his features were expressionless. She wanted to explain that she couldn't stay here, it wasn't her home. That if she'd come here to heal herself, then the process was only begun. It could only be completed at home. In the desert. But the words were locked in her throat. He had to stay; she had to go. It left them little room to get to know each other any better, less still to make a life together.

"What will happen to the house now?" she said instead.

El lobo shrugged. "Nuala will remain in it, of that we can be sure. A spirit such as she is difficult to exorcise. It won't matter who inherits the property now that the woman you called the Recluse is dead."

"The Recluse," Bettina repeated. "We left her by the pool."

"Yes . . ." *el lobo* said, drawing the word out.

"We can't just leave her there. She needs to be buried."

"If we're lucky," her wolf muttered, "the carrion birds will have done our work for us."

But he got a shovel from one of the sheds behind the house and led her back into *la época del mito* all the same.

Nothing had changed by the pool where *an bradán* slept. The hazel trees still leaned over the water. The low stone wall, haphazardly built of fieldstone and found rocks, still held its clutter of offerings. Antlers, posies of flowers, beaded bracelets and necklaces. The little bone and wood carvings that reminded her of her *milagros*. It was peaceful, a place that bespoke quiet wisdom and eased the spirit.

Or at least it would without the addition of the corpse.

Bettina sat by the pool, frustrated that she couldn't help her wolf with the task of burying the Recluse. He dug only a shallow grave some distance away and carried the body over to it, quickly filling in the grave once more. When he was done, all that remained was a long mound of dirt that made Bettina unhappy to look upon. She was unhappy the woman was dead, unhappy with all the Recluse had done, the lives she had ruined. And for what? To end up dead and buried unceremoniously, all her dreams turned to smoke and ash.

They walked back to the pool and sat on a clear space on the low stone wall. She gave him a small smile, then looked back into the pool, her gaze drawn to the salmon floating there, sleeping. It was all she could do to not reach in and stroke the shimmering scales. She couldn't have said why she felt the urge to touch it.

"It's still asleep," she said.

"What were you expecting?"

"Remember the first night we met?" she said. "You told me that if it woke, I would be changed forever."

"I remember."

"So that's why I thought it would be awake," Bettina told him.

Her wolf smiled. "Are you so different now?"

Bettina nodded.

Her wolf rolled a cigarette and offered it to her. When she shook her head, he lit it and leaned back, blowing a stream of smoke up into the boughs of the hazels. When he was finished, he ground the butt out in the dirt and put it in his pocket. Bettina asked him to bring over her backpack, to take out the small pouch in which she kept her *milagros* and asked him to look through them. He spread them on his hand, moving them about with a finger.

"That one," she said, pointing to a heart. "*El corazón*. There should be more than one."

"I can only find two."

"We only need two."

She had him put the rest away, then take out a spool wound round with a thin leather thong. Under her direction, he cut two lengths and threaded a heart-shaped *milagro* onto each one. When he was done she had him tie one around her neck. The *milagro* threaded onto it rested in the hollow of her throat. He held the other in his hand and looked at her.

"Do you want me to wear this?" he asked.

She studied him, trying to read what he was thinking, what he was feeling in that wolf's heart of his.

"Only if you want to," she said. "Consider it a promise. If you can wait for me, if you have the patience . . ."

"So you *will* return."

"We will be together," she promised him. "It's just . . . I need to understand these wings that flutter in my chest. I need to find Papá, to speak to him of our blood . . . of hawks. And then *los cadejos* . . ."

Her wolf nodded. "You are indebted to them now. I won't say that was ill-done, but . . ."

"You will think it."

He shrugged.

"So you will go now," he said.

"Soon. But first, I . . ."

Shyness overcame her courage for a moment. He gave her a quizzical look.

"That blanket you packed in my suitcase," she said. "Do you think you could take it out and lay it here on the grass? My . . . my hands are still tender, but perhaps you will let me hold you in other ways . . ."

A great stillness fell between them. Then her wolf smiled and lifted the thong to his neck, tying it in place so that his *milagro* hung just in the hollow of his own throat. He shook out the blanket and stood there on it, waiting until she rose from the stones by the pool to join him.

"*Mi lobo,*" she murmured as he lowered her to the blanket.

Then his lips were on hers and there was no more need for words.

8

Los cadejos

Endings are beginnings in disguise.

—Mexican saying

1

The ice storm lasted until the end of the week, driving the city completely to its knees. By the middle of the following week, basic services had been restored throughout most of the city, but there were still hundreds of homes in outlying regions without power and the cleanup of downed branches and utility poles, while progressing, seemed to operate at a snail's pace. There was simply so much damage and the onslaught of a new cold front didn't make anyone's job easier. The temperature dropped steadily through the weekend and by Monday they were gripped in a deep freeze as vicious as the one that had plagued the city in December.

Ellie immersed herself in the Angel Outreach program as soon as the Creek sisters let her off at her apartment. She went upstairs only long enough to have a shower and change before heading over to Angel's Grasso Street office to see if she could be of any use. She found the place in chaos and was soon working long days and nights, catching up on sleep when she could, which, as often as not, was on a cot in the back of the office.

The deep cold made her sojourn in some otherworldly desert all the easier to put on a backburner. The truth was she needed something like this—the cold and the hard work—to ground her after all she'd been through. She didn't want time to think. Not about Donal or monsters, mysterious otherworldly deserts, or this magic she was supposed to have inside her that had gotten her mixed up in all that craziness in the first place. Thinking could come later. Right now she only wanted to be busy, to fill every waking moment with work so that when she did catch some sleep, it was deep and dreamless.

With Tommy recuperating up on the rez and so much work for the volunteers to do, she usually found herself taking the van out on her own. Angel didn't like it; she always wanted her people paired and she especially didn't want women out alone in the vans, but everyone was overworked and there was simply too much that needed to get done for them to be able to follow protocol.

For her part, Ellie wasn't nervous being out on her own, but she couldn't explain why to Angel without sounding like an idiot. "You see," she would have had to say, "after facing down some huge tree monster in Neverneverland, it's kind of hard to get worked up about anything the streets could throw at me right now."

Besides, a general air of community seemed to have taken over the city, with everybody lending a hand to their neighbors, and even to strangers. There were stories about generators going missing, of lowlifes stealing from people they were pretending to help, but the numbers were far fewer than one might have expected in the chaos left behind the storm.

Most of the street people still weren't interested in the shelters, never mind the severe turn the weather had taken, but even they appeared to have acquired more of a Good Samaritan spirit. She found them actively keeping tabs on each other, steering her to people who needed help, and a couple of times she'd had a half-dozen of them pushing the van back onto the streets when she'd gotten stuck.

Not having to see her friends helped a lot. And even when she did, it was easy to put the haunted look in her eyes down to simple weariness.

"You okay?" Jilly asked her one afternoon when they were working side by side, washing up dishes in the makeshift soup kitchen that had been set up in the basement of St. Paul's. "You've got a look . . ."

If anyone could listen to her story with an open ear, it would be Jilly, and at some point Ellie knew she would talk to her about what she'd experienced, but she wasn't ready to do it yet.

"I'm just tired," she said.

Jilly nodded. "Tell me about it. I usually make do on four or five hours of sleep a night myself, but I'm not even getting that these days."

Ellie only smiled in response.

In the end, she'd done such a good job of putting aside the weird turn her life had taken prior to the ice storm that she was startled to get a call from Hunter that Wednesday afternoon when she was in the office on Grasso Street, putting together a new load of supplies for the evening's run in the van. Startled, but pleased, especially when she found out he was calling to ask if he could lend a hand after he'd closed the store that day.

"I could use some company in the van tonight," she told him.

"Okay. Sounds like a plan. Where should I meet you?"

"I'll pick you up at the store. What time do you close?"

"Six."

"I'll see you then."

"Great." She could almost feel his smile through the phone line as he added, "So is this, like, another one of our dates?"

She laughed. "Dress warm," she told him. "The van's heater is pretty much a rumor."

She was surprised at how happy she was to see him waiting for her when she pulled up in front of Gypsy Records at a little after six that evening, hands shoved deep into the pockets of his parka, hood up against the wind. The temperature had dropped even more this evening. Coupled with a fierce wind that had already rocked the van a few times on the drive over, it was serious frost-bite weather out there tonight.

"Hey," Hunter said as he got in on the passenger's side and fastened his seat belt. "It's great to see you."

"You, too."

"I tried calling you a bunch of times, but there was never any answer at your place."

"I've been working kind of non-stop with Angel since we got back."

Hunter nodded. "That's what I finally figured out. So I looked up Angel's office number."

"I'm glad you did."

And she was. She didn't know how committed he was to the work that she was doing for Angel—it was pretty obvious that he'd offered to help out with the Outreach program as an excuse to see her—but she was flattered by the attention and couldn't really blame him. She hadn't exactly made herself available to anybody since she'd gotten back.

Hunter dug in his pocket and pulled out a cassette.

"Here," he said, handing it to her. "I made this for you."

Ellie smiled. "Jilly's told me about this—it's like a record store guy thing, right?"

"I guess. Though Fiona makes them, too."

She looked at the label he'd made up for the cassette and started reading some of the names of the artists. "Ani DiFranco. Sonny Rollins. Solas. The Walkabouts. John Coltrane." She glanced at him. "This is . . . eclectic."

"Actually," Hunter said, "it's kind of a Miki tape. I got the feeling that you knew Donal a lot better than you did her and I thought maybe you'd understand her better if you could listen to some of the stuff she loves."

"More record store guy stuff."

"Well, you can tell a lot from the music a person listens to."

She smiled and put the cassette into the player. They listened to the first song, DiFranco singing against the minimal accompaniment of drums and a bass guitar. The song started and ended with:

i'm a pixie
i'm a paper doll
i'm a cartoon
i'm a chipper cheerful for all
and i light up a room
i'm the color me happy girl
miss live and let live
and when they're out for blood
i always give

When the song segued into Sonny Rollins blowing his horn, Ellie turned to Hunter.

"Everybody sees Miki like that, too," she said.

Hunter nodded. "She used to hide it well. She just compartmentalized all the crap and really did wake up to each day like it was, well, the first day of the rest of her life. But now . . ."

"Is she still going away?"

On the walk out of the otherworld, Miki had told them that as soon as she could, she was leaving town.

"She's already gone. She left this morning for Chicago in Donal's old VW minibus. Some booking agent she contacted had a band cancel out of this Irish club and she was in. She got a couple of her cohorts from Fall Down Dancing to go up with her and she's dead-serious about starting up a touring band."

"It seems so sudden," Ellie said.

"Well, she's leaving friends behind, but what else was left for her here? Everything she owns was trashed by the Gentry, Donal's . . . gone, and all's that left are a lot of weird memories."

"I don't know that running away's ever the best answer."

Hunter shook his head. "I think she's more running to something. She should have done this a long time ago. The difference now is she's traveling with a borrowed accordion and the handful of personal belongings she was able to buy with the money I fronted her, instead of also having to keep up a place back here."

"You really care about her, don't you?"

"Like a brother," Hunter said. "No, scratch that. Like a normal brother."

Ellie sighed. She hadn't even begun to deal with what all of this meant to her memories of her own relationship with Donal. She missed him terribly, but whenever she thought of him, all the horrors came flooding back into her head.

"Something like what happened to us all changes you big-time," Hunter said.

Ellie nodded. "I'm just trying not to think of it. For now."

"I can't do anything but. That's what I'm doing here with you tonight."

"How so?"

It was hard to tell with only the light from streetlamps coming into the van, but when she glanced at him, she'd swear he was blushing.

"I guess it taught me that life is short," he said, "so you'd better do something with it. I want to take chances. Do more with my life. Get out of the record store more often. Do things like this, where it makes a difference to other people."

So it wasn't just to see her, Ellie thought, unaccountably pleased. But then he added:

"And I want to be with you."

And that pleased her even more.

"No pressure," he said. "I mean, I don't even know how you feel about, you know, us. Or even the possibility of there being an 'us.' But I want to get to know you better and that's not going to happen sitting in my apartment reading magazines and listening to music. I . . ." He shrugged and smiled. "I'm talking too much."

"It's okay," Ellie said. "I'm enjoying it."

She pulled over to the curb where a few homeless men were sitting on a hot air grate, hunching their shoulders against the wind that came down the alley behind them. Hunter got out and went around to the side of the van, getting coffees and sandwiches to bring over to them. For awhile Ellie stood by the van, watching the easy way he had in talking to the men, treating them like individuals, like people, instead of looking down on them, before she walked over as well, offering them blankets, warmer clothes, a ride to a shelter.

"What about you?" Hunter asked when they were back in the van and driving once more.

"What about me what?"

"How did what happened to us affect you?"

"Like I said," she told him. "I'm trying not to think of it right now. I'm not trying to think of anything, really."

"Oh."

She smiled. "But so far I like this getting-to-know-each-other-better part a lot."

2

TUBAC, WEDNESDAY, JANUARY 28

Two weeks had passed in the World As It Is when Bettina and her wolf came out of *la época del mito* into the western bajada of the Santa Rita Mountains south of Tucson. The sun was just rising behind them, flooding their view with its dawn light. A wide plain stretched westward, grasslands dotted with mesquite, cholla, prickly pear, and tall, spindly ocatillos. With the early sun upon it, the plain appeared to be a vast luminescent field, glowing with its own inner light. In the distance they could see a band of lusher vegetation that followed the meandering banks of the Santa Cruz River. The temperature was in the high fifties, not warm, but not unpleasant. Bettina knew it would warm up before long.

"This is hardly a desert," *el lobo* said.

Bettina nodded. "My friend Ban says that life zones converge in Pima County. A hike from Tucson to the top of the Santa Catalina Mountains is like traveling from Mexico to Canada."

Her wolf smiled.

"*De verdad*. Someday I'll take you up Mount Lemmon—you'll think you're back home, walking under the oaks and pines."

"I would make *this* my home, wherever you are . . ."

His voice went soft and trailed off. His gaze remained on the distant view.

"But you can't," Bettina said after a moment. "I understand. I would not have you break your word."

They both had debts. At least her wolf knew the limits of his. She had no idea what *los cadejos* would ask of her.

"We can still make this work," she added.

She shifted the straps of her backpack so that it hung more comfortably, then took his free hand and led him off across the grasslands, the tall yellowed blades whispering against their light cotton pants. She could have carried her suitcase, but her wolf wouldn't let her.

"Let me be useful," he'd told her when she brought it up earlier.

"You are much more than useful," she'd replied and stood on her toes to kiss the corner of his mouth.

Two weeks in *la época del mito* had been time enough for her *brujería* to heal her hands. While her palms and the flats of her fingers remained scarred, the skin tight and still reddened, the pain was gone and she had regained most of her flexibility. But the look of them left her feeling terribly self-conscious. Her wolf's response was to hold them and kiss her palms, even when they weren't making love.

It took them the rest of the morning to reach the banks of the Santa Cruz. It was cool under the shade of the cottonwoods and willows and the water was chilly when they waded across.

"Your sister lives here?" *el lobo* asked as they came out from under the trees and walked up Bridge Road to the tiny central core of Tubac.

Bettina shook her head. "But she doesn't live far away. Her gallery is here."

The village was only three blocks long and three blocks wide and they soon reached Adelita's gallery, their pant legs still damp from their wade across the river. La Gata Verde was on Tubac Road, across from Tortuga Books and nestled in amongst a collection of shops and galleries selling pottery, clothing, jewelry, paintings, and Mexican folk art. The street was crowded with tourists, most of them snowbirds, migrating down to Arizona to take in the warmer weather that their own northern climes couldn't provide at this time of year.

A little bell chimed as they walked into the gallery and a small, dark-haired woman who could have been Bettina's twin looked up. Her welcoming smile broke into a huge grin when she recognized her sister.

"Bettina!" she cried, coming out from behind the counter, startling an eld-

erly couple who were browsing through the art prints. *"¡Dios mío!* What are
you doing here? And who is this handsome man?"

Bettina smiled and returned her sister's hug.

"He's . . . his name is Lobo," she said.

When she glanced at her wolf, there was a twinkle of amusement in his eye.

"Lobo," Adelita said, turning to look at him. "Such a fierce name. But better than Loco, *¿tu no crees?"*

"And this is my sister Adela," Bettina told her wolf.

"But everyone still calls me Adelita," her sister said.

El lobo set the suitcase down and reached out a hand, but Adelita gave
him a hug instead. Bettina smiled at his surprise.

"She can be very . . . exuberant," she said.

Adelita stepped back, smiling as well. "He is too handsome not to hug."

She started to draw them back behind the counter, taking *el lobo* by one
hand, Bettina by the other. The roughness of her sister's palm drew her gaze
down.

"¡Madre de Dios!" she cried. "What have you done to yourself?"

Bettina quickly pulled her hands away from her sister's scrutiny and thrust
them into the pockets of her pants.

"It's a very long story," she said. "I'm fine now."

"But, Bettina . . ."

"Verdaderos."

"And you're all wet," Adelita added. "Both of you."

"We waded across the river."

"But . . . whatever for? Where were you coming from?"

"The Santa Ritas."

Adelita shook her head. She was about to go on, but noticed her customers were leaving. Bettina couldn't help but feel guilty, sure that Adelita's
exuberant reaction to herself and her wolf had driven them away.

"Gracias," Adelita called after them. "Please come again."

When the couple had left, *el lobo* crossed to the door and locked it, turning the OPEN sign to CLOSED. Adelita didn't appear to notice. She looked from
one to the other, then shook her head again.

"Así," she said to *el lobo,* her voice bright, the way Bettina knew her own
went when she was ill at ease and didn't quite know what to say. "How do
you find Arizona? Or are you a native?"

"I'm a visitor," *el lobo* told her, amusement flickering in his eyes again.
"But I like it. There's an unusual smell in the air."

Adelita nodded. "It smells like rain."

At his puzzled look, she explained, "It's the resin on the leaves of the cre-
osote bushes. We had some rain last night." She turned to Bettina. "Have you
seen Mamá yet?"

Bettina shook her head. "We came here first."

"She'll be happy to see you. You can't imagine how much she talks about
you, considering how little you spoke with each other when you lived here.
And Janette will be delighted."

"I won't have time to see either of them this trip," Bettina told her.

Adelita regarded her worriedly. "Why *are* you here? You're not in trouble, are you?"

"No," Bettina told her. "We're finished with the trouble part. I was just hoping I could leave my things with you."

"Why? Where are you going?"

Bettina smiled. Adelita was more like their Mamá than she'd ever care to admit. Always worried. Always needing to know what was going on.

"To find Papá."

Adelita said nothing, but the look on her face spoke volumes.

"There has still been no word?" Bettina asked.

"You must understand," her sister said. "I loved him, too. But he left us, Bettina. He abandoned us."

Bettina shook her head. "I've been told that he has lost his way. That he has forgotten us—not because we mean nothing to him, but because he is in no position to remember."

It was hard to find a way to say this without speaking of *brujería* and spirits, but Bettina didn't wish to start another argument right now.

Adelita regarded her steadily. "Who told you this?"

"It doesn't matter who."

"*¿Quién?*" Adelita repeated, her voice sharper.

"You will not be happy with my answer."

Adelita sighed. "Just tell me what you have heard."

"*Bien,*" Bettina said. "He is in the desert. Living as a hawk who has forgotten he is a man. I want to find him. I need to remind him who he is."

Anger flashed in her sister's eyes.

"*¿Estás loca?*" she said. "How can you even begin to believe such things?"

"I told you the answer would not please . . ." Bettina began.

She paused when Adelita held up a hand. Her sister took a steadying breath.

"*Perdona,*" she said in a softer voice. "Here I promised you that I would try harder to keep an open mind and the first thing you tell me makes me want to shake the sense back into you."

"Adelita . . ."

"But it is hard, Bettina. *Está muy difícil.* These things you believe . . . the world you live in . . . it is so far from my own."

Bettina searched her sister's gaze. Of all the reactions she might have expected from her sister, this was the most surprising. But she saw that Adelita was truly trying to, if not exactly believe, to at least be willing to listen.

"I could show it to you," she said. "I could take you into it."

"No, no," Adelita told her. "It's too late for that. I have Chuy and Janette to think of. I have . . . my world."

You can have both, Bettina thought, but she left it unsaid.

"It should have been different," she said. "It should have belonged to both of us."

Adelita shook her head. "*Quizás*. But I might not have met Chuy, and we wouldn't have had Janette. I would not give up my daughter for anything."

Silence fell between them. Outside the gallery, the world went on, tourists happily exclaiming over this or that find, planning their lunches, looking for a washroom. Inside, the shadow of *la época del mito* hung thick in the air.

"*Así*," Adelita said finally. "So. You are going into the desert, then."

Bettina nodded, unwilling to trust her voice at this moment.

"What will I tell Mamá? And Janette?"

Bettina drew a ragged breath. She looked to her wolf and the kindness in his eyes gave her strength.

"Tell them nothing," she said. "I will be back as soon as I can."

With Papá, she thought, if all goes well. But she left that unsaid as well.

"You will be going far?"

Bettina considered *la época del mito*, how it could take one anywhere, anywhen.

"I don't know yet," she said.

"If you . . . if you come nearby again, you will stop and see me, yes? You could have a meal with us before you must go on once more. You know Janette would love to see you. Everyone misses you."

A film of tears blurred Bettina's vision.

"You know I love you all," she said. "But I love our *papá*, too."

Adelita swallowed hard. "If you can find him, bring him back to us."

"I will. I promise."

Adelita opened her arms and Bettina stepped into her embrace. When they pulled apart, both their eyes were wet with unshed tears.

"I will leave you with this," Bettina said.

Taking her wolf's hand, she reached out for her *bosque del corazón*. Then they stepped away, as though walking through a curtain of air, the hard tile surface of the gallery turning to dirt and pebbles under their feet. Bettina heard her sister gasp, just before the curtain closed behind them.

"Why did you do that?" her wolf asked.

They stood in *la época del mito* once more. Tubac, La Gata Verde, Adelita, the tourists . . . all were gone. There was only the desert, Bettina's *bosque del corazón* in the shadow of Baboquivari Peak. The lights that had risen from it the last time they were here had been replaced by a shroud of clouds, as though I'itoi had wrapped himself in a cloak of vapor.

"To let her know that her trust was not unfounded," Bettina said.

"How so?"

Bettina smiled. "It's hard to keep an open mind. So I gave her something to fill it. To keep the door of what might be ajar."

He nodded. "And now you've named me. Lobo."

He said the word as though tasting something unfamiliar. It was impossible to tell from his expression if the taste of it pleased him.

"That's how I've always thought of you," Bettina told him. "*El lobo*. The wolf. My wolf."

"I can be that," he said. "And gladly."

It wasn't easy to part with her wolf, but his responsibility to the *manitou* of the Kickaha Hills pressed on him and Bettina had her own obligations to fulfill. They tried to say goodbye quickly, but Bettina still clung to him for a long moment before she finally stepped back and let him go. *El lobo* appeared no more eager to leave himself. He held her hands, lifting them to his lips to kiss the palms, first one, then the other. Before she could speak, before she made the mistake of asking him to stay, or telling him she would go with him, he gave her a last, quick kiss on her lips and walked away.

He seemed to step into a heat mirage, a shimmering in the air, then just as they had departed from Adelita's gallery in Tubac, he was gone. Bettina sighed heavily. The minutes slipped away as she stood there, gaze on the place where he had vanished. Finally, she sighed again. Rolling her shoulders to loosen her muscles, she began the task she had not spoken of to either her wolf or Adelita.

First she went into Tucson to buy some staples: beans, squash, peppers, tomatoes, chiles, corn flour, tea. A container for water, a pot to cook and eat from. Bundles of twine. Matches. A small spade. A long-bladed folding knife. It was a short trip and she was soon back in her *bosque del corazón* under the shadow of Baboquivari Peak.

Her suitcase she had left with Adelita, but she had her backpack and the blanket that she and her wolf had lain on all those nights they had spent together in *la época del mito*. So she slept on her blanket, cooked meals on heated stones set on the edge of fires in which she burned mesquite and ironwood. And she worked.

She spent a few weeks gathering the long willowy ribs of toppled saguaros, wandering the desert, refamiliarizing herself with the land and its spirits. Every time she saw the red banded tail of a hawk, she paused, shading her eyes to study it. She would feel an answering whisper of wings move in her chest and she would reach out to the hovering shape high in the sky above, or perched on the topmost tip of a tall saguaro, searching for her father, for recognition, but finding neither.

When she thought she had gathered enough saguaro ribs, she measured out a square of flat ground, about eight by eight, and dug a hole in each corner. She stuck trimmed mesquite poles into each one, packing small boulders around the poles to keep them at a ninety-degree angle to the ground. Then she filled up the holes with dirt, watered it to pack it down better. She repeated the process a few times before she left the dirt around the poles to dry.

It wasn't until she began to lash a framework of saguaro ribs to the poles that *los cadejos* came to see what she was doing. Throughout that day they watched with interest as she tied the ribs in place with the twine she'd picked up in Tucson. She spoke to them a few times, but they kept to a reserved distance. Today they weren't the silly, singing dogs she'd first met so many years ago, but neither were they the more garrulous and certainly fierce animals who had protected her from the Glasduine.

By nightfall, she had the outline of a small building with a sloping flat roof completed. She sat by her fire as the moon rose, admiring her handiwork while eating bean tortillas that she washed down with tea. When *los cadejos* approached the fire, she offered them food, but they were only interested in the unfinished lean-to.

"*¿Qué es ésto?*" they asked. What is this?

"What are you making?"

"Are your hands sore?"

Bettina shook her head, replying to the last question first. "A little, but only from my work. The burns have healed."

The scars still made her self-conscious, but that had been easier to forget out here on her own for as long as she'd been. Now it took an effort not to hide them away in pockets.

"And as for what I'm building," she went on, "it's a house. *Una casa.*"

"A home?"

"For you?"

"No," Bettina told them. "But I hope to visit it often."

"Then whose will it be?"

"Yours," she said. "If you want it."

They gathered closer, the firelight flickering on their rainbow fur.

"Do you do this because of our bargain?" they asked.

"No," Bettina said. "You must decide what our bargain will be. I do this as would a friend."

"But why?"

Bettina shrugged. "I feel bad for how I ignored you all those years. I promised you a home, but gave you nothing. So now I am building one for you. Here, in the heart of my heart, *mi bosque del corazón.*" She smiled. "I am not a skilled builder, but I am doing my best."

"We think it is beautiful."

"*Sí. Muy bella.*"

A couple of them did little dances, cloven hooves clicking on the stones. And then they were all dancing around, making up a song about pretty mansions and the prettier *señoritas* who made them. Bettina laughed and clapped along with their nonsense, finally getting up and dancing with them, yipping at the moon like a *cadeja* or a coyote.

When she finally collapsed on her blanket, *los cadejos* sprawled in little rainbow-furred heaps all around her, still giggling and yipping quietly.

"*Es una cosa buena,*" one of them told her. It is a good thing.

"*Sí, sí.*"

"*Esta casa bella.*"

They came over and licked her hands or her cheek, one by one, then ran off into the darkened desert, laughter trailing behind them.

·   ·   ·

The next day she finished the roof, cutting the ribs to length and lashing them in place with her twine. She made two layers, placing the ribs of the second layer in the troughs made by the first to make it as waterproof as possible, given what she had to work with. *Los cadejos* came and went during the day, teasing her and telling her jokes. When she quit for the evening, they appeared carrying oranges which they dropped at her feet. She had no idea where they had gone to get them, but was happy to vary her fare.

That night they sat inside *"la casa del cadejos,"* as her companions insisted it be called and watched the sunset. Bettina was so tired that she fell asleep early. When she woke, *los cadejos* were gone, but they had pulled her blanket over her. She had a bean tortilla and the remainder of the oranges for breakfast, then got back to work.

A day later she had finished two sides, but she'd run out of saguaro ribs. The next morning she went out in search of more, this time accompanied by her raucous band of *cadejos*.

"Why did you come to me, that first time?" Bettina asked as they walked along.

"We didn't come to you."

"You came to us."

"You asked us in and gave us a home."

"But then you wouldn't play with us anymore."

Bettina thought back to that day in I'itoi's cave and realized that it was true. She *had* gone to them.

"I've been very rude, haven't I?" she said.

"Sí."

"Muy rudo."

"But now you are our friend."

"We like having friends."

"Yo, también," Bettina told them. Me, too.

They had to range farther and farther afield to gather the ribs, often walking all day, from dawn to dusk. But the weather was temperate and Bettina was enjoying this opportunity to ground herself once more in her beloved desert. A few days later, the lean-to was finished, three sides with a roof, a bench along the back wall to sit upon and a platform along one wall to lie upon.

They all sat inside again to watch the sunset. Bettina cupped her tea in one hand and leaned contentedly with her back against the wall of the lean-to, her other hand ruffling at the short stiff fur of the closest of her companions.

"Do you know my father?" she asked. "He is . . . an old spirit, I've been told. He can soar high above the desert like a hawk."

"We don't really know any birds," they replied.

"We are the oldest spirits that we know."

There was a general chorus of agreement.

"Salvo las muchachas del cuervo," one of them said.

"Y la Urraca."

"*Sí. La bella Señorita* Margaret."

Bettina didn't quite know what to make of their talk of crow girls and this woman Margaret who, from the sounds of it, was also a magpie. When she asked about them, she was simply told, "They were here when the world was born."

The cooking fire had long since died down and the night was dark, a cloud cover hiding the stars. Even with the night vision that was a part of the gift of her *brujería*, Bettina could not see far into the desert.

"Have you thought more of our bargain?" she asked. "What you would like in return for the help you gave me?"

"*Sí.* We want you to be our friend."

Bettina laughed and shook her head. "We are already friends."

"We want to be friends forever."

"That is not something friends bargain over," Bettina told them.

"That is all we want."

"Nothing more."

"*¡Nada, nada, nada!*"

"But you have this already," Bettina said.

"Then we are content."

"Here in the forest of your heart."

"Where we have our beautiful home."

"*La casa del cadejos.*"

"We are content."

Now that she had finished the house for *los cadejos*, Bettina began to search for her father in earnest. She journeyed in ever widening circles, sometimes accompanied by *los cadejos,* more often alone. She spoke to the spirits, tracked every hawk she saw, but there was no word, no sign of either Papá or his *peyoteros.* One afternoon, coming on to the sunset and many miles from her *bosque del corazón,* she heard a quiet weeping. When she turned in the direction from which she thought the sound was coming, she dislodged a pebble and there was immediate silence. She waited, listening.

"*¡Hola!*" she called after a moment. "Who is there?"

Still there was silence.

"Do not be frightened. I am Bettina San Miguel. A simple *curandera.*"

"*¿Verdaderos?*"

It was a woman's voice, soft, anxious.

"Truly," Bettina assured her. "Are you hurt? Can I help you?"

Another silence followed, then a fearful, "*Por favor.*"

Following the sound of the woman's voice, Bettina found her on the far side of a jumble of boulders, pressed up against the red stone, her eyes wide with fear. She seemed to be a Native woman, long of feature with dark braids hanging down either side of her face. She was dressed in a simple cotton shift, bare-legged and barefoot. She shivered and pressed closer to the boulders when Bettina moved towards her.

"Oh, no," Bettina said when she saw the ugly gash on the woman's leg. "What happened to you?"

"Coyote."

Bettina blinked in surprise. "I have never heard of a coyote attacking a person before."

"I . . . I was not a person when he attacked . . ."

"Ah . . ."

The woman began to tremble as Bettina approached, jerking when Bettina sat down and drew the woman's leg onto her lap.

"Don't be afraid," she said in a soothing voice. "I can mend this."

She looked over at the woman, her smile faltering for a moment. The woman's features had changed, nose and jaw extending into a long snout, a hare's long ears hanging where the braids had been. But there was still much human about her, as well. It was only the unexpected odd combination of animal and human features that had startled Bettina.

"What is your name?" she asked as she gently probed the woman's calf with her *brujería,* hands resting on either side of the wound, gently stroking the skin.

"Chuhwi."

Of course, Bettina thought. What else but "jackrabbit" in the language of the Tohono O'odham.

"Close your eyes, Chuhwi," she said, "and lie still for a moment. This shouldn't take long."

The gash was not nearly so bad as it looked. The bones weren't broken, which would greatly speed her ability to heal the wound.

"Will . . . will it hurt?"

"Not even for a moment."

As she concentrated on repairing the damage, Bettina marveled again on how much she had wasted this healing talent of hers with potions and charms. She wasn't sure if she'd be able to heal truly degenerative diseases—cancers and their like—but there were still many people with lesser complaints that she could ease.

As she promised, it didn't take long. Chuhwi regarded her with awe when it was done, running her fingers over and over the raised tissue of the scars.

"Try not to run on it for awhile," Bettina told her.

Chuhwi nodded. She was at ease now, her only sign of nervousness what Bettina assumed was a habitual twitch of her nose.

"You were in the shape of a rabbit when the coyote caught you?" she asked.

"You should have seen his face when I became a woman. I would have laughed if it hadn't hurt so much."

Bettina smiled. Somewhere a coyote was telling an impossible story to his companions, none of whom would believe him.

"You're the one looking for your father," Chuhwi said.

"*Sí.* Do you have word of him?"

"No, it's just . . . now that I have met you, I don't understand why you are looking for him."

"*Es mi papá.*"

"But surely you would understand why he would leave?"

Bettina shook her head.

"*Considerelo,*" Chuhwi said. Think about it. "He is an ancient spirit who has fallen in love with a mortal woman and raised a family with her. Year by year, she ages, yet he remains forever unchanged. When they finally die, when even the children of his grandchild's children dies, he will still be here, alive, unchanged. It hurts less to go away. The family can remember him as a man. And he, he can lose himself in another skin until finally the pain has faded to no more than a dull ache in his memory."

Bettina could only stare at the woman.

"Such spirits will swear never to fall in love again," Chuhwi went on, "but they always do. It is our nature. The flame of life burns so bright in humans, if brief. How can we ignore it?"

Bettina thought of her wolf. She knew that, circumstances being how they were, there would be many times when they would be apart. But if he were to simply walk away from her, disappear the way her *papá* had vanished, it would break her heart. A tightness grew in her chest. As it must have broken Mamá's heart.

"Is it better to have the brief time together," Chuhwi said, "or to have none at all? Which hurts more? I don't know. But there are many young men I cherish in my memory, and though I promise myself differently, I know there will be more."

Bettina was unable to speak. How could she not have realized this before? Papá must have tried to bring Mamá into *la época del mito,* to extend her life the way Abuela's had been extended, the way her own would probably be. But even such extended lives were no more than brief moments in the lifetime of an immortal, and Mamá . . . she had always been too devout. She would never have gone into *la época del mito,* with Papá. She might have been able to accept a being such as him into her world, but she would never have stepped outside of her world into his.

How things must have changed when they moved closer to town. When they exchanged the dirt floor for linoleum and wood. When they could ride in a bus or a car, instead of walk. Their two worlds had collided and the impact had eventually driven them apart. Mamá to her faith and the church, Papá to his beloved desert.

Oh, *mi lobo,* she thought, fingering the *milagro* that hung from the thong around her neck. How will it be with us?

Bettina camped that night with Chuhwi, leaving her the next morning when she was sure that her patient could manage on her own. Returning to her *bosque del corazón,* she sat outside the lean-to she had built for her *cadejos* and stared at the distant height of Baboquivari Peak. She was still sitting there late in the afternoon when *los cadejos* came ambling out of the desert and gathered around her. Most of them flopped on the dirt close by, but two of them lay down on either side of her and rested their heads on her knees. Bettina ruffled their short rainbow fur.

"When will you fly?" one of them asked her.

"Fly?" she said. "I don't know what you mean."

But the wings moved in her chest, feathers ruffling, and something shivered its way up her spine.

"Wake the hawk in you," *los cadejos* told her.

"Speak to your father's blood."

"Claim your birthright."

"You can't have forgotten so soon."

No, she hadn't forgotten. Even in the blur that made up her memories of their final confrontation with the Glasduine, she could remember how her flesh had twisted and shrunk, her bones had hollowed, the feathers bursting from her skin, the strange perspective as her eyes moved to the side of her head, the incredible sharpness of her vision, how the hawk spirit in her had recognized and greeted Aunt Nancy's spider spirit . . .

She stirred and the closest *cadejos* moved their heads from her knees. Standing up, she spread her arms wide and let her *brujería* fill her, twinning the involuntary shifting of her shape that had occurred in the struggle with the Glasduine, but this time she reached for the hawk spirit, greeted it, accepted its dominance. She gasped as the change came over her. She had time to wonder, where does the excess flesh go when woman becomes bird? Where does it come from when the bird shifts back once more? Then she was a red-tailed hawk standing in the dirt among a crowd of *cadejos,* wings outspread.

She flapped them, trying to take flight, but all it did was unbalance her.

"No, no," *los cadejos* told her.

"Don't fight the hawk."

"She knows how to fly."

"You don't."

No, she didn't. But she was afraid to let go too much. Afraid of forgetting herself in the shape of a hawk and becoming as lost to those she loved as had her *papá*.

She tried to convey her fears to *los cadejos,* but all that came from her beak was a loud, wheezing *kree-e-e.*

"Don't be afraid," *los cadejos* told her.

"We are always near."

So she let herself go, retreated in her mind until the hawk spirit was dominant. Under its guidance, she stepped forward to where the land dropped away into the arroyo and launched herself forward, into the air. Powerful wings beat at the air, lifting her up, up.

She cried out again, a joyful sound this time. Far below, her *cadejos* bounded in and out of the cacti, yipping and laughing as they chased the shadow of the hawk that raced across the desert floor ahead of them.

3

MANIDÒ-AKÌ, *MID-MARCH*

El lobo stood among the trees on a hill above the housing development that had proved too much to bear for the spirit whose body he now wore. On the edge of the development, the bulldozers were already at work, clearing trees and leveling the land for more houses. The roar of their engines was loud, even at this distance. The sky was gray overhead, loosing the odd flurry, the temperature hovering at the zero mark. The ground was frozen. But still they were out there.

Soon it would be all gone, all of Shishòdewe's territory, now his, consumed by houses and roads, by power lines, sewer and water pipes. Already the forest where he now stood was the playground of children and teenagers from down below. Pop cans and beer bottles lay under the snow, balled-up potato chip bags and candy wrappers, a thoughtless litter.

Sighing, he faded back into the trees and stepped across into *manidò-akì*, the spiritworld. Here it was late summer and quiet, the loudest sound the chittering of a pair of squirrels, high in the pines above him, the raucous caw of a crow, close, but out of sight. He rolled a cigarette and lit it, then walked deeper into the forest until he came to a clearing. The ground dropped at the far end, fifty feet down in a jumble of granite and limestone, dotted with stunted cedars.

When he was finished his cigarette, he put it out under the heel of his boot and pocketed the butt. From overhead he heard the sharp *kree-e-e* of a hawk and looked up to see a russet shape circling high above him. The sight of it depressed him, reminding him of Bettina. But then everything did.

A hundred times a day he thought of her, his fingers straying to the *milagro* she had given him, the tiny silver heart that symbolized the promise she had made. He would want to leave right then to be with her, go to her if she would not come to him, but he knew he couldn't. Shouldn't. He could leave his responsibility to Shishòdewe's territory for a few days. That wasn't the problem. It was that what Bettina needed to do, she needed to do on her own.

Still, it was hard, this waiting.

The hawk cried again, closer.

Looking up once more, he saw it dropping towards him. A spirit bird, then. Well, he could use some company.

But the relief of some diversion quickly gave way to astonishment as the hawk came in close to the ground. Just before it landed, it transformed into human form. A woman. But that it could shapeshift was not the surprise.

"Bettina," he said.

She gave him a grin. "*Está bueno—¿Sí?* I've been practicing."

"I've missed you," he told her.

"Oh, *mi lobo,* I've missed you, too."

When they embraced, he could feel a difference in her, as though the hawk's powerful muscles were still present, under the softness of her skin.

"You feel so strong," he said.

"But this is a good thing."

"Anything you do is a good thing."

She gave him a light punch on the shoulder. "Flatterer." But he could see she was pleased.

They walked then, hand in hand, while she told him of all she had managed to accomplish since they'd parted, of what still remained undone.

"I didn't know what to think anymore after meeting Chuhwi," she said when she came to the end of her story. "Embracing my hawk only made me miss Papá more. So I went to see my family. I met Mamá at mass, but—" She shrugged. "This is still something I can't share with her. Later, we ate at Adelita's house. She, at least, I can speak to now, but when I told her what Chuhwi told me, she could see no more of a solution to it than I can."

She paused and looked at him.

"So I've come to you," she said.

El lobo shook his head. "I only know of your father. We've never met."

"*Sí.* But you are a spirit, like him."

"Hardly. He is ancient and I—I don't know what I am."

"But you would know. Is this the way of it? Will it cause less heartbreak if I give up my search?"

"I can't answer that," he told her. "I have no answer."

She hesitated, then asked the question he realized was the true reason for her coming here to him today.

"And what of you?" she asked. "Will you vanish from my life when I grow old and you remained unchanged?"

He shook his head.

"But I'll be all wrinkled and feeble."

"Bettina," he said. "You are more like your father than I am. I should be asking you this question."

"Don't joke . . ."

"I'm not joking," he told her. "Many people carry the blood of the old spirits in them, but how many do you think can shift their shape as you can? Your father is one of the First People. His blood will run very pure in his children."

"In . . . in both of us? In Adelita as well?"

He nodded.

"But then why would he leave us? Wouldn't he have known that?"

"I can't speak for him," *el lobo* said. "But he is an old spirit, not necessarily a perfect one. I know of these things because I have reflected on them while trying to decipher the riddles of my own existence. He might never have had occasion to think of it himself. He might never have sired other children. Or

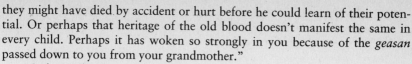
they might have died by accident or hurt before he could learn of their potential. Or perhaps that heritage of the old blood doesn't manifest the same in every child. Perhaps it has woken so strongly in you because of the *geasan* passed down to you from your grandmother."

"So he might not even know?"

"If he loved you as much as you've told me he did, why would he leave you if he *did* know?"

The happiness in her eyes made him leery of raising her hopes too high.

"But I can't be certain of this," he said.

"No. Of course not."

"So what will you do?"

"Continue to look for him," she said.

El lobo nodded and looked away. The world was large, the spiritworld, larger still. Her search could take many lifetimes of an ordinary man. He could wait. He would wait, but as he already knew, the waiting would be hard.

When he turned his gaze to her, he found her smiling at him.

"But not now," she said. "Not this moment."

"I'm glad."

She stood on her tiptoes and kissed his mouth.

"And I would rather do it with you," she said. "In the company of *mi lobo.*"

"But—"

She put a finger against his lips.

"There will be times when you can get away," she said. "We can search for him then. Besides, I want you to meet the rest of my family and get to know them better. And then there is the desert . . ."

El lobo nodded. Year by year the territory under his guardianship was shrinking. If the spread of housing developments continued at the pace it did, one day there would be nothing left of his responsibility. Shishòdewe had said as much when he lay dying. The *manitou* were bound to the wild places. When those-who-came tamed the last of them, spirits such as he could only move on or die. And *el lobo* was not ready to die. He was willing to become a wandering spirit, if Bettina was to be his company on the unending journey.

"But now I'm wondering," she said. "Where do you sleep?"

"You're tired?"

She gave him a mischievous smile. "No. Are you?"

"Let me show you," he said and led her back to his camp, deep in *manidò-akì*, under the boughs of the whispering pines.

Colorín colorado, este cuento se ha acabado.
The story has ended.